By Clarence E. Mulford from Tom Doherty Associates

Bar-20

Bar-20 Days

The Bar-20 Three

Buck Peters, Ranchman

The Coming of Cassidy

Hopalong Cassidy

Johnny Nelson

The Man from Bar-20

Tex

The Bar-20 Three

♦

Tex

♦

Clarence E. Mulford

FORGE®

A Tom Doherty Associates Book / New York

This is a work of fiction. All of the characters, organizations, and events portrayed in this novel are either products of the author's imagination or are used fictitiously.

THE BAR-20 THREE AND TEX

The Bar-20 Three was originally published in 1921. *Tex* was originally published in 1922.

All rights reserved.

A Forge Book
Published by Tom Doherty Associates, LLC
175 Fifth Avenue
New York, NY 10010

www.tor-forge.com

Forge® is a registered trademark of Tom Doherty Associates, LLC.

ISBN 978-0-7653-7779-1

Forge books may be purchased for educational, business, or promotional use. For information on bulk purchases, please contact the Macmillan Corporate and Premium Sales Department at 1-800-221-7945, extension 5442, or write to specialmarkets@macmillan.com.

First Mass Market Edition: April 2015

Printed in the United States of America

0 9 8 7 6 5 4 3 2 1

Contents

The Bar-20 Three

♦

I

♦

"Put a 'T' in It"

Idaho Norton, laughing heartily, backed out of the bar-room of Quayle's hotel and trod firmly on the foot of Ward Corwin, sheriff of the county, who was about to pass the door. Idaho wheeled, a casual apology trembling on his lips, to hear a biting, sarcastic flow of words, full of profanity, and out of all proportion to the careless injury. The sheriff's coppery face was a deeper color than usual and bore an expression not pleasant to see. The puncher stepped back a pace, alert, lithe, balanced, the apology forgotten, and gazed insolently into the peace officer's wrathful eyes.

"—an' why don't you look where yo're steppin'? Don't you know how to act when you come to town?" snarled the sheriff, finishing his remarks.

Idaho looked him over coolly. "I know how to act in any company, even yourn. Just now I ain't actin'—I'm waitin'."

The sheriff's eyes glinted. "I got a good mind—"

"You ain't got nothin' of th' sort," cut in the puncher, contemptuously. "You ain't got nothin' good, except, mebby, yore reg'lar plea of self-defense. I'm sayin' out loud that *that* ain't no good, here an' now; an' I'm waitin' to take it away from you an' use it myself. You been trustin' too cussed much to that nickel badge."

Bill Trask, deputy, who had a reputation not to be overlooked, now took a hand from the rear, eager to add to his list of victims from any of that outfit. The puncher was between him and the sheriff, and hardly could watch them both. Trask gently shook his belt and said three unprintable words which usually started a fight, and then glared over his shoulder at a sudden interruption, tense and angry.

"Shut up, you!" said the voice, and he saw a two-gun stranger slouching away from the hotel wall. The deputy took him in with one quick glance and then his eyes returned to those of the stranger and rested there while a slick prickling sensation ran up his spine. He had looked into many angry eyes, and in many kinds of circumstances, but never before had his back given him a warning quite so plainly. He grew restless and wanted to look away, but dared not; and while he hung in the balance of hesitation the stranger spoke again. "Two to one ain't fair, 'specially with the lone man in th' middle; but I'll make th' odds even, for I'm honin' to claim self-defense, myself. It's right popular. I saw it all—an' I'm sayin' you are three chumps to get all het up over a little thing like that. Mebby his toes *are* tender—but what of it? He ain't no baby, leastawise he don't look like one. An' I'm tellin' you, an' yore badge-totin' friend, that *I* know how to act, too." A twinkle came into the hard, blue eyes. "But what's th' use of actin' like four strange dogs?"

Somewhere in the little crowd a man laughed, others joined in and pushed between the belligerents; and in a minute the peace officers had turned the corner, Idaho was slowly walking toward the two-gun stranger and the crowd was going about its business.

"Have a drink?" asked the puncher, grinning as he pushed back his hat.

"Didn't I just say that I knowed how to act?" chuckled the stranger, turning on his heel and following his companion through the door. "You musta met them two before."

"Too cussed often. What'll you have? Make mine a cigar, too, Ed. No more liquor for me today—Corwin don't forget."

The bartender closed the box and slid it onto the backbar again. "No, he don't," he said. "An' Trask is worse," he added, looking significantly at the stranger, whose cigar was now going to his satisfaction and who was smilingly regarding Idaho, and who seemed to be pleased by the frank return scrutiny.

"You ain't a stranger here no longer," said Idaho, blowing out a cloud of smoke: "You got two good enemies, an' a one-hoss friend. Stayin' long?"

"About half an hour. I got a little bunch of cows on th' drive west of here, an' they ought to be at Twitchell an' Carpenter's corrals about now. Havin' rid in to fix up bed an' board for my little outfit, I'm now on my way to finish deliverin' th' herd. See you later if yo're in town tonight."

"I don't aim to go back to th' ranch till tomorrow," replied Idaho, and he hesitated. "I'm sorry you horned in on that ruckus—there's mebby trouble bloomin' out of that for you. Don't you get careless till yo're a day's ride away from this town. Here, before you go, meet Ed Doane. He's one of th' few white men in this runt of a town."

The bartender shook hands across the bar. "Pleased to meet up with you, Mr.— Mr—?"

"Nelson," prompted the stranger. "How do you do, Mr. Doane?"

"Half an' half," answered the dispenser of liquids, and then waved a large hand at the smiling youth. "Shake han's with Idaho Norton, who was never closer to Idaho than Parsons Corners, thirty miles northwest of here. Idaho's a good boy, but shore impulsive. He's spent most of his life practicin' th' draw, et cetery; an' most of his money has went for ca'tridges. Some folks say it ain't been wasted. Will you gents smoke a cigar with me?"

After a little more careless conversation Johnny nodded his adieus, mounted and rode south. Not long thereafter he came within sight of the Question-Mark, Twitchell and Carpenter's local ranch.

Its valley sloped eastward, following the stream winding down its middle between tall cottonwoods, and the horizon was limited by the tops of the flanking hills, which dipped and climbed and zigzagged into the gray of the east, where great sand hills reared their glistening tops and the hopeful little creek sank out of sight into the dried, salty bed of a one-time lake. Near the trail were two buildings, a small stockaded corral and a wire-fenced pasture of twenty acres; and the Question-Mark brand, known wherever cattlemen congregated, even beyond the Canadian line, had been splashed with red paint on the wall of the larger building. The glaring, silent interrogation-mark challenged every passing eye and had started many curious, grim, and cynical trains of thought in the minds of tired and thirsty wayfarers along the trail. To the north of the twenty-acre pasture a herd of SV cattle grazed, spread out widely, too tired, too content with their feeding to need much attention.

Johnny saw the great, red question-mark and instantly drew rein, staring at it. "Why?" he muttered, and then grew silent for a moment. Shaking his head savagely he urged the horse on again, and again glanced at the crimson interrogation. "Damn you!" he growled. "There ain't no man livin' can answer."

He passed the herd at a distance and rode up to the larger building, where a figure suddenly appeared in the doorway, looked out from under a shielding hand, and quickly stepped forward to meet him.

"Hello, Nelson!" came the cheery greeting.

"Hello, Ridley!" replied Johnny. "Glad to see you again. Thought I'd bring 'em down to you, an' save you goin' up th' trail after 'em. Why don't you paint out that glarin' question-mark on th' side of th' house?"

Ridley slapped his hands together and let out a roar of laughter. "Has it got you, too?" he demanded in unfeigned delight.

"Not as much as it would before I got married," replied Johnny. "I'm beginnin' to see a reason for livin'."

"Good!" exclaimed Ridley. "If I ever meet yore wife I'll tell her somethin' that'll make her dreams sweet." The expression of his face changed swiftly. "Do you know—" he considered, and changed the form of his words. "You'd be surprised if you knew th' number of people hit by that painted question-mark. I've had 'em ride in here an' start all kinds of conversations with me; th' gospel sharps are th' worst. One man blew his brains out in Quayle's hotel because of what that sign started workin' in his mind. Go look at it: it's full of bullet holes!"

"I don't have to," replied Johnny, and quickly answered his companion's unspoken challenge. "An' I can sleep under it, an' smile, cuss you!" He glanced at the distant cattle. "Have you looked 'em over?"

Ridley nodded. "They're in good shape. Ready to count 'em now?"

"Be glad to, an' get 'em off my han's."

"Bring 'em up in front of th' pasture, an' I'll wait for you there," said Ridley.

Johnny wheeled and then checked his horse. "What kind of fellers are Corwin an' Trask?" he asked.

Ridley looked up at him, a curious expression on his face. "Why?"

"Oh, nothin'; I was just wonderin'."

"As long as you ain't aimin' to stop around these parts for long, th' less you know about 'em th' better. I'll be waitin' at th' pasture."

Johnny rode off and started the herd again, and when it stopped it was compacted into a long V, with the point facing the pasture gate, and it poured its units from this point in a steady stream between the two horsemen at the open gate, who faced each other across the hurrying procession and built up another herd on the other side, one which spread out and grazed without restraint, unless it be that of a wire fence. And with the shrinking of the first and the expanding of the second the SV ownership changed into that of the Question-Mark.

The shrewd, keen-eyed buyer for Twitchell and Carpenter looked up as the gate closed after the last steer and smiled across the gap at the SV foreman as he announced his count.

Johnny nodded. "My figgers, to a T," he said. "That 2-Star steer don't belong to us. Joined up with us somewhere along th' trail. You know 'em?"

"Belongs to Dawson, up on th' north fork of th' Bear. I'll drop him a check in a couple of days. This feller musta wandered some to get in with yourn. Well, yourn is a good bunch of four-year-olds. You'll have to wait till I get to town, for I ain't got a blank check left, an' I shore ain't got no one thousand one hundred and forty-three dollars layin' around down here. Want cash or a check?"

"If I took a check I'd have to send somebody up to Sherman with it," replied Johnny. "I might take it at that, if I was goin' right back. Better make it cash, Ridley."

Ridley grinned. "I've swept up this part of th' country purty good."

Johnny shook his head. "I'm lookin' for weaners—an' not in this part of th' country. I'll see you in town."

"Before supper," said Ridley. "You puttin' up at Quayle's?"

"You called it," answered Johnny, wheeling. He rode off, picked up his small outfit and led the way to Mesquite, where he hoped to spend but one night. The little SV group cantered over the thin trail in the wake of their bobbing chuck wagon, several miles ahead of them, and reached the town well ahead of it, much to the cook's vexation. As they neared Quayle's hotel Johnny pulled up.

"This is our stable," he said. "Go easy, boys. We leave at daylight. See you at supper."

They answered him laughingly and swept on to Kane's place, which they seemed to sense, each for his favorite drink and game.

The afternoon shadows were long when Ridley, just from the bank, left his rangy bay in front of the hotel and entered the office, nodding to several men he knew. He went on through and stopped at the bar.

"Howd'y, Ed," he grunted. "That SV foreman around? Nelson's his name."

Ed Doane mopped up the bar mechanically and bobbed his head toward the door. "Here he comes now. Make a deal?"

Ridley nodded as he turned. "Hello, Nelson! Read this over. If it's all right, sign it, an' we'll let Ed disfigure it as a witness. I allus like a witness."

Johnny signed it with the pen the bartender provided and then the bartender labored with it and blew on it to dry the ink.

"Disfigure it, hey?" chuckled Ed, pointing to his signature, which was beautifully written but very much overdone. "That bill of sale's worth somethin' now."

Johnny admired it frankly and openly. "I allus did like shadin', an' them flourishes are plumb fetchin'. Me, now; I write like a cow."

"I'm worse," admitted Ridley, chuckling and giving Johnny a roll of bills. "Count 'em, Nelson. Folks usually turn my writin' upside down for th' first try. Speakin' of witnesses, there's another little thing I like. I allus seal documents, Ed. Take 'em out of that bottle you hide under th' bar.

Three of 'em. Somehow, Ed, I allus like to see you stoop like that. Well, Nelson; does it count up right? Then, business bein' over, here's to th' end of th' drought."

It went the rounds, Ed accumulating three cigars as his favorite beverage, and as the glasses clicked down on the bar Ridley felt for the makings. "Sorry th' bank's closed, Nelson. It might be safer there over night."

"Mebby—but it's safe enough, anyhow," smiled Johnny, shrugging his shoulders. "Anyhow th' bank wouldn't be open early enough in th' mornin' for us. Which reminds me that I better go out an' look around. My four-man outfit's got to leave at daylight."

"I'll go with you as far as th' street," said Ridley. As they neared the door Johnny hung back to let his companion pass through first and as he did so he heard a soft call from the bartender, and half turned.

"Come here a minute," said Doane, leaning over the bar. "It ain't none of my business, Nelson, but I'm sayin' *I* wouldn't go into Kane's with th' wad of money you got on you; an' if I did I shore wouldn't show it nor get in no game. You don't have to remember that I said anythin' about this."

"I never gamble with money that don't belong to me," replied Johnny, "nor not even while I've got it on me; an' already I've forgot you said anythin'. That place must be a sort of 'sink of iniquity,' as that sanctified parson called Abilene."

"Huh!" grunted Doane. "You can put a 'T' in that 'sink,' an' there's only one place where a 'T' will fit. Th' money would be enough, but in yore case there's more. Idaho said it."

"He's only a kid," deprecated Johnny.

" 'Out of th' mouths of babes—' " replied Doane. "I'm tellin' you—that's all."

Ridley stuck his head in at the door. "So-long, fellers," he said.

"Hey, Ridley!" called the bartender hurriedly. "Would you go into Kane's if you had Nelson's roll on you?"

"Not knowin' what I might do under th' infloonce of likker, I can't say," answered Ridley; "but if I did I wouldn't drink in there. So-long, an' I mean it, this time," and he did.

Johnny left soon afterward and wandered along the street toward the building on the northern outskirts of the town where Pecos Kane ran a gambling-house and hotel. Johnny ignored the hotel half and lolled against the door as he sized up the interior of the gambling-hall, and instantly became the center of well-disguised interest. While he paused inside the threshold a lean, tall man arose from a chair against the wall and sauntered carelessly out of sight through a narrow doorway leading to a passage in the rear. Kit Thorpe was not a man to loaf on his job when a two-gun stranger entered the place, especially when the stranger appeared to be looking for someone. Otherwise there was no change in the room, the bartender polishing his glasses without pause, the card players silently intent on their games and the man at the deserted roulette table who held a cloth against the ornate spinning wheel kept on polishing it. They seemed to draw reassurance from Thorpe's disappearance.

One slow look was enough to satisfy Johnny's curiosity. The room was about sixty feet long by half as wide and on his left-hand side lay the bar, built solidly from the floor by close-fitting planks running vertically, which appeared to be of hardwood and quite thick, and the top was of the same material. Several sand-box cuspidors lay before it. The backbar was a shelf backed by a narrow mirror running well past the middle half, and no higher than necessary to give the bartender a view of the room when he turned around, which he did but seldom. Round card-tables, heavy and crude, were scattered about the room and a row of chairs ran the full length along the other side wall. Several loungers sat at the tables, one of them an eastern tough, judging from his clothes, his peaked cap pulled well down over his eyes. At the farther end was a solid partition painted like a checkerboard and the few black squares which cunningly hid several peepholes were not to be singled out by casual observation. Those who knew said that they were closed on their inner side by black steel plates which hung on oiled pivots and were locked shut by a pin. At a table in front of the checkerboard were four men, one flung forward on it, his head resting on his crossed arms; another had slumped down on the edge of his chair, his chin on his chest, while the other two carried on a grunted, pessimistic conversation across their empty glasses.

Johnny's face flickered with a faint smile and he walked toward them, nodding carelessly at the man behind the bar.

Arch Wiggins looked up, a sickly grin on his flushed face. "Hullo," he grunted, foolishly.

"Not havin' nothin' else to do I reckoned I'd look you up," said Johnny. "Fed yet?"

Arch shrugged his shoulders and Sam Gardner sighed expressively, and then prodded the slumped individual into a semblance of intelligence and erectness. This done he kicked the shins of the prostrate cook until that unfortunate raised an owlish, agonized, and protesting countenance to stare at his foreman.

"Nelson wants to know if yo're hungry," prompted Sam, grinning.

"Take it—away!" mumbled the indignant cook. "I *won't* eat! Who's goin' to make me?" he demanded with a show of pugnacity. "I won't!"

Joe Reilly, painfully erect in his chair, blinked and focussed his eyes on the speaker. "Then don't!" he said. "Shut yore face—others kin eat!" He turned his whole body, stiff as a ramrod, and looked at each of the others in turn. "Don't pay no 'tention to him. I kin—eat th'—damned harness," he asserted, thereby proving that his stomach preserved family traditions.

Johnny laughed at them. "Yo're a hell of an outfit," he said without conviction. "What do you say about goin' up to th' hotel an' gettin' somethin' to eat? It's past grubtime, but let's see if they'll have th' nerve to try to tell us to get out. Broke?" he inquired, and as they silently arose to their feet, which seemed to take a great deal of concentration, he chuckled. Then his face hardened: "Where's yore guns?" he demanded.

Arch waved elaborately at the disinterested bartender. "That gent loaned us ten apiece on 'em," he said. "'Bligin' feller. Thank you, friend."

"Yo're a'right," said the cook, nodding at the dispenser of fluids.

"An' yo're a fine, locoed bunch, partin' with yore guns in a strange town," snapped Johnny. "You head for th' hotel *pronto!* G'wan!"

The cook turned and waved a hand at the solemn bartender. "Goo'-bye!" he called. "I *won't* eat! Goo'-bye."

Seeing them started in the right direction, Johnny went in and up to the bar. "Them infants don't need guns," he asserted, digging into a pocket, "but as long as they ain't shot themselves, yet, I'm takin' a chance. How much?"

The bartender, typical of his kind, looked wise when it was not necessary, finished polishing the glass in his hand and then slowly faced his inquisitor, bored and aloof. He had the condescending air of one who held himself to be mentally and physically superior to any man in town, and his air of preoccupation was so heavy that it was ludicrous. "Ten apiece," he answered nonchalantly, as behove the referee of drunken disputes, the adviser of sodden men, the student of humanity's dregs, whose philosophy of life was rotten to the core because it was based purely on the vicious and the weak, and whose knowledge, adjudged abysmal and cyclopedic by an admiring riffraff of stupefied mentality, was as shallow, warped, and perverted as the human derelicts upon which his observations were based. As Johnny's hand came up with the roll of bills the man of liquor kept his face passive by an act of will, but there crept into the ratlike eyes a strange gleam, which swiftly faded. "Put it 'way," he said heartily, a jovial, free-handed good fellow on the instant. "We got it back, an' more. It was worth th' money to have these where they wouldn't be too handy. We allus stake a good loser—it's th' policy of th' house. Take these instead of th' stake." He slid the heavy weapons across the bar. "What'll you have?"

"Same as you," replied Johnny, and he slowly put the cigar into a pocket. "Purty quiet in here," he observed, laying two twenty-dollar bills on the bar.

"Yeah," said the bartender, pushing the money back again; "but it's a cheerful ol' beehive at night. Better put that in yore pocket an' drop in after dark, when things are movin'. I know a blonde that'll tickle you 'most to death. Come in an' meet her."

"Tell you what," said Johnny, grinning to conceal his feelings. "You keep them bills. If I keep 'em I'll have to let them fools have their guns back for nothin'. I'm aimin' to take ten apiece out of their pay. If you don't want it, give it to th' blonde, with Mr. Nelson's compliments. It won't be so hard for me to get acquainted with her, then."

The bartender chuckled and put the bills in the drawer. "Yo're no child, I'm admittin'. Reckon you been usin' yore head quite some since you was weaned."

One of the card players at the nearest table said something to his two companions and one of them leaned back, stretched and arose. "I'm tired. Get somebody to take my place."

The sagacious observer of the roll of bills started to object to the game being broken up, glanced at Johnny and smiled. "All right; mebby this gent will sit in an' kill a little time. How 'bout it, stranger?"

Johnny smiled at him. "My four-man outfit ain't leavin' me no time to kill," he answered. "I got to trail along behind 'em an' pick up th' strays."

The gambler grinned sympathetically. "Turn 'em loose tonight. What's th' use of herdin' with yearlin's, anyhow? If you get tired of their company an' feel like tryin' yore luck, come in an' join us."

"If I find that I got any heavy time on my han's I'll spend a couple of hours with you," replied Johnny. As he turned toward the door he glanced at the bartender. "Don't forget th' name when you give her th' forty," he laughed.

The bartender chuckled. "I got th' best mem'ry of any man in this section. See you later, mebby."

Johnny nodded and departed, his hands full of guns, and as he vanished through the front door Kit Thorpe reappeared from behind the partition, grinned cynically at the bartender and received a wise, very wise look in return.

Reaching the hotel Johnny entered it by the nearest door, that of the barroom, walked swiftly through with the redeemed guns dangling from his swinging hands and without pausing in his stride, flung a brief remark over his shoulder to the man behind the bar, who was the only person, besides himself, in the room: "You was shore right. It should ought to have a 'T' in it," and passed through the other door, across the office and into the dining-room, where his four men were having an argument with a sullen waiter and a wrathy cook.

Ed Doane straightened up, his ears preserving the words,

his eyes retaining the picture of an angry, hurrying two-gun man from whose hands swung four more guns. He cogitated, and then the possible significance of the numerous weapons sprang into his mind. Ed did not go around the bar. He vaulted it and leaped to the door, out of which he hopefully gazed at the tranquil place of business of Pecos Kane. Slowly the look of hope faded and he returned to his place behind the bar, scratching his frowsy head in frank energy, his imagination busy with many things.

II

◆

Well-Known Strangers

The desert and a paling eastern sky. The penetrating cold of the dark hours was soon to die and give place to a punishing heat well above the hundred mark. Spectral agaves, flinging their tent-shaped crowns heavenward, seemed to spring bodily from the radiating circlet of spiny swords at their bases, their slender stems still lost in the weakening darkness. Pale spots near the ground showed where flower-massed yuccas thrust up, lance-like, from their slender, prickly leaves. Giant cacti, ghostly, bulky, indistinct, grotesque in their erect, parallel columns, reached upward to a height seven times that of a tall man. They are the only growing things unmoved by winds. The sage, lost in the ground-hugging darkness, formed a dark carpet, mottled by lighter patches of sand. There were quick rustlings over the earth as swift lizards scurried hither and yon and a faint whirring told of some "side-winder" vibrating its rattles in emphatic warning against some encroachment. Tragedies were occurring in the sage, and the sudden squeak of a desert rat was its swan song.

In the east a silvery glow trembled above the horizon and to the magic of its touch silhouettes sprang suddenly from vague, blurred masses. The agave, known to most as the century plant, showed the delicate slenderness of its arrowy stem and marked its conical head with feathery detail. The flower-covered spikes of the Spanish bayonets became studies in ivory, with the black shadows on their thorny spikes deep as charcoal. The giant cacti, boldly thrown against the silver curtain, sprang from their joining bases like huge, thick telegraph poles of ebony, their thorns not yet clearly revealed. The squat sage, now resolved into tufted masses, might have been the purplish leaden hollows of a great sea. The swift rustlings became swift movements and the "side-winder" uncoiled his graceful length to round a nearby sage bush. The quaking of a small lump of sand grew violent and a long, round snoot pushed up inquiringly, the cold, beady eyes peering forth as the veined lids parted, and a Gila monster sluggishly emerged, eager for the promised warmth. To the northeast a rugged spur of mountains flashed suddenly white along its saw-toothed edge, where persistent snows crowned each thrusting peak. A moment more, and dazzling heliographic signals flashed from the snowy caps, the first of all earthly things to catch the rays of the rising sun, as yet below the far horizon. On all sides as far as the eye could pierce through the morning twilight not a leaf stirred, not a stem moved, but everywhere was rigidity, unreal, uncanny, even terrifying to an imaginative mind. But wait! Was there movement in the fogging dark of the north? Rhythmic, swaying movement, rising and falling, vague and mystical? And the ghostly silence of this griddle-void was broken by strange, alien sounds, magnified by contrast with the terror-inspiring silence. A soft creaking, as of gently protesting saddle leather, interspersed with the frequent and not unmusical tinkle of metal, sounded timidly, almost hesitatingly out of the dark along the ground.

Silver turned into pink, pink into gold, and gold into crimson in almost a breath, and long crimson ribbons became lavender high in the upper air, surely too beautiful to be a portent of evil and death. Yet the desert hush tightened, constricted, tensed as if waiting in rigid suspense for a lethal stroke. Almost without further warning a flaming, molten arc pushed up over the far horizon and grew with amazing bulk and swiftness, dispelling the chill of the night, destroying the beauty of the silhouettes, revealing the purple sage as a mangy, leaden coverlet, riddled and thin, squatting tightly against the tawny sand, across which had sprung with instant speed long, vague shadows from the base of every object which raised above the plain. The still air shuddered into a slow dance, waving and quivering, faster and faster like some mad dance of death, the rising heat waves distorting with their evil magic giant cacti until their fluted, thorny columns weaved like strange, slowly undulating snakes standing erect on curving tails. And in the distance but a few leagues off blazed the white mockery of the crystal snow, serene and secure on its lofty heights, a taunt far-flung to madden the heat-crazed brain of some swollen, clawing thing in distorted human form slowly dying on the baking sands.

The movement was there, for the sudden flare of light magically whisked it out of the void like a rabbit out of a conjurer's hat. Two men, browned, leather-skinned, erect, silent, and every line of them bespeaking reliance with a certainty not to be denied, were slowly riding southward. Their horses, typical of their cow-herding type, were loaded down with large canteens, and suggested itinerant water ped-

dlers. Two gallons each they held, and there were four to
the horse. One could imagine these men counted on taking
daily baths—but they were only double-riveting a security
against the hell-fires of thirst, which each of them had known
intimately and too well. The first rider, as erect in his saddle
as if he had just swung into it, had a face scored with a
sorrow which only an iron will held back; his squinting
eyes were cold and hard, and his hair, where it showed beneath the soiled, gray sombrero, was a sandy color, all of
what was left of the flaming crimson of its youth. He rode
doggedly without a glance to right or left, silent, sullen, in-
scrutable. When the glorious happiness of a man's life has
gone out there is but little left, often even to a man of strength.
Behind him rode his companion, five paces to the rear and
exactly in his trail, but his wandering glances flashed far
afield, searching, appraising, never still. Younger in years
than his friend, and so very much younger in spirit, there
was an air of nonchalant recklessness about him, occasionally swiftly mellowed by pity as his eyes rested on the man
ahead. Now, glancing at the sun-cowed east, his desert cunning prompted him and he pushed forward, silently took
the lead and rode to a thicket of mesquite, whose sensitive
leaves, hung on delicate stems, gave the most cooling shade
of any desert plant. Dismounting, he picketed his horse and
then added a side-line hobble as double security against being left on foot on the scorching sands. Not satisfied with
that, he unfastened the three full canteens, swiftly examined them for leaks and placed them under the bush. Six gallons of water, but if need should arise he would fight to the
death for it. Out of the corner of his eye he watched his
companion, who mechanically was doing the same thing.
Red Connors yawned, drank sparingly and then, hesitating,
grinned foolishly and fastened one end of his lariat to his
wrist.

"That desiccated hunk of meanness don't leave this hombre afoot, not nohow," said Red, looking at his friend; but Hopalong only stared into the bush and made no reply.

Nothing abashed at his companion's silence, Red stretched out at full length under the scant shade, his Colt at his hand in case some Gila monster should be curious as to what flavor these men would reveal to an inquisitive bite. Red's ideas of Gilas were romantic and had no scientific warrant whatever. And it was possible that a "side-winder" might blunder his way.

"It's better than a lava desert, anyhow," he remarked as he settled down, having in mind the softness of the loose sand. "One whole day of hell-to-leather fryin', an' one more shiverin' night, an' this stretch of misery will be behind, but it shore saves a lot of ridin', it does. I'll bet I'm honin' for a swim in th' Rio Placer—an' I ain't carin' how much mud there is, neither. Ah, th' devil," he growled in great disgust, slowly arising. "I done forgot to sprinkle them cayuses' insides. One apiece, they get, which is only insultin' 'em."

Hopalong tried to smile, arose and filled his hat, which his thirsty horse frantically emptied. When the canteen was also empty he went back to the sandy couch, to lay awake in the scorching heat, fighting back memories which tortured him near to madness, his mental torments making him apathetic to physical ones. And so dragged the weary, trying day until the cooling night let them go on again.

Three days later they rode into Gunsight, made careless inquiries and soon thereafter drew rein before the open door of the SV, unconscious of the excited conjectures rioting in the curious town.

Margaret Nelson went to the door, her brother trying to push past her, and looked wonderingly up at the two smiling strangers.

Red bowed and removed his hat with a flourish. "Mrs.

Johnny?" he asked, and at the nodded assent smiled broadly. "My name's Red Connors, an' my friend is Hopalong Cassidy. He is th' very best friend yore fool husband ever had. We came down to make Johnny's life miserable for a little while, an' to give you a hand with his trainin', if you need it."

Margaret's breath came with a rush and she held out both hands with impulsive friendliness. "Oh!" she cried. "Come in. You must be tired and hungry—let Charley turn your horses into the corral."

Charley wriggled past the barrier and jumped for Hopalong, his shrill whoop of delighted welcome bringing a smile to the stern face of the mounted man. A swoop of the rider's arm, a writhing twist of the boy's body, coming a little too late to avoid the grip of that iron hand, and Charley shot up and landed in front of the pommel, where he exchanged grins at close range with his captor.

"I knowed you first look," asserted the boy as the grip was released. "My, but I've heard a lot about you! Yo're goin' to stay here, ain't you? I know where there's some black bear, up on th' hills—want to go huntin' with me?"

Hopalong's tense, wistful look broke into a smile, the first sincere, honest smile his face had known for a month. Gulping, he nodded, and turned to face his friend's wife. "Looks like I'm adopted," he said. "If you don't mind, Mrs. Johnny, Charley an' me will take care of th' cayuses while Red helps you fix up th' table." He reached out, grasped the bridle of Red's horse as its rider dismounted, and rode to the corral, Charley's excited chatter bringing an anxious smile to his sister, but a heartfelt, prayerful smile to Red Connors. He had great hopes.

Red paused just inside the door. "Mrs. Johnny," he said quietly, quickly, "I got to talk fast before Hoppy comes back. He lost his wife an' boy a month ago—fever—in four days. He's all broke up. Went loco a little, an' even came near shootin' me because I wouldn't let him go off by his-self. I've had one gosh-awful time with him, but finally managed to get him headed this way by talkin' about Johnny a-plenty. That got him, for th' kid allus was a sort of son to him. I'm figgerin' he'll be a lot better off down here on this south range for awhile. Even crossin' that blasted desert seemed to help—he loosened up his talk consider-able since then. An' from th' way he grabbed that kid, I'm sayin' I'm right. Where is Johnny?"

"Oh!" Margaret's breathed exclamation did not need the sudden moisture in her eyes to interpret it, and in that instant Red Connors became her firm, unswerving friend. "We'll do our best—and I think he should stay here, always. And Johnny will be delighted to have him with us, and you, too—Red."

"Here he comes," warned her companion. "Where is Johnny? When will he get here?"

"Why, he took a herd down to Mesquite," she replied, smiling at Hopalong, who limped slowly into the room with Charley slung under his arm like a sack of flour. "He should be back any day now. And won't he be wild with delight when he finds you two boys here! You have no idea how he talks about you, even in his sleep—oh, if I were inclined to jealousy you might not be so welcome!"

"Ma'am," grinned Red, tickled as a boy with a new gun, "you don't never want to go an' get jealous of a couple of old horned toads like us—well, like Hoppy, anyhow. We'll sort of ride herd on him, too, every time he goes to town. Talk about revenge! Oh, you wait! So he went off an' left you all alone? Didn't he write about some trouble that was loose down here?"

"It was—but it's cleaned up. He didn't leave me in any danger—every man down here is our friend," Margaret replied, quick to sense the carefully hidden thought which had prompted his words, and to defend her husband.

"Well, two more won't hurt, nohow," grunted Red. "You say he ought to get here any day?"

"I'm spending more time at the south windows every day," she smiled. "I don't know what will happen to the housework if it lasts much longer!"

"South windows?" queried Hopalong, standing Charley on his head before letting loose of him. "Th' trail is west, ain't it?" he demanded, which caused Red to chuckle inwardly at how his friend was becoming observant again.

"The idea!" retorted Margaret. "Do you think my boy will care anything about any trail that leads roundabout? He'll leave the trail at the Triangle and come straight for this house! What are hills and brush and a miserable little creek to *him,* when he's coming home? I thought you knew my boy."

"We did, an' we do," laughed Red. "I'm bettin' yore way—I hope he's got a good horse—it'll be a dead one if it ain't."

"He's saving Pepper for the homestretch—if you know what *that* means!"

"Hey, Red," said Charley, slyly. "Yore gun works, don't it?"

"Shore thing. Why?"

"Well, mine don't," sighed the boy. "Wonder if yourn is too heavy, an' strong, for a boy like me to shoot? *Bet* it ain't."

Margaret's low reproof was lost in Red's burst of laughter, and again a smile crept to Hopalong's face, a smile full of heartache. This eager boy made his memories painfully alive.

"You an' me an' Hoppy will shore go out an' see," promised Red. "Mrs. Johnny will trust you with us, I bet. Hello!

Here's somebody comin'," he announced, looking out of the door.

"That's my dad!" cried Charley, bolting from the house so as to be the first one to give his father the good news.

Arnold rode up laughing, dismounted and entered the house with an agility rare to him. And he was vastly relieved. "Well! Well! Well!" he shouted, shaking hands like a pump handle. "I saw you ride over the hill an' got here as fast as Lazy would bring me. Red an' Hopalong! Our household gods with us in the flesh! And that scalawag off seeing the sights of strange towns when his old friends come to visit him. I'm glad to see you boys! The place is yours. Red and Hopalong! I'm not a drinkin' man, but there are times when—follow me while Peggy gets supper!"

"Can I go with you, Dad?" demanded Charley.

"You help Peggy set the table."

"Huh! *I* don't care! Me an' Hoppy an' Red are goin' after bear, an' I'm goin' to use Red's gun."

"Seems to me, Charley," reproved Arnold, "that you are pretty familiar, for a boy; and especially on such short acquaintance. You might begin practicing the use of the word 'Mister.'"

"Or say 'Uncle Red' and 'Uncle Hopalong,'" suggested Margaret.

"'Red' is my name, an' I'm shore 'Red' to him," defended that person.

"Which goes for me," spoke up his companion. "I'm Hopalong, or Hoppy to anybody in this family—though 'Uncle' suits me fine."

"Then we'll have a fair exchange," retorted Margaret, smiling. "The family circle calls me 'Margaret' or 'Peggy.'"

"If you want to rile her, call her Maggie," said Charley. "She goes right on th' prod!"

"I'm plumb peaceful," laughed Red, turning to follow

his host. "You help Mrs. Margaret, an' when I come back you an' me'll figger on goin' after bear as soon as we can."

III

◆

A Question of Identity

Johnny sauntered into Quayle's barroom and leaned against the bar, talking to Ed Doane. An hour or two before he had finished his dinner, warned his outfit again about the early start on the morrow, advanced them some money, and watched them leave the hotel for one more look at the town, and now he was killing time.

"What do you think about Kane's?" asked Ed carelessly, and then looked up as a customer entered. When the man went out he repeated the question.

Johnny cogitated and shrugged his shoulders. "Same as you. Reg'lar cow-town gamblin'-hall, with th' same fixin's, wimmin', crooked games, an' wise bums hangin' 'round. Am I right?"

A group entered, and when they had been served they went into the hotel office, the bartender's eyes on them as long as they were in sight. He turned and frowned. "Purty near. You left a couple of things out. I'm not sayin' what they are, but I *am* sayin' this: Don't you ever pull no gun in there if you should have any trouble. Wait till you get yore man outside. Funny thing about that—sort of a spell, I reckon— but no stranger ever got a gun out an' workin' in Kane's place. They died too quick, or was put out of workin' order."

Johnny raised his eyebrows: "Mebby no good man ever tried to get one out, an' workin'."

"You lose," retorted Ed emphatically. "Some of 'em was shore to be good. It's a cold deck—with a sharpshooter. There I go again!" he snorted. "I'm certainly shootin' off my mouth today. I must be loco!"

"Then don't let that worry you. I ain't shootin' mine off," Johnny reassured him. "I'm tryin' to figger—"

A voice from the street interrupted him. "Hey, stranger! Yore outfit's in trouble down in Red Frank's!"

Johnny swung from the bar. "Where's *his* place?" he asked.

"One street back," nodded the bartender, indicating the rear of the room. 'Turn to yore right—third door. It's a dive—look sharp!"

Johnny grunted and turned to obey the call. Walking out of the door, he went to the corner, turned it, and soon turned the second corner. As he rounded it he saw stars, reached for his guns by instinct, and dropped senseless. Two shadowy figures pounced upon him, rolled him over, and deftly searched him.

Back in the hotel Idaho stuck his head into the barroom. "Seen Nelson?" he asked.

"Just went to Red Frank's this minute—his gang's in trouble there!" quickly replied Ed.

"I'll go 'round an' be handy, anyhow," said Idaho, loosening his gun as he went through the door. Rounding the first corner, he saw a figure flit into the darkness across the street and disappear, and as he turned the second corner he tripped and fell over a prostrate man. One glance and his match went out. Jumping around the corner, he saw a second man run across an open space between two clumps of brush, and his quick hand chopped down, a finger of flame spitting into the night. A curse of pain answered it and he leaped forward, hot and vengeful; but his search was in vain, and he soon gave it up and hastened back to his prostrate friend, whom he found sitting up against the wall with an open jackknife in his hand.

"What happened?" demanded Idaho, stopping and bending down. "Where'd he get you?"

"Somethin' fell on my head—an' my guns are gone," mumbled Johnny. "I—bet I've been robbed!" His slow, fumbling search revealed the bitter truth, and he grunted. "Clean! Clean!"

"I shoved a hunk of lead under th' skin of somebody runnin'—heard him yelp," Idaho said. "Lost him in th' dark. Here, grab holt of me. I'll take you to my room in th' hotel. Able to toddle?"

"Able to kill th' skunk with my bare han's," growled the unfortunate, staggering to his feet. "I'm goin' to Kane's!" he asserted, and Idaho's arguments were exhausted before he was able to have his own way.

"You come along with me—I want to look at yore head. An', besides, you ought to have a gun before you go huntin'. Come on. We'll go in through th' kitchen—that's th' nearest way. It's empty now, but th' door's never locked."

"You gimme a gun, an' I'll know where to go!" blazed Johnny, trembling with weakness. "I showed my roll in there, like a fool. Eleven hundred—hell of a foreman *I* am!"

"You can't just walk into a place an' start shootin'!" retorted Idaho, angrily. "*Will* you listen to sense? Come on, now. After you get sensible you can do what you want, an' I'll go along an' help you do it. That's fair, ain't it? How do you know that feller belongs to Kane's crowd? May be a Greaser, an' a mile away by now. Come on—be sensible!"

"Th' SV can't afford to lose that money—oh, well," sighed Johnny, "yo're right. Go ahead. I'll wash off th' blood, anyhow. I must be a holy show."

They got to Idaho's room without arousing any unusual interest and Idaho examined the throbbing bump with clumsy fingers, receiving frank statements for his awkwardness.

"Shucks," he grinned, straightening up. "It's as big as an egg, but besides th' skin bein' broke an' a lot of blood, there ain't nothin' th' matter. I'll wash it off—an' if you keep yore hat on, nobody'll know it. I reckon that hat just about saved that thick skull of yourn."

"What did you see when you found me?" asked Johnny when his friend had finished the job.

Idaho told him and added: "Hoped I could tell him by th' yelp, but I can't, unless, mebby, I go around an' make everybody in this part of th' country yelp for me. But I don't reckon that's hardly reasonable."

"Yo're right," grinned Johnny. "Well," he said, after a moment's thought, "I don't go back home without eleven hundred dollars, U.S., an' my guns; but I got to send th' boys back. They can't help me none, bein' known as my friends. Besides, we're all broke, an' they're needed on th' ranch. If I *knowed* that Kane had a hand in this, I'd cussed soon get that money back!"

"Yo're shore plumb set on that Kane idear."

"I showed that wad of bills in just two places: Ed's bar, an' Kane's joint."

"Ed's bar is out of it if nobody else was in there at th' time."

"Only Ridley, Ed, an' myself."

"Somebody could 'a' looked in th' window," suggested Idaho.

"Nobody did, because I was lookin' around."

"If you go in Kane's an' make a gunplay, you'll never know how it happened or who done it; an' if you go in, without a gunplay, an' let 'em know what you think, some Greaser'll hide a knife in you. Then you'll never get it back."

"Just th' same, that's th' place to start from," persisted
Johnny doggedly. "An' from th' inside, too."

Idaho frowned. "That may be so, but startin' it from
there means to end it there an' then. You can't buck Kane
in his own place. It's been tried more'n once. I ain't shore
you can buck him in this town, or part of th' country. Bigger people than you are suspected of payin' him money to
let 'em alone. You'd be surprised if I named names. Look
here: I better speak a little piece about this part of th' country. This county is unorganized an' ain't got no courts, nor
nothin' else except a peace officer which we calls sheriff.
It's big, but it ain't got many votes, an' what it has is one-
third Greaser. Most Greasers don't amount to much in a
stand-up fight, but their votes count. They are all for Kane.
We've only had one election for sheriff, an' although Corwin is purty well known, he won easy. Kane did it, an' when
anybody says 'Corwin,' they might as well say 'Kane.' He
is boss of this section. His gamblin'-joint is his headquarters, an' it's guarded forty ways from th' jack. His gang is
made up of all kinds, from th' near decent down to th' night
killer. When Kane wants a man killed, that man don't live
long. Corwin takes his orders before an' after a play like this
one. Yo're expected to report it to him. Comin' down to
cases, th' pack has got to be fed, an' they have got to make
a killin' once in a while. Even if Kane ain't in on it direct,
he'll get most of that money across his bar or tables. To
wind up a long speech, you better go home with yore men,
for that ain't enough money to get killed over."

"Mebby not if it was mine!" snapped Johnny. "An' I ain't
shore about that, neither. An' there's more'n money in this,
an' more than th' way I was handled. Somebody in this wart
of a town has got Johnny Nelson's two guns an' nobody
steals *them* an' keeps 'em! I got friends, lots of 'em, in Montanny, that would lend me th' money quick; but there ain't

nobody can give me them six-guns but th' thief that's got 'em. I'm rooted—solid."

"All right," said Idaho. "Yo're talkin' foolish, but cussed if I don't like to hear it. So me an' you are goin' to hog-tie that gang. If I get Corwin in th' ruckus, I'll be satisfied."

"Yo're th' one that's talkin' foolish," retorted Johnny, fighting back his grin. "An' I'm cussed if *I* don't like to hear it. But there's this correction: Me an' you ain't goin' to bulldog that gang at all. *I* am. Yo're goin' to sprawl on yore saddle an' light out for wherever you belong, an' stay there. Yo're a marked man an' wouldn't last th' swish of a longhorn's tail. Yore brand is registered—they got you in their brand books; but they ain't got mine. I'm not wearin' no brand. I ain't even ear-notched, 'though I musta been a 'sleeper' when I let 'em put this walnut on my head. I'm a plain, ornery maverick. Think I'm comin' out in th' open? I don't want no brass band playin' when I go to war. I'm a Injun."

"Yo're a little striped animal in this town—one of them kind that's onpleasant up-wind from a feller," snorted Idaho. "How can you play Injun when they know yo're hangin' 'round here lookin' for yore money? Answer me that, maverick!"

"I'm comin' to that. Can you get me an old hat? One that's plumb wore out?"

"Reckon so," grunted Idaho, in surprise. "Th' clerk might be able to dig one up."

"No, not th' clerk; but Ed Doane," corrected Johnny. "Now you think hard before you answer this one: Could you see my face plain when you found me? Could *they* have seen it plain enough to be shore it was me?"

Idaho stared at him and a cheerful expression drifted across his face. "I'm gettin' th' drift of this Injun business," he muttered. "Mebby—mebby—cuss it, it *will* work! I couldn't see nothin' but a bump on th' ground along that wall till I lit a match. I'll get you a hat an' I'll plant it, too."

Johnny nodded. "Plant anythin' else you want that don't look like anythin' I own. Be shore that hat ain't like mine."

Idaho raised his hand as a sudden tramping sounded on the stairs. "That yore outfit?" he asked as a loud, querulous voice was heard.

Johnny went to the door and called, whereupon Arch waved his companions toward their quarters and answered the summons, following his foreman into the room. Johnny was about to close the door when Idaho arose and pushed past him.

"We been talkin' too loud," whispered the departing puncher. "You never can tell. I'm goin' out to sit on th' top step where there's more air," and he went on again, the door closing after him.

Johnny turned and smiled at Arch's expression. "You boys leave at daylight on th' jump. I got to stay here. You can say I'm waitin' for th' chance to pick up some money— buyin' a herd of yearlin's cheap, or anythin' you can think of. Anythin' that'll stick. You'll have plenty of time to smooth it out before you get back home. I want you boys to scratch up every cent you've got an' turn it over to me. Any left of that I gave you after supper?"

"Shore—quite some," grinned Arch. "We had better luck, down th' street. You must be aimin' to get aplenty yearlin's, with that roll you got. What are *we* goin' to do, busted?"

"I want a couple of Colts, too," continued Johnny. "You won't need any money. Th' waggin is well stocked—an' when you get back you can draw on Arnold."

"We was goin' to stop at Highbank for a good time," protested Arch.

"Have it in yore old man's hotel an' owe it to him," suggested Johnny.

"Have a good time in my old man's place!" exclaimed Arch. "Oh, *hell!*" He burst out laughing. "That'll tickle th' boys, *that* will!" The puncher looked searchingly at his foreman. "Hey, what's all th' trouble?"

Johnny thought it would be wiser to post his companion and crisply told what had happened.

Arch cleared his throat, hitched up his belt, and looked foolish but determined. "It's been comin' rapid, but I got it all. Yo're talkin' to th' wrong man. You want to fix up that story for th' ranch with some soft-belly that's ridin' that way. Better send a letter. We're all stayin' here. *Fine* bunch of—"

"You can help me more by goin' back like nothin's happened," interrupted Johnny. "Th' ranch won't be worryin' me then, an' if you stayed here it might give th' game away. Besides, one man can live longer on th' money we got than four can, only have a quarter of th' chance to drink too much, an' only talk a fourth as much. That's th' natural play, an' everythin' has *got* to be natural."

"That's th' worst of havin' a smooth face," grumbled Arch, ruefully rubbing his chin. "If I only had whiskers, I could shave 'em off an' be a total stranger; but I don't reckon I could grow a good enough bunch to get back here in time."

Johnny laughed, his heart warming to the puncher. "Take *you* a year or two; an' there's more'n whiskers needed to hide from a *good* man. There's little motions, gait, voice—oh, lots of things. You can help me more if you go north. See Dave Green, tell him on th' quiet, an' ask him to send me down a couple hundred dollars. He can buy a check from th' Doc, payable to George Norton. There's a bank in this town. He's to send it to George Norton, general delivery."

"Dave will spread it far an' wide," objected Arch. "He tells all he knows."

"If he did," smiled Johnny, "it shore would be an eddication for th' man that heard it. He talks a lot—an' says nothin'.
If he told all he knew, hell would 'a' popped long ago on
them ranges. I'm only wishin' he could get a job in Kane's!"

"Gosh!" exclaimed Arch. "Mebby he can. He's a bang-
up bartender."

Johnny shook his head and laughed.

"Well, I reckon you know best," said Arch. "If you say
so, we'll go home—but it hurts bad as a toothache. An' as
long as we're goin', we can start tonight—this minute."

"You'll start at daylight, like honest folks," chuckled
Johnny. "Think I want Kane to sit down an' figger why a
lazy outfit got ambitious all at once? An' th' two boys that
lend me their guns want to be ridin' close to th' waggin, on
its left side, until they get out of town. I don't want anybody
noticin' they ain't got their guns. Mebby their coats'll hide
'em, anyhow. But before you do anythin' else, get me a copy
of that weekly newspaper downstairs. There's some layin'
around th' office. Shore you got it all?"

Arch nodded, and his foreman opened the door. Idaho
glanced around and then went down the stairs and through
the office, stopping at the bar, where he held a low-voiced
conversation with the man behind it. Ed looked a little surprised at the unusual request, but Idaho's earnestness and
anxiety told him enough and he asked no questions. A few
minutes later, after Idaho had disappeared into the kitchen,
Ed told the clerk to watch the bar, and went up to his room,
and dropped several articles out of the window before he
left it again.

When Idaho had finished scouting and planting the sombrero, a broken spur, and a piece torn from a red kerchief,
he went into the barroom and grinned at his friend Nelson,
who leaned carelessly back against the wall; and then his
eyes opened wide as he saw the size of the roll of bills from

which Johnny was peeling the outer layer. For two hours they sat and played California Jack in plain sight of the street as though nothing unusual had occurred, Johnny's sombrero pushed back on his head, the walnut handle of one of his guns in plain sight, his boots not only guiltless of spurs, but showing that they never had borne them, and his faded, soiled, blue neckerchief was as it had been all day. His mood was cheerful and his laughter rang out from time to time as his friend's witticisms gave excuse. To test his roll, he pulled it out again under his friend's eyes and thumbed off a bill, changed his mind, rolled it back again, and carelessly shoved the handful into his pocket.

Idaho leaned forward. "Who th' devil did *you* slug?" he softly asked.

"Tell you later—deal 'em up," grunted Johnny, a sigh of satisfaction slipping from him. It had been one of Tex Ewalt's maxims never to be broke, even if carefully trimmed newspapers had to serve as padding, and in this instance, at least, Johnny believed his old friend to be right. The world finds bluff very useful, and opulence seldom receives a cold shoulder.

At daylight three horsemen and a wagon went slowly up the little street, two men sticking close to each other and the vehicle, and soon became lost to sight. Two or three nighthawks paused and watched the outfit, and one of them went swiftly into Kane's side door. Idaho drew back from the corner of the hotel where he had been watching, nodded wisely to himself, and went into the stable to look after his horse.

The little outfit of the SV stopped when a dozen miles had been put behind and prepared and ate a hurried breakfast. As he gulped the last swallow of coffee, Arch arose and went to his horse.

"Thirty miles a day with a waggin takes too long," he said.

"One of you boys ride in th' waggin an' gimme a lead hoss. Nelson's a good man, an' it's our job to help him all we can. I can do it that way between sleeps, if I can keep my eyes open to th' end of it. By gettin' a fresh cayuse from my old man at Highbank, I'll set a record for these parts."

Gardner nodded. "Take my cayuse, Arch. I'm crucifyin' myself on th' cross of friendship. Cook, give him some grub."

Ten minutes later Arch left them in a cloud of dust, glad to get away from the wagon and keen to make a ride that would go down in local history.

After breakfast Johnny sauntered into the barroom, nodded carelessly to the few men there, and seated himself in his favorite chair.

"Thought mebby you might be among th' dear departed this mornin'," remarked Ed carelessly. "Heard a shot soon after you left last night, but they're so common 'round here that I didn't get none excited. Have any trouble in Red Frank's?"

"You better pinch yoreself," retorted Johnny. "You saw me an' Idaho settin' right in this room, playin' cards long after that shot. I was upstairs when I heard it. Didn't go to Red Frank's. Changed my mind when I got around at th' side of th' hotel, an' went through th' kitchen, upstairs lookin' for Idaho. What business I got playin' nurse to four growed-up men? A lot they'd thank me for cuttin' in on their play."

"Did they have any trouble?"

"No; they wasn't in Red Frank's at all—anyhow, that's what they said. Somebody playin' a joke, or seein' things, I reckon. Seen Idaho this mornin'?"

"No, I ain't," answered Ed sleepily. "Reckon he's still abed. Say, was that yore outfit under my winder before dawn? I come cussed near shootin' th' loud-mouthed fool that couldn't talk without shoutin'."

Johnny laughed. "I reckon it was. They was sore about havin' to go home. Know of any good yearlin's I can buy cheap?"

Ed yawned, rubbed his eyes, and slowly shook his head. "Too close to Ridley. Folks down here mostly let 'em grow up an' sell 'em to him. Prices would be too high, anyhow, I reckon. Better hunt for 'em nearer home."

"That's what I been doin'," growled Johnny. "Well, mebby yo're right about local prices an' conditions; but I'm goin' to poke around an' ask questions, anyhow. To tell you th' truth, a town looks good to me for a change, 'though I'm admittin' this ain't much of a town, at that. Sorta dead— nothin' happens, at all."

"That's th' fault of th' visitor, then," retorted Ed, another yawn nearly disrupting his face. "Ho-hum! Some day I'm goin' out an' find me a cave, crawl in it, close it up behind me, an' sleep for a whole week. An' from th' looks of you, it wouldn't do you no harm to do th' same thing." He nodded heavily to the other customers as they went out.

"I'll have plenty of time for sleep when I get home," grinned Johnny. "I got to get some easy money out of this town before I think of sleepin'. Kane's don't get lively till dark, does it?"

Ed snorted. "Was you sayin' easy money?" he demanded with heavy sarcasm.

"I was."

"Oh, well; if you must I reckon you must," grunted the bartender, shrugging his shoulders.

"A new man, playin' careful, allus wins in a place like Kane's, if he's got a wad of money as big as mine," chuckled Johnny, voicing another maxim of his friend Tex, and patting the bulging roll in his pocket.

Ed looked at the pocket, and frowned. "Huh! Lord help that wad!" he mourned.

"It's got all th' help it needs," countered Johnny. "I'm its guardian. I might change it for bigger bills, for it's purty prominent now. However, that can wait till it grows some more." He burst out laughing. "Big as it is, there's room for more."

"Better keep some real little ones on th' outside," suggested Ed wisely. "You show it too cussed much."

"Do you know there's allus a right an' a wrong way of doin' everythin'?" asked his companion. "A man that's got a lot of money will play safe an' stick a few little ones on th' outside; but a man that's got only little bills will try to get a big one for th' cover. One is tryin' to hide his money; th' other to run a bluff. Wise gamblers know that. I got little bills on th' outside of mine. You watch 'em welcome me."

Despite his boasts, he did not spend much time in Kane's, but slept late and hung around the hotel for a day or two, and then, one morning, he got a nibble on his bait. He was loafing on the hotel steps when he caught sight of the sheriff coming up the street. Corwin had been out of town and had returned only the night before. Seeing the lone man on the steps, the peace officer lengthened his rolling stride and headed straight for the hotel, his eyes fixed on the hat, guns, kerchief, and boots.

"Mornin'," he said, nodding and stopping.

"Mornin'," replied Johnny cheerily. "Bright an' cool, but a little mite too windy for this hour of th' day," he observed, watching a vicious little whirlwind of dust racing up the middle of the street. It suddenly swerved in its course, struck the sheriff, and broke, covering them with bits of paper and hurling dust and sand in their faces and mouths. Other furious little gusts sent the light debris of the street high in the air to be tossed about wildly before settling back to earth again.

"Yo're shore shoutin'," growled Corwin, spitting violently

and rubbing his lips. "Don't like th' looks of it. Ain't got no love for a sand storm." He let his blinking eyes rest for a moment on his companion's boots, noted an entire absence of any signs of spur straps, glanced at the guns and at the opulent bump in one of the trouser pockets, noted the blue neckerchief, and gazed into the light blue eyes, which were twinkling at his expression of disgust. "Damn th' sand," he grunted, spitting again. "How do you like this town of ourn, outside of th' dust, now that you've seen more of it?"

Johnny smiled broadly. "Leavin' out a few things besides th' dust—such as bein' too quiet, dead, an' lackin' 'most everythin' a town should have—I'd say it is a purty fair town for its kind. But, bad as it is, it ain't near as bad as that bed I've been sleepin' in. It reminds me of some of th' country I've rid over. It's full of mesas, ridges, canyons, an' valleys, an' all of 'em run th' wrong way. Cuss such a bed. I gave it up after awhile, th' first night, an' played Idaho cards till I was so sleepy I could 'a' slept on a cactus. After that, though, it ain't been so bad. It's all in gettin' used to it, I reckon."

The sheriff laughed politely. "Well, I reckon there ain't no bed like a feller's own. Speakin' of th' town bein' dead, that is yore fault; you shouldn't stay so close to th' hotel. Wander around a little an' you'll find it plumb lively. There's Red Frank's an' Kane's—they are high-strung enough for 'most anybody." The momentary gleam in his eyes was not lost on his companion.

"Red Frank's," cogitated Johnny. Then he laughed. "I come near goin' in there, at that. Anyhow, I shore started."

"Why didn't you go on?" inquired the sheriff, speaking as if from polite, idle curiosity. "You might 'a' seen some excitement in there."

"Somebody tried to play a joke on me," grinned Johnny, "but I fooled 'em. My boys are shore growed up."

"How'd yore boys make out?"

"They said they wasn't in there at all. Reckon somebody got excited or drunk if they wasn't tryin' to make a fool out of me. But, come to think of it, I *did* hear a shot."

"They're not as rare as they're goin' to be," growled the sheriff. "But it's hard to stop th' shootin'. Takes time."

Johnny nodded. "Reckon so. You got a bad crowd of Greasers here, too, which makes it harder—though they're generally strong on knifeplay. Mexicans, monte, an' mescal are a bad combination."

"Better tell yore boys to look sharp in Red Frank's. It's a bad place, 'specially if a man's got likker in him. An' they'll steal him blind."

"Don't have to tell 'em, for I sent 'em home," replied Johnny, and then he grinned. "An' there ain't no man livin' can rob 'em, neither, for I wouldn't let 'em draw any of their pay. Bein' broke, they didn't kick up as much of a fuss as they might have. I know how to handle my outfit. Say!" he exclaimed. "Yo're th' very man I been lookin' for, an' I didn't know it till just this minute. Do you know where I can pick up a herd of a couple or three hundred yearlin's at a fair figger?"

Corwin shook his head. "You might get a few here an' there, but they ain't worth botherin' about. Anyhow, prices are too high. Better look around on yore way back, up on some of them God-forsaken ranges north of here. But how'll you handle a herd with yore outfit gone?"

His companion grinned and winked knowingly. "I'll handle it by buyin' subject to delivery. Let somebody else have th' fun of drivin' a lot of crazy-headed yearlin's all that distance. Growed-up steers are bad enough, an' I've had all I want of them for awhile. Well," he chuckled, "not havin' no yearlin's to buy, I reckon I've got time to wander around nights. Six months in a ranchhouse is shore confinin'. I need a change. What do you say to a little drink?"

Corwin wiped more sand from his lips. "It's a little early in th' day for me, but I'm with you. This blasted wind looks like it's gettin' worse," he growled, scowling as he glanced about.

"It's only addin' to th' liveliness of yore little town," chuckled Johnny, leading the way.

"We ain't had a sand storm in three years," boasted the sheriff, hard on his companion's heels. "I see you know th' way," he commented.

Johnny set down his empty glass and brought up the roll of bills, peeled the outer from its companions, and tossed it on the bar. "You got to take somethin' with us, Ed," he reproved.

Ed shrugged his shoulders, slid the change across the counter, and became thoughtfully busy with the arrangement of the various articles on the backbar.

Corwin treated, talked a few moments, and then departed, his busy brain asking many questions and becoming steadily more puzzled.

Ed mopped the bar without knowing he was doing it, and looked at his new friend. "Where'd you pick *that* up?" he asked.

"Meanin'?" queried Johnny, glancing at the windows, where sand was beating at the glass and pushing in through every crack in the woodwork.

"Corwin."

"Oh, he rambled up an' got talkin'. Reckon I'll go out, sand or no sand, an' see if I can get track of any yearlin's, just to prove that you don't know anythin' about th' cow business."

"Nobody but a fool would go out into that unless they shore had to," retorted Ed. "It's goin' to get worse, shore as shootin'. I know 'em. Lord help anybody that has to go very far through it!"

Johnny opened the door, stuck his head out and ducked back in again. Tying his neckerchief over his mouth and nose, he went to the rear door, closed his eyes, and plunged out into the storm, heading for the stable to look to the comfort of his horse. Pepper rubbed her nozzle against him, accepted the sugar with dignity, and followed his every move with her great, black eyes. He hung a sack over the window and, finding nails on a shelf, secured it against the assaults of the wind.

"There, Pepper Girl—reckon you'll be right snug; but don't you go an' butt it out to see what's goin' on outside. I'm glad this ain't no common shed. Four walls are a heap better than three today."

"That you, Nelson?" came a voice from the door. Idaho slid in, closed the door behind him with a bang, and dropped his gun into the holster. "This is shore a reg'lar storm; an' that's shore a reg'lar hoss!" he exclaimed, spitting and blowing. He stepped toward the object of his admiration.

"Look out!" warned Johnny. "She's likely to brain a stranger. Trained her that way. She'll mebby kill anybody that comes in here; but not hardly while I'm around, I reckon. Teeth an' hoofs—she's a bad one if she don't know you. That's why I try to get her a stable of her own. What was you doin' with th' six-gun?"

"Keepin' th' sand out of it," lied Idaho. "Thiefproof, huh?" he chuckled. "I'm sayin' it's a good thing. Ever been tried?"

"Twice," answered Johnny. "She killed th' first one." He lowered his voice. "I'm figgerin' Corwin knows about that little fracas of th' other night. Did you tell anybody?"

"Not a word. What about yore outfit?"

"Tight as fresh-water clams, an', besides, they didn't have no chance to. They even left without their breakfast. But I'm dead shore he knows. How did he find it out?"

"Looks like you might be right, after all," admitted Idaho. "I kept a lookout that mornin', like I told you, an' th' news of yore outfit leavin' was shore carried, which means that somebody in Kane's gang was plumb interested. How much do you think Corwin knows about it?"

"Don't know; but not as much now as he did before he saw me this mornin'," answered Johnny. "When he sized me up, his eyes gave him away—just a little flash. But now he may be wonderin' who th' devil it was that got clubbed that night. An' he showed more signs when he saw my money. Say: How much does Ed know?"

"Not a thing," answered Idaho. "He's one of my best friends, an' none of my best friends ask me questions when I tell 'em not to. An' now I'm glad I told him not to, because, of course, you don't know anythin' about him. No, sir," he emphatically declared; "anythin' that Corwin knows come from th' other side. What you goin' to do?"

"I don't know," admitted Johnny. "I got to wrastle that out; but I *do* know that I ain't goin' out of th' hotel today. It looks like Californy Jack for us till this blows over. Yore cayuse fixed all right?"

"Shore; good as I can. Come on, if yo're ready."

"Hadn't you better carry yore gun in yore hand, so th' sand won't get in it?" asked Johnny gravely.

Idaho looked at him and laughed. "Come on—I'm startin'," he said, and he dashed out of the building, Johnny close at his heels.

IV

◆

A Journey Continued

Pounding into Highbank from the south, Arch turned the two fagged-out horses into his father's little corral, roped the better of the two he found there, saddled it, and rode around to the front of the hotel, where he called loudly.

Pete Wiggins went to the door and scowled at his son. "What you doin' with that hoss?" he demanded in no friendly tone.

"Breakin' records," impudently answered his young hopeful. "Left Big Creek, north of Mesquite, at six-twenty this mornin', an' I'm due in Gunsight before dark. Left you two cayuses for this one—but don't ride 'em too hard. Solong!" and he was off in a cloud of dust.

Pete Wiggins stepped forward galvanically and called, shaking his fist. "Come back here! Don't you kill *that* hoss!"

His beloved son's reply was anything but filial, but as long as his wrathful father did not hear it, perhaps it may better be left out of the record.

The shadows were long when Arch drew up in front of the "Palace" in Gunsight, and dismounted almost in the door. He looked at his watch and proudly shouted the miles and the time of the ride before looking to see who was there to hear it. As he raised his head and saw Dave Green, Arnold, and two strangers staring at him, he called himself a fool, walked stiffly to a chair, and lowered himself gently into it.

"That's shore some ridin'," remarked Dave, surprised. "What's wrong? What's th' reason for killin' cayuses?"

"Wanted to paste somethin' up for others to shoot at," grinned Arch, making the best of the situation.

"How'd you come to leave ahead of Nelson?" demanded Arnold, his easy-going boss. "Where is he? An' where's th' rest of th' boys?" The SV owner was fast falling into the vernacular, which made him fit better into the country.

"Oh, he's tryin' to make a fortune buyin' up a herd of fine yearlin's," answered the record-maker with confident assurance. "It ain't nothin' to him that th' owner don't want to sell 'em. I near busted laughin' at 'em wranglin'. They was near fightin' when I left. You should 'a' heard 'em! Anybody'd think that man didn't own his own cattle. But I'm bettin' on Nelson, just th' same, for when I left they had got to wranglin' about th' price, an' that's allus a hopeful sign. He shore will tire that man out. I used a lead hoss as far as Highbank, changin' frequent', an' got a fresh off th' old man. Nelson told us all to go home, where we're needed—but he'll be surprised when he knows how quick *I* got there. Sam an' th' others are with th' waggin, comin' slower."

"I should hope so!" snorted Arnold. "An' you ain't home yet. What's th' real reason for all this speed, an' for headin' here instead of goin' to th' ranch? A man that's born truthful makes a poor liar; but I'll say this for you, Arch—with a little practice you'll be near as good as Dave, here. Come on; tell it!"

Arch looked wonderingly at his employer, grinned at Dave, and then considered the two strangers. "I've done told it already," he affirmed, stiffly.

"Shake hands with Red Connors an' Hopalong Cassidy," said Arnold. "You've heard of them, haven't you?"

"Holy cats! I *have!*" exclaimed Arch, gripping the hands of the two in turn. "I certainly have. Have you two ever been in Mesquite?" he demanded, eagerly. "Good! Now, wait a minute; I want to think," and he went into silent consultation with himself.

"Mebby he's aimin' to improve on me," said Dave. "Judgin' from th' studyin', I figger he's trying to bust in yore class, Arnold."

Arch grinned from one to the other. "Seein' as how we're all friends of Nelson, an' his wife ought to be kept calm, I reckon I ought to spit it out straight. Here, you listen," and he told the truth as fully and completely as he knew it.

Arnold shook his head at the end of the recital. The loss of the herd money was a hard blow, but he was too much of a man to make it his chief concern. "Arch," he said slowly, "yo're so fond of breakin' records that yo're goin' to sleep in town, get another horse at daylight, an' break yore own record gettin' back to Mesquite. Tell that son-in-law of mine to come home right away, before Peggy is left a widow. It's no fault of his that he lost it—it's to his credit, goin' to the aid of his men. I wouldn't 'a' had it to lose if it wasn't for what he's done for th' SV. He earned it for me; an' if he's lost it, all right."

"Most generally th' East sends us purty poor specimens," observed Dave. "Once in awhile we get a thoroughbred. Gunsight's proud of th' one it got."

"Arnold," said Arch eagerly, "I'll get to Mesquite tomorrow if it's moved to th' other side of hell!"

Hopalong took the cigar from his mouth. "Wait a minute," he said. He slowly knocked the ashes from it and looked around. "While I'm appreciatin' what you just said, Arnold, I don't agree with it." He thought for a moment and then continued. "You don't know that son-in-law of yourn like I do. Somebody knocked him on th' head, stole his money an' his guns. Don't forget th' guns. Bein' an easterner, that mebby don't mean anythin' to you; but bein' an old

Bar-20 man, it means a heap to me. He won't leave till he's squared up, all around. I *know* it. Seein' how it is, we got to accept it; an' figger out some way to make his wife take it easy, an' not do no worryin'. Here!" he exclaimed, leaning forward. "Arnold, you sit down an' write him a letter. Write it now. Tell him to stay down there until he gets a good herd of yearlin's. Then Arch has got to start back in th' mornin' an' join th' waggin, an' come home like he ought to. He stays here tonight, an' nobody has seen him, at all."

"An' Dave don't need to bother with any check," said Red. "Hoppy an' me has plenty of money. We'll start for Mesquite at daylight, Arch, here, ridin' with us till we meet th' waggin. Of course, Hoppy don't mean that yo're really goin' to write a letter, Arnold," he explained.

"That's just what I *do* mean," said Hopalong. "He's goin' to write th' letter, but he ain't goin' to send it. He'll give it to Arch, an' then it can be torn up. What's th' use of lyin' when it's so easy to tell th' truth? 'Though I'm admittin' I wasn't thinkin' of that so much as I was that a man can allus tell th' truth better'n he can lie. When he tells about th' letter, he's goin' to be talkin' about a real letter, what won't get to changin' around in a day or two, or when he gets rattled. Mrs. Johnny is mebby goin' to ask a lot of questions."

"I'll give odds that she does," chuckled Dave, looking under the backbar. "Here's pen an' ink," he said, pushing the articles across the counter. "There's paper an' envelopes around here some—here it is. Go ahead, now: 'Dear Johnny: I take my—'"

"Shut up!" barked Arnold, glaring at him. "I guess I know how to write a letter! Besides, I don't take my pen in hand. It's your pen, you grinnin' chump! As long as we're ridin' on th' tail of Truth, let's stick to it, all th' way. Shut up, now, an' gimme a chance!" He glared around at the grinning faces, jabbed the pen in the ink, and went to work. When he

had finished, he read it aloud, and handed it to Arch, who
tore it up and threw the pieces on the floor.

Hopalong reached down, picked up the pieces, and
gravely, silently put them on the bar. Dave raked them into
his hand, dropped them into a tin dish, and put a match to
them. Arnold looked around the little group and snorted.

"Huh! You an' Dave musta gone to th' same school!"
Dave nodded. "We have, I reckon. Experience is a good
school, too."

"Th' lessons stick," said Hopalong, looking at Dave with
a new interest.

Arch chuckled. "Cuss it! I'll shore hate to stop at that waggin. I'm sayin' Mesquite is goin' to be terrible upset some
day soon. Why *ain't* I got whiskers? I'd like to see his face
when he sets eyes on you fellers. Bet he'll jump up an' down
an' yell!"

"Mebby," said Hopalong, "for if there's any yellin', he'll
shore have to start it. He sent you fellers away because you
was known to be friends of his, didn't he?"

Dave slapped the bar and laughed outright. "If I wasn't
so fat, I'd go with you! I'm beginnin' to see why he thought
so much of you fellers. Here—it's time for a drink."

"What are we goin' to tell Margaret?" asked Arnold.
"She may get suspicious if you leave so suddenly."

"You just keep repeatin' that letter to yoreself," laughed
Red, "an' leave th' rest to better liars. Yo're as bad a liar as
Arch, here. Me an' Hoppy may 'a' been born truthful, but
we was plumb spoiled in our bringin' up. Reckon we better
be leavin' now. Arch, where'll we meet you about two hours
after daylight tomorrow?"

Arch groaned. "Shucks! About daylight it'll take Fanning
that long to get me out of bed—oh, well," he sighed, resignedly. "I'll be at th' ford, waitin' for you to come along.
Come easy, in case I'm asleep."

"South of here, on this trail?" asked Red. "Thought so. All right. So-long," and he followed his slightly limping friend out to the horses.

Dave hurried to the door. "Hey!" he shouted. "Hadn't I better send him that check, anyhow? He may need it before you get there."

A roar of laughter from behind answered him, and he wheeled to face Arch. "When does th' mail leave?" asked the puncher.

"Day after tomorrow," answered Dave, and swung around as a voice from the street rubbed it in.

"You musta played hookey from that school, Dave," jeered Arnold.

"He's fat clean to th' bald spot," shouted Arch. "Come on in, Dave. We ain't got time to hold back for no mail to get there first." He stuck his head out of the window. "So-long, fellers! See you at th' ford."

Dave watched the three until they were well along the trail and then he turned slowly. "I never did really doubt th' stories Nelson told about that old outfit, but if I had any doubts I ain't got them no more. Did you see th' looks in their eyes when you was tellin' about Nelson?"

"I did!" snapped Arch. "Why in hell ain't I got whiskers?"

Reaching the SV, Arnold and his companions put up the horses and walked slowly toward the house, seeing a flurry of white through the kitchen door.

"Think it'll reach him in time?" asked Red, waiting outside the door for Arnold to enter first.

"Ought to. Slim said he would mail it at Highbank as soon as he got there," answered Arnold.

"I shore hope so," said Red. "I'd hate to have that ride for nothin'—an' it would just be our luck to pass him somewhere on th' way, an' get there after he left."

"He'd likely foller th' reg'lar trail up, anyhow," said Hopalong. "It ain't likely we'll miss him."

Margaret put down the dish and looked at them accusingly. "What are you boys talking about?" she demanded.

"Only wonderin' if yore father's letter will get to Johnny in time to catch him before he leaves," said Hopalong. "Dave says it will as long as that Slim feller is takin' it to Highbank with him. Slim live down there?" he asked his host.

"No; goin' down for th' Double X, I suppose," replied Arnold. "Supper ready, Peggy?"

"Not until I learn more about this," retorted Margaret, determinedly. "What letter are you talking about?"

"Oh, I told Johnny to look around and see if he could pick up a good herd of yearlings cheap," answered her father, going into the next room.

Margaret compressed her lips, but said nothing about it, whereupon Red silently swore a stronger oath of allegiance. "The table is waiting for you. I've had to keep the supper warm," she said.

Red nodded understandingly. "Men-folks are shore a trial an' tribulation," he said, passing through the door.

"Hadn't ought to take him very long, I suppose?" queried Arnold, passing the meat one way and the potatoes the other.

Red laughed. "You don't know him very well, yet," he replied. "Give him a chance to dicker over a herd an' he's happy for a week or more. He shore does like to dicker."

"I never saw anything in his nature which would indicate anything like that," said Margaret, tartly. "He always has impressed me with being quite direct. Perhaps I did not understand you correctly?"

"Peggy! Peggy!" reproved her father. "It means bread and butter for us."

"I can eat my bread without butter," she retorted. "As a matter of fact I've seen very little butter out in this country."

Red screwed his face up a little and wriggled his foot. "I don't reckon you've ever seen him buyin' a herd, ma'am?"

"You are quite right, Mr. Connors. I never have."

Red did not take the trouble to inform her that *he* never had seen her husband buy a herd. "I reckon it's his love for gamblin'," he said, carelessly, and instantly regretted it.

"Gambling?" snapped Margaret, her eyes sparking. "Did you say gambling?"

Hopalong flashed one eloquent look at his friend, whose hair now was not the only red thing about him, and removed the last of the peel from the potato. "Red is referrin', I reckon, to th' love of gamblin' that was born in yore husband, Margaret. It allus has been one of his, an' our, fears that it would get th' best of him. But," he said, proudly and firmly, "it never did. Johnny is gettin' past th' age, now, when a deck of cards acts strong on him. An' it's all due to Red. He used to whale him good every time he caught th' Kid playin'."

Red's sanctimonious expression made Hopalong itch to smear the hot potato over it, and the heel of his boot on Red's shin put a look of sorrow on that person's face which was not in the least simulated.

"We all had a hand in that, Margaret," generously remarked the man with the shuddering shin. "Tex Ewalt watched him closest. But, as I was sayin', out at th' corral, I don't believe he's got men enough to handle no herd of yearlin's. Them youngsters are plumb skittish, an' hard to keep on th' trail. Me an' Hoppy are aimin' to go down an' help him—an' see him all th' sooner, to tell you th' truth."

"That will please him," smiled Margaret. She looked at her father, whose appetite seemed to be ravenous, judging by the attention he was giving to the meal. "What did you write, Dad?"

Arnold washed down a refractory mouthful of potato, which suffered from insufficient salivation, and looked up. He repeated the letter carelessly and reached for another swallow of coffee, silently thanking Hopalong for insisting that the letter actually be written.

The meal over, they sat and chatted until after dark, Margaret doing up a bundle of things which she thought her husband might need. When morning came she had breakfast on the table at daylight for her departing friends, and she also had a fat letter for her husband, which she entrusted to Red, the sterling molder of her husband's manly character.

When they had ridden well beyond sight of the house Hopalong thoughtfully dropped the bundle to the ground, turned in the saddle and looked with scorn at his friend. "You shore are a hard-boiled jackass! For two bits I'd 'a' choked you last night. How'd you like to have somebody shoot off his mouth to yore wife about your gamblin'?"

"I've reformed, an' she knows it!"

"Yes, you've reformed! You've reformed a lot, you have!"

"You ain't got no business pickin' on th' man that taught th' Kid most all he knows about poker!" tartly retorted Red.

"Cussed little you ever taught him," rejoined Hopalong. "It was me an' Tex that eddicated his brain, an' fingers. He only used you to practice on."

And so they rode, both secretly pleased by this auspicious beginning of a new day, for the day that started without a squabble usually ended wrong, somehow. Picking up Arch, who yawningly met them at the ford, they pushed southward at a hard pace, relying on the relay which their guide promised to get at Highbank. Reaching this town Arch led them to his father's little corral, and exulted over the four fresh horses which he found there. Saddles were changed with celerity and they rolled on southward again.

Peter Wiggins in the hotel office held the jack of hearts over the ten of the same suit and cocked an ear to listen. Slowly making the play he drew another card from the deck in his hand, and listened again. Reluctant to bestir himself, but a little suspicious, he debated the matter while he played several cards mechanically. Then he arose and walked through the building, emerging from the kitchen door. Three swiftly moving riders, his son in the middle, were taking the long, gentle slope just south of town. Pete's laziness disappeared and he made good time to the corral. One look was enough and he shook a vengeful fist at his heir and pride.

"Twice!" he roared, kicking an inoffensive tomato can over the corral wall. "Twice! Mebby you'll try it again! All right; *I'm* willin'. I never heard of anybody around here thrashin' a twenty-three-year-old son, but as long as yo're bustin' records an' makin' th' Wigginses famous, I ought to do *my* share. Yo're bustin' ridin' records—I'm aimin' to bust th' hidin' records, if you don't smash th' sprintin' records, you grinnin' monkey!"

Pete went into the hotel, soon returning with the cards and a box; and for the rest of the morning played solitaire with the steadily rising sun beating on his back, and swarms of flies exploring his perspiring person.

The three riders were going on, hour after hour, their speed entirely controlled by what they knew of horseflesh, and when they espied the wagon Arch suggested another change of mounts, which was instantly overruled by Hopalong.

"Some of them Mesquite hombres will be rememberin' them cayuses," he said. "We're doin' good enough as we are."

When they reached the wagon and drew rein to breathe their mounts, Joe Reilly grinned a welcome. "Thought you was goin' to Gunsight!" he jeered.

Arch laughed triumphantly. "I've done been there, but got afraid you fellers might get lost. Meet Hopalong Cassidy an' Red Connors, friends of th' foreman."

"Why'n hell didn't you bring my hoss with you, you locoed cow?" blazed Sam Gardner from the wagon seat. "You never got to Gunsight. You musta hit a cushion an' bounced back."

"Forgot all about yore piebald," retorted Arch. "But if you must have a cayuse you can ask my old man for one when you get to Highbank. I'd do it for you, only me an' him ain't on th' best of terms right now." He turned to his two new friends. "All you got to do now is foller th' wagon tracks to town."

"So-long," said the two, and whirled away.

They spent the night not many miles north of Big Creek and were riding again at dawn. As they drew nearer to their objective the frisking wind sent clouds of dust whirling around them to their discomfort.

"That must be th' town," grunted Red through his kerchief as his eyes, squinting between nearly closed lids, caught sight of Mesquite through a momentary opening in the dust-filled air to the southeast.

"Hope so," growled his companion. "Cussed glad of it. This is goin' to be a whizzer. Look at th' tops of them sand hills yonder—streamin' into th' air like smoke from a roarin' prairie fire. Here's where we separate. I'm takin' to th' first shack I find. Don't forget our names, an' that we're strangers, for awhile, anyhow."

Red nodded. "Bill Long an' Red Thompson," he muttered as they parted.

Not long thereafter Hopalong dismounted in the rear of

Kane's and put his horse in the nearer of the two stables, doing what he could for the animal's comfort, and then stepped to the door. He paused, glanced back at the "P.W." brand on the horse and smiled. "Red's is a Horseshoe cayuse. That's what I call luck!" and plunged into the sand blasts. Bumping into the wall of Kane's big building he followed it, turned the corner, and groped his way through the front door.

At the sudden gust the bartender looked around and growled. "Close that door! *Pronto!*"

The newcomer slammed it shut and leaned against the wall, rubbing at his eyelids and face, and shed sand at every movement.

The bartender slid a glass of water across the bar. "Here, wash it out. You'll only make 'em worse, rubbin'," he said as the other began rubbing his lips and spitting energetically.

Bill Long obeyed, nodded his thanks and glanced furtively at the door, and became less alert. "Much obliged. I didn't get all there was flyin', but I got a-plenty."

The dispenser of drinks smiled. "Lucky gettin' in out of it when you did."

"Yes," replied Bill, nervously. "Yes; plumb lucky. This will raise th' devil with th' scenery."

"Won't be a trail left," suggested the bartender, watching closely.

Bill glanced up quickly, sighed with satisfaction and then glanced hurriedly around the room. "Whose place is this?" he whispered out of the corner of his mouth.

"Pecos Kane's," grunted the bartender, greatly pleased about something. His pleasure was increased by the quick look of relief which flashed across the other's face, and he chuckled. "Yo're all right in here."

"Yes," said Bill, and motioned toward a bottle. Gulping

the drink he paid for it and then leaned over the counter. "Say, friend," he whispered anxiously, "if anybody comes around askin' for Bill Long, you ain't seen him, savvy?"

"Never even heard of th' gent," smiled the other. "Here's where you should ought to lose yo're name," he suggested.

Bill winked at him and slouched away to become mixed up in the crowd. The checkerboard rear wall obtruded itself upon his vision and he went back and found a seat not far from it and from Kit Thorpe, bodyguard of the invisible proprietor, who sat against the door leading through the partition. Thorpe coldly acknowledged the stranger's nod and continued to keep keen watch over the crowd and the distant front door.

The day was very dull, the sun's rays baffled by the swirling sand, and the hanging kerosene lamps were lit, and as an occasional thundering gust struck the building and created air disturbances inside of it the lamps moved slightly to and fro and added a little more soot to the coating on their chimneys. Bill's natural glance at the unusual design of the rear wall caught something not usual about it and caused an unusual activity to arise in his mind. He knew that his eyes were sore and inflamed, but that did not entirely account for the persistent illusion which they saw when his roving glance, occasionally returning to the wall, swept quickly over it. There were several places where the black was a little blacker, and these spots moved on their edges, contracting and lengthening as the lamps swung gently. Pulling the brim of his hat over his eyes, he faced away from the wall and closed his burning eyelids, but his racing thoughts were keen to solve any riddle which would help to pass the monotonous time. Another veiled glance as he shifted to a more comfortable position gave him the explanation he sought. Those few black squares had been cut out, and the moving strips of black which had puzzled him were the shadows of the edges, moving across a black board which, set back from the thickness of the partition, closed them.

"Peekholes," he thought, and then wondered anew. Why the lower row, then, so low that a man would have to kneel to look through the openings? "Peekholes," persisted hide-bound Experience, grabbing at the obvious. "Perhaps," doubted Suspicion; "but then, why that lower row?" Suddenly his gunman's mind exulted. "Peekholes above, an' loopholes below." A good gunman would not try to look through such small openings, nearly closed by the barrel of a rifle. But why a rifle, for a *good* gunman? "He'd need all of a hole to look through, an' a *good* gunman likes a hip shot. That's it: Eyes to th' upper, six-gun at th' lower, for a range too short to allow a miss."

He stirred, blinked at the gambling crowd and closed his eyes again. The sudden, gusty opening of the front door sent jets of soot spouting from the lamp chimneys and bits of rubbish skittering across the floor; and it also sent his hand to a gun-butt. He grunted as Red Thompson entered, folded his arms anew and dozed again, as a cynical smile flickered to Thorpe's face and quickly died. Bill shifted slightly. "Any place as careful in thinkin' out things as *this* place is will stand a lot of lookin' over," he thought. "Th' Lord help anybody that pulls a gun in this room. An' I'll bet a man like Kane has got more'n loopholes. I'm shore goin' to like his place."

Kit Thorpe had not missed the stranger's alert interest and motion at the opening of the door, but for awhile he did not move. Finally, however, he yawned, stretched, moved restlessly on his chair and then noisily arose and disappeared behind the partition, closing the checkered door after him. It was not his intention to sit so close to anyone who gave signs which indicated that he might be engaged in a shooting match at any moment. It would be better to keep watch from the side, well out of the line of fire.

Bill Long did not make the mistake of looking at the holes again, but dozed fitfully, starting at each gust which was strong enough to suggest the opening of the door. "I got to find th' way, an' that's all there is to it," he muttered. "How am I goin' to be welcome around here?"

V

◆

What the Storm Hid

The squeaking of the door wakened Johnny and his gun swung toward the sound as a familiar face emerged from the dusk of the hall and smiled a little.

"Reckon it ain't no shootin' matter," said the sheriff, slowly entering. He walked over to a chair and sat down. "Just a little call in th' line of duty," he explained.

"Sorry there wasn't a bell hangin' on th' door, or a club, or somethin'," replied Johnny ironically. "Then you could 'a' waited till I asked you to come in."

"That wouldn't 'a' been in th' line of duty," chuckled Corwin, his eyes darting from one piece of wearing apparel to another. "I'm lookin' around for th' fellers that robbed th' bank last night. Yore clothes don't hardly look dusty enough, though. Where was you last night, up to about one o'clock?"

"Down in th' barroom, playin' cards. Why?"

"That's what Ed says, too. That accounts for you durin' an' after th' robbery. I've got to look around, anyhow, for them coyotes."

"You'd show more sense if you was lookin' around for hoss tracks instead of wastin' time in here," retorted Johnny, keeping his head turned so the peace officer could not see what was left of the bump.

"There ain't none," growled Corwin, arising. "She's still blowin' sand a-plenty—a couple of shacks are buried to their chimneys. I'm tellin' you this is th' worst sand storm that ever hit this town, but it looks like it's easin' up now. There won't be a trail left, an' th' scenery has shifted enough by this time to look like some place else. Idaho turn in when you did?"

"He did. Here he is now," replied Johnny, for the first time really conscious of the sand blasts which rasped against the windows.

Idaho peered around the door, nodded at Corwin and looked curious, and suspicious. "If I ain't wanted, throw me out," he said, holding up his trousers with one hand, the other held behind his back. "Hearin' voices, I thought mebby somebody was openin' a private flask an', bein' thirsty, I come over to help. My throat is shore dusty. An' would you listen to that wind? It shore rocked this old hotel last night. Th' floor of my room is near ankle deep in places."

"Th' bank was robbed last night," blurted Corwin, watching keenly from under his hat brim. "Whoever done it is still in town, unless he was a damned fool!"

Idaho grunted his surprise. "That so? Gee, they shore couldn't 'a' picked a better time," he declared. "Gosh, there's sand in my hair, even!"

Johnny rubbed his scalp, looked mildly surprised and slammed his sombrero on his head. "It ain't polite," he grinned, "but I got enough of it now." He sat up, crossed his legs under the sand-covered blankets and faced his visitors. "Tell us about it, Sheriff," he suggested.

"Wait till I get a belt," said Idaho, backing out of the

door. When he returned he carried the rest of his clothes and started getting into them as the sheriff began his recital.

"John Reddy, th' bank watchman, says he was a little careless last night, which nobody can hardly blame him for. He sat in his chair agin' the rear wall, th' whole place under his eyes, an' listened to th' storm. To kill time he got to makin' bets with hisself about how soon th' second crack in th' floor would be covered over, an' then th' third, an' so on. 'Long about a little after twelve he says he hears a moan at th' back door. He pulls his gun an' listens close, down at th' crack just above th' sand drift. Then he hears it again, an' a scratchin' an clawin'. There's only one thing he's thinkin' about then—how he'd feel if he was th' poor devil out there, lost an' near dead. I allus said a watchman should ought to have no feelin's, an' a cussed strong imagination. John ain't fillin' th' bill either way. He cleared away th' drift on his side of th' door an' opens it—an' beyond rememberin' somethin' sandy jumpin' for him, that's all he knows till he come to later on an' found hisself tied up, with a welt on th' head that felt big as a doorknob."

If the sheriff expected to detect any interchange of glances between his auditors at his reference to the watchman's bump on the head he was disappointed. Johnny was looking at him with a frank interest seconded by that of Idaho, and neither did anything else during the short pause.

"John got his senses back enough to know what had happened, an' one glance around told him that he was right," continued Corwin. "Finally he managed to get his legs loose enough to hobble, an' he butted out into th' flyin' sand with his eyes shut an' his nose buried agin' his shoulder so he could breathe; an' somehow he managed to hit a buildin' in his blind driftin'. It was McNeil's, an' by throwin' his weight agin' th' door an' buttin' it with his shoulders an' elbows, he woke up Sam, who let him in, untied his arms an' th' rest of him, fixed him up as well as he could in a hurry an' then left him there. Sam got Pete Jennings, next door, sent Pete an' a scatter-gun to watch over what was left in th' bank, an' then started out to find me. He had to give it up till it got light, so he waited in th' bank with Pete. Th' bank fellers are there now, checkin' up. Th' big, burglar-proof safe was blowed open neat as a whistle—but they plumb ruined th' little one. They overlooked the biggest of all, down in th' cellar. Well," he sighed, arising, "I got to go on with my callin'—an' it's one fine day to be wanderin' all over town."

"If I was sheriff I wouldn't have to do much wanderin'," said Idaho. "But, anyhow, it can't last," he grinned.

Johnny nodded endorsement. "Th' harder, th' shorter. It's gettin' less all th' time," he said, pivoting and sitting on the edge of the bed. "But, just th' same," he yawned, stretching ecstatically, "I'm shore-e-e—g-l-a-d _I_ can stay indoors till she peters out. Yo're plumb right, Corwin; them fellers never left town last night. An' if I was you I'd be cussed suspicious of anybody that seemed anxious to leave any time to-day."

"They never did leave town last night," said Idaho, a strange glint showing in his eyes.

"An' nobody can leave today, neither," said Corwin. "If they try it they will be stopped," he added, pointedly. "I've got a deputy coverin' every way out, sand or no sand. So-long," and he tramped down the bare stairs, grumbling at every step.

Johnny removed his hat to put on his shirt, and then replaced it. "You speakin' about sand in yore hair gave me what I needed," he grinned.

"That's why I said it," laughed his companion. "I saw that yore neck was stiff an' felt sorry for you. Now what th' devil do you think about that bank?"

"Kane," grunted Johnny, pouring sand from a boot.

"That name musta been cut on th' butt of th' gun that hit you," chuckled Idaho. "It's been drove in solid. Get a rustle on; I'm hungry, an' my teeth are full of sand. I'm anxious to hear what Ed knows."

An unpleasant and gritty breakfast out of the way, they went in to visit with the bartender and to while away a few hours at California Jack.

"Hello," grunted Ed. "Sheriff come pokin' his face in *yore* room?" he asked.

"He did," answered Johnny; "an' he'll never know how close he came to pokin' it into hell."

"My boot just missed him," regretted Ed. "He sung out right prompt when he felt th' wind of it. Damned four-flush."

"I'm among friends an' sympathizers," chuckled Idaho. "He says as how he's goin' wanderin' around in th' sand blasts doin' his duty. Duty nothin'! I'm bettin' he's settin' in Kane's, right now, takin' it easy."

"Then he can't get much closer to 'em," snorted Ed. "He can near touch th' men that did it." He paused as Johnny laughed in Idaho's face and, shrugging his shoulders, turned and rearranged the glasses on the backbar: "All right; laugh and be damned!" he snorted; "but would you look at that shelf an' them glasses? Cuss any country that moves around like that. I bet I got some of them Dry Arroyo sand hills in them glasses!"

"There was plenty in th' hash this mornin'," said Idaho; "but it didn't taste like that Dry Arroyo sand. It wasn't salty enough. Gimme a taste of that."

"Just because you'll make a han'some corpse ain't no reason why you should be in any hurry," retorted Ed. "Here!" he snorted, tossing a pack of cards on the bar. "Go over an' begin th' wranglin' agin—'though th' Lord knows I ain't got nothin' agin' Nelson." He glanced out of the window. "Purty near blowed out. It'll be ca'm in another half-hour; an' then you get to blazes out of here, an' stay out till dark!"

"I wish I had yore happy disposition," said Idaho. "I'd shore blow my brains out."

"There wouldn't be anythin' to clean up, anyhow!" retorted Ed. "Lord help us, here comes Silent Lewis!"

"Hello, fellers!" cried the newcomer. "Gee but it's been some storm. Sand's all over everythin'. Hear about th' bank robbery?"

"Bank robbery?" queried Ed, innocently. "What bank robbery? Sand bank?" he asked, sarcastically.

"Sand bank! Sand bank nothin'!" blurted Silent. "Ain't you heard it yet? Why, I live ten miles out of town, an' I know all about it."

"I believe every word you say," said Ed. "Tell us about it."

"Gee, where have you-all been?" demanded Silent. "Why, John Reddy, settin' on his chair, watchin' th' safe, hears a moanin', so he opened th' door—"

"Of th' safe?" asked Idaho, curiously.

"No, no; of th' bank. Th' bank door, th' rear one. He hears a moan—"

"Which moan; first, or second?" queried Ed, anxiously.

"Th' first—th' second didn't come till—hey, I thought you didn't hear about it?" he accused.

"I didn't; but you mentions two moans, separate an' distinct," defended Ed.

"You shore did," said Idaho, firmly.

Johnny nodded emphatically. "Yessir; you shore did. Two moans, one at each end."

"But I didn't get to th' second moan at all!"

"Now, what's th' use of tellin' us that?" flared the bartender. "Don't you think we got ears?"

"If you can't tell it right, shut up," said Idaho.

"I can tell it right if you'll shut up!" retorted Silent. "As I said, he hears a moan, so he leaves th' safe an' goes to th' door. Then he hears a second moan, scratchin', an'—"

"Hey!" growled Ed indignantly. "What you talkin' about? Who in hell ever heard of a second moan scratchin'—"

"It was th' first that scratched," corrected Idaho. "He said it plain. You must be listenin' with yore feet."

"If you'd gimme a chance to tell it—" began Silent, bridling.

"Never mind my hearin' you," snapped Ed at Idaho. "I know what I heard. An' lemme tell you, Silent, you can't cram nothin' like that down my throat. Before you go any further, just explain to me how a moan can scratch! I'm allus willin' to learn, but I want things explained careful an' full."

"He ain't quick-witted, like you an' me," said Johnny. "We understand how a scratch moans, but he's too dumb. Go on an' tell th' ignoramus."

"If yo're so cussed quick-witted, will you please tell me what'n blazes you are talkin' about?" demanded Silent, truculently. "What do you mean by a scratch moans?"

"That's what I want to know," growled Idaho. "You can't scratch moans. Cuss it, reckon I ought to know, for I've tried to do it, more'n once, too."

"Yo're dumber than Nelson," jeered Ed. "It's all plain to me."

"What is?" snapped Idaho.

"Moanin' scratches, that's what!"

"Of a safe?" asked Johnny. "Then why didn't you say so? How'd *I* know that you meant that. Go on, Silent."

"You was at th' second moan," prompted Ed.

"He scratched that," said Idaho. "He got as far as leavin' th' safe, 'though what he was doin' in there with it, I'd like to know. Reddy let you in?"

"Look here, Idaho," scowled Silent. "I wasn't in there at all. You'll get me inter trouble, sayin' things like that. I was ten miles away when it happened."

"Then why didn't you say so, at th' beginnin'?" asked Ed.

"Ah!" triumphantly exclaimed Johnny. "Then you tell us how you could hear th' scratchin' an' moanin'; tell us that!"

"That's all right, Nelson," said Idaho, soothingly. "He can hear more things when he's ten miles away than any man you ever knowed. Go ahead, Silent."

"You go to hell!" roared Silent, glaring. "You think yo're smart, don't you, *all* of you? I was goin' to tell you about th' robbery, but now you can cussed well find it out for yore-selves! An' don't let me hear about any of you sayin' I was in that bank last night, neither! Damned fools!" and he stamped out, slamming the door behind him. "Blow an' be damned!" he growled at the storm. "I'd ruther eat sand than waste time with them ijuts. 'Scratch moans!' Scratch *hell!*"

Silent's departure left a more cheerful atmosphere in the barroom. The three men he had forsaken were grinning at each other, the petty annoyances of the storm forgotten, and the next hour passed quickly. At its expiration the wind had died down and the storm-bound town was free again. Ed finished cleaning the bar and the glassware about the time that his two friends had swept the last of the sand into the street and cleared away a drift which blocked the rear door. They were taking a congratulatory drink when Ridley, coming to town for the mail himself because he would not ask any of his men to face the discomforts of that ride, stamped in, and his face was like a thunder cloud.

"Gimme a drink!" he demanded, and when he had had it he swung around and glared at Idaho. "Lukins have any money in that bank? Yes? You better be off to let him know about it. Hell of a note: Thirty thousand stole! An' Jud Hill holdin' a gun on *me* when I rode into town, askin' fool questions! An' let me tell you somethin'—judgin' from th' tools they forgot to take with 'em, it wasn't no amatachures that did that job. Diamond drills an' cow-country crooks don't know each other. An' that Jud Hill, a-stoppin' *me!*"

"Mebby he won't let you leave town," suggested Idaho. "Corwin's given orders like that."

Ridley crashed his fist on the bar, and then to better express his feelings he leaned over and stuck out his jaw. "Y-a-a-s? Then I'm invitin' you-all to Hill's funeral, an' Corwin's, too, if he cuts in! *Thirty thousand!* Great land of cows!"

"Corwin's out now, huntin' for 'em," said Ed.

"Is he?" sneered Ridley. "Then he wants to find 'em! Th' firm of Twitchell an' Carpenter owns near half of that bank—every dollar th' Question-Mark has was in it. There's a change comin' to this part of th' country!" and he stamped out, mounted his horse and whirled down the trail. When he reached the sentry he rode so close to him that their legs rubbed and Hill's horse began to give ground.

"Do I go on?" snapped Ridley.

Jud Hill nodded pleasantly. "Shore. Seein' as how you come in this mornin' I reckon you do."

Ridley urged his horse forward without replying, reached the ranchhouse, wrote a letter which was a masterpiece of its kind and gave it to one of his men to post in Larkinville, twenty miles to the south. That done, all he could do was impatiently await the reply.

After Ridley had left, Johnny went out to look after Pepper, found her all right, cleaned the sand out of the feed box and then went down to look at the bank. Four men with rifles were posted around it and waved him away. He could see several other men busy in the building, but beyond that there was nothing to claim his attention. Joining the small crowd of idlers across the street he listened to their conjectures, which were entirely vague and colorless, and then wandered back to look for Idaho in Quayle's. His friend was not to be seen and after exchanging a few words with the jovial proprietor he went in to talk with the bartender.

"No wind now, but my throat's dry. Gimme a drink, half water," and holding it untasted for the moment he jerked his head backward in the direction of the bank. "Nothin' to see, except some fellers inside lookin' for 'most anythin', an' four men with Winchesters on th' outside."

While he was speaking a man had entered and seated himself in the rear of the room. Johnny glanced carelessly at him, and the glass cracked sharply in his convulsive grip, the liquor squirting through his fingers and gathering a deeper color as it passed. A thin trickle of blood ran down his hand and wrist.

Ed had started at the sound and his head was bent forward, his unbelieving eyes staring at the dripping hand.

Johnny opened it slowly, shook the fragments from it and let it fall to his side, mechanically shaking off blood and liquor. "Cuss it, Ed," he gently reproved, looking calmly into the bartender's questioning face, "you should ought to pick out th' bad ones an' throw 'em away—yes, an' bust 'em first."

Ed picked up the bottom of the glass and critically examined it, noting a discolored strip along one of the sharp edges, where dirt had accumulated from numberless washings. The largest fragment showed the greasy line to the rounded brim. "I usually do," he growled. "Thought I had this one, too. Musta got back somehow. Hurt bad?"

"Nothin' fatal, I reckon," answered Johnny, drawing the injured member up his trousers leg. "But I'm sayin' you owe me another drink; an' leave th' water out, this time. Water in whisky never does bring good luck, nohow."

Ed smiled, pushing out bottle and glass. "We might say

that one was on th' house—all that didn't get on you." He instinctively reached for and used the bar cloth as he looked over at the stranger. "I can promise you one that ain't cracked," he smiled.

"I'll take mine straight," said Bill Long. "I don't want no more hard luck."

"Wonder where Idaho is?" asked Johnny. "Well, if he comes in, tell him I'm exercisin' my cayuse. Reckon I'll go down an' chin with Ridley this afternoon. Th' south trail is less sandy than th' north one."

"An' give Corwin a chance to say things about you?" asked Ed, significantly. "He'll be lookin' for a peg to hang things on."

"Then mebby he won't never look for any more."

"That may be true; but what's th' use?"

"Reckon yo're right," reluctantly admitted Johnny. "Guess I'll go up to Kane's an' see what's happenin'. If Idaho comes in, or any more of my numerous friends," he grinned, "send 'em up there if they're askin' for me. I'll mebby be glad to see 'em," and he sauntered out.

Ed smiled pleasantly at the other customer. "Bad thing, a glass breakin' like that," he remarked.

Bill Long looked at him without interest. "Serves him right," he grunted, "for holdin' it so tight. Nobody was aimin' to take it away from him, was they?"

Johnny entered Kane's too busy thinking to give much notice to the room and the suppressed excitement occasioned by the robbery, and sat down at a table. As he leaned back in the chair he caught sight of a red-headed puncher talking to one of Kane's card-sharps and he got another shock. "Holy maverick!" he muttered, and looked carelessly around to see if any more of his Montana friends had dropped into town. Then he smiled as the card-sharp, looking up, beckoned to him. As he passed down the room he noticed the quiet easterner hunched up in a corner, his cap well down over his eyes, and Johnny wondered if the man ever wore it any other way. He was out of place in his cow-town surroundings—perhaps that was why he had not been seen outside of Kane's building. Ridley's remark about the tools came to him and he hesitated, considered, and then went on again. He had no reason to do Corwin's work for him. Dropping into a vacant chair at the gambler's table he grunted the customary greeting.

"Howd'y," replied the card-sharp, nodding pleasantly. "No use bein' lonesome. Meet Red Thompson," he said, waving.

"Glad to meet you," said Johnny, truthfully, but hiding as well as he could the pleasure it gave him. "I once knowed a Thompson—short, fat feller. Worked up on a mountain range in Colorado. Know him?"

Red shook his head. "Th' world's full of Thompsons," he explained. "You punchin'?"

"Got a job on th' SV, couple of days' ride north of here. Just come down with a little beef herd for Twitchell an' Carpenter. Ain't seen no good bunch of yearlin's that can be got cheap, have you?"

Red shook his head: "No, I ain't."

The gambler laughed and poked a lean thumb at the SV puncher. "Modest feller, *he* is," he said. "He's foreman, up there."

Red's mild interest grew a little. "That so? I passed yore ranch comin' down. Need another man?"

The SV foreman shook his head. "I could do with one less. Them bank fellers picked a good time for it, didn't they?"

"They shore did," agreed the gambler. "Couldn't 'a' picked a better. Kane loses a lot by that, I reckon. Well, what do you gents say to a little game? Small enough not to cause no calamities; large enough to be interestin'? Nothin' else to do that I can see."

Red nodded and, the limit soon agreed upon, the game began. As the second hand was being dealt Bill Long wandered in, talked for a few moments with the bartender and then went over to a chair. Tipping it back against the wall he pulled down his hat brim, let his chin sink on his chest and prepared to enjoy a nap. Naturally a man wishing to doze would choose the darkest corner, and if he was not successful who could tell that the narrow slit between his lids let his keen eyes watch everything worth seeing? His attention was centered mostly on the tenderfoot stranger with the low-pulled cap and the cutout squares in the great checkerboard partition at the rear of the room.

The poker game was largely a skirmish, a preliminary feeling out for a game which was among the strong probabilities of the future. Johnny and the gambler were about even with each other at the breaking up of the play, but Red Thompson had lost four really worth-while jack pots to the pleasant SV foreman. As they roughly pushed back their chairs Bill Long stirred, opened his eyes, blinked around, frowned slightly at being disturbed and settled back again. "Red couldn't 'a' got that money to him in no better way," he thought, contentedly.

The three players separated, Johnny going to the hotel, Red seeking a chair by the wall, and the gambler loafing at the bar.

'An' how'd you find 'em?" softly asked the wise bartender. "Goin' after that foreman's roll?"

The gambler grunted and shifted his weight to the other leg. "Thompson ain't very much; but I dunno about th' other feller. Sometimes I think one thing; sometimes, another. Either he's cussed innocent, or too slick for me to figger. Reckon mebby Fisher ought to go agin' him, an' find out, for shore."

"How'd you make out, last night, with Long?"

"There's a man th' boss ought to grab," replied the gambler. "He didn't win much from me—but it's his first, an' last, chance with me. I don't play him no more. I'd like to see him an' Fisher go at it, with no limit. Fisher would have th' best of it on th' money end, havin' th' house behind him in case he had to weather a run of hard luck; but mebby he'd need it."

As the gambler walked away the easterner arose, slouched to the bar and held a short whispered conversation with the man behind it.

The bartender frowned. "You can't get away before night. Sandy Woods will take care of you before mornin', I reckon. Go upstairs an' quit fussin'. Yo're safe as hell!"

The bartender's prophecy came true after dark, when Sandy Woods and the anxious stranger quietly left town together; but the stranger had good reason to be anxious, for at dawn he was careless for a moment and found himself looking into his escort's gun. He had more courage than good sense and refused to be robbed, and he died for it. Sandy dragged the body into a clump of bushes away from the trail and then rode on to kill the necessary time, leading the other's horse. He was five thousand dollars richer, and had proved wrong the old adage about honor among thieves.

VI

♦

The Writing on the Wall

hen the senior member of the firm of Twitchell and Carpenter read Ridley's letter things began to happen. It was the last straw, for besides being half-owners in the bank the firm had for several years been annoyed by depredations committed by Mesquite citizens on its herds. The depredations had ceased upon payment of "campaign funds" to the Mesquite political ring, but the blackmail levy had galled the senior member, who was not as prone as Carpenter was to buy peace. Orders flew from the firm's office and the little printing-plant at Sandy Bend broke all its hazy precedents, with the result that a hard-riding courier, relaying twice, carried the work of the job-print toward Mesquite. Reaching Ridley's domain he turned the package over to the local superintendent, who joyously mounted and carried it to town.

Tim Quayle welcomed his old friend, listened intently to what Ridley had to say and handed over an assortment of tacks and nails, and a chipped hammer. " 'Tis time, Tom," he said, simply.

Ridley went out and selected a spot on the hotel wall, and the sound of the hammer and the sight of his unusual occupation caused a small crowd of curious idlers to gather around him. When the poster was unrolled there were sibilant whispers, soft curses, frank prophecies, and some commendations, which were entirely a matter of the personal viewpoint. Half an hour later, the last poster placed, Ridley took a short cut, entered the hotel through the kitchen and went into the barroom. What he had published for the enlightenment, edification, or disapprobation of his fellow-citizens was pointed and business-like, and read as follows:

$2,500.00 REWARD!

For Information Leading to the Capture
and Conviction of the Men Who Robbed
the Mesquite Bank.
STRICTLY CONFIDENTIAL
TWITCHELL & CARPENTER
Sandy Bend   TOM RIDLEY, Local Supt.

Quayle turned and smiled at the T & C man. "Ye've slapped their faces, Tom. Mind yore eye!"

"They've prodded th' old mosshead once too often," growled Ridley, looking around at Johnny, Idaho, and the others. "I reckon this stops th' blackmail to th' gang. When I wrote my letter I expected somethin' would happen, an' th' letter I got in return near curled my hair. Twitchell's fightin' mad."

"Th' reward's too big," criticized Idaho.

"I'm fearin' it ain't big enough," said Ed Doane, shaking his head.

Ridley laughed contentedly. "It's more than enough. There's men in this town, an' that gang, who would knife anybody for half of that. When they can get twenty-five hundred by simply openin' their mouths, without bein' known, they'll do it. Loyalty is fine to listen about, but there's few men in th' gang we're after that have any twenty-five hundred dollars' worth. This is th' beginnin' of th' end. Mark my words."

"A lot depends on how many were in on it," suggested Johnny, "an' how many of th' others know about it."

"He's throwin' money away," doggedly persisted Idaho. "A thousand would buy any of 'em, that an' secrecy."

"He ain't throwin' it away," retorted Ridley, "considerin' his letter. He's after results, amazin' results, an' he shore knows how to get 'em. It'll be sort of more pleasant if th' gang is sold out. He figgers a reward like that will save time an' be self-actin', for my orders are to stay in th' ranchhouse an' wait. That's what I'm goin' to do, too; an' I'll be settin' there with all guns loaded. No tellin' what'll happen now an', not bein' able to say how soon it will happen, I'm leavin' you boys. So-long."

He walked out to his horse and mounted. As he settled into the saddle there was a flat report, his hat flew from his head and he toppled from the horse, dead before he struck the ground.

Quayle swiftly reached over the desk and took a Winchester from its pegs, Irish tears in his eyes; and waited hopefully, Irish rage in his heart, watching the dirty windows and the open door. "It's to a finish, byes," he grated in a brogue thickened by his emotions, the veins of his forehead and neck swelling into serpentine ridges. "They read th' writin' on th' wall, an' they read ut plain. D'ye mind what some of thim divils would be after doin' for all that money? They'd cut their own mither's throat—an' Kane knows ut! An' I'm thinkin' they'll be careful now—Kane has served his notice."

The idlers in the street stood as if frozen, gaping, not one of them daring to approach the body, nor even to stop the horse as it kicked up its heels and trotted down the street. Ed Doane was the third man through the door and he brought in the dead man's hat as Johnny and Idaho placed the warm body on the floor of the office. They hardly had stepped back when hurried footsteps neared the door and the sheriff, with two of his deputies, entered the office, paused instinctively at sight of the rifle in Quayle's hands, and then slowly, carefully bent over to examine the body. The sheriff reached forth a hand to turn it over, but stopped instantly and froze in his stooped position, his arm outstretched.

"Kape ut off him!" roared Quayle, his eyes blazing. "What more d'ye want to see?"

"From behind?" asked Corwin, slowly straightening up, but his eyes fixed on the proprietor.

"An' where'd ye be thinkin' 'twas from?" snarled Quayle, the veins standing out anew. "No dirty pup of that pack would dare try ut from th' front, an' ye know ut! An' need ye look twice to see where th' slug av a buffalo-gun came out? Don't touch him, anny av ye! Kape yore paws off Tom Ridley! An' *I*'m buryin' him, mesilf."

"But, as sheriff—" began Corwin.

"Aye, *but!*" snapped Quayle. "We'll be after callin' things be their right names. Ye are no sheriff. Ye was choosed by th' majority av votes cast by th' citizens av an unorganized county, like byes choose a captain av their gangs. There's no laws to back ye up, an' ye took no oath. As long as th' majority will it, yore th' keeper av th' peace—an' no longer. Sheriff?" he sneered. "An' 'tis a fine sheriff ye'll be makin', rennin' in circles like a locoed cow since th' robbery, questionin' every innocent man in town, an' hopin' 'twould blow over, an' die a natural death. But it's got th' breath av life in it now! What do ye think old Twitchell will be sayin' to *this?*" he thundered, his rigid arm pointing to the body on the floor. "Clear out, th' pack av ye! Ye've seen all ye need to!"

Corwin glanced at the body again, from it around the ring of set and angry faces, shrugged his shoulders and motioned to his deputies to leave. "We'll hold th' inquest here," he said, turning away.

"Ye'll hold no inquest!" roared Quayle. "Show me yore coroner! Inquest, is ut? I've held yore inquest already.

There's plenty av us here an' we say, so help us God, Tom Ridley was murdered, an' by persons unknown. There's yer inquest, an' yer findin's. What do ye say, byes?" he demanded. A low growl replied to him and he sneered again. "There! There's your inquest! As long as yer playin' sheriff, go out an' do yer duty; but look out ye don't put yer han's on a friend! Clear out, an' run yer bluff!"

Corwin's eyes glinted as he looked at the fearless speaker, but with Idaho straining at a moral leash, Johnny's intent eagerness and the sight of the rifle in the proprietor's hands, he let discretion mold his course and slouched out to the street, where another quiet crowd opened silently to let him through.

Johnny passed close to Idaho. "Go to your ranch for a few days, or they'll couple you to me!" he whispered.

Bill Long, feeding his borrowed Highbank horse in the northernmost of the two stables at the rear of Kane's, heard the jarring crash of a heavy rifle so loud and near that he dropped instantly to hands and knees and crawled to a crack in the south wall. As he peered out he got a good, clear view of a pock-marked Mexican with a crescent-shaped scar over one eye and who, Sharps in hand, wriggled out of the north window of the adjoining stable, dropped sprawling within five feet of the watcher's eyes, scrambled to his feet and fled close along the rear of Bill's stable. The watcher sprang erect, sped silently back to his horse and stirred the grain in the feed box with one hand, while the other rested on a six-gun in case the Mexican should be of an inquisitive and belligerent frame of mind. His view of the street had been shut off by the corner of the southern stable and he had not seen the result of the shot. Wishing to show no undue curiosity he did not go down the street, but returned to the gambling-hall. He had not been seated more than a few minutes when one of Kane's retainers ran in from the street with the news of Ridley's death. There was a flurry of excitement, which quickly died down, but under the rippling surface Bill sensed the deeper, more powerful currents.

"This man Kane, whoever an' wherever he is," he thought, "has shore trained this bunch of scourin's. I'm gettin' plumb curious for a look at him. Huh!" he muttered, as the window-wriggling, pock-marked Mexican emerged from behind the partition, bent swiftly over Kit Thorpe and betook his tense and nervous self to the roulette table. "I've got yore ugly face carved deep in my mem'ry, you Greaser snake!" he growled under his breath. "If it wasn't for losin' bigger game I'd turn you over to Ridley's friends before night. You can wait."

Not long after the appearance of the Mexican, the sheriff came in by the front door, pushed through the crowd near the bar and walked swiftly toward the rear of the room. Speaking shortly to Kit Thorpe in a low voice he passed through the door of the checkerboard partition.

"I'm learnin'," muttered Bill. "I don't know who Kane is, but I'm dead shore I know *where* he is. An' I'm gettin' a better line on this killin'. I'll shore have to get a look behind that door, somehow."

Suddenly the doorkeeper arose and stuck his head around behind the partition and then, straightening up, closed the door, went up to the bar, spoke to several men there and led them to the rear. Opening the door again he let them through and resumed his vigil; and none of them reappeared before Bill went into the north building to eat his supper.

VII

◆

The Third Man

Kane's gambling-hall was in full blast, reeking with the composite odor of liquor, kerosene lamps, rank tobacco, and human bodies, the tables well-filled, the faro and roulette layouts crowded by eager devotees. The tenseness of the afternoon was forgotten and curses and laughter arose in all parts of the big room. The two-man Mexican orchestra strumming its guitars and the extra bartenders were earning their pay. Punchers, gamblers, storekeepers, two traveling men, a squad of cavalrymen on leave from the nearest post, Mexicans, and bums of several races made up the noisy crowd as Johnny Nelson pushed into the room and nodded to the head bartender.

"Well, well," smiled the busy barman without stopping his work. "Here's our SV foreman, out at night. Thought mebby you'd heard of some yearlin's an' hit th' trail after 'em."

"I don't reckon there was ever a yearlin' in this section," grinned Johnny.

"That so? There's several down at th' other end of th' bar," chuckled the man of liquor. "That blonde you left th' forty dollars for has shore been strainin' her eyes lookin' for you. Says she knows she's goin' to like you. Go back an' soothe her. Gin is her favorite."

"I ain't lookin' for her yet," replied Johnny. "That's somethin' you never want to do. It's th' wrong system. Don't pay no attention to 'em if you want 'em to pay attention to you. Let her wait a little longer. Where's that Thompson feller? I like th' way he plays draw, seein' as how I won some of his money. Seen him tonight?"

"Shore; he's around somewhere. Saw him a little while ago."

Johnny noticed a quiet, interested crowd in a far corner and joined it, working through until he saw two men playing poker in the middle. One was Bill Long and the other was Kane's best card-sharp, Mr. Fisher, and they were playing so intently as to be nearly oblivious of the crowd. On the other side of the ring, sitting on a table, was Red Thompson, his mouth partly open and his eyes riveted on the game.

The play was getting stiff and Fisher's eyes had a look in them that Johnny did not like. The gambler reached for the cards and began shuffling them with a speed and dexterity which bespoke weary hours of earnest practice. As he pushed them out for the cut his opponent leaned back, relaxed and smiled pleasantly.

"I allus like to play th' other fellow's game," Bill observed. "If he plays fast *I* like to play fast; if he plays 'em close, *I* like to play 'em close; if he plays reckless, *I* like to play reckless; if he plays 'em with flourishes, *I* like to play 'em with flourishes. I'm not what you might call original. I'm a imitator." He slowly reached out his hand, held it poised over the deck, changed his mind and withdrew it. "Reckon I'll not cut this time. They're good as they are. I like yore dealin'."

Fisher yanked the deck to him and dealt swiftly. "I'm not very bright," he remarked as he glanced at his hand, "so I'm gropin' about yore meanin'. Or didn't it have none?"

"Nothin', only to show that I'm so polite I allus let th' other feller set th' pace," smiled Bill. "As he plays, I play." He picked up the cards, squared them into exact alignment and slid them from the table and close against his vest, where a deft touch spread them for a quick glance at the pips. "They look good; but, I wonder?" he muttered. "Reckon that's best, after all. Gimme two cards when you get time."

Fisher gave him two and took the same number.

"I find I'm gettin' tired," growled Bill, "an' it shore is hot an' stiflin' in here. As it stands I'm a little ahead—not more'n fifty dollars. That bein' so, I quit after this hand and two more. There ain't much action, anyhow."

"If yo're lookin' for action mebby you feel like takin' off th' hobbles," suggested Fisher, carelessly.

"Hobbles, saddles an' anythin' else you can think of," nodded Bill. "Do we start now?"

Fisher nodded, saw the modest bet and doubled it.

Bill tossed his four queens and the ace of hearts face down in the discard and smiled. "Didn't get what I was lookin' for," he grinned into the set face across from him. "Got to have 'em before I can play 'em."

Fisher hid his surprise and carelessly tossed his four kings and the six of diamonds, also face down, into the discard, fumbled the deck as he went to pass it over and spilled it on top of the cards on the table. Cursing at his clumsiness, he scrambled the cards together and pushed them toward his opponent. "My fingers must be gettin' all thumbs," he growled as he raked in the money. What had happened? Had he bungled the deal, or wasn't four queens big enough for the talkative fool across from him?

Bill smilingly agreed. "They do get that way at times," he remarked, shuffling with a swift flourish which made Johnny hide a smile. He pushed the pack out, Fisher cut it, and the flying cards dropped swiftly into two neat piles almost flush on their edges, which seemed to merit a murmur of appreciation from the crowd. Johnny shifted his weight to the other leg and prepared to enjoy the game.

Fisher glanced at his hand and became instant prey to a turmoil of thoughts. Four queens, with an eight of clubs! He looked across at the calm, reflective dealer who was rubbing the disgraceful stubble on his chin while he drew two cards partly from his hand and considered them seriously. He seemed to be perplexed.

"I been playin' this game for more years than I feel like tellin'," Bill grumbled, whimsically; "but I ain't never been able really to decide one little thing." Becoming conscious that he might be delaying the game he looked up suddenly. "Have patience, friend. *Oh,* then it's all right! You ain't discarded yet," he finished cheerfully. Throwing away the two cards he waited.

"Gimme one," grunted Fisher, discarding, "an' I'm sayin' fifty dollars," he continued, shoving the money out without glancing at the card on the table. "How many you takin'?" he asked.

"Two," answered Bill, looking at him keenly. He glanced down at the single back showing on the table before him and grinned. "Th' other's under it," he explained needlessly. "Well, I'm still an imitator," he chuckled. "Here's yore fifty, and fifty more. I'm sorry I ain't playin' in my own town, so I could borrow when it all gets up."

Whatever Fisher's thoughts were he hid them well, and he was not to be the first one to weaken and look at the draw. He had a reputation to maintain, and he saw the raise and returned it. Bill pushed out a hundred dollars and Fisher came back, but his tenseness was growing.

Bill considered, looked down at his unknown draw, shook his head and picked up one card. "I'm feelin' the strain," he growled, seeing the raise and repeating it. He glanced up at the crowd, which had grown considerably, and smiled grimly.

Fisher evened up and raised again, watching his worried opponent, who scowled, sucked his lips, shook his head and then, with swift decision, picked up the other card. "I can't afford to quit now," he muttered. "Here goes for another boost!"

His opponent having wilted first and saved the gambler's face, Fisher picked up his own draw and when he saw it he stiffened, his thoughts racing again. It was no coincidence, he decided. In all of his experience he had known but two men who could do that, and here was a third! But still there was a hope that there was no third, that it was a coincidence. And there was quite a sum of money on the table. The doubt must be removed and the truth known, and another fifty, sent after its brothers was not too big a price to pay for such knowledge. He pushed the money out onto the table. "I calls," he grunted.

Bill dropped his little block of cards and spread them with a sweep of one hand, while the other was ready to make the baffling draw which had made him famous in other parts of the country. Fisher glanced at the four kings and nodded, all doubts laid to rest—the third man sat across from him.

He slowly pushed back as the crowd, not knowing just what to expect, scattered. "I'm tired. Shall we call it off for tonight?" he asked.

Without relaxing Bill nodded. "Suits me. I'm tired, too; an' near suffocated. See you tomorrow?"

Fisher grunted something as he arose and, turning abruptly, pushed through the thinning crowd to get a bracer at the bar, while the winner slowly hauled in the money. Gulping down the fiery liquor the gambler wheeled to go into the dark and deserted dining-room where he could sit in quiet and go over the problem again, and looked up to see the other gambler in his way.

"What did you find out?" asked the other in a low voice.

"I found th' devil has come up out of hell!" growled Fisher. "Come along an' I'll tell you about it. He's th' third man! Old Parson Davies was th' first, but he's dead; Tex Ewalt was th' second, an' I ain't seen him in years—cuss it! I wondered why this man's play seemed familiar! He's got some of Tex's tricks of handlin' th' cards."

"Shore he ain't Tex?"

"As shore as I am that you ain't," retorted Fisher; "but I'm willin' to bet he knows Tex. Come on—let's get out of this hullabaloo. He's got a nerve, pickin' *my* cards, an' dealin' 'em alternate off th' top an' bottom, with *me* watchin' him!"

"We got to figger how to get it back," thoughtfully muttered the other, following closely. "Everythin's goin' wrong. They went after Nelson an' got somebody else; they stirred up th' T & C by robbin' th' bank, an' then had to go an' make it worse by gettin' Ridley! I'm admittin' I'm walkin' soft, an' ready to jump th' country right quick."

Fisher sank into a chair in the dining-room. "An' if Long hangs around here much longer Kane'll ditch me like a wore-out boot. A couple more losses like tonight an' he'll plumb forget my winnin's for th' past two years. An' me gettin' all cocked to strike him for a bigger percentage!"

Out in the reeking gambling-hall Bill put his empty glass on the bar and slid a gold piece at the smiling head man behind the counter. "Spend th' change on th' ladies in th' corner," he said. "It allus gives me luck; an' I had such luck tonight that I ain't aimin' to take no chances losin' it. Reckon I'll horn in on th' faro layout," and he did, where he managed to lose a part of his poker winnings before he turned in for the night.

Up late the next morning he hastened into the dining-room to beat the closing of the doors and saw the head bartender eating a lonely breakfast. The dispenser of liquors beckoned and pushed back a chair at his table.

Bill accepted the invitation and gave his order. "Well," he remarked, "yo're lookin' purty bright this mornin'."

"I'm gettin' so I don't need much sleep, I reckon," replied the bartender. "Did yore folks use a poker deck to cut yore teeth on?"

Bill laughed heartily. "My luck turned, an' Fisher happened to be th' one that got in th' way."

"He says you play a lot like a feller he used to know."

"That so? Who was he?"

"Tex Ewalt."

"Well, I ought to, for me an' Tex played a lot together, some years back. Wonder what ever happened to Tex? He ain't been down this way lately, has he?"

"No. I never saw him. Fisher knew him. He says Tex was th' greatest poker player that ever lived."

"I reckon he's right," replied Bill. "I'm plumb grateful to Tex. It ain't his fault that I don't play a better game. But I got an idea playin' like his has got to be born in a man." He ate silently for a moment. "Now that I'm spotted I reckon my poker playin' is over in here. Oh, well, I ain't complainin'. I can eat an' sleep here, an' find enough around town to keep me goin' for a little while, anyhow. Then I'll drift."

"Unless, mebby, you play for th' house," suggested the bartender. "What kind of a game does that SV foreman play?"

"I never like to size a man up till I play with him," answered Bill. "I was sort of savin' him for myself, for he's got a fat roll. Now I reckon I'll have to let somebody else do th' brandin'." He sighed and went on with his breakfast.

"Get him into a little game an' see how good he is," suggested the other, arising. "Goin' to leave you now." He turned away and then stopped suddenly, facing around again. "Huh! I near forgot. Th' boss wants to see you."

"Who? Kane? What about?"

"He'll tell you that, I reckon."

"All right. Tell him I'm in here."

The other grinned. "I said th' *boss* wants to see *you*."

"Shore; I heard you."

"People he wants to see go to him."

"Oh, all right; why didn't you say so first off? Where is he?"

"Thorpe will show you th' way. Whatever th' boss says, don't you go on th' prod. If yore feelin's get hurt, don't relieve 'em till you get out of his sight."

"I've played poker too long to act sudden," grinned Bill, easily.

His breakfast over, he sauntered into the gambling-room and stopped in front of Kit Thorpe, whose welcoming grin was quite a change from his attitude of the day before. "I've been told Kane wants to see me. Here I am."

Thorpe opened the door, followed his companion through it and paused to close and bolt it, after which he kept close to the other's heels and gave terse, grunted directions. "Straight ahead—to th' left—to th' right—straight ahead. Don't make no false moves after you open that door. Go ahead—push it open."

Bill obeyed and found himself in an oblong room which ran up to the opaque glass of a skylight fifteen feet above the floor, and five feet below the second skylight on the roof, in both of which the small panes were set in heavy metal bars. The room was cool and well ventilated. Before him, seated at the far side of a flat-topped, walnut desk of ancient vintage sat a tall, lean, white-haired man of indeterminate age, who leaned slightly forward and whose hands were not in sight.

"Sit down," said Kane, in a voice of singular sweetness and penetrating timbre. For several minutes he looked at his visitor as a buyer might look at a horse, silent, thoughtful, his deeply-lined face devoid of any change in its austere expression.

"Why did you come here?" he suddenly snapped.

"To get out of th' storm," answered Bill.

"Why else?"

Bill looked around, up at the graven Thorpe and back again at his inquisitor, and shrugged his shoulders. "Mebby you can tell me," he answered before he remembered to be less independent.

"I think I can. Anyone who plays poker as well as you do has a very good reason for visiting strange towns. What is your name?"

"Bill Long."

"I know that. I asked, what *is* your name?"

Bill looked around again and then sat up stiffly. "That ain't interestin' us."

"Where are you from?"

Bill shrugged his shoulders and remained silent.

"You are not very talkative today. How did you get that Highbank horse?"

Bill acted a little surprised and anxious. "I—I don't know," he answered foolishly.

"Very well. When you make up your mind to answer my questions I have a proposition to offer you which you may find to be mutually advantageous. In the meanwhile, do not play poker in this house. That's all."

Thorpe coughed and opened the door, and swiftly placed a hand on the shoulder of the visitor. "Time to go," he said.

Bill hesitated and then slowly turned and led the way, saying nothing until he was back in the gambling-hall and Thorpe again kept his faithful vigil over the checkered door.

"Cuss it," snorted Bill, remembering that in the part he was playing he had determined to be loquacious. "If I told him all he wanted to know I'd be puttin' a rope around my neck an' givin' him th' loose end! So he's got a proposition to make, has he? Th' devil with him an' his propositions. I don't have to play poker in his place—there's plenty of it bein' played outside this buildin', I reckon. For two-bits I'd 'a' busted his neck then an' there!"

"You'd 'a' been spattered all over th' room if you'd made a play," replied Thorpe, a little contempt in his voice for such boasting words from a man who had acted far from them when in the presence of Kane. He had this stranger's measure. "An' you mind what he said about playin' in here, or I'll make you climb up th' wall, you'll be that eager to get out. You think over what he said, an' drift along. I'm busy."

Bill, his frown hiding inner smiles, slowly turned and walked defiantly away, his swagger increasing with the distance covered; and when he reached the street he was exhaling dignity, and chuckled with satisfaction—he had seen behind the partition and met Kane. He passed the bank, once more normal, except for the armed guards, and bumped into Fisher, who frowned at him and kept on going.

"Hey!" called Bill. "I want to ask you somethin'."

Fisher stopped and turned. "Well?" he growled, truculently.

Bill went up close to him. "Just saw Kane. He says he has got somethin' to offer me. What is it?"

"My job, I reckon!" snapped the gambler.

"Yore job?" exclaimed his companion. "I don't want yore job. If I'd 'a' knowed that was it I'd 'a' told him so, flat. I'm playin' for myself. An' say: He orders me not to play no more poker in his place. Wouldn't that gall you?"

"Then I wouldn't do it," said the gambler, taking his arm. "Come in an' have a drink. What else did he say?"

Bill told him and wound up with a curse. "An' that

Thorpe said he'd make me climb up th' wall! Wonder who he thinks he is—Bill Hickok?"

Fisher laughed. "Oh, he don't mean nothin'. He's a lookin'-glass. When Kane laughs, *he* laughs; when Kane has a sore toe, *he's* plumb crippled. But, just th' same I'm tellin' you Thorpe's a bad man with a gun. Don't rile him too much. Say, was you ever paired up with Ewalt?"

Bill put down his glass with deliberate slowness. "Look here!" he growled. "I'm plumb tired of answerin' personal questions. Not meanin' to hurt yore feelin's none, I'm sayin' it's my own cussed business what my name is, where I come from, who my aunt was, an' how old I was when I was born. I never saw such an' old-woman's town!"

Fisher laughed and slapped his shoulder. "Keep all four feet on th' ground, Long; but it *is* funny, now ain't it?"

Bill grinned sheepishly. "Mebby—but for a little while I couldn't see it that way. Have one with me, after which I'm goin' up an' skin that SV man before you can get a crack at him. He's fair lopsided with money. If I can't play poker in Kane's, I shore can send a lot of folks to his place with nothin' left but their pants an' socks!"

"Don't overdo it," warned Fisher. "Come on—I'm headin' back an' I'll leave you at Quayle's."

"How'd you ever come to let that yearlin'-mad foreman keep away from yore game?" asked Bill as they started up the street. "Strikes me you shore overlooked somethin'."

"Does look like it, from a distance," admitted Fisher, grinning. "Reckon we was goin' too easy with him; but we didn't know you was goin' to turn up an' horn in. We never like to stampede a good prospect by bein' hasty. We felt him out a little an' I was figgerin' on amusin' him right soon. There's somethin' cussed odd about him. We're all guessin', an' guessin' different."

"Yes?" inquired Bill carelessly. "I didn't notice nothin'

odd about him. He acts a little too shore of hisself, which is how I like 'em. You ain't got a chance to get him now, for I'm goin' to set on his fool head an' burn a nice, big BL on his flank. So any little thing that you know shore will come in handy. I'd do th' same for you. I'm through spoilin' yore game in Kane's, an' I didn't take yore job. What's so odd about him?"

Fisher glanced at his companion and shook his head. "It ain't nothin' about cards. He figgered in a mistake that was made, an' don't know how lucky he was. Th' boss don't often slip up—an' there's a white man an' some Greasers in this town that are cussed lucky too. They blundered, but they got what they went after. An' nobody's heard a word about th' gent that was *un*lucky, which makes me suspicious. I got a headache tryin' to figger it." He shook his head again and then exclaimed in sudden anger: "An' I've quit tryin'! Kane was all set to throw me into th' discard as soon as you come along. He can think what he wants to, for all I care. But let me tell you this: If you win a big roll in this town, an' th' one you got now is plenty big enough, be careful how you wander around after dark. I reckon I owe you that much, anyhow."

Bill stopped in front of the hotel. "I don't know what yo're talkin' about, but that don't make no difference. Th' last part was plain. Come in an' have somethin'."

Fisher looked at him and smiled. "Friend, I'd just as soon be seen goin' in there *now* as I would be seen rustlin' a herd; an' it might even be worse for me. Let it go till you come up to our place. *Adios*."

VIII

◆

Notes Compared

Entering the barroom of the hotel Bill bought a cigar, talked aimlessly for a few minutes with Ed Doane and then wandered into the office, where Johnny was seated in a chair tipped back against the wall and talking to the proprietor. Bill nodded, took a seat and let himself into the conversation by easy stages, until Quayle was talking to him as much as he was to Johnny, and the burden of his words was Ridley's death.

Bill spat in disgust. "*That* ain't th' way to get a man!" he exclaimed. "Looks like some Greaser had a grudge agin' him—somebody he's mebby fired off his payroll, or suspected of cattle-liftin'."

"You're a stranger here," replied the proprietor. "I can tell ut aisy."

"I am, an' glad of it," replied Bill, smiling; "but I'm learnin' th' ways of yore town rapid. I already know Fisher's poker game, Thorpe's nature, an' Pecos Kane's looks an' disposition. I cleaned Fisher at poker, Thorpe has threatened to make me climb up a wall, an' Kane told me, cold an' personal, to quit playin' poker in his place. I also learned that a white man an' some Greasers made a big mistake, but got what they went after; that Fisher figgers different from Kane an' th' others; an' that Kane won't slip up th' next time, after dark, 'specially if he don't use th' same fellers. All that I heard; but what it's about I don't know, or care."

Johnny was laughing at the humor of the newcomer, and waved from Bill to Quayle. "Tim, this is Bill Long, that we heard about, for I saw him clean out Fisher. Long, this is

Quayle, an' my name's Nelson. Cuss it man! *I'd* say you was gettin' acquainted fast. What was that you was sayin' about th' white man an' th' Greasers, an' some mistake? It was sort of riled up."

"It *is* riled up," chuckled Bill, crossing his legs. "I gave it out just like I got it. As I says to Fisher last night, I'm a imitator. Any news about th' robbery?"

Quayle snorted. "Fine chance! An' d'ye think they'd be after tellin' on thimselves? That's th' only way for any news to be heard."

"I may be a stranger," replied Bill; "but I'm no stranger to human nature, which is about th' same in one place as it is in another. If that reward don't pan out some news, then I'm loco."

Quayle listened to a call from the kitchen. "It's th' only chance, then," he flung over his shoulder as he left them. "It's that damned Mick. I'll be back soon."

Johnny, with a glance at the barroom door, leaned slightly forward and whispered one word, his eyes moist: "*Hoppy!*"

Bill Long squirmed and grinned. "*You flat-headed sage-hen!*" he breathed. "*I want to see you in secret.*"

Johnny nodded. "I reckon th' reward might start somethin' out in th' open, but I wouldn't want to be th' man that tried for it." His voice dropped to a whisper. "*We'll take a ride this afternoon from Kane's, plain an' open.*" In his natural voice he continued. "But, Twitchell an' Carpenter are shore powerful. An' they've got th' men an' th' money."

"Do you reckon anybody had a personal grudge?" asked Bill. "*I'll fix it.*"

"I'm near as much a stranger here as you are," answered Johnny, "though I sold Ridley some cattle. I met him before, on th' range around Gunsight. Nice feller, he was. *What time?*"

"He musta been a good man, to work for th' T & C," replied Bill. *"After dinner."*

"He was."

"Oh, well; it ain't *my* funeral. Feel like a little game?"

"I used to think I could play poker," chuckled Johnny; "but I woke up last night. Seein' as how I still got them yearlin's to buy, I don't feel like playin'."

Quayle's voice boomed out suddenly from the kitchen. "If yer fingers was feet ye'd be as good! *Hould* it, now—if ut slips this time I'll be after bustin' yer head. I've showed ye a dozen times how to put it back, an' still ye yell fer me. *There,* now—*hould* it! Hand me th' wire—annybody'd think—blast th' blasted man that made ut! Some Dootchman, I'll wager."

"Shure an' we ought to get a new wan—it's warped crooked, an' cracked—"

"We should, should we?" roared the proprietor. "An' who are 'we'? Only tin years old, an' it's a new wan we'd be gettin', is ut? What we ought to be gettin' is a new cook, an' wan that's *not* cracked. Now, th' nixt time ye poke ut, poke gintly—ye ain't makin' post holes with that poker. An' *now* look at me—" A door slammed and a washbasin sounded like tin.

Ed Doane's laugh sounded from the barroom and he appeared in the doorway, where he grinned. "I hear it frequent, but it's allus funny. Sometimes they near come to blows."

"Stove?" queried Bill.

"Shore—th' grate's buckled out of shape, an' it's a little short. Murphy gets mad at th' fire an' prods it good—an' then th' show starts all over again. It's funnier than th' devil when th' old man gets a blister from it, for he talks so that nobody but Murphy can understand one word in ten. Easy! Here he comes."

"Buy a new wan, is ut?" muttered the proprietor, his red

face bearing a diagonal streak of soot. "Shure—for him to spile, like he spiled this wan. Ah, byes, I'm tellin' ye th' hotel business ain't what it used to be."

"Yore face looks funny," said Ed.

Quayle turned on him. "Oh, it does, does ut? Well, if my face don't suit ye—now would ye look at that?" he demanded as he caught sight of his reflection in the dingy mirror over the desk. "But it ain't so bad, at that; th' black's above th' red!"

"Hey, Tim!" came from the kitchen. "Thought ye said ye fixed ut? Ut's down agin!"

"I—I—I!" sputtered Quayle wildly. He spread the soot over his face with a despairing sweep of his sleeve, leaped into the air and started on a lumbering run for the kitchen. "You—I—*damn* it!" he yelled, and the kitchen resounded to his bellowing demands for the cook.

Ed Doane wiped his eyes, looked around—and shouted, his out-thrust hand pointing to a window, where a red face peered into the room.

"Shure," said the cook, apologetically, "he's the divvil himself. If I stay here wan more day me name ain't Murphy. Will wan av yez, that ain't go no interest in th' dommed stove, tell that Mick to buy a new grate? An' would ye listen to him *now?*"

When he was able to Bill arose. "Well, I reckon I'll go up an' look in at Kane's. If I run this way, don't stop me."

Sauntering up the street he came to the south side of the gambling-hall and went along it, and when a certain number of paces beyond the fifth high window, the sill of which was above his head, he stumbled and fell. Swearing under his breath he picked up a Colt which had slipped from its holster and, arising to hands and knees, looked around and then stood up. He could see under the entire building except at the point where he had fallen, and there he saw that under Kane's private room the walls went down into the earth. When he reached the stables he entered the one which sheltered his horse, closed the door behind him and made a hasty examination of the building, but found nothing which made him suspect a secret exit. He came to the opinion that the boards went down to the earth below Kane's quarters for the purpose of not allowing anyone to crawl under his rooms. In a few minutes he led his horse outside, mounted and rode around to the front of the gambling-hall, where he dismounted and went in for a drink, scowling slightly at the vigilant and militant Mr. Thorpe, who returned the look with interest.

"Got a cayuse?" he asked the bartender.

The other shook his head. "No, why?"

"Thought mebby you'd like to ride along with me. That one of mine will be better for a little exercise. What's east of here?"

"Sand hills, dried lakes, an' th' desert."

"Then I'll go west," grinned Bill. "But mebby it's th' same?"

"It ain't bad over that way; but why don't you ride south? There's real good country down in them valleys."

"Ain't that where th' T & C is?"

The bartender nodded.

"West is good enough for me. Better get a cayuse an' come along."

"Can't do it, an' I ain't set a saddle in two years. I'd be a cripple if I stuck to you. Why don't you hunt up that Nelson feller? He ain't got nothin' to do."

"Just left him. Don't reckon he'd care to go. Huh!" he muttered, looking at the clock. "I reckon I'll eat first, an' ride after."

Shortly after dinner Johnny strolled in and nodded to the bartender, who immediately called to Bill Long.

"Here's Nelson now; mebby he'll go with you," he said.

"Go where?" asked Johnny, pausing.

"Ridin'."

"What for?"

"Exercise. He wants to take th' devilishness out of his horse. You got one, too, ain't you?"

"Shore have," answered Johnny. "An' she's gettin' mean, too. It ain't a bad idea. Where are you goin', Long?"

"Anywhere, everywhere, or nowhere," answered Bill carelessly. "I'm aiming to ride him to a frazzle, an' I got to cut down his feed more."

"All right, if you says so," agreed Johnny, joining the group.

Red Thompson rode up to the door and came in. "Hey, anybody that's goin' down th' trail wants to ride easy. That T & C gang are so suspicious that they're insultin'. Got four men ridin' along their wire, with rifles across their pommels. Looks like they was goin' on th' prod."

Thorpe silently withdrew, to reappear in a few minutes and resume his watch.

Bill arose and nodded to Johnny as he went out. "Ready, Nelson?" he asked.

In a few minutes they met in front of the gambling-hall, and the SV foreman's black caused admiring and covetous looks to show on the faces of the idle group.

"Foller th' trail leadin' to Lukins' ranch, over west," suggested Fisher. "It's better than cross-country. You'll strike it half a mile above."

Long nodded and led the way, both animals prancing and bucking mildly to work off some of their accumulated energy. Reaching the cross trail they swung along it at a distance-eating lope.

"Tell me about everythin'," suggested Johnny. "How'd you come to ride south?"

"Kid," said Hopalong, "you got th' best cayuse ever raised in Montanny. That Englishman was shore right: it pays to cross 'em with thoroughbreds." Moodily silent for a moment, he slowly continued. "Kid, I've lost Mary, an' William, Junior. Fever took 'em in four days, an' never even touched *me!* I'm all alone. Either you move up north, or I stay with you till I die. An' if I do that I'll miss Red an' th' others like th' devil. I'm goin' to have a good look at that Bar-H, that you chased them thieves off of. Montanny is too far north, an' I'm feelin' th' winters too hard. An' it's gettin' settled too fast, an' bein' ploughed up more every year. But all of this can wait: what's goin' on down here that I don't know?"

Johnny told him and when he had finished and listened to what his friend knew they spent the rest of the time discussing the situation from every angle and arranged a few simple signals, resurrected from the past, to serve in the press of any sudden need. They met two punchers riding in from Lukins' ranch, exchanged nods and then turned south into the cattle trail, crossed a crescent arroyo and turned again, when below the town, under the suspicious eyes of a Question-Mark sentry hidden in a thicket. Following the main trail north they entered the town and parted at Quayle's.

The evening passed uneventfully in Kane's and when the group began to break up Bill Long went up to his room. Gradually man after man deserted the gambling-hall, until only Johnny and the head bartender were left, and after half an hour's dragging conversation the dispenser of liquids yawned and nodded decisively.

"Nelson, I'm goin' to lock up after you. See you tomorrow."

"Most sensible words said tonight," replied Johnny, and he stepped out, the door closing behind him. The lights went out, one by one, with a tardiness due to their height from the floor, and he stood quietly for a moment, scrutinizing the sky and enjoying the refreshing coolness. Moving out into the middle of the street he sauntered toward the dark hotel, every sense alert as a previous experience came back to him. Suddenly a barely audible sound, like the cracking of a toe joint, caused him to leap aside. An indistinct figure plunged past him, so close that he felt the wind of it. His gun roared while he was in the air and when he alighted he was crouched, facing the rear, where another figure blundered into the second shot and dropped. Swiftly padding feet came nearer and he slipped further to the side, letting the sound pass without hindrance. Moving softly forward he turned and crept along the wall of a building, smiling grimly at the low Spanish curses behind him on the street. Again the kitchen door served him well and the deeper blackness of the interior silently engulfed him.

Up at Kane's, Red Thompson, who was awake and waiting until the building should be wrapped in sleep, heard the shots and crept to the window. He could see nothing, but he heard whispers and heavy, slow and shuffling steps, which drew steadily nearer. The Mexican tongue was no puzzle to Red, whose years largely had been spent in a country where it was constantly used and his fears, instantly aroused, were soon followed by a savage grin.

"That Nelson, he is a devil," floated up to him, the words a low growl.

"Again he got away. I will not face the Big Boss. It is the second failure, and with Anton dead, an' Juan's arm broken, I shall leave this town. Put him here, at the door. May God forgive his sins! *Adios!*"

"Wait, Sanchez!" called a companion. "We will all go, even Juan, for he'd better ride than remain. There will be trouble."

"What's all th' hellabaloo?" came Thorpe's truculent voice in English from the corner of the building, where he stood, clad only in boots and underwear, a six-shooter in his upraised hand. At the sudden soft scurrying of feet he started forward, and then checked himself.

"If them Greasers bungled it *this* time, may th' Lord help 'em. They'll shore get aplenty. I wouldn't be—" he stopped and stared at the door, and then moved closer to it. "By God, they *got* him!" he whispered, and bent down, his hand passing over the indistinct figure. "Huh! I take it all back," he muttered in disgust. "That's a Greaser, by feel an' smell. They made more of a mess of it this time than they did before. Well, you ain't no fit ornament for th' front door. Might as well move you myself," and, grumbling, he grabbed hold of the collar and dragged the unresisting bulk around to the rear, where he carelessly dropped it and went back into the building. Soon two Mexicans, rubbing sleepy eyes, emerged with shovel and spade, that the dawn should find nothing more than a carefully hidden grave.

Red waited a little longer and then, knowing better than to go on his feet along the old floor of the hall, inched slowly over it on his stomach, careful to let each board take his weight gradually. Reaching the second door on his left he slowly pushed it open, chuckling with pride at his friend's forethought in oiling the one squeaking hinge. Closing it gently he scratched on the floor twice and then went on again toward the answering scratch. An hour passed in the softest of whispering and when he at last entered his own room again and carefully stood up, the darkness hid a rare smile on his tanned and leathery face, which an exultant thought had lighted.

"Th' Old Days: They're comin' back again!" he gloated. "Me, an' Hoppy, an' the Kid! Glory be!" and the smile persisted until he awakened at dawn, when it moved from the wrinkled face to the secrecy of his heart.

IX

♦

Ways of Serving Notice

If Sandy Bend had been seized with a local spasm when the senior member of the T & C had learned of the robbery of the Mesquite bank, it now was having a very creditable fit. The little printing-shop was the scene of bustling activities and soon a small bundle of handbills was on its way to the office of the cattle king. McCullough, drive-boss *par excellence* and one of the surviving frontiersmen who not only had made history in several localities, but had helped to wear the ruts in the old Santa Fe Trail until the creeping roadbed of the railroad had put the trail with other interesting relics of the past, was rudely torn from his seven-up game with his cronies by one of the several couriers who lathered horses at the snapping behest of the senior partner. He hastened to the office, rumbled across the outer room and pushed open the door of the holy of holies without even the semblance of a knock. He was blunt, direct, and no respecter of persons.

"Hello, Charley!" he grunted. "What's loose now?"

"Hell's loose!" snapped Twitchell. "Ridley's been murdered by one of Kane's gang. Shot in th' back—head near blowed off. There's only four men up there now, an' they may be dead by this time. Take as many men as you need an' go up there—we just bought a herd of SV cows, if there's any left. But I want th' man that killed Ridley. That's first. I want th' man who robbed th' bank—that's second. An' I want Pecos Kane—that's first, second, an' third. Damn it! I growed up with Tom Ridley!"

"I'll take twenty men an' bring you th' whole gang—but

some of 'em will shore spoil before we can get 'em here, this kind of weather. Do I burn that end of th' town?"

"You'll burn nothin'," retorted Twitchell. "You'll not risk a man until you have to. You'll stay on th' ranch an' watch th' cattle. I've lost one good man now, an' I'm spendin' money before I risk losin' any more. There's a bundle of handbills. When they've been digested by that bunch of assassins you can sit in th' bunkhouse an' have yore game delivered to you, all tied up, an' tagged."

"Orders is orders," growled McCullough; "but some are damned fool orders. If you want somebody to set on th' front porch an' whittle, why'n hell are you cuttin' *me* out of th' herd for th' job?"

"I'm cuttin' you out because I want my best man out there!" retorted the senior member heatedly. "You may find it lively settin', an' have to do yore whittlin' with rifles an' six-guns. Look out that somebody don't whittle you at eight hundred while yo're settin' on th' front porch! You talk like you think yo're goin' to a prayer meetin'!"

"I'm hopin' they come that close," said McCullough, picking up the package of bills. "So Tom's gone, huh? Charley, there ain't many of us left no more. Remember how you an' Ridley an' me used to go off trappin' them winters, hundreds of miles into th' mountains, with only what we could easy carry on our backs? That was livin'."

"You get out of here, you old fraud!" roared Twitchell. "Ain't I got enough to bother me now? Take care of yore-self, Mac; an' my way's worth tryin', an' tryin' good. If it don't work, then we'll have to try yore way."

"All right; I'll give it a fair ride, Charley; but it will be time wasted," replied the trail-boss. "In that case I'm takin' a dozen men. We relay at th' Squaw Creek corrals, an' again at Sweetwater Bottoms. Send a wagon after us— you'll know what we'll need. You send a new boss to th'

Sweetwater, for I'm pickin' up Waffles. He's one of th' best men you got, an' he's been picketed at that two-bits station long enough."

"Good luck, Mac. Take who you want. Yo're th' boss. Any play you make will be backed to th' limit by th' T & C."

When McCullough got outside he found a crowd of men which the hard-riding couriers had sent in from all parts of the town. They shouted questions and got terse answers as he picked his dozen, the twelve best out of a crowd of good men, all known to him in person and by deeds. The lucky dozen smiled exultantly at the scowling unfortunates and dashed up the street in a bunch after their grizzled pace-maker. One of the last, glancing behind him, saw a stern-faced, sorrowful man in a black store suit standing in the office door looking wistfully after them; and the rider, gifted with understanding, raised his hand to his hat brim and faced around.

"Th' old man's sorry he's boss," he confided to his near-est companion.

"An' there's plenty up in Mesquite that will be th' same," came the reply.

Despite his years McCullough held his lead without crowding from the rear, for he was of the hard-riding breed and toughened to the work. When the first relay was obtained at Squaw Creek that evening there were several who felt the strain more than the leader. A hasty supper and they were gone again, pounding into the gathering dusk of the north-west. All night they rode along a fair trail, strung out behind a man who kept to it with uncanny certainty. Dawn found them changing mounts in Sweetwater Bottoms, but without the snap displayed at the Squaw. Waffles, one-time foreman of the O-Bar-O, needed all his habitual repression to keep from favoring them with a war dance when he heard his luck. Impatiently waiting for the surprised but enthusiastic cook to prepare their breakfasts, they made short work of the meal when it appeared and rolled on again, silent, grim, heavy-lidded, but cheerful. They gladly would do more than that for McCullough, Twitchell—and Tom Ridley. The second evening found them riding up to the buildings of the Question-Mark, guns across their pommels, and they were thankfully received.

Mesquite awakened the next morning to a surprise, for handbills were scattered on its few streets and had been pushed under doors, one of them under the front door of Kane's gambling-hall. When Johnny came down to breakfast the proprietor handed him the sheet, pointing to its flaming headline.

"Read that, me bye!" cried Quayle.

Johnny obeyed:

$2,500.00 REWARD!
For Information Leading to the Capture and
Conviction of the Murderer of Tom Ridley
STRICTLY CONFIDENTIAL
TWITCHELL & CARPENTER, Sandy Bend
JOHN McCULLOUGH, Gen'l. Supt., Mesquite

He thoughtlessly shoved it into his pocket and shrugged his shoulders. "That man Twitchell thinks a lot of his money," he said. "But, if it's his way, it's his way. I'm glad to say it ain't mine."

Quayle looked at him from under heavy brows and smiled faintly. "Mac's here, hisself," he said. "They've raised th' ante, an' if I was as young as you I'd have a try at th' game. An', me bye, it isn't only th' money; 'tis a duty, an' a pleasure. Go in an' eat, now, before that wild Mick av a cook scalps ye."

Hoofbeats pounded up the street from the south and a

Mexican galloped past toward Kane's, followed on foot by several idlers.

"There ye go!" savagely growled the proprietor; "an' I hope ye saw aplenty, ye Greaser dog!"

After a hurried breakfast Johnny went up to Kane's and found an air of tension and suspicion. Men were going in and out of the door through the partition and the half-friendly smiles which he had received the night before were everywhere missing. Feeling the chill of his reception did not blunt his powers of observation, for he saw that both Red Thompson and Bill Long, being unaccredited strangers, drew an occasional suspicious glance. The former was seated in a chair at the lower end of the bar, his back to the wall and only a step from the dining-room door. Bill Long was leaning against the upper end of the counter, where it turned at right angles to meet the wall behind it. At Bill's back and only two steps away was the front door. His chin was in his hand and his elbow rested on the bar, where he appeared to be moodily studying the floor behind the counter, but in reality his keen, narrowed eyes were watching Thorpe and the loopholes in the checkerboard. From his position he caught the light on them at just the right angle to see the backing plates. He let Johnny go past him without more than a casual glance and nod.

Thorpe moved forward, cleaving a straight path through the restless crowd and stopped in front of the newcomer. "Nelson," he said, tartly; "th' boss wants to see you, *pronto!*" As he spoke he let his swinging hand rest against the butt of his gun.

Johnny took plenty of time for his answer, his mind working at top speed. If Kane had caused inquiries to be made around Gunsight concerning him he knew that the report hardly would please any man who was against law and order; and he knew that Kane had had plenty of time to make the inquiries. The thinly veiled hostility and suspicions on the faces around him settled that question in his mind. He slouched sidewise until he had Thorpe in a better position between him and the partition.

"You shore made a mistake," he drawled. "Th' boss never even heard of me."

"I said *pronto!*" snapped Thorpe.

"Well, as long as yo're so pressin'," came the slow, acquiescent reply, "you can *go to hell!*"

Thorpe's gun got halfway out, and stopped as a heavy Colt jabbed into his stomach with a force which knocked the breath out of him and doubled him up. Johnny's other gun, deftly balanced between his palm and the thumb on its hammer, freezing the expressions as it had found them on the faces of the crowd. "Stick up yore han's! All of you! You, in the chair!" he roared. "Stick 'em up!" and Red lost no time in making up for his delinquency. Bill Long, being out of the angry man's sight, raised his only halfway.

"I was welcome enough last night," snapped Johnny; "but somethin's wrong today. If Kane wants to see me, he can send somebody that can talk without insultin' me. An' as for this sick cow, I'm warnin' him fair that I shoot at th' first move, *his* move or anybody *else's.* Stand up, *you!*" he shouted; "an' foller me outside. Keep close, an' plumb in front of me. I'll turn you loose when I get to cover. *Come on!*"

As he backed toward the door, Thorpe following, Bill Long, seeing that Johnny was master of the situation, got his hands all the way up, but the motion was observed and Johnny's gun left Thorpe long enough to swing aside and cover the tardy one. "You keep 'em there!" he gritted. "You can rest 'em later!" and he cautiously backed against the door, moved along it the few inches necessary to gain the opening, and felt his way to the street. "Don't you gamble, Thorpe!" he warned. "Stick closer!"

Being furthest from the front door and soonest out of Johnny's sight, Red Thompson let his hands fall to his hips and cautiously peered over the top of the bar, ready to cover the crowd until Bill Long could drop his upraised hands.

Bill was unfortunate, since he would have to be the last man to assume a more natural position; but he was growing tired and suddenly flung himself sidewise beyond the door opening. As he left the bar there came a heavy report from the street and the bullet, striking the edge of the counter where he had stood, glanced upward and entered the ceiling, a generous cloud of dust moving slowly downward.

"He's a mad dog," muttered Bill, shrinking against the wall. "An' he can shoot like hell! I reckon he's itchin' to get me on sight, *now*. Somebody look out an' see where he is. But what'n blazes is it all about, anyhow?"

The chief bartender's head reappeared farther down the counter. "You fool!" he yelled. "Why didn't you let me know what you was goin' to do? Don't you never think of nobody but yourself? That parted my hair!"

Fisher swore disgustedly. "Look out, yourself, Long, if yo're curious! But why didn't you get him?" he demanded. "You was behind him!"

"I wasn't neither behind him; I was on th' side!" retorted Bill. "He was watchin' me out of th' corner of his eye, like th' damned rattler he is! I could see it plain, I tell you!"

"You can see lots of things when yo're scared stiff, can't you?" sneered a voice in the crowd.

"I wasn't scared," defended Bill. "But I wasn't takin' no chances for th' glory of it. He never done nothin' to me, an' I ain't on Kane's payroll—yet."

"An' you ain't goin' to be, I reckon," laughed another.

Fisher's face proclaimed that he had solved whatever problem there might be in Bill's lack of action. "Ain't had a chance to get it from him yet, huh?" he asked. Sneering, he gave a warning as he turned away. "An' don't you try for it, neither. If he won't come back here no more, I can get him playin' somewhere else."

Red arose fully and stretched, hearing a slight grating noise at a loophole in the partition behind him, where the slide dropped into place. "I'm dry; bone dry," he announced. "I never was so dry before. All in favor of a drink, step up. I'm payin' for *this* round."

All were in favor of it, and the bartender moved slowly behind the counter toward the front door, his head bent over far to the right. "Don't see him; but we better wait till Thorpe comes back. Great guns! Did you *see* it!" he marveled.

"I can see it better now than I could then," said Red, leaning against the bar. "Come on, boys; he's done gone. This means you, too, Long; 'though I ain't sayin' you hardly earned it. If he saw you before he backed up, I says he's got eyes in his ears. Why, cuss it, he was lookin' plumb at *me* all th' time. You got too hefty an imagination, Long."

Out in the street Johnny, backing swiftly from the building, saw Bill Long's sudden leap and fired, for moral effect, at the place vacated. Yanking his captive's gun from its holster, he was about to toss it aside when his fingers gripped the telltale butt and a colder look gleamed in his eyes. Slipping his right-hand gun into its holster he gripped the captured weapon affectionately, and then hazarded a quick glance around him. Someone was riding rapidly down the trail from the north, and a second sidewise glance told him that it was Idaho.

"Faster, you!" he growled to the doorkeeper. "Keep a-comin'—keep a-comin'. One false move an' Kane'll

need another sentry. You may be able to make Bill Long
climb up a wall, but I ain't in his class."

Idaho, who was riding in to appease his burning curiosity, felt its flames lick instantly higher as he saw his friend
back swiftly from Kane's front door, with Thorpe apparently
hooked on the sight of the six-gun. Drawing rein instantly
in his astonishment, he at once loosened them and whirled
into the scanty and scrawny vegetation on the far side of the
trail. Going at a dead run he sent the wiry little pony over
piles of cans, around cacti and other larger obstructions
until he reached the rear of Red Frank's, facing on the next
street. Here he pulled up and drew the Winchester from its
scabbard, feeling that Johnny was capable of taking care
of Kane's if not interfered with from behind.

Johnny, reaching the rear of the building which he had
sought the night before, leaped back and to one side as he
came to the end of the wall, glanced along the rear end and
then curtly ordered Thorpe back to his friends.

"There'll be more to this," snarled Thorpe, white from
anger, his face working. His courage was not of the fineness
necessary to let him yield to the mad impulse which surged
over him and urged him to throw himself, hands, feet, and
teeth, in a blind and hopeless attack upon the certain death
which balanced itself in the gun in Johnny's hand. His blazing eyes fixed full on his enemy's, he let discretion be his
tutor and slowly, grudgingly stepped back, his dragging feet
moving only inches at each shuffle, while their owner,
poised and tense and ready to take advantage of any slip on
Johnny's part, backed toward the sandy street and the scene
of his discomfiture. At last reaching the front of the building
he paused, stood slowly erect and then wheeled about and
strode toward Kane's. At the door he glanced once more at
his waiting adversary and then plunged into the room, strid-

ing straight for the partition door without a single sidewise glance.

Idaho's voice broke the spell. "I thought he was goin' to risk it," he muttered, a deep sigh of relief following the words. "He was near loco, but he just about had enough sense left to save his worthless life. You would 'a' blowed him apart at that distance."

"I'd 'a' smashed his pointed jaw!" growled Johnny. "I ain't shootin' nobody that don't reach for a gun. An' if I'd had any sense I'd 'a' chucked th' guns to you an' let him have his beatin'. Next time, I will. Fine sort of a dog he is, tellin' me what I'm goin' to do, an' when I'm goin' to do it!"

"Wait till payday, when I'll have more money," chuckled Idaho. "I can easy get three to two around here. He's th' champeen rough-an'-tumble fighter for near a hundred miles, but I'm sayin' any man with th' everlastin' nerve to pull Kit Thorpe out from his own kennel an' pack ain't got sense enough to know when he's licked. An' that bein' so, I'm bettin' on yore condition to win. He's gettin' fat an' shortwinded from doin' nothin'. Besides, I'm one of them fools that allus bets on a friend." He laughed as certain memories passed before him. "I've done had a treat—come on, an' let me treat you. How many was in there when you pulled him out? An' why didn't th' partition work like it allus did before?"

"Because th' man that worked it was out in front," answered Johnny. "Things went too fast for anybody else to get behind it." A sudden grin slipped to his face. "Hey, I got one of my pet guns back! He was wearin' it. I knowed it as soon as my fingers closed around th' butt, for I shaped it to fit my hand several years ago. Did you see th' handbills? Twitchell's put up another reward, this one for Ridley; an' McCullough is down on th' Question-Mark. Things ought to step fast, now."

X

Twice in the Same Place

Thorpe reappeared through the partition door armed anew with the mate to the gun he had lost, too enraged to notice that it was better suited to a left than to a right hand. An ordinary man hardly would have noticed it, but a gunman of his years and experience should have sensed the ill-fitting grip at once. He glared over the room, suspiciously eager to catch some unfortunate indulging in a grin, for he had been so shamed and humiliated that it was almost necessary to his future safety that he redeem himself and put his shattered reputation back on its pedestal of fear. There were no grins, for however much any of his acquaintances might have enjoyed his discomfiture they had no lessened respect for his ability with either six-guns or fists; and there was a restlessness in the crowd, for no man knew what was coming.

Fisher conveyed the collective opinion and broke the tension. *"Any* man would 'a' been fooled," he said to the head bartender, but loud enough for all to hear it. His voice indicated vexation at the success of so shabby a trick. "When he answered Thorpe I shore thought he was goin' prompt an' peaceful—why, he even *started!* Nobody reckoned he was aimin' to make a gunplay. How could they? An' I'm sayin' that it's cussed lucky for him that *Thorpe* didn't!"

"Anybody can be fooled th' *first* time," replied the man of liquor. He looked over at the partition door and nodded. "Come over an' have a drink, Thorpe, an' forget it. I got money that says there ain't no man alive can beat you on th' draw. He tricked you, actin' that way."

"He's th' first man on earth ever shoved a gun into me like that," growled Thorpe, slowly moving forward. "An' he's th' last! Seein' as there's some here that mebby ain't shore about it, I'll show 'em that I was tricked!" He stopped in front of Bill Long and regarded that surprised individual with a look as malevolent as it was sincere. "Any squaw dog can tote *two* guns," he said, his still raging anger putting a keener edge to the words. "When he does he tells everybody that he's shore bad. If he ain't, that's *his* fault. I tote one—an' yo're not goin' to swagger around these parts with any more than I got. Which one are you goin' to throw away?"

Bill blinked at him with owlish stupidity. "What you say?" he asked, as though doubting the reliability of his ears.

"Oh," sneered Thorpe, his rage climbing anew; "you didn't hear me th' first time, huh? Well, you want to be listenin' *this* time! I asked, which gun are you goin' to throw away, you card-skinnin' four-flush?"

"Why," faltered Bill, doing his very best to play the part he had chosen. "I—I dunno—I ain't goin' to—to throw any of 'em away. What you mean?"

"Throw one away!" snapped Thorpe, his animal cunning telling him that the obeyance of the order might possibly be accepted by the crowd as grounds for justification, if any should be needed.

Bill changed subtly as he reflected that the crowd had excused Thorpe's humiliation because he had been tricked, and determined that no such excuse should be used again. He looked the enraged man in the eyes and a contemptuous smile crept around his thin lips. "Thorpe," he drawled, "if yo're lookin' for props to hold up yore reputation, you got th' wrong timber. Better look for a sick cow, or—"

The crowd gasped as it realized that its friend's fingers were again relaxing from the butt of his half-drawn gun and that three pounds of steel, concentrated on the small circumference of the barrel of a six-gun, had been jabbed into the pit of his stomach with such speed that they had not seen it, and with such force that the victim of the blow was sick, racked with pain and scarcely able to stand, momentarily paralyzed by the second assault on the abused stomach, which caved, quivered, and retched from the impact. Again he had failed, this time after cold, calm warning; again the astonished crowd froze in ridiculous postures, with ludicrous expressions graven on their faces, their automatic arms leaping skyward as they gaped stupidly, unbelievingly at the second gun. Before they could collect their numbed senses the master of the situation had backed swiftly against the wall near the front door, thereby blasting the budding hopes of the bartender, whose wits and power of movement, returning at equal pace, were well ahead of those of his friends. It also saved the man of liquor from being dropped behind his own bar by the gun of the alert Mr. Thompson, who felt relieved when the crisis had passed without calling forth any effort on his part which would couple him with the capable Mr. Long.

"Climb that wall!" said Bill Long, his voice vibrating with the sudden outpouring of accumulated repression. "I'm lookin' for a chance to kill you, so I ain't askin' you to throw away no gun. This is between you an' me—anybody takin' cards will drop cold. You got it comin', an' comin' fair. Climb that wall!"

Thorpe, gasping and agonized, fought off the sickness which had held him rigid and stared open-eyed, openmouthed at glinting ferocity in the narrowed eyes of the two-gun man.

"Climb that wall!" came the order, this time almost a whisper, but sharp and cutting as the edge of a knife, and there was a certainty in the voice and eyes which was not to be disregarded. Thorpe straightened up a little, turned slowly and slowly made his way through the opening crowd to the wall, and leaned against it. He had no thought of using the gun at his hip, no idea of resistance, for the spirit of the bully within him had been utterly crushed. He was a broken man, groping for bearings in the fog of the shifting readjustments going on in his soul.

"Climb!" said Bill Long's voice like the cracking of a bull-whacker's whip, and Thorpe mechanically obeyed, his finger-nails and boot toes scraping over the smooth boards in senseless effort. He had not yet had time to realize what he had lost, to feel the worthlessness which would be his to the end of his days.

The two-gun man nodded. "I told you boys I was a imitator," he said, smiling; "an' I am. I imitated him in his play to kill me. I imitated that SV foreman, an' now I'm imitatin' Thorpe again. It's his own idea, climbin' walls."

Fisher, watching the still-climbing Thorpe, was using his nimble wits for a way out of a situation which easily might turn into anything, from a joke to a sudden shambles. He now had no doubts about the real quality of Bill Long, and he secretly congratulated himself that he had not yielded to certain temptations he had felt. Besides, his arms were growing heavy and numb. There came to his mind the further thought that this two-gun, card-playing wizard would be a very good partner for a tour of the country, a tour which should be lucrative and safe enough to satisfy anyone.

"Huh," he laughed. "We're imitatin', too; only we're imitatin' ourselves, an' we're gettin' tired of holdin' 'em up. I'm sayin', fair an' square, that I ain't aimin' to draw no cards in any game that is two-handed. I reckon th' rest of th' boys feel th' same as I do. How 'bout it, boys?"

Affirmation came slowly or explosively, according to the individual natures, and the two-gun man was confident enough in his ability to judge character to accept the words. He slowly dropped his guns back in the holsters and smiled broadly. Even the lower class of men is capable of feeling a real liking, when it is based on audacious courage, for any-one who deserves it; and he knew that the now shifting crowd had been caught in the momentum of such a feeling. There was also another consideration to which more than one man present gave grave heed: They scarcely had quit marveling at the wizardy of one two-gun man when the sec-ond had appeared and made them marvel anew.

"All right, boys," he said. "Thorpe, you can quit climbin', seein' that you ain't gettin' nowhere. Come over here an' gimme that gun. I'm still imitatin'. This ain't been no lucky day for you, an' just to show you that you can make it luckier," he said as he took the Colt, "I'm goin' to im-press somethin' on yore mind." He threw the barrel up and carelessly emptied the weapon into the checkerboard partition with a rapidity which left nothing to be desired. The distance was nearly sixty feet. "Reckon you can cover 'em all with th' palm of one hand," he remarked as he shifted the empty gun to his left hand, where he thought it would fit better. He looked at it and turned it over. Three small dots, driven into the side of the frame, made him repress a smile. His own guns had two, while Red Thomp-son's lone Colt had four. He opened the flange and shoved the gun down behind the backstrap of his trousers, where a left-handed man often finds it convenient to carry a weapon, since the butt points that way. Letting his coat fall back into place he walked slowly to the door and out onto the street, the conversation in the room buzzing high after he left.

He next appeared in Quayle's, where he grinned at Idaho, Quayle, Johnny, and Ed Doane.

"I just made Thorpe climb th' wall," he said. "He looked

like a pinned toad. Do you ever like to split up a pair of aces, Nelson?"

Johnny considered a moment and then slowly shook his head.

"Neither do I," replied the newcomer. His left hand went slowly around under his coat and brought out the captured Colt. "An' I ain't goin' to begin doin' it now. Here," and he handed the weapon to Johnny.

Johnny took it mechanically and then quickly turned it over and glanced at the frame. Weighing it judicially he looked up. "Th' feel an' balance of this Colt just suits me," he said. "Want to sell it?"

"I don't hardly own it enough to *sell* it," answered Bill; "but I reckon I can give it away, seein' that Thorpe set th' fashion. I'm warnin' you that he *might* want it back. But you should 'a' seen him a-climbin' that wall!" and he burst into laughter.

"I'll gamble," grinned Johnny. "I'll get you a new one for it."

"No, you won't," replied Bill, still laughing. "I got more'n th' value of a wore-out six-gun watchin' yore show up there. Besides, if it was better'n mine I would 'a' kept it myself. I ain't expectin' you'll be there, tonight," he finished.

"Suits me right here," replied Johnny. "Much obliged for th' gun." He looked at Idaho and grinned. "I aim to clean out this sage-hen at Californy Jack, tonight."

"Which same you might do," admitted Idaho, slowly looking at the Colt in his friend's hand; "for you shore are a fool for luck."

♦

A Job Well Done

Pecos Kane looked up at the sound of shooting and signaled for the doorkeeper. Getting no response he pulled another cord and waited impatiently for the man who answered it.

"What was that shooting, and who did it?" demanded the boss. He cut the wordy recital short. "Tell Bill Trask to assume Thorpe's duties and send Thorpe to me."

Thorpe soon appeared, slowly closed the door behind him and faced the boss, who studied him for a silent interval, the object of the keen scrutiny squirming at the close of it.

"You are no longer suited for my doortender," said Kane's hard voice. "Report to the dining-room, or kitchen, or leave the hotel entirely. But first find Corwin and send him to me. That is all."

Thorpe gulped and shuffled out and in a few minutes the sheriff appeared.

"Sit down, Corwin," said Kane, pleasantly. "Trask has Thorpe's job now. Wait a moment until I think something out," and he sat back in his chair, his eyes closing. In a few moments he opened them and leaned forward. "I have come to a decision regarding some strangers in this town. I have reason to believe that Long and Thompson know each other a great deal better than they pretend. I want to know more about Nelson, so you will send a good man up to his country to get me a report on him. Do it as soon as you leave me, and tell him to waste no time. That clear?"

Corwin nodded.

"Very well," continued the boss. "I want you to arrest both Long and Thompson before tomorrow, and throw them into jail. Since Long's exhibition today it will be well to go about it in a manner calculated to avoid bloodshed. There is no use of throwing men away by sending them against such gunplay. You are to arrest them without a shot being fired on *either* side. It is only a matter of figuring it out, and I will give you this much to start on: Whatever suspicions may have been aroused in their minds about their welcome here not being cordial must be removed. Because of that there should be no ill-advised speed in carrying out the arrests. They could be shot down from behind, but I want them alive; and it suits my purpose better if they are taken right here in this building. They are worth money, and a great deal more than money to me, to you, and to all of us. Twitchell and Carpenter are very powerful and they must be placated if it can be done in such a way as not to jeopardize us. I think it may be done in a way which will strengthen us. You follow me closely?"

The sheriff nodded again.

"All right," said Kane. "Now then, tell me where each of the three men, Nelson, Long, and Thompson, were on the occasions of the robbery of the bank and the death of Ridley. Think carefully."

Corwin gazed at the floor thoughtfully. "When th' bank was robbed Nelson was playin' cards with Idaho Norton in Quayle's saloon. Quayle an' Doane were in there with 'em. Long an' Thompson were here, upstairs, asleep."

"Very good, so far," commented Kane; "go on."

"When Ridley was shot Nelson was with Idaho Norton in Quayle's hotel, for both of them rustled into th' street an' carried him indoors. Thompson was in th' front room, here, an' Long come in soon after the shot was fired."

"Excellent. Which way did he come?"

"Through th' front door."

"Before that?" demanded the boss impatiently.

"I don't know."

"Why don't you?" blazed Kane. "Have I got to do *all* th' thinking for this crowd of dumbheads?"

"Why, why should I know?" Corwin asked in surprise.

"If you don't know the answer to your own question it is only wasting my time to tell it to you. Now, listen: You are to send four men in to me—but not Mexicans, for the testimony of Mexicans in this country is not taken any too seriously by juries. The four are not all to come the same way nor at the same time. The dumbheads I have around me necessitate that each be instructed separate and apart from the others, else they wouldn't know, or keep separate their own part. Is this plain?"

"Yes," answered the arm of the law.

"Very well. Now you will go out and arrange to arrest and jail those two men. And after you have arranged it you will *do* it. Not a shot is to be fired. When they are in jail report to me. That is all."

Corwin departed and did not scratch his head until the door closed after him, and then he showed great signs of perplexity. As he went up the next corridor he caught sight of a friend leaning against the back of the partition, and just beyond was Bill Trask at his new post. He beckoned to them both.

"Sandy, you are to report to th' boss, right away," ordered the sheriff. "He wants four white men, an' yo're near white. Trask, send in three more white men, one at a time, after Woods comes out. An' let me impress *this* on yore mind: It is strict orders that you ain't to fire a shot tonight, when somethin' happens that's goin' to happen; you, nor nobody else. Got that good?"

"What do you mean?" asked the sentry, grinning.

"Good God!" snorted the sheriff. "Do I have to do *all* th' thinkin' for this crowd of dumbheads?"

"Yo're a parrot," retorted Trask. "I know that by heart. You *don't* have to. You don't even do yore *own*. You may go!"

Corwin grunted and joined the crowd in the big room and when Bill Long wandered in and settled down to watch a game the sheriff in due time found a seat at his side. His conversation was natural, not too steady and not too friendly and neither did he tarry too long, for when he thought that he had remained long enough he wandered up to the bar, joked with the chief dispenser, and mixed with the crowd. After a while he went out and strolled over to the jail, where a dozen men were waiting for him. His lecture to them was painfully simple, in the simplest words of his simple vocabulary, and when he at last returned to the gambling-hall he was certain that his pupils were letter-perfect.

Meanwhile Kane had been busy and when the first of the four appeared the clear-thinking boss drove straight to his point. He looked intently at the caller and asked: "Where were you on the night of the storm, at the time the bank was robbed?"

"Upstairs playin' cards with Harry."

"Do you know where Long and Thompson were at that time?"

"Shore; they was upstairs."

"I am going to surprise you," said Kane, smiling, and he did, for he told his listener where he had been on that night, what he had seen, and what he had found in the morning in front of the door of Bill Long's room. He did it so well that the listener began to believe that it was so, and said as much.

"That's just what you must believe," exclaimed Kane. "Go over it again and again. Picture it, with natural details, over and over again. Live every minute, every step of it. If you forget anything about it come to me and I'll refresh your memory. I'll do so anyway, when the time comes. You may go."

The second and third man came, learned their lessons and departed. The fourth, a grade higher in intelligence, was given a more difficult task and before he was dismissed Kane went to a safe, took out a bundle of large bills and handed two of them to his visitor, who nodded, pocketed them, and departed. He was to plant them, find them again and return them so that the latter part of the operation would be clear in his memory.

Supper was over and the big room crowded. Jokes and laughter sounded over the quiet curses of the losers. Bill Long, straddling a chair, with his arms crossed on its back, watched a game and exchanged banter with the players during the deals. Red Thompson, playing in another game not far away, was winning slowly but consistently. Somebody started a night-herding song and others joined in, making the ceiling ring. Busy bartenders were endeavoring to supply the demand. The song roared through the first verse and the second, and in the middle of the following chorus, at the first word of the second line there was a sudden, concerted movement, and chaos reigned.

Unexpectedly attacked by half a dozen men each Bill and Red fought valiantly but vainly. In Bill's group two men had been told off to go for his guns, one to each weapon, and they had dived head-first at the signal. Red's single gun had been obtained in the same way. Stamping feet, curses, grunts, groans, the soft sound of fist on flesh, the scraping of squirming masses of men going this way and that, the heavy breathing, and other sounds of conflict filled the dusty, smoky air. Chairs crashed, tables toppled and were wrecked by the surging groups and then, suddenly, the turmoil ceased and the two bound, battered, and exhausted men swayed dizzily in the hands of their captors, their chests rising and falling convulsively beneath their ragged shirts as they gulped the foul air.

Two men rocked on the floor, slobbering over cracked shins, another lay face down across the wreck of a chair, his gory face torn from mouth to cheekbone; another held a limp and dangling arm, cursing with monotonous regularity; a fifth, blood pouring from his torn scalp and blinding him, groped aimlessly around the room.

Corwin glanced around, shook his head and looked at his two prisoners in frank admiration. "You fellers shore can lick hell out of th' man that invented fightin'!"

Bill Long glared at him. "I didn't see—you—nowhere near!" he panted. "Turn us—loose—an' we'll clean—out th' place. We was—two-thirds—licked before we—knew it was comin'."

"Don't waste yore—breath on th'—damned bastard," snarled Red. "There's a few I'm aimin' to—kill when I—get th' chance!"

"What's th' meanin' of—this surprise party?" asked Bill Long.

"It means that you an' Thompson are under arrest for robbin' th' bank; an' you for th' murder of Ridley," answered the peace officer, frowning at the ripple of laughter which arose. A pock-marked Mexican, whose forehead bore a crescent-shaped scar, seemed to be unduly hilarious and vastly relieved about something.

Thorpe came swiftly across the room toward Bill Long, snarled a curse, and struck with vicious energy at the bruised face. Bill rolled his head and the blow missed. Before the assailant could recover his balance and strike again a brawny, red-haired giant, whose one good eye glared over a battered nose, lunged swiftly forward and knocked Thorpe backward over a smashed chair and overturned table. The prostrate man groped and half arose, to look dazedly into the giant's gun and hear the holder of it give angry warning.

"Any more of that an' I'll blow you apart!" roared the giant. "An' that goes for any other skunk in th' room. Bearbaitin' is barred." He looked at Corwin. "You've got 'em—now get 'em out of here an' into jail, before I has to kill somebody!"

Corwin called to his men and with the prisoners in the middle the little procession started for the old adobe jail on the next street, the pleased sheriff bringing up the rear, his Colt swinging in his hand. When the prisoners had been locked up behind its thick walls he sighed with relief, posted two guards, front and rear, and went back to report to Kane that a good job had been well done.

The boss nodded and bestowed one of his rare compliments. "That was well handled, Sheriff," he said. "I am sorry your work is not yet finished. A zealous peace officer like you should be proud enough of such a capture as to be anxious to inform those most interested. Also," he smiled, "you naturally would be anxious to put in a claim for the reward. Therefore you should go right down to McCullough and lay the entire matter before him, as I shall now instruct you," and the instructions were as brief as thoroughness would allow. "Is that clear?" asked the boss at the end of the lesson.

"It ain't only clear," enthused Corwin; "but it's gilt-edged; I'm on my way, now!"

"Report to me before morning," said Kane.

Hurrying from the room and the building the sheriff saddled his horse and rode briskly down the trail. Not far from town he began to whistle and he kept it up purposely as a notification of peaceful and honorable intentions, until the sharp challenge of a hidden sentry checked both it and his horse.

"Sheriff Corwin," he answered. "What you holdin' *me* up for?"

A man stepped out of the cover at the edge of the trail. "Got a match?" he pleasantly asked, the rifle hanging from the crook of his arm, both himself and the weapon hidden from the sheriff by the darkness. "Where you goin' so late? Thought everybody was asleep but me."

Corwin handed him the match. "Just ridin' down to see McCullough. Got important business with him, an' reckoned it shouldn't wait 'til mornin'."

The sentry rolled a cigarette and lit it with the borrowed match in such a way that the sheriff's face was well lighted for the moment, but he did not look up. "That's good," he said. "Reckon I'll go along with you. No use hangin' 'round up here, an' I'm shore sleepy. Wait till I get my cayuse," and he disappeared, soon returning in the saddle. His quiet friend in the brush settled back to resume the watch and to speculate on how long it would take his companion to return.

McCullough, half undressed, balanced himself as he heard approaching voices, growled profanely and put the freed leg in the trousers. He was ready for company when one of the night shift stuck his head in at the door.

"Sheriff Corwin wants to see you," said the puncher. "His business is so delicate it might die before mornin'."

"All right," grumbled the trail-boss. "If you get out of his way mebby he can come in."

Corwin stood in the vacated door, smiling, but too wise to offer his hand to the blunt, grim host. "Got good news," he said, "for you, me, an' th' T & C."

"Ya-as?" drawled McCullough, peering out beneath his bushy, gray eyebrows. "Pecos Kane shoot hisself?"

"We got th' fellers that robbed th' bank an' shot Ridley," said the sheriff.

"The hell you say!" exclaimed McCullough. "Come in an' set down. Who are they? How'd you get 'em?"

"That reward stick?" asked Corwin anxiously.

"Tighter'n a tick to a cow!" emphatically replied the trail-boss. "Who are they?"

"I got a piece of paper here," said the sheriff, proving his words. He stepped inside and placed it on the table. "Read it over an' sign it. Then I'll fill in th' blanks with th' names of th' men. If they're guilty, I'm protected; if I've made a mistake, then there's no harm done."

McCullough slowly read it aloud:

"'Sheriff Corwin was the first man to tell me that
_____ and _____ robbed the Mesquite bank, and
that _____ killed Tom Ridley. He will produce the
prisoners, with the witnesses and other proof in Sandy
Bend upon demand. If they are found guilty of the
crime named the rewards belong to him.'"

The trail-boss considered it thoughtfully. "It looks fair; but there's one thing I don't like, Sheriff," he said, putting his finger on the objectionable words and looking up. "I don't like 'Sandy Bend.' I'm takin' no chances with them fellers. I'll just scratch that out, an' write in, 'to me.' How 'bout it?"

"They've got to have a fair trial," replied Corwin. "I'm standin' for no lynchin'. I can't do it."

"Yo're shore right they're goin' to have a fair trial!" retorted the trail-boss. "Twitchell ain't just lookin' for two men—he wants th' ones that robbed th' bank an' killed Ridley. You don't suppose he's payin' five thousan' out of his pocket for somebody that ain't guilty, do you? Why, they're goin' to have such a fair trial that you'll need all th' evidence you can get to convict 'em. Lynch 'em?" He laughed sarcastically. "They won't even be jailed in Sandy Bend, where they shore *would* be lynched. You take 'em to Sandy Bend an' you'll be lynched out of yore reward. You know how it reads."

Corwin scratched his head and a slow grin spread over his face. "Cuss it, I never saw it that way," he admitted. "I guess yo're shoutin' gospel, Mac; but, cuss it, it ain't reg'lar."

"You know me; an' I know you," replied the trail-boss, smiling. "There's lots of little things done that ain't exactly reg'lar; but they're plumb sensible. Suppose I change this here paper like I said, an' sign it. Then you write in th' names an' let me read 'em. Then you let me know what proof you got, an' bring down th' prisoners, an' I'll sign a receipt for 'em."

"Yes!" exclaimed Corwin. "I'll deputize you, an' give 'em into yore custody, with orders to take 'em to Sandy Bend, or any other jail which you think best. That makes it more reg'lar, don't it?" he smiled.

McCullough laughed heartily and slapped his thigh. "That's shore more reg'lar. I'm beginnin' to learn why they elected you sheriff. All right, then; I'm signin' my name." He took pen and ink from the shelf, made the change in the paper, sprawled his heavy-handed signature across the bottom and handed the pen to Corwin. "Now, damn it: Who are they?"

The sheriff carefully filled in the three blanks, Mc-Cullough peering over his shoulder and noticing that the form had been made out by another hand.

"There," said Corwin. "I'm spendin' that five thousand right now."

" 'Bill Long'—'Red Thompson'—'Bill Long' again,"

growled the trail-boss. "Never heard of 'em. Live around here?"

Corwin shook his head. "No."

"All right," grunted McCullough. "Now, then; what proof you got? You'll never spend a cent of it if you ain't got 'em cold."

Corwin sat on the edge of the table, handed a cigar to his host and lit his own. "I got a man who was in th' north stable, behind Kane's, when th' shot that killed Ridley was fired from th' other stable. He was feedin' his hoss an' looked out through a crack, seein' Long sneak out of th' other buildin', Sharps in hand, an' rustle for cover around to th' gamblin'-hall. Another man was standin' in th' kitchen, gazin' out of th' winder, an' saw Long turn th' corner of th' north stable an' dash for th' hotel buildin'. He says he laughed because Long's slight limp made him sort of bob sideways. An' we know why Long done it, but we're holdin' that back. That's for th' killin'.

"Now for th' robbery: I got th' man that saw Long an' Thompson sneak out of th' front door of th' dinin'-room hall into that roarin' sand storm between eleven an' twelve o'clock on th' night of th' robbery. He says he remembers it plain because he was plumb surprised to see sane men do a fool thing like that. He didn't say nothin' to 'em because if they wanted to commit suicide it was their own business. Besides, they was strangers to him. After a while he went up to bed, but couldn't sleep because of th' storm makin' such a racket. Kane's upstairs rocked a little that night. I know, because I was up there, tryin' to sleep."

"Go on," said the trail-boss, eagerly and impatiently, his squinting eyes not leaving the sheriff's face.

"Well, quite some time later he heard th' door next to his'n open cautious, but a draft caught it an' slammed it shut. Then Bill Long's voice said, angry an' sharp: 'What th' hell you doin', Red? Tellin' creation about it?' In th' mornin', th' cook, who gets up ahead of everybody else, of course, was goin' along th' hall toward th' stairs an' he kicks somethin' close to Long's door. It rustles an' he gropes for it, curious-like, an' took it downstairs with him for a look at it, where it wasn't so dark. It was a strip of paper that th' bank puts around packages of bills, an' there was some figgers on it. He chucks it in a corner, where it fell down behind some stuff that had been there a long time, an' don't think no more about it till he hears about th' bank bein' robbed. Then he fishes it out an' brings it to me. I knowed what it was, first glance."

"Any more?" urged McCullough. "It's *good;* but, you got any more?"

"I shore have. What you think I'm sheriff for? I got two of th' bills, an' their numbers tally with th' bank's numbers of th' missin' money. You can compare 'em with yore own list later. I sent a deputy to their rooms as soon as I had 'em in jail, an' he found th' bills sewed up in their saddle pads. Reckon they was keepin' one apiece in case they needed money quick. An' when th' sand was swept off th' step in front of that hall door, a gold piece was picked up out of it."

"When were you told about all this by these fellers?" demanded the trail-boss.

"As soon as th' robbery was known, an' as soon as th' shootin' of Ridley was known!"

"When did you arrest them?"

"Last night; an' it was shore one big job. They can fight like a passel of cougars. Don't take no chances with 'em, Mac."

"Why did you wait till last night?" demanded McCullough. "Wasn't you scared they'd get away?"

"No. I had 'em trailed every place they went. They wasn't either of 'em out of our sight for a minute; an' when they slept there was men watchin' th' stairs an' their winders. You see, Kane lost a lot of money in that robbery, bein' a director; an' I was hopin' they'd try to sneak off to where they cached it an' give us a chance to locate it. They was too wise. I got more witnesses, too; but they're Greasers, an' I ain't puttin' no stock in 'em. A Greaser'd lie his own mother into her grave for ten dollars; anyhow, most juries down here think so, so it's all th' same."

"Yes; lyin' for pay is shore a Greaser trick," said Mc-Cullough, nodding. "Well, I reckon it's only a case of waitin' for th' reward, Sheriff. Tell you what I wish you'd do: Gimme everythin' they own when you send 'em down to me, or when I come up for 'em, whichever suits you best. Everythin' has got to be collected now before it gets lost, an' it's got to be ready for court in case it's needed."

"All right; I'll get back what I can use, after th' trial," replied Corwin. "I'll throw their saddles on their cayuses, an' let 'em ride 'em down. How soon do you want 'em? Right away?"

"First thing in th' mornin'!" snapped McCullough. "Th' sooner th' better. I'll send up some of th' boys to give you a hand with 'em, or I'll take 'em off yore hands entirely at th' jail. Which suits you?"

"Send up a couple of yore men, if you want to. It'll look better in town if I deliver 'em to you here. Why, you ain't smoked yore cigar!"

McCullough looked at him and then at his own hand, staring at the crushed mass of tobacco in it. "Shucks!" he grunted, apologetically, and forthwith lied a little himself. "Funny how a man forgets when he's excited. I bet that cigar thought it was in a vise—my hand's tired from squeezin'."

"Sorry I ain't got another, Mac," said Corwin, grinning,

as he paused in the door. "I'll be lookin' for yore boys early. *Adios.*"

"*Adios,*" replied McCullough from the door, listening to the dying hoofbeats going rapidly toward town. Then he shut the door, hurled the remains of the cigar on the floor and stepped on them. "He's got 'em, huh? An' strangers, too! He's got 'em too damned pat for me. It takes a good man to plaster a lie on me an' make it stick—an' he ain't no good, at all. He was sweatin' before he got through!" Again the trousers came off, all the way this time, and the lamp was turned down. As he settled into his bunk he growled again. "Well, I'll have a look at 'em, anyhow, an' send 'em down for Twitchell to look at," and in another moment he was asleep.

XII

◆

Friends on the Outside

While events were working out smoothly for the arrest of the two men in Kane's gambling-hall, four friends were passing a quiet evening in Quayle's barroom, but the quiet was not to endure.

With lagging interest in the game Idaho picked up his cards, riffled them and listened. "Reckon that's singin'," he said in response to the noise floating down from the gambling-hall. "Sounds more like a bunch of cows bawlin' for their calves. Kane's comin' to life later'n usual. Wonder if Thorpe's joinin' in?" he asked, and burst out laughing. "Next to our hard-workin' sheriff there ain't nobody in town that I'd rather see eat dirt than him. Wish I could 'a' seen him a-climbin' that wall!"

"Annybody that works for Kane eats dirt," commented Quayle. "They has to. He'll learn how to eat it, too, th' blackguard."

"There goes *somethin'*," said Ed Doane as the distant roaring ceased abruptly. "Reckon Thorpe's makin' another try at th' wall." He laughed softly. "They're startin' a fandango, by th' sound of it."

"'Tis nothin' to th' noise av a good Irish reel," deprecated the proprietor.

"I'm claimin' low this hand," grunted Idaho. "Look out for yore jack."

Johnny smiled, played and soon a new deal was begun.

"Th' dance is over, too," said Doane, mopping off the bar for the third time in ten minutes. "Musta been a short one."

"Some of them *hombres* will dance shorter than that, an' harder," grunted Idaho, "th' next time they pay *us* a visit. They didn't get many head th' last time, an' I'm sayin' they'll get none at all th' next time. Where they take 'em to is more'n we can guess: th' tracks just die. Not bein' able to track 'em, we're aimin' to stop it at th' beginnin'. You fellers wait, an' you'll see."

Quayle grunted expressively. "I been waitin' too long now. Wonder why nobody ever set fire to Kane's. 'Twould be a fine sight."

"You'll mebby see that, too, one of these nights," growled the puncher.

"Then pick out wan when th' wind is blowin' *up* th' street," chuckled Quayle. "This buildin' is so dry it itches to burn. I'm surprised it ain't happened long ago, with that Mick in th' kitchen raisin' th' divvil with th' stove. If I didn't have a place av me own I'd be tempted to do it meself."

The bartender laughed shortly. "If McCullough happens to think of it I reckon it'll be done." He shook out the bar cloth and bunched it again. "Funny he ain't cut loose yet. That ain't like him, at all."

"Waitin' for th' rewards to start workin', I reckon," said Johnny.

Idaho scraped up the cards, shaped them into a sheer-sided deck and pushed it aside. "I'm tired of this game; it's too even. Reckon I'll go up an' take a look at Kane's." He arose and sauntered out, paused, and looked up the street. "Cussed if they ain't havin' a pe-rade," he called. "This ain't th' Fourth of July, is it? I'm goin' up an' sidle around for a closer look. Be back soon."

Johnny was vaguely perturbed. The sudden cessation of the song bothered him, and the uproar which instantly followed it only served to increase his uneasiness. Ordinarily he would not have been affected, but the day's events might have led to almost anything. Had a shot been fired he swiftly would have investigated, but the lack of all shooting quieted his unfounded suspicions. Idaho's remark about the parade renewed them and after a short, silent argument with himself he arose, went to the door and looked up the street, seeing the faint, yellow patch on the sand where Kane's lamps shone through the open door and struggled against the surrounding darkness, and hearing the faint rumble of voices above which rang out frequent laughter. He grimly told himself that there would be no laughter in Kane's if his two friends had come to any harm, and there would have been plenty of shooting.

"Annythin' to see?" asked Quayle, poking his head out of the door.

"No," answered Johnny, turning to reenter the building. "Just feelin' their oats, I reckon."

"'Tis feelin' their *ropes* they should be doin'," replied Quayle, stepping back to let his guest pass through. "An' 'twould be fine humor to swing 'em from their own. Hist!" he warned, listening to the immoderate laughter which came rapidly nearer. "Here's Idaho; he'll know it all."

Idaho popped in and in joyous abandon threw his sombrero against the ceiling. "Funniest thing you ever heard!" he panted. "Corwin's arrested that Bill Long an' Red Thompson. Took a full dozen to do it, an' half of 'em are cripples now. Th' pe-rade I saw was Corwin an' a bunch escortin' 'em over to th' jail. Ain't we got a ripsnortin' fool for a sheriff?" His levity died swiftly, to give way to slowly rising anger. "With this country fair crowded with crooks he can't find nobody to throw in jail except two friendless strangers! Damn his hide, I got a notion to pry 'em out and turn 'em loose before mornin', just to make things right, an' take some of th' swellin' out of his flat head. It's a cussed shame."

The low-pulled brim of Johnny's sombrero hid the glint in his eyes and the narrowed lids. He relaxed and sat carelessly on the edge of the table, one leg swinging easily to and fro as conjecture after conjecture rioted through his mind.

"They musta stepped on Kane's toes," said Ed, vigorously wiping off the backbar.

Idaho scooped up his hat and flung it on the table at Johnny's side. "You'd never guess it, Ed. Even th' rest of th' gang was laughin' about it, all but th' cripples. I been waitin' for them rewards to start workin', but I never reckoned they'd work out like this. Long an' Thompson are holdin' th' sack. They're scapegoats for th' whole cussed gang. Corwin took 'em in for robbin' th' bank, an' gettin' Ridley!"

Ed Doane dropped the bar cloth and stared at the speaker and a red tide crept slowly up his throat and spread across his face. Johnny slid from the table and disappeared in the direction of his room. He came down again with the two extra Colts in his hands, slipped through the kitchen and ran toward the jail. Quayle's mouth slowly closed and then let out an explosive curse. The bartender brought his fist down on the bar with a smash.

"Scapegoats? Yo're right! It's a cold deck—an' you bet Kane never would 'a' dealt from it if he wasn't dead shore he could make th' play stick. Every man in th' pack will swear accordin' to orders, an' who can swear th' other way? It'll be a strange jury, down in Sandy Bend, every man jack of it a friend of Ridley an' th' T & C. Well, I'm a peaceable man, but this is too much. I never saw them fellers before in my life; but on th' day when Corwin starts south with 'em I'll be peaceable no longer—an' I've got friends! There's no tellin' who'll be next if he makes this stick. Who's with me?"

"*I* am," said Quayle; "an' *I* got friends."

"Me, too," cried Idaho. "There's a dozen hickory knots out on th' ranch that hate Corwin near as much as I do. They'll be with us, mebby even Lukins, hisself. Hey! Where'd Nelson go?" he excitedly demanded. "Mebby he's out playin' a lone hand!" and he darted for the kitchen.

Johnny, hidden in the darkness not far from the jail, was waiting. The escort, judging from the talk and the glowing ends of cigarettes, was bunched near the front of the building, little dreaming how close they stood to a man who held four Colts and was fighting down a rage which urged their use. At last, thoroughly master of itself, Johnny's mind turned to craftiness rather than to blind action and formulated a sketchy plan. But while the plan was being carried through he would not allow his two old friends to be entirely helpless. Slipping off his boots he crept up behind the jail and with his kerchief lowered the two extra guns through the window, softly calling attention to them, which redoubled the prisoners' efforts to untie each other. Satisfied now that they were in no immediate danger he slipped back to his boots, put them on and waited to see what would happen, and to listen further.

"There ain't no use watchin' th' jail," said a voice, louder than the rest. "They're tied up proper, an' nobody ever got out of it before."

"Just th' same, you an' Harry will watch it," said Corwin. "Winder an' door. I ain't takin' no chances with this pair."

A thickening on the dark ground moved forward slowly and a low voice called Johnny's name. He replied cautiously and soon Idaho crawled to his side, whispering questions.

"Go back where there ain't no chance of anybody hearin' us, or stumblin' over us," said Johnny. "When that gang leaves there won't be so much noise, an' then they may hear us."

At last reaching an old wagon they stood up and leaned against it, and Johnny unburdened his heart to a man he knew he could trust.

"Idaho," he said, quietly, "them fellers are th' best friends I ever had. They cussed near raised me, an' they risked their lives more'n once to save mine. 'Most everythin' I know I got from them, an' they ain't goin' to stay in that mud hut till mornin', not if I die for it. They come down here to help me, an' I'm goin' to get 'em out. Did you ever hear of th' old Bar-20, over in th' Pecos Valley?"

"I shore did," answered Idaho. "Why?"

"I was near raised on it. Bill Long is Hopalong Cassidy, an' Red Thompson is Red Connors, th' whitest men that ever set a saddle. Rob a bank, an' shoot a man from *behind!* Did Bill Long act like a man that had to shoot in th' back when he made Thorpe climb his own wall, with his own crowd lookin' on? Most of their lives has been spent fightin' Kane's kind; an' no breed of pups can hold 'em while I'm drawin' my breath. It's only how to do it th' best way that's botherin' me. I've slipped 'em a pair of guns, so I got a little time to think. Why, cuss it: Hoppy knows th' skunk that got Ridley! An' before we're through we'll know who robbed th' bank, an' hand 'em over to Mac. That's what's keepin' th' three of us here!"

"Bless my gran'mother's old gray cat!" breathed Idaho. "No wonder they pulled th' string! I'm sayin' Kane's got hard ridin' ahead. Say, can I tell th' boys at th' ranch?"

"Tell 'em nothin' that you wouldn't know except for me tellin' you," replied Johnny. "I know they're good boys; but they might let it slip. Me an' Hoppy an' Red are aimin' for them rewards—an' we're goin' to get 'em both."

"It's a plumb lovely night," muttered Idaho. "Nicest night I think I ever saw. I don't want no rewards, but I just got to get my itchin' paws into what's goin' on around this town. An' it's a lovely town. Nicest town I think I ever was in. That 'dobe shack ain't what it once was. I know, because, not bein' friendly with th' sheriff, an' not bein' able to look all directions at once, I figgered I might be in it, myself, some day. So I've looked it over good, inside an' out. Th' walls are crumbly, an' th' bars in th' window are old. There's a waggin tongue in Pete Jarvis' freight waggin that's near twelve foot long, an' a-plenty thick. Ash, I think it is; that or oak. Either's good enough. If it was shoved between th' bars an' then pushed sideways that jail wouldn't be a jail no more. If Pete ain't taken th' waggin to bed with him, bein' so proud of it, we can crack that little hazelnut. I'm goin' back an' see how many are still hangin' around."

"I'm goin' back to th' hotel, so I'll be seen there," said Johnny.

"I'll do th' same, later," replied his friend as they separated.

Quayle was getting rid of some of his accumulated anger, which reflection had caused to soar up near the danger point. "Tom Ridley wasn't killed by no strangers!" he growled, banging the table with his fist. "I can name th' man that done it by callin' th' roll av Kane's litter; an' I'll be namin' th' bank robbers in th' same breath." He looked around as Johnny entered the room. "An' what did ye find, lad?"

"Idaho was right. They've got 'em in th' jail."

"An' if I was as young a man as you," said the proprietor, "they wouldn't kape 'em there. As ut is I'm timpted to go up an' bust in th' dommed door, before th' sheriff comes back from his ride. Tom Ridley's murderer? Bah!"

"Back from his ride?" questioned Johnny, quickly and eagerly.

"Shure. He just wint down th' trail. Tellin' Mac, I don't doubt that he's got th' men Twitchell wants. I was lookin' around when he wint past. This is th' time, lad. I'll help ye by settin' fire to Red Frank's corral if th' jail's watched. It'll take their attention. Or I'll lug me rifle up an' cover ye while ye work." He arose and went into the office for the weapon, Johnny following him. "There she is—full to th' ind. An' I know her purty ways."

"Tim," said Johnny's low voice over his shoulder. "Yo're white, clean through. I don't need yore help, anyhow, not right now. An' because you are white I'm goin' to tell you somethin' that'll please you, an' give me one more good friend in this rotten town. Bill Long an' Red Thompson are friends of mine. They did not rob th' bank, nor shoot Ridley; but Bill knows who *did* shoot Ridley. He saw him climbin' out of Kane's south stable while th' smoke was still comin' from th' gun that shot yore friend. I can put my hand on th' coyote in five minutes. Th' three of us are stayin' here to get that man, th' man who robbed th' bank, an' Pecos Kane. I'm tellin' you this because I may need a good friend in Mesquite before we're through."

Quayle had wheeled and gripped his shoulder with convulsive force. "Ah!" he breathed. "Come on, lad; point him out! Point him out for Tim Quayle, like th' good lad ye are!"

"Do you want him so bad that yo're willin' to let th' real killer get away?" asked Johnny. "You only have to wait an' we'll get both."

"What d'ye mean?"

"You don't believe he shot Ridley without bein' told to do it, do you?"

"Kane told him; I know it as plain as I know my name."

"Knowin' ain't provin' it, an' provin' it is what we got to do."

"'Tis th' curse av th' Irish, jumpin' first an' thinkin' after," growled Quayle. "Go wan!"

"Yo're friends with McCullough," said Johnny. "Mac knows a little; an' I'm near certain he's heard of Hopalong Cassidy an' Red Connors, of th' Bar-20. Don't forget th' names: Hopalong Cassidy an' Red Connors, of th' old Bar-20 in th' Pecos Valley. Buck Peters was foreman. I want you to go down an' pay him a friendly visit, and tell him this," and Quayle listened intently to the message.

"Bye," chuckled the proprietor, "ye leave Mac to me. We been friends for years, an' Tom Ridley was th' friend of us both. But, lad, ye may die; an' Bill Long may die—life is uncertain anywhere, an' more so in Mesquite, these days. If yer a friend av Tim Quayle, slip me th' name av th' man that murdered Ridley. I promise ye to kape han's off—an' I want no reward. But it fair sickens me to think his name may be lost. Tom was like a brother."

"If you knew th' man you couldn't hold back," replied Johnny. "Here: I'll tell Idaho, an' Ed Doane. If Bill an' I go under they'll give you his description. I don't know his name."

"Th' offer is a good wan; but Tim Quayle never broke his

word to anny man—an' there's nothin' on earth or in hiven I want so much as to know who murdered Tom Ridley. I pass ye my word with th' sign av th' cross, on th' witness of th' Holy Virgin, an' on th' mem'ry av Tom Ridley—I'll stay me hand accordin' to me promise."

Johnny looked deeply into the faded blue eyes through the tears which filmed them. He gripped the proprietor's hand and leaned closer. "A Greaser with a pock-marked face, an' a crescent-shaped scar over his right eye. He is about my height an' drags one foot slightly when he walks."

"Aye, from th' ball an' chain!" muttered Quayle. "I know th' scut! Thank ye, lad: I can sleep better nights. An' I can wait as no Irishman ever waited before. Annythin' Tim Quayle has is yourn; yourn an' yore friends. I'll see Mac tomorrow. Good night." He cuddled the rifle and went toward the stairs, but as he put his foot on the first step he stopped, turned, and went to a chair in a corner. "I'm forgettin'," he said, simply. "Ye may need me," and he leaned back against the wall, closing his eyes, an expression of peace on his wrinkled face.

XIII

◆

Out and Away

Idaho slipped out of the darkness of the kitchen and appeared in the door. "All right, Nelson," he called. "There's two on guard an' th' rest have left. They ain't takin' their job any too serious, neither. Just one apiece," he chuckled.

Johnny looked at the proprietor. "Got any rope, Tim?" he asked.

"Plenty," answered Quayle, arising hastily and leading the way toward the kitchen. Supplying their need he stood in the door and peered into the darkness after them. "Good luck, byes," he muttered.

Pete Jarvis was proud of his new sixteen-foot freighter and he must have turned in his sleep when two figures, masked to the eyes by handkerchiefs, stole into his yard and went off with the heavy wagon tongue. They carried it up to the old wagon near the jail, where they put it down, removed their boots, and went on without it, reaching the rear wall of the jail without incident, where they crouched, one at each corner, and smiled at the conversation going on.

"I'm hopin' for a look at yore faces," said Red's voice, "to see what they looked like before I get through with 'em, if I ever get my chance. Come in, an' be sociable."

"Yo're doin' a lot of talkin' *now,* you red-headed coyote," came the jeering reply. "But how are you goin' to talk to th' judge?"

"Bring some clean straw in th' mornin'," said Bill Long, "or we'll bust yore necks. Manure's all right for Greasers, an' you, but we're white men. Hear me chirp, you mangy pups?"

"It's good enough for you!" snapped a guard. "I was goin' to get you some, but now you can rot, for all I care!"

Johnny backed under the window, raised up and pressed his face against the rusty bars. "It's th' Kid," he whispered. "Are you untied yet?"

The soft answer pleased him and he went back to his corner of the wall, where he grudged every passing minute. He had decided to wait no longer, but to risk the noise of a shot if the unsuspecting guards could get a gun out quickly enough, and he was about to tell Idaho of the change in plans when the words of a guard checked him.

"Guess I'll walk around again," said one of them, arising slowly. "Gettin' cramped, an' sleepy, settin' here."

"You spit in that window again an' I'll bust yore neck!" said Red's angry voice, whereupon Johnny found a new pleasure in doing his duty.

"You ain't bustin' nobody, or nothin'," jeered the guard, "'less it's th' rope yo're goin' to drop on." He yawned and stretched and sauntered along the side of the building, turned the corner and then raised his hands with a jerk as a Colt pushed into his stomach and a hard voice whispered terse instructions, which he instantly obeyed. "You fellers ain't so bad, at that," he said, with only a slight change in his voice; "but yo're shore playin' in hard luck."

"Keep yore sympathy to yoreself!" angrily retorted Bill Long.

Idaho, having unbuckled the gun-belt and laid it gently on the ground, swiftly pulled the victim's arms down behind his back and tied the crossed wrists. Johnny now got busy with ropes for his feet, and a gag, and they soon laid him close to the base of the wall, and crept toward the front of the building, one to each wall. Johnny tensed himself as Idaho sauntered around the other corner.

"Makin' up with 'em?" asked the guard, ironically. "You don't want to let 'em throw a scare into you. They'll never harm nobody no more." He lazily arose to stretch his legs on a turn around the building. "You listen to what *I'm* goin' to tell 'em," he said. Then he squawked and went down with Johnny on his back, Idaho's dive coming a second later. A blow on his head caused him to lose any impertinent interest which he might have had in subsequent events and soon he, too, lay along the base of the rear wall, bound, gagged, and helpless.

"I near could feel th' jar of that in here," said Red's cheerful voice. "I'm hopin' it was th' coyote that spit through th' window. What's next?" he asked, on his feet and pulling at bars. He received no answer and commented upon that fact frankly and profusely.

"Shut yore face," growled Bill, working at his side. "He's hatchin' somethin' under his hat."

"Somethin' hatchin' all over me," grunted Red, stirring restlessly. "I'm a heap surprised this old mud hut ain't walkin' off some'ers."

Bill squirmed. "You ain't got no call to put on no airs," he retorted. "Mine's been hatched a long time. I wouldn't let a dog lay on straw as rotten as that stuff. Oh!" he gloated. "Somebody's shore goin' to pay for this little party!"

"Wish th' sheriff would open that outside door about now," chuckled Red, balancing his six-chambered gift. "I'd make him pop-eyed."

Hurrying feet, booted now, came rapidly nearer and soon the square-cornered end of a seasoned wagon tongue scraped on the adobe window ledge. Bill Long grabbed it and drew it between two of the bars.

"Go toward th' south," he said. "That's th' boy! Listen to 'em scrape!" he exulted. "Go ahead—she's startin'. I can feel th' 'dobe crackin' between th' bars. Come back an' take th' next—you'll have a little better swing because it's further from th' edge of th' window. Go ahead! It's bendin' an' pullin' out at both ends. Go on! Whoop! There goes th' 'dobe. Come back to th' middle an' use that pry as a batterin'-ram on this bar. Steady; we'll do th' guidin'. All ready? Then let her *go!* Fine! Try again. That's th' stuff—she's gone! Take th' next. Ready? Let her *go!* There goes more 'dobe, on *this* side. Once more: Ready? Let her *go!* Good enough: Here we come."

"Wait," said Johnny. "We'll pass one of these fellers in to you. If we leave 'em both together they'll mebby roll together an' untie each other."

"Like we did," chuckled Red.

"Give us th' first one you got," said Bill. "He's th' one that spit through th' window. I want him to lay on this straw, too. He's tied, an' can't scratch."

The guard was raised to the window, pushed and pulled through it and carelessly dumped on Red's bed, after which it did not take long for the two prisoners to gain their freedom.

"Good Kid!" said Bill, gripping his friend's hand. "An' you, too, whoever you are!"

"Don't mention no names," whispered Idaho. "We couldn't find no ear plugs," he chuckled, shaking hands with Red. "I'm too well known in this town. What'll we do with this coyote? Let him lay here?"

"No," answered Johnny. "He might roll over to Red Frank's an' get help. Picket him to a bush or cactus. Here, gimme a hand with him. I reckon he's come to, by th' way he's bracin' hisself. Little faster—time's flyin'. All right, put him down." Johnny busied himself with the last piece of rope and stood up. "Come on—Kane's stables, next."

As they crossed the street above the gambling-house, where in reality it was a trail, Bill Long took a hand in the evening's plans.

"Red," he said, "you go an' get our cayuses. Bring 'em right here, where we are now, an' wait for us. Idaho, you an' Johnny come with me an' stand under th' window of my room to take th' things I let down, an' free th' rope from 'em. I'm cussed shore we ain't goin' to leave all of our traps behind, not unless they been stole."

"I like yore cussed nerve!" chuckled Idaho. "Don't blame you, though. I'm ready."

"His nerve's just plain gall!" snapped Red, turning to Hopalong. "Think yo're sendin' me off to get a couple of cayuses, while yo're runnin' that risk in there? Get th' cayuses yoreself; *I'll* get th' fixin's!"

"Don't waste time like this!" growled Johnny. "Do as yo're told, you red-headed wart! Corwin will shore go to th' jail before he turns in. Come on, Hoppy."

"That name sounds good again," chuckled Hopalong, giving Red a shove toward the stables. "Get them cayuses, Carrot-Top!"

Red obeyed, but took it out in talking to himself as he went along, and as he entered the north stable he stepped on something large and soft, which instantly went into action. Red dropped to his knees and clinched, getting both wrists in his hands. Being in a hurry, and afraid of any outcry, he could not indulge in niceties, so he brought one knee up and planted it forcefully in his enemy's stomach, threw his weight on it and jumped up and down. Sliding his hands down the wrists, one at a time, he found the knife and took it from the relaxing fingers. Then he felt for the victim's jaw with one hand and hit it with the other. Arising, he hummed a tune and soon led out the two horses.

"Don't like to leave th' others for them fellers to use," he growled, and forthwith decided not to leave them. He drove them out of both stables, mounted his own, led Hopalong's, and slowly herded the other dozen ahead of him over the soft sand and away. When he finally reached the agreed-upon meeting place he reflected with pleasure that anyone wishing to use those horses for the purpose of pursuit, or any other purpose, would first have to find, and then catch them. They were going strong when he had last heard them.

Idaho had stopped under the window pointed out to him, and his two companions, leaving their boots in his tender care, were swallowed up in the darkness. They opened the squeaking front door, cautiously climbed the squeaking stairs and fairly oozed over the floor of the upper hall, which wanted to squeak, and did so a very little. Hopalong slowly opened the door of his room, thankful that he had oiled its one musical hinge, and felt cautiously over the bed. It was empty, and his sigh of relief was audible. And he was further relieved when his groping hand found his possessions where he had left them. He was stooping to loosen the coil of rope at the pommel of his saddle when he heard a sleepy, inquiring voice and a soft thud, and anxiously slipped to the door.

"Kid!" he whispered. *"Kid!"*

"Shut yore fool face," replied the object of his solicitude, striking a match for one quick glance around. The room was strange to him, since he never had been in it before, and he had to get his bearings. The inert man on the bed did not get a second glance, for the sound and weight of the blow had reassured Johnny. There were two saddles, two rifles, two of everything, which was distressing under the circumstances.

Hopalong had just lowered his own saddle to the waiting Idaho when the catlike Johnny entered the room with a saddle and a rifle. He placed them on the bed, where they would make no noise, and departed, catlike. Soon returning he placed another saddle and rifle on the bed and departed once more.

Hopalong, having sent down both of Johnny's first offerings, felt over the bed for the rest of Red's belongings, if there were any more, and became profanely indignant as his hand caressed another rifle and then bumped against another saddle.

"What'n hell is he doin'?" he demanded. "My God! There's more'n a *dozen* rooms on this floor, an' men in all of 'em! Hey, Kid!" he whispered as breathing sounded suddenly close to him.

"What?" asked Johnny, holding two slicker rolls, a sombrero, a pair of boots, and a suit of clothes. Two belts with their six-guns were slung around his neck, but the darkness mercifully hid the sight from his friend.

"Damn it! We ain't *movin'* this hotel," said Hopalong with biting sarcasm. "It don't *belong* to us, you know. An' what was that whack I heard when you first went in?"

"Somebody jumped Red's bed, an' wanted to know some fool thing, or somethin', an' I had to quiet him. An' what'n blazes are *you* kickin' about? I've moved *twice* as much as you have, more'n twice as *far*. Grab holt of some of this stuff an' send it down to Idaho. He'll think you've went to sleep."

"You locoed tumble-bug!" said Hopalong. "Aimin' to send down th' bed, with th' feller in it, too?"

A door creaked suddenly and they froze.

"Quit yore damned noise an' go to sleep!" growled a sleepy, truculent voice, and the door creaked shut again.

After a short wait in silence Hopalong put out an inquiring hand. "Come on," he whispered. "What you got there?"

Johnny told him, and Hopalong dropped the articles out of the window, all but the hat, boots, and clothes. "Don't you know Red's wearin' his clothes, boots an' hat, you chump?" he said, gratis. "Leave them things here an' foller me," and he started for the head of the stairs.

They were halfway down when they heard a horse galloping toward the hotel. It was coming from the direction of the jail and they nudged each other.

Sheriff Corwin, feeling like he was master of all he surveyed, had ridden to the jail before going to report to Kane for the purpose of cautioning the guards not to relax their vigil. Not being able to see them in the darkness meant nothing to him, for they should have challenged him, and had not. He swept up to the door, angrily calling them by name and, receiving no reply, dismounted in hot haste, shook the door and then went hurriedly around the building to feel the bars. One sweep of his hand was enough and as he wheeled he tripped over the wagon tongue and fell sprawling, his gun flying out of his hand. Groping around he found it, jammed it back into the holster, darted back to his horse and dashed off at top speed for Kane's to spread the alarm and collect a posse.

There never had been any need for caution in opening the hotel door and his present frame of mind would not have heeded it if there had been. Flinging it back he dashed through and opened his mouth to emit a bellow calculated almost to raise the dead. The intended shout turned to a choking gasp as two lean, strong hands gripped his throat, and then his mental sky was filled with lightning as a gunbutt fell on his head. His limp body was carried out and dropped at the feet of the cheerful Idaho, who helped tear up portions of the sheriff's clothing for his friends to use on the officer's hands, feet, and mouth.

"Every time I hit a head I shore gloat," growled Johnny, his thoughts flashing back to his first night in town.

"Couldn't you send *him* down, *too?*" Idaho asked of Hopalong. "An' how many saddles do you an' Red use generally?"

"He wasn't up there," answered Hopalong. "We run into him as we was comin' out."

Johnny's match flashed up and out in one swift movement. "Corwin!" he exulted. "An' I'm glad it was *me* that hit him!"

Idaho rolled over on the ground and made strange noises. Sitting up he gasped: "Didn't I *say* it was a lovely night? Holy mavericks!"

"You fellers aim to claim squatter sovereignty?" whispered Red from the darkness. "If I'd 'a' knowed it I'd 'a' tied up somethin' I left layin' loose."

"We got to get a rustle on," said Hopalong. "Some cusses

come to right quick. That gent in Red's bed is due to ask a lot of questions at th' top of his voice. Come on—grab this stuff, *pronto!*"

"I left another in th' stable that's goin' to do some yellin' purty soon," said Red. "Reckon he's a Greaser."

They picked up the things and went off to find the horses and as they dropped the equipment Red felt for his saddle. "Hey! Where's *mine?*" he demanded.

"Here, at my feet," said Johnny.

Red passed his hand over it and swore heartily. "This ain't it, you blunderin' jackass! Why didn't you get *mine?*" he growled.

"Feel of this one," grunted Johnny, kicking the other saddle.

Red did so. "That's it. Who's th' other belong to?"

"*I* don't know," answered Johnny, growing peeved. "Yo're cussed particular, you are! Here's two rifles, two six-guns, an' two belts. Take 'em with you an' pick out yore own when it gets light. *I* don't want 'em."

Red finished cinching up and slipped a hand over the rifles. He dropped one of them into its scabbard. "Got mine. Chuck th' other away."

"Take it along an' chuck it in th' crick," said Idaho. "Now you fellers listen: If you ride up th' middle of Big Crick till you come to that rocky ground west of our place you can leave th' water there, an' yore trail will be lost. It runs southwest an' northeast for miles, an' is plenty wide an' wild. If you need anythin' ride in to our place any night after dark. I'll post th' boys."

"We ain't got a bit of grub," growled Red. "Well, it ain't th' first time," he added, cheerfully.

"We're not goin' up Big Crick," said Hopalong, decisively. "We're ridin' like we wanted to get plumb out of this country, which is just what Bill Long an' Red Thompson would do. When fur enough away we're circlin' back east of town, on th' edge of th' desert, where nobody will hardly think we'd go. They'll suspect that hard ground over yore way before they will th' desert. Where'll we meet you, Kid, if there's anythin' to be told; an' when?"

Johnny considered and appealed to Idaho, whose knowledge of the country qualified him to speak. In a few moments the place had been chosen and well described, and the two horsemen pulled their mounts around and faced northward.

"Get a-goin'," growled Johnny. "Anybody'd reckon you thought a night was a week long."

"Don't like to leave you two boys alone in this town, after tonight's plays," said Hopalong, uneasily. "Nobody is dumb enough to figger that we didn't have outside help. Keep yore eyes open!"

"Pull out!" snapped Johnny. "It'll be light in two hours more!"

"So-long, you piruts," softly called Idaho. "Yessir," he muttered, joyously; "it's been one plumb lovely night!"

Not long after the noise of galloping had died in the north a Mexican staggered from the stable, groping in the darkness as he made his erratic way toward the front of the gambling-hall, his dazed wits returning slowly. Leaning against the wall of the building for a short rest, he went on again, both hands gripping his jaw. Too dazed to be aware of the disappearance of the horses and attentive only to his own woes, he blundered against the bound and gagged sheriff, went down, crawled a few yards and then, arising again to his feet, groped around the corner of the building and sat down against it to collect his bewildering thoughts.

Upstairs in the room Red had used, the restless figure on the bed moved more and more, finally sitting up, moaning softly. Then, stiffening as memory brought something back to him, he groped about for matches, blundering against the walls and the scanty furniture, and called forth profane language from the room adjoining, whose occupant, again disturbed, arose and yanked open his door.

"What you think yo're doin', raisin' all this racket?" he demanded.

"Somebody near busted my head," moaned the other. "I been robbed!" he shouted as the lack of impedimenta at last sank into his mind.

"Say!" exclaimed his visitor, remembering an earlier nocturnal disturbance. "Wait here till I get some matches!"

He returned with a lighted lamp, instead, which revealed the truth, and its bearer swiftly led the way into the second room down the hall. A pair of boots which should not have been there and the absence of the equipment which should have been there confirmed their fears. The man with the lamp held it out of the window and swore under his breath as a bound figure below him gurgled and writhed.

"Looks like Corwin!" he muttered, and hastened down to make sure, taking no time to dress. The swearing Mexican received no attention until the sheriff staggered back with the investigator, and then the vague tale was listened to.

A bellowing voice awakened the sleepers in the big building and an impromptu conference of irate men, mostly undressed, was held in the hall. Sandy Woods returned front the stables, reporting them bare of horses; the investigator from the jail came back with the angry guards, one of whom was too shaky to walk with directness. Others came from a visit to Red Frank's corral, leading half a dozen borrowed horses, and, a hasty, cold breakfast eaten, the posse, led by a sick, vindictive sheriff, pounded northward along a plain trail.

Those who were not able to go along stood and peered through the paling darkness and two deputies left to take up positions in the front and rear of Quayle's hotel where they could see without being seen, while a third man crept into the stable to look for a lineup horse. Had he been content with looking he would have been more fortunate, but thinking that the master would have no further use for the animal, he decided to take it for himself, trusting that possession would give him a better claim when the new ownership was finally decided by Kane. Reassured by the earliness of the hour and by the presence of the hidden deputy, he went ahead with his plans.

Pepper's flattened ears meant nothing to the exultant thief, for it had been his experience that all horses flattened their ears whenever he approached them, especially if they had reason to know him; so, with a wary eye on the trim, black hoofs, he slipped along the stable wall to gain her head. He had just untied the rope and started back with the end of it in his hand when there was a sudden, sidewise, curving swerve of the silky black body, a grunt of surprise and pain from the thief, pinned against the wall by the impact, and then, curving back again and wheeling almost as though on a pivot, Pepper's teeth crunched flesh and bone and the sickened thief, by a miracle escaping the outflung front hoofs, staggered outside the stable and fell as the whizzing hind feet took the half-open door from its flimsy hinges. Rolling around the corner, the thief crawled under a wagon and sank down unconscious, his crushed shoulder staining darkly through his torn shirt.

The watching deputy arose to go to his friend's assistance, but looked up and stopped as a growled question came from Ed Doane's window.

"Jim's hurt," he explained to the face behind the rifle. "Went in to see if his cayuse had wandered in there, an' th' black near killed him. Gimme a hand with him, will you?"

Quayle had nearly fallen off the chair he had spent the

night on when the crash and the scream of the enraged horse awakened him. He ran to the kitchen door, rifle in hand, and looked out, hearing the deputy's words.

"I'll give ye a hand," he said, "but more cheerful if it's to dig a grave. *Mother av God!*" he breathed as he reached the wagon. "I'm thinkin' it's a priest ye want, an' there's none within twenty miles." He looked around at the forming crowd. "Get a plank," he ordered, "an' get Doc Sharpe."

Ed Doane, followed by Johnny and Idaho, ran from the kitchen and joined the group. One glance and Johnny went into the stable, calling as he entered. Patting the quivering nozzle of the black he looked at the rope and came out again.

"That man-killer has got to be shot," said the deputy to Ed Doane.

"I'll kill th' man that tries it," came a quiet reply, and the deputy wheeled to look into a pair of frosty blue eyes. "Th' knot I tie in halter ropes don't come loose, for Pepper will untie any common knot an' go off huntin' for me. It was untied. If you want to back up a hoss thief, an' mebby prove yore part in it, say that again."

"Yo're plumb mistaken, Nelson," said the deputy. "Jim was huntin' his own cayuse, which Long an' Thompson stampeded out of th' stable last night. He was goin' over th' town first before he went out to look for it on th' plain."

"That's *good!*" sneered Johnny. "Long an' Thompson are in jail. I'm standin' to what th' knot showed. Do you still reckon Pepper's got to be shot?"

"They broke out an' got away," retorted the deputy, "an' they shore as hell had outside help." He looked knowingly into Johnny's eyes. "Nobody that belongs to this town would 'a' done it."

"That's a lie," said Quayle, his rifle swinging up carelessly. "I belong to this town, an' I'd 'a' done it, mesilf, if I'd thought av it. Seein' that I didn't, I'm cussed glad that somewan had better wits than me own."

"I was aimin' to do it," said Idaho, smiling. "I was goin' out to get th' boys, an' bust th' jail tonight. I was holdin' back a little, though, because I was scared th' boys might get a little rough an' lynch a few deputies. They're on set triggers these days."

The cook started to roll up his sleeves. "I'll lick th' daylight out av anny man that goes to harm that horse, or me name's not Murphy," he declared, spitting. "I feed her near every mornin', an' she's gintle as a baby lamb. But she's got a keen nose for blackguards!"

Dr. Sharpe arrived, gave his orders and followed the bearers of the improvised stretcher toward his house. As the crowd started to break up Johnny looked coldly at the deputy. "You heard me," he said. "Pass th' word along. An' if she don't kill th' next one, *I* will!"

North of town the posse reached Big Creek and exulted as it saw the plain prints going on from the further bank. Corwin, sitting his saddle with a false ease, stifled a moan at every rise and fall, his head seeming about to split under the pulsing hammer blows. When he caught sight of the trail leading from the creek he nodded dully and spoke to his nearest companion.

"Leavin' th' country by th' straightest way," he growled. "It'll mebby be a long chase, damn 'em!"

"They ain't got much of a start," came the hopeful reply. "We ought to catch sight of 'em from th' top of th' divide beyond Sand Creek. It's fair level plain for miles north of that. Their cayuses ain't no better than ourn, an' *some* of ourn will run theirs off their feet."

Sand Creek came into sight before noon and when it was reached there were no tracks on the farther side. The posse was prepared for this and split without hesitation, Corwin leading half of it west along the bank and the other half going east. Five minutes later an exclamation caused the sheriff to pull up and look where one of his men was pointing. A rifle barrel projected a scant two inches from the water and the man who rode over to it laughed as he leaned down from the saddle.

"It lit on a ridge of gravel an' didn't slide down quite fur enough," he called. "An' it shore is busted proper."

"Bring it here," ordered Corwin. He took it, examined it and handed it to the next man, whose head ached as much as his own and who would not have been along except that his wish for revenge over-rode his good sense.

"That yourn?" asked the sheriff.

The owner of the broken weapon growled. "They've plumb ruined it. It's one more score they'll pay. Come on!" and he whirled westward. Corwin drew his Colt and fired into the air three times at counted intervals, and galloped after his companions when faint, answering shots sounded from the east.

"They're makin' for that rocky stretch," he muttered; "an' if they get there in time they're purty safe."

Not long after he had rejoined his friends the second part of the posse whirled along the bank, following the trail of the first, eager to overtake it and learn what had been discovered.

Well to the east Hopalong and Red rode at the best pace possible in the water of the creek, now and then turning in the saddle to look searchingly behind them. Following the great bend of the stream they went more and more to the south and when the shadows were long they rode around a ridge and drew rein. Red dismounted and climbed it, peering over its rocky backbone for minutes. Returning to his companion he grinned cheerfully.

"No coyotes in sight," he said. "Some went west, I reckon, an' found that busted rifle where we planted it. No coyotes, at all; but there's a black bear down in that little strip of timber."

"I can eat near all of it, myself," chuckled Hopalong. "Let's camp where we drop it. A dry wood fire won't show up strong till dark. Come on!"

XIV

♦

The Staked Plain

Pecos Kane sat behind his old desk in the inner room and listened to the reports of the night's activities, his anger steadily mounting until ghostly flames seemed to be licking their thin tongues back in his eyes. The jail guards had come and departed, speaking simply and truthfully, suggesting various reasons to excuse the laxity of their watch. The Mexican told with painful effort about the loss of the horses, growing steadily more incoherent from the condition of his jaw and from his own rising rage. Men came, and went out again on various duties, one of them closely interrogating the owner of the freight wagon, whose anger had died swiftly by the recovery of the great tongue, which was none the worse for its usage except for certain indentations of no moment. A friend of Quayle and hostile to Kane and for what Kane stood for, the wagon owner allowed his replies to be short, and yet express a proper indignation, which did not exist, about the whole affair. When again alone in the sanctity of his home he allowed himself the luxury of low-voiced laughter and determined to put his crowbar where any needy individual of the future could readily find it.

Bill Trask, because of his short-gun expertness temporarily relieved of guarding the partition door, led three companions toward Quayle's hotel, his face and the faces of the others tense and determined. Two went around to the stable, via Red Frank's and the rear street and one of them stopped near it while the other slipped along the kitchen wall and crouched at the edge of the kitchen door. The third man went silently into the hotel office as Trask sauntered carelessly into the barroom and nodded at its inmates.

"Them fellers shore raised hell," he announced to Ed Doane as he motioned for a drink.

"They did," replied Doane, spinning a glass after the sliding bottle, after which he flung the coin into the old cigar box and assiduously polished the bar, wondering why Trask patronized him instead of Kane's.

"They shore had nerve," persisted the newcomer, looking at Johnny.

"They shore did," acquiesced the man at the table, who then returned to his idle occupation of trying to decipher the pattern of the faded-out wall paper. Wall paper was a rarity in the town and deserved some attention.

"Them guards was plumb careless," said Kane's hired man. Not knowing to whom he was speaking there was no reply, and he tried again, addressing the bartender.

"They was careless," replied Doane, without interest.

Johnny was alert now, the persistent remarks awakening suspicion in his mind, and a slight sound from the wall at his back caused him to push his chair from the table and assume a more relaxed posture. His glance at the lower and nearer corner of the window let him memorize its exact position and he waited, expectant, for whatever might happen. The surprise and capture of his two friends had worked, but that had been the first time; there would be no second, he told himself, especially as far as he was concerned.

"Is th' boss in?" asked the visitor.

"Th' boss ain't in," answered Ed Doane as Johnny glanced at the front door, the front window and the door of the office, which the bartender noticed. "Too dusty," said Doane, going around the bar to the front wall and closing the window.

"When will he be in?"

"Dunno," grunted the bartender, once more in his accustomed place.

"I got to see him."

"I handle things when he ain't here," said Doane. "See me," he suggested, looking through the door leading to the office, where he fancied he had heard a creak.

"Got to see him, an' *pronto*," replied the visitor. "He made some remarks this mornin' about gettin' them fellers out. We know it was done by somebody on th' outside, an' we got a purty good idea of who it was since Quayle shot off his mouth. He's been gettin' too swelled up lately. If he don't come in purty quick I'm aimin' to dig him out, myself."

Johnny was waiting for him to utter the cue word and knew that there would be a slight change in facial expression, enunciation, or body posture just before it came. He was not swallowing the suggestions that it was Quayle who was wanted.

"You shore picked out a real job to handle all alone," said Doane, not letting his attention wander from the hotel office. "Any dog can dig out a badger, but that's only th' beginnin'," he said pleasantly, his hand on the gun which always lay under the bar. He expected a retort to his insult, and when none came it put a keener edge to his growing suspicions.

"I'm diggin' him out, just th' same," said Trask. "There's law in this town, an' everybody's on one side or th' other. Bein' a deputy it's my job to see about them that's on th' other side. Gettin' arrested men out of jail is serious an' I got to ask questions about it. Of course, Quayle don't allus say what he means—we none of us do. We all like to have our jokes; but I got to do my duty, even if it's only askin' questions. Is he out, or layin' low?"

"He's out," grunted Doane, "but he'll be back any minute, I reckon."

"All right; I'll wait," said Trask, carelessly, but he tensed himself. "How's business?" and at the words he flashed into action.

A chair crashed and a figure leaped back from it, two guns belching at its hips. The face and hand which popped up into the rear window disappeared again as the smoking Colt swung past the opening and across Johnny's body to send its second through the office doorway, and curses answered both shots. Trask, bent over, held his right arm with his left hand, his gun against the wall near the front door. The first shot of Johnny's righthand Colt had torn it from Trask's hand as it left the holster and the second had rendered the arm useless for the moment. A shot from the corner of the stable sang through the window and barely missed its mark as Johnny leaned forward, but his instant reply ended all danger from that point.

"Trask," he said, "I'm leavin' town. I ain't got a chance among buildin's again' pot-shooters. I'm leavin'—but th' Lord help Kane an' his gang when I come back. You can tell him I'm comin' a-shootin'. An' you can tell him this: I'm goin' to get him, Pecos Kane, if I has to pull him out of his hell-hole like I pulled Thorpe. Go ahead of me to th' stable— I'll blow you apart if any pot-shooter tries at me. G'wan!"

Trask obeyed, the gun against his spine too eloquent a persuader to be ignored. He knew that there were no pot-shooters yet, and he was glad of it, for if there had been one, and his captor was killed, the relaxation of the tense thumb holding back the hammer of a gun whose trigger was tied back would fire the weapon. The man who held it would fire one shot after his own death, however instantaneous it might be.

Passing through the kitchen Johnny picked up his saddle and ordered his captive to carry the rifle and slicker roll. They disappeared into the stable and when they came out again Johnny ordered Trask into the saddle, mounted behind him and rode for the arroyo which lay not far from the hotel. At last away from the buildings he made Trask dismount, climbed over the cantle and settled himself in the vacated saddle.

"I'm goin' down to offer myself to McCullough," he said. "You can tell Kane that, too. They'll need men down there, an' I'll be th' maddest man they got. An' th' next time me an' you have any gun talk, I'm shootin' to kill. *Adios!*"

He left the cursing deputy and went straight for the trail, where the rising wind played with the dust, and along it until stopped by a voice in a barranca.

"I'm puttin' 'em up," he called. "My name's Nelson an' I'm mad clean through. Get a rustle on; I want to see Mac."

"Go ahead, Bar-20," drawled the voice. "I wasn't dead shore. There's a good friend of yourn down there."

"Quayle?" asked Johnny.

"There's another: Waffles, of th' O-Bar-O," came the reply, and a verse of a nearly forgotten song arose on the breeze.

I've swum th' Colorado where she runs down clost
  to hell,
  I've braced th' faro layouts in Cheyenne;
I've fought for muddy water with a howlin' bunch
  of Sioux,
  An' swallered hot tamales, an' cayenne.

"There's more, but I've done forgot most of it," apologized the singer.

Johnny laughed with delight. "Why, that's Lefty Allen's old song. Here's th' second verse":

> *I've rid a pitchin' broncho till th' sky was underneath,*
> *I've tackled every desert in th' land;*
> *I've sampled Four-X whisky till I couldn't hardly see,*
> *An' dallied with th' quicksands of th' Grande.*

"That's shore O-Bar-O. Lefty made it up hisself, an' that boy could sing it. It all comes back to me now—he called it 'Th' Insult.' Why—here, *you!*" he chuckled. "I said I was mad an' in a hurry. I ain't mad no more, but I *am* in a hurry. See you tonight, mebby. So-long."

Riding on again he soon reached the Question-Mark bunkhouse and dismounted as a puncher turned the corner of the house. They grinned at each other, these good, old-time friends.

"You son-of-a-gun!" chuckled Johnny, holding out his hand.

"You son-of-a-gun!" echoed Waffles, gripping it, and so they stood, silent, exchanging grins. It had been a long time since they last had seen each other.

McCullough loomed up in the doorway and grinned at them both.

"Hear yo're married," said Waffles.

"Shore!" bragged Johnny.

"It ain't spoiled you, *yet*. How's Hoppy an' Red?"

"Fine, now they're out of jail."

Waffles threw his head back and laughed heartily. "I near laughed till I busted when Quayle told us who they was. Hoppy an' Red in *jail!* It was *funny!*"

"Hello, Nelson," said McCullough. "What are you doin' down here?"

"Had to leave town; too many corners, an' too much cover. I'm lookin' for a job, if it don't cut me out of th' rewards."

"She's yourn."

"Wait a minute," said Johnny. "I can't take it. I got to be free to do what I want; but I'll hang out here for awhile."

"You've got th' job instanter," said the appreciative trail-boss smiling broadly. "It's steady work of bossin' yoreself. I've heard of yore work, up Gunsight way. Feed yet? Then come on."

"Shore will. Where's Quayle?"

"Rode back, roundabout; him not courtin' bein' seen; but I reckon everybody in town knows he's been here. He swears by you."

Despite Idaho's boasts to the contrary his ranch again had nocturnal visitors, and there was no lead-flying welcome accorded them. Having spied out the distribution of Lukins' riders the visitors chose a locality free from guards and with the coming of night drifted a sizable herd of Diamond L cattle across an outlying section of the range and with practiced art and uncanny instinct drove the compacted herd onto and over the rocky plateau, where the chief of the raiders obtained a speed with the cattle which always bordered upon a panicky flight, but never quite reached it. All that night they rumbled over the rocky stretch and as dawn brightened the eastern sky the running herd passed down a gentle slope, picked up the waiting caviya and not long thereafter moved over the hard bottom of a steep-walled ravine which could have been called a canyon without unduly stretching the meaning of the word.

The chief of the raiding party cared nothing for the fat-

ness of the animals, or other conditions which might operate against the possibilities of a lucrative sale. There later
would be time for improving their condition, plenty of time
in a valley rich with grass. All he cared for now was to put
miles speedily behind him, and this he was accomplishing
like the master cattleman he was. After a mid-day breathing space they went on again, alternately walking and running, and well into the second night, stopping at a water-hole
known only to a few men other than these. Some miles north
of this water-hole was another, and very much smaller, one,
being only a few feet across, and there also was a difference
between the waters of the two. The larger was of a nature to
be expected in such a locality, but much better than most
such holes, for the water was only slightly alkaline and the
cattle drank it eagerly. The other was sweet and pure and
cold, but rather than cover the distance to it and back again,
it was ignored by all but one man, for the others stayed with
the herd. There was grass around both; not enough to feed
a herd thoroughly, but enough to keep it busy hunting over
the scanty growth. With more than characteristic thought
these holes had been named in a manner to couple and yet
to keep them separate, and to Kane's drive crew they were
known as "Sweet" and "Bitter."

Again on the trail before the sun had risen above the horizon, the herd was sent forth on another day's hard drive,
which carried it, with the constantly growing tail herd of
stragglers, far into the following night, despite all dumb re-
monstrances. No mercy was shown to it, but only a canny
urging, and if no mercy was shown the cattle none was accepted by the drivers, who rode and worked, swore and
panted on wiry ponies which, despite frequent changing,
began to show the marks of their efforts under the pitiless
sun and through the yielding sands. Both cattle and horses
had about reached their limits when the late afternoon of the

next day brought them to a rocky ledge sticking up out of the desert's floor, which now was hard and stony; and upon turning the south end of the ridge an emerald valley suddenly lay before their eyes, from whence the scent of water had put a new spirit into cattle and horses for the last few miles; and now it nearly caused a fatal stampede at the entrance to the narrow ledge which slanted down the steep, rock walls.

To a stranger such a sight would have awakened amazed incredulity, and strong suspicion that his sanity had been undermined by the heat-cursed, horror-laden desert miles; or he might have sneered wisely at so palpable a mirage, scorned to be tricked by it in any attempt to prove it otherwise and staggered on with contemptuous curses. But Miguel and the men he so autocratically bossed knew it to be no vision, no trick of air or mind, and sighed with relief when it finally lay before them. While they all knew it was there and had visited it before, none of them, except Miguel, had ever learned the way, try as they might, for until the high ledge of rock, hidden on the west by a great, upslanting billow of sand, came into sight there were no landmarks to show them the way. Each new journey across the simmering, shimmering plateau found fears in every heart but the guide's that he would lose his way. That their fears may be justified and to show them blameless in everything but their lack of confidence in him, it may be well to have a better understanding of this desert and what it meant; and to show why men should hold as preposterous any claim that a cattle herd could safely cross it. Some went even further and said no man, mounted or not, could make that journey, and confessed to themselves a superstitious fear and horror for it and everything pertaining to it.

Before the deep ruts had been cut in the old Santa Fe Trail

in that year of excessive rains; before the first wheel had
rolled over the prairie soil to prove that wagons could safely
make the long and tiresome trip; before even the first pack
trains of heavily laden mules plodded to or from the Missouri frontier, and even before the pelt-loaded mules of the
great fur companies crossed Kansas soil to the trading
posts of the East, Mexican hunters rode from the valley of
Taos and Santa Fe to procure their winter meat from the
vast brown herds of buffalo migrating over their curious,
crescent-shaped course to and from the regions of the
Arkansas, Canadian, and Cimarron. They dried the strips of
succulent meat in the sun or over fires, the fuel for the
latter having been supplied by the buffalo themselves on previous migrations; they stripped the hides from the prostrate
bodies and cured them, and trafficked with the bands of
Indians which followed the herds as persistently as did
the great, gray wolves. Of these *ciboleros,* swarthy-skinned
hunters of Mexico, some more hardy and courageous than
their fellows, or by avarice turned trader, ventured farther
afield and were not balked by the high, beetling cliffs which
bordered a great, forbidding plateau lying along and below
the capricious Cimarron, in places a river of hide-and-seek
in the sands, wet one day and dry the next.

From the mesa-like northern edge, along the warning
arroyos of the Cimarron, where erosion, Nature's patient
sculptor, carved miracles of artistry in the towering clays,
shales, and sandstones, to the great sand hills billowing
along its far-flung other edges, this barren waste of dreary
sand and grisly alkali was a vast, simmering playground for
dancing heat waves and fantastic mirage, and its treacherous
pools of nauseous, alkaline waters shrunk daily from their
encrusted edges and gleamed malignantly under a glow-
ering, molten sun. Arroyos, level plain, shifting sand, and

imponderable dust, with a scrawny, scanty, hopeless vegetation which the whimsical winds buried and then dug up again, this high desert plateau lay like a thing of death, cursing and accursed. It sloped imperceptibly southward, its dusty soil gradually breaking into billowy ridges constantly more marked and with deeper troughs, by insensible gradations becoming low sand hills, ever growing more separate and higher until at last they were beaten down and strewn broadcast by more persistent winds, and limited by the firmer soils which were blessed with more frequent rains to coax forth a thin cover of protecting, anchoring vegetation. To the west they intruded nearly to the Rio Pecos, a stream which in almost any other part of the country would have been regarded as insignificant, but here was given greatness because its liquid treasure was beyond price and because it was permanent, though timid.

Of the first of the Mexicans to push out over this great desolation perhaps none returned, except by happy chance, to tell of its tortures and of the few serviceable water holes leagues apart, the permanency of which none could foretell. But return some eventually did, and perhaps deprecated the miseries suffered, in view of the saving in miles; but their experience had been such as to impel them to drive a line of stakes along the happily chosen course to mark in this manner the way from each more trustworthy water hole to the next, be they reservoirs or furtive streams which bubbled up and crept along to die not far from their hopeful springs, sucked up by palpitant air and swallowed by greedy sands, their burial places marked by a shroud of encrusted salts. In the winter and spring an occasional rain filled hollows, ofttimes coming as a cloudburst and making a brave showing as it tumultuously deepened some arroyo and roared valiantly down it toward swift effacement. The trail was staked, if not by the swarthy traders, then by their red-skinned brothers, and from this line of stakes the tableland derived its name, and became known to men as the Lano Estacada, or Staked Plain.

Of this accursed desert no one man had full knowledge, nor thirsted for it if it were to be had only through his own efforts. There were great stretches unknown to any man, and there were other regions known to men who had not brought their knowledge out again; and what knowledge there was of its south-central portions was not to be found in men with white skins, but in certain marauding redmen fitted by survival to cope with problems such as it presented, and to live despite them. One other class knew something of its mysteries, for among the Mexicans there were some who had learned by bitter pilgrimages, but mostly from the mouths of men long dead who had passed the knowledge down successive generations, each increment a little larger when it left than when it came, who had a more comprehensive, embracing knowledge of the baking tableland; and these few, because what they knew could best be used in furtive, secretive pursuits bearing a swift penalty for those caught in them, hugged that knowledge closely and kept it to themselves. A man who has that which another badly needs can drive shrewd bargains. And of the few Mexicans who were enriched by the possession of this knowledge, those who knew most about it had mixed blood flowing through their veins, for the vast grisly plateau had been a short cut and place of refuge for marauding bands of Apaches, Utes, and Comanches while civilization crawled wonderingly in swaddling clothes.

Of the knowing few Pecos Kane owned two, owned them body and soul, and to make his title firmer than even proof of murder could assure, he threw golden sops to the wise ones' avarice and allowed them seats in the sun and privileges denied to their fellows. One of them, by name

Miguel, a small part Spaniard and the rest Mescalero Apache, was a privileged man, for he knew not only the main trails across the plain but certain devious ways twisting in from the edges, one of which wandered for accursed miles, first across rock, then over sand and again over rock and unexpectedly turned a high, sharp ridge to look upon his Valle de Sorprendido, deep and green, whose crystal spring wandered musically along its gravelly bed from the graying western end of the canyon-like ravine to sink silently into the thirsty sands to the east and be seen no more. Manuel, also, knew this way.

Surprise Valley was no terminal, but a place for tongue-lolling, wild-eyed cattle to pause and rest, drink and eat before the fearful journey called anew. No need for corral, fence, or herders here to keep them from straying, but an urgent need for pressing riders to throw the herd back on the trail again, to start the dumbly protesting animals on the thirty-six-hour drive to the next unfailing water, against the instinct which bade them stay. A valley of delight it was, a jewel, verdant and peaceful, forced by man to serve a vicious purpose; but as if in punishment for its perversion the glistening sand hills crept slowly nearer, each receding tide of their slow advance encroaching more and more each year until now the valley had shrunk by half and a stealthy grayness crept insidiously into its velvety freshness like the mark of sin across a harlot's cheek.

Near the fenced-in spring was an adobe building, deserted except when a drive crew sought its shelter, and it served principally as a storehouse should a place of refuge suddenly be needed. It lay not far from the sloping banks of detritus which now ran halfway up the sheer, smooth stone walls enclosing the valley. Across from it on the southern side of the depressed pasture a broad trail slanted up the rock cliffs to the desert above. The cabin, the trail, and the valley itself long ago would have been obliterated by sand but for the miles of rocks, large and small, which lay around it like a great, flat collar. Should some terrific sand storm sweep over it with a momentum great enough to bridge the rocky floor the valley would cease to be; and smaller storms raging far out on the encircling desert carried their sands farther and farther across the stubborn rock, until now its outer edge was closer by miles. Already each rushing wind retained sand enough to drop it into the valley and powder everything.

The pock-marked guide, disdaining the precarious labors of getting the herd down the ledge with no fatalities among the maddened beasts, lolled in his saddle on the brink of the precipice and watched the struggle on the plain behind him, where hard-riding, loudly yelling herders were dashing across the front of the weaving, shifting, stubborn mass of tortured animals, letting them through the frantic restraining barrier in small groups, which constantly grew larger. Here and there a more determined animal slipped through and galloped to the descending ledge, head down and tail up. The cracking of revolvers fired across the noses of the front rank grew steadily and Miguel deemed it safer to leave the brim of the cliff. It was possible that the maddened herd might break through the desperate riders and plunge to its destruction. Had the trail been a few hours longer nothing could have held them.

"Give a hand here!" shouted the trail-boss as the guide rode complacently out of danger. "Ride in there an' help split 'em!"

"I weel be needed w'en we leeve again," replied Miguel. "To run a reesk eet ees foolish. I tol' you to stop 'em a mile away an' spleet 'em there. Eet ees no beesness of Miguel's, theese. You deed not wan' to tak' the time? Then tak' w'at you call the consequence."

Eventually the last of the herd, which mercifully was composed of stragglers whose lack of strength made them more tractable, were successfully led to the ledge and stumbled down it to join their brothers standing or lying in the little brook as if to appease their thirst by absorption before drinking deeply. The frantic, angry bawling of an hour ago was heard no more, for now a contented lowing sounded along the stream, where the quiet animals often waited half an hour before attempting to drink. They stood thus for hours, reluctant to leave even to graze and after leaving, left the grass and returned time after time to drink. There were a few half-blinded animals among the weaklings, but water, grass, and rest would restore their sight. Here they would stay until fit for the second and lesser ordeal, and the others in turn.

The weary riders, turning their mounts loose to join the rest of the horse herd, piled their saddles against the wall of the hut and waited for the cook to call them to fill their tin plates and cups. One of them, more energetic and perhaps hungrier than the rest, unpacked the load of firewood from a spiritless horse and carried it to the hut.

The perspiring Thorpe looked his thanks and went on with his labors and in due time a well-fed, lazy group sprawled near the hut, swapping tales or smoking in satisfied silence. At the other side of the building Miguel sat with those of his own kind, boasting of his desert achievements and in reply to a sneering remark from the other group he showed his teeth in a mocking smile, raised his eyebrows until the crescent scar reached his sombrero and shrugged his shoulders.

"Eet ees not good to say sooch theengs to Miguel," he complacently observed. "Eef he should get ver' angree an' leeve een the night eet would be ver' onluckie for Greengos. *Quien sabe?*"

"He got you there, Jud," growled a low voice. "He shore hurts me worse'n a blister, but I'm totin' my grudge silent."

"Huh," muttered another thoughtfully. "A man can travel fast without no cattle to set th' pace. He shore can 'leeve' an' be damned for all *I* care. An' I'm sayin' that if he does there'll be a damned dead Greaser in Mesquite right soon after I get back. Th' place for him to 'leeve' us is at Three Ponds—for then we shore would be in one bad fix."

"I ain't shore I'd try to get away," said Sandy Woods slowly. "There's good grass an' water here, no herdin', no strayin', nobody to bother a feller. A man can live a long time on one steer out here, jerkin' th' meat. Th' herd would grow, an' when it came time to turn 'em into money he'd only have to drive plumb west. It wouldn't be like tryin' to find a little place like this. Just aim at th' sunset an' keep goin'."

"How long would this valley feed a herd like th' one here now?" ironically demanded the trail-boss. "You can tell th' difference in th' grass plain at th' end of a week. Yo're full of loco weed."

"Eef you say sooch things to me I may leeve in the night," chuckled the other. "Wish they'd stampeded an' knocked him over th' eege! One of these days some of us may be quittin' Kane, an' then there'll be one struttin' half-breed less in Mesquite. Tell you one thing: I won't make this drive many more times before I know th' way as well as he does; an' from here on we could stake it out."

Soft, derisive laughter replied to him and the trail-boss thoughtfully repacked his pipe. "It ain't in you," he said. "You got to be born with it."

"You holdin' that a white man ain't got as much brains as a mongrel with nobody knows how many different kinds of blood in him?" indignantly demanded Sandy.

"He's got generations behind him, like a setter or a pointer, an' it ain't a question of brains. It's instinct, an' th' lower down yore stock runs th' better it'll be. There ain't no human brains can equal an animal's in things like that. I doubt if you could leave here an' get off this desert, plumb west or not. You got a big target, for it's all around you behind th' horizon; but I don't think you'd live till you hit it at th' right place. Don't forget that th' horizon moves with you. If there wasn't no tracks showin' you th' way you'd die out on this fryin' pan."

"An' th' wind'll wipe them out before mornin'," said one of the others.

The doubter laughed outright. "Wait till we come back. I'll give you a chance to back up yore convictions. Don't forget that I ain't sayin' that I'd try it afoot. I'd ride an' give th' horse its head. There ain't nothin' to be gained arguin' about it now. An' I'm free to admit that I'm cussed glad to be settin' here lookin' out instead of out there some'ers tryin' to get here to look in. Gimme a match, Jud."

The trail-boss snorted. "Now yo're takin' *my* end," he asserted. "If you ride a cayuse an' give it its head it ain't a white man's brains that yo're dependin' on. That ain't yore argument, a-tall. I'll bet you, cayuse or no cayuse, you can't leave Three Ponds an' make it. A cayuse has to drink once in a while or he'll drop under you an' you'll lose yore instinct-compass."

"I'll take that when we start back," retorted Sandy, "if you'll give me a fair number of canteens. I'm figgerin' on outfittin' right."

"Take all you want at Cimarron corrals," rejoined the trail-boss. "After we leave there I'm bettin' nobody will part with any of theirs." He looked keenly at the boaster and took no further part in the conversation, his mind busy with a new problem; the grudge he already had.

XV

♦

Discoveries

Hopalong and Red liked their camp and were pleased that they could stay in it another day and night. They jerked the bear meat in the sun and smoke and took a much-needed bath in the creek, where the gentle application of sand freed them from the unwelcome guests which the jail had given them. Clothing washed and inspected quickly dried in the sun and wind. Neither of them had anything on but a sombrero and the effect was somewhat startling. Red picked up his saddle pad to fling it over a rock for a sun bath and was about to let go of it when he looked closer.

"Hey, did you rip open this pad?" he asked, eying his friend speculatively.

Hopalong added his armful of fuel to the pile near the fire and eyed his friend. "For a growed man you shore do ask some childish questions," he retorted. "Of course I did. I allus rip open saddle pads. All my life I been rippin' open every saddle pad I saw. Many a time I got mad when I found a folded blanket instead of a pad. I've got up nights an' gone wanderin' around looking for pads to rip open. You look like you had sense, but looks shore is deceivin'. Why'n blazes would I rip open yore saddle pad? I reckon it's plumb wore out an' just nat'rally come apart. You've had it since Adam made th' sun stand still."

"You musta listened to some sky pilot with yore feet!" retorted Red. "Adam didn't make th' sun stand still. That was Moses, so they'd have longer light for to hunt for him in. An' you needn't get steamed up, neither. Somebody ripped this pad, with a knife, too. Seein' that it was in th' same camp all night with you, I nat'rally asked. I'm shore *I* didn't do it. Then *who* did?" He swaggered off to get his friend's pad and picked it up. "Of course you wouldn't rip yore own. That—" he held it closer to his eyes and stared at it. "Cussed if you *didn't,* though! It's ripped just like mine. I reckon you'll be startin' on th' saddles, next!"

Hopalong's amusement at the ripping of his companion's pad faded out as he grabbed his own and looked at it. "Well, I'm cussed!" he muttered. "It shore was ripped, all right. It never come apart by itself. *Both* of 'em, huh?" He pondered as he turned the pad over and over.

"They didn't play no favorites, anyhow," growled Red. "Wonder what they thought they'd find? Jewels?"

Hopalong pushed back his hat and gently scratched a scalp somewhat tender from the sand treatment. "Things like that don't just happen," he said, reflectively. "There's allus a reason for things." He grew thoughtful again and studied the pad. "Mebby they wasn't lookin' for anythin'," he muttered, suspiciously.

Red snorted. "Just doin' it for practice, mebby?" he asked, sarcastically. "Not havin' nothin' else *to* do, somebody went up to our rooms an' amused themselves by rippin' open our pads. You got a head like a calf, only it's a hull lot smaller."

"We was accused of robbin' th' bank, Reddie," said Hopalong in patient explanation. "They knowed we didn't do it—so they musta wanted us to be blamed for it. Th' best proof they could have, not seein' us do it, was to plant somethin' to be found on us. This is past yore A B C eddication, but I'll try to hammer it into you. If it makes you dizzy, hold up yore hand. What does a bank have that everybody wants? Money! Why do people rob banks? To get money, you sagehen! What would bank robbers have after they robbed a bank? Money, you locoed cow! Now, Reddie, there's *two* kinds of money. One is hard, an' th' other is soft like yore head. Th' soft has pretty pictures on it an' smells powerful. It also has numbers. Th' numbers are different, Reddie, on each bill. Some banks keep a list of th' numbers of the biggest bills. Reckon I better wait an' let you rest up."

"Too bad they got us out of jail—*both* of us," said Red. "I should 'a' stayed behind. It wouldn't 'a' been half as bad as hangin' 'round with you."

"Now," continued his companion, looking into the pad, "if some of them numbered bills was found on us they'd have us, wouldn't they? We wasn't supposed to have no friends. An' where would a couple of robbers be likely to carry dangerous money? On their hats? No, Reddie; *not* on their hats. In their pockets, where they might get dragged out at th' wrong time? Mebby; but not hardly. Saddle pads, says th' little boy in th' rear of the room. Right you are, sonny. Saddle pads, Reddie, is a real good place. While you go all over it again so you can get th' drift of it I'll put on some clothes. I'm near baked."

"It started some time ago," said Red innocently.

"What did?"

"Th' bakin'. You didn't get that hat on quick enough," his friend jeered. "I've heard of people eatin' cooked calves' brains, but they'd get little nourishment an' only a moldy flavor out of yourn. An' you'd shore look better with *all* yore clothes on. I can see th' places where you've stopped washin' yore hands, feet, an' neck all these years."

Hopalong mumbled something and slid into his underwear. "Gee!" he exulted. "These clean clothes shore do feel good!"

"*You'd* nat'rally notice it a whole lot more than I would," said Red, following suit. As his head came into sight again he let his eyes wander along the eastern and southeastern horizon. "You know, them bluffs off yonder remind me a hull lot of parts of th' Staked Plain," he observed. "We hadn't ought to be very far away from it, down here."

"They're its edge," grunted Hopalong, rearranging the strips of meat over the fire. Both became silent, going back in their memories to the events of years before, when the Staked Plain had been very real and threatening to them.

At daylight the following morning they arose and not much later were riding slowly southward and as near the creek as the nature of its banks would allow. When the noon sun blazed down on them they found the creek dwindling rapidly and, glancing ahead down the sandy valley they could make out the dark, moist place where the last of it disappeared in the sands. They watered their horses, drank their fill and went on again toward the place where they were to meet Johnny, riding on a curving course which led them closer and closer to the forbidding hills. In mid-afternoon they came to a salt pond and instead of arguing about the matter with their thirsty mounts, let them go up to it and smell it. The animals turned away and went on again without protest. A little later Red squinted eastward and nodded in answer to his own unspoken question.

"Shore it is," he muttered.

Hopalong followed his gaze and grunted. "Shore." He regarded the distant bulk thoughtfully. "Strikes me no sane cow ever would go out there, unless it was drove. It's our business to look into everythin'. Comin'?"

"I shore am. Nobody can buffalo me an' chuck me into jail without a comeback. I'm lookin' for things to fatten it."

"It can't get too fat for me," replied his friend. "Helpin' th' Kid get his money back was enough to set me after some of that reward money; but when I sized up Kane an' his gang it promised to be a pleasure; now, after that jailin', it's a yelpin' joy. If there's no other way I'm aimin' to ride into Mesquite an' smoke up with both guns."

As they neared the carcass Red glanced at his cheerful friend. "Head's swelled up like a keg," he said. "Struck by a rattler."

"Reckon so; but cows dead from snakebite ain't common."

They pulled up and looked at it at close range.

"Shot," grunted Hopalong.

"Then somebody was out here with it," said Red swinging down. "He was tender-hearted, *he* was. Gimme a hand. We'll turn it over an' look at th' brand."

Hopalong complied, and then they looked at each other and back to the carcass, where a large piece of hide had been neatly trimmed around and skinned off.

"Didn't dare let it wander, an' they plugged it after it got struck," said Red.

"Careful, they was," commented his companion. "They was too careful. If they'd let it wander it wouldn't 'a' told nothin', 'specially if it wandered toward home. But shootin' it, an' then doin' *this*—I reckon our comeback is takin' on weight."

"It shore is," emphatically said Red. "Cuss this hard ground! It don't tell nothin'. They went north or south—an' not long ago, neither. Which way are you ridin'?"

Hopalong considered. "If they went either way they'd be seen. I got a feelin' they went right across. Greasers an' Injuns know that desert, an' there's both kinds workin' for Kane. It allus has been a shore-thing way for 'em. Remember what Idaho said?"

"It can't be done," said Red.

"Slippery Trendly an' Deacon Rankin did it."

"But they only crossed one corner," argued Red.

"McLeod's Texans did it!"

"They didn't cross much more'n a corner," retorted Red. "An' look what it *did* to 'em!"

"It's a straight drive for them valleys along th' Cimarron," mused Hopalong. "Nobody to see 'em come or go, good grass to fatten 'em up after they got there, an' plenty of time for blottin' th' brands. I'll bet Kane's got men that knows how to get 'em over. There's water holes if you only know where to look, an' how to head for 'em; an' some of these half-breeds down here know all of that. If they went north or south on a course far enough east to keep many folks from seein' 'em they'd find it near as dry. Well, we better go down an' meet th' Kid before we do anythin' else. We got our bearin's an' can find th' way back again. What you say?"

Red mounted and led the way. "If I'm goin' to ride around out here I'm goin' to have plenty of water, an' that means canteens. I'm near chokin' for a drink; an' this cayuse is gettin' mean. Come on."

"We might pick up some tracks if we hunt right now," said Hopalong. "If we wait longer this wind'll blot 'em out. I ain't thirsty," he lied. "You go down an' meet th' Kid an' I'll look around east of here. We can't gamble with this: if I find tracks they'll save us a lot of ridin' an' guessin'. Go ahead."

"If you stay I stay," growled Red.

"Listen, you chump," retorted Hopalong. "It's only a few hours more if I stay out here than if I go with you. Get canteens an' supplies. Th' Kid can bring us more tomorrow. I'm backin' my guess: get a-goin'."

Red saw the wisdom of the suggestion and wheeled, riding at good speed to the southwest while his friend went eastward, his eyes searching the desert plain. It was night when Red returned, picking his way with a plainsman's instinct to the carcass of the cow, and he softly replied to a low call which came from behind a billow of sand.

Hopalong arose. "You made good time," he said.

"Reckon so," replied Red, riding toward him. "I only got

two canteens an' not much grub. Th' Kid'll be ready for us tomorrow. What about yore cayuse?"

"Don't worry," chuckled Hopalong. "It's th' cayuses that's been botherin' me most. They're all right now. I found a little hole with cold, sweet water, an' there's grass around it for th' cayuses. There ain't much, but enough for these two goats. Th' water hole ain't more'n three feet across an' a foot deep, but it fills up good an' has wet quite a spot around it. An' Red, I found somethin' else!"

"Good; what is it?"

"There's clay around it an' a thin layer of sand over th' clay," replied Hopalong. "I found th' prints of a cayuse an' a man, an' they was fresh—not more'n twenty-four hours old if I'm any judge. I cast around on widenin' circles, but couldn't pick up th' trail any distance from th' hole. Th' wind that's been blowin' all day wiped 'em out; but it didn't wipe out much at th' edge of th' water. I could even make it out where he knelt to drink. There you are: a dead cow, with th' brand skinned off; tracks of a man an' a cayuse at that water hole; no herd tracks, no other cayuse tracks—just them two, an' *our* suspicions. What you think?"

Red chuckled. "I think we're gettin' somewhere, cussed slow an' I don't know where; but I'm playin' up that skinned cow. If it was all skinned I'd say a hide hunter might 'a' done it, an' that he made th' tracks you saw; but it wasn't. You should 'a' looked better near th' carcass instead of huntin' up th' water hole. You might 'a' seen th' tracks of a herd, or what th' wind left of 'em, 'though I reckon they drove that cow off quite a ways before they dropped it."

"Did you cross any herd tracks after you left me?" asked Hopalong.

"No; why?"

"An' we didn't cross any before you left," said Hopalong. "If there's been any to see runnin' east an' west we'd 'a' found 'em. That was all hard ground; an' there was th' wind. There wasn't none to find."

"Huh!" snorted Red, and after a moment's thought he looked up. "Mebby that feller found th' cow all swelled up with snakebite, away off from water as he thought, an' just put an end to its misery?"

"Then why did he cut out th' brand?" snapped Hopalong.

"What are you askin' *me* for?" demanded Red, truculently. "How'd *I* know? You shore can ask some damn fool questions!"

"Yo're half-baked," growled his companion. "I will be, too, before I get any answer to what I'm askin' myself. I'm aimin' to squat behind a rise north of that water hole an' wait for my answer if it takes a month. I can get a good view from up there."

Red, whose hatred for deserts was whole-hearted, looked through the darkness in disgust at his friend. "You've picked out a fine job for us!" he retorted. "If yo're right an' they did drive a herd across to th' other side it'll shore be a wait. Be more'n a week, an' mebby two."

"They've got to drive hard between waters," replied Hopalong. "They'll waste no time; an' they won't waste time comin' back again, when they won't have th' cows to hold 'em down. There's one thing shore: They won't be back tomorrow or th' next day, an' we both can ride down an' see th' Kid, an' mebby McCullough. It's too good a lead to throw away. But before we meet Johnny we're goin' to have a better look around, 'specially south an' east."

"All right," agreed Red. "How'd you come to find th' hole?"

"Rode up on a ridge an' saw somethin' green, an' knowin' it wasn't you I went for it," answered his friend. "If it had been made for us it couldn't be better. With water, an' grass enough for night grazin', an' a good ridge to look from, it's a fine place for us. We'll take turns at it, for it won't feed two cayuses steady. Th' off man can ride west to grass, mebby back to our camp, an' by takin' shifts at it we can mebby save most of th' grass at th' hole."

"An' mebby get spotted while we're ridin' back an' forth?"

"Th' ridge will take care of that, an' I reckon when it peters out there'll be others to hide us. I'm dead set on this: I'm so set that I'll stick it out all alone rather than pass it by. I tell you I got a *feelin'*."

"I ain't quittin'," growled Red; "I ain't got sense enough to quit. Desert or *no* desert I'm aimin' to do my little gilt-edged damndest; but I'm admittin' I'll be plumb happy when it's my time off. We'll get supplies an' more canteens from th' Kid tomorrow, an' be fixed so we can foller any other lead that sticks up its head. I shore can stand more than ridin' over a desert if it'll give us anythin' on them fellers."

"Here we are," grunted his companion, swinging from the saddle. "Finest, coldest water you ever drunk. I'm puttin' double hobbles on my cayuse tonight, just to make shore."

"Me, too," said Red, dismounting.

In the morning they rode up for a look along the ledge, found that it would answer their requirements and then went southeast, curving farther into the desert, and it was not long before Red's roving glance caught something which aroused his interest and he silently rode off to investigate, his companion going slowly ahead. When he returned it was by another way and he rode with his eager eyes searching the desert beneath and ahead of him. Reaching his friend, who had stopped and also was scanning the desert floor with great intentness, he nodded in quiet satisfaction.

"Think you see 'em, too?" he smilingly inquired. "They're so faint they can't hardly be seen, not till you look ahead, an' then it's only th' difference between this strip of sand that we're on an' th' rest of th' desert. It's a cattle trail, Hoppy; I just found another water hole, a big one. Th' bank was crowded with hoof marks, cattle an' cayuses. Looks like they come from th' west, bearin' a little north. Th' only reason we didn't see 'em when we rode down was because they was on hard ground. That shore explains th' dead cow."

"An' in a few hours more," said his companion, "this powdery dust will blot 'em out. If they was clearer I'd risk follerin' them, even if we only had a canteen apiece. We can ride as far between waters as they can drive a herd, an' a whole lot farther. It's only fearin' that th' trail will disappear that holds me back."

"We don't have to risk it yet," said Red, grimly. "We've found out where they cut in an' how they start across; an' all we got to do is to lay low up there an' wait for 'em to come back, or start another herd across, to learn who they are."

"If we wait for their next drive we can foller 'em on a fresh, plain trail, an' be a lot better prepared," supplemented Hopalong. "I reckon we're shore goin' to fatten our comeback!"

"It's pickin' up fast," gloated his friend. "All we got to do is watch that big water hole an' we got 'em. There ain't so many water holes out on this skillet that they can drive any way they like. We'll camp at th' little one, of course, but we can lay closer to th' big one nights."

"An' from th' ridge up yonder th' man on day watch can see for miles."

"Yes; an' fry, an' broil, an' sizzle, an' melt!" muttered Red. "Damn 'em!"

Hopalong had wheeled and was leading the way into the southwest as straight as he could go for the meeting with Johnny, and Red pushed up past him and bore a little more to the west. They had seen all they needed to see for the day, and they had made up their minds.

At last after a long, hot ride they reached the bluffs marking the side of the plateau and soon were winding down a steep-walled arroyo which led to the plain below, and the country began to change with such insensible gradations that they hardly noticed it. Sage and greasewood became more plentiful and after an hour had passed an occasional low bush was to be seen and the ground sloped more and more in front of them. A low fringe of greenery lay along the distant bottom, where Sand Creek or some other hidden stream came close to the top of the soil, later to issue forth and become the stream into which the Question-Mark's creek later emptied. They crossed this and breasted an opposing slope, followed around the base of a low ridge of hills and at last stopped under a clump of live-oak and cottonwoods in the extreme east end of the Question-Mark valley.

While the two friends were riding toward the little clump of trees west of the Question-Mark ranch visitors rode slowly up to the door of the ranchhouse and one of them dismounted. The shield he wore on his open vest shone in the sun with nickel brightness, but his face was anything but bright. The job which had been cut out for him was not to his liking and had destroyed his peace of mind, and the peace of mind of the two deputies, who needed no reflection upon their subordinate positions to keep them in the sheriff's rear. What little assurance they might have started with received a jolt soon after they had left town, when a gruff and unmistakably unfriendly voice had asked, with inconsiderate harshness and profanity, their intended destination and their business. At last allowed to pass on after quite some humiliation from the hidden sentries, they now were entering upon the dangerous part of their mission.

Corwin stepped up to the door and knocked, a formality which he never dispensed with on the Question-Mark. Other visitors usually walked right in and found a chair or sat at the table, but it never should be said to Corwin's discredit that an officer of the law was rude and ignorant in such a well-known and long-established form of etiquette. So Sheriff Corwin knocked.

"Come in!" impatiently bawled a loud and rude voice. The sheriff obeyed and looked around the door casing. "Ah, hello, Mac," he said in cheery greeting.

"Mac *who?*" roared the man at the table.

"McCullough," said the man at the door, correcting himself. "How are you?"

"Yo're one full-blooded damn fool of a sheriff," sneered the trail-boss. "Where's them two prisoners I been waitin' for?"

"They got away. Somebody helped 'em bust th' jail. I sent word back to you by yore own men."

"Shore, I got it; I know that. That's no excuse a-tall!" retorted the trail-boss. "I went an' sent word down to Twitchell on th' jump that his fool way worked an' that I was goin' to send him th' men he wanted. Then you let 'em bust out of jail! Fine sort of a fool you made of me! Where's yore reward now, that you was spendin' so fast? An' what'll Twitchell say, an' *do?* He wants th' bank robbers, not excuses; an' more'n all he wanted th' man that shot Ridley. It ain't only a question of pertectin' th' men workin' for him, but it's personal, too. Ridley was an old friend of his'n—an' he'll raise hell till he gets th' man that killed him. What about it? What have you done since they got away?"

"We trailed 'em, but they lost us," growled Corwin. "Reckon they got up on that hard ground an' then lit out, jumpin' th' country as fast as they could. Kane had it on 'em, cold an' proper—but I had my doubts, somehow. I ain't quittin'; I'm watchin' an' layin' back, an' I'm figgerin' on deliverin' th' man that got Ridley."

"You mean Long an' Thompson are innocent?" demanded McCullough with a throaty growl. "Yo're sayin' it yoreself! What was you tryin' to run on me, then?"

"They musta robbed th' bank," replied the sheriff; "but I got my own ideas about who killed yore friend. This is between us. I'm waitin' till I get th' proof; an' after I get it, an' th' man, I'll mebby have to leave th' country between sunset an' dawn. I ain't no dog, an' I'm gettin' riled."

"Then it was Kane who cold-decked them two fellers?" demanded McCullough.

"I ain't sayin' a word, now," replied the sheriff. "Not yet, I ain't, but I'm aimin' to get th' killer. Where's that Nelson?"

"What you want with him?" asked the trail-boss. "Reckon he done it?"

"No; he didn't," answered Corwin. "He only helped them fellers out of jail, an' I'm goin' to take him in."

"What?" shouted McCullough, and then burst out laughing. "I'm repeatin' what I said about you bein' full-blooded! Say, if you can turn that trick I won't raise a hand—not till he's in jail; an' then I'll get him out cussed quick. He's workin' for me, an' he didn't do no crime, gettin' a couple of innocent men out of that mud hut; an', besides, I don't know that he did get 'em out. Go after him, Corwin; go right out after him." He glanced out of the window again and chuckled. "I see you brought some of yore official fam'bly along. Shucks! That ain't no way to do, three agin' one. An' I heard you was a bad hombre with a short gun!"

"It ain't no question of how bad I am!" retorted the sheriff. "We want him alive."

"Oh, I see; aim to scare him, bein' three to one. All right; go ahead—but there ain't goin' to be no potshootin'. Tell yore fam'bly that. I mean it, an' I cut in sudden th' minute any of it starts."

"There won't be no pot-shootin'," growled the sheriff, and to make sure that there wouldn't be any he stepped out and gave explicit instructions to his companions before going toward the smaller corral. When part way there he heard whistling, wheeled in his tracks and went back to the bunk-house, hugging the wall as he slipped along it, his gun raised and ready for action.

Johnny turned the corner, caught sight of the two deputies, who held his suspicious attention, and had gone too far to leap back when he saw Corwin flattened against the wall and the sheriff's gun covering him. Presumably safe on a friendly ranch, he had given no thought to any imminent danger, and now he stood and stared at the unexpected menace, the whistling almost dying on his pursed lips.

"Nelson!" snapped the sheriff, "yo're under arrest for helpin' in that jail delivery. I'll shoot at th' first hostile move! Put up yore hands an' turn 'round!"

Johnny glanced from him to the deputies and thought swiftly. Three to one, and he was covered. He leaned against the wall and laughed until he was limp. When he regained control of himself he blinked at the sheriff and drew a long breath, which nearly caused Corwin to pull the trigger; but the sheriff found it to be a false alarm.

"What th' devil makes you think I was mixed up in that?" he asked, laughing again. He drew another long breath with unexpected suddenness, and again the nervous sheriff and the two deputies nearly pulled trigger; and again it was a false alarm.

"I've done my thinkin'!" snapped Corwin. "Watch him, boys!" he said out of the corner of his mouth. "An' if you wasn't mixed up in it you won't come to no harm."

"No; not in a decent town," rejoined Johnny, leaning against the wall again, where Corwin's body somewhat sheltered him from the deputies. The sheriff tensed again at the movement. "But Mesquite's plumb full of liars," drawled Johnny, "trained by Kane. How do I know I'll get a square deal?"

"You'll get it! Put 'em up!" snapped Corwin, raising his gun to give the command emphasis, and it now pointed at the other's head.

"Long an' Thompson—" began Johnny, and like a flash he twisted sidewise and jerked his head out of the line of fire, the bullet passing his ear and the powder scorching his hair. As he twisted he slipped in close, his left hand flashing to Corwin's gun-wrist and the right, across his body, tore the weapon from its owner's hand. The movement had been done so quickly that the sheriff did not realize what had occurred until he found himself disarmed and pressing against his own weapon, which was jammed into his groin. Johnny's left-hand gun had leaped into the surprised deputies' sight at the sheriff's hip and they lost no time in letting their own guns drop to the ground in instant answer to the snapped command. Corwin's momentary surprise died out nearly as quickly as it was born and, scorning the menace of the muzzle of his own gun, he grabbed Johnny. As he shifted his foot Johnny's leg slipped behind it and a sudden heave turned the sheriff over it, almost end over end, and he struck the ground with a resounding thump. Johnny sprang back, one gun on the sheriff, the other on the deputies.

"Get off them cayuses," he ordered and the two men slowly complied. "Go over near th' corral, an' stay there." In a moment he gave all his attention to the slowly arising officer.

"All this was unnecessary," he said. "You put us all in danger of bein' killed. Don't you *never* again try to take me in till you *know* why yo're doin' it! My head might 'a' been blowed off, an' all for nothin'! You don't know who busted that jail, judgin' by yore fool actions, an' you cussed well know it. You got plenty of gall, comin' down here an' throwin' a gun on me, for that! I'm sayin', frank, that whoever done that trick did th' right thing; but that ain't sayin' that *I* did it. Hope I didn't hurt you, Corwin; but I had to act sudden when you grabbed me."

"Don't you do no worryin' on my account!" snapped the sheriff.

"I ain't blamin' you for doin' your duty, if you was doin' it honest," said Johnny; "but you ain't got no business jumpin' before yo're shore. I ain't holdin' th' sack for nobody, Corwin; Kane or nobody else. Now then: you can tell what proof you got that it was me that busted th' jail."

Corwin was watching the smiling face and the accusing eyes and he saw no enmity in either. "Then who did?" he demanded.

Johnny shrugged his shoulders. *"Quien sabe?"* he asked. "There's a lot of people down here that would have more reason to do a thing like that, even for strangers, than *I* would. You ain't loved very much, from what I've heard. I don't want any more enemies than I got; but I'm tellin' you, flat, that I ain't goin' back with you; an' neither would you, if you was in my place, in a strange town. Here," he said, letting the hammer down and tossing the gun at the sheriff's feet, "take your gun. I'm glad you ain't hurt; an' I'm cussed glad I ain't. But somebody's shore goin' to be th' next time you pull a gun on me on a guess. You want to be *dead shore,* Corwin. We've had enough of this. Did you get any trace of them two?"

The sheriff watched his opponent's gun go back into its holster and slowly picked up his own. "No; I ain't," he admitted, and considered a moment as he sheathed the weapon with great care. "I *ain't* got nothin' flat agin' you," he said; "but I still think you had a hand in it. That's a good trick you worked, Nelson; I'm rememberin' it. All right; th' next time I come for you I'll *have* it cold; an' I'm shore expectin' to come for you, an' Idaho, too."

"That's fair enough," replied Johnny, smiling; "but I don't see why you want to drag Idaho in it for. He didn't have no more to do with it than *I* did."

"I'm believin' that, too," retorted the sheriff; "since you put it just that way. I haven't heard you say that you *didn't* do it. Before I go I want to ask you a question: Where was you th' night th' Diamond L lost them cows?"

"Right here with Mac an' th' boys."

"He was," said McCullough. "Yo're ridin' wide of th' trail, Corwin."

"Mebby," grunted the sheriff. "There's two trails. I mebby am plumb off of *one* of 'em, as long as you know he was down here that night; but I'm ridin' right down th' middle of th' other. When did you meet Long an' Thompson first?" he asked, wheeling suddenly and facing Johnny.

"Thinkin' what you do about me," replied Johnny, "I'd be a fool to tell you anythin', no matter what. So, as long as yo're ridin' down th' middle you'll have to read th' signs yoreself. Some of 'em must be plumb faint, th' way yo're guessin', an' castin' 'round. Get any news about them rustlers?"

"What's th' use of makin' trouble for yoreself by bein' stubborn?" asked McCullough. He looked at Corwin. "Sheriff, I know for shore that he never knowed any Bill Long or Red Thompson until after he come to Mesquite. What news did you get about th' rustlers?"

"Huh!" muttered Corwin, searching the face of the trail-boss, whose reputation for veracity was unquestioned. "I ain't got any news about 'em. Once they got on th' hard stretch they could go for miles an' not leave no trail. I'm figgerin' on spendin' quite some time north of where Lukins' boys quit an' turned back. There's three cows missin' that are marked so different from any I've ever seen that I'll know 'em in a herd of ten thousan' head; an' when they're cut out for me to look at there's some marks on horns an' hoofs that'll prove whose cows they are. I'm takin' a couple of his boys with me when I go, to make shore. Of course, I don't know that we'll ever see 'em, at all. Well," he said, turning toward his horse, "reckon I'll be goin'." He waved to the deputies, who approached, picked up their guns under Johnny's alert and suspicious scrutiny, and mounted. "As for you, Nelson, *next* time I'll be dead shore; an' I'll mebby shoot first, on a gamble, an' talk afterward. So-long."

Watching the three arms of the law ride away and out of sight, Johnny swung around and faced the grinning trail-boss. "You told th' truth, Mac; but I wonder if Corwin heard it like I did?"

McCullough shrugged his shoulders. "Who cares? I'm thankin' you for an interestin' lesson in how to beat th' drop; but I reckon I'm gettin' too old to be quick enough to use it. I reckon Waffles has been tellin' th' truth about yore Bar-20 outfit. Where you goin' now?"

"Off to see a couple of better men from that same outfit," grinned Johnny.

He went on with his preparations and soon rode Pepper toward a gap in the southern chain of hills, leading a loaded pack horse behind him. Emerging on the other side of the pass he followed the chain westward and in due time rounded the last hill and headed for the little clump of trees where he saw his two friends waiting. They waved to him and he replied, chuckling with pleasure.

Red looked critically at the pack animal. "Huh! From th' looks of that cayuse I reckon he figgers we're goin' to be gone some months, like a prospector holin' up for th' winter."

"He never underplays a hand," grunted Hopalong, a

warm light coming into his eyes. "Desert or no desert, it's shore good to be with him again. He never should 'a' left Montanny."

Johnny soon joined them, dismounted, picketed the pack horse, pushed back his sombrero and rolled a cigarette, grinning cheerfully. "If you want any more canteens you can have th' pair on my cayuse," he said. "Find anythin'?"

They told him and he nodded in quiet satisfaction. "You shore ain't been asleep," he chuckled. "You've just about found out somethin' that's been puzzlin' a lot of folks down here for some years. I wonder how close they ever come to them water holes when they was scoutin' around? But mebby they never scouted over that way much—everybody was bankin' on 'em stayin' on th' hard stretch over Lukins' way, instead of crossin' it so close to town. You'd never thought of lookin' for 'em over east if you hadn't remembered Slippery Trendly, now would you?"

"We wasn't lookin' for nothin' nor nobody except you," admitted Hopalong. "But when Red saw a dead cow as far out on th' desert as *it* was, we just had to take a look at it. An' when we saw it had been shot we couldn't do nothin' else but look for th' brand. That bein' cut out made us plumb suspicious. One thing just nat'rally led to th' next, as th' mule said when its tail was pulled."

"What you bet that missin' brand wasn't a Diamond L?" Johnny asked.

"Ain't that th' ranch Idaho works for?" queried Red.

Johnny nodded. "They raided Lukins th' night of th' day you an' Hoppy left town. That outfit put in two days ridin' along th' hard ground, half of 'em up an' half of 'em down. They lost over a hundred head."

His friends exchanged looks, each trying to visualize the all but obliterated trail, and both nodded.

"Mebby it *was* a Diamond L," said Hopalong, and he explained their plans to some length.

"That's goin' to win if you can stick it out," said Johnny. "McCullough's steamin' a little, but he's still carryin' out Twitchell's wishes; an' I been arguin' with him, too, to give you fellers a chance. Hey!" he exclaimed, grinning. "I allus knowed I'd get a bad name for hangin' out with you two coyotes; an' I done got it. I'm suspected strong of bein' a criminal, like you fellers, an' I'll mebby be an outlaw, too. Sheriff Corwin just said so, an' he ought to know if anybody does. He arrested me for helpin' to get you fellers out of jail, but he didn't say how he aimed to keep me in it, busted like it is."

"How'd you get away?" asked Red. "Wouldn't you go with him?"

"Mebby he didn't have th' rest of th' dozen," suggested Hopalong.

"Oh, he wasn't real shore about it really bein' me he wanted, so he turned me loose," replied Johnny. "Anyhow, I couldn't 'a' gone with him: I had to get this stuff out to you fellers. An' besides, I knowed if I got in that 'dobe hut you wouldn't have th' nerve to bust me out again."

"I'm honin' to bust Corwin's 'dobe head," growled Red.

"There's four canteens an' plenty of grub, with Mac's compliments," said Johnny, waving at the pack horse. "When am I to meet you again?"

Hopalong considered a moment. "There's too much ridin', comin' down here unless we has to," he said. "Tell you what: We'll find a hill, or a ridge up on th' plateau where a fire can be lit that won't show to nobody north of them hills you just come around. Take that white patch up yonder: we can see it plain for miles. You ride up to it every day about two hours after sun-up; an' every night just after dark. If you see smoke puffs in daylight, or a winkin' fire at night, ride toward that split bluff behind us. We'll meet you there. If you get news for us, do th' same thing on th' other slope, so it can't be seen from across this valley. As long as it can be seen on a line with th' split bluff we won't miss it."

Johnny scratched his head. "Strings of six puffs or six winks means trouble: come a-latherin'," he suggested. "Strings of three means news, an' take yore time. Better have a signal for grub an' supplies: it'll mebby save ridin'. Say groups of two an' five, alternate?"

Hopalong nodded and repeated the signals to make certain that he had them right. "Two an' five, alternate, for supplies; strings of six, come a-runnin'; strings of three, news, an' take our time. Couple of hours after sun-up an' just after dark. All right, Kid."

"Mac's got an old spyglass. Want it, if I can get it?" asked Johnny.

"Shore!" grunted Red.

"Bring it next time you come," said Hopalong.

"All right. Where you goin' now?"

"Up on Sand Creek, where we're camped," answered Red. "We got a couple of days before we move out on th' fryin' pan, an' we're aimin' to make th' most of it."

"Wait till I get th' glass, an' I'll go along," suggested Johnny, eagerly.

"Get a rustle on—an' take this pack animal back with you," smiled Hopalong as Johnny started without it. "We'll empty out th' canteens, an' we can tote th' supplies without it."

XVI

♦

A Vigil Rewarded

The days passed quietly for the two watchers after Johnny had gone back to the Question-Mark, the hours dragging in monotonous succession. In the Sand Creek camp time passed pleasantly enough, but out on the great, up-slanting billow of sand north of Sweet Spring, devoid of shelter from the blazing sun and from the reflected glare of the gray-white desert around it, was another matter. Prone on his stomach lay Hopalong on the northward slope, his face barely level with the crest of the ridge. Down in the hollow behind him was his horse, picketed and hobbled as well, and at his side on his blanket to keep the cutting sand and clogging dust from barrels and actions lay his rifle and his six-guns, so hot that their metal parts could not be touched without a grimace of discomfort coming to his face. The telescope at intervals swung around the shimmering horizon, magnifying the dancing heat waves until the distortion of their wavering, streaming currents at times rendered the view chaotic and baffling. Strange sights were to be seen in the air and knowing what they were he watched them as his only source of amusement. A tree-bordered lake appeared, its waters sparkling, arose into the air, became vague and slowly dissolved from view, calling from him caustic comment. Inverted mountains reached down from the heavens, standing on snow-covered tops, writhed more and more from their outer edges and melted down from the up-flung bases, slowly fading from view. They were followed by a silvery, winding river, certain features which caused him to think that he recognized it and while he studied it a herd of cattle upside down, and greatly magnified, pushed through into sight as the river scene faded away. Another hour passed and then a steep-walled, green valley inverted itself before his gaze. He could make out a hut and a few trees and then as mounted men began to ride up its slanting bluff trail his attention became riveted on it and he reached for the hot telescope. One look through the instrument made him grunt with disgust, for the figures danced and shrunk and expanded, weaved and became like shadows, through which he looked as though through a rare, discolored vapor. He was mildly excited and tried in vain to search his visual image of the sight for the faces of the men; but it was in vain, and he opened his eyes as the image faded and then closed them again to better search the memory picture. This, too, availed him nothing and he realized that he had not really seen the faces. He was perplexed and vexed, for there was something familiar about some of those riders. About to move for a look around through the telescope, he yielded to a humorous warning and lay quiet for awhile. Was it possible that the mirage had been double-acting, and had revealed each to the other?

"Mebby they won't put as much stock in theirs as I did in mine," he said, and slowly picked up the telescope for a final look all around the horizon before Red should relieve him. East, south, west he looked and saw nothing. Swinging it toward the Sand Creek camp he grunted in satisfaction as a figure very much like Red wavered and danced as it emerged over a ridge of sand. Farther north he swung it and slowly swept the northern horizon. Swearing suddenly he stopped its slow progress and brought it back searchingly over ground it had just covered. Rigid he held it and looked with unbelieving eyes.

"Mirage?" he growled, questioningly. "It's too solid for that—I'm goin' up to see."

Getting his horse he gingerly slipped the hot rifle into its scabbard, hastily dropped the six-guns into their holsters and, mounting, rode to meet his nearing friend.

"Cooked?" queried Red, grinning. "You shore didn't lose no time gettin' started after you saw me! Ain't it hell out here?"

"Hell is right," answered Hopalong, handing over the telescope. "But we got cayuses, full canteens, an' know where we are. Swing that blisterin' tube over yonder," he said, pointing, "an' tell me what you see?"

Red obeyed and the moving glass suddenly stopped and swung back a little. After long scrutiny he raised his head and gazed steadily over the rigid tube as though along a rifle barrel. "I see him, now, without it," he said. "A-foot, he is, staggerin' every-which way. Comin'?"

His companion replied by pushing into the lead and setting a stiff pace through the soft sand and alkali dust. As they drew near they both shivered at the sight which steadily was being better revealed.

The figure of a man, and scarcely more than a figure, stumbled crazily across the sand, hatless, his bare feet covered with dust which had become pasty with the blood exuding through the deepening clefts in the skin and flesh. Progress on such feet would have made him mad from pain if he had not already become so from other causes. His trousers were ripped and frayed to the swollen, dust-plastered knees, the crimson fissures running up and down his swollen legs. Shirt he had none, save the strip which hung stiff and crimson from his belt. His upper body was a thing of horror, swollen, matted with crusts of dried blood, from beneath which more oozed out to in turn coagulate. His burning eyes peered through slits in the puffed face and his tongue, blackened and purplish, stuck out of his mouth.

"God!" muttered Red, glancing awesomely at the tense face of his companion.

"He's gone," said Hopalong, softly. "Nothing can save him. It would be a mercy—" but he checked the words, searching Red's acquiescent eyes.

"Can't do it," said Red. "Can you?"

Hopalong drew in a deep breath and shook his head. "We got to try th' other first," he said. "It's wrong—but there's nothin' else. We ain't doctors, an' there may be a fightin' chance. Hobble th' cayuses. We'll both tackle him—one alone might have to be too rough, for he'll mebby fight."

"He's down," said Red as he swung from his saddle. "Lookin' right at us, too, an' don't see us."

The figure groveled in the sand, digging with blundering fingers worn to the bone by previous digging, and choked sounds came from the swollen throat. Red talked to himself as he hobbled his horse and pushed down the picket pin.

"Lost his cayuse, somehow, or went crazy an' chased it away. Used up his last water an' then threw away everythin' he had. Tore off his shirt because th' neckband got too tight an' th' cloth stuck to th' blood clots an' pulled at 'em. I've seen others, but they warn't none of 'em as bad as him," growled Red more to himself than to his companion.

Hopalong pushed home his own picket pin and stood up. "Comin'?" he asked, starting slowly for the groveling, digging thing on the sand.

They stepped up to him and lifted the unfortunate from the ground. Dazed and without understanding, the pitiful object of their assistance suddenly snarled and reached its bleeding fingers for Red's throat, and for the next few minutes two rational, strong men had as hard a fight on their hands as they ever had experienced; and when it was over and the enraged unfortunate became docile from exhaustion they were covered with blood. Letting a few drops of water trickle down the side of the protruding tongue, which they forced to one side when the drops were stopped by it, they worked over the dying man as long as they dared in the sun and then, carrying him to Hopalong's horse they put him across the saddle, lashing him securely, and covered him with a doubled blanket to cheat the leering sun.

"Go ahead to th' water hole," said Hopalong, straightening up from tying the last knot. "I'll take him to camp an' do what I can. There won't be no trouble handlin' him, tied like he is. Got to try to save him—'though I hope somebody puts a bullet through my head if I ever get like him."

"Bein' crazy, he mebby ain't feelin' it as much as he might," replied Red. "Seems to me he's the one they called Sandy Woods; but he's so plumb changed I ain't shore."

Hopalong thought of the last mirage he had seen, was about to speak of it, but abruptly changed his mind. He conveyed his warning in another way. "Keep a-lookin' sharp, Red," he said. "Th' poor devil shore was one of them rustlers; an' they mebby ain't far behind him. It's gettin' nearer an' nearer th' time they ought to come back. I'll stay with him in camp an' let th' Kid's signal go, if he makes one. This feller ain't got long to live, I'm figgerin'."

"It's a wonder he lived this long," said Red, riding off to take up the vigil.

Hopalong swung his belts and guns over the pommel of the saddle to lighten him, drank sparingly from a canteen and started on foot for the camp, leading his dispirited horse. After a walk through the hot, yielding sand which became a punishment during the last mile he sighed with relief as he stopped the horse on the bank of Sand Creek and tenderly placed its burden on the ground in the shade of a tree. More water, in judicious quantities, and at increasingly frequent intervals brought no apparent relief to the sufferer, and in mid-afternoon Sandy Woods lost all need of earthly care. Kane's thieving trail-boss had won his bet.

Hopalong looked down at the body freed of its suffering and slowly shook his head. "Th' other way would 'a' been th' best," he said. "*I* knowed it; *Red* knowed it—yet, both plumb shore, an' *knowin'* it was better, we just couldn't do it. A man's trainin' is a funny thing."

He looked around the little depression and walked toward a patch of sand lying near a mass of stones which had rolled down the slope; and before the evening shadows had reached across the little creek, a heaped-up pile of rocks marked the place of rest of one more weary traveler. At the head, lying on the ground, was a cross made of stones. Why he had placed it there Hopalong could hardly have told, but something within him had stirred through the sleep of busy and heedless years, and he had unthinkingly obeyed it.

He looked up at the sun and found it was time to go on watch again. He had been given no opportunity to sleep, but did not complain, carelessly accepting it as one of the breaks in the game. When he reached his friend, ready to go on duty again, Red looked up at him and scrutinized his face.

"Lots of sleep you musta got," said Red. "How's our patient?"

"Gettin' all th' sleep there is," came the reply. "We was right—both ways."

"Spread yore blanket here," said Red. "I'm stickin' to th' job till you have a snooze. Anyhow, somethin' tells me that two won't be more'n we need out here at night, from now on."

"It's my trick," replied Hopalong, decisively. "Spread yore own blanket."

"Him turnin' up like he did was an accident," retorted Red, "an' accidents are shared between us both. Anyhow,

I ain't sleepy—an' th' next few hours are pleasant. Get some sleep, you chump!"

"Well, as long as we're both handy, it don't make much difference," replied Hopalong, spreading the blanket. "We can spell each other any time we need to. Hope th' Kid ain't tryin' to signal nothin'."

"We got more to signal than he has," growled Red. "Shut up, now; an' go to sleep," and his companion, blessed by one of the prized acquirements of the plainsman, promptly obeyed; but it seemed to him that he scarcely had dozed off when he felt his friend's thrusting hand, and he opened his eyes in the darkness, staring up at the blazing stars, in surprise.

"Yes?" whispered Hopalong, without moving or making any other sound, again true to his training.

His companion's whisper, a whisper by force of habit rather than for any good reason, reached him: "Turn over, an' look over th' ridge."

Hopalong obeyed, threw off the blanket which Red had spread over him when the chill of the desert night descended, and became all eyes as he saw the faint glow of a distant fire, which rapidly grew and became brighter. "It's them, down at th' other water hole," he said, arising and feeling to see if his Colts had slid out of their holsters while he slept. "I'm goin' down for a better look," and he glanced at the northern sky just above the horizon, memorized a group of stars and disappeared noiselessly into the night.

Nearing the larger water hole he went more slowly and finished by wriggling up to the crest of a sand billow, his head behind a lone sage bush, and his eyelids closed to a thin crack, lest the light of the fire should reflect from his eyes and reveal him to some keen, roving glance.

The greasewood fire blazed under a pair of skillets, while a coffeepot imitated the Tower of Pisa on the glowing coals at one edge. Around it, reclining on the powdery clay, or squatting in the more characteristic attitude of men of the saddle, were a half-dozen of Kane's pets, Miguel and his cronies well to one side. The hidden watcher knew them all by sight and saw several men who had helped the sheriff trick him and Red. In the darkness behind the group he heard their horses moving about as they grazed.

"Do you reckon he made it, Miguel?" asked the trail-boss, apropos of the conversation around the fire.

Miguel turned his face to the light, the scar over his eye glistening against the duller skin around it. "I say no," he drawled. "He change hees horrse at the corrals, no? Thee horrse he took was born at thee Cimarron corral an' foaled eet's firrst colt there. I would not lak' sooch a horrse eef I did not know my way. But, *quien sabe?*"

The trail-boss looked at him searchingly, wondering how much the half-breed knew about Sandy's reasons for making the change. Kane would not allow fighting in the ranks, and grudges live long in some men. Besides, to lose the bet was to lose his share of the drive profits to a man he secretly hated, and this did not suit the trail-boss.

Miguel smiled grimly into the cold, searching eyes and shrugged his shoulders, his soft laugh turning the cold stare into something wanner. "Eef he deed, then eet ees ver' good," he said; "eef he deed not, then eet hees own fault. But he should not change hees horrse."

"We'll know tomorrow night, anyhow," said a voice well back from the fire. "Get a rustle on you, Thorpe," it growled. "You move around like an old woman."

"Ain't no walls to climb," said another, laughing.

The red-faced cook did not raise his head or retort, but in his memory another name was deeply carved, to replace the one he was certain would be erased when they reached Mesquite. Sandy Woods' dislike for the horse given to him at the corrals had been overcome by the smooth words of the unforgiving cook, who also had a score to pay.

"When do we rustle next?" asked a squatting figure. "We been layin' low too long, an' my pile has done faded; I wasn't lucky, like you, Trask, an' the sheriff," he said, looking at the trail-boss. "Next time a bank is busted *I* aim to be in on it. You fellers can't hog *all* th' good things."

"Don't do no good to talk about it," snapped the trail-boss. "Kane names them he wants. Trask an' me was robbed of half of our share—I ain't forgettin' it, neither. An' as for th' next raid, that's settled. As long as all of us are in it, you might as well know. We're cleanin' up on McCullough's west range, an' there won't be much of a wait." Neither the speaker, his companions, nor the man behind the sage brush knew that Kane already had changed his mind, and because of Lukins' activity had decided to raid McCullough's east range.

"*How* soon?" demanded the questioner.

"Some night this week, I reckon," came the answer. "If we get a good bunch we'll sit back an' take things easy for awhile. Too many drives may cut a trail that'll show, an' we can't risk *that*."

"Too bad we have to drive west an' north before we hit for the plain," said Jud Hill. "Takes two days more, that way."

The trail-boss smiled. "I know a way that would suit you, Jud," he said. "So does Miguel—but we've been savin' it till th' old route gets too risky. It joins th' regular trail right here. Well, at last th' cook has really cooked—pass it this way, Thorpe. I'm eatin' fast an' I'm turnin' in faster. Th' more we beat th' sun gettin' away from here, th' less it'll beat on us. We're leavin' an hour ahead of it."

Not waiting until the camp should become silent, when any noise he might make would be more likely to be heard,

Hopalong crept away while the rustlers ate and returned to his friend, who waited under a certain group of stars.

Red cocked his head at the soft sound, his Colt swinging to cover it, when he heard his name called in his friend's voice, and he replied.

Hopalong sat down on the blanket and related what he had seen and heard without comment from his listener until the end of the narrative.

"Huh!" said Red. "You learned a-plenty. An' I'm glad they reached that water hole after dark, an' are goin' to go on again before it gets light. They missed our tracks. I call that luck," he said in great satisfaction. "We wasn't doin' much guessin'. That's shore their drive trail, an' th' best thing about it is that it's th' bottom of th' Y. They've got two ways of leavin' th' ranges without showin' tracks, but they both come together down yonder. I reckon mebby we'll have a piece to speak when they come this way again. Goin' to tell McCullough what's bein' hatched?"

"We ought to," answered his companion, slowly. "We'll tell th' Kid an' leave it to him. They must be purty shore of themselves to rustle Question-Mark cattle at *this* time. If th' Kid tells Mac, an' they try it, Mesquite shore is goin' to be a busy little town. I think I know his breed."

"They ain't takin' much of a chance, at that, if they try it," said Red. "They don't know that we know anythin' about it an' that McCullough will know it, if th' Kid tells him. Mebby they figger that by springin' it right now when th' feelin' is so strong agin' 'em, that it would make folks think they didn't do it, because they oughten't to—oh, pshaw! You know what I'm gettin' at!"

"Shore," grunted Hopalong. He was silent a moment and then stirred. "We ain't got no reason to stay out here for a day or two. Let's pull out an' go down where we can signal th' Kid after sun-up. We'll ride well to th' east past their camp. What wind is stirrin' is comin' from th' other way, an' there's no use makin' any fresh tracks in front of 'em."

An hour or so after daylight a small fire sent a column of smoke straight up, the explanation of its smoking qualities suggested by the canteen lying near it. Hopalong and Red slid a blanket over the fire and drew it suddenly aside, performing this operation three times in succession before letting the column mount unmolested for brief intervals. In the west, above and behind a bare spot on a ridge of hills an answering column climbed upward, and then a series of triple puffs took its place. Scattering the fire over the ground the two friends absent-mindedly kicked sand over the embers, and suddenly grinned at each other at the foolishness of their precautions.

When they reached the little grove they found Johnny waiting for them, his horse well loaded with more provisions. As they transferred the supplies to their own mounts they told him what had occurred and he decided that McCullough should be informed of the forthcoming raid, whether or not it would in any way jeopardize the winning of the rewards.

"It's a toss-up whether Mac will wait for them to run it off," he said, "when I tell him. He's gettin' more riled every minute, but he seemed to calm down a little after Corwin visited him. Somethin' sort of pulls him back when he gets to climbin' onto his hind legs, an' he ends up by leanin' agin' th' wall an' swearin'. I'm not tellin' him nothin' about anythin' but th' raid. You aimin' to go back to that water hole?"

Hopalong shook his head. "No, sir," he answered. "There ain't no reason to till th' raid happens. We're campin' on Sand Creek till you signal that it's been run off. Time enough then for us to watch on that cussed griddle."

"Have special signal for that?" suggested Red. "Say two,

two an' three, repeated. Mebby won't have time to hear what th' news is. When you get our answer don't bother ridin' down here to tell us anythin'—we'll be makin' tracks *pronto*."

Johnny nodded. "Two, two an' three is OK. I'll be ridin' back to tell Mac there's goin' to be a party on his west range some night soon. I'm bettin' it'll be a bloody party, too. Say," he exclaimed, pulling up, "Lukins an' Idaho was down last night. They're mad as hell, an' they're throwin' a cordon of riders plumb across th' hard stretch every night. Lukins an' Mac are joinin' forces, an' from now on th' two ranches are workin' together as one. With us scoutin' around east of town somethin' shore ought to drop." He pressed Pepper's sleek sides and started back to the sheltering hills.

"Somethin's *goin'* to drop," growled Red, the memory of the jailing burning strongly within him. "Don't forget, Kid— two, two an' three."

Johnny turned in his saddle, waved a hand and kept on going. Rounding the westernmost hill he rode steadily until opposite the white patch of sand on the northern slope and then, dismounting, collected firewood, and built it up on the dead ashes of his signal fire, ready for the match. Going on again he rode steadily until he reached the place in the arroyo which lay directly behind the ranchhouse.

McCullough returned from a ride over the range to find his cheerful friend smoking some of his tobacco.

"Want a job, Nelson?" asked the trail-boss, swinging from the saddle with an easy agility belying his age and weight.

Johnny smiled at him. "Anythin' that don't take me away from th' ranch too far or too long. Call it."

"One of th' boys, ridin' south of th' hills on a fool's errand, this mornin', thought he saw smoke signals back of

White Face," said McCullough. "He says he reckons he's loco. I ain't goin' that far. Think you could find out anythin' about 'em?"

Johnny considered, and chuckled. "Huh!" he snorted. "He's plumb late. *I* saw them before he did, an' know all about 'em. You stuck a couple of jabs into me about bein' lazy, an' likin' to set around all day doin' nothin'. Any chump can wear out cayuses ridin' around discoverin' things, but th' wise man is th' feller that can set around all day, lazy an' no-account, an' figger things out. I don't have to go prowlin' around to find out things. I just set in th' shade of th' house, roll cigarettes an' hold powwows with my medicine bag. You'd be surprised if you knowed what I got in that bag, an' what I can get *out* of it. You shore would."

McCullough looked at him with an expression which tried to express so many uncomplimentary things at once that the composite was almost neutral; at least, it was somewhat blank.

"Ye-ah?" he drawled, his inflection in no way suggesting anything to Johnny's credit.

"Ye-ah," repeated the medicine man somewhat belligerently.

"Oh," said the trail-boss, eyeing his victim speculatively. "You know all about 'em, huh?"

"Everythin'," placidly replied Johnny, rolling another cigarette.

"I wish to heaven you'd quit smokin' them cussed things around here," said McCullough plaintively. "Yo're growed up now, purty near; an' you *ain't* no Greaser. I'll buy you a pipe if you'll promise to smoke it."

"Pipes, judgin' from yourn," sweetly replied Johnny, calmly lighting the cigarette, "are dangerous, unless a man hangs around th' house *all* th' time. When I used to go off scoutin', I allus wished th' other fellers smoked pipes, corncob pipes, like Mister McCullough carries around. Why, cuss it, I could smell 'em out, *up*-wind, if they did. It would 'a' saved me a lot of crawlin' an' worryin'. I knowed you was comin' back ten minutes before I saw you. Now, you can't blame a skunk—he was born that way, an' he's got good reasons for keepin' on th' way he was born. But a human, goin' out of his way, to smell like *some* I knows of," he broke off, shrugging his shoulders expressively.

McCullough slowly produced the corncob, blew through the stem with unnecessary violence, gravely filled and lit it, his eyes twinkling. "Takes a *man,* I reckon, to enjoy its aromer," he observed. "Goin' back to yore medicine bag, let's see what you can get out of it," he challenged.

Johnny drew out his buckskin tobacco pouch, placed it on the floor, covered it with his sombrero and chanted softly, his eyes fixed on the hat. "I smell a trail-boss an' his pipe. They went to th' bend of th' crick, an' they says to Pete Holbrook, who rides that section, that he ought to ride on th' other side of th' crick after dark." He was repeating information which he had chanced to overhear near the small corral the night before, when he had passed unobserved in the darkness.

McCullough favored the hat with a glance of surprise and Johnny with a keen, prolonged stare.

"Pete, he said that wouldn't do no good unless he went far enough north to leave his section unprotected. He borrowed a chew of tobacco before th' man an' th' pipe went away an' let th' air get pure again." The medicine man knew Pete's thrifty nature by experience.

"Yo're shore a good guesser," grunted McCullough. "What about them smoke signals, that you know all about?"

Johnny readjusted the hat a hairsbreadth, passed his hands over it and closed his eyes. "I see smoke signals," he chanted. "There's palefaces in 'em, ridin' cautious at night over a hard plain. They're driftin' cows into a herd. Th' herd is growin' fast, an' it drifts toward th' hard ground. Now it's goin' faster. Th' brands are Diamond L. I see more smoke signals an' more ridin' in th' dark. Another herd, bigger this time, is runnin' hard over that same plain. Th' brands are SV, vented; an' plain Question-Mark. It seems near—within a week—an' it's on yore west range." He opened his eyes, kicked the hat across the room and pocketed the tobacco pouch.

"Mac," he said, gravely. "That's a shore-enough prophecy. Leavin' out all jokin', it's true. Hoppy an' Red told me, a little while ago, that they overheard some of Kane's gang talkin'. They're goin' to raid you like I said. Th' smoke signals was me answerin' theirs. They say Sandy Woods is dead. They ought to know because they buried him. They know three of th' men that robbed th' bank an' they've knowed ever since Ridley was shot, who killed him. They've seen Kane's drive trail crew an' they know a whole lot that I ain't goin' to tell you now; mebby I'll not tell you till we get th' rewards; but if it'll make you feel any better, I'm sayin' that we're goin' to get them rewards right soon. When Kane raids you he springs th' trap that'll clear a lot of vermin off this range."

"How much of all that do you mean?" demanded the trail-boss, his odorous pipe out and reeking more than ever. He was looking into his companion's eyes with a searching, appraising directness which many men would have found uncomfortable.

"All of it," complacently answered the medicine man, rolling a new cigarette. "There's only one thing I'm doubtful about, 'though it was what Hoppy overheard, so I gave it to you that way. They said yore west range. If Kane learns how th' Diamond L riders are spread out, an' I'm bettin' he knew it near as soon as Lukins did, he'll be a fool to drive that way. If it was me, I'd split my outfit an' put half of 'em on th' east end! But I'm a gambler."

McCullough considered the matter. "They'll leave a plain trail if they raid th' east section," he muttered; "an' th' desert'll hold 'em to a narrow strip north or south. There's water up th' north way, but there's people scattered all around, an' they're nat'rally near th' water. South, there's less water, an' more people th' further they go. They might tackle th' desert, but Lukins an' me figger they go west from th' hard ground. I ain't agin' gamblin', but I don't gamble with anythin' *I* don't own. If yore friends heard them coyotes say 'west,' I'm playin' my cards accordin' to their case-rack. I may call it wrong, I may get a split, or I may win—but I'm backin' th' case-keepers, 'specially when they're keepin' th' rack for *me*. West it is an' west is where hell will pop when they pay their visit. An' lemme tell you this, Nelson: Win, lose or split on th' raid, if it comes off within a week, I'll be dead shore who's behind it, an' there's a cyclone due in Mesquite right soon after. Twitchell had his chance. His game's no good—I'm playin' th' cards I've drawn in my own way when they show their hand in this raid. I'm bein' cold-decked by Corwin—but I'll warm it aplenty. You hang around an' see th' fireworks!"

Johnny stretched, relaxed, and grinned. "I'm aimin' to touch some off, myself," he replied, "an' I reckon Hoppy an' Red will send up a couple of rockets on their own account. Rockets?" He grinned. "No; not rockets—there's allus burned sticks comin' down from rockets. Besides, they're too smooth an' easy. Reckon they'll touch off some pinwheels. Whizzin', tail-chasin' pinwheels; or mebby jumping-jacks. Most likely they'll be jumping-jacks, th' way some folks'll be steppin' lively to get out of th' way. Don't you bank on this bein' *yore* celebration—you'll only own th' lot an' make th' noise. Th' grand display, th' glorious finish is Bar-20. Just plain, old-fashioned Bar-20. Gee, Mac, it makes me a kid again!"

"It's got an easy job, then!" snorted the trail-boss.

XVII

♦

A Well-Planned Raid

On night shift again Pete Holbrook reached the end of his beat, waited until his fellow-watcher on the east bulked suddenly out of the darkness, exchanged a few words with him and turned back under the star-filled sky, his horse having no difficulty in avoiding obstructions, but picking its way with ease around scattered thickets, grass-tufted hummocks, and across shallow ravines and hollows. Objects close at hand were discernible to eyes accustomed to the darkness and Pete's range of vision attained the enviable limits enjoyed by those who live out-of-doors and look over long distances. An occasional patch of sand moved slowly into his circumscribed horizon as he rode on; vague, squatting bulks gradually revealed their vegetative nature and an occasional more regular bulk told him where a cow was lying. These latter more often were catalogued by his ears before his eyes defined them and from the contentment in the sounds he nodded in satisfaction. Soon he felt the gentle rise which swept up to the breeze-caressed ridge which projected northward and forced the little creek to follow it for nearly a mile before the rocky obstruction could be passed.

There had been a time when the ridge had forced the creek again as far out of its course, but on quiet nights a fanciful listener could hear the petulant grumblings of the stream and its constant boast. Placid and slow above the ridge, the waters narrowed and deepened when they reached the insolent bulk as if concentrating for the never-ending assault. They had cut through softer resistance along the edges and now gnawed noisily at the stone itself. Narrower grew the stream and deeper, the pools clear and with clean rock bottoms and sides where the hurrying water, now free from the last vestige of color imposed by the banks further up, became crystal in the light of day. Hurrying from pool to pool, singing around boulders it ran faster and faster as if eager for the final attempt against its bulky enemy, and hissed and growled as it sped along the abrupt rock face. Loath to leave the fight, it followed tenaciously along the other side of the ridge and at last gave up the struggle to turn sharply south again and flow placidly down the valley on a continuation of the line it had followed above.

This forced detour made the U-Bend, so called by Question-Mark riders, and the sloping ground of the ridge was as much a favorite with the cattle as were its bordering pools with the men. Here could be felt every vagrant breeze, and while the grass was scantier than that found on the more level pastures round about, and cropped closer, the cattle turned toward it when darkness came. It was the best bed-ground on the ranch.

The grunting, cud-chewing, or blowing blots grew more numerous as Holbrook went on and when he had reached the crest of the ridge his horse began to pick its way more and more to avoid them, the rider chanting a mournful lay and then followed it with a song which, had it been rightfully expurged, would have had little left to sing about. Like another serenade it had been composed in a barroom, but the barroom atmosphere was strongly in evidence. It suddenly ceased.

Holbrook stopped the song and his horse at the same instant and his roving glances roved no more, but settled into a fixed stare which drew upon itself his earnest concentration, as if the darkness could better be pierced by an act of will.

"Did I, or didn't I?" he growled, and looked around to see if his eyes would show him other lights. Deciding that they were normal he focussed them again in the direction of the sight which had stopped the song. "Bronch, I shore saw it," he muttered. "It was plain as it was short." He glanced down at the horse, saw its ears thrust rigidly forward and nodded his head emphatically. "An' so did you, or I'm a liar!"

He was no liar, for a second flash appeared, and it acted on him like a spur. The horse obeyed the sudden order and leaped forward, careening on its erratic course as it avoided swiftly appearing obstacles.

"Seems to me like it was further west th' last time," muttered Holbrook. "What th' devil it is, I don't know; but I'm goin' to show th' fambly curiosity. Can't be Kane's coyotes—folks don't usually show lights when they're stealin' cows. An' it's on Charley's section, but we'll have a look anyhow. Cuss th' wind."

The light proved to be of will-o'-the-wisp nature, but he pursued doggedly and after a time he heard sounds which suggested that he was not alone on the range. He drew his six-gun in case his welcome should take that course and swung a little to the left to investigate the sounds.

"Must be Charley," he soliloquized, but raised the Colt to a better position. One would have thought Charley to be no friend of his. The Colt went up a little higher, the horse stopped suddenly and its rider gave the night's hailing signal, so well imitated that it might easily have fooled the little animal to whom Nature had given it. It came back like a double echo and soon Charley bulked out of the dark.

"You follerin' that, too?" he asked, entirely reassured now that his eyes were all right, for he had had the same doubts as his friend.

"Yes; what you reckon it is?"

"Dunno," growled Charley. "Thought mebby it was some fool puncher lightin' a cigarette. It wasn't very bright, an' it didn't last long."

"Reckon you called it," replied Holbrook. "Well, th' only animal that lights them is humans; an' no human workin' for this ranch is lightin' cigarettes at night, *these* nights. Bein' a strange human where strange humans shouldn't ought to be, I'm plumb curious. All of which means I'm goin' to have a closer look."

"I'm with you," said Charley. "We better stick together or we'll mebby get to shootin' each other; an' I'm frank in sayin' I'm shootin' quick tonight, an' by ear. There ain't no honest human ridin' around out here, day *or* night, that don't belong here; an' them that does belong ain't over there, lightin' cigarettes nor nothin' else. That lightnin' bug don't belong, but he may *stay* here. Look! There she is again— *this* side of where I saw it last!"

"Same place," contradicted Holbrook, pushing on.

"Same place yore hat!"

"Bet you five it is."

"Yo're on; make it ten?"

"It is. Shut yore face an' keep goin'. Somethin's happenin' over there."

Minute after minute passed and then they swore in the same breath.

"It's south!" exulted Charley. "You lose."

"He crossed in front of us, cuss him," said Holbrook.

As he spoke an answering light flashed where the first

ones had been seen and Holbrook grunted with satisfaction. "You lose; there's two of 'em. We was bettin' on th' other."

"They're signalin', an' there's mebby more'n two. What's th' difference? Come on, Pete! We'll bust up this little party before it starts. But what are they lightin' lights for if they're rustlin'? An' if they ain't rustlin' what'n blazes *are* they doin'?"

"Head over a little," said his companion, forcing his horse against his friend's. "We'll ride between th' flashes first, an' if there's a herd bein' collected we'll mebby hit it. Don't ask no questions; just shoot an' jump yore cayuse sideways."

South of them another puncher was riding at reckless speed along the chord of a great arc and although his section lay beyond Holbrook's, he was now even with them. When they changed their course they drew closer to him and some minutes later, stopping for a moment's silence so they could listen for sounds of the enemy, they heard his faint, far-off signal and answered it. He announced his arrival with a curse and a question and the answer did not answer much. They went on together, eager and alert.

"Heard you drummin' down th' ridge—you know that rocky ground rolls 'em out," the newcomer explained. "Knowed somethin' was wrong th' way you was poundin', an' follered on a gamble till I saw th' lights. Reckon Walt ain't far behind me. I'm tellin' you so you'll signal before you shoot. He's loose out here somewhere."

When the light came again it was much farther west and the answering flash was north. The three pulled up and looked at each other.

"There ain't no cayuse livin' can cover ground like that second feller," growled Holbrook. "He was plumb south only a few minutes ago, an' *now* will you look where he is!"

"Mebby they're ghostes, Bob," suggested Charley, who harbored a tingling belief in things supernatural.

" 'Ghostes'!" chuckled Holbrook. "Ghosts, you means! Th' same as 'posts'! Th' 'es' is silent, like in 'cows.' I never believed in 'em; but I shore don't claim to know it all. There's plenty of things *I* don't understand—an' this is shore one of 'em. My hair's gettin' stiff!"

"Yo're a couple of old wimmin!" snorted Bob. "There's only one kind of a ghost that'll slow me up—that's th' kind that packs hardware. Seein' as they ain't supposed to tote guns, I'm goin' for that coyote west of here. He don't swap ends so fast. Mebby I can turn him into a *real* ghost. Look out where you shoot. So-long!"

"We'll assay his jumpin' friend," called Charley.

Again the flashes showed, one to the south, the other to the north, and while the punchers marveled, the third appeared in the southwest.

"One apiece!" shouted Holbrook. "I'll take th' last. Go to 'em!" and drumming hoofbeats rolled into silence in three directions.

Soon spitting flashes in the north were answered in kind, the reports announcing six-guns in action; in the west a thinner tongue of flame and a different kind of report was answered by rapid bursts of fire and the jarring crashes of a Colt. Far to the south three stabbing flashes went upward, Walt's signal that he was coming. From beyond the U-Bend, far to the east, the triple signal came twice, flat and low. Beyond them a yellow glow sprang from the black void and marked the ranchhouse, where six sleeping men piled from their bunks and, finishing their dressing as they ran, chased the cursing trail-boss to the saddled, waiting horses, their tingling blood in an instant sweeping the cobwebs of sleep from their conjecturing brains. There was a creaking of leather, a soft, musical jingling of metal and a sudden thunderous rolling of hoofbeats as seven bunched horses leaped at breakneck speed into the darkness, the tight-lipped riders eager, grim, and tense.

Through a bushy arroyo leading to Mesquite three Mexicans rode as rapidly as they dared, laughing and carrying on a jerky, exultant conversation. A mile behind them came a fourth, his horse running like a frightened jack rabbit as it avoided the obstructions which seemed to leap at them. A bandage around the rider's head perhaps accounted for his sullenness. The four were racing to get to Red Frank's, and safety. Out on the plain the fifth, and as Fate willed it, the only one of the group openly allied to Kane, lay under his dead horse, his career of thieving and murder at an end. Close to him was a dead Question-Mark horse, and the wounded rider, wounded again by his sudden pitch from the saddle as the horse dropped under him, lay huddled on the ground. Slowly recovering his senses he stirred, groped and sat up, his strained, good arm throbbing as he shakily drew his Colt, reloaded it and fired into the air twice, and then twice more. A burst of firing answered him and he smiled grimly and settled back as the low rumbling grew rapidly louder. It threatened to pass by him, but his single shot caused a quick turn and soon his friends drew up and stopped.

"Who is it?" demanded McCullough, dismounting at his side.

"Holbrook," came the answer, shaky and faint. "They got me twice, an' my cayuse, too. Reckon I busted my leg when he went down—I shore sailed aplenty afore I lit."

"You got one!" called an exultant voice. A match flared and in a moment the cheerful discoverer called again. "Sanchez, that Greaser monte dealer of Kane's. Plumb through th' mouth an' neck, Pete! I call that *shootin'*, with th' dark an' all—" his voice trailed off in profane envy of the accomplishment.

But Pete, hardy soul that he was, had fainted, a fractured leg, the impact from his flying fall and three bullet holes excuse enough for any man.

The flaring of the match brought a distant report and a bullet whined above the discoverer's head. Someone hurriedly fired into the air and a little later the group heard hoofbeats, which stopped abruptly when still some distance away. A signal reassured the cautious rider and soon Walt joined the group, Bob and Charley coming up later. Two of the men started back to the ranchhouse with Holbrook, the rest of the group riding off to search the plain for the two riders who had not put in an appearance, and to see what devilment they might discover. Both of the missing men were found on the remote part of the western range, one plodding stolidly toward the ranchhouse, his saddle and equipment on his shoulders; the other lay pinned under his dead horse, not much the worse, as it luckily happened, for his experience.

While the outfit concentrated on the western part of the ranch, events of another concentration were working smoothly and swiftly east of the ranchhouse, where mounted men, now free from interference, thanks to their Mexican friends, rode unerringly in the darkness, and drifted cattle into a herd with a certainty and dispatch born of long experience. Steadily the restless nucleus grew in size and numbers, the few riders who held it together chanting in low tones to keep the nervous cattle within bounds. The efficiency of these night raiders merited praise, nefarious as their occupation was, and the director of the harmonious efforts showed an uncanny understanding of the cattle, the men, and the whole affair which belongs to genius. Not a step was taken in uncertainty, not an effort wasted. Speed was obtained which in less experienced hands would have resulted in panic and a stampede. Steadily the circle of riders grew shorter and shorter; steadily, surprisingly, the

shadowy herd grew, and as it grew, became more and
more compact. Farther down the creek a second and smaller
herd was built up at the same time and with nearly the same
smoothness, and waited for the larger aggregate to drift
down upon it and swallow it up. The augmented trail herd
kept going faster and faster, the guarding and directing riders in their allotted places and, crossing the creek, it swung
northeast at a steadily increasing pace. The cattle had fed
heavily and drunk their fill and to this could be ascribed
the evenness of their tempers. Almost without realizing it
they passed from the Question-Mark range and streamed
across the guarding hills, flowing rapidly along the northern side. Gradually their speed was increased and they accepted it obediently, and with a docility which in itself was
a compliment to the brains of the trail-boss. Compacted
within the close cordon of the alert riders it maintained a
speed on the very edge of panic, but went no further. Shortly
before dawn two hard-riding rustlers pounded up from the
rear, reported all clear, and fell back again, to renew their
watch far back on the trail. For three hours the herd had
crossed hard ground and as it passed over a high, dividing
ridge and down the eastern slope the trail-boss sighed with
relief, for now dawn held no terrors for him. He had passed
the eastern horizon of any keen-eyed watchers of the pil-
laged range. On went cattle and riders, and the paling dawn
saw them following the hard bottom of a valley which led
to others ahead, and kept them from dangerous sky lines.
When the last hard-floored valley lay behind and sloping
holows of sand lay ahead, the trail-boss dropped back, un-
corked his canteen of black coffee tempered with brandy,
and drank long and deep. It was interpreted by his men to
mean that the danger zone had been left in the rear, and
they smilingly followed his example, and then leisurely and

more critically looked over the herd to see what they had gained. The entire SV trail herd was there, a large number of Question-Mark cattle and a score or more miscellaneous brands, which Ridley from time to time had purchased at bargain prices from needy owners. The trail-boss grinned broadly and waved his hand. It was a raid which would go down in the annals of rustler history and challenge strongly for first honors. At noon the waiting caviya was picked up, and Miguel and his three friends added four more riders to the ranks. He took his place well ahead of the hurrying cattle, and remained there until the first, and seldom visited, water hole was reached, where a short rest was taken. Then he led the way again, abruptly changing the direction of the herd's course and, following depressions in the desert floor, struck for Bitter Spring, which would be reached in the early morning hours. By now the raid was a successful, accomplished fact, according to all experience, and the matter of speed was now decided purely upon the questions of water and food, which, however, did not let it diminish much.

The trail-boss dropped back to his *segundo* and smiled. "Old Twitchell's got somethin' to put up a holler over *now*."

The other grinned expansively. "He'll mebby ante up another reward—he shore is fond of 'em."

Back on the Question-Mark a sleepy rider jogged along the creek, idly looking here and there. Suddenly he stiffened in the saddle, looked searchingly along the banks of the little stream, glanced over a strangely deserted range and ripped out an oath as he wheeled to race back to the ranch-house. His vociferous arrival caused a flurry, out of which emerged Johnny Nelson, who ran to the corral, caught and saddled his restive black, and scorning such a thing as a signal fire, especially when he feared that he could not start it within the limits of the time specified, raced across the valley, climbed the hills at a more sedate pace, dropped down the farther slopes like a stone, and raced on again for the little camp on Sand Creek.

XVIII

◆

The Trail-Boss Tries His Way

McCullough watched the racing horseman for a moment, a gleam of envious appreciation in his eyes at the beautiful action of the black horse, nodded in understanding of the rider's journey and wheeled abruptly to give terse orders.

Charley swung into the saddle and started in a cloud of dust for the Diamond L, to carry important news to Lukins and his outfit; two men sullenly received their orders to stay behind for the protection of the ranch and the care of Pete Holbrook, their feelings in no way relieved by the remark of the trail-boss, prophesying that Kane and his gang would be too busy in town to disturb the serenity of the Question-Mark. The rest of the outfit, procuring certain necessaries for the visit to Kane's headquarters, climbed into their saddles and followed their grim and taciturn leader over the shortest way to town.

Far back on the west end of the northern chain of hills a Mexican collapsed his telescope, hazarded a long-range shot at the hard-riding Charley and, mounting in haste, sped to carry disturbing news to his employer. The courier looked around as the singing lead raised a puff of dust in front of him, snarled in the direction from whence he thought it had come and, having no time for personal grievances, leaned forward and quirted the horse to greater speed. Whirring across the Diamond L range Charley caused another Mexican, watching from a ridge overlooking the ranch buildings, to run to the waiting horse and mount it, after which he delayed his departure until he saw the Diamond L outfit string out into a race for town, whereupon he set a pace which promised to hold him his generous lead.

In Mesquite a Mexican quirted a lathered horse for a final burst of speed up the quiet street, flung himself through Kane's front door, shouted a warning as he scrambled to his feet and dashed through the partition door to make his report direct to his boss. As he bolted out of sight behind the partition, other men popped from the building like weasel-pursued rabbits from a warren and scurried over the town to spread the alarm to those who were most vitally concerned by it. Two streams forthwith flowed over their trails, the first and larger heading for Kane's; the other, composed entirely of Mexicans, flowed toward Red Frank's, which had been allotted the role of outlying redoubt, to help keep harmless the broken ground between it and Kane's front wall, and was now being put in shape to withstand a siege.

Around Kane's was the noisy activity of a beehive. Hurrying men pulled thick planks from the piles under the floor and hauled them, on the jump, to windows and doors, feeding them into eager hands inside the building. Numbers of empty sacks grew amazingly bulky from the efforts of sand shovelers and were carried, shoulder high, in an unending line into the building. Great shutters were unfastened and swung away from the outer walls, their cobwebbed loopholes soon to play their ordained parts. A feverish squad emptied the stables of horses and food, taking both into the diningroom, and returned, posthaste, to remove doors and certain planks which turned the stables into sieves of small use to an attacking force, even if they were won. That the need for haste was pressing was proved by the sound of a handbell on the roof, where a selected group of riflemen lay behind the double-planked parapet to give warning, and exhibitions of long-range shooting. The shovelers hurled their tools through open windows, the plank carriers shoved the last board into the building and leaped to the shutters, slamming them shut as they hastened along the side of the building, and poured hastily through the front door, which now was protected by a great, outer door of planks, mortised, bolted, and braced in workmanlike manner. From the roof sounded two heavy reports, and grim iron tubes slid into loopholes along the walls. The bartenders carried boxes of ammunition and spare weapons, leaving their offerings below every oblong hole. To threaten Kane was one thing; to carry it to a successful end, another.

Puffs of gray-white smoke broke unexpectedly from points around the building, to thin out as they spread and drifted into oblivion. The cracking of rifles and the echo-awakening, jarring reports of heavy six-guns, were punctuated at intervals by the booming roar of old-time buffalo guns, of caliber prodigious. Punchers, guns in their hands, made the rounds of the town, going from building to building to pick up any of Kane's men who might have loitered, or who planned to hide out and open fire from the rear. Their efforts were not entirely wasted, for although Kane's brood had flocked to its nest, there were certain of the town's inhabitants who were neither flesh nor fish and might become one or the other as expediency urged. These doubtful ones were weeded out, disarmed, and escorted to their horses with stern injunctions as to the speed of their departure and their continued absence. Some of the neutrals, seeing that the mastery of the town at present lay with the ranchmen, trimmed their sails for this wind and numbered themselves with the offense in spirit if not in deeds. Of these human pendulums Quayle had a fair mental list and the owners of certain names were well watched.

The first day passed in perfecting plans, assigning men to strategic stations, several of these vantage-points remaining tenantless during the daylight hours because of the alertness and straight shooting of the squad on Kane's roof, who speedily made themselves obnoxious to the attackers. The owner of the freight wagon, remembering a smooth-bore iron cannon of more than an inch caliber, a relic of the prairie caravans which had followed the old Santa Fe and other trails a generation past, exulted as he dragged it from its obscurity and spent a busy hour scaling the rust from bore and touchhole. Here was the key to the situation, he boasted, and rammed home a generous charge of rifle powder. To find a suitable missile was another question, but he solved it by falling upon bar-lead with ax and hammer. Wheeled into position, its rusty length protruding beyond the corner of an adobe building, it was sighted by spasmodic glances, an occupation not without danger, for which blame could be given to the argus-eyed riflemen on the roof of the target. Consternation seized the defenders, who had not allowed for artillery, and they awaited its thundering debut with palpitant interest.

The discoverer and groom of the relic was unanimously elected gunner, not a dissenting voice denying his right to the honor, a right which he failed either to mention or press. The powder heaped over the touchhole was jarred off by the impact of a Sharps bullet and to replace it required a kitchen spoon fastened to a stick, which was an alluring if small target to the anxious aerial riflemen. At last heaped up again, the gunner declined methods in vogue for the firing of such ancient muzzleloaders and used a bundle of kerosene-soaked paper swinging by a wire from the end of the spoon. A few practice swings were held to be fitting preliminaries to an event of such importance, and then the nervous cannoneer, screwing his courage to the sticking-point, swept the blazing mass across the scaly breach and shrunk behind the sheltering corner. He escaped thunderous destruction by an eyelash, for what he afterward found was a third of the doughty weapon whizzed past his corner, taking a large chunk of sun-dried brick with it. From the besiegers arose guffaws; from the defenders, howls of derision; and from the owner of the adobe hut, imprecation and denouncement in fluent Spanish. The wall of his habitation closest to the fieldpiece justified all he said and even all he thought.

"You should ought 'a run it under Kane's before you touched her off," bawled a hilarious voice from cover. "Got another?" he demanded. "Tie it together an' try again."

The cannoneer without a job affected gaiety, drew inspiration from the taunts and hastened home to fashion bombs out of anything he could which would answer his purpose, finally deciding upon a tomato can and baling wire, and soon had a task to occupy the flaming fires of his genius.

Red Frank's, being the weaker of the two defenses and only point-blank range from the old adobe jail whose walls, poor as they were, could be relied upon to stop bullets, formed the favorite point of attack while the offense settled down into better-ordered channels. Idaho and others of his exuberant youth decided that it was their "pudding" and favored it with attentions which were as barren of results as they were full of enthusiasm. Discovering that their bullets passed entirely through the frame second-story and whirred, slobbered, and screamed into the air, they wasted ammunition lavishly, ignorant that for three feet above the second-story floor the walls were reinforced with double planking of hard wood, each layer two inches thick. They might turn the upper two-thirds of walls into a bird cage and do no one any material damage. And so passed the first day,

McCullough's efforts unavailing in face of the careless enthusiasm of his men, caused by the novelty of the situation; and not until one man had died and several others received serious wounds did the larking punchers come fully to realize that the game was deadly, and due to become more so.

XIX

♦

A Desert Secret

While McCullough argued and swore and waited for sanity to return to his frisking men, three punchers lay on the desert sands north of Sweet Spring, and baked. The telescope occasionally swept the southern horizon and went back between the folds of the blanket, which also hid the guns from the rays of the molten sun. The situation and most of the possible variations had been gone over from every angle and a course of action yet had to be agreed upon. Knowing that a fight in town was imminent, each feared he would miss it and that the reward would be lost to them. From their knowledge of deserts in general they did not wish to assume the labors of driving a herd back across it, even if they were able to capture it; but neither did they wish to let it get entirely away and be lost to McCullough. And so they continued to discuss the problem, jerkily and without enthusiasm, writhing under the sun like frogs on a gridiron. The afternoon dragged into evening and with the coming of twilight came quick relief from the heat, soon to be followed by a cold undreamed of by the inexperienced. The stars appeared swiftly and blazed with glittering brilliance through the chill air and the three watchers sought their blanket rolls for relief.

Hopalong unrolled from his covering and arose. "Dark enough, now," he said. "I'm goin' down to th' other water hole to wait for 'em. May learn somethin' worth while." He rolled his rifle in the blanket to protect it from sand and stretched gratefully.

"I'm goin' with you," said Johnny, covering his own rifle.

"I reckon I'll have to lay up here an' hold th' sack, like a fool," growled Red, who longed for action, even if it were no more than a tramp through the sand.

"You shore called it, Reddie," chuckled Johnny. "Somebody has got to stay with th' cayuses; an' I don't know anybody as reliable as you. Don't forget, an' build a camp fire while we're gone," and with this parting insult Johnny melted into the darkness after his leader and plodded silently behind him until Hopalong stopped and muttered a command.

"We're not far away now," he said. "Reckon we oughtn't get too close till they come to th' hole an' get settled down. Some of 'em may have to ride far an' wide if th' herd's ornery, an' run onto us. We've got th' trumps, an' they're worth twice as much if they don't know we got 'em. They shoot off their mouths regardless out here."

Johnny grunted his acquiescence and squatted comfortably on his haunches, the tips of the fingers of one hand in the sand. "Never felt more like smokin' than I do now," he chuckled. "Got any chewin'?"

His friend passed over the desired article and Johnny worried off a generous mouthful. "It's got too many stems in it; but bein' th' first chew I've had since I got married I ain't kickin'," he complacently remarked. "Margaret says it sticks to me for hours."

Hopalong grunted. "Gettin' to be real lady-like, ain't you?" he jeered. "Put perfumery on yore shirt bosom?"

"I would if she wanted me to," retorted his companion. "I don't just know what I wouldn't do if *she* wanted me to."

Hopalong snorted. "That so?" he demanded, pugnaciously. "Reckon she might like to know what yo're doin' down here, how much longer you aim to stay, an' if yo're still alive—an' other little foolish things like that. Let me tell you, Kid, you don't know how big a woman fills up yore life till you've lost her."

"I can imagine what it would be without her," said Johnny, slowly and reverently, his heart aching for his friend's loss. "She knows all about it; nearly all, anyhow. I've writ to her every third day, when I could, an' sometimes oftener. She may be worryin', but I'm bettin' every cent I'll ever have that she ain't doin' no cryin'! There ain't many wimmen like her, even in this kind of country."

"Then she's shore got Red an' me figgered for a fine pair of liars," murmured Hopalong; "but just th' same I'm feelin' warmer toward you than I have for a week," he announced. "When did you tell her all about this scrambled mess?"

"When I found that I couldn't tell how much longer I'd have to stay here," confessed Johnny. "I couldn't write letters an' lie good enough to fool her; an' I had to write letters, didn't I?"

"I'll take everythin' back, Kid," said his companion, grinning in the dark.

Johnny grunted and the silence began again, a silence which endured for several hours, such a silence that can exist between two real friends and be full of understanding. It endured between them and was not even broken by the distant, dim flare of a match, nor when low sounds floated up to them and gradually grew into the clicking and rattle of horns against horns, and the low rumble of many hurrying hoofs—hoofs hurrying toward the water which bovine nostrils had long since scented. The rumble grew rapidly as the thirst-tortured herd stampeded for Bitter Spring. A revolver flashed here and there on the edges of the animated avalanche and then a sweet silence came to the desert, soon to be tunefully and pleasantly broken by the soft lowing of cattle leg deep in the saving water.

> *Let th' air blow in up-on m-e-e,*
> *Let me see th' mid-night s-k-y;*
> *Stand back, Sisters, from around m-e-e:*
> *God, it i-s s-o-o h-a-r-d to d-i-e.*

wailed a cracked voice, the owner relieving his feelings.

"Thorpe, if you don't wrastle a hot snack damned quick, I'll eat yore ears!"

"Give him anythin' to stop that yowlin'," bellowed another. "Can't he learn nothin' but 'Th' Dyin' Nun'? Thank heaven he never learned no more of it. A sick calf ain't no cheerfuller than him."

"You'll have to eat lively, boys," sang out the trail-boss. "Everythin' is on th' move in an hour. If yo're in such a cussed hurry, Jud, get some wood for him. Take it from that lame pack horse. Reckon we'll have to shoot him if he don't get better in a hurry."

> *Up to my knees in mud I go*
> *An' water to my middle;*
> *Whenever firewood's to be got*
> *I'm Cookie's second fid-dle*

chanted Jud, splashing out to where the lame pack horse conducted an experiment in saturation. "Hot, cussed hot," he enlightened the cheerful, but tired group on the bank. "Hot *an'* oozy. Hello, hoss," he greeted, slapping the shrinking shoulder. "You heard what th' boss said about you? Pick up, Ol' Timer; pick up or you'll get shot. What? Don't blame you a bit, not a cussed bit. *I*'d ruther be shot, too, than tote wood over this part of hell. Oh, well; life's plumb funny. You'll fry if you do, an' you'll die if you don't. What's th' difference, anyhow, Ol' Timer?"

"Hey, Jud," called a voice. "Got a new bunkie?"

"I could have worse than a cayuse," replied Jud. "A cussed sight worse."

"There's moccasins, rattlers, copperheads, tarantulas, an' scorpions in that pond!" warned another.

"You done forgot Gila monsters, tigers an'—an'—Injuns," retorted Jud. "Now comes a job. With both arms full of slippin', criss-crossin' firewood, th' rest slidin' from th' pack, l got to hang on to what I got, put th' rest back like it ought to go an' make everythin' tight. Come out here, some damned fool, an' gimme a hand. Better move lively—only got four arms an' six hands. There!" he exploded. "There goes th' shootin'-match off th' hoss. Th' wind'll blow 'em ashore an' we can pick up th' whole caboodle."

"Wind?" jeered the snake-enumerator. "Where's th' wind? Yo're a fool!"

"On th' bank, where yo're settin', you thick-headed ass!" yelled Jud. "You got so cussed much to say, suppose you muddy yore lily-white pants an' do somethin' besides bray!"

"Did you spill any of 'em, Jud?" anxiously asked a voice. "I heard a splash."

Jud's reply was such that the trail-boss snapped a warning which checked some of the conversation, and promised his help. "Wait for me, Jud; I'm comin'," he said.

"Why don't you send that white-washed idol?" asked Jud. "I'll show him who's th' fool; an' what a splash sounds like!"

Hopalong nudged his companion and they crept forward,

feeling before them for anything which might make a sound if stepped on. A vibrant *whir* made them spring back and go around the warning snake, and soon they reached the little, sandy ridge which had sheltered Hopalong on his other visit.

"I'm glad you hung on to what you had, Jud," came Thorpe's thankful voice as his match caught the sunbaked wood and sent a tiny flame licking upward among the shavings whittled by his knife. "What you do you allus do right. It's dry as a bone."

"An' so am I," grunted the horse wrangler. "Who's got their canteen?"

"He's askin' for a canteen, with th' whole pond in front of him!" laughed a squatting rustler. "Here; take mine."

The fire grew quickly and a coffeepot, staunch friend of weary travelers, was placed in the flame, no one caring what it looked like or how hot the handle got. Time passed swiftly in talking of the raid and in consuming the light, hurried meal and soon the wrangler argued to his charges from the bank, and then waded in for his own horse, after which the matter was much simplified. He had them bunched, the next change of horses had been cut out by the men and they were ready to resume the drive when a distant voice hailed them. Soon a lathered horse glistened in the outer circle of light, and the hard-riding courier dashed up to the fire.

"They've hit th' town, boys!" he shouted. "Th' Question-Mark an' th' Diamond L have joined hands agin' us. Their friends in town are backin' 'em. Kane says to drive this herd hell-to-leather to th' valley, leave it there an' burn th' trail back. Where's Hugh Roberts?"

"Here," answered the trail-boss, stepping forward. "Hello, Vic."

"Got strict orders from th' boss," said Vic, leaning over and whispering in the ear of the trail-boss.

Roberts stiffened and swore angrily. "Is *that* all he says for us to do?" he sneered. "I got a notion to tell him to go to hell!"

Eager questions assailed him from the pressing group and he pushed himself free. "He says we are to take Quayle's hotel, their headquarters, from th' rear at dawn of th' day we get back—an' *hold* it! *That's* all!"

An angry chorus greeted the announcement and the shouting courier had a hard time to make himself heard, "That's wins for us!" he yelled. "You get their leaders, you split 'em in two—an' Kane'll turn his boys loose to hit 'em during th' confusion. He's got a wise head, I'm shoutin'. Red Frank's gang smashes from th' west end, an' they'll never know what happened. We'll have 'em split three ways, leaderless, not knowin' what's happened. It'll be a stampede an' a slaughter. Cuss it, *I*'ll be with you! That shows what *I* think of it!"

"Throw th' herd back on th' trail," ordered the boss. "We'll drive hard, an' turn th' rest of it over in our minds as we go. So we can have yore valuable assistance yo're goin' with us. Get a fresh cayuse from th' caviya. I say, *yo're goin' with us,* savvy?"

Covered by the noise of the renewed drive Hopalong and Johnny wriggled back until they could with safety arise to their feet, when they hastened back to Red and tersely reported what they had learned. Red's reply was instant.

"One of us has got to learn where that herd is kept; th' others light out for McCullough. Th' herd trailer can go to town when he gets it located. We can't lose them cattle, now."

"Right!" said Hopalong. "I'm puttin' cartridges in my hand. Th' worst guesser goes after th' herd. Odd or even. Red, you first," and he placed his clenched fist in Red's hand.

"Even," said Red, and then he opened the fist, felt of the cylinders and chuckled. There were two.

Hopalong fumbled at his belt and placed his fist in Johnny's hand. "Call it, Kid," he said.

"Even," said Johnny, carelessly. He felt the closed hand slowly open and cast his fingers over its palm, finding two cartridges, and he grunted. "Better take th' extra canteens, Hoppy; an' that spyglass. It'll mebby come in handy. Want Pepper?"

"Just 'cause she's a good cayuse for you don't say that she is for me," chuckled the loser. "She knows you; I'm a stranger," and he led the way to the picketed and hobbled horses. In a few minutes he swung into the saddle, the telescope under his arm, cheerily said his good-byes and melted into the darkness, bound farther into the desert, where or how far he did not know. Passing the southern water hole he drew two cartridges from his belt, placed one in the palm of his right hand and held the other between his fingers. Slowly opening the clenched fist he relaxed the fingers and the second cartridge dropped onto its mate with a little click. There was no need to cough now and hide that slight, metallic noise, so he grinned instead and slowly pushed them back into the vacant loops.

"Fine job, lettin' th' Kid go out on this skillet," he snorted, indignant at the thought. "Me, now—it don't matter a whole lot what happens to me these days; but th' Kid's got a wife, an' a darned fine one, too. Go on, you lazy cow yore work's just *startin'*."

It was not long before he caught the noise of the hard-driven herd well off to his right and he followed by sound until dawn threatened. Then, slowing his horse, he rode off at an angle and hunted for low places in the desert floor, where he went along a course parallel to that followed by the herd. Persistently keeping from sky lines, although

added miles of twisting detours was the price, and keeping
so far from his quarry that he barely could pick out the small,
dark mass with the aid of the glass, he feared no discovery.
So he rode hour after weary hour under the pitiless sun,
stopping only once to turn his sombrero into a bucket, from
which his horse eagerly drank the contents of one huge canteen, its two gallons of water filling the hat several times.

"Got to go easy with it for awhile, bronch," he told it.
"Water can't be so terrible far ahead, judgin' from that herd
pushin' boldlike across this strip of hell—but cows can go
a long time without it when they has to; an' out here they
shore has to. I'm not cheatin' you—there's four for you an'
one for me, an' we won't change it."

Mile upon burning mile passed in endless procession as
they plodded through hard sand, soft sand, powdery dust,
and over stretches of rocky floor blasted smooth and slippery by the cutting sands driven against it by every wind
for centuries. An occasional polished boulder loomed up,
its coat of "desert-varnish" glistening brown under the pale,
molten sun. He knew what the varnish was, how it had been
drawn from the rock and the mineral contents left behind
on the surface as its moisture evaporated into the air. An
occasional "sidewinder," diminutive when compared to the
rattlesnakes of other localities, slid curiously across the
sand, its beady, glittering eyes cold and vicious as it watched
this strange invader of its desert fastness.

Warned at last by the fading light after what had seemed
an eternity of glare, he gave the dejected horse another canteen of water and then urged it into a brisker pace, to be
within earshot of the fleeing herd when darkness should
make safe a nearer approach.

With the coming of twilight came a falling of temperature and when the afterglow bathed the desert with magic
light and then faded as swiftly as though a great curtain had

been dropped the creeping chill took bold, sudden possession of the desert air to a degree unbelievable. So passed the night, weary hour after cold, weary hour; but the change was priceless to man and beast. The magic metamorphosis emphasized the many-sided nature of the desert, at one time a blazing, glaring thing of sinister aspect and death-dealing heat; at another cold, almost freezing, its considerable altitude being good reason for the night's penetrating chill. The expanse of dim gray carpet, broken by occasional dark blots where the scrawny, scattered vegetation arose from the sands, stretched away into the veiling dark, allowing keen eyes to distinguish objects at surprising distances. Overhead blazed the brilliant stars, blazed as only stars in desert heavens can, seeming magnified and brought nearer by the dry, clear air. His eyes at last free from the blinding glare of quivering air and glittering crystals of salts in the sand; his dry, parched, burning skin free from the baking heat, which sucked moisture from the pores before perspiration could form on the surface; he sucked in great gulps of the vitalizing, cold air and found the night so refreshing, so restful as to almost compensate for the loss of sleep.

The increased pace of his mount at last brought reward, for there now came from ahead and from the right the low, confused noise of hurrying cattle, as continuous, unobtrusive, and restful as the soft roar of a distant surf. So passed the dark hours, and then a warning, silver glow on the eastern horizon caused him to pull up and find a sandy depression, there to wait until the proper distance was put behind it by the thirsty herd, still reeling off the miles as though it were immune to fatigue. The silver band widened swiftly, changed to warmer tints, became suffused with crimson and cast long, thin, vague, warning shadows from sage bush and greasewood—and then a molten, quivering orb pushed up over the prostrate horizon and bathed the shrinking sands with its light.

The cold, heavy-lidded rider glowered at it and removed the blanket which had been wrapped around him, rolling it tightly with stiff fingers and fumblingly made it secure in the straps behind the cantle of his saddle.

"There it is again, bronch," he growled. "We'll soon wonder if th' cold was all a dream."

He stood up in the stirrups and peered cautiously over the bank of the depression, making out the herd with unaided eyes.

"They can't go on another day," he muttered. "This ain't just dry trail—it's a chunk out of hell. They can't stand much more of it without goin' blind, an' that's th' beginnin' of th' end on a place like this. I'm bettin' they get to water by noon—an' then *we* got to wait till th' coast is clear? He shook the canteen he had allotted himself and growled again. "About a quart, an' I could drink a gallon! All right, bronch; get a-goin'," and on they plodded, keeping to the hollows and again avoiding all elevations, to face the torments of another murderous day. Again the accursed hours dragged, again the horse had a canteen of water, a sop which hardly dulled the edge of its raging thirst. Earth, air, and sky quivered, writhed and danced under the jelly-like sun and the few, soft night noises of the desert were heard no more. The leveled telescope kept the herd in sight as mile followed mile across the scorched and scorching sand.

The sun had passed the meridian only half an hour when the sweeping spyglass revealed no herd, but only a distant ridge of rock, like a tiny island on a stilled sea.

"It shore is time," muttered the rider, dismounting. "Seein' as how we're nearly there, I reckon you can have th' last canteen. You shore deserve it, you game old plodder. An' I'm shore glad them rustlin' snakes have their orders to get back *pronto;* but it would just be our luck if that bull-headed trail-boss held a powwow in that valley of theirs. His name's Roberts, bronch; Hugh Roberts, it is. We'll remember his name an' face if he makes us stay out here till night. You an' me have got to get to that water before another sunrise if all th' thieves in th' country are campin' on it—we *got* to, that's all."

An hour passed and then the busy telescope showed a diminutive something moving out past the far end of the distant ridge. Despite the dancing of the heat-distorted image on the object-glass the grim watcher knew it for what it was. Another and another followed it and soon the moving spots strung out against the horizon like a crawling line of grotesque, fantastic insects, silhouetted against the sky.

"There they go back to Mesquite to capture Quayle's hotel an' win th' fight," sneered Hopalong. "I could tell 'em somethin' that would send them th' other way—but we'll let 'em ride with Fate; an' get to that water as quick as yore weary legs can take us. Th' herd is there, bronch; all alone, waitin' for us. It's our herd now, if we want it, which we don't. Huh! Mebby they left a guard! All right, then; he's got a big job on his hands. Come on; get a-goin'!"

Swinging more and more to the south he soon forsook the windings of the hollows and struck boldly for the eastern end of the valley, and when he reached it he hobbled and picketed the horse, frantic with the heavy scent of water in its crimson, flaring nostrils, and went ahead on foot, the hot Sharps in his hands full cocked and poised for instant action. Crawling to the edge of the valley he inched forward on his stomach and peered over the rim. An exclamation of surprise and incredulity died in his throat as the valley lay under his eyes, for it was the valley he had seen in the mirage only a few days before.

The stolen herd filled the small creek, standing like stat-

ues, soaking in the life-giving fluid and nosing it gently. One
or two, moving restlessly, blundered against those nearest
them and the watcher knew that they had gone blind. The
sharpest scrutiny failed to discover any guard, and he knew
that his uncertain count of the kaleidoscopic riders had been
correct. Hastening back to the restless horse he soon found
that it had in reserve a strength which sent it flashing to the
trail's edge and down the dangerous ledge at reckless speed.
At last in the creek it, too, stood as though dazed and nosed
the water a little before drinking.

Hopalong swung into the stream, removed saddle and
bridle and then splashed across to the hut, dumping his
load, canteens, and all against the front wall. To make assurance doubly sure he scouted hurriedly down one side of
the little valley, crossed the creek and went back along the
other wall.

Thorpe's carefully stacked firewood provided fuel for a
cunningly built-up fire; one of Thorpe's discarded tomato
cans, washed and filled in the spring near the hut's walls
sizzled and sputtered in the blazing fire and soon boiled
madly. Picking it out of the blaze with the aid of two longer
sticks the hungry cook set it to one side, threw in a double
handful of Thorpe's coffee, covered it with another washed
can and then placed Thorpe's extra frying pan on the coals,
filling it with some of Thorpe's bacon. A large can of
Thorpe's beans landed close to the fire and rolled a few
feet, and the cheerful explorer emerged from the hut with
a sack of sour-dough biscuits which the careless Thorpe
had forgotten.

"Bless Thorpe," chuckled Hopalong. "I'll never make
him climb no more walls. I wouldn't 'a' made him climb
that one, mebby, if I'd knowed about this."

Looking around as a matter of caution, his glance embracing the stolid herd and his own horse grazing with the

jaded animals left behind by the rustlers, he fell to work turning the bacon and soon feasted until he could eat no more. Rolling a cigarette he inhaled a few puffs and then, picking up telescope and rifle, he grunted his lazy way up the steep trail and mounted the ridge, sweeping the western horizon first with the glass and then completed the circle. Satisfied and drowsy he returned to the valley, spread his folded blanket behind the hut, placed the saddle on one end of it for a pillow and lay down to fall asleep in an instant.

When he awakened he stretched out the kinks and looked around in the dim light. He felt unaccountably cold and he looked at the blanket which he had pulled over him some time during his sleep, wondering why he had felt the need for it during the daylight hours in such a place as this.

"Well, I'll cook me some more bacon before it gets dark, an' then set up with a nice little fire, with a 'dobe wall at my back. It'll be a treat just to set an' smoke an' plan, th' night chill licked by th' fire an' my happy stomach full of bacon, beans, an' biscuits—an' coffee, cans an' cans of coffee."

It suddenly came to him that the light was growing stronger instead of weaker, that it was not the afterglow, and that the chill was dying instead of increasing. Shocked by a sudden suspicion he glanced into the eastern sky and stared stupidly, surprised that he had not noticed it before.

"I was so dumb with sleep that I didn't savvy east from west," he muttered. "It's daylight, 'stead of evenin'—I've slept all afternoon an' night! Well, I don't see how that changes th' eatin' part, anyhow. No wonder I pulled th' blanket over me, an' no wonder I was stiff."

With the coming of the sun a disagreeable journey loomed nearer and nearer but, as he told the horse when cinching the saddle on its back, the return trip would not be one of uncertainty; nor would they be held down to such a slow pace by any clumsy herd. A further thought hastened his movements: there was a big fight going on in Mesquite, and his two friends were in it without him. Looking around he saw that he had cleaned up and effaced all signs of his visit and, filling the canteens and fastening them into place, he mounted and rode up the steep slope, turned his back to the threatening sun and loped westward along a plain and straight trail, a grim smile on his face.

XX

♦

The Redoubt Falls

After Hopalong had ridden off on his desert trailing, Johnny and Red rode to the Question-Mark, reaching it a little after daylight and were promptly challenged when near the smaller corral. The sharp voice changed to a friendly tone when the sentry had a better look at the pair.

"Thought you'd be up with th' circus," said the Question-Mark puncher.

"On our way now," replied Johnny. "Come down here to learn what was happenin'. Meet Red Connors, an old friend of Waffles."

"Howd'y," grunted the puncher, looking at Red with a keener interest. "You fellers are lucky—*we* got to stay here an' miss it all. Walt come down last night an' said Kane's goin' to be a hard nut to crack. He's fixed up like a fort."

"Reckon we'll take a look at it," said Johnny, wheeling.

"Hey! If you want to find Mac, he's hangin' out at Quayle's."

Johnny waved his thanks and rode on with his cheerful

companion. In due time they heard the distant firing and not much later rode up to Quayle's back door and went in. Mc-Cullough was raging at the effectiveness of the sharpshooters on Kane's roof who had succeeded in keeping the fight at long range and who dominated certain strategic positions which the trail-boss earnestly desired to make use of; all of which made him irritable and unusually gruff.

"Where *you* been?" he demanded as Johnny entered.

"Locatin' a missin' herd of yore cattle," retorted Johnny, nettled by the tone. "They're waitin' for you when you get time to go after 'em. Now we'll locate them sharpshooters. Anythin' else you can't do, let us know. Come on, Red," and he went out again, his grinning friend at his heels. At the door Red checked him.

"Looks like a long-range job, Kid. My gun's all right for closer work, but I ought to have a Sharps for this game."

Johnny wheeled and went back. "Gimme a Sharps," he demanded.

"Take Wilson's—they got him yesterday," growled the trail-boss, pointing.

Johnny took the gun and the cartridge belt hanging on it, joined Red and led the way to a place he had in mind. Reaching the selected spot, an adobe hut on the remote outskirts of the sprawled town, he stopped. "This is good enough for me," he grunted, "except th' range is too cussed long. Well, we'll try it from here, anyhow."

"I'm goin' to th' next shack," replied Red, moving on. "We'll use our old follow-shootin'—an' make 'em sick. Ready? I'm goin' to cross th' open." At his friend's affirmative grunt Red leaned over and dashed for the other adobe. A bullet whined in front of him, barely heard above the roar of Johnny's rifle. He settled down, adjusted the sights and proceeded to prove title to his widely known reputation on other ranges of being the best rifle-shot of many square miles. "Make a hit, Kid?" he called. "It's mebby further than you figger."

"It is," answered Johnny. "Like old times, huh? Lord help 'em when you get started! Are you all set? I'm ready to draw 'em."

"Wind gentle, from th' east," mumbled Red. "Dirty gun—got to shoot higher. All right," he called, nestling the heavy stock.

Johnny pushed his rifle around the corner of the building, aimed quickly and fired. A hatted head arose above Kane's roof and a puff of smoke spurted into the air above it as Red's Sharps roared. The hat flew backward and the head ducked down again, its owner surprised by the luck of the shot.

Johnny laughed outright. "For a trial shot I'm admittin' that was a whizzer. I ain't no slouch with a Sharps—but how th' devil you can make one behave like *you* do is a puzzle to me."

"I'm still starin'," said a humorous, envious voice behind them and they looked around to see Waffles hugging the end of the building. "If I can get over on Red's right I'll help make targets for him."

"Walk right over to that other shack," called Johnny. "Yo're safe as if you was home in yore bunk. Cover him, Red."

Waffles' mind flashed back into the past and what it presented to him greatly reassured him, but to walk was tempting Providence; he ran across the open and again Red's rifle roared.

"Got him!" yelled Johnny, staring at the body lying over the distant parapet. It was swiftly pulled back out of sight. The rest of Johnny's words were profanely eulogistic.

"Shut yore face," growled Red. "It was plumb luck."

"*Shore* it was," laughed his friend in joyous irony; "but yo're allus makin' 'em. That's what counts."

Waffles, having gained the shelter he coveted, looked around. "Heads was plentiful up there yesterday. There was allus one or two bobbin' up. I'm bettin' they'll be scarcer today."

"They'll be scarcer tomorrow, when we are behind them other shacks," replied Red. "They're easy three hundred paces nearer, an' that's a lot sometimes."

'An' twice as much to them," rejoined Johnny. "Th' nearer you get th' more you make it even terms. You stay where you are—me an' Waffles'll go out there tonight."

When the afternoon dragged to an end Red had another sharpshooter to his credit, and the dominating group on the roof were much less dominant. They cursed the long-range genius who shot hats off of heads, clipped ears, and had killed two men. The shooting, with a rest and plenty of time to aim, would have been creditable enough; but to hit a bobbing head meant quick handling. They were properly indignant, for it was a toss-up with Death to show enough of their heads to sight a slanting rifle. One of their number, whose mangled ear was bound up with a generous amount of bandage, savagely hammered the chisel with which he was cutting a loophole through four inches of seasoned wood, vowing vengeance on the man who had ruined his looks.

The light failing for close shooting, the three friends left their positions and went to the hotel for a late supper, Red receiving envious, grinning looks as he entered the dining-room. Idaho promptly forsook his bosom friends and went over to finish his meal at the table of the newcomers.

"We got Red Frank's place plumb full of holes—you can see daylight through th' second floor," he announced; "but it don't seem to do no good. If I could get close enough to use a bomb I got, we might clean 'em up."

"Crawl up in th' dark," suggested Waffles.

"Can't; they spread flour all around th' place, an' th' minute a man crosses it he shows up plain. Two of us found out *all* about *that!*"

"Go through or over th' buildin's this side of th' place," said Johnny, visualizing the street. "They lead up close to Red Frank's."

Idaho stared, and slapped his thigh in enthusiastic endorsement. "I reckon you called it!" he gloated. "Wait till I tell th' boys," and he hastened back to his friends. Judging from the sudden noise coming from the table, his friends were of the same opinion and, bolting the rest of the meal, they hastened away to forthwith try the plan.

McCullough entered the dining-room and strode straight to Johnny. "Did I hear you say you know where my cattle are?" he asked, sitting down.

Johnny nodded, chewed hurriedly and replied. "I didn't finish it. *I* don't know where they are, but Hopalong is trailin' 'em, an' *he*'ll know when he comes back. Pay us them rewards now, instead of later, an' I'll do some high an' mighty guessin' about yore head—an' bet you th' rewards that I guess right."

The trail-boss laughed. "You've shore got plenty of nerve," he retorted. "When this fight is over there won't be no rewards paid. We got th' whole gang in them two buildin's, an' we got 'em good. You've had yore trouble for nothin', Nelson."

"How 'bout th' gang that are with th' herd?" asked Johnny, a note of anger edging his words.

McCullough shrugged his shoulders. "I ain't worryin' about them—they'll never come back to Mesquite."

"That so?" queried Johnny, sarcastically. "I ought to keep my mouth shut, th' way yo're talkin', but I hate to see good men killed. I'll bet you they'll come back just at dawn, some time in th' next five days. An' I'll bet you they'll sneak up on this hotel an' raise th' devil, while Kane starts a bunch from his place and Red Frank's, to help 'em. Th' minute they start shootin' in here their friends'll sortie out an' carry th' fight to you. Want to bet on it?"

McCullough regarded the speaker through narrowed lids. "How do you figger that?" he demanded suspiciously. "You gettin' that out of your medicine bag, too?" and then he eagerly drank in every word of the explanation. After a moment's thought he looked around the room and then back to the smiling Johnny. "Much obliged, Nelson. I'm beginnin' to see that I owe you fellers somethin', after all. If them fellers we want were loose an' you got 'em, then of course th' reward would stand; but you can't win it very well when we've got 'em corraled. Who-all is in that bunch with th' herd?"

Johnny smiled but shook his head.

"Didn't you say you knowed who killed Ridley?" persisted the trail-boss.

"I know him, an' how he did it. Hopalong saw him while his gun was smokin', but didn't know what he had shot at till later."

"Why didn't you tell me, an' earn that reward right away?"

"That's only half of th' rewards," replied Johnny. "There's money up for th' fellers that robbed th' bank. If we got Ridley's murderer th' others might 'a' smelled out what we was after. You see, I was robbed of more than eleven hundred dollars th' first night I was in town. Th' money belonged to th' ranch. Th' only chance I had of gettin' it back was to make th' rewards big enough to stand three splits that would be large enough to cover it. An' I'm still goin' to do that,

Mac. Pay it now an' we'll stick with you till you get th' men an' yore herd. Of course, yo're going to get th' herd, anyhow, as far as we are concerned. I ain't holdin' that over yore head; I'm only tryin' to show you why I can't be open an' free with you."

"I couldn't pay th' rewards now even if I wanted to," said the trail-boss.

"I know that, an' I didn't think you would. I was only showin' you how things are with us."

McCullough nodded, placed a hand on the speaker's shoulder and arose, turning to Red. "Connors," he said, "yo're a howlin' wonder with a Sharps. Much obliged for holdin' down that roof. If you can clean 'em up there this fight'll go on a cussed sight faster. Th' cover on th' north side of Kane's is so poor that we can't do much out there, but we can do a little better when them sharpshooters are driven down. From what I know of you two, yore friend Cassidy is shore able to trail that herd. I've quit worryin' about everythin' but th' fight here in town. An' lemme make a long speech a little longer: if you fellers can earn them rewards I won't waste no time in payin' up; but there ain't a chance for you. We got 'em under our guns."

"Who was right about where that raid on you was goin' to take place?" asked Johnny. "You was purty shore about that, too, wasn't you?"

The trail-boss smiled and shook his head. "Yo're a good guesser," he admitted, and went out to consult with Lukins.

The next day found the line a little tighter around the stronghold, thanks to Red's shooting, which increased in accuracy after he had decided to use closer cover and cut three hundred paces out of the range. Better positions had been gained by the attackers during the night, some of the more daring men now being not far from pointblank range, which enabled them to make the use of Kane's loopholes hazardous.

To the north another rifleman lay in a hollow of the sandy plain, but too far away to do much damage. The north parapet of the building was hidden from Red by the one on the south and the aerial marksmen made free use of it.

Red Frank's place was in jeopardy, for Idaho and his enthusiastic companions were in the building next on the south, separated from the Mexican's house by less than twenty feet. There was an open window facing the gambling-house and Idaho, chancing quick glances through it, noticed that one of the heavy, board shutters of a window of the upper floor sagged out a little from the top. Signaling the men behind the jail to increase their fire, he coiled his rope and cast it through the window. It struck the upper edge of the shutter, dropped behind it and grew swiftly taut. Two of his companions added their strength to his, while the other two covered them by pouring a heavy revolver fire at the two threatening loopholes. The shutter creaked, twisted, and then slowly gave way, finally breaking the lower hinge and sailing over against the other house to a cheer from the jail. Heavy firing came through the uncovered window, the bullets passing through the opposing wall and driving the Diamond L men to other shelter. Here they waited until it died down and then, picking up the bomb made by the owner of the new freight wagon, Idaho lit the jumpy, uncertain fuse, waited as long as he dared and hurled it across the intervening space and through the shutterless window as the opening was being boarded up. There was a roar, jets of smoke spurt from windows and holes and the wild cursing of injured men rang out loudly. A tongue of flame leaped through a trapdoor on the roof and grew rapidly brighter. At intervals the smoke pouring up became suddenly heavy and thick, but cleared quickly between the onslaughts of the water buckets. Fire now crept through the side of the frame structure and mounted rapidly, and such a hail of lead poured through the smoke-spurting, upper loopholes that it became impossible for the buckets to be properly used. It was only a matter of time before the blazing roof and floor would fall on the defenders in the adobe-walled structure below, and through a loophole Red Frank suddenly shoved out a soiled towel fastened on the end of a rifle barrel.

"Come ahead, with yore hands up!" shouted a stentorian voice from the jail. "Quit firin', boys; they're surrenderin'." Almost on the tail of his words a hurrying line of choking Mexicans, bearing their wounded, streamed from the front door. They were promptly and proudly escorted by the hilarious attackers to safe quarters on the southern outskirts of the town.

XXI

♦

All Wrapped Up

McCullough and Lukins drew men from the cordon around the gambling-hall until the line was thinned and stretched as much as prudence allowed, covering only the more strategic positions, while the men taken from it were placed in an ambuscade at the rear of Quayle's hotel. Both leaders would have preferred to have placed their reception committee nearer the outskirts of the rambling town but, not knowing from which direction the attack would come and not being able to spare men enough for outposts around the town, they were forced to concentrate at the object of the attack. When night fell and darkness hid the movement they set the trap, gave strict orders for no one to approach the rear of the hotel during the dark hours, and waited expectantly.

The first night passed in quiet and the following day found the cordon reenforced until it contained its original numbers. By nightfall of the second day Red, Johnny, and Waffles had cleared the parapet and made it useless during daylight, and as the moon increased in size and brightness the parapet steadily became a more perilous position at night for the defenders. All three marksmen, now ensconced within three hundred yards of the gambling-house and out of the line of sight of every lower loophole, had the range worked out to a foot. Red and Waffles had discarded their borrowed Sharps and were now using their own familiar Winchesters, and it was certain death to any man who tried to shoot from Kane's roof on any side but the north one.

Evening came and with it came a hare-brained attempt by Idaho and his irrepressibles to capture and use the stables. Despite McCullough's orders to the contrary the group of youngsters, elated by their success against Red Frank's, made the attempt as soon as darkness fell; and learned with cost that the stables were stacked decks. One man was killed and all the others wounded, most of them so badly as to remove them from the role of combatants; but one dogged, persistent, and vindictive unit of the foolish attack managed to set fire to the sun-dried structures before crawling away.

The baked wood burned like tinder and became a mass of flames almost in an instant, and for a few minutes it looked as though they would take the gambling-hall with them. It was a narrow squeak and missed only because of a slight shift of the wind. The scattered line of punchers to the north of the building, not expecting the sudden conflagration, had crawled nearer to the gambling-hall in the encroaching darkness, only to find themselves suddenly revealed to their enemies by the towering sheets of flame. They got off with minor injuries only because the north side of the building was not well manned and because the stables were holding the attention of most of the besieged. When the flames died down almost as swiftly as they had grown, the smouldering ashes gave a longer and less obstructed view to the guards of Kane's east wall and rendered useless certain positions cherished by McCullough.

The trail-boss, seething with anger, stamped up to Lukins and roared his demands, with the result that Idaho and the less injured of his companions were sent to take the places of cooler heads in the ambush party and were ordered to stay in Quayle's stable until after the expected attack.

In Quayle's kitchen four men waited through the dragging hours, breaking the silence by occasional whispers as they watched the faintly lighted open spaces and the walls of certain buildings newly powdered with flour so as to serve as backgrounds and to silhouette any man passing in front of them. Only the north walls had been dusted and there was nothing to reveal their freshly acquired whiteness to unsuspecting strangers coming up from the south. In the stable Idaho and his restless friends grumbled in low tones and cursed their inactivity. Three men at the darkened office windows, and two more on the floor above watched silently. Outside an occasional shot called forth distant comment, and laughter arose here and there along the alert line.

On the east end of the line a Diamond L puncher, stretched out on his stomach in a little depression he had scooped in the sand during the darker hours of the second night, stuck the end of his little finger in a bullet hole in his canteen and rimmed the hole abstractedly, the water soaking his clothes and making him squirm.

"Cuss his hide," he growled. "Now I got to stay thirsty." He slid a hand down his body and lifted the clinging clothing from the small of his back. "If it was only as cold as that when I *drink* it, I wouldn't grumble. An' I wasn't thirsty till he spilled it," he added in petulant afterthought.

To his right two friends crouched behind the aged ruins of an adobe house, paired off because one of them shot left-handed, which fitted each to his own corner. "Got any chewin'?" asked Righthand. "Chuck it over. Seems to me that they—" he set his teeth into the tobacco, tore off a generous quantity and tossed the plug back to its owner—"ain't answerin' as strong as they was this afternoon."

"No?" grunted Lefthand, brushing sand from the plug. He shoved it back into a pocket and reflected a moment. "It was good shootin' while th' stable burned." Another pause, and then: "Did you hear Billy yell when them fools started th' fire?"

Righthand laughed, stiffened, fired, and pumped the lever of the gun. "I'm gettin' so I can put every one through that loophole. Hear him squawk?" He dropped to his knees to rest his back, and chuckled. "Shore did. Billy, he was boastin' how near he could crawl to them stables. I reckon he done crawled *too* close. Lukins ought to send them kids home."

In a sloping, shallow arroyo to their right Walt and Bob of the Question-Mark lay side by side. Behind them two shots roared in quick succession. Walt lazily turned his head from the direction of the sounds and peeped over the edge of the bank.

"I reckon some coyote took a look over th' edge of th' roof," he remarked.

"Uh-huh," replied Bob without interest and without relaxing his vigil.

"I don't lay out here one little minute after Connors

leaves that 'dobe," said Walt. He spat noisily and turned the cud. "I'm sayin' shootin' like his is a gift. I'm some shot, myself, but hell—"

"You'd shore 'a' thought so," replied Bob, grinning as he reviewed something, "if you'd seen that sharpshooter flop over th' edge of th' roof th' other day. I'd guess it was close to fifteen hundred." He changed his position, grunted in complacent satisfaction and continued. "Some folks can't see a man's forehead at that distance, let alone *hit* it. Of course, th' sky was behind it."

"Which made it plainer, but harder to figger right," observed Walt. "Waffles says Connors can drive a dime into a plank with th' first, an' push it through with th' second, as far away as he can see th' dime. When it's too far away to be seen, he puts it in th' middle of a black circle, an' aims for th' middle of th' circle. But I put plenty of salt on th' tails of *his* stories."

"Which holds 'em down," grunted Bob. "Who's that over there, movin' around that shack?"

Walt looked and cogitated. "Charley was there when I came out," he answered. "Cussed fool—showin' hisself like that." He swore at a thin pencil of flame which stabbed out from a loophole, and fired. "Told you so!" he growled. "Charley is down!"

Both fired at the loophole and hazarded a quick look at the foolish unfortunate, who had dragged himself behind a hummock of sand. Rapid firing broke out behind them and, sensing what it meant, they joined in. A crouched figure darted from a building, sprinted to the hummock, swung the wounded man on its back, and staggered and zigzagged to cover.

"That was Waffles," said Walt, reloading the magazine of his rifle. "It's a cussed shame to make a man take chances like that by bein' a fool."

Behind the building Waffles lowered his burden to the ground, ripped off the wet shirt and became busy. He fastened the end of the bandage and stood up. "Fools *are* lucky sometimes," he growled; "an' I says you are lucky to only have a smashed collar bone. You try a fool trick like that again an' I'll bust yore head. Ain't you got no sense?"

"Don't *you* go to put on no airs, Waffles," said Red Connors. "I can tell a few things on *you*. I *know* you."

Johnny chuckled. "Tread easy," he warned. "We *both* know you."

"Go to hell!" grunted the ex-foreman of the O-Bar-O, grinning. "Fine pair of sage-hens *you* are to tell tales on me! I got you throwed and hog-tied before you even start." He wheeled at a noise behind him, and glared at the wounded man. "Where'n hell are *you* goin'?" he demanded, truculently.

"Without admittin' yore right to ask fool questions," groaned Charley, still moving, "I'll say I'm goin' to join th' ambush party at Quayle's, an' relieve somebody else." He gritted his teeth and stood erect. "I can use a Colt, can't I?" he demanded.

"Yo're so shaky you can't hit a house," retorted Waffles.

"Which I ain't aimin' to do," rejoined the white-faced man. "You'll show more sense if you'll tie my left arm like it ought to be, instead of standin' with yore mouth open. You'll shore catch a cold if you don't shut it purty soon."

"You stubborn fool!" growled Waffles, but he fixed the arm to its owner's satisfaction.

"If he gets smart, Charley," suggested Johnny, "pull his nose. He allus *was* an old woman, anyhow."

With the coming of midnight the cordon became doubled in numbers as growling men rubbed the sleep from their eyes and took up positions for the meeting of Kane's sortie in case the hotel was attacked by his expected drive outfit.

The hours dragged on, the silence of the night infrequently broken by bits of querulous cursing by some wounded puncher, an occasional taunt from besieger or besieged and sporadic bursts of firing which served more for notifications of defiance and watchfulness than for any grimmer purpose. Patches of clouds now and then drifted before the moon and sailed slowly on. Nature's denizens of the dark were in active swing and filled the night with their soft orchestration. The besiegers, paired for night work, which let one man doze while his companion watched, hummed, grumbled, or snored; in the gambling-hall fortress weary men slept beside the loopholes, the disheartened for a few hours relieved of their fears or carrying them across the borderland of sleep to make their slumbers restless and broken, while scowling, disheartened sentries kept a keener watch, alert for the rush hourly expected.

South of town a group of horsemen pulled up, dismounted, tied their mounts to convenient brush and slipped like shadows toward the nearest house, approaching it round-about and with animal wariness. From house to house, corral to corral, cover to cover they crept, spread out in a fan-shaped line, silent, grim, vindictive and desperate. Not a shadow passed unsearched and unused, not a boulder or thicket was above suspicion nor below being utilized. Nearer and nearer they worked their way, eyes straining, ears tuned for every sound, high-strung with nerves quivering, keyed to swift reflex and instant decision. The scattered, infrequent firing grew steadily nearer, every flat report was searched for secret meanings and the sharp squeak of a gyrating bat overhead sent every man flat to the earth. The last in the group became cannily slower as opportunity offered and soon managed to be so far behind that his quick, furtive desertion was unnoticed in the tenseness of conjecture as to what lay immediately ahead.

Kane's trail-boss slanted his watch under the moon's rays and gave a low, natural signal, whereupon to right and left a man detached himself and left the waiting group. Minutes passed, their passing marked on nervous foreheads by the thin trickle of cold sweat. Any instant might a challenge, a shot, a volley ring out on any side; hostile eyes might be watching every movement, hostile guns waiting for the right moment, like ravenous hounds in leash. The scouts returned as silently as they had departed and breathed their reassuring words in Roberts' ear. The town lay unsuspecting, every waking eye bent on the bulking gambling-hall. Not a hidden outpost, not a pacing sentry to watch the harmless rear. To the right showed the roof of a two-story building, bulking above the low, thick roofs of scattered, helter-skelter adobes, in any one of which Death might be poised.

Again the slow advance, and breathed maledictions on the head of any unfortunate who trod carelessly or let his swinging six-gun click against buckle or button. Roberts, peering around the end of an adobe wall, held his elbows from his sides, and progress ceased while a softly whistling figure strode across the street and became lost to sight. This was the jumping-off place, the edge of a black precipice of fate, unknown as to depth or what lay below. The savage, thankful elation which had possessed every man at his success in making this border line of life and death faded swiftly as his mind projected itself into the unknown on the other side of the house. Roberts knew what might follow if hesitation were allowed here, and that the conjecturing minds might have scant time to waver he nerved himself and snapped his fingers, leaping around the corner for Quayle's kitchen door, his men piling after him, still silent and much more tense, yet tortured to shout and to shoot. Ten steps more and the goal would have been reached, but even as the leaping group exulted there came a shredded sheet of flame and the deafening crash of spurting six-guns worked at top speed at pointblank range. The charging line crumpled in mid-stride, plunged headlong to the silvered sands and rolled or flopped or lay instantly still. At the head of his men the rustler trail-boss offered a target beyond the waiting punchers' fondest hopes, yet he bounded on unscathed, flashed around the hotel corner, turned again, doubling back behind the smoke-filled stable and scurried like a panic-stricken rabbit for the brush-filled arroyo, while hot and savage hunters searched the street for him until a hail of lead from Kane's drove them to any shelter which might serve.

When the sheltering arroyo led him from his chosen course Roberts forsook it and ran with undiminished speed toward where the horses waited. At last he reached them and as he stretched out his arm his last measure of energy left him and he plunged forward, rolling across the sand. But a will like his was not to be baffled and in a few moments he stirred, crawled forward, clawed himself into a saddle, jerked loose the restraining rope and rode for safety, hunched over and but half conscious. Gradually his pounding heart caught up with the demand, his burning lungs and spasmodic breathing became more normal, his head steadied and became a little clearer and he looked around to find out just where he was. When sure of his location he turned the horse's head toward Bitter Spring, and beyond it, to follow the tracks he knew were still there to the only safe place left for him in all the country.

He seemed to have been riding for days when he caught sight of something moving over a ridge far ahead of him and he closed his eyes in hope that the momentary rest would clear his vision. After awhile he saw it push up over another low ridge and he knew it to be a horseman riding in the same direction as himself. Again he closed his eyes and unmercifully quirted the tired and unwilling horse into a pace it could not hold for long. Another look ahead showed him that the horseman was a Mexican, which meant that he was hardly a foe even if not a friend. And he sneered as he thought how little it mattered whether the Mexican was an enemy or not, for one enemy ahead and a Greaser at that was greatly to be preferred to those who might be following him. Soon he frowned in slowly dawning recognition. It was Miguel and he had obtained quite a start. Conjecturing about how he had managed to be so far in the lead stirred up again the vague suspicions which had been intruding themselves upon him while he had been unable to think clearly; but he was thinking clearly now, he told himself, and his eyes glinted the sudden anger.

He thought he now knew why the town had been entered so easily, why they had been allowed to penetrate unopposed to its center. It was plain enough why they had been permitted to get within a few feet of Quayle's back door, and then be stopped with a volley at a murderously short range. As he reviewed it he almost was stunned by the thought of his own escape and he tried to puzzle it out. It might be that every waiting puncher thought that others were covering him—and in this he was right. The compact group behind him had drawn every eye. It had been one of those freakish tricks of fate which might not occur again in a hundred fights; and it turned cold, practical Hugh Roberts into a slave of superstition.

On the way to town he had sneered when Miguel had pointed out a chaparral cock which raced with them for several miles and claimed that it was an omen of good luck; but from this time on no "roadrunner" ever would hear the angry whine of his bullets. Thinking of Miguel brought him back to his suspicions and he looked at the distant rider with an expression on his face which would have caused chills to race up and down the Mexican's back, could he have seen them. Miguel, unhurt, riding leisurely back to the herd, with a head-start great enough to be in itself incriminating. And then the Mexican turned in his saddle and looked back, and Roberts let his horse fall into a saner pace.

The effect upon Miguel was galvanic. He reined in, flung himself off on the far side of his horse and cautiously slid the rifle from its scabbard while he pretended to be tightening the cinch. His swarthy face became a pasty yellow and then resumed its natural color, a little darker, perhaps, by the sudden inrush of blood. After what he had done in town Hugh Roberts would be on his trail for only one thing. Miguel's racing imagination and his sudden feeling of guilt for his deliberate, planned desertion found a sufficient reason for the pursuing horseman. Sliding the rifle under his arm he waited until the man came nearer, where a hit would be less of a gamble. The Mexican knew what had happened, for he had delayed until he heard that crashing volley, and knew it to be a volley. Knowing this he knew what it meant and had fled for Surprise Valley and the big herd waiting there. That Roberts should have escaped was a puzzle and he wrestled with it while the range was steadily shortened, and the more he wrestled the more undecided he became. Finally he slipped the gun back, mounted, and waited for the other to come up. He had a plausible answer for every question.

Roberts slowed to a walk and searched the Mexican's eyes as he pulled up at his side. "How'd you get out here so far ahead of *me?*" he demanded, his eyes cold and threatening.

Miguel shrugged his shoulders, but did not take his hand from his belt. "Ah, eet ees a miracle," he breathed. "The good Virgin, she watch over Miguel. An' *paisano,* the roadrunner—deed I not tell you eet was good luck? An' you, too, was saved! How deed eet happen, that you are save?"

"They none of them looked at me, I reckon," replied Roberts. "They got everybody but me—an' *you*. How is it that yo're out here, so far ahead of me?"

"Jus' before the firs' shootin'—the what you call vol-ley—I stoomble as I try not to step on Thorpe. I go down—the volley, eet come—I roll away—they do not see me—an' here I am, like you, save."

"Is that so?" snapped Roberts.

"Eet ees jus' so, so much as eet ees that somewan tell we are comin' to Quayle's," answered Miguel. "For why they do not see us, in the town, when we come in? For why that vol-ley, lak one shot? Sometheeng there ees that Miguel he don' understan'. An' theese, please: Why ees there no sortie wen we come in? We was on the ver' minute—eet ees so?"

"Right on th' dot!" snarled Roberts, his thoughts racing along other trails. "Huh!" he growled. "Our shares of th' herd money comes to quite a sizable pile—mebby that's it. Take th' shares of *all* of us, an' it's more'n half. Well, I don't know, an' I ain't carin' a whole lot now. Think we can swing that herd, Miguel, an' split *all* th' money, even shares?"

The Mexican showed his teeth in a sudden, expansive smile. "For why not? Theese horses are ver' tired; but the others—they are res' now. We can wait at Bitter Spring to-night, an' go on tomorrow. There ees no hurry now."

"We don't hang out at Bitter Spring all night," contra-dicted Roberts flatly. "We'll water 'em an' breath 'em a spell, an' push right on. Th' further I get away from Mes-quite th' better I'm goin' to like it. Come on, let's get goin'."

"There ees no hurry from Bitter Spring," murmured the Mexican. "They ees only one who know beyond; an' Man-uel, he ees weeth Kane."

"I don't care a damn!" growled his companion, stubbornly. "I'm not layin' around Bitter Spring any longer than I has to."

Neither believed the other's story, but neither cared, only each determined to be alert when the drive across the desert was completed. Before that there was hardly need to let their mutual suspicions have full play. Each was necessary to the success of the drive—but after? That would be another matter. Fate was again kind to them both, for as they hurried east Hopalong Cassidy hastened west along his favorite trail, the rolling sand between hiding them from him.

Back in the town the elated ambushers buried the bodies, marveled at the escape of Roberts and drifted away to take places on the firing line, which soon showed increased activity. Here and there a more daring puncher took chances, some regretting it and others gaining better positions. Red, Johnny, and Waffles attended strictly to the roof, which now had been abandoned on all sides but the north, where lack of cover prohibited McCullough's men from getting close enough to do any considerable damage. The few punchers lying far off on the north were there principally to stop a sortie or an attempt at escape. As the day passed the defenders' fire grew a little less and the Question-Mark foreman was content to wait it out rather than risk unnecessary casualties in pushing the fighting any more briskly.

Evening came, and with it came Hopalong, tired, hungry, thirsty, and hot, which did not add sweetness to his disposition. Eager to get the men he wanted and to return for the herd, he listened impatiently to his friends' account of the fight, his mind busy on his own account. When the tale had been told and McCullough's changing attitude touched upon he shoved his hat back on his head, spread his feet and ripped out an oath.

"Bastard!" he growled. "All these men, all this time, to clean up a shack like that?"

"Mac's playin' safe—it's only a matter of time, now," apologized Waffles, glaring at his two companions, who already had worn his nerves ragged by the same kind of remarks.

"Hell!" snorted Hopalong impatiently. "We'll all grow whiskers at this rate, before it's over!" He turned to Johnny and regarded him speculatively. "Kid, let Red an' Waffles handle that roof an' come along with me. I'm goin' to start things movin'."

"You'll find Mac plumb set on goin' easy," warned Waffles.

"Th' hell with Mac, an' Lukins, an' you, an' everybody else," retorted Hopalong. "We're not workin' for nobody but ourselves. All I got to do is keep my mouth shut an' Mac loses a plumb fine herd. Let me hear him talk to me! Come on, Kid."

Johnny deserted his companions as though they were lepers and showed his delight in every swaggering movement. A whining bullet over his head sent his fingers to his nose in contemptuous reply, but nevertheless he went on more carefully thereafter. As they reached the rear of a deserted adobe Hopalong pulled him to a stop.

"I'm tired of this blasted country, an' you ought to be, for you've got a wife that's havin' dull days an' sleepless nights. I'm goin' to touch somethin' off that'll put an end to this fool quiltin' party, an' let us get our money an' go home. By that I'm meanin' th' SV, for it's goin' to be home for me. Besides, it's our best chance of gettin' them rewards. So he's aimin' on cuttin' us out of 'em, huh? All right; I'm goin' to Quayle's, an' while I'm holdin' their interest you fill a canteen with kerosene an' smuggle it into th' stable."

"What you goin' to do?" demanded his companion with poorly repressed eagerness.

"I'm goin' to set fire to that gamblin'-joint an' drive 'em out, that's what!"

"Th' moon won't let you," objected Johnny, but as he looked up at the drifting clouds he hesitated and qualified his remark. "You'll have times when it won't be so light, but it'll be too light for that."

"When I start for th' hotel gamblin'-joint I go agin' th' northeast corner, where there ain't but one loophole that covers that angle. I got it figgered out. When I start, you an' Red won't be loafin' back there where I found you, target-practicin' at th' roof."

Reaching the hotel they found a self-satisfied group complacently discussing the fight. Quayle looked up at their entry, sprang to his feet and heartily shook hands with both.

"Welcome to Mesquite, Cassidy," he beamed. " 'Tis different now than whin ye left, an' it won't be long before honest men have their say-so in this town."

"Couple of weeks, I reckon, th' way things are driftin'," replied Hopalong, smiling as Johnny left the office to invade the kitchen, where Murphy gave a grinning welcome and looked curiously at the huge canteen held out to him.

"Couple of days," corrected Quayle.

McCullough arose and shook hands with the newcomer. "Hear you been trailin' my herd," he said. "Locate 'em?"

"They're hobbled, an' waitin' for yore boys to drive 'em home. Wish you'd tell yore outfit an' th' others not to shoot at th' feller that heads for Kane's northeast corner tonight, but to cut loose at th' loopholes instead. I'm honin' to get back home, an' so I'm aimin' to bust up this little party tonight. To do that I got to get close."

"That's plumb reckless," replied the trail-boss. "We got

this all wrapped up now, an' it'll tie its own knots in a day or two. What's th' use of takin' a chance like that?"

"To show that bunch just who they throwed in jail! Somebody else might feel like tryin' it some day, an' I'm aimin' to make that 'some day' a long way off."

"Can't say I'm blamin' you for that. Whereabouts did you leave th' herd?"

"Where nobody but me an' my friends, on this side of th' fence, knows about," answered Hopalong. "I'll tell you when I see you again—ain't got time now." He nodded to the others, went out the way he had come in and walked off with Johnny, who carried the innocent canteen instead of putting it into the stable.

As they started for the place where Hopalong had left his horse, not daring to ride it into town, they chose a short-cut and after a few minutes' brisk walking Hopalong pointed to a bunch of horses tied to some bushes.

"Th' fellers that owned them played safer than I did," he said, "leavin' 'em out here. I reckon they're all Question-Mark."

Johnny put a hand on his friend's arm and stopped him. "I got a better guess," he said. "I know where all their cayuses are. Hoppy, that rustlin' drive crew musta come in this way. What you bet?"

"I ain't bettin'," grunted his companion, starting toward the little herd, "I'm lookin'. I don't hanker to lose that cayuse of mine, an' they'll mebby get th' hoss I ride after I start for their buildin' tonight. He's so mean I sort of cotton to him. An' he's got some thoroughbred blood in his carcass, judgin' from what Arch said. In a case like this it's only fair to use theirs. Besides, they're fresh; mine ain't."

Johnny pushed ahead, stopped at the tethered group and laughed. "Good thing you didn't bet," he called over his shoulder.

Hopalong untied a wicked-looking animal. "He looks like he'd burn th' ground over a short distance, an' that's what I'm interested in. I'm goin' down an' turn mine loose. If things break like I figger they will there's no tellin' when I'll see him again, an' I don't want him to starve tied up to a tree. He's so thirsty about now that he'll head for Mc-Cullough's crick on a bee line."

Johnny nodded, considered a moment and went toward the tie ropes. "Shore, an' not stray far from that grass, neither." He released the horses except the one he mounted and then rode up so close to his friend that their knees rubbed. "No tellin' when anybody will be comin' this way or when they'll get a drink. You look like you been hit by an idea. That's so rare, suppose you uncork it?"

"It's one I've been turnin' over," replied his friend, "an' it looks th' same on both sides, too."

"Turn it over for me an' lemme look."

"Kid, I'm lookin' for somethin' to happen that shore will bother Mr. McCullough a whole lot if he happens to think of it. When that buildin' starts burnin' it's shore goin' to burn fast. They can't fight th' fire like they should with them punchers pourin' lead into them lighted loopholes. Once it starts nothin' can stop it; an' I'm tellin' you it's shore goin' to start right. Th' south side is goin' first. They know there's only a few men watchin' th' north side, an' them few are layin' too far back. It won't take a man like Kane very long to learn that he's got to jump, an' jump quick; an' when he does he'll jump right. Right for him an' right for us. He can't do nothin' else. You said they got their cayuses in there with 'em?"

Johnny nodded. "So I was told. I'm seein' yore drift, Hoppy; an' when Kane an' his friends jump me an' Red shore will have jammed guns an' not be able to shoot at 'em."

"Marriage ain't spoiled yore head," chuckled his

companion. "Kane havin' us jailed that way riled me; an' McCullough tryin' to slip out of payin' them rewards has riled me some more. I'm washin' one hand with th' other. Do you think you an' Red could get yore cayuses an' an extra one for me, in case they get this one, around west somewhere back of where yo're goin'?"

"How'll this one do for you?" asked Johnny slapping the horse he was on.

"Plenty good enough."

"Then he'll be there, ready to foller th' jumpers," laughed Johnny.

"Good for you, Kid. You shore have got th' drift. Now, seein' that I may get into trouble an' be too late to go after 'em when they jump, you listen close while I tell you where to ride, an' all about it," and the description of the desert trail and the valley was as meaty as it was terse. He told his friend where to take the horses and where to look for him before the night's work began, and then went back to Kane and his men. "They're bound to head for that valley. There ain't no place else for 'em to go. I'll bet they've had that figgered for a refuge ever since they learned about it."

Johnny laughed contentedly. "An' Mac tellin' me that he's got 'em all tied up an' ain't aimin' to pay no rewards! But," he said, becoming instantly grave, "there's one thin' I don't like. I'm admittin' it's yore scheme, but we ought to draw lots to see who's goin' to use that kerosene. After all, yo're down here to help me out of a hole. Dig up some more cartridges, you maverick!"

"Don't you reckon I got brains enough to run it off?" demanded his friend.

"An' some to spare," replied Johnny; "but I ain't no idjut, myself. Here; call yore choice," and he reached for his belt.

"Yo're slow, Kid," chuckled Hopalong, holding out his hand. "Call it yourself."

Johnny hesitated, pushed back the cartridges and placed his hand on those of his friend. "You went at that like you was pullin' a gun: an' I can't say nothin' that means anythin' faster. Why th' hurry?"

"Habit, I reckon," gravely replied his friend. "Savin' time, mebby; *I* dunno why, you chump!"

"It's a good habit; an' I'm shore you saved considerble time, which same I'm aimin' to waste," replied Johnny. He thought swiftly. Last time he had called "even," and lost. He was certain that Hopalong wanted the task. How would his friend figure? The natural impulse of a slow-witted man would be to change the number. Hopalong was not slow-witted; on the contrary so far from slow-witted that he very likely would be susicious of the next step in reasoning and go a step further, which would take him back to the act of the slow-witted, for he knew that the cogitating man in front of him was no simpleton. Odd or even: a simple choice; but in this instance it was a battle of keen wits. Johnny raised his own hand and looked down at his friend's, the upper one clasping and covering the lower; and then into the night-hidden eyes, which were squinting between narrowed lids to make their reading hopeless. Being something of a gambler Johnny had the gambler's way of figuring, and this endorsed the other line of reasoning: he believed the chances were not in favor of a repetition.

"Cuss yore grinnin' face," he growled. "I said 'even' last time, an' was wrong. Now I'm sayin' 'odd.' Open up!"

Hopalong opened the closed hands and his squinting eyes at the same instant and laughed heartily. "Kid, I cussed near raised you, an' I know yore ways. Mebby it ain't fair, but you was tryin' hard to outguess me. There they are— pair of aces. Count 'em, sonny; count 'em."

"Count 'em yourself," growled Johnny; "if you can count that far!" He peered into the laughing eyes and thrust out his jaw. "You know my ways, do you? Well, when we get back to th' SV, me an' you are goin' in to Dave's, get a big stack of two-bit pieces an' go at it. I'll cussed soon show you how much you know my ways! G'wan! Get out of here before I get rough!"

"He's too old to spank," mused Hopalong, kneeing the horse, "an' too young to fight with—reckon I'll have to pull my stakes an' move along." Chuckling, he looked around. "Ain't forgot nothin' about tonight, have you, child?"

"No!" thundered Johnny. "But for two-bits I *would!*" Hopalong's laugh came back to him and sent a smile over his face. "There ain't many like you, you old son-of-a-gun!" he muttered, and wheeled to return to the town and to Red.

His departing friend grinned at the horse. "Bronch," he said, confidently, "he shore had me again. I'm gettin' so cheatin's second nature; an' worse'n that, I'm cheatin' my best friends, an' likin' it. Yessir, *likin'* it! Ain't you ashamed of me? You nod that ugly head of yourn again an' I'll knock it off you! G'wan: This ain't no funeral *yet!*"

XXII

♦

The Bonfire

Johnny rode up to the hotel, got a Winchester and ammunition for it from the stack of guns in the kitchen and then went to the stable for Red's horse and Pepper. As he led them out he stopped to answer a pertinent question from the upper window of the hotel and rode off again, leading the extra mounts.

Ed Doane lowered the rifle and scratched his head. "Goin' for a moonlight ride," he repeated in disgust as he drew back from the window. "Cussed if punchers ain't gettin' more locoed every day. Moonlight ride! Shore—go out an' look at th' scenery. Looks different in th' moonlight—bah! To me a pancake looks like a pancake by kerosene, daylight, wood fire or—or moonlight. I suppose th' moonlight'll get into 'em an' they'll be singin' love-songs an' harmonizin'; but thank th' Lord I don't have to go along!" He glanced around at a sudden *thap!*, grinned in the darkness at the double planking on that side wall and sat down again. "Shoot!" he growled. "Shoot twice! Shoot an' be damned! Waste 'em! Reckon th' moonlight's got into you, you cow-stealin', murderin' pup." Filling his pipe he packed and lit it, blew several clouds through nose and mouth and scratched his head again. "Goin' for a moonlight ride, huh? Well, mebby you are, Johnny, my lad; but Ed Doane's bettin' there's more'n a ride in it. You didn't go for no moonlight rides before that missin' friend of yourn turned up; an' then, right away, you ride up on one hoss, collect two more an' go gallivantin' off under th' moon. I'm guessin' close. Eddie Doane, I'll bet you a tenspot them three grizzlies are out for to put their ropes on them rewards. An' I hope they collect, cussed if I don't. That Scotch trail-boss is puttin' on too many airs for me—an' he's rilin' Nelson slow but shore. Go get it, Bar-20: I'm bettin' on you."

There came steps to his door. "Ar-re ye there, Ed?" called a voice.

"Shore; come in, Murphy."

The door opened and closed as the cook entered. "Have ye a pipeful? Mine's all gone."

"Help yourself," answered Doane, tossing the sack. "There it is, by yore County Cork feet."

"I have ut," grunted Murphy. 'An' who was th' lad ye was talkin' to from th' windy just now?"

"Nelson. He's goin' ridin' in th' moonlight. Must aim to go far, for he's got three horses."

"Has he, now?" Murphy puffed in quiet satisfaction for a moment. "He's a good la-ad, Ed. Goin' ridin', is he? Well, ridin' is fine for them as likes it. But I'm wonderin' what he's doin' with th' kerosene I gave him?"

"Kerosene? When?"

"Whin he come in with his friend Cassidy—an' a fine bye *that* man is, too. Shure: a hull canteen av it. Two gallons. He says for me to kape it quiet: as if I'd be tellin'! Quayle would have me scalp if he knowed it—givin' away his ile like that. Now where ye goin' so fast?"

"For a walk, under th' moonlight!" answered Doane. "Yo're goin' too—an' we're goin' with our mouths shut. Not a word about th' horses or th' kerosene. You remember what Cassidy said about goin' agin' Kane's northeast corner? Come on—an' see th' bonfire!"

"Shure, an' who's fool enough to have anny bonfires now?"

"Murphy, I said *with our mouths shut.* Come on, up near th' jail!"

The cook scratched his head and favored his companion with a sidewise glance, which revealed nothing because of the darkness of the room. "Th' jail?" he muttered. "He's crazy, he is. Th' jail won't make no bonfire. It's mud. But as long as he has th' 'baccy, I'll go wid him. *Whist!*" he exclaimed as another *thap!* sounded on the wall. "An' what's that?"

"This room's haunted," explained Ed.

"Lead th' way, thin; or let me," said Murphy in great haste. "I'll watch yore mud bonfire."

After leaving the hotel Johnny kept it between himself and Kane's building, rose to the arroyo which Roberts had found so useful and followed it until out of sight of anyone in town. When he left it he turned east, crossed the main trail and dismounted east of the place where he and Red had kept watch on the gambling-house roof. Working his way on foot to his sharpshooting friends he lay down at Red's side and commented casually on several subjects, finally nudging the Bar-20 rifleman.

"I'm growin' tired of this spot an' this game," he grumbled. "They know where we are now, an' that roof's plumb tame."

Red stirred restlessly. "You musta read my mind," he observed. "You've had a spell off—stay here while I take a rest."

"Stay nothin'!" retorted Johnny. "This ain't our fight, anyhow."

"Somebody's got to stay," objected Red.

"Let Waffles, then," rejoined Johnny. "You don't care if we look around?"

"I'd just as soon stay here as go any place else," said the ex-foreman of the O-Bar-O. "Where you fellers aimin' to go?"

"Over west to cover Hoppy," answered Johnny, remembering that this much was generally known. "He aims to make a dash for th' hotel, an' he's so stubborn nobody can stop him. He says th' fight's been goin' on too long; an' you know how he can use six-guns. To use 'em right he'll have to get plumb close."

"Cussed fool!" snorted Red, arising to his knees. "How can he end it by makin' a dash, an' usin' his short guns? Mebby he's aimin' to put his rope on it an' pull it over, shootin' as they pop out from under!" he sarcastically suggested.

"Mebby; better ask him," replied Johnny. "*I* did. Mebby you can get it out of him. When he wants to keep his mouth shut, he shore can keep it shut tight. There's no use wastin' our breath on it. He's got some fool scheme in his head an' he's set solid. All we can do is to try to save his fool skin. Waffles can hold down this place till we come back. Come on, Red."

Red grumbled and stretched. "All right. See you later mebby, Waffles."

Johnny turned. "Don't forget an' shoot at th' feller runnin' for th' east end of th' buildin'," he warned.

"Mac sent th' word along a couple of hours ago," replied Waffles, settling down in the place vacated by Red to resume the watch on the hotel roof, which was fairly well revealed at times by the moon. He seemed to be turning something over in his mind, but finally shrugged his shoulders and gave his attention to the roof. "They've got somethin' better'n six-guns at close range," he muttered. "Well, a man owes his friends somethin', so I'm holdin' my tongue."

Reaching the horses Johnny and his companion mounted and rode northward, leading the spare mount.

"What's he up to?" demanded Red.

"Goin' to set fire to th' shack," answered Johnny, and he forthwith explained the whole affair.

"Huh!" grunted Red. "There ain't no doubt in my mind that it'll work if he can get there an' get th' fire started." He was silent for a moment and then pulled his hat more firmly down on his head. "If he don't get there, I'll give it a whirl. Anyhow, I'd have to leave cover to get to him if he went down—so it ain't much worse goin' th' rest of th' way. An' I'm tellin' you this: That lone loophole is shore goin' to be bad medicine for anybody tryin' to use it after he starts. I'll put 'em through it so fast they'll be crowdin' each other."

"An' while yo're reloadin' I'll keep 'em goin'," said Johnny, patting his borrowed Winchester. "They'll shore think somebody's squirtin' 'em out of a hose."

Some time later he stopped his horse and peered around in the faint light.

Red stopped, also. "This th' place?"

"Looks like it—we ought to get some sign of Hoppy purty soon. Anyhow, we'll wait awhile. Glad that moon ain't very bright."

"An' cussed glad for th' clouds," added Red. "Clouds like them ain't th' rule in this part of the country." He leaned over and looked down at the sand. "Tracks, Kid," he said. "Follow 'em?"

"No," answered his companion slowly. "I'm bettin' they're Hoppy's. Stay with th' cayuses—I'm goin' to look around," and as he dismounted they heard a hail. Red swung to the ground as their friend appeared.

"You made good time," said Hopalong, advancing. "I been off lookin' things over. We can leave th' cayuses in a little hollow about long rifle-shot from th' buildin'. From there you two can get real close by travelin' on yore bellies from bush to bush. Th' cover's no good in daylight, but on a night like this, by waitin' for th' clouds, it'll be plenty good enough."

"How close did you get?" asked Johnny.

"Close enough to send every shot through that loophole, if I wanted to."

"Did they see you? Did you draw a shot?"

"No. They ain't watchin' that loophole very close. Ain't had no reason to since th' stables burned. There ain't no-body been layin' off in this direction. Th' cover wasn't good enough to risk it, with only a blank wall to watch, an' with them fellers on th' roof to shoot down. Red couldn't cover th' north part of it from where he was. I been wonderin' if I ought to use a cayuse at all."

"There's argument agin' usin' one," mused Johnny.

"Th' noise, an' a bigger object to catch attention," remarked

Red. "If you walked th' cayuse to soften its steps, it still looms up purty big; an' if you cut loose an' dash in, th' noise shore will bring a shot. Me an' th' Kid would have to start shootin' early an' keep it up a long while—an' we're near certain to leave gaps in th' string."

"What moonlight there is shines on this end of th' buildin'," observed Johnny. "That loophole show up plain?" he asked.

"You can't see nothin' else," chuckled Hopalong. "It's so black it fair hollers."

Red drew the Winchester from its sheath and turned the front sight on its pivot, which then showed a thin white line. He never had regretted having it made, for since it had been put on he had not suffered the annoyance of losing sight of it against a dark target in poor light. "Bein' bull-headed," he remarked, "you chumps has to guess; but little Reddie ain't doin' none of it. I told you long ago to have one put on."

"Shut up!" growled Johnny, turning his own Winchester over in his hands.

"I reckon I'm travelin' flat on my stomach," said Hopalong, slinging the big canteen over his head. "I'll go with you till we has to stop, let you get set an' then make a run for it. Seein' that th' Kid has got a repeater, too, you'll be able to keep lead flyin' most of th' time I'm in th' open if you don't pull too fast; an' when you run out of cartridges I'll start with my Colts. I'll be close enough, then, to use 'em right. When you see that I'm under th' buildin' go back quite a ways so th' fire won't show you up too plain, an' *watch th' roof.* I'll start a fire under that loophole before I leave, an' that'll spoil their view through it; an' I ain't leavin' before I've fixed things so them fellers will have so much to do they won't have much time for sharpshootin'. That buildin' will burn like a pine knot."

"Then yo're comin' back th' way you go in?" asked Red.

"Shore," answered Hopalong. "Everythin' plain?"

"Watch me," ordered Red, his hand rising and falling. "If we space our shots like this we ought to be able to reload while th' other is emptyin' his gun. Is it too slow?"

"No," said Johnny, considering.

"No," said the man with the canteen, watching closely. "It'll take that long to throw a gun into th' loophole an' line it up, in this light."

"Not bein' used to a repeater like Red is," suggested Johnny, "I'd better shoot th' second string—that'll give us three of 'em before it's my time to reload. Red can slide 'em in as fast as I can shoot 'em out, timin' 'em like that."

"You can put 'em through that hole as good as I can," said Red. "It's near point-blank shootin'. You do th' shootin' an' I'll take care of loadin' both guns. We can't make no blunders, with Floppy out there runnin' for his life."

"That's why I ought to do th' runnin'," growled Johnny. "I can make three feet to his two."

"It's all settled," said Hopalong, decisively. "I got th' kerosene, an' I'm keepin' it. Come on. No more talkin'."

They followed him over the course he had picked out and with a caution which steadily increased as they advanced until at length they went ahead only when the crescent moon was obscured by drifting clouds. Ahead loomed the two-story gambling-hall, its windowless rear wall of bleached lumber leaden in the faint light. An occasional finger of fire stabbed from its south wall to be answered by fainter stabs from the open, the reports flat and echoless. A distant voice sang a fragment of song and a softened laugh replied to a ribald jest. A horse neighed and out of the north came quaveringly the faint howl of a moon-worshiping coyote.

The three friends, face down on the sand, now each behind a squat bush, wriggled forward silently but swiftly, and gained new and nearer cover. Again a cloud passed before the moon and again they wriggled forward, their eyes fixed on the top of the roof ahead, two of them heading for the same bush and the other for a shallow gully. The pair met and settled themselves to their satisfaction, heads close together as they consulted about the proper setting of the rear sights. One of them knelt, the rifle at his shoulder reaching out over the top of the bush, his companion sitting cross-legged at his side, a pile of dull brass cartridges in the sombrero on the ground between his knees to keep the grease on the bullets free from sand.

The kneeling man bent his head and let his cheek press against the stock of the heavy weapon, whispered a single word and waited. Twice there came the squeak of a frightened rat from his companion and instantly from the right came an answering squeak as the figure of a man leaped up from the gully and sprinted for the lead-colored wall, the heavy, jarring crash of a Winchester roaring from the bush, to be repeated at close intervals which were as regular as the swing of a pendulum. A round, dark object popped up over the flat roof line and the cross-legged man on the ground threw a gun to his shoulder and fired, almost in one motion. The head dropped from sight as the marksman slid another cartridge into the magazine and waited, ready to shoot again or to exchange weapons with his kneeling friend.

The runner leaped on at top speed, but he automatically counted the reports behind him and a smile flashed over his face when the count told him that the second rifle was being used. He would have known it in no other way, for the spacing of the shots had not varied. Again the count told of the second change and a moment later another extra report confirmed his belief that the roof was being closely watched by his friends. A muffled shout came from the building and a spurt of fire flashed from the loophole, but toward the sky and he fancied he heard the sound of a falling body. Far to his left jets of flame winked along a straggling line, the reports at times bunched until they sounded like a short tattoo, while behind him the regular crashing of an unceasing Winchester grew steadily more distant and flatter.

His breath was coming in gulps now for he had set himself a pace out of keeping with the habits of years and the treacherous sand made running a punishment. During the last hundred feet it was indeed well for him that Johnny shot fast and true, that the five-hundred grain bullets which now sang over his aching head were going straight to the mark. He suddenly, vaguely realized that he heard wrangling voices and then he threw himself down onto the sand and rolled and clawed under the building, safe for the time.

Gradually the jumble of footsteps over his head impressed themselves upon him and he mechanically drew a Colt as he raised his head from the earth. Suddenly the roaring steps all went one way, which instantly aroused his suspicions, and he crawled hurriedly to the black darkness of a pile of sand near the bottom of the south wall, which he reached as the steps ceased. No longer silhouetted against the faint light of the open ground around the building, a light which was bright by contrast with the darkness under the floor, he placed the canteen on the ground and felt for chips and odds and ends of wood with one hand while the other held a ready gun.

There came the sharp, plaintive squeaking of seldom-used hinges, which continued for nearly a minute and then a few unclassified noises. They were followed by the head of a brave man, plainly silhouetted against the open sand. It turned slowly this way and that and then became still.

"See anythin'?" came a hoarse whisper through the open trap.

There was no reply from the hanging head, but if thoughts could have killed, the curious whisperer would have astonished St. Peter by his jack-in-the-box appearance before the Gates.

"If he did, we'd know by now, you fool," whispered another, who instantly would have furnished St. Peter with another shock.

"He'd more likely feel somethin', rather than see it," snickered a third, who thereupon had a thrashing coming his way, but did not know it as yet.

The head popped back into the darkness above it, the trapdoor fell with a bang, and sudden stamping was followed by the fall of a heavy body. Furious, high-pitched cursing roared in the room above until lost in a bedlam of stamping feet and shouting voices.

"He ought to kill them three fools," growled Hopalong, indignant for the moment; and then he shook with silent laughter. Wiping his eyes, he fell to gathering more wood for his fire, careless as to noise in view of the free-for-all going on over his head. Removing the plug from the canteen he poured part of the oil over the piled-up wood, on posts, along beams and then, saturating his neckerchief, he rubbed it over the floor boards. Wriggling around the pile of sand he wet the outer wall as far up as his arm would reach, soaked two more posts and another pile of shavings and chips and then, corking the nearly empty vessel, he felt for a match with his left hand, which was comparatively free from the kerosene, struck it on his heel and touched it here and there, and a rattling volley from the besiegers answered the flaming signal. Backing under the floor he touched the other pile and wriggled to the wall directly under the loophole. Again and again the canteen soaked the kerchief and the kerchief spread the oil, again a pile of shavings leaned against a wetted post, and another match leaped from a mere spot of fire into a climbing sheet of flame, which swept up over the loophole and made it useless. As he turned to watch the now well-lighted trapdoor, there came from the east, barely audible above the sudden roaring of the flame, the reports of the rifles of his two friends, the irregular timing of the shots leading him to think that they were shooting at animated targets, perhaps on the roof.

The trapdoor went up swiftly and he fired at the head of a man who looked through it. The toppling body was grabbed and pulled back and the door fell with a slam which shook the building. Hopalong's position was now too hot for comfort and getting more dangerous every second and with a final glance at the closed trapdoor he scrambled from under the building, slapped sparks from his neck and shoulders and sprinted toward his waiting, anxious friends, where a rifle automatically began the timed firing again, although there now was no need for it. Slowing as he left the building farther and farther behind he soon dropped into a walk and the rifle grew silent.

"Here we are," called Johnny's cheery voice. "I'm admittin' you did a good job!"

"An' *I'm* sayin' you did a good one," replied Hopalong. "Them shots came as reg'lar as th' tickin' of a clock."

"Quite some slower," said Red. "That gang can't stay in there much longer. Notice how Mac's firin' has died down?"

"They're waitin' for 'em to come out an' surrender," chuckled Hopalong. "Keep a sharp watch an you'll see 'em come out an' make a run for it."

"Better get back to th' cayuses, an' be ready to foller," suggested Red.

"No," said Johnny. "Let 'em get a good start. If we stop 'em here Mac may get a chance to cut in."

"An' we'll mebby have to kill some of th' men we want alive," said Hopalong. "Let 'em get to that valley an' think they're safe. We can catch 'em asleep th' first night."

The gambling-hall was a towering mass of flames on the south and east walls and they were eating rapidly along the other two sides. Suddenly a hurrying line of men emerged from the north door of the doomed structure, carrying wounded companions to places of safety from the flames. Dumping these unfortunates on the ground, the line charged back into the building again and soon appeared leading blind-folded horses, which bit and kicked and struggled, and turned the line into a fighting turmoil. The few shots coming from the front of the building increased suddenly as McCullough led a running group of his men to cover the north wall. A few horses and a man or two dropped under the leaden hail, the accuracy of which suffered severely from the shortness of breath of the marksmen. The group expanded, grew close at one place and with quirts rising and falling, dashed from the building, pressing closely upon the four leaders, and became rapidly smaller before the steadying rifles of its enemies took much heavier toll. Before it had passed beyond the space lighted by the great fire only four men remained mounted, and these were swiftly swallowed up by the dim light on the outer plain.

McCullough and most of his constantly growing force left cover and charged toward the building to make certain that no more of their enemies escaped, while the rest of his men hurried back to get horses and form a pursuing party.

XXIII

♦

Surprise Valley

Hopalong turned and crawled away from the lurid
scene, his friends following him closely. As soon as
they dared they arose to their feet and jogged toward where
their horses waited, and soon rode slowly northeastward,
heading on a roundabout course for Sweet Spring.

"Take it easy," cautioned Hopalong. "We don't want to
get ahead of 'em yet. If my eyes are any good th' four that
got away are Kane, Corwin, Trask, an' a Greaser. What you
say?"

Reaching the arid valley through which Sand Creek
would have flowed had it not been swallowed up by the
sands, they drew on their knowledge of it and crossed on
hard ground, riding at a walk and cutting northeastward so
as to be well above the course of the fleeing four, after which
they turned to the southeast and approached the spring
from the north. Reaching the place of their former vigil they
dismounted, picketed the horses in the sandy hollow, and lay
down behind the crest of the ridge. Half an hour passed and
then Johnny's roving eyes caught sight of a small group of
horsemen as it popped up over a rise in the desert floor. A
moment later and the group strung out in single file to round
a cactus chaparral and revealed four horsemen, riding
hard. The fugitives raced up to Bitter Spring, tarried a few
moments, and went on again, slowly growing smaller and
smaller, and then a great slope of sand hid them from sight.

Hopalong grunted and arose, scanning their back trail.
"They've been so long gettin' out here that I'm bettin' they
did a good job hidin' their trail. I can see Mac an' his gang

ridin' circles an' gettin' madder every minute. Well, we can go on, now. By goin' th' way I went before we won't be seen."

"How long will it take us?" asked Red, brushing sand from his clothes as he stood up.

"Followin' th' pace they're settin' we ought to be there tonight," answered Hopalong. "Give th' cayuses all they can drink. If them fellers hold us off out there we'll have to run big risks gettin' our water from that crick. Well, let's get started."

The hot, monotonous ride over the desert need not be detailed. They simply followed the tracks made by Hopalong on his previous visit and paid scanty attention to the main trail south of them, contenting themselves by keeping to the lowest levels mile after burning mile. It was evening when they stopped where their guide had stopped before and after waiting for nightfall they went on again in the moonlight, circling as Hopalong had circled and when they stopped again it was to dismount where he had dismounted behind a ridge. They picketed and hobbled the weary, thirsty horses and went ahead on foot. Following instructions Red left them and circled to the south to scout around the great ridge of rock before taking up his position at the head of the slanting trail from the valley. His companions kept on and soon crawled to the rim of the valley, removed their sombreros and peered cautiously over the edge. The faint glow of the fire behind the adobe hut in the west end of the sink shone in the shadows of the great rock walls and reflected its light from boulders and brush. Below them cattle and the horses of the caviya grazed over the well-cropped pasture and a strip of silver told where the little creek wandered toward its effacement. Moving back from the rim they went on again, looking over from time to time and eventually reached the point nearly over the fire, where they could hear part of the conversation going on around it, when the voices raised above the ordinary tones.

"You haven't a word to say!" declared Kane, his out-stretched hand leveled at Trask, the once-favored deputy-sheriff. "If it wasn't for your personal spite, and your damned avarice, we wouldn't be in this mess tonight! You had no orders to do that."

Trask's reply was inaudible, but Corwin's voice reached them.

"I told him to let Nelson alone," said the sheriff. "He was dead set to get square for him cuttin' into th' argument with Idaho. But as far as avarice is concerned, you got yore part of th' eleven hundred."

"Might as well, seeing that the hand had been played!" retorted Kane. "What's more, I'm going to keep it. Anybody here think he's big enough to get any part of it?"

"Nobody here wants it," said Roberts. "Th' boys I had with me, an' Miguel, an' myself have reasons to turn this camp fire into a slaughter, but we're sinkin' our grievances because this ain't no time to air 'em. I'm votin' for less squabblin'. We ain't out of this yet, an' we got four hundred head to get across th' desert. Time enough, later, to start fightin'. I'm goin' off to turn in where there ain't so much fool noise. I've near slept on my feet an' in th' saddle. Fight an' be damned!" and he strode from the fire, keen eyes above watching his progress and where it ended.

The hum around the fire suffered no diminution by his departure, but the words were not audible to the listeners above. Soon Corwin angrily arose and left the circle, his blankets under his arm. His course also was marked. Then the two Mexicans went off, and the eager watchers chuck-led softly as they saw the precious pair take lariats from the saddles of two picketed horses and slip noiselessly toward the feeding caviya. Roping fresh mounts, and the pick of the lot, they made the ropes fast and went back to the other horses. Soon they returned with their riding equipment and blankets, saddled the fresh mounts and, spreading the blankets a few feet beyond the radius of the picket ropes, they rolled up and soon were asleep.

"Sensitive to danger as hounds," muttered Johnny.

"Cunnin' as coyotes," growled Hopalong, glancing at the clear-cut, rocky rim across the valley, where Red by this time lay ensconced. "I hope he remembers to drop their cayuses first—Miguel's worth more to us alive."

"An' easier to take back," whispered Johnny. "We want 'em *all* alive—an' we'd never get 'em that way if they wasn't so played out. They'll sleep like they are dead—luck is with us."

Down at the dying camp fire Kane, his back to the hut, talked with Trask in tones which seemed more friendly, but the deputy was in no way lulled by the change. He sensed a flaming animosity in the fallen boss, who blamed him for the wreck of his plans and the organization. Muttering a careless good night, Trask picked up his blankets and went off, leaving the bitter man alone with his bitterness.

Tired to the marrow of his bones, so sleepy that to remain awake was a torture, the boss dared not sleep. In the company of five men who were no longer loyal, whose greed exceeded his own, and each of whom nursed a real or fancied grudge against him and who searched into the past, into the days of his contemptuous treatment of them for fuel and yet more fuel to feed the fires of their resentment, he dared not close his eyes. On his person was a modest fortune compacted by the size of the bills and so well distributed that unknowing eyes would not suspect its presence; but these men knew that he would not leave his wealth behind him, to be perhaps salvaged from a hot and warped safe in the smoking ruins of his gambling-house.

He stirred and gazed at the glowing embers and an up-shooting tongue of flame lighted up the small space so vividly that its portent shocked through to his dulled brain and sent him to his feet with the speed and silence of a frightened cat. He was too plain a target and too defenseless in the lighted open, and like a ghost he crept away into the darker shadows under the great stone cliff, to pace to and fro in an agonizing struggle against sleep. Back and forth he strode, his course at times erratic as his enemy gained a momentary victory; but his indomitable will shook him free again and again; and such a will it was that when sleep finally mastered him it did not master his legs, for he kept walking in a circular course like a blind horse at a ginny.

When he had leaped to his feet and left the hut the watchers above kept him in sight and after the first few moments of his pacing they worked back from the valley's rim and slipped eastward.

"Here's th' best place," said Hopalong, turning toward the rim again. They looked over and down a furrow in the rock wall. "We'll need two ropes. It'll take one, nearly, to reach from here to that knob of rock an' go around it. Red's got a new hemp rope—bring that, too. If he squawks about us cuttin' it, I'll buy him a new one. Got to have tie ropes."

Johnny hastened away and when he returned he threw Red's lariat on the ground, and joined the other two. Fastening one end around the knob of rock he dropped the other over the wall and shook it until he could see that it reached the steep pile of detritus. Picking up the hemp rope he was about to drop it, too, when caution told him it would make less noise if carried down. Slinging it over his shoulder he crept to the edge, slid over, grasped the rope and let himself down. Seeing he was down his companion was about to follow when Johnny's whisper checked him.

"Canteens—better fill 'em while it's easy."

Hopalong drew his head back and disappeared and it was not much of a wait before the rope was jerking up the wall and returned with a canteen. To send down more than one at a time would be to risk them banging together. When they all were down Johnny took them and slipped among the boulders, Hopalong watching his progress. For caution's sake the water carrier took two trips from the creek and sent them up again one at a time. Soon his friend slid down, glanced around, took the hemp rope and cut it into suitable lengths, giving half of the pieces to Johnny and then without a word started for the west end of the valley, treading carefully, Johnny at his heels.

Roberts, sleeping the sleep of the exhausted, awoke in a panic, a great weight on his legs, arms, and body, and a pair of sinewy thumbs pressing into his throat. His struggles were as brief as they were violent and when they ceased Hopalong arose from the quiet legs and released the limp arms while his companion released the throat hold and took his knees from the prostrate chest. In a few minutes a quiet figure lay under the side of a rock, its mouth gagged with a soiled neckerchief and the new hemp rope gleaming from ankles, knees, and wrists.

Corwin, his open mouth sonorously announcing the quality of his fatigue, lay peacefully on his back, tightly rolled up in his blankets. Two faint shadows fell across him and then as Johnny landed on his chest and sunk the capable thumbs deep into the bronzed throat on each side of the windpipe, Hopalong dropped onto the blanket-swathed legs and gripped the encumbered arms. This task was easy and in a few minutes the sheriff, wrapped in his own blankets like a mummy, also wore a gag and several pieces of new hemp rope, two strands of which passed around his body to keep the blanket rolled.

The two punchers carried him between two boulders,

chuckled as they put him down, and stood up to grin at each other. The blanket-rolled figure amused them and Johnny could not help but wish Idaho was there to enjoy the sight. He moved over against his companion and whispered.

"Shore," answered Hopalong, smiling. "Go ahead. It's only fair. He knocked you on th' head. I'll go up an' spot Kane. Did it strike you that he must have a lot of money on him to be so hell-bent to stay awake? I don't like him pacin' back an' forth like that. It may mean a lot of trouble for us; an' them Greasers are too nervous to suit me. When yo're through with Trask slip off an' watch them Mexicans. Don't pay no attention to me no matter what happens. Stick close to them two. I'll give you a hand with 'em as soon as I can get back. If you have to shoot, don't kill 'em," and the speaker went cautiously toward the hut.

Johnny removed his boots and, carrying them, went toward the place where he had seen the deputy bed down; but when he reached the spot Trask was not there. Thanking his ever-working bump of caution for his silent and slow approach he drew back from the little opening among the rocks and tackled the problem in savage haste. There was no time to be lost, for Hopalong was not aware that any of the gang was roaming around and might not be as cautious as he knew how to be. Why had Trask forsaken his bed-ground, and when? Where had he gone and what was he doing? Cursing under his breath Johnny wriggled toward the creek where he could get a good view of the horses. Besides the two picketed near the sleeping Mexicans none were saddled nor appeared to be doing anything but grazing. Going back again Johnny searched among the boulders in frantic haste and then decided that there was only one thing to do, and that was to head for the hut and get within sight of his friend. Furious because of the time he had lost he started for the new point and finally reached the hut. If Trask was inside he had to know it and he crept along the wall, pausing only to put his ear against it, turned the corner and leaped silently through the door, his arms going out like those of a swimmer. The hut was empty. Relieved for the moment he slipped out again and started to go toward Kane.

"I'll bet a month's pay—" he muttered and then stopped, his mind racing along the trail pointed out by the word. Pay! That was money. Money? As Hopalong had said, Kane must have plenty of it on him—money? Like a flash a possible solution sprang into his mind. Kane's money! Trask was a thief, and what would a thief do if he suspected that the life savings of a man like Kane might easily be stolen? And especially when he had been so angered by the possessor of the wealth?

"I got to move *pronto!*" he growled. "I'm no friend of Kane's but I ain't goin' to have him killed—not by a coyote like Trask, anyhow. We got to have him alive, too. An' Hoppy?" His reflections were such that by the time he came in sight of Kane his feelings were a cross between a mad mountain lion and an active volcano. He stopped again and looked, his mind slowly forsaking rage in favor of suspicion. Kane was walking around in a circle, his eyes closed; his feet were rising and falling mechanically and with an exaggerated motion.

"War dancin'?" thought Johnny. "What would he do that for? He ain't no Injun. I'm sayin' he's loco. Kane loco? Like hell! Fellers like him don't get loco. Makin' medicine? I just said he ain't no Injun. Prancin' around in th' moonlight, liftin' his feet like they had ropes to 'em to jerk 'em. An' with his eyes close shut! I'm gettin' a headache—an' I'm settin' tight till I get th' hang of this walkin' Willy. Mebby he thinks he's workin' a charm; but if he is he ain't goin' to run it on me!"

He pressed closer against the boulder which sheltered

him and searched the surroundings again, slowly, painstakingly. Then there came a low rustling sound, as though a body were being dragged across dried grass. It was to his left and not far away. If it is possible to endow one sense with the total strength of all the others, then his ears were so endowed. Whether or not they were strengthened to an unusual degree they nevertheless heard the rubbing of soft leather on the boulder he lay against, and he held his breath as he reversed his grip on the Colt.

"Hoppy, or Trask?" he wondered, glad that his head did not project beyond the rock. A quick glance at the milling Kane showed no change in that person's antics and he felt certain that he had not been detected by the boss. He froze tighter if it is possible to improve on perfection, for his ears caught a renewal of the sounds. Then his eyes detected a slow movement and focussed on a shadowy hand which fairly seemed to ooze out beyond the rock. When he discerned a ring on one of the fingers he knew it was not Hopalong, for his friend wore no ring. That being so, it only could be Trask who was creeping along the other side of the rock. Johnny glanced again at the peripatetic gang leader and back to the creeping hand, and wondered how high in the air its owner would jump if it were suddenly grabbed. Then he mentally cursed himself, for his independent imagination threatened to make him laugh. He could feel the tickle of mirth slyly pervading him and he bit his lip with an earnestness which cut short the mirth. The hand stopped and the heel of it went down tightly against the earth as though bearing a gradual strain. Johnny was reassured again, for Trask never would be stalking Kane if he had the slightest suspicion that enemies, or strangers, were in the valley, and he hazarded another glance at Kane.

The mechanical walker was drawing near the rock again and in a few steps more would turn his back to it and start away. By this time Johnny had solved the riddle, for although such a thing was beyond any experience of his, his wild guess began to be accepted by him: Kane was walking in his sleep. Where was Hopalong? He hoped his friend would not try to capture the boss until he, himself, had taken care of Trask. This must be his first duty, and knowing what Trask would do very shortly he prepared to do it.

He got into position to act, moving only when the slight sound of Kane's footfalls would cover the barely audible noise of his own movements. Kane's rounding course brought him nearer and then several things happened at once. The owner of the hand leaped from behind the rock and as his head popped out into sight a Colt struck it, and then Johnny started for Kane; but as he reached his feet something hurtled out of the shadows to his right and bore the boss to the ground. Then came the sound of another gun-butt meeting another head and the swiftly moving figure seemed to rebound from the boss and sail toward Johnny, who had started to meet it. He swerved suddenly and muttered one word, just as Hopalong swerved from his own course. They both had turned in the same direction and came together with a force which nearly knocked them out. Holding to each other to keep their feet, they recovered their breath and without a word separated at a run, Hopalong going to Kane and Johnny to Trask. Less dazed by the collision than his friend was, Johnny finished his work first and then helped Hopalong carry Kane to the shelter of the rock.

"Good thing you forgot what I said about watchin' them Greasers," grunted Hopalong. "It's them next, if—" his words were cut short by two quick shots, which reverberated throughout the valley, and without another word he followed his running companion, and scorned cover for the first few hundred yards.

When they got close to the trail they saw two bulks on it, which the moonlight showed to be prostrate horses.

"Where are they, Red?" shouted Johnny. "They're th' only ones free!"

"Down near you somewhere," answered the man above, and his words were proved true by a bullet which hummed past Johnny's ear. He dropped to his stomach and began to wriggle toward the flash of the gun, Hopalong already on the way.

Cut off from escape up the trail the two Mexicans tried to work toward the hut, from which they could put up a good fight; but their enemies had guessed their purpose and strove to drive them off at a tangent.

Red, watching from the top of the cliff, noticed that the occasional gun flashes were moving steadily northwest-ward and believed it safe to leave his position and take an active hand in the events below. After their experience on the up-slanting trail the Mexicans would hardly attempt it again, even though they managed to get back to the foot of it, which seemed very improbable. The thought became ac-tion and the trail guard started to wriggle down the decliv-ity, keeping close to the bottom of the wall, where the shadows were darkest. Because of the necessity for not be-ing seen his progress was slow and quite some time elapsed before he reached the bottom and obtained cover among the scattered rocks. The infrequent reports were farther away now, and they seemed to be getting farther eastward. This meant that they were nearer to the hut, and his decision was made in a flash. The hut must not be won by the fugitives, and he arose and ran for it, bent over and risking safety for speed. After what seemed to be a long time he reached the little cleared space among the rocks, bounded across it, and leaped into the black interior of the hut. Wheeling, he leaned against the rear wall to recover his breath, watching the open door, a grim smile on his face. While keeping his weary watch up on the rim he had craved action, and congratulated himself that he now was a great deal nearer to it than he was before.

Meanwhile the two fugitives, not stomaching a real stand against the men whom they had seen exhibit their abilities in Kane's gambling-hall, had managed to work on a circular course until they were northwest of the hut and not far from it. This they were enabled to do because they were not held to a slow and cautious advance by enemies ahead of them, as were the old Bar-20 pair. They were moving toward the hut, not far from the north wall of the valley, when they blundered upon Trask. In a moment he was released and began a frantic search for his gun, which he found among the rocks not far away. Losing no time he hurried off to release the man he would have robbed, glad to have his assistance. Kane went into action like a spring released and began a hot search for his Colt. When he found it, the cylinder was missing and suspicious noises not far away from him forced him to abandon the search and seek better cover, armed only with a deadly and efficient steel club.

Hopalong and Johnny, guided entirely by hearing, followed the infrequent low sounds in front of them, thinking that they were made by the Mexicans, and drew steadily away from the hut. The Mexicans, motionless in their cover, exulted as their scheme worked out and finally went on again with no one to oppose them. Reaching the last of the rocky cover they arose and ran across the open, leaped into the hut and turned, chuckling, to close the door, leaving Trask to his fate.

Warned by instinct they faced about as Red leaped. Miguel dropped under a clubbed gun, but Manuel, writhing sidewise, raised his Colt only to have it wrenched from his hand by his shifty opponent. Clinching, he drew a knife and strove desperately to use it as he wrestled with his sinewy enemy. At last he managed to force the tip of it against Red's side, barely cutting the flesh; and turned Red into a raging fury. With one hand around Manuel's neck and the other gripping the wrist of the knife-hand, Red smashed his head again and again into the Mexican's face, his knee pressing against the knifeman's stomach. Suddenly releasing his neck hold Red twisted, got the knife-arm under his armpit, gripped the elbow with his other hand and exerted his strength in a twisting heave. The Mexican screamed with pain, sobbed as Red's knee smashed into his stomach and dropped senseless, his arm broken and useless. Red dropped with him and hastily bound him as well as possible in the poor light from the partly opened door.

He had just finished the knot in the neckerchief when a soft, swift rustling appraised him of danger and he moved just in time. Miguel's knife passed through his vest and shirt and pinned him to the hard-packed floor. Before either could make another move the door crashed back against the wall and Kane hurtled into the hut, landing feet first on the wriggling Mexican. He put the knife user out of the fight and pitched sprawling. His exclamation of surprise told Red that he was no friend and now, free from the pinning knife, Red pounced on the scrambling boss.

The other struggles of the crowded night paled into insignificance when compared to this one. Red's superior strength and weight was offset by the fatigue of previous efforts, and Kane's catlike speed. They rolled from one wall to another, pounding and strangling Kane as innocent of the ethics of civilized combat as a maddened bobcat, and he began to fight in much the same way, using his fingernails and teeth as fast as he could find a place for them. Red wanted excitement and was getting it. Torn and bleeding from nails and teeth, his blows lacking power because of the closeness of the target and his own fatigue, Red shed his veneer of civilization and fought like a gorilla. Planting his useful and well-trained knee in the pit of his adversary's stomach, he gripped the lean throat with both hands and hammered Kane's head ceaselessly against the hard earth floor, while his thumbs sank deeply on each side of the gang leader's windpipe. Too enraged to sense the weakening opposition, he choked and hammered until Kane was limp and, writhing from his victim's body, he knelt, grabbed Kane in his brawny arms, staggered to his feet and with one last surge of energy, hurled him across the hut. Kane struck the wall and dropped like a bag of meal, his fighting over for the rest of the night.

Red stumbled over the Mexicans, fell, picked himself up, and reeled outside, fighting for breath, his vision blurred and kaleidoscopic, staring directly at two men among the rocks but seeing nothing. "Come one, come all—damned you!" he gasped.

Trask, thrice wounded, hunted, desperate, fleeing from a man who seemed to be the devil himself with a six-gun, froze instantly as Red appeared. Enraged by this unexpected enemy and sudden opposition where he fondly expected to find none, Trask threw caution to the winds and raised the muzzle of the Colt. As he pulled the trigger a soaring bulk landed on his shoulders, knocking the exploding weapon from his hand and sending him sprawling. Snarling like an animal he twisted around, wriggled from under and grabbed Johnny's other Colt from its holster. Before he could use it Johnny's knee pinned it and the hand holding it to the ground. A clubbed six-gun did the rest and Johnny, calling to Red to watch Trask, hurried away to see if Roberts and Corwin were loose. The latter was helpless in the blanket, but Roberts had freed his feet and was doing well with the knots on his wrists when Johnny's appearance and growled command put an end to his efforts. He put the rope back on the kicking feet and arose as Hopalong limped up.

"Phew!" exclaimed Johnny. "This has been a reg'lar night! Here, you stay with Corwin while I tote this coyote to th' hut." He got Roberts onto his back and staggered away, soon returning for the sheriff.

Dawn found six bound men in varying physical condition sitting with their backs to the hut, their wounds crudely dressed and their bonds readjusted and calculated to stay fixed. Kane was vindictive, his eyes snapping, and he seethed with futile energy, notwithstanding the mauling he had received. His lean face, puffed, discolored, and wolfishly cruel, worked with a steadily mounting rage, which found vent at intervals in scathing vituperative comments about Trask, whom he still blamed for the predicament in which he found himself. Corwin, sullen and fearful, kept silent, his fingers picking nervously at the buckle and strap on the back of his vest. Roberts was angry and defiant and sneered at his erstwhile boss, sending occasional verbal shafts into him in justification of Trask. The two Mexicans had sunk into the black depths of despair and acted as though they were stunned. Trask, a bitter sneer on his face, glared unflinchingly at the storming boss and showed his teeth in grim, ironical smiles.

"Th' crossbreed shows th' cur dog when th' wolf is licked," he sneered in reply to a particularly vicious attack of Kane's. "What you blamin' me for? You took yore share of Nelson's money, an' took it eager. *You* heard me!" he snarled. "I don't care who knows it—I got it, an' you took yore part of it. It was all right *then,* wasn't it? An' you didn't *know* it was his—you let him make a fool of you an' wouldn't listen to me. But as long as you got yourn you didn't care a whole lot *who* lost it. Serves you right."

"Shut up!" muttered Roberts.

"Shut up nothin'," jeered Trask. "Think I'm goin' to swing to save a mad dog like him? Look at him! Look at th' dog breakin' through th' wolf! *Wolf?* Huh! Coyote would be more like it. Don't talk to me!" He looked at the camp fire and at the man busy over it. "I can eat some of that, Nelson," he said.

Johnny nodded and went on with the cooking.

Sounds of horses clattering down the steep trail suddenly were heard and not much later Red rode up on a horse he had captured from the rustlers' caviya and dismounted near the fire. His face was a sight, but the grin which tried to struggle through the bruises was sincere. He dropped two saddles to the ground, the saddles belonging to the Mexicans, which he had stopped to strip from the dead horses on the trail up the wall.

"Our cayuses went loco near th' crick," he said. "I left Hoppy to take off th' saddles an' let 'em soak themselves," referring to the three animals they had left up on the desert the evening before. "I'm all ready to eat, Kid. How's it shapin' up?"

"Grab yore holt," grunted Johnny. He stood up to rest his back. "Mebby it would be more polite to feed our guests first," he grinned.

Red looked at the line-up. "We'll *have* to feed 'em, I reckon. I ain't aimin' to untie no hands. Who's first?"

"Don't play no favorites," answered Johnny. "Go up an' down th' line an' give 'em all a chance." He faced the prisoners. "You fellers like yore coffee smokin'?" Only two men answered, Roberts and Trask, and they did not like it smoking hot. "Let it cool a little, Red; no use scaldin' anybody."

The prisoners had all been fed when Hopalong appeared on another horse from the rustlers' caviya and swung down. "Smells good, Kid! An' looks good," he said. "I got all th' saddles on fresh cayuses, waitin'—all but these here. We'll lead our own cayuses. That Pepper-hoss of yourn acts lonesome. She ain't lookin' at th' grass, at all." He sat down, arose part way and felt in his hip pocket, bringing out the cylinder of a six-gun. Glancing at Kane, to whom it belonged, he tossed it into the brush and resumed his seat.

Johnny's face broke into a smile and he whistled shrilly. Quick hoofbeats replied and Pepper, her neck arched, stepped daintily across the little level patch of ground and nosed her master.

"Ha!" grunted Trask. "That's a *hoss!*" A malignant grin spread over his face and he turned his head to look at Kane. "Kane, how much money, that money you got on you now, would you give to be on that black back, up on th' edge of th' valley? *All* of it, I bet!"

"Shut up!" snapped Roberts, angrily.

"Go to hell," sneered Trask, and he laughed nastily. "You wait till I speak my little piece before you tell me to shut up! No dog is goin' to ride me to a frazzle, blamin' me for this wind-up, without me havin' somethin' to say about it!" He looked at Red. "What was them two shots I heard, up there on top? They was th' first fired last night."

"That was me droppin' th' Greasers' cayuses from under 'em on th' ledge," Red answered. "They was pullin' stakes for th' desert."

"Leavin' us to do th' dancin', huh?" snapped Trask. "All right; I know another little piece to speak. Where you fellers takin' us?"

Red shrugged his shoulders and went off to get horses for the crowd.

A straggling line of mounted men climbed the cliff trail, the horses of the inner six fastened by lariats to each other, and three saddleless animals brought up the rear. They pushed up against the sky line in successive bumps and started westward across the desert.

XXIV

♦

Squared Up All Around

Mesquite, still humming from the tension of the past week felt its excitement grow as Bill Trask, bound securely and guarded by Hopalong, rode down the street and stopped in front of Quayle's, where the noise made by the gathering crowd brought Idaho to the door.

"Hey!" he shouted over his shoulder. "Look at this!" Then he ran out and helped Hopalong with the prisoner.

Quayle, Lukins, Waffles, McCullough, and Ed Doane fell back from the door and let the newcomers enter, Idaho slamming it shut in the face of the crowd. Then Ed Doane had his hands full as the crowd surged into the barroom.

"Upstairs!" said Hopalong, steering the prisoner ahead of him. In a few minutes they all were in Johnny's old room, where Trask, his ropes eased, began a talk which held the interest of his auditors. At its conclusion McCullough nodded and turned to Hopalong.

"All this may be true," he said; "but what does it all amount to without th' fellers he names? If you'd kept out of th' fight an' hadn't set fire to that buildin' we would 'a' got every one of them he names. Gimme Kane an' th' others an' better proof than his story an' you got a claim to that reward that's double sewed."

Hopalong seemed contrite and downcast. He looked around the group and let his eyes return to those of the trail-boss. "I reckon so," he growled. "But have you got th' numbers of th' missin' bills?" he asked, skeptically.

"Yes, I have; an' a lot of good it'll do me, *now!*" snapped McCullough. "We was countin' on them for th' real proof, but that fool play of yourn threw 'em into th' discard! What'n hell made you set that place afire?"

Hopalong shrugged his shoulders. "I dunno," he muttered. "Was you aimin' to find th' missin' bills on them fellers?" he asked. "Would that 'a' satisfied you?"

"Of course!" snorted the trail-boss. "An' with Trask, here, turnin' agin' 'em like he has it would be more than enough. Any fool knows that!"

Hopalong arose. "I'm glad to hear you come right out an' say that for that's what I wanted to know. I've been bothered a heap about what you might ask in th' line of proof. You shore relieve my mind, Mac. If you fellers will straddle leather we'll ride out where Kane an' th' others Trask named are waitin' for visitors. I don't reckon they none of them got away from Johnny an' Red."

"What are you talkin' about?" demanded McCullough, his mouth open from surprise.

"I mean we've got Kane, Roberts, Corwin, Miguel, an' another Greaser all tied up, waitin' to turn 'em over to you an' collect them rewards. As long as we know just what you want, an' can give it to you, I don't see no use of waitin'. I'm invitin' Lukins an' th' rest along to see th' finish. What you goin' to do with Trask?"

McCullough was looking at him through squinting eyes, his face a more ruddy color. Glancing around the group he let his eyes rest on Trask. Shrugging his shoulders he faced Hopalong. "Take him south, I reckon, with th' others. If he talks before a jury like he's talked up here I reckon he won't be sorry for it." He walked to a window and looked down into the street. "Hey!" he called. "Walt, get a couple of th' boys an' come up here right away. We got somebody for you to stay with," and in a few minutes he and the others left Walt and his companions to guard and protect the prisoner.

The sun was at the meridian when Hopalong led his companions into the Sand Creek camp and dismounted in front of Red, who was watching the prisoners.

"Where's th' Kid?" he asked curiously.

"Don't you do no worryin'," answered Red. He lowered his voice and put his mouth close to his friend's ear. "Th' Greaser on th' end is goin' to pieces. Pound him hard an' he'll show his cards."

The information was conveyed to McCullough, who stood looking at the downcast group. He strode over to Miguel, grabbed his shoulders and jerked him to his feet. Running his hands into the Mexican's pockets he brought out a roll of bills. Swiftly running through them he drew out a bill, compared it with a slip which he produced from his own pocket, whirled the bound man around and glared into the frightened eyes.

"Where'd you get this?" he shouted, shaking his captive.

"Kane geeve eet to me—he owe me money," answered the Mexican.

"What for?" demanded McCullough, shaking him again.

"I lend heem eet."

"You loaned *him* money?" roared the trail-boss. "That's likely! Why did he give it to you?"

Miguel shrugged his shoulders and did not answer.

McCullough jerked him half around and pointed to Hopalong. "This man here saw you sneakin' from Kane's south stable with a smokin' Sharps in yore hand after you shot Ridley. Trask says you did it. Is *this* all Kane gave you for that killin'?"

"I could no help," protested Miguel, squirming in the trail-boss' grip. "W'en Kane he say do theese or that theeng, I mus' do eet. I no want to but I mus'."

McCullough whirled around and faced Corwin. "That story you told me down in th' bunkhouse that night about how Bill Long shot Ridley is near word for word what Bill says about th' Greaser, an' Trask's story backs him up. How did you come to know so much about it? Come on, you coyote; spit it out! Who told you what to say?" Corwin's silence angered him and he showed his teeth. "There's a lynchin' waitin' for you in town, Corwin, if you don't stop it by speakin' up. Who told you that?"

Corwin looked away. "Miguel," he muttered. "I told you I was hopin' to get th' real one."

"He lie! I never say to heem one word!" shouted the Mexican. "He lie! Kane, he was the only one who know like that beside me!"

"Stand up, *Sheriff!*" snapped McCullough. He searched the sullen prisoner and found two rolls of bills. Going quickly over them he removed and grouped certain of them, and then compared them with his list. "There's five here that tally with th' bank's numbers," he said, looking up. "Where'd you get 'em?"

"Won 'em at faro-bank."

"Won five five-hundred-dollar bills at faro, when everybody knows yo're a two-bit gambler?" shouted the trailboss. "I'm no damned fool! Don't you forget what I said about th' lynchin', Corwin. I'm all that stands between you an' it. Where'd you get 'em? Like Trask said?"

Corwin's hunted look flashed despairingly around the group. "No," he said. "Kane gave 'em to me, to get changed into smaller bills!"

"Reckon Kane musta robbed that bank all by hisself," sneered McCullough. "I never knowed he had diamond drills an' could bust safes. Didn't you go along to protect an' keep an eye on that eastern safe-blower that Kane had come to do th' job? *Pronto!* Didn't you?"

"I had to," growled Corwin, in a voice so low that the answer was lost to all but the man to whom he was talking.

McCullough gave him a contemptuous shove and wheeled to question Roberts. "Get up," he ordered, and searched the rustler trail-boss. "By God!" he exclaimed when he saw the size of the roll. "You coyotes was makin' money fast! There's near three thousand here! Let's see how they compare with my list." In a few moments he nodded. "How'd you get these five-hundred-dollar bills? Kane give 'em to you, too?"

"No, Kane didn't give 'em to me!" snapped Roberts in angry contempt. "I earned 'em as my share of th' bank robbery, along with Corwin, th' white-livered snake! Kane didn't give 'em to either of us." He glared at the one-time sheriff. "I'm sayin' plain that if I ever get a chance I'm aimin' to shoot this skunk, along with Trask. You hear me?"

"If you ain't got a gun, hunt me up an' I'll lend you one," offered Idaho.

"Shut up!" snapped McCullough, glaring at the puncher. Whirling he pushed Roberts away. "It'll be a long time before you shoot anybody or anythin'. Now, then," he said, stepping up in front of Kane: "Get up!"

Kane arose slowly, his eyes burning with rage. He submitted to the exploring fingers of the trail-boss and maintained a contemptuous silence as his shirt was whipped up out of his trousers and the two money belts removed from around his waist.

McCullough opened the belts and his eyes at the same time. Neatly folded bunches of greenbacks followed each other in swift succession from the pockets of the belts and, scattering as they were tossed into a pile, made quite an imposing sight. Staring eyes regarded them and more than one observer's mouth gaped widely.

"Seven thousand," announced McCullough, reaching for another handful. "I'm sayin' you wasn't leavin' nothin' behind." He looked up again after a moment. "Eighteen thousand five hundred," he growled and picked up another handful. "Holy mavericks!" he breathed as the last bill was counted and placed on the new pile. "Forty-nine thousand eight hundred and seventy! You was takin' chances, totin' all that with this gang of thieves! Fifty thousand dollars, U.S.!"

Handing his written list to Quayle, he selected the five-hundred-dollar bills and called off the numbers laboriously, Quayle as laboriously hunting through the list. It took considerable time before they were checked off and put to one side, and then he looked up.

"There's still a-plenty of them bills missin'," he announced. "Where did *they* get to?"

Hopalong stepped forward and drew a roll from his pocket. "Here's what I found on Sandy Woods when he died in this camp," he said, offering it to the astonished trail-boss.

McCullough took it, opened and counted it, and called the numbers off to the excited holder of the list.

"They're all on th' list—th' Lord be praised!" said Quayle.

"Where'd Sandy Woods come in this?" demanded Mc-Cullough, looking around from face to face.

Roberts sneered. "Huh! He was th' man that took th' safe-blower out of th' country. He didn't have no hand in th' bank job. I'm glad th' skunk died, an' I'm glad it was me that planned his finish. He shore musta held up that feller. How much is there, in th' bank's bills?"

"Five thousand," answered the trail-boss.

"He got it all, cuss him!" snorted Roberts.

McCullough looked at Kane. "I never hoped to meet you like this," he said. "I ain't goin' to ask you no questions—you can talk in court, an' explain how you came to have so many of th' registered bills; an' there's other little things you can tell about, if somebody don't tell it all first." He turned to Hopalong. "We'll be takin' these fellers to th' ranch now."

"Better take th' reward money out of that bundle," replied Hopalong, nodding at the money in the hands of the trail-boss. "We've dealt 'em like you asked, an' gave you th' cards you want. Our part is finished."

McCullough looked from him to the prisoners and then at his friends. "How can I hand it to *you?*" he asked. "Where's Nelson? He's settin' in this."

"He'll show up after th' money's paid," said Red innocently as he arose.

McCullough hesitated and looked around again. As he did so Idaho carelessly walked over to Red, smoothing out a cigarette paper, and took hold of a paper tag hanging out of Red's pocket and pulled it. Carelessly rolling a cigarette he shoved the tobacco sack back where he had found it, but he did not leave Red's side. Blowing a lungful of smoke into the air he smiled at McCullough.

"Shucks, Mac," he said. "You shouldn't ought to have no trouble findin' them rewards in that unholy wad. An' mebby you could find Nelson's missin' eleven hundred on Trask, if you looked real hard. I like a man that goes through with his play."

"I'm not lookin' for no eleven hundred at all!" snapped McCullough. "An' I ain't shore that they've earned th' reward, burnin' that buildin' like they did! They let these fellers get away, first!"

"I just handed you th' money I found on Sandy Woods," said Hopalong. "That's like givin' it to you to pay us with. Hell! You act like you hated to make good Twitchell's bargain. Well, of course, you don't have to take this bunch, nor th' money, neither; but I'm sayin' they don't go separate. Suits us, Mac—we'll keep th' whole show—money an' all, if you say so."

"Fine chance you got!" retorted the trail-boss, bridling. "They're here—an' I'm takin' 'em, *with* th' money."

"There ain't nobody takin' nothin'," rejoined Hopalong calmly, "until th' bargain's finished. Don't rile Johnny, off there in th' brush; he's plumb touchy." His drawling voice changed swiftly. "Come on—a bargain's a bargain. Five thousand, *now!*"

"Mac!" said Quayle's accusing voice.

The trail-boss looked at the money in his hand and slowly counted out the reward amount, careful not to include any of the registered bills. "Here," he said, handing them to Hopalong. "You give us a hand gettin' 'em to th' ranch?"

"If three of us could catch 'em, an' bring 'em here," said Hopalong, coldly, "I reckon you got enough help to take 'em th' rest of th' way—if you steer clear of town."

"Don't worry, Mac," said Idaho, cheerfully. "*I'll* go along with you."

The trail-boss growled in his throat and began, with Lukins, Waffles, and Quayle, to get the prisoners on the horses. This soon was accomplished and he headed them south, Lukins on the other side, Quayle and Waffles and Idaho bringing up the rear.

"Better come to town for a celebration," called the proprietor, disappointment in his voice. "Ye can leave at dawn."

Johnny shook his head. "There's a celebration waitin' at th' ranch," he shouted, and turned to find his two companions mounted and his black horse waiting impatiently for him. Mounting, he wheeled to face northward, but checked the horse and turned to look back in answer to a faint hail from Idaho, and grinned at the insulting gesture of the distant puncher.

He replied in kind, chuckled, and dashed forward to overtake his moving friends.

"Home!" he exulted. "Home—an' *Peggy!*"

Tex

♦

I

♦

The Trail Calls

Memory's curtain rises and shows a scene softened by time and blurred by forgetfulness, yet the details slowly emerge like the stars at twilight. There appears a rain-washed, wind-swept range in Montana, a great pasture level in the center, but rising on its sides like a vast, shallow saucer, with here and there a crack of more somber hue where a ravine, or sluggish stream, leads toward the distant river. Green underfoot, deep blue overhead, with a lavender and purple rim under a horizon made ragged and sharp by the not too distant mountains and foothills. An occasional deep blue gash in the rim's darker tones marks where some pass or canyon cuts through the encircling barriers. A closer inspection would reveal a half-dozen earthy hollows, the rutting holes of the once numerous buffalo which paused here on their periodic migrations. In the foreground a white ranchhouse and its flanking red buildings, framed by the gray of corral walls, nestles on the southern slope of a rise and basks in the sunlight. From it three faint trails grow more and more divergent, leading off to Everywhere. Scattered over the vast, green pastures are the grazing units of a great herd, placid and content, moving slowly and jerkily, like spilled water down a gentle, dusty slope. But in the total movement there is one thread with definite directness, even though it constantly turns from side to side in avoiding the grazing cattle. This, as being different and indicating purpose, takes our instant attention.

A rider slowly makes his way among the cattle, by force of habit observing everything without being fully conscious of it. His chaps of soft leather, worn more because of earlier associations than from any urgent need on this northern range, have the look of long service and the comfort coming from such. His hat is a dark gray sombrero, worn in a manner suggesting a cavalier of old. Over an open vest are the careless folds of a blue kerchief, and at his right hip rubs a holster with its waiting, deadly tenant. A nearer approach reveals him to be a man in middle life, lean, scrupulously neat, clean shaven, with lines of deep humor graven about his eyes and mouth, softening a habitual expression which otherwise would have been forbiddingly hard and cynical.

His roving glances reach the purple horizon and are arrested by the cerulean blue of a pass, and he checks his horse with a gesture hopelessly inadequate to express the restlessness, the annoying uncertainty of his mood, a mood fed unceasingly by an inborn yearning to wander, regardless of any aim or other condition. Here is a prospect about him which he knows cannot be improved upon; here are duties light enough practically to make him master of his time, yet heavy enough to be purposeful; his days are spent in the soothing solitudes of clean, refreshing surroundings; his evenings with men who give him perfect fellowship, wordless respect, and repressed friendship, speaking when the mood urges, or silent in that rare, all-explaining silence of strong men in perfect accord. His wants are few and automatically supplied: yet for weeks the longing to leave it all daily had grown stronger—to leave it for what? Certainly for worse: yet leave it he must.

He sat and pondered, retrospective, critical. The activities of his earlier days passed before him, with no hypocritical hiding or blunting of motives. They revealed few redeeming features, for he carelessly had followed the easy trails through the deceptive lowlands of morality, and among men and women worse even than himself in overt acts and shameless planning, yet better because they did not have his intelligence or moral standards. But he slowly rose above them as a diver rises above treacherous, lower currents, and the reason was plain to those who knew him well. First he had a courage sparkling like a jewel, unhesitant, forthright, precipitate; next he had a rare mixture of humor and cynicism which better revealed to him things in their right proportions and values; and last, but hardly least by any means, an intelligence of high order, buttressed by facts, clarified by systematic study, and edged by training. In his youth he had aimed at the practice of medicine, but gave too much attention to more imaginative targets and found, when too late, that he had hit nothing. His fondness for drinking, gambling at cards, and other weedy sowings resulted from, rather than caused, the poor aim. Certain unforgivable episodes, unforgivable because of their notoriety more than because of the things themselves, brewed a paternal tempest, upon which he had turned a scornful back, followed Horace Greeley's famous advice, and sought the healing and the sanctuary of the unasking West.

In his new surroundings he soon made a name for himself, in both meanings, and quickly dominated those whose companionship he either craved or needed. An inherent propensity for sleight of hand provided him an easy living at cards; and his deftness and certainty with a six-gun gave him a pleasing security. However, all things have an end. There came a time when he nearly had reached the lowest depths of moral submersion when he met and fought a character as strong as his own, but in few other ways resembling him; and from that time on he swam on the surface. It would be foolish to say that the depths ceased to lure him, for they did, and at times so powerfully that he scarcely could resist them. For this he had to thank to no small degree one of the bitterest experiences of his life: his disastrous marriage. Giving blind love and unquestioning loyalty, he had lost both by the unclean evidence unexpectedly presented to his eyes. In that crisis, after the first madness, his actions had been worthy of a nature softer than his own and he had gone, by devious ways, back to his West and started anew with a burning cynicism. But for the steadying influence of his one-time enemy, and the danger and the interest in the task which Hopalong Cassidy had set before him, the domestic tragedy certainly would have sent him plunging down to his former level or below it.

Time passed and finally brought him news of the tragic death of his faithless wife, and he found that it did not touch him. He had felt neither pity, sorrow, nor relief. It is doubtful if he ever had given a thought to the question of his freedom, for with his mental attitude it meant nothing at all to him. He had put among his belongings the letter from his former employer, who had known all about the affair and the names and addresses of several of his western friends, telling him that he was free; and hardly gave it a second thought.

Turning from his careless scrutiny of the distant pass he rode on again and soon became aware of the sound of hoofbeats rapidly nearing him. As he looked up a rider topped a rise, descried him, and waved a sombrero. The newcomer dashed recklessly down the slope and drew rein sharply at his side, a cheerful grin wreathing his homely, honest face. Pete was slow-witted, but his sterling qualities masked this defect even in the eyes of a man as sharp as his companion, who felt for him a strong, warm friendship.

"Hello, Tex!" said the newcomer. "What's eatin' you? You shore look glum."

Tex thought if it was plain enough for Pete Wilson to notice it, it must be plain, indeed. "Mental worms an' moral cancer, Pete," replied the cynic, smiling in spite of himself at the cogitation started in his friend by the words.

"Whatever that means," replied Pete, cautiously. "However, if it's what I reckon it is, there's just two cures." Pete was dogmatic by nature. "An' that's likker, or a new range."

"Somethin's th' matter with you today, Pete," rejoined Tex. "Yo're as quick as a reflex." He studied a moment, and added: "An' yo're dead right, too."

"There ain't no reflection needed," retorted Pete; "an' there ain't nothin' th' matter with me a-tall. I'm tellin' you common sense; but it's shore a devil of a choice. If it's likker, then *you* lose; if it's driftin' off som'ers, then *we* lose. Tell you what: Go down to Twin River an' clean 'em out at stud, if you can find anybody that ain't played you before," he suggested hopefully. "Mebby there's a stranger in town. You'll shore feel a whole lot better, then." He grinned suddenly. "You might find a travelin' man: they're so cussed smart they don't think anybody can learn 'em anythin'. Go ahead—try it!"

Tex laughed. "Where you goin'?" he abruptly demanded. He could not afford to have any temptations thrown in his way just then.

"Over Cyclone way, for Buck. Comin' along?"

Tex slowly shook his head. "I'm goin' th' other way. Wonder why we haven't got word from Hoppy or Red or Johnny?" he asked, and the question acted like alum in muddy water, clearing away his doubts and waverings, which swiftly precipitated and left the clear fluid of decision.

"Huh!" snorted Pete in frank disgust. "You wait till any of them fellers write an' there'll be a white stone over yore head with nice letterin' on it to tell lies forever. You know 'em. Comin' along with me?" he asked, wheeling, and was answered by an almost imperceptible shake of his friend's head.

"I'll shake hands with you, Pete," said Tex, holding out his deft but sinewy hand. "In case I don't see you again," he explained in answer to his friend's look of surprise. "I'm mebby driftin' before you get back."

"Cuss it!" exploded Pete. "I'm allus talkin' too blamed much. Now I've gone an' done it!"

"You've only hastened it a little," assured Tex, gripping the outstretched hand spasmodically. "Cheer up; I don't aim to stay away forever!" He spurred his mount and shot away up the incline, Pete looking after him and slowly shaking his head.

When the restless puncher stopped again it was at the kitchen door of the white ranchhouse. As he swung from the saddle something stung him where his trousers were tight and he stopped his own jump to grab the horse, which had been stung in turn. A snicker and a quick rustle sounded under the summer kitchen and Tex took the coiled rope from his saddle, deftly unfastening the restraining knot. The rustling sounded again, frantic and sustained, followed by a half-defiant, half-supplicating jeer.

"You can't do it, under here!" said Pickles, reloading the bean-shooter from a bulging cheek. "I can shoot yore liver out before you can whirl it!" Pickles was quite a big boy now, but threatened never to grow dignified; and besides, he had been badly spoiled by everybody on the ranch.

"Whirling livers never appealed to me," rejoined Tex, putting the rope back. "Never," he affirmed decidedly; "but I'm goin' to whirl yourn some of these days, an' you with it!"

"Those he loves, he annoys," said a low, sweet voice, its

timbre stimulating the puncher like a draught of wine. His sombrero sweeping off as he turned, he bowed to the French Rose, wife of the big-hearted half-owner of the ranch. If only he had chosen a woman like this one!

"I seem to remember him annoyin' Dave Owens, at near half a mile, with Hoppy's Sharps," he slowly replied. "Nobody ever told me that he loved Dave a whole lot." At the momentary cloud the name brought to her face he shook his head and growled to himself. "I'm a fool, ma'am, these days," he apologized; "but it strikes me that you ought to smile at that name—it shore played its unwilling part in giving you a good husband; an' Buck a mighty fine wife. Where *is* Buck?"

"Inside the house, walking rings around the table—he seems so, so—" she shrugged her shoulders hopelessly and stepped aside to let Tex enter.

"I don't know what he seems," muttered Tex as he passed in; "but I know what he is—an' that's just a plain, ornery fool." He shook his head at such behavior by any man who was loved by the French Rose.

Buck stopped his pacing and regarded him curiously, motioning toward an easy chair.

"Standin's good enough for me, for I'm itchin' with th' same disease that you imagine is stalkin' you," said Tex, looking at his old friend with level, disapproving gaze. "It don't matter with me, but it's plain criminal with you. I'm free to go; yo're not. An' I'm tellin' you frank that if I had th' picket stake that's holdin' you, all hell couldn't tempt me. Yo're a plain, damned fool—an' you know it!"

Buck leaned back against the edge of the table and thoughtfully regarded his companion. "It ain't so much that, as it is Hoppy, an' Red, an' Johnny," he replied, spreading out his hands in an eloquent gesture. "They could write, anyhow, couldn't they?" he demanded.

"Shore," affirmed Tex, grinning. "How long ago was it that you answered their last letters?" He leaned back and laughed outright at the guilty expression on his friend's face. "I thought so! Strong on words, but cussed poor on example."

"I reckon yo're right," muttered Buck. "But that south range shore calls me strong, Tex."

"'Whither thou goest, I go' was said by a woman," retorted Tex. "'Yore people are my people; yore God, my God.' I'm sayin' it works both ways. You ought to go down on yore knees for what's come to you. An' you will, one of these days. Think of Hoppy's loss—an' you'll do it before mornin'. But I didn't come in to preach common sense to a lunatic—I come to get my time, an' to say good-bye."

Buck nodded. Vaguely disturbed by some unnamed, intermittent fever, he had been quick to read the symptoms of restlessness in another, especially in one who had been as close to him as Tex had been. He went over to an old desk, slowly opened a drawer and took out a roll of bills and a memorandum.

"Here," he said, holding both out. "Far as I know it's th' same as when you gave it to me. Ought to be seven hundred, even. Count it, to make shore." While Tex took it and shoved it into his pocket uncounted and crumpled the memorandum, Buck also was reaching into a pocket, and counted off several bills from the roll it gave up. These he gravely handed to his companion, smiling to hide the ache of losing another friend.

"I shore haven't earned it all," mused Tex, looking down at the wages in his hand. "I reckon I'm doin' this ranch a favor by leavin', for there ain't no real job up here no more for any man as expensive as I am. You got th' whole country eatin' out of yore hand, an' th' first thing you know th' cows will catch th' habit an' brand an' count 'emselves to save you th' trouble of doin' it."

"You'll be doin' us a bigger favor when you come back, one of these days," grinned Buck. "You shore did yore share in trainin' it to eat out of my hand. For a while it looked like it would eat th' hand—an' it would 'a', too. Aimin' to ride down?"

Tex's eyes twinkled. "How'd you come to figger I'm goin' down?"

Buck smiled.

"No, reckon not," said Tex. "Ridin' as far's th' railroad. I'll leave my cayuse with Smith. When one of th' boys goes down that way he can get it. I'll pay Smith for a month's care." Reading the unspoken question in his friend's eyes, he carelessly answered it. "Don't know where I'm goin'. Reckon I'll get down to th' SV before I stop. That'd be natural, with Red an' Hoppy stayin' with Johnny."

"They might need you, too," suggested Buck, hopefully. If he couldn't be with his distant friends himself, he at least wished as many of them to be together as was possible.

"I'm copperin' that," grunted Tex. His eyes shone momentarily. "Yo're forgettin' that our best three are together. Lord help any misguided fools that prod 'em sharp. Well, I'm dead shore to drift back ag'in some day; but as you say, those south ranges shore do pull a feller's heart." He looked shrewdly at his friend and his face beamed from a sudden thought. "We're a pair of fools," he laughed. "You ain't got th' wander itch! You don't want to go jack-rabbitin' all over th' country, like me! All you want is that southwest country, with yore wife an yore friends on th' same ranch; down in th' cactus country, where th' winters ain't what they are up here. I'm afraid my brain's atrophied, not havin' been used since Dave Owens rolled down from his ambush with Hoppy's slugs in him for ballast."

Buck looked at him with eager, hopeful intentness and his sigh was one of great relief and thankfulness. He need not be ashamed of that longing, now vague and nameless no longer. His head snapped back and he stood erect, and his voice thrilled with pride. Tex had put his finger on the trouble, as Tex always did. "I've been as blind as a rattler in August!" he exclaimed.

"Not takin' th' time to qualify that blind-rattler-in-August phrase, I admits yo're right," beamed Tex. He arose, shoved out his hand for the quick, tight grasp of his friend and wheeled to leave, stopping short as he found himself face to face with Rose Peters. "A happy omen!" he cried. "Th' first thing I see at th' beginnin' of my journey is a rose."

She smiled at both of them as she blocked the door, and the quick catch in her voice did not escape Tex Ewalt.

"I was but in the other room," she said, her face alight. "I could not but hear, for you both speak loud. I am so glad, M'sieu Tex—that now I know why my man is so—so restless. Ruth, she said what I think, always. We are sorry that you mus' go—but we know you will not forget your friends, and will come back again some day."

Buck put his arm around his wife's shoulders and smiled. "An' if he brings th' other boys back with him, we'll find room for 'em all, eh Rose?" He looked at his friend. "We're shore goin' to miss you, Tex. Good luck. We'll expect you when we see you."

Tex bowed to Rose and backed into the curious Pickles, whom he lightly spanked as a fitting farewell; and soon the noise of his departure drummed softer and softer into the south.

II

◆

Refreshed Memories

The dusty, grimy, almost paintless accommodation train, composed of engine, combination smoking-baggage car, and one day coach, rumbled and rattled, jerked and swayed over the uneven roadbed, the clicking at the rail joints sensible both to tactual and auditory nerves, and calling attention to the disrepair into which the whole line had fallen. In the smoking compartment of the baggage car sat Tex Ewalt, sincerely wishing that he had followed his first promptings and chosen the saddle in preference to this swifter method of traveling.

All day he had suffered heat, dust, cinders, and smoke after a night of the same. It had been bad enough on the main line, but after leaving the junction conditions had grown steadily worse. All day he had crossed a yellow gray desolation, flat and unending, under a dirty blue sky and a dust-filled air shimmering with heat waves. He had peered at a drab, distant horizon which seemed hardly to change as it crept eastward past him, at all times barely more than a thin circle about as interesting and colorful as a bleached hoop from some old, weather-beaten barrel. Wherever he had looked, it had been to see sun-burned grass and clouds of imponderable dust, the latter sucked up by the train and sent whirling into every crack and crevice; occasional white spots darting rearward he knew to be the grim, limy skulls of herbiverous animals; arrow-like trails cut deep into the drought-cursed earth, and not too frequently a double line of straggling, dispirited willows, cottonwoods, and box elders, marked the course of some prairie creek, whose characteristic, steep earth banks, often undermined, now enclosed sun-dried mud, curling like heated scales, with here and there pools of noisome water hidden under scabs of scum. Mile after mile of this had dulled him, familiar as he had once been with the sight, and he sat apathetic, dispirited and glum, too miserable to accept the pressing invitation of a traveling cardsharp to sit into a game of draw poker. Gradually the mild, long swells of the prairie had grown shorter, sharper, and higher; gradually the soil had become rockier and the creek beds deeper below the rims of their banks. The track wound more and more as it twisted and turned among the hills, and for some hours he had noticed a constant rising, which now became more and more apparent as the top of the watershed drew nearer.

He dozed fitfully at times and once the sharper had roused him by touching his shoulder to ask him again to take cards in a game. To this invitation Tex had opened his eyes, looked up at the smiling poker devotee and made a slight motion, dozing off again as the surprised gambler moved away from one he now knew to be of the same calling as himself. Towns had followed each other at increasingly long intervals, insensibly changing in their aspect, and the horizon steadily had been narrowing. Here and there along the dried beds of the creeks were rude cabins and shacks, each not far from an abandoned sluice and cradle. Between the hills the pastures grew smaller and smaller, their sides more precipitous, but as they shrunk, the number of cattle on them seemed to increase. Rough buildings of wood or stone began to replace the low sod dugouts of a few hours ago, and he knew that he was rapidly nearing his destination.

Suddenly a ribbon-like scar on the horizon caught his eye. It ran obliquely from a northeastern point of his vista southwesterly across the pastures, hills, and valleys, like a lone spoke in some great wheel, of which the horizon was both felloe and tire. At this he sat up with a show of interest. Judging from its direction, and from what he remembered of it at this section of its length, it would cross the track some miles farther on. He nodded swiftly at this old-time friend of his cattle-driving days—he had been a fool not to have remembered it and the cow-town not far ahead, but the names of all the mushroom towns he had been in during his career in the West had not remained in his memory. Years rolled backward in a flash. He could see the distant, plodding caravans of homesteaders, or the long, disciplined trains of the freighters, winding over the hills and across the flats, their white canvas wagon covers flashing against the sky, the old, dirty covers emphasizing the newness and whiteness of their numerous patches. But on this nearing trail, winding into the southwest there had been a different migration. He almost could see the spread-out herd moving deliberately forward, the idling riders, the point and swing men, and the plodding, bumping chuck wagon with its bumptious cook. This trail, a few hundred yards wide, beaten by countless hoofs, had deepened and deepened as the wind carried away the dust, and if left to itself would be discernible after the passing of many years.

The name of the town ahead and on this old trail brought a smile to his lips, a smile that was pleasantly reminiscent; but with the name of the town came nearly forgotten names of men, and the smile changed into one that was not pleasant to look upon. There was Williams, Gus Williams, often referred to as "Muttonhead." He had been a bully, a sure-thing gambler, herd trimmer, and cattle thief in a small way, but he had been only a petty pilferer of hoofed property, for his streak of caution was well developed. Tex had not seen him, or heard of him, for twenty years, never since he had shot a gun out of Williams' hand and beat him up in a corner of his own saloon.

The rapidly enlarging ribbon drew nearer and more distinct, and soon it crossed the track and ran into the south. He remembered the wide, curving bend it took here: there had been a stampede one rainy night when he was off trick and rolled up in his blanket under the chuck wagon. They had reason to suspect that the cattle were sent off in their mad flight through the dark by human agency. Two days had been spent in combing the rough plain and in rounding up the scattered herd, and there had been a sizable number lost.

A deeper tone leaped into the dull roar of the train and told of a gully passing under the track. It ran off at a slight angle, the dried bed showing more numerous signs of human labors and habitations, and when the train came to a bumping, screeching stop at a ramshackle one-room station he knew that he was at the end of his ride and within three stations from the end of the line, which here turned sharply toward the northwest, baffled by the treacherous sands of the river, whose bank it paralleled for sixty miles. Had he gone on in the train he would have come no closer to his objective and would have to face a harder country for man and horse. Gunsight, where his three friends were located, lay about a hundred miles southwest of the bend in the track; but because of the sharp bend it lay farther from the station beyond. From where he now was, the riding would not be unpleasant and the ford across the river was shallower, the greater width of the stream offset by a more sluggish current. This ford was treacherous in high water and not passable after sudden rises for a day or two, because the force of the swollen current stirred up the unstable sands of the bottom. As a veteran of the old cattle trails he knew what a disturbed river bottom often meant.

The wheezing exhaust and the complaining panting of the

all but discarded engine added dismal sounds to a dismal view. He stiffly descended the steps, a bulging gunny sack over his shoulder and a rolled blanket and a sheathed rifle fully utilized his other arm and hand. Dropping his burdens to the ground he paused to look around him.

It was just a frontier town, ugly, patched, sprawling, barely existent, and an eyesore even to the uncritical; and cursed further by Kansas politics which at this time were not as stalwart as they once had been, reminding one of the mediocre sons of famous fathers. In place of the old daring there now were trickery and subtle meannesses; in place of hot hatreds were now smoldering grudges; where once old-time politicians "shot it out" in the middle of the street, there now were furtive crawlings and treacherous shots from the dark. Like all towns it had a name—it will suffice if we know it as Windsor. Being neither in the mining country nor on the cattle range, and being in an out-of-the-way position even on the merging strip between the two, it undoubtedly would have died a natural death except for the fortuitous chance which had led the branch-line railroad to reach its site. The shifting cattle drives and a short-lived townsite speculation had been the causes for the rails coming; then the drives stopped at nearer terminals and the speculation blew up—but the rails remained. This once flamboyantly heralded "artery of commerce" swiftly had atrophied and now was hardly more than a capillary, and its diurnal pulsation was just sufficient to keep the town about one degree above coma.

Tex sneered openly, luxuriously, aggressively, and for all the world to see. He promised himself that he would not remain here very long. Before him lay the squalid dirt street with its cans and rubbish, the bloated body of a dog near the platform, a dead cat farther along. There were several two-story frame buildings, evidently built while the townsite game was on. The rest were one-story shacks, and he remembered most of them.

He picked up his belongings and sauntered into the station to wait until the agent had finished his business with the train crew, and that did not take long.

The agent stepped into the dusty, dirty room, coughed, nodded, and passed into his partitioned office. In a moment he was out again, looked closely at the puncher and decided to risk a smile and a word: "Is there anything I can do for you?" he hazarded.

Tex put his sombrero beside him on the bench and wiped his forehead with a sleeve. He saw that his companion was slight, not too healthy, and appeared to be friendly and intelligent; but in his eyes lay the shadow of fear.

"Mebby you can tell me th' best place to eat an' sleep; an' th' best place to buy a horse," he replied.

"Williams' hotel is the best in town, and I'd ask him about the horse. You might do better if you didn't say I recommended him to you."

"Not if you don't want me to," responded Tex, smiling sardonically for some inexplicable reason. "Reckon he'd eat you because yo're sendin' him trade? Don't worry; I won't say you told me."

"So far as I am concerned it don't matter. It's you I'm thinking about."

Tex stretched, crossed his legs, and smiled. "In that case I'll use my own judgment," he replied. "Been workin' for th' railroad very long?"

"Little too long, I'm afraid," answered the agent, coughing again, "but I've been out here only two months." He hesitated, looked a little self-conscious, and continued. "It's my lungs, you know. I got a transfer for my health. If I can stick it out here I have hopes of slowly improving, and perhaps of getting entirely well."

"If you can stick it out? Meanin' yo're findin' it too monotonous an' lonely?" queried Tex.

The agent laughed shortly, the look of fear again coming into his eyes. "Anything but the first; and so far as being lonely is concerned, I find that my sister is company enough."

Tex cogitated and recrossed his legs. "From what I have already seen of this town I'd gamble she is; but a man's allus a little better off if he can herd with his own sex once in a while. So it ain't monotonous? Have many trains a day?" he asked, knowing from his perusal of the time-table that there were but two.

"One in and one out. You passed the other on the siding at Willow, if you've come from beyond there."

"Reckon I remember it. Much business here to keep you busy?"

"Not enough to tire even a—lunger!" He said the word bitterly and defiantly.

"That's a word I never liked," said Tex. "It's too cussed brutal. Some people derive a great deal of satisfaction in calling a spade a spade, and that is quite proper so far as spades are concerned; but why go further? A man can't allus help a thing like tuberculosis—especially if he's makin' a livin' for two. Yo're not very high up here, but I reckon th' air's right. It's th' winter that's goin' to count ag'in' you. You got to watch that. You might do better across th' west boundary. Any doctor in town?"

"There's a man who calls himself a doctor. His favorite prescription is whiskey."

"Yeah? For his patients?"

"For his patients and himself, too."

"Huh," grunted the puncher. He cleared his throat. "I once read about yore trouble—in a dictionary," he explained, grinning. "It said milk an' aigs, among other things; open air, both capitalized, day *an'* night; plenty of sleep, no worryin', an' no excitement. Have many heavy boxes to rustle?"

"No," answered the agent, looking curiously at his companion. "I had plenty of milk and eggs, but the milk is getting scarce and the eggs are falling off. I—" he stopped abruptly, shrugging his shoulders. "Damn it, man! It isn't so much for myself!"

"No," said Tex, slowly arising. "A man usually feels that way about it. I'm goin' up to th' hotel. May drop around to see you tomorrow if I'm in town."

"I'll be mighty glad to see you; but there's no use for you to make enemies," replied the agent, leading the way outside. He stopped and took hold of a trunk, to roll it into the building.

"Han's off," said Tex smiling and pushing him aside. "You forgot what th' dictionary said. Of course this wouldn't kill you, but I'm stiff from ridin' in yore palatial trains, mile after weary mile." Rolling the trunk through the door and against the wall, he picked up his belongings, gravely saluted and went on his way whistling cheerily.

The agent looked after him wistfully, shook his head and retired into his coop.

Tex rambled down the street and entered Williams' hotel, held a brief conversation with the clerk, took up his key, and followed instructions. The second door on the right-hand side, upstairs, let him into a small room which contained a chair, bed, and washstand. There was a rag rug before the bed, and this touch of high life and affluence received from him a grave and dignified bow. "Charmed, I'm sure," he said, and went over to the window to view the roofs of the shacks below it. He sniffed and decided that somewhere near there was a stable. Putting his belongings in a corner, he took out his shaving kit and went to work with it, after which he walked downstairs, bought a drink and treated its dispenser to a cigar, which he knew later would be replaced and the money taken instead.

"Hot," said Tex as though he had made a discovery. "An' close," he added in an effort not to overlook anything.

"Very," replied the bartender. This made the twenty-third time he had said that word in reply to this undoubted statement of fact since morning. He did not know that his companion had used it because it was colorless and would stamp him, sub-consciously, as being no different from the common human herd in town. "Hottest summer since last year," said the bartender, also for the twenty-third time. He grinned expectantly.

Tex turned the remark over in his mind and laughed suddenly, explosively. "That's a good un! Cussed if it didn't nearly get past me! 'Hottest summer since last year!' Ha-ha-ha! Cuss it, it *is* good!" He was on the proper track to make a friend of the second man he had met. "Have another cigar," he urged. Good-will and admiration shone on his face. "Gosh! Have to spring that un on th' boys! Ha-ha-ha!"

"Better spring it before fall—it might not last through th' winter, though some'r tougher'n others," rejoined the bartender, his grin threatening to inconvenience his ears.

Tex choked and coughed up some of the liquor, the tears starting from his eyes. He had meant it for an imitation choke, but misjudged. Coughing and laughing at once he hung onto the bar by his elbows and writhed from side to side. "Gosh! You oughter—warn a fel—ler!" he reproved. "How'd'y think of 'em like that?"

"Come easy, somehow," chuckled the pleased dispenser of liquor. "Stayin' in town long?" he asked.

"Cussed if I know," frankly answered Tex. He became candid and confidential. "Expectin' a letter, an' I can't leave till it comes. Where's th' post office? Yeah? Guess I can find it, then. Reckon I'll drift along an' see if there's anythin' come in for me. See you tonight."

Crossing the street he sauntered along it until he came to the building which sheltered the post office, and he stopped, regarded the sign over its door with open approval, and then gravely salaamed.

"'Williams's Mecca,'" he read. "Sign painters are usually generous with their esses. Wonder why? Must be a secret sign of th' guild. Why are monument works usually called 'monumental'? Huh: Wonder if it is th' same Williams? If it is, where did *he* ever hear of 'Mecca'?" It was a refreshing change from the names so common to stores in towns of this kind and size. "An' cussed if it ain't appropriate, too!" he muttered. "In a place like this what could more deserve that name than the general store and post office, unless it be the saloons, hotels, and gambling houses?" He started for the door, eager to see whom he would meet.

A burly, dark-visaged individual looked up at his entry. He would have been amazed had he known that a score of years had slipped from him and that he was a callow, furtive-eyed man in his early twenties, cringing in a corner with his present visitor standing contemptuously over him and daring him to get up again.

Tex's face remained unchanged, except for a foolish smile which crept over it as he gave greeting. "Though I ain't goin' to pray, I shore am turnin' my face to th' birthplace of th' Prophet," he said. "Yeah, I'm even enterin' its sacred portals." He watched closely for any signs for recognition in the other, but failed to detect any; and he was not surprised.

The heavy face stared at him and a tentative smile tried to change it. The attempt was abortive and the expression shifted to one of alert suspicion, shaded by one of pugnacity. He was not accustomed to levity at his expense. "What you talkin' about?" he slowly asked.

"Why, th' faith of all true believers: *There is but one God, and Mohammed is his Prophet.* May th' blessin's of Allah be on thee. Incidentally I'm askin' if there's a letter for th' pilgrim, Tex Jones?" He cast a careless glance at a cold-eyed individual who lounged in the shadow of a corner, and instantly classified him. Besides the low-slung holster, the man had the face of a cool, paid killer. Tex's interest in him was not to be correctly judged by the careless glance he gave him.

"Then why in hell didn't you say so in th' first place, 'stead of wastin' my valuable time?" growled the proprietor, reluctantly shuffling toward the mail rack in a corner. He wet his thumb generously, not caring about the color given to it by the tobacco in his mouth, and clumsily ran through the modest packet of mail. Shaking his head he turned. "There ain't nothin'," he grunted.

"It is Allah's will," muttered Tex in pious resignation. He would have fallen over had there been anything for him.

"Look here, stranger," ominously remarked the proprietor, "if yo're aimin' to be smart at *my* expense, look out it don't become yourn. Just what's th' meanin' of all these fool remarks?"

"Why, yore emporium is named 'Mecca,' ain't it?" asked Tex innocently, but realizing that he somehow had got on the wrong trail.

"What's that got to do with it?" demanded Williams, who could talk as mean as he cared to while the quiet, cold man sat in the corner.

"Everythin'. Ain't you th' proprietor, like th' barkeep of th' hotel said? Ain't you Mr. Williams?"

"I am."

Tex scratched his head, frankly puzzled. "Well," he said. "Mohammed came out of Mecca to startle th' world, an'—"

"He didn't do nothin' of th' kind!" interrupted the proprietor. "Mecca was out of Prophet, by Mohammed; an' a cussed good hoss she was, too. Though she didn't startle no world, she was my filly, an' plenty good enough for this part of th' country. Of course, mebby back from where you came from, mebby she wouldn't have amounted to much," he sneered. "Now, if you got any more smart-Aleck remarks to make, you'll be wise if you save 'em till you get outside."

Tex burst out laughing. "It's all my mistake, Mr. Williams. I thought you named yore store after a poem I read once, that's all. No offense on my part, sir. Are you th' Mr. Williams that keeps th' ho-tel?"

"I am: what about it?"

"I'm puttin' up there," answered Tex. "If a letter comes for me, would you mind puttin' it in yore pocket an' bringin' it over when you go there? It'll save me from botherin' you every day. Yore friend at th' station said I'd find you right obligin'. An' he knows a good ho-tel when he sees it. He sent me there."

"That scut!" bellowed Williams, his face growing red. "You'll come after yore own mail, my man; an' you'll do it polite. There ain't no mail here for you. Good day!"

"I'm patient an' I can wait. I didn't hardly expect to get any letter so quick, anyhow. After th' recent experience of reasonin' right from th' wrong premises, however, I'll not be a heap surprised if I get a letter on tomorrow's train. Thank you kindly, sir. I bid you good day."

"An' mind you don't call that cussed agent no friend of mine, th' job stealer!"

"Whatever you say; but, don't forget to bring over that letter when it comes," sweetly replied Tex, and he carefully slammed the door as he went out. Going down the street he grinned expansively and snapped his fingers because of a strange elation.

"Th' old thief!" he muttered. "Heavier, more ill tempered, and downright autocratic—an' how he has prospered! Regular, solid citizen, the bulwark of the commonwealth. An' cussed if he ain't got himself a bodyguard; a regular, no-mistake gunman with as mean an eye as any I ever saw. Of course, his brains have improved with the years, for they couldn't go the other way and keep him out of an asylum. 'Muttonhead' Williams! All right: once a sheep, always a sheep. I'm going to enjoy my stay in Windsor. Good Lord!" he exclaimed as a sudden fancy hit him. "Wouldn't it be funny if the old fool has been working hard and saving hard all these years for his old enemy, Tex Ewalt? He always was crazy to play poker, and I got a notion to make it come true. Gosh, if a man ever was tempted, I'm tempted now! Muttonhead Williams, allus stuck on his poker playing. Get behind me, Satan!"

III

◆

Tempted Anew

A hand bell, ringing thin and clamorous somewhere below caused Tex to gather up the cards with which for two hours he had been assiduously practicing shuffling, cutting, and dealing. Putting them away he washed his face and hands in the tin basin, combed his hair without slicking it with water, and went down to supper.

He paused momentarily in the doorway to size up the dining-room. The long table was crowded by all sorts and conditions of men. Miners down on their luck and near the end of their resources because of the long drought which had dried up the streams and put an end to placer mining operations, rubbed elbows with more fortunate men of their own calling, who had longer purses. Two cowpunchers from a distant ranch sat next to two cavalrymen on a prized leave from the iron discipline of a remote frontier post, both types dangerous because free from the restraint which had held them down for so long a time. A local tin-horn gambler and the traveling card-sharp were elbow to elbow, and several other men, evidently belonging to the town, nearly filled both sides of the table.

At the head sat Gus Williams, most influential citizen and boss of the town, and he made no attempt to hide his importance. Next to him on the left was a lean, hard-looking, shifty-eyed man who seemed to shine in reflected light, and who showed a deference to the big man which he evidently expected to receive, in turn, from the others. If it was true that there was only one boss, it was also true that he had only one nephew. To the right of the boss was the cold-eyed person whose seat in the general store was well back in the corner. No one moved or spoke except under his critical observance. His cocksure confidence irritated Tex, who was strongly tempted to try the effect of a hot potato against a cold eye. He thought of his friend Johnny Nelson and grinned at how that young man's temper would steam up under such an insolent stare. Moving forward under the gunman's close scrutiny Tex dropped into the only vacant chair, one near the nephew, and fell to eating, his vocal chords idle, but his optic and auditory apparatus making up for it. The conversation, jerky and broken at first, grew more coherent and increased as the appetites of the hungry men yielded to the bolted food. The protracted drought was referred to in grunts, growls, monosyllables, sentences, and profane speeches. It was discussed, rediscussed, and popped up at odd moments for new discussion.

"Never saw it so bad since th' railroad came," said a miner.

"Never saw it so bad since th' first trail herd ended here," affirmed the nephew.

"*I* never saw it so dry, for so long a spell, since th' first trail herd *passed* here," said the uncle, his remark the strongest by coming last; but he was not to enjoy that advantage for long.

"Hum!" said a cattleman, apologetically clearing his throat. "I never saw it as dry as it is now since I located out here."

The miner frowned, the nephew scowled, and the uncle snorted. The last named looked around belligerently and smote the table with his fist. "I remember, howsomever, that I did see it near as dry, that year I strayed from th' Santa Fe Trail, huntin' buffalers for th' caravan. We passed right through this section an' circled back. I come to remember it because when we crossed th' Walnut I jumped right over it, dry-shod. Them was th' days when men was men, or soon wasn't nothin' a-tall."

"I reckon they wasn't th' kind that would play off sick so they could get another man's job away from him, anyhow," growled the nephew, introducing his pet grievance. "I run that station a cussed sight better than it's bein' run now; an' anybody's likely to make mistakes once in a while."

"A few dollars, one way or another, ain't bustin' no railroad," asserted the uncle. "It was only th' excuse they was a-waitin' for."

"Nobody can tell me no good about no railroad," said the freighter, his fond memory resurrecting a certain lucrative wagon haul which had vanished with the advent of the first train over the line.

"Hosses are good enough for me," said Tex, looking around. "Which remark reminds me that a rider afoot is a helpless hombre. Bein' a rider, without no cayuse, I'm a little anxious to get me a good one. Anybody know where I can do it reasonable?"

All eyes turned to the head of the table, where Williams was washing down his last mouthful of food with a gulp of hot, watery coffee. He cleared his throat and peered closely, but pleasantly, at the stranger. "Why, it's Mr. Jones," he said. "I reckon I have such a hoss, Mr. Jones. Mebby it ain't any too well broken, but that hadn't oughter bother a *rider.*"

Tex grinned. "If that's all that's th' matter with it I reckon it'll suit me; but I can tell better after I ride it, an' learn th' price."

"Want it tonight?" frowned Williams.

"No; I ain't in no hurry. Tomorrow'll be plenty of time, when you ain't got nothin' else to do but show it. Speakin' of railroads like we was, I reckon they ain't done nothin' very much for this town. While I'm new to these parts, I'm betting Windsor was a whole lot better when th' drive trail was alive an' kickin'."

Williams nodded emphatically. "I've seen these plains an' valleys thick with cattle," he said, regretfully. "There was a time when I could see th' dust clouds rollin' up from th' south an' away in th' north, both at once, day after day. This town was a-hummin' every day an' night. Money come easy an' went th' same way. Men dropped in here, lookin' like tramps, almost, who could write good checks for thousands of dollars. Th' buyers bought whole herds on th' seller's say-so, without even seein' a hoof, an' sold 'em ag'in th' same way. Money flowed like water, an' fair-sized fortunes was won an' lost at a single sittin'. I've seen th' faro-bank busted three days hand-runnin'—but, of course, that was very unusual. Mostly it was th' other way 'round. All one summer an' fall it was like that. Then th' winter come, an' that was th' end of it so fur's Windsor was concerned. Th' Kiowa Arroyo branch line was pushed further an' further southwest until th' weather stopped it; but it went on ag'in as soon as spring let it. By th' time th' first herds crossed th' state line, headin' for here, that line of rails was ready for 'em, an' not another big herd went past this town. Of course, there was big herds drivin' north, just th' same, bound for th' Yellowstone region on government contract, an' some was bein' sent out to stock ranges in th' West, but they followed a new trail found by Chisholm, or old McCullough. I've heard lately that Mac is workin' for Twitchell an' Carpenter. But if you'd seen this town then you shore wouldn't know it now. Damn th' railroads, says I!"

Tex frowned honestly at the thought of the passing of this once great cattle trail, for the memories of those old trails lay snug and warm in the hearts of the men who have followed them in saddle. He looked up at Williams, a congratulatory look on his face. "Well, that shore was hard; but not as hard, I reckon, as if you had been a cattleman, an' follered it. It sort of hurts an old-time cowman to think of them trails."

"That's where yo're wrong," spoke up the nephew. "He *is* a cattleman. Th' GW brand is known all over th' state, an' beyond. It was knowed by every puncher that followed that old trail."

"There wasn't no such brand in them days," corrected Williams. He did not think it necessary to say that the GW mark was just starting then, far back in the hills and well removed from the trail; that it grew much faster by the addition of fully grown cattle than it did by natural increase; or that a view of the original brands on the fullgrown cattle would have been a matter of great and burning interest to almost every drive boss who followed a herd along the trail. Later on, when he threw his herd up for a count, the drive boss was likely to have re-added his tally sheet and asked heaven and earth what had happened to him. "Well, them days has gone; but when they went this town come blamed near goin' with 'em. It shore ain't what it once was."

Tex thought that it was just as well, since the town was mean enough and vicious enough as it was; he remembered vividly its high-water period; but he nodded his head.

"It ain't hardly fair to judge it after such a long dry spell," he said. "Th' whole country, south an' west of th' Missouri is fair burnin' up. Th' Big Muddy herself was a-showin' all her bars."

"That's th' curse of this part of Kansas," said the nephew. "That an' job jumpers."

"Yes?" asked Tex. "How's that?"

"Station agent a friend of yourn?"

It became evident to Tex that the uncle and the nephew had been discussing him. Gus Williams was the only man to whom he had mentioned the agent. He shook his head. "Never saw him before I stepped off th' train today," he answered, looking vexed about something. "We up an' had some words, an' I told him I reckoned he might find healthier towns further west, across th' line. I'm a mild man, gents: but I allus speak my mind."

"An' you gave him some cussed good advice," replied the nephew warmly. "This ain't no place for any man as plays off sick an' does low-down tricks to turn another man out of a job. If it wasn't for his sister I'd 'a' buffaloed him *pronto*. Which reminds me, stranger," he warned with an ugly leer. "She's a rip-snortin' fe-male—but I shore saw her first. I'm just tellin' you so you won't get any notions that way. I'm fencin' that range."

"Don't you worry, Hen," consoled a friend. "Yo're able to run herd on her, balky as she is, an' when th' time's ripe you'll put yore brand on her. So fur's th' job's concerned, yore uncle'll get it back for you when he gets ready to move. We ought to ride that Saunders feller out of town, *I* say!"

"There's plenty of time for that," said Williams, as he turned to address another diner. "John, show Mr. Jones that gray when he gits around tomorrow. Aimin' to stay in town long, Mr. Jones?"

Tex shrugged his shoulders. "Got to wait for a letter— don't know what to do; but I shore could be in worse places than this here hotel, so I ain't worryin' a lot. Bein' a stranger, though, I reckon time'll drag a little evenin's."

Various kinds of smiles replied to this, and Williams laughed outright. "I reckon you understand th' inner-cent game of draw?" he chuckled.

Tex froze: "Sometimes I think I do," he said, and laughed to hide his struggle against the pressure of the old temptation. He fairly burned to turn his poker craft against this blowhard's invitation, to wipe from that self-complacent face its look of omniscience. "An' then, sometimes I reckon I don't," he continued; "but I'm admittin' she's plumb fascinatin'. From th' pious expressions around me I reckon mebby I've shocked somebody."

Williams led in the laughter that followed, his bull voice roaring through the room. "You'd better buy that hoss before you assist in th' evenin's worship," he cried in boisterous good humor, "for I'm sayin' a puncher ain't nowhere near in th' prospector's class when it comes to walkin'; though I reckon th' boys will play you for th' hoss, at that, an' you'd be no better off in th' end. My remarks as how this town has slid back didn't have nothin' to do with our poker playin', Mr. Jones. If you feel like settin' in ag'in' a Kansas cyclone, you can't say I didn't warn you."

Tex wondered what the crowd would say if he should lean over and pull a royal flush out of Williams' ear, or a full-house from the nephew's nose. They might be surprised if they found out that the cold-eyed gunman at Williams' elbow carried a handful of Colt cartridges in his tight-shut mouth. He had no rabbits to lift out of hats, but that trick was threadbare from being overworked, anyhow. He waved both hands, a smart-Aleck grin sweeping across his face. "I've rode cayuses, punched cows, an' played draw from Texas to Montanny, an' near back ag'in. So far I ain't throwed, rolled under, or cleaned out; an' I'm allus willin' to be agreeable. Where you gents lead I'll foller, like a hungry calf after its ma." His voice had grown loud and boastful and he joined the swiftly forming card group with a swagger as it settled around the table in the barroom, his bovine conceit hiding the silent struggle going on within him.

Tex of the old days was fighting Tex of the new. The smug complacency of the local boss stirred up the desire to break him to his last cent, to make a fool of him in the way others had been broken and made ridiculous; but the new Tex won: As usual he would play Hopalong's game—which was as his opponents played, straight or crooked, as they showed the way. He had no real wish for large winnings, for if he made his expenses as he went along he would be satisfied, and he could do that from his knowledge of psychology, a knowledge gained outside of classrooms. He now had no reputation to defend or maintain, for Tex Jones was not Tex Ewalt, famed throughout the cow-country. The new name meant nothing. But how pleasant it would be to repeat history in this town, so far as Williams was concerned!

He always had claimed that he could learn a man's real nature more quickly in a game of poker than in any other way in the same length of time, and he did not mean some one more prominent trait, but the man's nature as a whole;

and now he set himself to study his new acquaintances against some future need. The game itself would not engross him to the exclusion of all else, for while he was Tex Jones externally, it would be Tex Ewalt who played the hands, the Tex Ewalt who as a youth had discovered an uncanny ability in sleight of hand and whose freshman and sophomore years had given so much time to developing and perfecting the eye-baffling art that every study had suffered heavily in consequence; the Tex Ewalt who had found that his ability was peculiarly adaptive to cards, and who had given all his attention to that connection when once he had started to travel along the line of least resistance. So well had he succeeded that seasoned gamblers from the Mexican line north to Canada had been forced to admit his mastery.

Before the end of the second deal he had learned the rest of the nephew's more prominent characteristics, but had not bothered to retaliate for the cheating. On the third deal he was forced to out-cheat a miner to keep even with the game. Before the evening's play was over he had renewed his knowledge of Gus Williams, and now knew him as well as that loud-voiced individual knew himself; and he had not incurred the enmity of the boss, because while Tex had won from the others he had lost to him. While not yielding to the temptations rampant in him, he had compromised and left Williams in a ripe condition for a future skinning. At the end of the play only he and Williams had won.

As the others pushed back their chairs to leave the table, Williams ignored them and looked at Tex. "You an' me seem to be th' best," he said loudly. "So there won't be no doubt about it, let's settle it between us."

Tex raised a belated hand too late to hide his yawn, blinked sleepily, and squinted at the clock. "I'm surprised

it's so late," he said. "It takes a lot out of a man to play ag'in'
this crowd. My head's fair achin'. What you say if we let it
go till tomorrow night? I been travelin' for three days an'
three nights an' ain't slept much. You'd take it away from
me before I could wake up."

Williams laughed sarcastically. "You shore been crossin'
a lot of sand since you left th' Big Muddy, but I don't reckon
none of it got inter yore system." He paused to let the words
sink in, and for a reply, and none being forthcoming he
laughed nastily as he arose. "Texas is a sandy state, too.
Reckon you was named before anybody knowed very much
about you."

Tex paled, fought himself to a standstill and shrugged his
shoulders. Out of the corner of his eye he saw Bud Haines,
the cold-eyed bodyguard, become suddenly more alert.

"Windsor's got a hell of a way of welcomin' strangers,"
he said. "You'll have a different kind of kick to make
tomorrow night, for you'll be eatin' sand. I play poker when
I feel like it: just now I don't feel like it. I'll say good night."

"Ha-ha-ha!" shouted Williams. "He don't feel like it,
boys! Ha-ha-ha!"

Tex stopped, turned swiftly, pulled out a roll of bills that
was a credit to his country and slammed it on the table,
reaching for the scattered deck. "Mebby you feel like
puttin' up seven hundred dollars ag'in' mine, one cut, th'
highest card, to take both piles? Ha-ha-ha!" he mimicked.
"Here's action if that's what yo're lookin' for!"

Williams' face turned a deep red and he cursed under
his breath. "That's a baby game: I said poker!" he retorted,
making no effort to get nearer to the table.

"That's mebby why I picked it," snapped Tex, stuffing the
roll back into his pocket. "You can wait till tomorrow night
for poker." Turning his back on the wrathful Williams
and the open-mouthed audience, he yawned again, muttered

something to express his adieus, and clomped heavily and slowly up the stairs, his body shaking with repressed laughter; and when he fell asleep a few minutes later there was a placid smile on his clean-shaven face.

IV

♦

A Crowded Day

After a late breakfast about noon Tex got the gunny sack, threw it over his shoulder and went to the Mecca, nodding to the proprietor in a spirit of good-will and cheerfulness. Bud Haines did not appear to be about.

"I come in to see about that cayuse," he said. "Where'll I find it?"

"Go down to th' stable an' see John," growled Williams. "You'll find it next to Carney's saloon, across th' street. Got rested up yet?" The question was not pleasantly asked.

Tex threw the sack over the other shoulder, hunched it to a more comfortable position, and grinned sheepishly. "Purty near, I reckon; anyhow, I got over my grouch. I was shore peevish last night; but th' railroad's to blame for that. They say they are necessary, an' great blessin's; but I ain't so shore about it. Outside of my personal grudge ag'in' 'em, I'm sore because they've shore played th' devil with th' range. Cut it all up—an' there ain't no more pickin' along th' old trails no more, like there once was. I don't reckon punchers has got any reason to love 'em a whole lot."

Williams flashed him a keen look and slowly nodded. "Yo're right: look at what they've done to this town. We ain't seen no real money since they came."

Tex shifted the sack again. "Everybody had money in

them days," he growled. "If a feller went busted along th' trails he allus could pick up a few dollars, if he had a good cayuse an' a little nerve. Why, among them hills—but that ain't concernin' us no more, I reckon." He shook his head sadly. "What's gone is gone. Reckon I'll go look at that cayuse. You ain't got no letter for me yet, have you?"

"Le's see—Johnson?" puzzled the storekeeper, scratching his unshaven chin.

"No; Jones," prompted Tex innocently, hiding his smile.

"Oh, shore!" said his companion, slowly shaking his head. "There ain't nothin' for you so far."

Tex did not think that remarkable not only because there never would be anything for him, but also because there had been no mail since he had asked the day before; but he grunted pessimistically, shifted the sack again, and turned to the door. "See you later," he said, going out.

He easily found the stable, grinned at the bleached, weather-beaten "Williams" painted over the door and going into the smelly, cigar-box office, dumped the sack against the wall and nodded to John Graves. "Come down to look at that cayuse Williams spoke about last night," he said, drawing a sleeve across his wet forehead.

"Shore; come along with me," said Graves, arising and passing out into the main part of the building, Tex at his heels. "Here he is, Mr. Jones—as fine a piece of hossflesh as a man ever straddled. Got brains, youth, an' ginger. Sound as a dollar. Cost you eighty, even. You'll go far before you'll find a better bargain."

Tex looked at the teeth, passed a hypnotic hand down each leg in turn as he talked to the gray in a soothing voice. Children, horses, and dogs liked him at first look. He frankly admired the animal from a distance, but sadly shook his head.

"Fine cayuse, an' a fair price," he admitted; "but I'm

dead set ag'in' grays. Had two of 'em once, one right after th' other—an' come near to dyin' on 'em both. If I didn't get killed, they did, anyhow. It's sort of set me ag'in' grays. Now, there's a roan that strikes me as a hoss I'd consider ownin'. Of course, he ain't as good as th' gray, but he suits me better." He walked over to the magnificent animal, which was far and away superior to the gray and talked to it in a low, caressing voice as he made a quick examination. "Yes, this cayuse suits me if th' price is right. If we can agree on that I'll lead him down th' street an' see how he steps out. Ain't got nothin' else to do, anyhow."

Graves frowned and slowly shook his head. "Rather not part with that one—an' he's a two-hundred-dollar animal, anyhow. It's a sort of pet of th' boss—he's rid it since it was near old enough to walk. That gray's th' best I've got for sale, unless, mebby, it might be that sorrel over there. Now, there's a mighty good hoss, come to think of it."

Tex glanced at the beautiful line of the roan's back and thought of the massive weight of Williams, and of the sway-back bay standing saddled in front of his store. He shook his head. "Two hundred's too high for me, friend," he replied. "As I said, I don't like grays, an' that sorrel has shore got a mean eye. It ain't spirit that's showin', but just plumb treachery. If you got off him out on th' range he'd head for home an' leave you to hoof it after him. I got an even hundred for th' roan. Say th' word an' we trade."

Graves waved his arms and enumerated the roan's good points as only a horse dealer can. The discussion was long and to no result. Tex added twenty-five dollars to the hundred he had offered and the whole thing was gone over again, but to no avail. He picked up the sack, slung it onto his back, and turned to leave.

"I'm shore surprised at th' prices for cayuses in this part of th' country," he said. "Mebby I can make a dicker with

somebody else. Of course, I'm admittin' that th' roan ain't
got a sand crack like th' sorrel, or a spavin like th' gray—but
that's too much money for a saddle hoss for a puncher out
of a job. See you tonight, mebby."

Graves waved his arms again. "I'm tellin' you that you
won't find no hoss in town like that roan—why, th' color of
that animal is worth half th' price. Just look at it!"

"All of which I admits," replied Tex; "but, you see, I'm
buyin' me a hoss to ride, not to put on th' parlor table for
to admire. Comin' right down to cases, any hoss but a gray,
that's sound, an' not too old, is good enough for any
puncher. You should 'a' seen some that I've rode, an' been
proud of!"

"Seein' that yo're a lover of good hossflesh, I'll take a
chance of Gus gettin' peeved, an' let you have th' roan for
one-ninety. That's as low as I can drop. Can't shave off another dollar."

"It's too rich for Tex Jones," grumbled the puncher. "See
you tonight," and the sack bobbed toward the door just as a
sudden brawl sounded in the street. Tex took two quick steps
and glanced.

A miner and a cowpuncher were rolling in the dust, biting, hitting, gouging, and wrestling and, as Tex looked he
saw the puncher's gun slip out of its open-top sheath. The
fighting pair rolled away from it and someone in the closely
following crowd picked it up to save it for its owner. The
puncher, pounds lighter than his brawny antagonist, rapidly was getting the worst of the rough-and-tumble in which
the other's superior weight and strength had full opportunity to make itself felt. Suddenly the miner, thrown from
his victim by a tremendous effort, leaped to his feet, snarling like a beast, and kicked at the puncher's head. The
heavy, hob-nailed boot crashed sickeningly home and as the
writhing man went suddenly limp, the victor aimed another

kick at his unconscious enemy. His foot swung back, but it never reached its mark. A forty-pound saddle in a sack shot through the air with all of a strong man's strength behind it and, catching the miner balanced on one foot, it knocked him sprawling through ten feet of dust and debris. Following the sack came Tex, his eyes blazing.

The miner groped in the dust, slowly sat up, moving his head from side to side as he got his bearings. At once his eyes cleared and his hand streaked to the knife in his belt as he half arose. Tex leaped aside as the heavy weapon cut through the air to sink into a near-by wall, where it quivered. The thrower was on his feet now, his face working with rage, and he sprang forward, both arms circling before him. Tex swiftly gripped one outstretched wrist, turned sharply as he pushed his shoulder under the armpit and suddenly bent forward, facing away from his antagonist. The miner left the ground on the surging heave of the puncher's shoulder, shot up into the air, turned over once as Tex, not wishing him to break his neck, pulled down hard on the imprisoned arm, and landed feet first against the wall, squarely under the knife. Bouncing up with remarkable vitality, the miner wrenched at the wicked weapon above him and then cursed as the steel, leaving its point embedded in the wood, flew out of his hand.

Tex shoved the smoking Colt back into his holster and peered through the acrid, gray fog. "If you don't know when yo're licked, you better take my word for it," he warned. "Seein' as how yo're a rubber ball, I'll make shore th' third time!"

A snarl replied and the miner leaped for him, the hairy hands not so far extended this time. Tex broke ground with two swift steps and then, unexpectedly slipping to one side and forward in two perfectly timed motions, swung a rigid, bent arm as the charging miner went blunderingly past. The bony fist landed fair above the belt buckle and it was nearly half an hour later before the prospector knew where he was, and then he was too sick to care much.

Tex turned and faced the crowd with insolent slowness. His glance passed from face to face, finding some friendliness, much surprise, and a few frank scowls. He stepped up to the man who had retrieved the puncher's gun and, ignoring the crowd altogether, took the weapon from the reluctant fingers which held it and went back to the front of the stable, where Graves had succeeded in bringing the prostrate puncher back to consciousness. Tex ran his fingers over the wobbly man's head and face, grunted, nodded, and smiled.

"Bad bruise, but nothin' is busted. Why there ain't I'm shore *I* don't know. I figgered you was a goner. Here, take your gun, an' let us help you into th' stable."

Once on his feet the puncher pushed free from the sustaining hands and staggered to a box just inside the door, where he carefully seated himself, drew the Colt, and rested it on his knees, his blurred, throbbing eyes watching the street.

Tex grinned. "You can put that up ag'in—he's had all he can digest for a little while. Punchin' for Williams?"

"I'm ridin' for Curtis: C Bar. Over northeast, a couple of hours out. I'm keepin' th' gun where it is: th' miners run this town. Where do you fit in? One of th' GW gang?"

"Nope; I'm all of th' Tex Jones outfit. Stranger here, but shore gettin' acquainted rapid. Got any good cayuses for sale out at yore place? Our mutual friend, here, wants th' Treasury for th' only good animal he's got. Bein' a stranger is a handicap."

Graves leaned forward. "That hoss is worth—" he began in great earnestness.

"—not one red cent to me, now," interrupted Tex, smiling. "Come to think of it, I ain't goin' to buy no hoss a-tall. I've changed my mind."

"We got th' usual run out on th' ranch," said the injured man. "You know 'em, I reckon. Poor on looks, mean as all hell, with hearts crowded with sand. I'll be leavin' in half an hour if th' miners don't interfere—borry a cayuse an' ride out with me."

"Nope," replied Tex. "I ain't goin' to buy, a-tall, as I just said." He turned. "Good luck to you, friend. Barrin' th' soreness, an' yore looks yo're all right," and he went out, picked up the bulging sack, and passed down the street. Leaving the sack with the bartender in the hotel he went on to the station and smiled at the agent, who was joking with a red-headed Irishman.

"Hello; here he is now," exclaimed the boss of the depot. "Friend, shake hands with Tim Murphy. Tim, this is Mr.—Mr.—"

"Jones," supplied Tex: "Tex Jones, of Montanny, Texas, an' New York."

"Pleased to meet you, Mr. Geography," grinned Murphy. "Th' lad here was a-tellin' me ye gave him a friendly word an' some good advice. From that I was knowin' ye didn't belong around here. I'll shake yer hand if ye don't mind. Th' sack wint like an arrow, th' wrestlin' trick couldn't be bate, I never saw a nicer shot, an' th' finish does ye proud. Ye fair tickled me when ye wint for th' soft spot. 'Tis a rare sight in street fights, an' in th' ring, too, for that matter. Welcome to Windsor!"

Tex laughed heartily and gripped the hairy fist. He liked the feel of the great, calloused hand, and the look on the smiling, tanned face, from which twinkled a pair of blue eyes alight with humor, honesty, and courage. "But did you ever see a man come back as quick as he did?" he asked.

"'Twas surprisin' for a bully," admitted Murphy, grudgingly.

"That's where yo're wrong: he's no bully," contradicted Tex. "He's a brute, all right, savage as th' devil, an' foul in his fightin'—but he ain't any coward. It fair stuck out of his eyes."

"Trust me to miss anything like that," growled the agent; "and trust Tim not to," he added.

"Hist, now!" warned Murphy, motioning with his thumb held close to his vest. "Here comes th' lass. An' what do ye be thinkin' av th' town now, Mr. Jones?"

"Just what you do," laughed Tex, turning slowly.

"An' how are ye this day, miss?" asked Murphy, his hat in his hand and his red face beaming.

"Very well, indeed, Tim," replied the girl. She glanced at Tex as she turned to her brother, holding out the lunch basket. "Jerry, I couldn't get any decent eggs—and they had no milk for me." There was a poorly hidden note of distress in her voice, and a faint look of anxiety momentarily clouded her face. Neither was lost to the observant puncher.

Tex liked her instantly. Her voice was full and sweet, of resonant timbre—a voice one would not easily tire of. Her figure was slender, and yet full and rounded, promising a wiry strength and great vitality. The sunbonnet she wore hid most of the chestnut-brown hair, but set off the face within it with a bewitching art. Altogether she made a very pretty picture.

"It doesn't matter, Jane," smiled her brother, quick to sense her worry. He pinched the full lips with caressing playfulness. "I'm getting stronger every day, and food isn't as critical a subject as it once was. The credit is all yours—Jane, meet Mr. Jones. I was speaking about him last night."

Tex bowed gravely. "How do you do?" he murmured.

"Conscientious care is more than half of the battle. The credit he gave you appears to be well deserved."

Jane Saunders, accustomed to embarrassed self-consciousness or stammering volubility, smiled faintly as she acknowledged the introduction. The man was as impersonal and as sure of himself as any she ever had met. She looked him fairly in the eyes.

"How did you come to advise my brother to go farther west?" she asked, but while her voice was casual, her look challenged him.

"It was given upon certain conditions of the weather this winter, Miss—I do not believe I caught the name."

"No fault of yours," she laughed. "Jerry always ignores it in his introductions. It is Jane Saunders. Then it was only in the nature of a physician's advice?" she persisted, her eyes searching his soul for the truth.

Tex nodded. "My knowledge of his complaint is very sketchy; but like all amateurs I paraded what little I had. I thought that perhaps the winters out here might not be as dry as they are farther west. No doubt it was entirely uncalled for. We will hope so, anyway."

"Are you a physician, Mr. Jones?"

"No, indeed; although I went part way through the course. What little time I had left from more interesting activities, I gave to study."

"Ye was speakin' about th' aigs an' milk, miss," said Murphy, his face alight with eager anticipation. He chuckled. "Ye needn't be askin' no more favors av Williams' black heart. I've a little somethin' to show ye all, if ye'll step down th' track a bit. An' Costigan is goin' to get him a cow. Th' missus said th' word, an' divvil a bit Mike can wiggle out av it. Ye'll have first call on th' milk, so I hear. Mr. Jones, if ye'll be kind enough to escort Jerry, I'll lead th' march with th' lass."

"Oh, well," sighed Tex, gravely offering his arm to the station agent, "I suppose it *is* yore party; but I'm admittin' yo're not overlookin' Number One. Lead on, MacDuff." He caught her quick glance at the abrupt change in his language, and smiled to himself. It never paid to be too well understood by a woman.

"Th' Irish are noted for bein' judges av good whiskey, fine hosses, an' fair wimmin," retorted Murphy. "I'll take no chances of any pearls bein' cast careless."

"I notice you put th' wimmin last," countered Tex. "Grunt, Jerry! Quick, man! Before Miss Saunders looks around!"

"He said pearls, Mr. Jones," said Jane, laughingly. "I'm afraid he intended it all to be plural."

"It was wrongly written in th' first place," complained Tex. "Tim has an uncanny instinct; he only met me about ten minutes ago."

"Ten is a-plenty, sometimes," chuckled Murphy. "But I'll own to havin' a previous sight av ye. Wait now: here we are."

They stopped in front of the toolhouse and watched Murphy walk along one of the two ties spanning the drainage ditch at the edge of the roadbed. He unlocked the doors and flung them wide open as a clamorous cackling broke out in the building. On one end of a hand car was a crate of chickens and leaning against it were several bundles of long stakes. A pile of new lumber could be seen in the back of the shed, while a fat spool of wire rested near the stakes.

Murphy turned, his face red with delight at his surprise. "There ye are, miss," he cried proudly. "A round dozen av them, with their lord an' master. I couldn't let that Mike Costigan go puttin' on his airs over his boss, so now there'll be aigs for aignoggs that I'll have a claim to. For safe-keepin' we'll build th' coop in yore back yard where it will be right handy for ye. Ye can now tell Williams to kape his aigs. If he don't understand yer soft language, I'll be tellin' him in a way he can't mistook."

"You angel!" whispered Jane, tears in her eyes. She was not misled by his remarks about eggnoggs. "Oh, Tim—you shouldn't have done it! Why didn't *I* think of it? And how is it that Mrs. Costigan suddenly needs a cow? If I've heard her aright, she has stalwart, old-fashioned ideas, bless her, about nursing children. And I never knew she was partial to eggnoggs. Jerry, what shall we do to them?"

Jerry blew his nose with energy. "For a cent I'd lick Murphy right now, and Mike immediately afterward," he laughed, sizing up the huge bulk of bone, sinew, and toil-hardened muscle of the section-boss. "Tim, you and your boys are the one redeeming feature of this country. And you redeem it fully. How long have you been plotting this?"

"G'wan with ye, th' pair av ye!" chuckled the section-boss, his face flaming. "If Casey hadn't stopped th' train down by this shed yesterday we couldn't 'a' surprised ye. Ye never saw a consignment handled quicker or more gintly."

"And I was wondering why he did it," confessed Jerry. "The brakeman said he was trying his brakes. Tim, you should be ashamed of yourself!"

"An' I've been that, many a time," retorted Murphy. He turned to Tex. "I'll be leavin' it to ye, Mr. Jones, if a man hasn't certain rights after bein' nursed for three weeks by a brown-haired angel, an' knowin' that th' same angel nursed Mrs. Costigan an' th' twins whin they was all down with th' measles. Patient an' unselfish, she was, with never a cross word, day or night—an' always with a smile on her pretty face, like th' sun on Lake Killarney."

Tex looked gravely and judicially at Jane Saunders. "You haven't a word to say, Miss Saunders. The verdict of the court is for the defendant. Case dismissed, without costs of either party against the other." He turned to the section-boss. "When are we buildin' that coop, Murphy?" he asked.

"Tomorrow, Tex," answered the Irishman. "We'll be after runnin' th' darlin's up there right away, an' come back for th' lumber an' wire. That'll give us an early start. Th' sidin' will let us ride 'em near halfway an' save a lot of flounderin' in th' sand."

"We'd better come back for th' darlin's after th' coop is ready for 'em," said Tex, grinning. "If I know coyotes as well as I reckon I do, th' harem will be a lot safer in this here shed; an' I'm glad it's got a board floor, too. Lend a hand here an' we'll change th' cargo on this meek steed. *Gently, brother, gently pray.* Now for th' lumber." He burst into a chant: *"I once was a bloody pirate bold, an' I sailed on th' Spanish Main, yo-ho! Th' treasure chests were full of gold, which gave us all a pain you know."* He glanced at one of his hands and grimaced. "Blast th' splinters. An' would you look at that corn? Blessed if th' man hasn't got enough to feed another Custer expedition! Murphy, you certainly do grow on one!"

Murphy paused with a huge armful of lumber, and looked suspicious. "On one what?" he demanded.

"Prickly pear plant, I reckon, in lieu of anything else; or on a mesquite tree, perhaps, for you shore do know beans when th' pod's open. *An' it stopped—short—never to go again, when th' old—man—died,"* hummed Tex. "All aboard. Clang-clang! Clang-clang! I can still hear that bell in my sleep. Yo're th' engineer, Murphy; I'll act in an advisory capacity, at th' same time pushing hard on my very own handle. Ladies first! Miss Saunders, if you please! That's right, for you might as well ride in state. Up you go. From your elevated position you may scan the country roundabout and give us warning of the approach of redskins. *A Book of Verses underneath the Bough, a Jug of Wine, a Loaf of Bread*—and fried eggs—*Oh, Wilderness were Paradise enow!*"

"I see no redskins, Advisory Capacity," called Jane, who thoroughly was enjoying herself; "but hither rides a horseman on a horse."

Tex looked up and saw a recklessly riding puncher coming toward them. He slyly exchanged grins with Murphy and kept on pushing.

The rider, smiling as well as a swollen face and throbbing temples would permit, slid to a stand, removed his sombrero and bowed.

"My name's Tom Watkins," he said. "I just come down to tell you, friend, that I've learned what you done for me, awhile back. I'm—"

Tex interrupted him. "You just came down in time, Thomas, to drop yore useful rope over that bobbin' handle an' head west at a plain, unornamental walk. High-heeled boots was never made for pushin' han' cars over ties an' rocks. An' I suspect Murphy of stealin' a ride every time my head goes down."

"Then I'd be cheatin' myself," retorted Murphy, looking upon the newcomer with strong favor. "Th' car would be after stoppin' every time I rode, like th' little boat with th' big whistle." He turned to the agent. "Jerry, there's no tellin' how fast this car will be goin', for I misdoubt that animal's intentions. Suppose ye run along an' throw th' switch for us. Hadn't ye better get down, miss?"

"Not for the world, Tim!"

The disfigured puncher grinned even wider, dropped his rope over the handle with practiced art and wheeled his horse. "What'll I do when I git to th' end of th' rails?" he asked, mischievous deviltry, unabashed by what had befallen him, shining in his eyes, and there was an eager curiosity revealed by his voice.

"What'll he do, Murphy?" demanded Tex.

"He'll stop, blast him!" emphatically answered the section-boss.

'You'll stop, Thomas," said Tex. "As Hamlet said: 'Go on, I'll follow thee!'"

"But he's not nearly a ghost yet," objected Jane. Her cheeks were flushed, her eyes sparkling from the fun she was having. Many days had passed since she had had so good a time. It was a treat to get away from the ever-lasting "Yes, ma'am" and "No, ma'am" which had been the formula for conversation with everyone to whom she had talked except her brother and Murphy.

"No, ma'am," said the puncher. "Not yet."

Jane shuddered and grimaced at Tex as the rider turned away. "That's all I've heard since I've been out here," she softly called down to him.

"Yes, ma'am," he replied, not daring to look up.

The procession wended onward to the edification of sundry stray dogs, and Costigan's goats, tethered near the tool-shed, promptly went into consultation as to what measures to pursue, apparently deciding upon a defensive course of action if the worst came to pass.

The end of the rails reached, the engineer of the motive power stopped, sized up the ground roundabout and then looked hopefully at his companions. "Reckon we can manage th' haul. Totin' them boards afoot shore will be tirin'. Where we drivin' to?"

Jerry pointed out the little house, but shook his head. "We can't make it."

"Cowboy," said Tex, "that ain't no plowhorse. When she feels th' drag of this vehicle in th' sand she'll display her frank an' candid thoughts about it."

"Then blindfold her," suggested Tom Watkins. "She

won't know it ain't a steer she's fastened to. You fellers can git behind an' push, too."

" 'Sic transit gloria mundi'," murmured Jane, preparing to descend to earth.

" 'Sic transit' glorious Monday," repeated Tex, stepping to assist her. "Only it ain't Monday. Take my honest hand, lady, and jump." He turned and looked at the grinning engineer. "Now, you cactus-eatin' burro, try yore hand-kerchief. If *our* idea works, all right; if *yore* idea don't work, it's Murphy's fault. Commence!"

"I'm thinkin' it would work better if th' car was off th' track," caustically commented Murphy. "I misdoubt if we can climb that buffer; th' flanges on these wheels are deep an' strong an' I'm shore we can't pull th' rails over. If th' engineer will lend a hand here we mebby can clear th' track without unloadin'. I'll take th' off side; ye byes take th' other, which makes it even, for it is a well-known fact that one Irish section-boss is worth two punchers. Are ye ready, now?"

"I've heard they can run faster than two cowpunchers," retorted Tex. "For the ashes of your fathers, *lift!* Try it again—*now.* Inch her over—that's the way. Now then, *lift!* Once more—*lift!* Phew! All right: proceed, cowboy," he grunted.

"Hold yer horses!" shouted Murphy. "What's th' good av a section-boss that can't lay a track?" he demanded, taking up a two-by-four, Tex following his lead. The car was lifted onto the timbers and the procession went on again. "Will they spread, now?" queried Murphy doubtfully, watching them closely. He had just decided they would not when they did. After numerous troubles the little house was reached, the lumber unloaded, and the car sent back without rails.

"Goin' to make any more hauls?" asked the horseman.

"We are not," said Tex with emphasis. "We could 'a' toted this stuff over in half th' time. *Tempus* fidgets, an' I'm catchin' it. Yore ideas are plumb fine till they're put in practice."

"*My* ideas?" queried the disfigured rider, his rising eyebrows pushing wrinkles onto his forehead. "Didn't you tell me to chuck my rope over that bobbin' handle?"

"Do you allus have to do what yo're told?" retorted Tex. "Answer me that! Do you?"

The rider looked down at Jane, who was nearly convulsed, and sighed with deep regret, and because her presence forbade the only appropriate retort, he shook his head sorrowfully and turned to haul the car back to the track.

"Hey!" called Tex. "Sling them spools of barb wire across yore saddle. We might as well get more of that stuff while we have yore good-natured assistance. Just chuck it on any place an' bring it here."

"You just can't chuck a spool of wire on a saddle any place," retorted the puncher. "Was you speakin' about ideas?"

"An while yer about it," said Murphy, "ye might bring back a spade, th' saws, three hammers, that box av nails, an' them staples. Th' staples are in a little keg—th' one without th' handle. I've a mind to start buildin' today. What do ye say, Tex? Good for ye: yer a man after me own heart."

Despite his aches and bruises the puncher's feet left the stirrups and slowly went up until he stood with his shoulder on the saddle. He waved his legs three times and resumed the correct posture for riding. Words were hopelessly inadequate. He looked at Jane, who was shrieking and pointing at the ground under the horse. Thomas craned his neck and looked down. He thereupon dismounted and picked up one Colt's .45, one pocket-knife, one watch which now needed expert attention, various coins, a plug of tobacco, and three horseshoe nails. Murphy stared at him, spat disgustedly, and attacked the pile of lumber.

After the puncher's return the work went on rapidly, and when the roof of the coop was finished, the three perspiring workmen stepped back to admire it.

"We've got to slat them windows," said Tex, thinking of coyotes.

"An' we got thirteen nests to build," said Thomas Watkins.

"Th' saints be praised!" ejaculated Murphy, staring incredulously at the battle-scarred recruit. "Mebby there'll be a coincidence about twelve layin' all at once, but there won't be no thirteenth on th' job. Mebby yer thinkin' th' Sultan will nest down alongside them to set them a good example? Six boxes will be a-plenty, Tommy, my lad."

Tommy tilted his sombrero to scratch his head. "Well, if you reckon there won't be no stampedin', mebby six will be enough, 'though I'd hate to think of 'em milling frantic for their turn on th' nests. An' while we're speakin' of calamities, I'm sayin' good chickens will fly over th' fence you fellers aim to build. Six feet ain't high enough, nohow."

"We clip their wings, Tommy," enlightened Tex.

"We clip one wing close up," corrected Murphy. "That lifts 'em on one side an' flops 'em around in a circle. I can easy see you ain't no *hen puncher*."

"Th' principle is sound in theory an' proved by practice," said Tex. "Just like when you saw off th' laigs on one side of a steer. That allus keeps 'em from jumpin' fences."

"Too cussed bad you stopped that miner," growled Watkins. "I'd 'a' been a whole lot better off dead."

"We're sorry, too," retorted Murphy. "Now, then; we got a four-sided fence to build, three posts to a side. That's a dozen holes to dig."

"Tell you what," suggested Tommy, winking at Tex.

"You can handle a spade all around us, one Irish section-boss bein' worth two punchers. Besides we only got one spade for th' three of us. You dig th' north an' south sides while me an' Tex start on nests an' put up th' roosts. Then we'll dig th' east an' west sides while yo're settin' yore posts an' tampin' 'em."

"An' I'll have mine set while you fellers git ready to start on yer roosts," boasted Murphy, grabbing the spade and starting to work. Jane Saunders, who had come up unobserved, suddenly stuffed her handkerchief in her mouth and fled back to the house.

There ensued great hammering and frantic dirt throwing. Tex and his companion were hampered by mirth and were only building the last nest when Murphy stuck his head in the door.

"Ye wouldn't last in no gang av mine!" he jeered. "I got me holes dug an' th' posts set. Set 'em single-handed an' they're true as a plumb line."

"All right, Murphy," said Tommy without looking up. "Run along an' do th' other two while we're finishin' up. It's gettin' late."

"Tryin' to lay it onto me, eh?" demanded Murphy. "You an' yer two post holes! Ye must think—" he stopped short, thought a moment, and then slyly glanced out at the unfinished sides of the enclosure. "Hivin save us!" he muttered and slipped out without another word.

Tommy wiped his eyes and leaned against the wall for support. "Four sides," he babbled. "Three to a side: that's a dozen holes to dig! He will make smart remarks about my thirteen nests, will he?"

"Figures don't lie, an' logic is logic," laughed Tex. "Reckon we can't finish th' fence today; but it don't make no difference, anyhow. Them chickens are as safe in th' toolshed as they'd be up here. Did you close th' doors when you left?" he demanded anxiously.

"Yes; too many hungry, stray dogs around. I'd like to 'a' gone to th' finish with you boys, but I got to get back to th' ranch. Climb up behind me an' I'll let you off at th' hotel."

"I'll wait for Murphy," replied Tex. "He'll mebby need help about somethin'. I'm cussed glad to know you, Watkins; an' I've shore had a circus today."

"You pulled me out of a bad hole, Tex; an' you shore as shootin' dug one for yoreself. This town's run by th' miners, a lot of hoof-poundin' grubs, with pack mules for pardners. There's been feelin's between us an' them walkin' fools"—here he voiced the riders' contempt for men who walked—"for a long time. Yo're a puncher, an' you shore come out flat an' took sides today. Tell you what—either you come out to th' ranch with me, or I'll stay here in town with you. Come along: we'll find you a good cayuse, an' not rob you, neither."

"Can't do it, Tommy," replied Tex, warming to his new acquaintance. "I got my eye on a roan beauty an' I'm goin' to own him by tomorrow. He won't cost me a red cent. So far's danger is concerned, I ain't in none that my tongue or my six-gun can't get me out of. But I'll ride out an' pay yore outfit a visit after I get th' roan."

"That's th' third best cayuse in this section," replied Tommy. "Williams owns all three of 'em, too. There ain't nothin' on th' ranch that can touch any of 'em." He paused and looked closely at his companion. "You heard any war-talk ag'in' th' agent?"

"Only a rumblin', far off," answered Tex. "Th' dust ain't plain yet, so I can't tell how it's headin'. What do you know about it?"

"Not half as much as Murphy, I bet," replied Watkins.

"You ask him. It's a cussed shame for a man to be hounded by a pack of dogs. Well, I'm off. Remember that you got friends on th' C Bar when you need 'em, which you shore as shootin' will. We'll come a-runnin'." He shook hands and went out, Tex loafing after him as far as the door. "Tim, I reckon you an' Tex can manage to get along without me now, so I'll drift along. I'm due at th' ranch."

"Whose?" asked Murphy carelessly, trying a post to see if it was well set.

"Julius Caesar Curtis: Judy, for short," answered Watkins, holding out his hand. "You can leave th' other four posts for me to set when I come in again," he grinned.

"For a bye's-sized chew av tobaccy I'd skin ye," chuckled Tim, shaking the hand heartily. "Much obliged, Thomas, me son. Come in an' see us when ye can. There's so few decent men in this part av th' country that ye'll be welcome as th' flowers av spring."

Tommy swung into the saddle, raised his hat to the woman who appeared in the kitchen door, and whirled around to leave.

"Mr. Watkins!" called Jane, running toward the little group. "You are not going to leave without your supper? Your place is set and Jerry is pouring the coffee."

Tommy Watkins flushed, swallowed his Adam's apple, looked blankly at Tex and Tim, stammered gibberish, and managed to convey the impression that the salvation of the ranch and its outfit depended on his immediate departure. His mute appeal for moral support was coldly received by his fellow-builders.

"I do not wish to be rude, Mr. Watkins," smiled Jane, "and I would not wish to turn you from your duty. But I shall be a little disappointed if you won't allow me to show my poor appreciation of what you have done for us. But I will not press you: if not tonight, then some other time?"

The savior of the C Bar flushed deeper, received scowling looks from his late bosom companions, who knew a liar when they heard one, and he ducked his head quickly. "Yes, ma'am," he blurted eagerly. "I'd admire to stay, but Curtis shore is dependin' on me to git back. If you'll excuse me, ma'am—I—so—by," and he was whirling away in a cloud of dust, his sombrero held out at arm's length.

Murphy looked gravely at Tex and flushed slightly. "He has an important job, miss," he said.

Tex looked gravely at Murphy and did not flush. "A great weight for shoulders so young," he lied, suspecting, however, that Tommy might have acquired, during the course of the day, a very great weight, indeed. He had observed his glances at Jane.

She smiled inscrutably and turned to look at the coop, clapping her hands in delight. "Isn't it fine, and new, and piney!" she exclaimed, sniffing the tangy odor. "And it looks so strong—I must peek in for a moment."

There was not much room to spare when they all had entered, a fact which Tex easily explained.

"You see, Miss Saunders," he said, waving his hands, "it is to serve only as a nesting place and a shelter from predatory animals. During the day your flock will roam about the enclosure outside; but at twilight, without fail, it must be confined securely in this coop. No self-respecting coyote will be restrained for five minutes by the wire—he either will force himself between the strands, or dig under; and there are any number of those thieves around this town. They cannot be trapped or baffled—they will outwait or outwit any watcher. The only thing that will stop them is something physically impregnable.

"Tim and I intend to weave slats and laths between the lower strands of wire, running them vertically up from the ground, in which their lower ends will be driven. They will offer some protection, but their chief value will be to keep the chickens from getting outside. No coyote will be bothered by them for very long, and in order to save yourself the labor of filling up the tunnels they surely will dig if they can get in in no other way, I'd advise you to leave the fence gate wide open every night.

"We lay this floor for that reason. No matter what they are able to do, they can't get into the coop. I'll wager that you will find tunnels running under it before long. Don't fail to close this building before nightfall, and your flock will be safe."

"Amen," said Murphy. "They're cunnin' divvils, coyotes are!"

"I don't know how to thank you," said Jane, impulsively putting her hands on the arms of her companions. "Think what it will mean to Jerry—a dozen fresh eggs a day!"

Murphy chuckled. "Four a day will be doin' good, an' not that many for awhile. I'll get ye some grit, an' make a batch av whitewash."

"Hey!" called a voice. "Everything's getting cold!"

"There's Jerry, playing domestic tyrant," laughed Jane. "Isn't it remarkable what a difference it makes to the cook? He thinks nothing of making me wait. Come on—you can tell me all about chicken raising after supper." She cast a furtive glance at Tex, and past him at the twilight-softened range beyond, where Tommy Watkins somewhere rode to save his ranch and outfit.

V

◆

A Trimmer Trimmed

About ten o'clock that night Murphy and Tex neared the station and stopped short at the former's sudden ejaculation.

"Th' switch is open," he said. "Not that anythin' serious might happen, unless th' engineer went blind; but either av them would have plenty to say about it. Trust 'em for that. An' tomorrow is Overton's trick eastbound. He's worse than Casey. Wait here a bit," and the section-boss went over, threw the switch, and returned.

Soon they stopped again at the station to say good night to each other. Murphy seemed a little constrained and worried and soon gave the reason for it.

"Tex," he said in a low voice, "yer takin' sides with th' weakest party, an' yer takin' 'em fast an' open. Right now yer bein' weighed an' discussed, an' to no profit to yerself. I can see that yer a man that will go his own way—but if th' hotel gets unpleasant an' tirin', yer more than welcome in my shanty. 'Tis only an old box car off its wheels, but there's a bunk in it for ye any time ye want to use it. Tread easy now, an' keep yer two eyes open; an' while I'm willin' to back ye up, I daren't do it unless it's a matter av life an' death. I'm Irish, an' so is Costigan. There's a strong feelin' out here ag'in' us—an' when a mob starts not even wimmin an' childer are safe. Costigan has both, an' there's th' lass, as well. I've urged Mike to send his family back along th' line somewhere, but his wife says *no*. She's foolish, no doubt, but I say, God bless such wimmin."

"She's not foolish," replied Tex with conviction. "She's

wise, riskin' herself mebby, on a long chance. While she stays here Costigan will use a lot of discretion—if she goes, he might air his opinions too much, or get drunk and leave her a widow. I'll do what I can to stave off trouble, even to eatin' a little dirt; but, Tim, I'd like nothing better than to send for a few friends an' let things take their natural course. Every time I look at that nephew I fair itch to strangle him. It can't be possible that Miss Saunders gives him any encouragement? I'm much obliged about yore offer. I'd take it up right now except that it would cause a lot of talk an' thinkin'. Here, you better hand me two dollars for my day's work—there ain't no use lyin' about anythin' if th' truth will serve. I'll return it th' next time I see you."

"Th' lass won't look at that scut. He follers her around like a dog," Murphy growled, and then a grin came to his face as he dug into his pocket. "Here. Yer overpaid, but I should 'a' dickered with ye before I let ye go to work."

"Thanks, boss," chuckled Tex. "You'll need me tomorrow, for th' wire stringin'?"

"Yer fired!" answered Murphy, his voice rising and changing in timbre. "Yer a loafin', windy, clumsy, bunglin' no-account. By rights that ought to make ye mad. Does it?"

Tex could not fail to read the answer he was expected to make, for it lay in the section-boss' tones; and he thought that he had seen something move around the corner of the station. He stepped on the toe of one of his companion's boots to acknowledge the warning.

"Am I?" he demanded, angrily. "Yo're so d—d used to bossin' Irish loafers that you don't know a good man when you see one. You don't have to fire me, you Mick! I'm quittin', an' you can go to hell!"

Murphy's arm stopped in mid-air as Tex's gun leaped from its sheath.

"You checked it just in time," snapped Tex. "Any more

of that an' I'll blow you wide open. Turn around an' hoof it to yore sty!"

Murphy, strangling a chuckle, backed warily away. "If ye was as handy with tools as ye are with that damned gun—" he growled. "'Tis lucky for ye that ye have it!"

"This *is* my tool," retorted Tex. "Shut up an' get out before you make me use it. Fire me, hey? You got one —— gall!"

He stood staring after the shuffling Irishman, muttering savagely to himself, until the section-boss had been swallowed up by the darkness. Then he turned, slammed the gun back into its holster and stamped toward the hotel; but he stopped in the nearest saloon to give the eavesdropper, if there had been one, a chance to get to the hotel before him.

The bar was deserted, but half a dozen prospectors were seated at the tables, and they greeted his entrance with scowls. The two cavalrymen present glanced at him in disinterested, momentary curiosity and resumed their maudlin conversation. Some shavetail's ears must have been burning out at their post.

Tex stormed up to the bar and slammed two silver dollars on it. "Take this dirty money an' give th' boys cigars for it," he growled. "Me, I'm not smokin' any of 'em. Fire me, huh? I'd like to see th' section-boss that fires me! 'Overpaid,' he says, an' me workin' like a dog! 'I don't need ye tomorry,' he says: I cussed soon told him what he needed, but he didn't wait for it. Fire me?" he sneered. "Like hell!"

The cavalrymen grinned sympathetically and nodded their thanks for the cigars, which they had no little difficulty in lighting. The other men in the room took their gifts silently, two of them abruptly pushing them across the table, away from them.

"There'll be others that'll mebby git what they're needin'," said a rasping, unsteady voice from a corner table. "'Specially if he sticks his nose in where it ain't wanted."

Tex casually turned and nodded innocently. "My sentiments exactly," he agreed, waiting to receive unequivocal notification that it was he for whom the warning was meant. A little stupidity was often a useful thing.

"Nobody asked you for yore sentiments," retorted the prospector. "Strangers can't come into this town an' carry things with a high hand. Next time, Jake will kill you."

Tex looked surprised and then his eyes glinted. "That bein' a little job he can start 'most any time," he retorted. "When a man fights worse'n a dog he makes me mad; an' he fought like a cur. I'd do it ag'in. He got what he was needin', that's all."

The miner glowered at him. "An' he's got friends, Jake has," he asserted.

"Tell him that he'll need 'em—all of 'em," sneered Tex. "Our little session was plumb personal, but I'll let in his friends. Th' gate's wide open. They don't have to dig in under th' fence, or sit on their haunches outside an' howl. An' let me tell you somethin' for yore personal benefit—I've swallered all I aim to swaller tonight. I'm peaceable an' not lookin' for no trouble—you hold yore yap till I get through talkin'—but I ain't dodgin' none. Somehow I seem to be out of step in this town; but I'm whistlin' that I'm cussed particular about who sets me right. I ain't got no grudges ag'in' nobody; I'm tryin' to act accordin' to my lights, but I ain't apologizin' to nobody for them lights. Anybody objectin'?"

"Fair enough," said one of the cavalrymen. "I like his frank ways."

"That rides for me, too," endorsed his companion, aggressively.

"Shut up, you!" cried the bartender.

"For two bits—" pugnaciously began a miner, but he was cut short.

"An' you, too!" barked the man behind the counter, a gun magically appearing over the edge of the bar. "This has gone far enough! Stranger, you spoke yore piece fair. Tom," he said, looking at the angry miner, "you got nothin' more to say: yo're all through. If you think you has, then go outside an' shout it there. Th' subject is closed. What'll you-all have?"

Tex tarried after the round had been drunk but he did not order one on his own account, feeling that it would be a mistake under the circumstances. It might be regarded as a sign of weakness, and was almost certain to cause trouble. Turning his back on the sullen miner he talked casually with the bartender and the cavalrymen, and then one of the miners cleared his throat and spoke.

"Did you have a run-in with th' big Irishman?" he asked.

Tex leaned carelessly against the bar, grinned and frankly recounted the affair, and before he had finished the narrative, answering grins appeared here and there among his audience. The sputter of a sulphur match caught his eyes as his late adversary slowly reached for and lit the cigar he had pushed from him a few minutes earlier, but Tex did not immediately glance that way. When he had finished the story he looked around the room, noticed that all were smoking and he nodded slightly in friendly understanding. A little later he said good night, smiled pleasantly at the once sullen prospector, and went carelessly out into the night. The buzz of comment following his departure was not unfavorable to him.

When he entered the hotel barroom all eyes turned to him, and he noticed a grim smile on Williams' face and that the evil countenance of the nephew was aquiver with suspicion. Walking over, he stepped close to the table, watching the play, and from where he could keep tabs on Bud Haines' every move. During the new deal Williams leaned back, stretched, and glanced up.

"Had yore supper?" he carelessly asked.

Tex nodded. "Shore: reg'lar home-cooked feed. It went good for a change. I reckon I shore earned it, too." He drew out a sack of tobacco, filled a cigarette paper and held the sack in his teeth while he rolled himself a smoke. "What's paid around here for a good, half-day's work?" he mumbled between his teeth.

"What kind of work?" judicially asked Williams.

Tex removed the sack, moistened the cigarette and held it unlighted while he answered "Freightin' on foot, carpenterin', diggin', an' doin' what I was told to do."

"Dollar to a dollar four bits," replied Williams. "What you doin'? Hirin' out?"

"I was; but I ain't no more," replied Tex, lighting up. He exhaled a lungful of smoke and dragged up a chair. "I asked two dollars, an' there was an argument. That's all."

The hands lay where they had been dealt, Williams having let his own lay, and the players were idly listening until he should pick it up.

"What's it all about?" asked Williams. "You talk like a dish of hash."

The eager nephew squirmed closer to the table and his assumed look of indifference was a heavy failure.

Tex laughed, leaned back, and with humorous verbal pigments painted a rapidly changing picture to the best of his by no means poor ability. He took them up to the digging of the post holes, and then leaned forward. "Murphy said we'd build a four-sided fence, three posts to th' side, makin twelve in all. That suited us, an' as there was only one spade, we told him to go ahead an' dig his holes while we worked on th' nest boxes. He was to do th' north an' th' south sides, which he said was fair." The speaker paused a moment, leaning back in his chair, his eyelids nearly closed. Between their narrowed openings he looked swiftly around. The card players grinned in expectation of some joke about to appear, Williams looked suspicious and puzzled, but the bartender's eyes popped open and he choked back a sudden burst of laughter. Tex drew in a long breath, pushed back into his chair and glanced around at the players. "I was honest an' fair enough to say th' diggin' wasn't evenly divided, us bein' two and' him only one. What do you boys say?"

"What's it all amount to anyhow?" snarled the nephew. "Who cares if it was or not? What did you think of th' gal?" he demanded.

Tex breathed deeply, relaxed, and gravely considered his boots. "Well, if I was aimin' to start a kindergarten I might have took more notice of her—an' you, too, bub. Can't you do yore own lookin'?" he plaintively demanded. "Anyhow, I was warned fair, wasn't I? Huh! When you get to be my age an' have had my experience with this fool world you won't be takin' no more interest in 'em than I do. Beggin' yore pardon for interruptin' th' previous conversation we was holdin'. I'll perceed from where I was." He looked back at the card players. "We was debatin' th' fairness of th' offer to dig them holes. What you boys say?"

The man nearest to him pursed his lips and cogitated. The subject was no more frivolous than the majority of subjects which had furnished bones of contention many a night. Most barroom arguments start on even less. "I reckon it was, him bein' more used to diggin'."

His partner leaned forward. "What did *he* say about it, at first?"

"He was shore satisfied," answered Tex as the bartender, turning his back on the room, shook with the ague.

The last questioner bobbed his head decisively. "Then it shore was fair."

Williams nodded slowly, for his opinions were not lightly given. "I'd say it was. What about it?"

"Oh, nothin' much," growled Tex. "I reckon he changed his mind later on." He looked over at the gambler leaning against the wall, the same gambler he had seen on the train. At this notice Denver Jim, sensing possible bets, straightened up, winked, and made a sign which among his class was a notification that he had declared himself in for half the winnings of a game. Tex shook his head slightly and frowned, as if deeply puzzled over Murphy's conduct. The gambler repeated the sign and moved forward.

Tex did some quick thinking. He could not afford to be linked to a tin-horn and he did not intend to make any money out of his joke. Whatever he won in this town he would win at cards, and win it alone. His second signal of refusal was backed up by his hand dropping carelessly and resting on the butt of his gun. The gambler scowled, barely nodded his acquiescence and went to the bar for a drink. Bud Haines glanced up from the weekly paper he was reading, saw nothing to hold his interest, and returned to his reading.

Tex went on with his story, telling about the supper and his scene with Murphy at the station, repeating the latter word for word as nearly as he could from the time when he detected the approach of the eavesdropper. From the constantly repeated looks of satisfaction on Williams' face he knew that the local boss had been given a detailed account of the incident, and that he was checking it up, step by step. Briefly sketching his trouble in the saloon, Tex threw the cigarette butt at a distant box cuspidor and stretched. "An' here I am," he finished.

Williams picked up his hand, glancing absentmindedly at the cards. "Yes," he grunted, "here you are." Putting the cards back on the table he carelessly pushed them from him, squaring the edges with zealous care. "You come near not bein' here, though," he said, his level look steady and accusing. "Whatever made you jump on Jake that way?" he demanded coldly.

"Shucks! Here it comes again!" said Tex. He looked suspicious and defiant. "I did it to stop a murder, an' a lynchin'," he answered shortly.

"Very fine!" muttered Williams. "You was a little mite overanxious—there wouldn't 'a' been no lynchin' of Jake; but there might 'a' been one, just th' same. I had to do some real talkin' to stop it. It ain't wise for strangers to act sudden in a frontier town—'specially in this town. That's somethin' you hadn't ought to forget, Mr. Jones."

"If I get yore meanin' plain, yo're intendin' me to think I was in danger of bein' lynched?"

"You shore was."

"Then yo're admittin' that this town of Windsor will lynch a man because he keeps a murder from bein' committed, by lickin' th' man who tried to do it?"

"Exactly. Jake has lots of friends."

"He's plumb welcome to 'em, an' I reckon, if he's that kind of a man, he shore needs 'em bad. But from what I saw of Jake he ain't that kind of a man. I'm a friend of his'n, too. I'm so much a friend of Jake's that if he treads on my toes I'll save him from facin' th' trials an' hardships that come with old age. His existence is precarious, anyhow. He's allus just one step ahead of poverty an' grub stakes. Life for Jake is just one placer disappointment after another. He allus has to figger on a hard winter. Then he has to dodge sickness an' saddles, wrestlin' tricks, boxin' tricks, an' fast gunplay. But Jake is th' kind of a man that does his own fightin' for hisself. Yo're plumb mistaken about him."

"Mebby I am," admitted Williams. "I didn't know you

was acquainted with anybody around here, 'specially th' C Bar outfit."

"I wasn't," replied Tex. "It ain't my nature to be distant an' disdainful, however." He grinned. "I get acquainted fast."

"You acted prompt in helpin' that Watkins," accused Williams.

"I shore had to, or he'd 'a' quit bein' Watkins," retorted Tex. "You look here: We'll be savin' a lot of time if we come right down to cases. I saw a big man tryin' to kick th' head off another man, a smaller one, that was down. I stopped him from doin' it without hurtin' him serious. If it'd been th' other way 'round I'd done th' same thing. As it stands, it's between Jake an' me. We'll let it stay that way until th' lynchin' party starts out. Then anybody will be plumb welcome to cut in an' stop it. Excuse me for in- terferin' with yore game—but th' fault ain't mine. Talkin' is dry work—bartender, set 'em up for all hands. Who's winnin'?"

Williams picked up his cards again, looked at them, puckered his lips and glanced around at his companions. He cleared his throat and looked back at Tex. "I reckon I was, a little. Want to sit in? After all, Jake's troubles are his own: we got enough without 'em."

Tex looked at the table and the players, shrugged his shoulders and answered carelessly. "Don't feel like playin' very much—ate too much supper, I reckon. Later on, when I ain't so heavy with grub, mebby I'll take cards. I'd rather play ag'in' fewer hands, tonight, anyhow."

Williams looked up and sneered. "Think you got a better chance, that way?"

"I get sort of confused when there's so many playin'," con- fessed Tex; "but I shore can beat th' man that invented th' game, playin' it two-handed. I used to play for hosses, two-handed. Allus had luck, somehow, playin' for them. Why, once I owned six cayuses at one time, that I'd won."

"That so? You like that gray: how much will you put up ag'in' him?"

"I wouldn't play for no gray hoss—they're plumb unlucky with me. I ain't superstitious, but I shore don't like gray hosses."

"Got anythin' ag'in' sorrels?" Williams asked with deep sarcasm.

"Nothin' much; but I'm shore stuck on blacks an' roans. I call *them* hosses!" Tex grinned at the crowd and looked back at Williams. "Yes, sir; I shore do."

"How much will you put up ag'in' a good roan, then?"

"Ain't got much money," evaded Tex, backing away.

"Got two hundred dollars?"

"Not for no cayuse. Besides, I don't know th' hoss yo're meanin'."

"That roan you saw today," replied Williams. "John said you liked him a lot. I'll play you one hand, th' roan ag'in' two hundred."

Tex glanced furtively at the front door and then at the stairway. "Let it go till tomorrow night," he mumbled.

"Yo're a great talker, ain't you?" sneered Williams. "I'll put up th' roan ag'in' a hundred an' fifty. One hand, just me an' you."

"Well, mebby," replied Tex. "Better make her th' best two out of three. I might have bad luck th' first hand."

Williams' disgust was obvious and a snicker ran through the room. "I wouldn't play that long for a miserable sum like that ag'in' a stranger. One hand, draw poker, my roan ag'in' yore one-fifty. Put up, or shut up!"

"All right," reluctantly acquiesced Tex. "We allus used to make it two out of three up my way; but I may be lucky. After you get through—I ain't in no hurry."

Williams laughed contemptuously: "You shore don't have to say so!" He smiled at his grinning companions and resumed his play.

Tex dropped into the seat next to the sneering nephew, from where he could watch the gun-fighter. Bud's expression duplicated that of his boss and he paid but little attention to the wordy fool who was timid about playing poker for a horse.

"Hot, ain't it?" said Tex pleasantly. "Hot, an' close."

"Some folks find it so; reckon mebby it is," answered the nephew. "What did you people talk about at supper?" he asked.

"Hens," answered Tex, grinning. "She's got a dozen. You'd think they was rubies, she's that stuck up about 'em. Kind of high-toned, ain't she?"

The nephew laughed sneeringly. "She'll lose that," he promised. "I don't aim to be put off much longer."

"Mebby yo're callin' too steady," suggested Tex. "Sometimes that gives 'em th' idea they own a man. You don't want to let 'em feel too shore of you."

Henry Williams shifted a little. "No," he replied; "I ain't callin' too often. In fact, I ain't done no callin' at all, yet. I've sort of run acrost her on th' right-of-way, an' watched her a little. I get a little bit scary, somehow—just can't explain it. But I aim to call at th' house, for I'm shore gettin' tired of ridin' wide."

"Ain't they smart, though?" chuckled Tex; "holdin' back an' actin' skittish. I cured a gal of that, once; but I don't reckon you can do it. It takes a lot of nerve an' will-power. You feel like playin' show-downs, two-bits a game?"

"Make it a dollar, an' I will. How'd you cure that one of yourn?"

"Dollar's purty steep," objected Tex. "Make it a half." He

leaned back and laughed reminiscently. "I worked a system on her. Lemme deal first?"

"Suit yourself. Turn 'em face up—it'll save time. What did you do?"

"Made her think I didn't care a snap about her. Want to cut? Well, I didn't know—some don't want to," he explained. "Saves time, that's all. Reckon it's yore pot on that queen. Deal 'em up."

"How'd you do it? Snub her?"

"Gosh, no! Don't you ever do that: it makes 'em mad. Just let 'em alone—sort of look at 'em without seein' 'em real well. You dassn't make 'em mad! You win ag'in. Yo're lucky at this game: want to quit?"

"Give you a chance to get it back," sneered the nephew. "Think it would work with her?"

"Don't know: she got any other beaux?"

"I've seen to that. She ain't. Take th' money an' push over yore cards. Do you think it will work with her?" Henry persisted.

"Gosh, sonny: don't you ask me that! No man knows very much about wimmin', an' me less than most men. It's a gamble. She's got to jump one way or th' other, ain't she? How was you figgerin' to win?"

"Just go get her, that's all. She'll tame down after awhile."

"But you allus can do that, can't you? Now, if it was me I'd try to get her to come of her own accord, for things would be sweeter right at th' very start. But, then, I'm a gambler, allus willin' to run a risk. A man's got to foller his own nature. I got you beat ag'in: this shore is a nice game."

"Too weak," objected the nephew. "Dollar a hand would suit me better. My eights win this. Want to boost her?"

Tex reflected covetously. "Well, I might go high as a dollar, but not no more."

"Dollar it is, then. What's yore opinion of that gal?"

"Shucks," laughed Tex. "She's nice enough, I reckon; but she ain't my style. Yore uncle's game is bustin' up an' he's lookin' at me. See you later. You win ag'in, but I allus have bad luck doublin' th' stakes, 'though I ain't what you might call superstitious. See you later."

Tex arose and went over to the other table, raked in the cards, squared them to feel if they had been trimmed, thought they had been, and pushed them out for the cut, watching closely to see how the face cards had been shaved. Williams turned the pack, announced that high dealt, grasped the sides of the pack and turned a queen. Tex also grasped the sides of the pack remaining and also turned a queen. He clumsily dropped the deck, growled something and bunched it again, shoving it toward his companion in such a way that Williams would have to show a deliberate preference for the side grip. This he did and Tex followed his lead. The ends of the face cards and aces had been trimmed and the sides of the rest of the deck had been treated the same way. Because of this the sides of the face cards stuck out from the deck and the ends of the spot cards projected. Yet so carefully had it been done that it was not noticeable. Williams cut again, turning another queen. Tex cut a king and picked up the pack. As he shuffled he was careful not to show any of his characteristic motions, for although his opponent had forgotten his face in the score of years behind their former meeting, it might take but very little to start his memory back-tracking.

"My money ag'in' th' roan," said the dealer, pushing out the cards for the cut. "Hundred an' fifty," he explained.

Williams cut deep and nodded. "This one game decides it: a discard, a draw, an' a show-down. Right?"

"Right," grunted Tex, swiftly dropping the cards before them. Williams picked up his hand, but gave no sign of disappointment. There was not a face card in it. He made his selection, discarded, and called for three cards. Tex had discarded two. Williams wanted no face cards on the draw, since he held a pair of nines. One more nine would give him a fair hand, and another would just about win for him. He drew a black queen and a pair of red jacks.

"Well," he said, "ready to show?"

Tex grunted again, glanced at Bud Haines, and lay down three queens, a nine, and a jack. "What you got?" he anxiously asked.

"An empty box stall, I reckon," growled his adversary, spreading his hand. He pushed back without another word to Tex, looked at his stableman and spoke gruffly. "John, give that roan to Mr. Jones when he calls for it. He's to keep it somewhere else. I'm turnin' in. Good night, all."

VI

◆

Friendly Interest

Freshly shaven, his boots well rubbed, and his clothes as free from dust as possible, Tex sauntered down the street after breakfast the next morning and stepped into the stable. John Graves met him, nodded, and led the way to the roan's stall.

"You got a fine hoss, Mr. Jones," he said, opening the gate.

"Yes, I have; an' you've taken good care of him. His coat couldn't be better. I like a man that looks after a hoss."

"I ain't sayin' nothin' about nobody, but I'm glad to see him change owners," said Graves, glancing around. "Rub yore hand on his flank. I got th' coat so it hides 'em real well."

Tex stroked the white nose, rubbed the neck and shoulders, and slowly passed his hand over the flank. The scars were easily found. He wheeled and looked at the stableman. "Who in hell did that, an' why?" he demanded.

"That ain't for me to say, an' sayin' wouldn't do no good; but I'm plumb glad he's in other hands. Just because a hoss fights back when he's bein' abused ain't no reason to cut him to pieces. An' a big man can kick hard when he's mad."

Tex held a lump of sugar to the sensitive, velvety lips before replying. "Yes, he can," he admitted. "Anybody in town that'll treat this hoss right, an' give him a stall?"

"Better see Jim Carney in his saloon. He's a good, reliable man an' likes hosses. He'll take good care of Oh My."

Tex stared at him. "Of what?"

"Oh My," replied the stableman. "Th' rest of th' name is Cayenne."

" 'Suffer little children!' " exclaimed Tex. "Who named him that, an' why?"

"I reckon Williams did, because he's peppery an' red."

"Good heavens!" ejaculated Tex. He thought a moment. "Huh! Prophet! Mecca! Mohammed!" he muttered. Suddenly seeing a great light, he flipped his sombrero into the air, caught and balanced it on his nose when it came down, sidestepped, and as it fell, punched it across the stable. Turning gravely he shook hands with the surprised stableman, slapped him on the shoulder and burst out laughing. "Where'n blazes did he dig 'em up? He don't know what one of them names means; *There was the Veil through which I might not see.* Come, John: *Oh, many a Cup of this forbidden Wine must drown the memory of that insolence!* Wait till I get my hat: *Better be jocund with the fruitful Grape than sadden after none, or bitter, Fruit.*"

Carney gave them a nonchalant welcome and displayed little interest in them until Graves told him about the horse.

"Th' roan, eh?" exclaimed the saloonkeeper. "I'll shore find a place for it, but I'm afraid it'll miss th' beatin's.

There's a closet built across one corner of th' stable: I'll give you a key to it, Mr. Jones. It'll be handy for yore trappin's."

After a few rounds Tex went out, mounted bareback and, leaving Graves in front of the stable, rode to the hotel to get his saddle. Soon thereafter he dismounted at the station and smiled at the agent.

"'Richard is himself again,'" he chuckled, affectionately patting Omar. "An' I still have my kingdom."

"He looks fit for a king to ride," replied Jerry.

"He'd honor a king. How's th' hen ranch comin' along? Got th' fence up yet?"

"Yes; Murphy just finished it. That looks like Williams' roan."

"It was. I won it at poker. I could feel in my fingers that I was goin' to be lucky. Hello!" he exclaimed, looking at a box across the track. On it were painted irregular, concentric circles. "Looks like it might be a target."

Jerry laughed. "It is; and so far, unhit."

Tex glanced at the other's low-hung belt and gun. "Have you shot at it yet?"

Jerry nodded.

"From where?"

"Right here."

"Great mavericks!" said Tex. "Here: let's see how fast you can get that gun out, an' empty it at that box. I got a reason for it."

At the succession of reports the toolshed door flew open and a huge Irishman, rifle in hand, popped into sight. Seeing Tex he grunted and slowly went back again.

Tex looked from the box to the marksman, shook his head, silently unbuckled the belt from its owner's waist, took the empty gun from the agent's hand, and tossed the outfit on a near-by box.

"Don't you carry it, Jerry," he said. "Load it up an' leave

it home. Popular feelin', even in this town, frowns at th' shootin' of an unarmed man. It's somethin' that's hard to explain away."

"But then I'll be defenseless!" expostulated Jerry. "It's *some* protection."

"You were defenseless before I took it from you," said Tex.

"But it is some protection," Jerry reiterated.

Tex shook his head. "It's a screaming invitation for a killin', that's what it is. Here: That's you," pointing to the target. "You got somethin' I want plumb bad. You try to stop me from gettin' it, an' I won't listen to you. I force th' hand an' you make a move that I can claim was hostile. Yo're armed, ain't you? I might even slap yore face. Then this happens."

The spurting smoke enveloped them both, the stabs of flame and the sharp reports coming with unbelievable rapidity. Stepping from the gray fog, Tex pointed. The box was split and turned part way around. The inner two circles showed six holes.

"I did it in self-defense. What chance did you have?" demanded the puncher.

"Great guns! What shooting!" marveled Jerry, his mouth open.

"That's good shootin'," admitted Tex. "Better mebby, than most men in this town can do, quite a lot better than th' average. There's plenty of men who can't do as good. Th' draw was more'n fair, too; better than most gun-toters; but I know two men that would 'a' killed me before I jerked loose from th' leather. I wasn't showin' off: I was answerin' yore remark about a gun bein' some protection to you. While we're speakin' about guns, can Miss Saunders use one? Bein' a woman I hardly thought so, unless Hennery has taught her."

"Henry!" growled Jerry. "Why would he teach her?"

"Why a young woman like her would be right popular,

out here or anywhere else," replied Tex. "House full of admirers, an' others taggin' along. I reckoned Hennery might have showed her how to shoot."

"The devil had a better chance," retorted Jerry. "If Henry ever calls at our house she'll scald him. She thinks about as little of Henry as she does of a snake."

"I'm admirin' Miss Saunders more every day," said Tex. "Havin' disposed of th' interpolation, we'll get at th' main subject. As I was sayin', bein' a woman, she's not likely to be shot at. But I'm sorry yore Colt is so big: she couldn't drag a gun like that around with her. Besides, th' caliber needn't be so big."

"I got a short-barreled .38 at home," said Jerry. He looked a little worried. "What makes you talk like that?"

"Bein' a gunman, I reckon; an' my ornery, suspicious nature," answered Tex. "Bein' a poker player for years, readin' faces is a hobby with me. I've read some in this town that I don't like. 'Taint nothin' to put a finger on, but I'm so cussed suspicious of every male biped of th' genus Homo that I allus look for th' worst. Anyhow, it wouldn't be no crime if Miss Saunders knew how to use that snub-nosed .38, would it? Sort of give her a sense of security. Then, if Murphy or our adolescent Watkins took her out ridin' an showed her how to get th' most out of its limited possibilities, it ought to relieve yore mind."

"I don't know of anyone better qualified to get the most out of a gun than yourself," replied Jerry. "If it ain't asking too much," he hastily added.

"Havin' a brand-new, Cayenne pepper cayuse to learn about, an' show off," laughed Tex, "it wouldn't set on me like a calamity. Shall I bring a horse for Miss Saunders, or saddle up her own?"

"She hasn't any; but—"

"—me no buts," interrupted Tex. "I'll now pay my

respects to yore sister, with yore permission, an' invite her to ride out with me, tomorrow, an' view th' lovely brown hills an' dusty flats, where every prospect pleases, an' only man is vile. Procrastination never was a sin of mine: it's th' one I overlooked. We'll likely go far enough from town so there won't be no panicky fears of a hostile raid. Does Miss Saunders favor any particular hoss?"

"No, and she can ride, so you won't have to get one that's nearly dead."

Tex laughed. "All right; but when she gets it, it won't be as ornery as it might be. How is it that nobody but Murphy paid any attention to our shootin'?"

"They're used to it by this time."

"Well, so-long," and Tex swung into the saddle and rode off.

Jane showed her pleasure at his visit and smilingly accepted his invitation to go riding. They examined the coop and yard, talked of numerous things and after awhile Tex turned to leave, but stopped and grinned.

"Bring your six-gun, Miss Saunders, and we'll have a match," he said. "The great western target, the ubiquitous tin can, is sure to be plentiful, despite the killing drought."

"My gun?" she laughed. "I have no gun. Do you think that I go around with a gun?"

He tapped his forehead significantly. "I'm so used to carrying one that I forgot. Shucks, that's too bad. Well, if we overtake any wild cans you can use mine, although a smaller gun would be more pleasant for you. Too bad you haven't a short-barreled gun—a .32, for instance. Shooting is really great sport. Then I'm to call at two o'clock?"

"If there was some place where we could enjoy a lunch," she murmured. "We could leave earlier and get back earlier."

"There is sure to be," assured Tex, smiling. "Say ten o'clock, then?"

"That will be much better. I'll have everything ready when you come. Is there anything in the eating line which you particularly fancy?"

Tex fanned himself with the sombrero, a happy expression on his face. "Yes, there is," he admitted. "Mallard duck stuffed with Chesapeake oysters. Plenty of cold, crisp, tender celery, and any really good brand of dry champagne. I'll enjoy anything you prepare, and I'll have a round-up appetite."

"I'll try to give you a change from hotel food," she laughed as he swung into the saddle.

She watched him ride away and walked slowly back to the house. Then her face brightened a little as she thought of the revolver in Jerry's room. Jerry had said it was a .38.

The station agent answered the hail and went out to the edge of the platform.

"All fixed?" he asked.

Tex nodded. "You get her to bring that gun. I paved the way for it, but you know her better than I do, and how to persuade her without making her frightened. What's it shoot: longs, or shorts? That's good; shorts are O.K. Is Murphy in th' toolshed?"

"He's married to it," smiled Jerry.

"If you see him, tell him I'm goin' to call on him late tonight. If his light's *out* I'll know he's home. Any fool would know it if it was lit. Well, so-long."

Jerry looked after him and shook his head, a peculiar, baffled, friendly light in his eyes. "I don't know when you are most serious: when you *are* serious, or when you are joking. Was your warning about my gun just a general one, or did it have a special meaning? And about Jane learning to shoot? What do you know, how much do you know, and why are you bothering about us? The Heathen Chinee was simple beside you, Tex Jones."

He coughed and turned to enter the station, but stopped in his tracks as a possible solution came to him. "I wonder, now," he cogitated, and fell into the vernacular. "She's a fine girl, sis is; but headstrong. Cuss it, if it ain't one thing it's another. I don't even know his name is Jones, or how many wives he may have. Oh, well: I'll have to wait and see how it heads."

Tex rode slowly down the street, very well satisfied with himself. He had warned the agent, owned a fine horse that cost him nothing, and was going riding on the morrow with a very interesting and pretty young woman. Suddenly he took cognizance of a thought which had been trying to get his attention for quite some time: Where was Jake and what was he doing?

"I'm gettin' careless," he reproved himself. "I ain't seen my little playmate since I paralyzed his nerve system. He didn't act like a man who would go into retirement with a thing like that tagged to him. I reckon he's plannin' a comeback: but a man like him usually acts quicker. All right, Jake: you take plenty of time an' work it out well. An' that's shore good advice."

There came a sudden yelping from the other side of a nearby building, so high-pitched, continuous, and full of agony that something moved along his spine. He reacted to the misery in the sound without giving it any thought, and when he turned the corner of the store and saw a chained dog being beaten by one of the town's ne'er-do-wells his hand of its own volition loosened the coiled rope at the saddle and swung it twice around his head. The soft lariat leaped through the air like a striking snake, and as it dropped over its victim, the roan instantly obeyed its training.

Jerked off his feet, his arms imprisoned at his sides, the

dog beater slid, rolled, and bumped along the ground, at first too startled to protest. Then his voice arose in a stream of blasphemous inquiry, finishing with a petition.

Tex rode along without a backward glance, deeply engrossed by some interesting problem and nearly had reached Carney's saloon before he became conscious of his surroundings. A miner, cursing, leaped to the roan's head and checked her, shouting profanely at the rider.

Tex checked the horse, looked curiously down at the protestor and then, sensing the burden of the other's remarks and becoming aware of the maledictions behind him, turned languidly in the saddle and looked back in time to see a dust-covered figure stagger to its feet and throw off the slackened rope.

"Hey!" shouted Tex indignantly. "What you doin' with my rope? Think it's worth th' price of a few drinks, eh? You drop it, *pronto!* An' as for you, my Christian friend," he said to the man at the roan's head, "if you ever grab my cayuse like that again me an' you are shore goin' to have an impolite little party all to ourselves. Drop that hackamore."

"You was killin' that man!" yelled the miner, loosening his hold and showing fight.

"Well, what of it?" demanded Tex. "Any man that chains up a dog an' then beats it like he was, ain't got no right to live. If I don't kill him, somebody else will. What you raisin' all th' hellabaloo about?"

"I reckon you ain't far from wrong," said the other, by this time fully aware of the identity of the dog beater. "I'm nat'rally for law an' order. Whiskey Jim ain't no good, I'm admittin'!"

"If yo're for law an' order you must be lonesome associatin' all by yoreself in this squaw town," replied Tex, grinning, but not for one moment losing sight of Whiskey Jim, who at that moment was stooping to pick up a stone lying against the corner of a building. Tex sent a shot over his head and the incident was closed. "What do you do for company?"

"I ain't hankerin' for none," answered the miner, smiling grimly. "I only come in for supplies, an' don't stay long. You a stranger here?"

"That's unkind; but, seein' as how I ain't as much a stranger now as I was when I come, I won't hold it ag'in' you. Mebby I am gettin' to look like I belonged here." He laughed. "I don't know very many, but everybody knows me. They point with pride when they see me comin'; an' cock their guns behind their backs with their other hand. Where you located, friend?"

"Second fork on Buffaler Crick, th' first crick west of town. Quickest way is to foller th' track. Be glad to see you any time. Mine's th' shack above Jake's."

"I envy you," replied Tex. "See much of our mutual friend?"

"Only when he wants to borry somethin'," grinned the other. "I see you got th' pick of Williams' animals under yore saddle."

"I *was* lucky pickin', I admits," beamed Tex. "Nice feller, Williams."

"For them as likes him. Well, friend, I'm mushin' on. Name's Blascom."

"Tex Jones is my *nom de guerre*," replied Tex. "Th' north is a better country than this for minin'. How'd you ever come to leave it?"

Blascom looked at him questioningly. "Yes, reckon it is; but how'd you know I come from there?"

"They don't *mush* nowhere else that I know of," chuckled Tex. He coiled the dusty lariat, shook it, and brushed his chaps where it had touched, waved his farewell; and went on to Carney's, where he dismounted and went in.

"Just met Whiskey Jim," he said across the bar.

"I congratulate you."

"Who's he livin' on?"

"Th' whole town," answered Carney. "He used to hang around here, seein' what he could steal, but I kicked his pants around his neckband an' he ain't favorin' me no more. Reckon he belongs to Williams."

"Then he must do somethin' for his keep," suggested Tex. "Our friend Gustavus Adolphus ain't no philanthropist, I'm bettin'."

"No; Gus is a Republican," replied Carney. "Whiskey Jim used to ride for him, an' mebby Gus is scared not to look after him a little."

Tex nodded. "Good reason; good, plain, practical, common-sense reason. Now, Carney—I want a good hoss for a lady, an' I'll have a little ride on it before I turn it over. Want it tomorrow mornin' at eight o'clock."

"Miss Saunders won't thank you much for tirin' it out."

"You couldn't help guessin' right th' first time," accused Tex. "There ain't no other ladies that I've seen or heard about. What th' lady don't know won't hurt her pride or spoil her appetite. Cuss it, man; I ain't aimin' to kill th' beast!"

"I reckon you know what yo're goin' to do with th' hoss," replied Carney, thoughtfully; "but I wonder do you know what yo're doin', goin' ridin' with that little lady?"

Tex regarded him with level gaze. "Meanin'?" he coldly demanded.

"Meanin' that claim is staked, th' notices posted, an' trespassers warned off; which is a d—d shame!"

"Hearsay ain't no good. I ain't been formally notified in writin'," replied Tex. "Until I am, I act natural; an' after I am, twice as natural, bein' mean by nature an' disposition. All of which reminds me that this is a re-markable town, an' that there's a re-markable man in it."

His companion studied him for a moment. "You should keep yore hat on when yo're ridin' around in th' sun. Th' only remarkable thing about this town is that it's still alive. Th' only remarkable man in it has been buried these last twenty years, up yonder on Boot Hill."

"I'm joinin' issue with you on that," replied Tex. "Th' sense of loyalty an' affection of this town for its leadin' citizen is a great an' beautiful thing for these degenerate, money-mad days. Parenthetically, I wonder if there was ever a time when th' days were anythin' else? Why, everybody is his friend! There's Jake, an' th' nephew, Whiskey Jim, Tim Murphy, Jerry Saunders, John Graves, Blascom, you, an' me. I don't know any more at this writin'. An' that leadin' citizen, a man of culture, wealth, and discernment, is our most esteemed Mr. Gus Williams. Hear! Hear!"

"There's some names you can scratch, Carney among 'em," growled the saloonkeeper, spitting in violent disgust. "Yore touchin' paregoric near makes me weep, an' I'm hard-shelled, like a clam. Two-thirds of th' people here do what he says, because he either scares or fools 'em. Th' rest dassn't lynch him because they ain't strong enough. Wealth? Shore. He got most of it when th' trail was in full swing. His brands, an' he had a-plenty, were copied from some on th' south ranges near th' old trail. A herd comin' up, grazin' wide, or passin' through that scrub an' hill country would near certain pick up a few local head on th' way, cattle bein' gregarious. Whiskey Jim was th' local herd trimmer. He'd throw up a herd, claim any of th' stray brands as belongin' around here. He had th' authority an' th' drawin's of them brands. If it was a herd of Horseshoe an' Circle Dots he claimed every other brand with them that was found this side of th' Cimarron. You know th' rules. He got 'em. Then there was stampedes, an' cattle run off at night. One time it got so bad that there was talk of a third Texan

Expedition to clean it up. Only this one would 'a' been for a different purpose than th' other two."

"You better keep off th' Texas Expedition," said Tex. "That was a covered invasion for th' freedom of th' pore, robbed, browbeaten New Mexicans; an' it come to a terrible end."

"Not th' one I'm referrin' to," retorted Carney, his face set and determined. "Th' second one—that plundered caravans on th' old Santa Fe. I called this other one th' third only because of th' number of men who would have been in it, an' because it was a Texas idea. But we'll not quarrel. I had a good friend in th' second, avengin' th' first."

"I won't quarrel about Texas," said Tex. "Not bein' a Texan, my withers are unwrung. What did Williams do in th' face of that threat?"

"Drifted his herds off before snow flew, to a distant winter range an' let th' trail herds alone."

"That story ain't unusual," observed Tex. "He's a strange man. Picks queer names for his hosses. I never heard such names. Take my roan, now: his name is Oh My Cayenne. That's a devil of a name for anythin', let alone a hoss. Where'd he ever git it?"

Carney laughed. "I'm agreein' with you, but he didn't name th' roan. That hoss was named by Windy Barrett, when he was blind drunk. Windy was a peculiar cuss; allus spoutin' poetry an' such nonsense. Read books while he was line ridin'. Well, he woke up one mornin' after a spree in Williams' stable. As he turned his head to see where he was, th' roan, then a colt, poked its nose over th' stall an' nuzzled him. One of th' boys was just goin' in th' stable an' saw th' whole thing. Windy pushes th' hoss away an' says, sadlike: 'Yo're dead wrong, Oh My Cayenne; it don't banish th' sorrers with its whirlwind sword.' Th' boys thought it was such a good joke they let th' name stick."

Tex looked dubious. "Mebby they thought so, but I'm not admittin' that I do; an' it's no joke for any cayuse to have a name like that. There goes Bud Haines, ridin' out of town: he ain't earnin' his pay. Well, reckon I'll drift up an' see Williams. I allus like to be sociable. So-long."

VII

♦

Weights and Measures

The proprietor of the general store glanced out of the window as the roan stopped before his door and he frankly frowned at Tex's entry.

"Ain't no letters come for no Joneses," he said brusquely.

"Hope springs eternal," replied Tex. He sauntered up to the counter and was about to turn and lean against it when his roving glance passed along a line of widenecked bottles. They looked strangely familiar and he glanced at them again. A label caught his eye. "Chloral Hydrate" he read silently. He looked at Williams and chuckled. "I don't claim to be no Injun, but just th' same I got a lot of patience when it comes to waitin'. Looks like I'm goin' to need it, far as that letter is concerned." He looked along the walls of the store. "You shore carry a big stock for a town like this, Mr. Williams," he complimented, his eyes again viewing the line of bottles with a sweeping glance. "Strychnine," he read to himself, nodding with understanding. "Shore, for wolves an' coyotes. Quinine, Aloes, Capsicum, Laudanum— quite a collection for a general store. Takes me back a good many years." Aloud he said, "I was admirin' that there pipe, an' I've got to have it; but that ain't what I'm lookin' so hard for." Again he searched shelves, up and down, left and right, and shook his head. "Don't see 'em," he complained. His mind flashed back to one word, and his medical training prompted him. "Chloral hydrate—safe in the right hands and very efficient. Ought to be tasteless in the vile whiskey they sell out here. You never can tell, an' I might need every aid." He shook his head again, and again spoke aloud. "Too bad, cuss it."

"If you wasn't so cussed secret about it I might be able to help you find what yo're lookin' for," growled Williams. "Bein' th' proprietor I know a couple of things that are in this store. Yore article might be among 'em."

"I'm loco," admitted Tex. "What I want is some center-fire .38 shorts. Couple of boxes will be enough."

Williams flashed a look at the walnut handle of the heavy Colt at his customer's thigh. He could see that it was no .38. Suspicion prompted him and he wondered if his companion was a two-gun man, with only one of them being openly worn. Such a combination was not a rarity. A gun in a shoulder holster or a derringer on an elastic up a sleeve might well use such a cartridge. This would be well to speak to Bud Haines about.

"You would 'a' saved yore valuable time, an' mine, if you'd said so when you first come in," ironically replied Williams. "Got plenty of .45's, quite some .44's, less .41's, and a few .38's in th' long cat'ridges. I ain't got no .38 shorts, nor .32's, nor .22's, nor no putty for putty blowers. Folks around these diggin's as totes guns mostly wants 'em man-size."

"I reckon so," agreed Tex pleasantly. "Don't blame 'em. Failin' in th' other qualifications they'd naturally do th' best they could to make up for them they lacked. I'm shore sorry you ain't got 'em because my rifle cat'ridges are runnin' low. That's what comes of havin' to buy a gun that don't eat regulation food. It was th' only one he had, an' I had to take it quick, bein' pressed hard at th' time. Time, tide, an' posses wait for no man. Yo're dead shore you ain't got 'em, huh?"

"Well, lemme see," cogitated the proprietor, scratching his head. "I did have some—they sent me some shorts by mistake an' I never took th' time to send 'em back. You wait till I look."

"Then you've got 'em now," said Tex. "You never could sell 'em in these diggin's, where folks as totes guns mostly wants 'em man-size. I'll wait till you see." He idly watched the scowling proprietor as he went behind the counter and dropped to one knee, his back to his customer. As he started to pull boxes from against the wall Tex silently sat on the counter as if better to watch him.

Williams was talking more to himself than to Tex, intent on trying to remember what he had done with the shorts, and save himself a protracted search. "Kept 'em with th' rest of th' cat'ridges till I got mad from nearly allus takin' 'em down for longs. I think mebby I put 'em about here."

Tex leaned swiftly backward, his hand leaping to one of the wide-mouthed bottles on the shelf. "They shore are a nuisance," he said in deep sympathy. "I allus have more or less trouble gettin' 'em," he admitted, his hands working silently and swiftly with the cork. "Didn't hardly hope to get 'em here," he confessed as he swung back and replaced the depleted bottle. He assumed an erect position again, one hand resting in a coat pocket. "Shore sorry to put you to all this trouble," he apologized; "but if you got 'em you are lucky to git rid of 'em, in this town."

Williams turned his head, saw his customer perilously balanced on the edge of the counter, and watching him with great interest. "I can find 'em if they're here, Mr. Jones," he growled. "You might strain yore back, leanin' that way— yep, here they are, four boxes of 'em. Only want two?"

"Reckon I better take all I can git my han's on," answered

Tex. "No tellin' where I can git any more, they're that scarce."

"Yore rifle looks purty big an' heavy for these," observed Williams, craning his neck in vain to catch a glimpse of it. It lay on the other side of the horse.

"Yes, it's one of them *sängerbund,* or shootin'-fest guns," replied Tex. "Made for German target clubs, back in th' East. Got fine sights, an' is heavy so it won't tremble none. Two triggers, one settin' th' other for hair-trigger pullin'. Cost me fifty-odd. Don't bother to tie 'em up; they carry easier if they ain't all in one pocket. Don't forget that pipe."

Williams did some laborious figuring. "I see yo're gettin' acquainted fast," he remarked, pushing the change across the counter. "Them Saunders are real interestin'."

"Oh, so-so," grunted Tex. "Tenderfeet allus are. But I reckon she'll make yore nepphey a good wife."

"Hennery is a fortunate boy," replied Williams complacently, so complacently that Tex itched to punch him. "He'll make her a good husban', bein' nat'rally domestic an' affectionate. An' he's so sot on it that I'm near as much interested in their courtship as they are. I shore would send anybody to dance in hell as interfered with it. Gettin' cooler out?"

"Warmer out, an' in," answered Tex. "Well, they ought to be real happy, bein' young an' both near th' same age. I'm sayin' age is more important than most folks admit. Me an' you, now, would be makin' a terrible mistake if *we* married a woman as young as she is. We got too much sense. An' I'm free to admit that I'm rope shy—don't like hobbles of any kind, a-tall. I'm a maverick, an' aim to stay so. When is th' weddin' comin' off?"

"Purty soon, I reckon," replied Williams, his voice pleasanter than it had been since Tex had appeared in town. "She's nat'rally a little skittish, an' Hennery is sort of shy. Young folks usually are. He was tellin' me you gave him some good advice."

Tex laughed and shrugged his shoulders. "Don't know how good it is," he replied. "An' it wasn't no advice. I just sort of mentioned to him somethin' I found worked real well; but what works with one woman ain't got no call to get stuck on itself—th' odds ain't in favor of its repeatin'. If it was me, howsomever, I'd shore try it a whirl. It can't do no harm that I can see."

"He's goin' to back it a little," responded Williams, "till he sees how it goes."

"A little ain't no good, a-tall," replied Tex. "It might not show any results for awhile, an' then work fast an' sudden. Well, see you later mebby. This cayuse of mine needs some exercise. So-long."

Williams followed him to the door, hoping for a glimpse of the German shooting-club rifle, but Tex mounted and rode away without turning that side of the horse toward the store.

His next stop was the hotel, where he had a few sandwiches put up for him and then he left town, heading for Buffalo Creek. He had no particular object in choosing that direction, the main thing being to get out of town and to stay out of sight until after dark. As he rode he cogitated:

"Chloral hydrate. Twenty to thirty grains is the dose soporific. Yes; that's right. In a hydrous crystal of this nature that would just about fill—what?" He rode on, oblivious to his surroundings, trying to picture the size of a container that would hold the required weight of crystals. "In our rough-and-ready weights a silver half-dime was twenty grains; a three-cent piece was forty grains, and I think my three-cent silver piece of '51 weighed ten grains. But not havin' any of 'em now, all that does me no good. Shucks— there's plenty of miners' scales in this country. Bet Blascom has one that'll help me out: an' a grain is a grain, all th' way through." He hitched up his heavily loaded belt and as his hand came into contact with the ends of the cartridges he chuckled and slapped the horse in congratulation.

"Omar, we're gettin' close. Bet a .45 shell will hold the dose. However, not wantin' to kill nobody, we'd better make shore. Yo're a willin' cayuse, an' I like yore gait: suppose you let it out a little? We got business ahead."

When he came to the dried bed of a creek he followed it at a distance and had not gone far before he espied the first fork. On the north side of the gully was a miserable hut. "That must be Jake's: we'll detour so he won't see us." Twenty minutes later he came to the second fork and a second hut, not much better than the first. A familiar figure was just emerging from it, and soon Tex rode down the steep bank and hailed.

The prospector looked up and waved, turning to face his visitor. "Glad to see you," he called. "Hope Whiskey Jim ain't run you out of town."

"He might if he kept close to me, up wind," laughed Tex. "Busy doin' nothin?"

"Busy as a hibernatin' bear. Git off an' come in th' house, where th' sun ain't so hot. An' I reckon yo're thirsty."

Tex accepted the invitation and found a box to sit on. The interior of the shack was not out of keeping with the exterior, and it was none too clean. His roving glances saw and passed the gold scales, two metal cups hanging by three threads each from a slender, double-taper bar. Beside it was a tin box which he guessed contained weights.

"Washin' out lots of gold, Blascom?" asked Tex, smiling.

"Can't even wash my face without totin' water, or goin' up to th' sump. Th' crick's like it is out there for as far up as I've been. If it wasn't for a sump I've dug in a sandy place in its bed I'd had no water at all." He reached into his pocket and produced several bits of gold, none of them much larger than a grain of wheat. "Found these when I was gettin' water just now. That sump's goin' to go deeper right quick, 'though I'm scared I'll lose my water."

"What'll they weigh?" asked Tex curiously, handing them back.

"About a pennyweight, I reckon," replied Blascom.

Tex shook his head. "Not them. You've got too trustin' a nature. Yo're too hopeful: but I reckon that's what makes miners."

Blascom arose, dropped the flecks into a scale pan and dug around in the tin box. There was a metallic clink and the two pans slowly sought the same level. "Couple of grains under," he announced. "About twenty-two, I'd say. That's close figgerin', close enough for a guess."

"Cussed good," complimented Tex as the prospector put back the weights and dumped the gold out into his hand. "I ain't never dug out no hunks of gold an' I'm curious. If you aim to put that sump down farther I'm just itchin' to give you a hand. Come on—what you say?"

"You'd be a mess, sloppin' around with me," laughed Blascom. He shook his head. "Better set down an' watch me, lendin' yore valuable advice; or stay here an' keep out of th' sun."

"I can do that in town."

Blascom considered, looking dubiously at his guest's clothes. "Here," he said, finally. "You can help me more by carryin' water an' fillin' up everythin' in here that'll hold it. After I get through wrastlin' with a pan in that sump th' water won't be fit to drink before mornin'. That suit you?"

"Good enough," declared Tex, arising and picking up the buckets. "Come on: reveal yore gold mine. I'm a first-class claim jumper. You had yore dinner yet?"

Blascom shook his head, picked up a shovel and his gold

pan and led the way. "That can wait. It ain't often I have any free help forced on me an' I'd be a sucker to let an empty belly cut in."

"I can cook, too," said Tex. "After I fill th' hut with water I'll get you a meal that'll make you glad yo're livin'; but you got to come after it to eat it; an' when I yell, you come a-runnin'. If you don't I'll eat it myself."

The sump lay about a hundred yards up the creek bed, around a bend which was covered with a thin growth of sickly willows and box elders. It was a hole about two feet square, the sandy sides held up by a cribwork of sticks, pieces of boxes, and barrel staves. Blascom dipped both pails in and started back with them.

"Wait a minute," objected Tex, reaching for them. "Thought you was goin' after nuggets while I toted th' water?"

"I thought so, too," answered Blascom, "till I had sense enough to think that I couldn't go rammin' around in there with my shovel until after th' water was saved. You can carry 'em th' next trip. Sit down an' do th' gruntin' for me, this time. A dozen buckets will empty her, almost."

Tex shrugged his shoulders and obeyed, rolled a cigarette, and then plucked a .45 from its belt loop. Wiping off the grease, he placed his thumb against the lead and pushed, turning the cartridge slowly as he worked. When he heard Blascom's heavy, careless tread nearing the bend he slipped the loosened cartridge into his vest pocket and lazily arose.

"There ain't nothin' else to fill but these here buckets," said the prospector as he appeared. Filling them again he passed them to Tex and reached for the shovel and the gold pan. "There's beans you can warm up, an' some bacon. There's also some sour-doughs. Make a good pot of coffee an' yell when yo're ready. I'm surprised at th' way this hole's fillin' up, but I ain't mindin' that. As long as I dump it close by it's bound to get back again."

Tex picked up the buckets and departed clumsily, his high-heeled boots not aiding his progress. Reaching the house he set down his load and wheeled swiftly toward the swaying balance. The pennyweight disk slid into one pan as his other hand brought from his pocket a generous quantity of the whitish, translucent crystals. Sniffing them, he smiled grimly and then nodded as the biting odor gripped his nostrils. He let them drop slowly into the other pan and when the balance was struck he added one more crystal and put the rest back into his pocket. Glancing around the hut he saw a torn, discarded pamphlet in a corner and he removed some of the inner sheets. When he had finished weighing and wrapping he had a dozen little packages of more than twenty-four, and less than thirty, grains. Wiping out the little tray he replaced the weight, drank deeply from a bucket and then started a fire in the home-made rock-and-clay stove. While it caught he went out, picked up some clean pebbles and returned to the scales, soon selecting the pebble that weighed the same as his powders. He might have use for it sometime in the future. Taking another piece of paper he emptied into it the rest of the crystals from his pocket and, sorting out pieces of thickened lint and bits of tobacco, wrapped the chloral up securely. Then he got busy with the meal and when the coffee was ready he went to the door and shouted the old bunkhouse classic: "Come an' get it!"

Blascom soon appeared, his clothing wet and sandy, and in his hand were several rice grains of gold with quite some dust. "Looks fair to me," he said. "I can't hardly tell what I'm doin', th' sump fills up so fast, an' th' sand is washed in with th' water, fillin' it up from th' bottom as fast as I can dig it out an' pan it. I can't understand where all that water comes from. I know there's cussed little of it further down th' crick bed. When she dried up I nat'rally wanted a sump nearer th' hut, but I couldn't get one nearer than I have. Must be a spring somewhere under it." He sniffed cheerfully. "That coffee shore smells good," he declared, going out to wash his hands.

The meal was eaten rapidly, without much talking, but when it was finished Blascom packed his pipe and passed the pouch to his companion. "New pipe?" he asked. "Then wet yore finger an' rub it around in th' bowl before you light her. You don't want a job cookin', do you? I never drunk better coffee."

The new pipe going well, Tex leaned back and smiled. "I'll cook th' supper if you want. I ain't anxious to get back to town before dark. An' I'll put on them old clothes over there an' help you at th' sump th' rest of th' day. Let's get goin'."

"All right; it's a two-man job with that water comin' in so fast," answered the prospector. "We'll not do any pannin'— just get th' sand out an' dump it up on th' bank, out of th' way of high water. I can pan it any time. You see, this dry spell is due to end 'most any time, an' when it does it'll be a reg'lar cloud-burst. That'll mean no more placerin' near th' sump. Ever see these creek beds after a cloud-burst? They're full from bank to bank an' runnin' like bullets."

Tex nodded and looked steadily out of the door, his mind going back some years and vividly presenting an arroyo and the great, sheer wall of water which swept down it on the day when he and his then enemy, Hopalong Cassidy, were fighting it out in the brush. His eyes glowed as the details returned to him and went past in orderly array. From that sudden and unexpected danger, and the impulsive chivalry of the man who had had him at the mercy of an inspired six-gun, had come his redemption.

"Yes," he said slowly. "I've seen 'em. They're deadly

when they catch a man unawares." He drew a deep breath and returned to the main subject. "Why don't you hire somebody, Jake for instance, an' clean up that sump as quick as you can?"

"An' have a knife in my back?" exclaimed Blascom, "or be killed in my sleep? I don't know much about Jake, but what little I do know about him, th' less he, or any of th' fellers in town know about that sump, th' better I'll like it. There ain't one I'd trust, an' most of 'em are busted an' plumb desperate. I've been pannin' a lot better than fair day's wages out here, but I'm doin' without everythin' that I can because I dassn't look so prosperous. Let me show much dust in town an' I'd be raided an' jumped th' same night. They're like a pack of starvin' coyotes. I don't even keep my dust in this shack. I cache it outside at night."

"Suppose you was to buy things in town with coin or bills, lettin' on that it is yore bedrock reserve that yo're livin' on," suggested Tex. "That ought to help some."

"But I ain't got 'em," objected Blascom. "Got nothin' but raw gold."

Tex laughed and dug down into his pocket. "That's easy solved. Here," he said, bringing up a handful of double eagles. "Gold weighs as much in one shape as it does in another—even less, bulk for bulk, without th' alloy. I'll change with you if you want." Then he drew back his hand and grinned quizzically. "It's allus well to think of th' little things. It might be better if we didn't swap. You fellers ain't likely to have a currency reserve: more likely to have it just as you dug it out. That right?"

Blascom nodded. "Yes; 'though I knowed a feller that allus carried big bills in place of gold when he could get 'em, an' when he wasn't broke. They weighed a lot less. Raw gold would be better, out here."

"All right; how'd you like to drop into th' hotel about

eleven tonight an' win heavy from me in a two-hand game of draw? Say as much as we can fix up? How much you want to change? Couple of hundred?" He chuckled. "We can fix it either way: raw gold or currency."

"Make it raw gold, then; better yet, mix it," said Blascom, arising, his face wrinkled with pleasure. He nodded swiftly. "Be back in a minute," and he went out. When he returned he went into a corner where he could not be seen by anyone passing the hut and took several sacks from his pocket. It did not take him long to verify the weights and the cleanness of the gold, he put the odd gold back into a sack and handed the other to his companion.

"Two hundred even," he said. "Keep yore money till I take it away from you tonight. Much obliged to you, Jones."

"How do you know I'll be there?" asked Tex, smiling. "I got th' gold an' a cussed good cayuse. With such a good start it'll be easy."

Blascom chuckled and shrugged his shoulders. "Yore little game with Whiskey Jim an' your soiree with Jake tell me different," he answered. "I've rubbed elbows with all sorts of men for forty-odd years—ever since I was a boy of sixteen. A man's got to back his best judgment: an' I'm backin' mine. If I wasn't shore about you do you reckon I'd be tellin' you anythin' about that sump? Now then: what you say about settin' here an' takin' things easy for th' rest of th' day? I don't want you to get all mucked up."

Tex arose, took the boxes of .38 shorts out of his pockets and lay them on a shelf. He put the heavy little sacks in their places and turned. "It'll do me good; an' I might learn somethin' useful," he said. "A man can't never learn too much. Come on; we'll tackle that sump." As he changed his clothes for those of his host the latter's words of confidence in him set him thinking. To his mind came scenes of long ago. "Deacon" Rankin, "Slippery" Trendley, "Slim"

Travennes, and others of that savage, murderous, vulture class returned on his mental canvas. Of the worst class in the great West they had stood in the first rank; and at one time he had stood with them, shoulder to shoulder, had deliberately chosen them for his friends and companions, and in many of their villainies he had played his minor parts. He stirred into renewed activity and dressed rapidly. Changing the gold sacks into the clothes he now wore and putting on his host's extra pair of boots, he stepped toward the door and then thought of Jake, who reminded him somewhat of his former friends, lacking only their intelligence. He turned and swept up his gun and belt, buckling it around him as he left the shack to help his new friend.

VIII

◆

After Dark

Murphy's blocked-up box car was dark and showed no signs of life, making only a blacker spot in the night. To any prowler who might have investigated its externals, the raised shades and the closed doors would have left him undecided as to whether or not its tenant was within; but the closed windows on such a night as this would have suggested that he was not, for the baked earth radiated heat and the walls of the modest habitation were still warm to the touch. Inside the closed car the heat must have been well-nigh intolerable.

The silence was natural and unbroken. The brilliant stars seemed rather to accentuate the darkness than to relieve it. An occasional breath of heated air furtively rustled the tufts of drought-killed grass, but brought no relief to man or beast; but somewhere along the branch line a stronger wind was blowing, if the humming of the telegraph wires meant anything. In the west gleamed a single glowing eye of yellow-white, where the switch light told that the line was open. To the right of it blotches of more diffused and weaker radiance outlined the windows and doors of the straggling buildings facing the right-of-way. An occasional burst of laughter or a snatch of riotous song came from them, mercifully tempered and mellowed by the distance. From the east arose the long-drawn vocal atrocity of some mournful coyote who could not wait for the rising of the crescent moon to give him his cue. Infrequent metallic complaints told of the contradiction of the heat-stretched rails.

In the south appeared a swaying thickening of the darkness, an elongated concentration of black opacity. Gradually it took on a more definite outline as its upper parts more and more became silhouetted against a sky of slightly different tone and intensity. First a moving cone, then a saucer-like rim, followed slowly by a sudden contraction and a further widening. Hat, head, and shoulders loomed up vaguely, followed by the longer bulkiness of the body.

This apparition moved slowly and silently toward the rectangular blot at the edge of the right-of-way, advancing in a manner suggesting questionable motives, and it paused frequently to peer into the surrounding void, and to listen. After several of these cautious waits it reached the old car, against whose side it stood out a little more distinctly by contrast. The gently rolling tattoo of finger nails on wood could scarcely be heard a dozen feet away and ceased before critical analysis would be able to classify it. Half a minute passed and it rolled out again, a little louder and more imperative. Another wait, and then came a flat *clack* as a tossed pebble bounced from the wall at the waiter's side. Its effect was magical. The figure wheeled, crouched, and a hand spasmodically leaped hip high, a soft, dull gleam tipping it. While one might slowly count ten its rigid posture was maintained and then a rustling not far from the door drew its instant attention.

"What ye want?" demanded a low, curious voice. "If it's Murphy, he's sleepin' out, this night av hell."

The figure at the door relaxed, grew instantly taller and thinner and a chuckle answered the query of the section-boss. "Don't blame you," it softly said, and moved quietly toward the owner of the car.

"To yer left," corrected the Irishman. "Who's wantin' Murphy at this time av night, an' for what?"

"Yore fellow-conspirator," answered Tex, sinking down on the blanket of his companion. "Didn't Jerry tell you to expect me?"

"Yes, he did; but I wasn't shore it was you," replied Murphy. "So I acted natural. Th' house is past endurin' with th' winders an' door closed; an' not knowin' what ye might have to talk about I naturally distrusted th' walls. This whole town has ears. Out here in th' open a man will have more trouble fillin' his ear with other people's business. How are ye?"

"Hot, an' close," chuckled Tex. "Also curious an' lonesome." He crossed his legs tailor fashion, and then seemed to weigh something in his mind, for after a moment he changed and lay on his stomach and elbows. "I don't stick up so plain, this way," he explained.

"I hear ye trimmed old Frowsyhead at poker," said Murphy, "an' won a good hoss. Beats all how a man wants to smoke when he shouldn't. Have a chew?"

"I'll own to that vice in a limited degree and under cer-

tain conditions," admitted Tex, taking the huge plug. "An'
I'll confess that to my way of thinkin' it's th' only way to get
th' full flavor of th' leaf; but I ain't sayin' it's th' neatest."

"'Tis fine trainin' for th' eye," replied Murphy, the twinkle
in his own hidden by the night.

"An' develops amazin' judgment of distance," supplemented Tex, chuckling. "There's some I'd like to try it on—
Hennery Williams, for instance."

"Aye," growled Murphy in hearty accord. "He'll be lucky
if he ain't hit by somethin' solider than tobaccy juice. I fair
itch to twist his skinny neck."

"A most praiseworthy longing," rejoined Tex, a sudden
sharpness in his voice. "How long has he been deservin' such
a reward?"

"Since *she* first came here," growled his companion.
"That was why I wanted Mike Costigan to get his family
out av th' way, for I'm tellin' ye flat, Costigans or no Costigans, that little miss will be a widder on her weddin' day, if
it gets that far. Th' d—d blackguard! I've kept me hand hid,
for 'tis a true sayin' that forewarned is forearmed. They'll
have no reason to watch me close, an' then it'll be too late.
Call it murder if ye will, but I'll be proud av it."

"Hardly murder," murmured Tex. "Not even homicide,
which is a combination of Latin words meanin' th' killin'
of a human bein'. To flatter th' noble Hennery a little, I'd go
as far as to admit it might reach th' dignity of vermicide.
An' no honest man should find fault with th' killin' of a
worm. Th' Costigans should be persuaded to move."

"Ye try it," grunted Murphy sententiously. "Can ye dodge
quick?"

"Nobody ever justly accused me of tryin' to dodge a
woman," said Tex. "There must be a way to get around her
determination."

"Yes?" queried Murphy, the inflection of the monosyllables leaving nothing to be learned but the harrowing details.

"Coax her to go to Willow," persisted Tex.

"She don't like th' town."

"Yore inference is shore misleadin'," commented Tex. "I'd take it from that that she does like Windsor."

"Divvil a bit; but she stays where Mike is."

"Then you've got to shift Mike. There's not enough work here for a good man like Costigan," suggested Tex.

"Yer like a dog chasin' his tail. Costigan stays where th' lass an' her brother are."

"Huh! Damon an' Pythias was only a dual combination," muttered the puncher. "Cussed if there ain't somethin' in th' world, after all, that justifies Nature's labors."

"An'," went on Murphy as though he had not been interrupted, "th' lass sticks to her brother, an' he stays where he's put. He's not strong an' he has a livin' to make for two. Ye can take yer change out av that, Mr. Tex Jones."

Tex grunted pessimistically. "Well, anyhow," he said, brightening a little, "mebby Miss Saunders won't be pestered for a little while by Hennery—an' then we'll see what we see. I'm unlucky these days: I'm allus with th' under dog," and he went on to tell his companion of his suggestions to the nephew.

"'Tis proud av ye I am," responded Murphy. "May th' saints be praised for th' rest she'll be gettin'. We can all av us breathe deep for a little while; an' meanwhile I'll be tryin' my strength with Lefferts, th' boss at th' Junction. I've hated to leave town even that long, but now I can make th' run; 'though I know it will do no good. Ye'll be stayin' in town tomorry?"

"Why, no; I'm goin' ridin' with Miss Saunders," and Tex explained that, to his companion's admiration and delight.

"It'll be a pleasure for her to be able to leave th' house without bein' tagged after by that scut," said the section-boss. "Yer a bye with a head. An' I see where ye not only get th' suspicions av that Tommy lad, but run afoul of that Henry an' his precious uncle. Haven't ye been warned yet?" The gleam of hope in his eyes was hidden by the darkness. "Ye'll mebby have trouble with th' last two—an' if ye do, keep an eye on Bud Haines. Ye'll do well to watch him, anyhow. Why don't ye slip out quiet-like, straight southwest from her house? Less chance av bein' seen; but a mighty slim one. They've eyes all over town."

"We are shore to be seen," quietly responded Tex. "If we sneak out it will justify their suspicions. I don't want to do that. I'm aimin' to ride plumb down th' main street, through th' middle of town, an' pay Tommy a little visit out at his ranch. *There is no shuffling, there th' action lies in his true nature.* Like Caesar's wife, you know. An', by th' way, Tim: we have some friends in town, an' I'm addin' an ally from Buffalo Crick. Time works for us." He paused and then asked, curiously: "Who is our friend Bud Haines, an' what does he do for a livin'? I've my suspicions, but I'd rather be shore."

Murphy swore softly under his breath. "He used to ride for Williams till he earned a reputation as a first-class gunman; but now he follows old Frowsyhead around like a shadder. Cold blooded, like th' rattlesnake he is; a natural-born killer. They say he's chain lightnin' on th' draw."

"I've heard that said of better men than him; some of them now dead," said Tex. "Must be a pleasant sort of a chap." He cogitated a bit. "An' how long has he been playin' shadow to friend Williams? Since I come to town, or before?" he asked as casually as he could, but tensely awaited the answer.

"Couple av years," answered Murphy; "an' mebby

longer." He tried to peer through the darkness. "Was ye thinkin' ye made th' job for him?"

"Well, hardly," replied Tex. "I'm naturally conceited, suspicious, and allus lookin' out for myself. Th' thought just happened to hit me."

Their conversation began to ramble to subjects foreign to Windsor and its inhabitants, and after a little while Tex arose to leave. He melted out of sight into the night and half an hour later rode into town from the west, along the railroad, and soon stopped before the hotel.

The customary poker game was in full swing and he nodded to the players, received a civil greeting from Gus Williams, and after a short, polite pause at the table, wandered over to the bar, where Blascom leaned in black despondency.

"How'd'y," said Tex affably. "Fine night, but hot, an' close."

"Fine, hell!" growled Blascom, sullenly looking up. "Not meanin' you no offense, stranger," he hastily added. "I'm grouchy tonight," he explained.

"Why, what's th' trouble?" asked Tex after swift scrutiny of the other's countenance. "Barkeep, give us two drinks, over yonder," and he led his companion to the table. "No luck?"

Blascom growled an oath. "None at all. My stake's run out, all but this last bag," and he slammed it viciously onto the table. "Th' claim's showin' nothin'." He scowled at the bag and then, avarice in his eyes and desperation in his voice, he looked up into the face opposite him. "This is next to no good: I'll double it, or lose it. What you say to a two-hand game?"

Tex looked a little suspicious. "I don't usually play for that much, rightaway, ag'in' strangers." He looked around the room and flushed slightly at the knowing smiles and sarcastic grins. "Oh, I don't care," he asserted, swaggering a little. "Come on; I'll go you. Deck of cards, friend," he called to the dispenser of drinks, and almost at the words they were sailing through the air toward his hands. "You've got as much chance as I have; an' if I don't win it, somebody else will. Draw, I reckon?" he asked nervously. "All right; low deals," and the game was on.

Blascom won the first hand, Tex the second. For the better part of an hour it was an up-and-down affair, the ups for Tex not enough to offset the downs. Finally, with a big pot at stake he pressed the betting on the theory that his opponent was bluffing. Suddenly becoming doubtful, he let a palpable fear master him, refused to see the raise, and slammed his hand down on the table with a curse. Blascom laughed, grandiloquently spread a four-card flush under his adversary's nose, and raked in his winnings.

"Shuffle 'em up," chuckled the prospector. "Things are lookin' better."

Glancing from the worthless hand into Blascom's exultant face Tex kicked the chair in under him, arose and went to the bar where he gulped his drink, glanced sullenly around the room, and strode angrily to the stairs to go to his room. Wide and mocking grins followed him until he was hidden from sight, the expressions on the faces of Williams and his nephew transcending the others.

The prospector gleefully pocketed the money and dust, sighed with relief and swaggered over to the other table, one thumb hooked in an armhole of his vest. He stopped near Williams and beamed at the players, patting his pocket, but saying nothing until the hand had been played and the cards were being scooped up for a new deal.

"Williams," he said, laughing, "my supplies are cussed low, but now that I can pay for what I want I'm comin' in tomorrow mornin' an' carry off 'most all yore grub."

The storekeeper had glanced meaningly at one of the players and now he lazily looked up, his face trying to express pleasure and congratulation. The man he had glanced at arose, yawned and stretched, mumbled something about being tired and out of luck and pushed back his chair. As he slouched away from the table he turned the chair invitingly and nodded to Blascom.

"Take my place; I'm goin' to turn in soon," he said.

"Why, shore," endorsed Williams. "Set in for a hand or two, Blascom. It's early yet, too early to head for yore cabin. This game's been draggin' all evenin'; mebby it'll move faster if a new man sets in." Waiting a moment for an answer and none being forthcoming, he leaned back and stretched his arms. "How you makin' out on th' crick—bad?"

"Couldn't be much worse," answered the prospector, his face becoming grave. "I can't do much without water, an' th' only water I got is a sump for drinkin' an' cookin' purposes. You know that I ain't th' one to put up no holler as long as I'm gettin' day wages out of it; but when I can't make enough to pay my way, then I can't help gettin' a little mite blue."

"We all have our trials," replied Williams. He waved his hand toward the vacant chair. "Better set in for a little while. You've had good luck tonight: give it its head while it's runnin' yore way. Besides, a little fun an' company will shore cheer you up. You ain't got no reason to be hot-footin' off to yore cabin so early in th' evenin'."

The prospector smilingly shook his head. "I ain't needin' no cheerin' now," he asserted, again slapping the pocket. "I got a little stake that'll let me stick it out till we get rain. I got too much faith in that claim to clear out an' leave it; but now I got still more faith in my luck. It broke for me tonight an' I'm bettin' it's th' turnin' point; an' if a man ain't willin' to meet a turn of good luck at sunrise, with a smile, he shore don't deserve it. At sunup I'll be in that crick bed with a shovel in my hand, ready to go to work. I've been busted before; more'n once; but I don't seem to get used to it, at all. Well, good luck, everybody, an' good night," and he turned and strode briskly toward the door and disappeared into the darkness.

Williams looked disappointed and cautiously pushed the substitute deck farther back in its little slot under the table. Looking around, he beckoned to the unselfish player and motioned for him to resume his seat. The lamb having departed, the regular friendly game for small stakes would now go on again.

"You fellers heard what I said about sand, th' very first night that Jones feller showed up," remarked Williams, chuckling. "I'm sayin' it ag'in: he figgered Blascom was bluffin', played that way until th' stakes got high an' then got scared out an' quit. Quit cold without even feedin' in a few more dollars to see th' hand. Left th' table in a rage just because he lost a hundred or two. I was watchin' him as much as I could, an' I could see he was gettin' madder an' madder, nervouser an' nervouser all th' time; an' when a man gets like that he can't play poker good enough to keep warm in hell. He ain't no poker player; an' as soon as I can buffalo him into a good, stiff game, I'll show you he ain't!"

He paused and looked around knowingly. "He didn't win that roan. I just sorta loaned it to him. Might have to bait him ag'in, too; but before he leaves this town I'll git it back, with all he's got to-boot. There ain't no call for nobody to start yappin' around about what I'm sayin'," he warned.

"I was a-wonderin' about him winnin' that hoss," said the unselfish player as he resumed his seat and drew up to the table. A broad grin spread itself across his face. "Prod him sharp, Gus: we'll get him playin' ag'in th' gang, some night, an' win him naked."

The subject of their conversation was upstairs behind his closed door. He had taken off his coat and vest and was seated facing the washstand, from which he had removed the basin and pitcher. On the bench was a pile of .45s, their bullets greaseless, and he was working assiduously at the slug of another cartridge, his thumb pressing this way and that, and from time to time he turned the shell for assaults on the other side. It was hard on the thumb, but no other way would do, for no other way that he could take advantage of would leave the soft lead entirely free from telltale marks.

Time passed, but still he labored, changing thumbs at intervals. At last, all the leads removed and each one standing against its own shell, he emptied the powder from the brass containers and made a little paper package of it. Going to his coat and taking out the packets of chloral, he put the powder package in their place and returned with them to the bench.

The translucent crystals were of all sizes, some of them too large to be economically contained by the shells, which he had cleaned of powder marks. These crystals were larger only in two dimensions, for in thickness they were practically the same as the others. Doubtful whether the shells would hold a full dose and permit the leads to be replaced, he felt some anxiety as he placed the chloral in the folds of a clean kerchief and began crushing them by the steady pressure of the butt of his Colt. This was slower than pounding, but the latter was too noisy a process under present conditions. Dumping the reduced crystals into a shell lined with paper against possible chemical action on the brass, he gently tapped the outside of the container and watched the granules settle until there was room for the lead. He did not dare tamp it for fear it would not easily empty when inverted.

Pushing home the bullet he up-ended the cartridge and tapped it again to loosen the contents. Shaking it close to his ear, he smiled grimly. The dose was loose enough to fall out readily, large enough to insure its proper effect, and the granules of a size small enough to dissolve quickly. When he had filled and reloaded the last shell he chuckled as he made a slight notch on the rim of each, for they would bear close inspection by weight, sight, and sound, and it was necessary that he mark them to keep from fooling himself.

He put them back into the pocket of the coat and grinned. "As I remember the action of chloral hydrate somebody may lose consciousness and muscular power and sensibility. Their expanding pupils as they wake up will expand under sore and inflamed eyelids. They'll sleep tight and not be worth very much for an hour or two after they do awaken. And these men gulp their whiskey without waiting to taste it, and it is so vile that they'll never suspect an alien flavor, 'specially if it's not too strong. Gentlemen, I bid you all good night: and may you sleep well and soundly."

IX

◆

A Pleasant Excursion

After an early breakfast, early for him these days, Tex went down the street toward Carney's. As he passed Williams' stable he heard hammering, and paused to glance in at the door to see what his friend, Graves, was doing.

The stableman looked up and turned halfway around at the hail. "Hello!" he mumbled through a mouthful of nails. Removing them he nodded at the door. "Tryin' to fasten that lock so it'll do some good. It must 'a' been forced off more'n once, judgin' by th' split wood, which is so old that it ain't much good, anyhow. Th' nails sink into it like it was putty."

Tex was about to suggest the sawing out of the poorest part of the plank and the in-letting of a new piece in its place, but some subconscious warning bade him hold his peace.

"Much ado about nothin', Graves," he said, smiling ironically. "Hoss stealin' is a bigger risk in these parts than it is a profit; an' anyhow, th' slightest noise will wake you up, sleepin' like you do right next to th' door." He examined the wood. "Huh; them splits were made when th' wood was tough—it wouldn't split as dead as it is now: th' nails would just pull out. So you see it was done years ago. Hoss stealin' has gone out of style since then. All you want is a catch to hold it shut ag'in' th' wind." He winced suddenly and held a hand gently against his jaw. "That's all it wants."

"Reckon yo're right," agreed the stableman, glancing curiously at his companion's hand. "What's th' matter? Toothache?"

Tex growled a profane malediction and nodded. "Reckon I'll have to go around an' see th' doc, an' get some laudanum."

"An' pay that thief three prices!" expostulated Graves indignantly. "Chances are he's so drunk he'll give you strychnine instead. Why don't you go up to Williams' store? He's got th' laudanum, an' knows how to fix it up for toothaches an' earaches, I reckon."

"Williams?" queried Tex in moderate surprise. "What you talkin' about? He ain't runnin' no drugstore! What's he doin' with drugs an' such stuff?"

Graves laughed and contemplated the lock with strong disapproval. "No, it ain't no drug-store," he replied. "But th' doc drinks so hard he ain't got no money left to carry a full line of drugs, so Williams carries 'em for him, an' sells him stuff as he needs it. Besides, he allus did sell strychnine to th' ranchers, for coyotes an' wolves—though I ain't never heard it said that any wolves was ever poisoned. Sometimes they do get a coyote—but not no wolves. They've been hunted so hard they just about know as much as th' hunters." He stepped forward and felt of the wood around the lock. "I reckon yo're right," he admitted; "'though while I ain't nat'rally a sound sleeper, it would take quite some racket to wake me up if I'd had a couple of drinks before goin' to bed, which I generally do have. I'll just let her stay like she is."

Tex looked at the lock and at the bolt receptacle on the door jamb. The lock was fastened securely for most people, seeing that the pressure from being pushed inward would not work against it very much; but the receptacle, the keystone of the door's defense, was nailed to even poorer wood than the lock itself and he saw at once that any real strain would force it loose.

"Shore; good enough," he said. "Have an eye-opener?"

Graves accepted with alacrity and in a moment they were smiling across Carney's bar at the good-natured proprietor.

"That hoss ready?" asked Tex when the conversation lulled.

"In th' stall next to th' roan," answered Carney. "Th' stable boys went to Europe last night an' won't be back till tomorrow; but I reckon you can saddle her yoreself."

"I'd rather do it myself," replied Tex.

"Labor of love?" queried Carney, grinning.

"Measure of precaution," retorted Tex, a slight frown on his face.

Carney nodded endorsement. "Can't take too much," he rejoined. "That goes for every kind, too. Nice gal, she is—though a little mite stuck up. I reckon she—"

"Nice day," interrupted Tex, looking straight into the

eyes of the proprietor; "though it's hot, an' close," he added slowly.

"It is that," muttered Carney. "As I was sayin', you'll find both hosses ready for saddles," he vouchsafed with slight confusion.

"Much obliged," answered Tex with a smile, turning toward the rear door. "See you boys later," he said, going out. In a few minutes they saw him ride past on a nettlesome black which put down its white feet as though spurning contact with the earth.

"Whitefoot shore glistens," observed Graves.

"She ought to," replied Carney. He mopped off the bar and looked up. "Beats all how them fellers ride," he observed. "They sit a saddle like they'd growed there. An'," he cogitated, "beats all how touchy some of 'em are. I can't figger him, a-tall," whereupon ensued an exhaustive critique of cowpunchers, their manners, and dispositions.

Meanwhile the particular cowpuncher who had started the discussion was riding briskly northeastward along the trail which he knew led to the C Bar, and after he had put a few miles behind him he took a package from his pocket and sowed black powder along the edge of the trail. After a short while he turned and rode back again.

Jane Saunders answered the knock and smiled at the self-possessed puncher who faced her, hat in hand. "Come in a moment," she invited, stepping aside. "This coffee is hardly cool enough to be put into the bottles, but it won't be long before it is. I am so glad you have brought Whitefoot. I have ridden her before."

"She's quite a horse," he replied. "Gaited as easy as any I ever rode."

She flashed him a suspicious glance. "Then you've ridden her? When, and what for?"

"I thought it would do no harm to learn her disposition,"

he answered carelessly. "She hasn't been out of the stable for two weeks. We had a nice five-mile ride, and she took it with plenty of spirit. She's a good hoss."

After awhile Jane filled two bottles with coffee and placed them with the lunch on the table. Tex took down a blackened tin pail from a hook over the stove and, picking up the bottles and the lunch, went out to his horse, followed by Jane, who had at the last moment buckled on a cartridge belt and the .38 Colt.

Tex looked at them and cogitated. "That'll be quite heavy and annoying, bobbing up and down at every step," he observed. "Why not leave the belt behind and let me slip the gun into my pocket?"

"But I should get accustomed to it," she protested.

"Intend to wear it steadily?"

"No; hardly that," she laughed.

"Then there's no reason to get accustomed to it," he replied. "Surprise is a great factor, because what is known can be guarded against. Will you allow me to advise you in a matter of this kind?"

"Jerry says I couldn't have a better adviser," she replied. She regarded him with level gaze. "Of course, Mr. Jones; but I want to carry it: you have too much without taking it. Frankly, I'm amused by your suggestion that I learn to use it, by Jerry's earnestness that I do learn, and by Tim's fear that I will not. Let us start out by being frank: Why do you think it necessary that I do?"

"Necessary?" asked Tex. "Why, I am not claiming that it is necessary; but I do know that it is a very pleasant diversion. Miss Saunders, there is a great deal said and written about the chivalry of western men. I won't say that most of it, or even nearly all of it is not deserved, for I believe that it is; but I will say that there are men who have no idea of chivalry, honesty, or even decency. You find them wherever men are, be it any point of the compass, or in any stratum of society. The West has some of them, even if less than its proportionate share; and this town of Windsor was not overlooked in their distribution. I know of no particular reason why you should learn the use of a revolver; but we are dealing with generalities. They suffice. With the odds a hundred to one that you never will have need to call upon knowledge of firearms, why refuse that knowledge when it is so easily acquired; and when the acquirement not only will be a pleasure but will lead to further pleasures? Shooting calls for that coordination of nerves and muscles which make all sports sport. And let me say, further, that the feeling of confidence, of security, which comes from the proper handling of a six-shooter is well worth what little effort has been expended to learn its use. Later I hope you will make use of my rifle—after I reduce the powder charges a little—but the short gun should come first. And I would much prefer that you carry it yourself, and make its carrying a habit rather than an exception."

"You are a very difficult man to argue against successfully, Mr. Jones," she said smiling. "I believe, quite the hardest I ever have met."

She took off the belt, slipped the gun inside her waist and hung the belt on a branch of a small tree beside her.

Tex dismounted, took the belt and carried it into the house and, returning, lifted her into the saddle, which she wisely sat astride. Swinging onto the roan he led the way toward town. She was about to speak of the direction when she decided to keep silent, and, glancing sidewise at him, smiled to herself at his easy assurance and rather liked his open defiance of the townspeople. She had no illusions as to what effect their ride together might have in certain minds, and she allowed her feelings, if not her thoughts, to choose her words.

"What a relief it is to have a day's freedom," she exulted, patting the black.

Tex nodded understandingly. "Yes," he said. "Being cooped up and hedged around does get tiresome, I suspect. Well," he laughed, "the fences are all down today. We ride where we listeth and let no man say us nay."

She looked at him smilingly. "Do you know that you are something of an enigma? I'm curious to know what's going on in your head," she daringly declared. "You just said the fences are all down, you know."

He laughed and glanced down the main street, into which they at that moment turned, and a certain grimness came to his face, which she did not miss. "Why allow yourself to be disappointed?" he asked. "Illusions have their worth; and a mystery solved loses its interest. As a matter of fact, the less that is known of what goes on in my head, the better for my reputation for wisdom and common sense. It reminds me of the mouse in the cave."

"Yes?"

"Yes. It was such a big cave and such a little mouse," he explained. "And except for the little mouse the cave was empty."

"I admire your humility; it is refreshing, especially in this country; but I fear it is a very great illusion. Like the other illusions to which you just referred, has it its worth?"

"Confession is good for the soul, and always has worth."

While he spoke he saw a lounger before the hotel come to startled life and hurry inside. Down the street three conversing miners stopped their words to stare open-mouthed at the two riders nonchalantly jogging their way. The door of the hotel became jammed and curious, surprised faces peered from its dirty windows, among them the angry countenance of Henry Williams.

The ordeal of proceeding naturally and carelessly down

that street under such frank scrutiny would have tried the balance of any poise, and Jane, flushing and trying to ignore the stares, flashed a searching glance at her companion and felt a quick admiration for him. She could imagine Tommy under these conditions. For all she could detect, her companion might have been riding across the uninhabited plains with no observing eyes within a day's ride of him. Swaying rhythmically to the motion of his horse, relaxed, unconcerned, and natural, he talked with ease and smoothness; and unknowingly made an impression on her which time never would efface.

"That simile of the mouse in the cave," he was saying, "naturally sets up a train of thought—all thought being an unbroken, closely connected, although not necessarily manifest to us, concatenation—and leads to the ass in the lion's skin, being helped materially by the great number of asses in sight, despite the scarcity of even the skins of the nobler beasts. The dual combination does not end there, however; there are jackals in lobos' hides, and vultures posing as eagles. Even the lowly skunk has found a braver skin and bids for a reputation sweeter to bear than the one earned by his own striking peculiarity. For such a one there is nothing so disconcerting as a six-gun appearing from a place where no six-gun should be—and it loses none of its potency even if the bore be small and the charge light. Have you ever had the opportunity to study animals at close range, Miss Saunders?"

His companion, bent over the saddle horn in her mirth, gasped that she never had enjoyed such an opportunity, especially before today, whereupon he continued.

"The ass in the lion's skin was all right and got along famously until he brayed," he explained; "but the skunk fools no one for one instant, not even himself. He can't even fool Oh My, here," and he slapped the glossy neck of the roan.

"Who?" demanded Jane, her face red from laughter.

"Oh My; my horse," he answered. "He was named by one Windy Barrett, when that person awakened from a stupor acquired by pouring libations to Bacchus. The rest of the name is Cayenne."

"Why, that's an exclamation, not a name—Oh!" Jane went off into another fit of laughter. "*Omar Khayyam!* Isn't that rich! Whatever did you do when you heard it?"

"I led Graves to the tavern door agape," answered Tex, grinning.

By this time they had swung into the trail leading to the C Bar and the miles rolled swiftly behind them. Suddenly Tex touched his companion's arm, both reining in abruptly. Squarely in the middle of the trail was a rattlesnake, huge for the prairie, and it coiled swiftly, the triangular head erect and the tail whirring.

"Ugh!" exclaimed Jane, a wave of revulsion sweeping over her. "What a monster! Can you shoot it from here?"

Tex nodded. "Yes, but while I usually do, I rather dislike the job. He's a snake all right, man's hereditary enemy since the world was young, and the hatred for him comes to us naturally. Sinister, repellant, and all that, that chap is as square as any enemy in the wild, and he is coolly business-like. He hasn't a friend outside his own species, and even in that is to be found one of his chief enemies. There he lies, for all to see, his gauntlet thrown, whirring his determination to defend himself, and to depart if given a chance. Look at those coils, their grace and power, not an ungainly movement the whole length of him. Look at his markings— from the freshness of his skin and its vivid coloration I'd say he has very recently parted with his old skin, and the parasites which infected it. You shed your skin in vain, Old-Timer—you'll not enjoy it long," and his hand dropped to the holster. A flash and a roar, a rolling burst of smoke, and the defiant head jerked sidewise, hanging by a few shreds of muscle to the writhing coils. "'Dead for a ducat, dead!'" quoted Tex, leading the way past his victim.

A little farther on he pointed to a track along the side of the trail.

"Dog or wolf," he said. "They're identical except for directness. A dog's track wavers, a wolf's does not. From the fact that it follows the trail I'd say that was a dog; but it may puzzle us before we lose it. He was a big animal, though, and if a wolf he's a lobo, the gray buffalo wolf, cunning as Satan and brave as Hector. And what a killer! No carrion for him, no meat killed by anyone but himself, and usually he's shy about returning to that. He creates havoc on a cattle range. Poison he sneers at, and it takes mighty shrewd trapping to catch him. To avoid the scent of man is his leading maxim. Before the snow comes he is safe—afterwards his troubles begin if a tracer crosses his trail."

"Why I thought he was a big coyote," said Jane. "You make him out to be quite a remarkable animal."

"And justly," responded her companion. "Coyote? They shouldn't be mentioned together in the same breath. The buffalo gray is a king—the coyote a crawling scavenger, with wits in place of courage. The difference in the natures is indicated graphically by the way they hold their tails. The coyote's droops at a sharp angle, but the lobo's is held straight out. A single wolf is more expensive to ranchers now than he once was, because he has been hunted so hard with traps and poison that he now has learned not to eat dead animals, and in some cases even to ignore his own kill after once he has left it. I've heard of several wolves, each of which have been blamed for the killing of sixty cows in a year, and their score might have run quite some higher. Have you been watching this track? I'd say it's wolf—and as direct as an arrow. And there is the great western target—tomato, from the color of it. Suppose you try your hand at it?"

Jane produced the pistol and listened intelligently (and how rare a gift that is!) to all her companion had to tell her. When the pistol was emptied the can was still untouched. Laughing, Tex dismounted, and drew a long rectangle in the sand, with the can in the median line and to one end.

"The ground laying flat instead of standing up like a man," he explained, "I had to figure on your line of vision. If the upper half of a man's body were placed on the line nearer you, his head would just about intercept your view of the farther line. Now your third and sixth shots, having struck inside the four lines, would have hit a man at that distance. I'd say you hit his stomach with the third shot, and his right shoulder with the other. The can is of no moment, for cans are not dangerous; but when I show you how to reload, I want you to aim at the can, as if it were the buckle of a belt. You take to that Colt like a duck takes to water—and by the way, Miss Saunders, if I were you, carrying that gun as you must carry it, I'd leave one cartridge out, and let the hammer rest on the empty chamber."

The lesson went on, his pupil slowly becoming enthused and finding that it truly was a sport. When she had made four out of five in the marked-off space she was greatly elated and would have continued shooting after she was tired, but her tutor refused to let her.

"That is enough for now," he laughed. "On our way back you may try a few more rounds if you wish. No use to tire yourself, especially after such a creditable showing. In these few minutes you graduated out of the defenseless-woman class, and may God help anybody who discounts your defense. You see, the main thing is not the shooting, but the freedom from fear of weapons and knowing how to use them. There is nothing mysterious about a Colt—it won't blow up, or shoot behind. Whatever timidity you may have had about handling one has been overcome, and in a few minutes you have learned to hold it right and to shoot it. The bare threat of a gun held in capable hands is in most cases enough. Now, if you please, I'll try my left hand at the can. I wear only one gun, but it may be necessary to wear two—and while my left hand has been trained to shoot well, this is a good opportunity to exercise it."

Filling the can with sand and dirt to weigh it against rolling, he stepped back twenty paces, tossed his own Colt into his left hand, dropped the butt to his hip and sent six shots at the crimson target. Stepping from the smoke cloud he advanced and examined the can. One bullet had clipped its upper edge, another had grazed one side, while the other four were grouped in the sand within a radius only a little larger than that of the target.

"That wouldn't do for two of my friends," he laughed, "but it's good enough for me. Not a shot would have missed the target I had in mind. Had I shot as quickly as I could, I might have missed the target altogether, but close enough for practical purposes. On the other hand, had I taken a little more time, the score would be better."

Jane's mouth still was open in delighted surprise. "Do you mean to tell me that anyone can do better than that, from the hip, without sighting at all?" she demanded incredulously.

"Oh, yes," he replied, reloading the weapon. "Quite some few, notably those two friends of whom I spoke. You see I am satisfied in attaining practical perfection in my left hand, knowing that my other is skilled to a higher degree; but my friends must spend their time and cartridges painting the lily. Either Johnny or Hopalong would feel quite chagrined if at least five hadn't cut into the can. You should see them shooting against each other, breaking matches to get the exact measurements and arguing as if a fortune depended on it. Why, Miss Saunders, either of them could walk into Williams' hotel on a busy night, give warning, and empty two guns in less than ten seconds, every shot hitting a man. They have faced greater odds than that, both of them."

"You mean that one man could defeat a crowd like that?"

"Exactly; but they would not have to fire a shot," he said, smiling. "You see, such a man would only have to throw down on the crowd to hold them in check, if they know he will go through with his play. It isn't unlike an arch. The keystone in this case is the fear of certain death to the man who leads. The first man in the crowd to make a play would die. To some people martyrdom has a morbidly pleasant appeal as an abstract proposition; but in a concrete state, where the suffering is not vicarious, it really has few devotees. And here is a psychological fact: every man in the front rank of such a crowd is fully convinced that he has been selected for the target if the rush starts. Hopalong and Johnny would go through with their play if their hand was forced, and they are the kind of men whose expressions assure that they will. It is a great comfort to have them with you if you must enter a hostile town. It's a gift, like the gift of keener, swifter reflexes."

"It seems so impossible," commented Jane. "Won't you please try your other hand at a can? Somehow I felt that the snake was killed by accident more than skill. It seemed absurd, the offhand way you did it."

"This really is no test," he responded, filling another can and stepping back as he shifted the weapon to the right hand. "There is not the tenseness which a great stake causes; but, on the other hand, there is not the high-tension signals to the muscles. Watch closely," and the jarring crashes sounded like a loud ripping. One hole through the picture of a perfect tomato, two just above it, two lower down, and the sixth on the upper edge of the can gave mute testimony that he shot well.

She fairly squealed with delight and clapped her hands in spontaneous enthusiasm. "Wonderful! Wonderful! Oh, if I ever could shoot like that! I don't believe those friends can even equal it, and I don't care how good they are." Her face beamed. "But that must have taken a great deal of practice."

"Years of it," he replied, "coupled to a natural aptitude. While the accuracy is good enough, that is of secondary consideration. Had only one bullet struck the target, or grazed it, the other five would not have been necessary. The speed of the draw is the great thing. Any man used to shooting a revolver can hit that mark once in six—but he is far from a real gunman if he can't beat ninety-nine men out of a hundred in firing the first shot. That is what counts with a gunfighter. His target is almost any place between the belt and the shoulders. If he strikes there and does not kill his man he will have time for a second shot if it is needed. My left hand is as deadly as my right against a living target so far as accuracy is concerned; but pit it against my right and it would be hopelessly lost, dead before it could get the gun out of the holster. And Hopalong Cassidy twice gave me lessons in the fine art of drawing—once in an exhibition and the second time in what would have been mortal combat if he had not allowed his heart to guide his head. I did not in the least merit his mercy. I had lived a wild, careless life, Miss Saunders; but it changed from that day."

"Jerry told me why you made him give up wearing his revolver," she said, thoughtfully. "I did not fully appreciate his words; but the graphic exposition lacks nothing to be convincing. Was your interest in his welfare another of your generalities?"

Her companion laughed. "Jerry is a very likable chap, Miss Saunders. Knowing that some feeling against him existed, and not knowing into what it might develop, I only followed the promptings of caution. He is a gentleman and a man infinitely finer grained than the rest of the inhabitants of Windsor. He is honorable and he lacks insight into the common motives which impel many men to perform acts he would not countenance. I have knocked about the West for twenty years, seeing it at its best and at its worst—and you simply cannot conceive what that worst is. I have met many Gus Williamses and Jakes and Bud Haineses and Henry Williamses. They are almost a distinct variation of the human species; they are a recognized and classified type. I knew them all as soon as I saw them. Bud Haines is a natural killer. He'd kill a man at a nod from the man who hired him. Gus Williams hires him, knowing that. Henry, the nephew, is foul, a sneak, and a coward. I'd rather see a sister of mine in her grave than married to him. But he is Gus Williams' nephew, the second power in town and must not be overlooked; and he never will know how close to death he has been these last few days. It fairly has breathed in his face. But we've had enough of this: not far ahead is a fairly good place for our lunch, unless you would prefer to go on to the C Bar."

"Why have you mentioned the nephew to me?" demanded Jane, her cheeks flushed and a fear in her eyes.

"Did I single him out?" asked Tex in surprise. "Why, I only mentioned him, along with the others, while giving examples of a detestable type and to explain why Jerry should not go about armed. I hope I have not frightened you, Miss Saunders?"

"You have not frightened me," she answered. "I have been frightened for a long time. We are so helpless! Things which bother me, I dare not speak to him about them, for he only would get into trouble and to no avail. He cannot pick and choose; and I must stand by him, no matter where he goes, or what he does. Is there mercy in heaven, is there justice in God, that we should be so circumscribed, forced by ills hard enough in themselves to bear, into still greater ills? Jerry's lungs would be tragedy enough for us to bear; but when I look around at times and see—do you believe in God, Mr. Jones?"

"What I may or may not believe in is no aid to you, Miss Saunders," replied Tex, amazed at his reaction to her distress. It was all he could do to keep from taking her in his arms. It was a lucky thing for Henry Williams that he finally abandoned the idea of following them. "If you have been taught to believe in a Divine Power, then don't you turn away from it. To say there is no God is to be as dogmatic as to say there is; for every reasoning being must admit a First Cause. It is only when we characterize it, and attempt to give It attributes that differences of opinions arise. I am not going to enter into any discussion with you on subjects of this nature, Miss Saunders. Nor am I going to tell you what my convictions are. They do not concern us. If you have any religious belief, cling to it: this is when it should begin paying dividends."

"Have you read Kant?"

"Yes; and Spencer tears him apart."

"You are familiar with Spencer?"

"As I am with my own name. To my way of thinking his is the greatest mind humanity ever produced—but, with your permission, we will change the subject."

"Not just yet, please," she said. "You admire his logical reasoning?"

"I refuse to answer," he smiled. "Here, let me give you an example of logical reasoning, Miss Saunders. Here are two coins," he said, digging two double eagles out of his pocket, "which, along with thousands of others, we will say, were struck from one die. You and I would say that they are identical, especially after the most thorough and minute examination failed to disclose any differences. I hardly believe that any man, no matter how much he may be aided by instruments of precision, can take two freshly minted coins from the same die and find any difference. But what does pure logic say?"

"Certainly not that there is any difference?" she challenged in frank surprise.

He chuckled. "That is just what it claims, and here is the reasoning: No one will deny that the die wears out with use, which is the same as saying that the impressions change it. To deny that they do is to say that it does not wear out, which is absurd. Therefore each impression, being a part of the total impressions, must have done its share in the changing. And each impression, having changed it, must be different from those preceding and following it. Now, if the die changes, as we have just proved that it does, so must the coins struck off from it, for to say otherwise is to claim that effects are not produced by causes, and that a changed die will not make changed coins. Therefore, there are no two coins absolutely alike, never have been, and never can be, even at the moment they leave the die. Put them into circulation and the hypothetical differences rapidly increase, since no two of the coins can possibly receive the same treatment in their travelings. There you have it, in pure logic: but does it get you any place? On the strength of it, would you persist in denying that these coins are dissimilar? Are they so practically? And it is from practical logic that we draw the deductions by which we think and move and live. So you take my word that it will be better for you to cling to whatever faith you may have. If it is not practical enough for you, I'll look after that end for you; and between your faith and the cunning of my gun-hand I'll warrant that your brother will come to no harm. Shall we lunch at the C Bar, or in that little clump of burned and sickly timber on the bank of that dried-up creek?"

"I'm really too hungry to postpone the lunch," she said, smiling; "besides I want to watch you in camp, and to listen to you. It seems to me that you have too keen a brain to be spending your life where it all is wasted."

"Your compliment is disposed of by the fact that I am what I am," he responded. "The return compliment of not being able to be in a better place, under present conditions, is so obvious that I'll not spoil its effect by saying it. Anyhow, a fair vocabulary and a veneer of knowledge are not the measures of wisdom, but rather a disguising coat. To come right down to elementals, I heartily agree with you about the lunch. I'll be better company after the inner man has been properly attended to, for food always leavens my cynicism. Did I hear you ask why I do not eat continually?"

The clump of browned trees reached, it took but little time to unpack the lunch and start a cunningly built fire of twigs and broken branches, over which the coffee quickly heated. Depressing as the surroundings were, barren and sun-baked as far as eye could see, the bed of the creek dried and cracked and curling, this scene was destined to live long in the memory of Tex Ewalt. The food, better cooked and far more daintily prepared than any he could recall, tasted doubly good in the presence of his intelligent, good-looking companion. The subjects of their interested discussions were wide in range and neither very long maintained a certain restraint which had characterized their earlier conversations. She led him to talk of the West as it was, as he had seen it, and as he hoped it would become; a skillful question starting him off anew, and her intelligent comments keeping him at his best. So absorbed were they that even he failed to hear the step of a horse and did not know of its presence until an eager, if timid, hail stopped him short.

"Gosh, you people look cheerful," called Tommy Watkins, gazing at Jane with his heart in his eyes.

"Sorry I can't say the same about your looks," chuckled Tex, his quick glance noting the boyishness of their visitor, his youthful freshness and the rebellious admiration in his unblinking eyes. Tex took himself in hand and crushed the feeling of jealousy which tingled in him and threatened to show itself in words, looks, and actions. He looked inquiringly at his companion and at her slight nod, he beckoned to the youth. "Come over here an' make it three-handed, cowboy," he called. "We'll salvage what we can of th' lunch an' feed it to you. Did you find the ranch there, when you got home th' other night?"

Tommy rode up and gravely dismounted. "Yes, it was there. They said you hadn't been around so far as they knew, so I had my hasty ride for nothin'. How'd'y do, ma'am?" he asked, his hat going under his arm.

"Very well, indeed," replied Jane, smiling and fixing a place for him at her other side. "I'm sorry you did not come while there was more to eat, although I'll confess that I am not apologizing for my share of the havoc. It has been a long time since I have enjoyed a meal as I have this lunch. Sit here, Mr. Watkins—I am glad that there is some coffee left."

"That's what I get for being thrifty and thinking of the future," laughed Tex. "It's like the men who work hard and save all their lives, so that someone else can spend for them. Here you go, Thomas: look out—it's still hot."

"Thank you ma'am," said Tommy, flushing and embarrassed, as he dropped onto the spot indicated. "I ain't a bit hungry, though."

"You will be after the first bite," assured Tex. "The cups

have been used, and there's no water for washing them. That's excuse enough for any man to drink out of the pail, and I envy you there, Tommy Watkins. Cattle gettin' along all right in spite of the drought? Expect to have a big gain this round-up? They ought to bring top-notch prices if they're in good shape."

Steered easily into familiar channels of conversation, Tommy got on well, so well that his embarrassment gradually disappeared and he was nearly his natural self; but he did envy his friend's ability to think coherently and to talk with fluent ease on any subject mentioned. Jane Saunders learned more about cows, cattle, steers, calves, cows, cattle, riding, roping, round-ups, branding, cows, calves, horses, cattle, and other ranch subjects than she thought existed to be learned. And she shot a glance of grateful appreciation at Tex Jones for the way in which he put their guest on his feet and kept him there through several vocal flounderings. It was so tactfully done that Tommy did not realize it.

Gradually Tex worked out of the conversation and studied his companions. He saw clean youth entertaining clean youth; a bubbling mirth free from suspicion or irony; an absence of cynicism, and an unbounding faith in the future. He hid his smile at how Tommy was led to talk of himself and of his ambitions. They looked to be about the same age, Tommy perhaps a few years her senior; and when she looked at Tommy there was friendliness in her eyes; and when Tommy looked at her there was a great deal more in his.

The keen, but apparently careless, observer silently and fairly reviewed the years that had passed since he had been at Tommy's age; the lack of illusions, the cold, cynical practicality of his thoughts and actions; the laws, both civil and moral, which he contemptuously had shattered. He could not remember the time when he had had Tommy's faith in men, nor his enthusiasm. Tommy was looking forward to a life of clean, hard work, and actually with a fierce eagerness. Never had such a thing been an impelling motive in the life of Tex Ewalt. Instead he had planned shrewdly and consistently how to avoid working for a living, and when it was solved, then how to live higher and higher with the least additional effort. And he now admitted that if he had the chance to live that period over again, under the same circumstances, he would repeat his course in the major things. He felt neither regret nor remorse at the contrast—he had lived as it pleased him, and the Tex Ewalt of today had no censure for the Tex Ewalt of yesterday. But he was fair, at all events; and to draw true deductions from accepted facts was an art not to be perverted because expediency might beckon. After all, he did not try to fool himself; and he was no hypocritical whiner. Being fair, he calmly realized that he was the unfitting unit of this triangle, that he did not belong there. But there would be time enough for such cogitation later on.

"Shore," Tommy was dogmatically asserting. "Th' rattler gets all cramped up an' tired, an' there is an instant when he can't turn fast enough to keep his nasty little eyes on th' other, that's racin' around him like a flash. That's th' end of th' rattler. Th' kingsnake darts in, grabs th' rattler behind th' head, an' after a great thrashin' around, kills him dead. *Ain't* that so, Mr. Jones?"

Tex lazily turned his head and looked at the doubting auditor and then at the anxious Tommy. He gravely nodded. "Yes that's th' end. That's the enemy within the snake's own species which I mentioned back on the trail, Miss Saunders."

The look of doubt faded from her face and a nebulous smile transformed it. She was certain of it now.

Tex flamed at what that change told him, tingling to his finger tips with a surging elation. He felt that he had but to speak three words to put her vague feelings into a coherent wonder of wonders; but to crystallize them into an everlasting passion by the alchemy of his avowal, or the touch of his lips. The lulled storm within him broke out anew and blazed fiercely. He arose, kicked an inoffensive tin can over the bed of the creek and spun it in mid-air by a vicious, eye-baffling shot from his Colt. Realizing how he had forgotten himself, and his resolutions, he, the cool, imperturbable Tex Ewalt, he recovered his poise and bowed, smilingly, to the surprised pair.

"That's shootin', Tex!" cried Tommy.

"It's more than that," smiled Tex. "It's notice that it's time to try that .38, Miss Saunders," he announced. "She is learning to use a gun, Tommy—I've been telling her how much fun it is. I'll call th' shots while you stand by her to answer questions. Suppose we have a more suitable target, this time. What can we use?"

Tommy grinned expansively. "Who's goin' to do th' shootin'?" he demanded.

"Miss Saunders," answered Tex. "Why?"

"Oh; all right then—here, prop up my hat," offered Tommy; "But not too all-fired close!" he warned.

"There's chivalry for you, Mr. Jones!" triumphantly exclaimed Jane, her eyes dancing.

"Think so?" queried Tex, grinning. "Huh!" He shook his head. "I'd say he is not paying you any compliment. Just for that I hope you shoot it to pieces."

He took the sombrero from Tommy's extended hand, went down and crossed the creek bed, and placed the hat against the opposite bank. Stepping off twenty paces he drew a line on the earth with the side of his boot sole and beckoned to the flushed markswoman.

"That hat is a pressing danger," he warned. "You've got

to get it, or it'll get you. Don't be careless, and don't waste any sympathy on the grinning wretch who owns it."

"But I don't want to ruin it," she protested. "Surely something else will answer?"

"You go ahead an' ruin it, if you can," chuckled Tommy. "Don't *you* worry none—I ain't!"

"I do believe it wasn't a compliment, or chivalry, at all," she laughed. "All right, Mr. Watkins: here goes for a new hat!" Slowly, deliberately, holding her arm as she had been instructed, she aimed and fired until the weapon was empty. The hat had a hole near one edge of the crown and another near the edge of the brim.

"Glory be!" exclaimed Tommy. "I'm votin' for a new target! Why that's plumb fine, Miss Saunders—if it ain't an accident!"

"Let's see if it was," suggested Tex, handing her another round of cartridges. "Here!" he exclaimed, glancing at Tommy. "Where you goin' so fast?"

"To collect th' ruins," retorted the puncher over his shoulder. "*You* got a hat, ain't you?"

"I have, and I'm keeping it right where it belongs," rejoined Tex. "I didn't suggest that it was any accident, did I?"

Speed and Guile

Tex and Tommy said their adieus, watched Jane enter the house, and then rode slowly toward the station where, after a few words with Jerry Saunders, Tommy went on alone, leaving Tex talking with the agent.

The C Bar puncher rode down the main street full of more kinds of emotion than he ever had known before, and among them was a strong feeling of his inability to gain Jane's attention while Tex Jones was around. Jealousy was working in the yeasty turbulence of his heart and mind. Taking off his perforated sombrero he gazed at it as though it were something sacred. There they were, two of them, made by her blessed bullets! Reverently pushing the ragged felt of their rims back into place, he patted the nearly closed holes and put the sombrero on his head again. There would be no new hat for Tommy Watkins, as she had laughingly said. No, sir! No, sir-e-e!

Opposite the hotel he became aware of his surroundings and suddenly decided that he needed a drink to steady himself, to shock himself into a more natural condition of mind. As he made the decision, he idly observed Bud Haines emerge from the door of the general store and start toward him on the peculiar, bow-legged, choppy stride he so much affected. And as Tommy swung off the horse and carelessly tossed the reins across the tie-rail he caught sight of Tex Jones waving to the agent and slowly wheeling the roan.

Tommy made his way through the card-table end of the room, noticing without giving any particular weight to the fact, that he was the cynosure of all eyes. Still strange to himself and very much occupied by his thoughts, he did not note whether there were six or two dozen men in the room; nor that their eager and low-voiced conversation abruptly ceased upon his entry, and that there was an air of expectancy which seemed to fill the room. He passed Henry Williams, who was seated at a small table, with a nod and rested his elbows on the bar. Silently a bottle and glass were placed before him, silently he poured out a drink and downed it mechanically. Then Henry spoke, his ratlike eyes for a moment not shifting.

"That's a fenced range," he said in a low, tense voice. "You keep off it!"

Tommy, not realizing that the words were intended for him, still rested his elbows on the bar, his back to the speaker and the rest of the room, buried in his abstractions. He neither saw nor heard the quiet, quick entry of Bud Haines through the front door, nor knew that the gunman stopped suddenly and leaned against the jamb. Neither he, nor anyone else, caught the quiet step nearing that same door from the street.

Henry Williams, finding his warning totally ignored, let his anger leap to rage.

"You!" he snarled. "I'm talking to *you,* Watkins!"

Tommy started and swung around, momentarily out of touch with his surroundings. The meanness in the voice, the deadly timbre of it, warned him subconsciously rather than acutely, and he stared at the speaker.

"What you say, Williams?" he asked, rapidly sensing the hostility in the air. "I was thinkin' of something'," he explained.

"I'm givin' you somethin' to think about!" retorted Henry, slowly arising and slowly leaning forward on the table. "You don't want to stop thinkin' about it, neither—unless you want to join th' dead uns on Boot Hill. I said that range is fenced—*you keep off!*"

Tommy, alert as a coiled snake now, watched the angry man while he considered. A fenced range. He was to keep off. "I ain't gettin' th' drift of that," he said, slowly. "Any reason why you shouldn't talk so I'll know what yo're meanin'?"

"Yo're dumb as hell, ain't you?" sneered Henry, his voice rising shrilly and the little, close-set eyes beginning to flame. "I wouldn't have nobody say you wasn't warned plain. I'm tellin' you for th' last time, to do yore courtin' somewhere else! I'm claimin' that Saunders gal. Keep away, that's all!"

Tommy went a little white around his stiffening lips. When his words came they sounded the spirit of the C Bar, but where they came from he did not know; perhaps he had heard them or read them somewhere. Certainly they did not by right belong to his direct method of conveying thought. He knew Henry Williams, his baseness, his petty villainies, his bestial nature. The picture of Jane, innocent and sweet, came to him and made a contrast which sickened him. Looking straight into Henry's eyes his voice rasped its insulting, deadly reply.

"It's bad enough for a coyote like me to admire a rose; but I'm d—d if any polecat's goin' to pluck it!"

Before the words were all spoken and before either of the disputants could move they heard the startling crash of a gun and instinctively glanced toward the sound. They saw Bud Haines, his smoking revolver forced slowly up behind his back, higher and higher, the gun wrist gripped in the sinewy fingers of Tex Jones, whose right hand held his own Colt at his hip, the deadly muzzle covering the two in front of the bar, without a tremble of its steely barrel. His gripping fingers kept on twisting, while one knee held the killer from writhing sidewise to escape the grip of the punishing bending of the imprisoned arm. Slowly the tortured muscles grew numb, slowly beads of perspiration stood out on the killer's forehead, and as his throbbing elbow neared the snapping point, he gasped, released his hold on the Colt and then went spinning across the room from the power of his captor's whirling shove. When he stopped he froze in his tracks, for Tex carelessly held two guns now, the captured weapon covering its owner.

"Phew!" sighed Tex, a grin slowly spreading across his red face. "That was close, *that* was! Reckon I done saved quite a mess in here." He glared at Tommy. "You get th' hell out of here an' don't come back till you know how to act! Runnin' around like a mad dog, tryin' to kill men that never done you no harm! G'wan, or I'll let Hennery loose at you! I heard what you said, an' I wouldn't blame him if he blowed you wide open! G'wan! Shove that gun back where it belongs, an' git: *Pronto!* You've gone an' got Bud an' me bad friends, I reckon, an' I can't hardly blame him, neither."

Henry's eyes were riveted on the menacing Colt, his hand frozen where it had stopped, a few inches above the butt of his own. Bud Haines leaned forward, balanced on the balls of his feet, but not daring to leap. The spectators were staring, open-mouthed, quite content to let things take their course without any impetus from them.

Tommy sullenly slid the gun back into its holster and walked toward the door, too angry to speak. Glaring at Tex he went out, mounted and rode toward the ranch; and it was half an hour later before he came to the realization that his life had been saved from a shot from the side, and by the time he had reached the ranchhouse he was grinning.

Tex flipped the captured gun into the air, caught it by the barrel, and tossed it, butt first, to the killer. "I shore am apologizin' to you, Bud," he said, "for cuttin' in that way— but I had to act sudden, an' rough."

As the weapon settled into its owner's hand it roared and leaped, the bullet cutting Tex's vest under the armpit. Before a second shot could follow from it Bud twisted sidewise and plunged face down on the floor.

Tensed like a panther about to spring, Tex peered through the thinning cloud of smoke rising from his hip, his attention on the others in the room. "Sorry," he said. "You saw it all. I gave him his gun, butt first, an' he shot at me with it. Clipped my vest under my left shoulder. I couldn't do nothin' else. I'm sayin' that doin' favors for strangers is risky business—but is anybody findin' any fault with this shootin'?" He glanced quickly from face to face and then nodded slightly. "It was plain self-defense. If I'd 'a' thought he was a-goin' to shoot I shore wouldn't 'a' chucked him his loaded gun. Reckon I'm a plain d—d fool!"

There were no replies to him. The tense faces stared at the man who had killed Bud Haines in a fight after the killer had shot first. While there were no accusations in their expressions, neither was there any friendliness. The killing had been justified. This seemed to be the collective opinion, for in no way could the facts be changed. Bud had been man-handled in a manner which to him had been an unbearable insult, the fight could be considered as of his adversary's starting, but the actual shooting was as the victor claimed; and it was the shooting which they were to judge.

Tex, feeling ruefully of the bullet-torn vest, shoved his gun into its sheath and went over to Henry's table. The nephew hardly had moved since the first shot.

"I got somethin' to talk to you about, Henry," said Tex in a low, confidential voice. "'Tain't for everybody's ears, neither; so sit down a minute. That fool Watkins came cuttin' in as we was ridin' back, or I might have more news."

Henry slowly followed his companion's movements and straddled his chair. He motioned to the bartender for drinks and then let his suspicious eyes wander over his companion's face. He had a vast respect for Tex Jones.

"I reckon he's been cured of cuttin' in," he growled, a momentary gleam showing. "That's a habit of yourn, too," he said. "An' it's a cussed bad one, here in Windsor."

Tex spread his hands in helpless resignation. "I know it. Ever since I've been in this town I been puttin' my worst foot forward. I'm allus bunglin' things; an' just when I was beginnin' to make a few friends, Bud had to go an' git blind mad an' spoil everythin'. I didn't have nothin' ag'in' Bud; but I reckon mebby I was a little mite rough."

"Oh, Bud be d—d!" coldly retorted Henry. "He had th' edge, an' lost. That's between him an' you. What I'm objectin' to, Jones, is th' way you spoiled my plans. Don't you never cut into my affairs like you did just now. I'm tellin' you fair. I'm admittin' yo're a prize-winnin' gun-thrower; but there's other ways in this town. Savvy?"

Tex shook his head apologetically and nodded. "You an' me ain't goin' to have no trouble, Hennery," he declared earnestly. "If you want that C Bar fool, go git him. It ain't none of my business. But I'm worryin' about what yore uncle's goin' to say about me shootin' Bud," he confessed with plain anxiety. "He's a big man, Williams is; an' me, shucks: I ain't nothin' a-tall."

"He'll take my say-so," assured Henry, "after he cools down. Now what you got to tell me?"

"It's about that Saunders gal," answered Tex. He hitched his chair a little nearer to the table. "You remember what I told you, couple of nights ago? Well, I got to thinkin' about it when I was near th' station yesterday, so I went in an' got friendly with her brother." He rubbed his chin and grinned reminiscently. "There was a box across th' track that he had been using for a target. I asked him what it was an' he told me, an' he said he couldn't hit it. I sort of egged him on, not believin' him; an' shore enough he couldn't—an', Hennery, it was near as big as a house! I cut loose an' made a sieve of it—you must 'a' heard th' shootin'? His eyes plumb stuck out, an' we got to talkin' shootin'. Finally he ups an' asks me can I show his sister how to throw a gun an', seein' my chance to learn somethin' about her, I said I shore could show anybody that wasn't scared to death of one, an' that had any sense. 'How much will you charge for th' lessons?' says he. I had a good chance to pick up some easy money, but that wasn't what I was playin' for. I just wanted to get sort of friendly with her, an' him, too. I says, 'Nothin'.' Well, we fixed it up, an' today we goes off practicin'—you should 'a' seen that lunch, Hennery! I'm cussed near envyin' you!" He laughed contentedly, leaned back, and rubbed his stomach.

"Well?" demanded Henry, grinning ruefully.

"Well," echoed Tex. "You know that sewin' an' crochetin' is a whole lot different from shootin' a .45; an' so does she, now. I reckon a .22 would 'most scare her to death. Did you ever shoot with yore eyes shut? You don't have to try: it can't be done, an' hit nothin'. Six-guns an' wimmin wasn't never made to mix; an' they shore don't. We ate up th' lunch an' started back ag'in, an' I was just gettin' set to swing th' conversation in yore direction, carelesslike, but real careful, an' see what I could find out for you, when cussed if that C Bar coyote didn't come dustin' up, an' I don't know any more than I did before. But I'm riskin' one thing, Hennery: I'm near shore she ain't got nothin' ag'in' you; an' on th' way out, when I refers to you she speaks up quicklike, with her nose turned up a little, an' says: 'Henry Williams? Why, he'll be a rich man some day, when his uncle dies. Ain't some folks born lucky, Mr. Jones?' Hennery, there ain't none of 'em that are overlookin' th' good old pesos, U.S. You keep right on like you are; an' save me a front seat at th' weddin'."

Henry sat back, buried in thought. He glanced at the huddled figure near the door and then looked quickly into his companion's bland eyes. "Her brother's dead set ag'in' it. He knows he done me a dirty trick, stealin' my job, an' like lots of folks, instead of hatin' hisself, he hates me. Human nature's funny that way. So he can't hit a box, hey?"

Tex chuckled and nodded. "He up an' says he's so plumb disgusted with hisself that he ain't never goin' to tote a gun again, not never. Seems to me yo're doin' a lot of foolish worryin' about losin' that job. That ain't no job to worry about. If I was Gus Williams' only relation, you wouldn't see me lookin' for no jobs! You shore got th' wrong idea, Hennery. What do *you* want to work for, anyhow?"

"Well," considered the nephew of the uncle who some day would die, "that *is* one way of lookin' at it; but, Tex, he did me out of it. That's what's rilin' me!"

Tex leaned back and laughed heartily. "Hennery, you make me laugh! If I got mad an' riled at every dog that barked at me I'd be plumb soured for life by this time. A man like you should be above holdin' grudges ag'in' fellers like Saunders. It ain't worth th' risk of spoilin' yore disposition. Let him have his dried-out bone: you would 'a' dropped it quick enough, anyhow. An' if it wasn't for him gettin' that two-by-nothin' old job you wouldn't never 'a' seen his sister, would you? Ever think about it like that? Well, what you think? Had I better try to go ridin' with her ag'in an' git her to talkin'? Or shall I set back an' only keep my eyes an' ears open?"

"What's interestin' you so much in this here affair?" questioned Henry, his glance resting for a moment on the face of his companion.

"Well, I ain't got that letter," confessed Tex, slyly; "an' what's more, I'm afraid I ain't goin' to get it, neither, th' coyote. He lets me come out here, near th' end of th' track, an' then lets me hold th' sack. Time's comin' when I'll be needin' a job; an' yo're aces-up with yore uncle." He grinned engagingly. "My cards is face up. I got to look out for myself."

Henry laughed softly. "You shore had me puzzled," he replied. "Well, we'll see what we see. I don't hardly know, yet, what kind of a job you ought to have. There's good jobs, an' poor jobs. An' while I think of it, Tex, you'd mebby better go ridin' with her ag'in. But don't you forget what I was sayin' about there bein' other ways than gun-throwin' in Windsor. I—"

The low hum of conversation about them ceased as abruptly as did Henry's words. He was looking at the door, and sensing danger, Tex pushed back quietly and followed his companion's gaze. Jake, under the influence of liquor, stood in the doorway, a gun in his upraised hand, staring with unbelieving eyes at the body of Bud Haines.

"Stop that fool!" whispered Tex. "I've done too much killin' today: an' he's drunk!"

Henry arose and walked quietly, swiftly toward the vengeful miner, who now turned and looked about the room. A spasm of rage shot through him and his hand chopped down, but Henry knocked it aside and the heavy bullet scored the wall. Two men near the door leaped forward at the nephew's call and after a short struggle, Jake was disarmed, pacified, and sent on his way again.

Tex dropped his gun back into the holster and went up to the nephew. "Much obliged, Hennery," he said. "I've been expectin' him most every minute an' I'm glad you handled it so good. Where's he been keepin' hisself, anyhow?"

"Out in his cabin, nursin' his grudge," answered Henry. "He's one of them kind. He's got it chalked up ag'in' you, Tex, an' it'll smolder an' smolder, no tellin' how long. Then it'll bust out ag'in, like it did just now. Keep out of his way—he's a good man, Jake is. He's a friend of mine."

"That's good enough for me," Tex assured him. "I ain't got no grudge ag'in' Jake. It's th' other way 'round. Reckon I'll put up my cayuse. See you later."

XI

◆

Empty Honors

The dramatic death of Bud Haines created a ripple of excitement in Windsor which ran a notch higher than any killing of recent years. The late gunman posed as a gunman, swaggeringly, exultantly. Himself a contributor of victims to Boot Hill, his going there aroused a great deal more satisfaction than resentment. He was unmourned, but not unsung, and the question raised by his passing concerned the living more than the dead. How would his conqueror behave?

Bud was an out-and-out killer, cold, dispassionate, calculating; one whose gun was for hire and salary. He had no sympathy, no softer side to his nature, if his fellow-townsmen knew him right. The crooked mouth, grown into a lop-sided sneer, had been a danger signal to everyone who saw him, and through his up-to-then invincible gun Williams had passed his days in confidence, his nights in sleep. He had been taciturn, unsmiling, grim, and the few words he occasionally uttered were never cryptic. On the other hand Tex Jones was voluble, talked loosely and foolishly and had shown signs at poker that his courage was not what it should be to wrap the mantle of the fallen man about him and play his part; but had it been truly shown? Was his poker playing a true index to his whole nature? There was his brief, high-speed, complete mastery over Jake, himself a man bad enough to merit wholesome respect; there was the cool killing of Bud, and the nonchalant actions of the victor after the tragedy. He scarcely had given his victim a second look.

This question, as all questions do, provided argument. Gus Williams, sullen and morose at losing a valuable man in whose fidelity he could place full trust, and on whose prowess his own power largely rested, maintained that Tex Jones had pulled the trigger mechanically, and that it had been for him a lucky accident. His nephew took issue with him and paid his new companion full credit. The miners were about evenly divided, while Carney openly exulted and made the victory his principal topic of conversation. It helped him in another way, for there are some who blindly follow a champion, and the Windsor champion kept his horse and spent many of his spare hours at Carney's. John Graves sighed with relief at Bud's passing, due to an old score he had feared would be reopened, and he urged the appointment of Tex Jones for city marshal, a position hitherto unfilled in Windsor. Carney was for this heart and soul, and offered a marshal's office rent free. It was a lean-to adjoining his saloon.

The railroad element breathed easier now. Tim Murphy wanted to bet on the new man against anyone, at any style, and he glowed with pride as he realized that he, perhaps, was nearer to Tex Jones than any man in town. He had no trouble in persuading Costigan to look with warm favor on the successor to Bud Haines. Jerry Saunders, remembering a bit of gun practice, said he was not surprised and he exulted secretly. Tex Jones had been the first man outside of the railroad circle to give him a kind word and to show friendship; but he had little to say about it after the door of his home closed upon him.

Jerry's sister puzzled him. He saw traces of tears, strange moods came over her which swept her from gaiety to black despondency in the course of an hour or two, and no matter how he figured, he could not understand her. The story of how the affair had started and of Tommy Watkins' part in it made her moods more complex and unfathomable. Jane, he decided, was not only peculiar, but downright foolish. Bud Haines, being but a free member of Williams' own body, executing his wishes and the wishes of the detestable nephew, had been an evil whose potentiality could only be conjectured. He had been swept off the board and his conqueror was at heart very friendly to the Saunders family. They no longer were the most helpless people in town.

When Jerry had gone home on the day of the tragedy he had been full of the exploit, for Murphy and he had discussed it from every angle, and he had absorbed a great deal of the big Irishman's open delight.

Stunned at first, Jane flatly refused to talk about it, and had fled from the supper table to her room. Later on when he had cautiously broached the subject again, quoting the enthusiastic Murphy almost entirely, to show that his own opinions were well founded, she had listened to all he had to say, but had remained dumb. The evening was anything but pleasant and he had gone to bed in an unconcealed huff. She gave credit to Watkins but withheld it from Jones, who had earned it all. "Damn women, anyhow," had been his summing up.

The following morning he ate a silent breakfast and hurried to the station as he would flee to an oasis from the open desert. He found Tim waiting for him, eager to talk it all over again.

Hardly had the station been opened when Tex rode up, leaped from the magnificent roan, and sauntered to the door. His face was grave, his manner dignified and calm. "How'd'y, boys," he said in greeting.

"Proud I am this mornin'," beamed Murphy, his thick, huge hand closing over the lean, sinewy one of the gunman. "'Twas a fine job ye done, Tex, my boy; an' a fine way ye did it! Gave th' beast th' first shot! There's not another man could do it."

"There's plenty could," answered Tex. "I can name two, an' there's many more. I'm no gunman, understand: I'm just plain Tex Jones. But I didn't come here to hold any pow-pow—I'm wonderin' if you'd let me look in th' toolhouse—I might 'a' left it there when we loaded th' hand car."

"An' what's 'it'?" asked Murphy.

"My knife."

"Come along then," said the section-boss, swinging his keys and leading the way. They found no knife, but Murphy was given some information which he considered worth while. As they reached the station door again Tex burst out laughing.

"I know where it is! Cuss me for a fool, I left it in Carney's stable, stickin' in th' side of th' harness closet. Oh, well; there's no harm done." He turned to Jerry. "I wonder if Miss Saunders would like another bit of practice today?"

Jerry's face clouded. No matter how much he might admire Bud Haines' master in the late Bud's profession of gun-throwing, and no matter how much he might admire him for sundry other matters, nevertheless none of them qualified the new-found friend as an aspirant for his sister's hand. He did not wish to offend Tex, and certainly he did not want his enmity. To him came Jane's inexplicable behavior and in coming it brought an inspiration. Jane, he thought, could handle this matter far better than he could.

"She didn't seem to be feeling well this morning," he answered. "Still, I never guess right about her. If you feel like riding again, go up and ask her."

"I hear there's some talk about them makin' you marshal of this town," said Tim. "Don't you shelve it. This town needs a fair man in that job. It's been quiet of late, but ye can't allus tell. Wait till th' rains come an' start th' placerin' a-goin'. They'll have money to spend, then, an' trouble is shore to follow that. You take that job, Tex."

Jerry nodded eagerly, pointed to some bullet holes in the frame of one of the windows of the office and, grasping Tex by the arm, led him closer to the window. "See that bullet hole in there, just over the table an' below the calendar? The first shot startled me and made me drop my pen—I stooped to pick it up. When I sat up again there was a hole in the glass and under the calendar. When I stooped I saved my life. Just a drunken joke, a miner feeling his oats. One dead man a week was under the average. This town, under normal conditions, is a little bit out of hell. Take that job, Jones: the town needs you."

Tex laughed. "You better wait till it's offered to me, Jerry. There's quite some people in this town that don't want any marshal. Gus Williams is the man to start it."

"He will," declared Tim. "Bud was his bodyguard, but he was more. Williams has a lot of property to be protected, an' now Bud is gone, th' saints be praised. He'll start it."

While they spoke, a miner was seen striding toward the station and soon joined them. "How'd'y," he said, carelessly, glancing coldly at Tim and Jerry. His eyes rested on Tex and glowed a little. "Th' boss wants to talk with you, Jones. Come a-runnin'."

"Come a-runnin'," rang in Tex's ears and it did not please him. If he was going to be the city marshal it would be well to start off right.

"Th' boss?" he asked nonplussed.

"Shore; Gus—Gus Williams," rejoined the messenger crisply and with a little irritation. "You know who I mean. Git a move on."

"Mr. Jones' compliments to Mr. Williams," replied Tex with exaggerated formality, "an' say that Mr. Jones will call on him at Mr. Jones' convenience. Just at present I'm very busy—good day to you, sir."

The miner stood stock-still while he reviewed the surprising words.

Tex ignored him. "No," he said, "I ain't lookin' for no change in th' weather till th' moon changes," he explained to the two railroad men. "But, of course, you know th' old sayin': 'In times of drought all signs fail.' An' there never was a truer one. I wouldn't be surprised if it rained any day; an' when it comes it's goin' to rain hard. Still, I ain't exactly lookin' for it, barrin' the sayin', till th' moon changes. That's my prophecy, gents; you wait an' see if I ain't right. Well, I reckon I'll be amblin'. Good day."

They watched him walk to the roan, throw the reins over an arm, and lead it slowly down the street, followed by the conjecturing messenger. Tex Jones evidently was in no hurry, for he stopped in two places before entering the hotel, and in there he remained for a quarter of an hour. When premature congratulations were offered him he accepted them with becoming modesty and explained that he was not yet appointed.

Gus Williams looked up with some irritation when the door opened and admitted Tex into the store. The newcomer leaned against the counter, nodded to Gus and grinned at Henry. "Hear you want to see me about somethin'," he said, flickering dust from his boots with a softly snapping handkerchief.

"What made you shoot Bud Haines?" growled the proprietor, turning on the stepladder against the shelves.

Tex shook his head in befitting sorrow. "I shore didn't want to shoot Bud," he answered slowly. "Bud hadn't never done nothin' to me; but," he explained, wearily, "he just made me do it. I dassn't let him shoot twice, dast I?"

Williams growled something and replaced several articles of merchandise.

"Hennery says you had to do it," he grudgingly admitted. "I reckon mebby you did—*but,* I don't see why you went at Bud like that, in th' first place."

"I aimed to stop a killin'," muttered Tex, contritely; "an', instead of doin' it, I went an' made one. I ain't none surprised," he said, sighing resignedly, "for I generally play in bad luck. Ever since I shot that black cat, up at Laramie, I've had bad luck—not that I'm what you might call superstitious," he quickly and defiantly explained.

"Well, a man can't allus help things like that," admitted Williams. "I had streaks of luck that looked like they never would peter out." He shifted several articles, leaned back to study their arrangement, and slowly continued. "You see, Bud had a job that ain't very common; an' men like Bud ain't very common, neither. He allus was plumb grateful because I saved his life once in a—stampede," he naively finished. "I got a lot of valuable property in this here town, and Windsor gets quite lively when th' placerin' is going good. I shore feel sort of lost without Bud." He wiped his dusty hands on his trousers and slowly climbed down. "Now, I remembered that Scrub Oak an' Willow both has peace officers, an' Windsor shore ain't taking a back seat from towns like them. Hennery was sayin' that folks here sort of been talkin' about a city marshal, an' mentionin' you for th' office. We ought to have our valuable property pertected, an' me, bein' the owner of most of th' valuable property here an' here-abouts, nat'rally leans to that idea; but, bein' th' biggest owner of valuable property, I sort of got to look the man over purty well before I appoint him. I got to have a good man, a man that'll pertect th' most property first. What you think about it?"

Tex removed his sombrero, turned it over slowly in his hands and stared at its dents. Punching them out and punching in new ones, he gravely considered them. "Well," he drawled, "you see, if that letter comes—I don't know how long I'm goin' to stay in town; but if I *did* stay, I'd shore do my damndest to pertect property, an' you havin' the most of it, you'd nat'rally be pertected more'n others that had less."

Williams glanced swiftly at his nephew. "You still expectin' that letter, Jones?" he slyly demanded.

Tex hesitated and turned the hat over again. "Can't hardly say I am," he admitted, frowning at Henry. "But there's a sayin' that hope springs infernal—an' I reckon that's th' hell of it; a man never knows when to quit waitin' for it to spring. Meanwhile I got to eat—an' I like a game of poker once in awhile. Here, tell you what—I'll take the job as long as I can hold it, if the pay is right. What you reckon the job's worth, in a lawless, desperate town like this, where no man's life or property is worth very much?"

Williams scowled. "This here town ain't lawless an' desperate," he denied. "There ain't a more peaceable town in Kansas!"

"Which same ain't payin' no compliments to Kansas towns, once the rains come," chuckled Tex. "I'm admirin' your humor, Mr. Williams—I ain't never heard dryer," he beamed in frank admiration. "But, wet or dry, there's allus them mean low-down cow-wrastlers comin' to town to likker up—an' them an' miners are as friendly as a badger and a dog. Let's name over them as would want the pertection of a marshal, an' then figger how much they'd sweeten the pot. Take Carney, now—he ought to be willin' to ante up han'some, his business bein' so healthy."

"Carney," sneered Williams in open contempt. "Huh! Here, gimme that pencil an' that old envelope!" He worked laboriously, revised the figures several times and then looked up. "I reckon two hundred a month ought to be enough. Scrub Oak pays that—Willow does likewise. You got your outfit. We furnish th' office, ammernition, an' pay extra expenses. That's th' best Windsor can do. Yore office will be next door to this store."

Tex looked questioningly at Henry, who nodded decisively, and carefully put the hat back on his head. "All right," he said. "When do I start in?"

"Right now," answered Williams, fumbling under the counter. "We ain't got no marshal's badge, but I got a sheriff's star somewhere around. He was killed up on Buffaler Crick last spring. Yep—here it is: this'll do for awhile. Lean over here, Marshal," he chuckled. "There: It ain't every marshal that's a sheriff, too." Smiling at Henry he said, jokingly, "Now let her rain!"

Tex nodded. "Let it come," he said. "Everybody that deserves it will have a slicker ag'in' th' rain. As marshal I'm playin' no favorites—there's no strings to a city marshal. My job's to keep th' peace of Windsor, an' let th' devil whistle." He smiled enigmatically, hitched up his belt, and then looked at Henry. "You know where Bud's belt an' gun are?"

Henry nodded. "Baldy's got 'em, behind th' bar. Want 'em?"

"Yes," answered Tex, slowly turning. "When it starts rainin', two guns will keep me on an even keel. My left hand feels empty-like. Reckon I'll go git Bud's outfit an' have th' harness-maker turn th' holster so it'll set right for th' left side; or mebby he's got a cavalry sheath, which won't need so much changin'."

"But you ought to have a rifle heavier than a .38 short," suggested Gus Williams. "That ain't no gun for this country."

Tex smiled. "For town use that's plenty heavy enough. But

we won't argue about that because I ain't got it no more. I swapped with that section-boss, paying him fifteen dollars to-boot. To a thick Mick like him there ain't much difference between a .38 short and a .45-90. He can't use either one worth a cuss, anyhow. I'd say I was lucky stumblin' on him." He turned and walked toward the door, glanced up at the cloudless sky, and chuckled. "No signs of rain, yet. Oh, well; it'll come when it gets here. *Adios,*" and the slow steps of the walking roan grew softer down the street.

The harness-maker looked from the belt and holster to an up-ended box and waved at the latter. "Set down, Mr. Jones. 'Twon't take a minute, but you might as well set. Many a one I've turned. A new cut here, a new strap, an' a scallop out of th' top on th' other side so yore fingers'll close on th' butt first thing. Let's see th' other. Yep; deep cut down to th' guard. Now, if I put back on th' belt at th' same place, it'll throw th' buckle around back—all right, then. They won't match each other, but that don't make no difference, I reckon. Ain't there been some talk of appointin' you city marshal?"

Tex nodded. "This star was th' only one they had," he explained.

"Well, you may be workin' both jobs afore long if Gus Williams has th' say-so," commented the harness-maker. "Funny, but I never work on a gun sheath but I think of th' one I made to order for Jack Slade after he got around ag'in from Old Jules' shotgun. Jack blamed it on his holster, an' it shore made him particular. That was back in Old Julesburg when I was a harness-apprentice there. Soon after that he was sent up to take charge of th' Rocky Ridge division of th' stage line, which was th' worst division of th' whole line. Holdups was a reg'lar thing. They soon stopped after he took charge. He was th' best man with a short gun I ever saw. I heard that he wore that holster to th' day th' vigilantes got him, up in Virginia City, Montanny. Now, Mr. Marshal, strap this on you an' see if th' gun comes out right. Sometimes they got to be shaped a little mite—ah, that looks all right. Reckon it'll do?"

With the newly acquired belt hanging over the old one, sloping loosely from the right hip across his body to a point below the left, the marshal went out, mounted the roan, and rode carelessly down to the toolshed, where he told Murphy of his appointment and of the fictitious swapping of rifles, and then went up to the station. As he neared it Jerry came out of the door, caught the flash of the sun on the nickel-plated star and turned, grinning, to await the coming of the new marshal.

"That looks mighty good to the station agent," Jerry laughed. "An' so you're wearin' two guns instead of one? Gosh, that looks business-like!"

Tex reined in and grinned down at him. "Any time you feel urged to shoot up th' town, Mr. Agent, you'll find out that it *is* business-like. Better start by gettin' th' marshal first: it'll be a lot safer, that way."

"That's good advice, and I won't forget it," replied Jerry. "I'll notify the company of your appointment. That ought to make it feel good, and it might want to pay its share of your salary. I'm certainly wishing you luck."

"I may be needin' it," responded the marshal. "Reckon I'll go on to th' house an' show off my new bright an' shinin' star." He glanced down at the badge and grinned. "Seein' how you reads 'Sheriff' instead of 'Marshal' she'll mebby wonder what you are. So-long, Jerry!"

Reaching the little house, Tex swung gravely off Omar and proceeded to the door in mock dignity. Knocking heavily, he assumed a stern demeanor and waited. When the door opened he removed his sombrero, bowed, and grinned. "Behold the Law, Miss Saunders, in the person of the marshal of Windsor."

"I congratulate you, Marshal," she coldly replied. "Doubtless you may now take life with legal authority. It is too bad it comes a little late."

"I did not need legal authority, Miss Saunders, if I rightly interpret your remark," he rejoined. "The authority of Nature ever precedes and transcends it. Self-preservation is the first law. He fired, and I did not dare let him fire again."

"You provoked his attack!" she flashed. "He could do nothing else."

"That was because I preferred to risk his life than the certainty of him taking that of Tommy Watkins, who was being deliberately baited. Bud lost his rights when he drew his gun against an unsuspecting man. I am sorry if you look upon the unfortunate incident in any other light; but I am so sure of my position that I would repeat it today under the same conditions. Besides I am naturally prejudiced against assassins."

"Why did you give him his gun before he had time to master his anger?" she demanded, her eyes flashing.

"Because I wanted to show him how impersonal my interference was, and to help smooth over a tense situation. It was one of those high-tension moments when a false move might easily precipitate a shambles. There were a dozen armed men in the room, a ratio of ten to two. I followed my best judgment. I am not apologizing, Miss Saunders, even to you; I am merely explaining the situation as it existed. When Bud Haines drew his gun from the side to shoot a man who did not know of his danger, he broke our rules. I would have been justified in shooting him down at the move. Instead I tried to stop his shot and give him a way out of it." While he spoke his right hand had risen to his belt and now hung there by a crooked thumb, a position he was in the habit of assuming when he spoke earnestly.

She glanced down at it involuntarily, shuddered, and slowly closed the door.

"I am very sorry, Mr. Jones, but—" the closing of the door ended the conversation for both.

He studied the warped, weather-beaten panel and the white, china knob for a full minute, and then slowly replaced his hat and slowly walked back to his horse. Patting the silky neck he shook his head. "Omar, it's been comin' to me for twenty years—but it might have waited till I really deserved it. Come on—we'll go back to th' herd, where we belong."

Thoughtfully he rode away, his face older and sterner, its lines seemingly a little deeper.

XII

♦

Closer Friendships

In the selection of the marshal's office Williams was overruled and rather than make a contest of it, since he could not deny the economy in using a building already erected, and knowing that his store was nearly as well protected, he gave his slow assent to Carney's offer; and soon the lean-to was cleared out, a table, some chairs, and a rough bunk put in it, the latter at the marshal's insistence. Over the door were two words, newly painted: CITY MARSHAL. The question of a jail came next, and was quickly solved by the addition to the lean-to of a room constructed of two-inch planks, walls, floor, and roof. Two pairs of new, shining handcuffs and a new badge, appropriately labeled, completed the civic improvements in the way of law and order. All prisoners guilty of major offenses were to be taken down to Willow and there tried; while minor offenders could sit in the jail until a suitable time had elapsed.

From his chair in the door of his office, Tex could keep watch of nearly all of the main street, and the trail leading in from the C Bar for half a mile. The end of his first week as peace officer found him in his favorite place, contentedly puffing on his pipe, despite the heat of the day. A few miners straggled past, grinning and exchanging shafts of heavy wit with the smiling officer. Blascom drifted into town a little later, learned of the appointment, and hurried down from the hotel to congratulate his new friend.

Tex reached behind him and pulled a chair outside the door. "Sit down, Blascom," he invited. "How's th' sump comin' along?"

Blascom glanced around before replying. "I'm sorry you ain't sheriff, as well," he replied. "I reckon I'm out of bounds, out there on Buffalo, an' I'm shore to be rushed if I'm figgerin' right on that crick. Anybody in th' new jail?"

"Not yet," smiled Tex. "Talk low an' nobody'll hear you. Strike somethin'?"

"I'll gamble on it. I'm so shore of it, I'm filin' a new claim: th' old one didn't quite cover it. You know where th' sump's located, of course; an' you remember how rapid it filled up with water every time I tried to bail it out?"

Tex nodded and waved carelessly at the C Bar trail as though discussing something far from placering. "Send th' location papers off through Jerry Saunders—tell him they're from me. Ever follow a trail herd day after day?" he asked.

"No; why?"

"Ever do anythin', out here, except minin'?"

"Shore; why?"

"What was it?"

"Freightin' from Atchison to Denver an' back: why?"

"Then yo're tellin' me about it now," prompted Tex, handing him a cleaning rod. "Trace th' old trail in th' sand an' keep referrin' to it while you talk. You don't know me good enough to talk long an' steady an' earnest. Here, gimme that rod—" and the marshal took it and drew a line. "This end is Atchison—from there you went up th' Little Blue, like this. Then, crossin' that divide south of th' Platte, you rolled down to that river near Hook's Station, an' follered it past Ft. Kearney, Plumb Crick, an' O'Fallon's Bluffs, an' so on. Here's Hook's Station, th' Fort, Plumb Crick, an' O'Fallon's—now you go on with it."

Blascom took the rod and finished the great curve. "As I was sayin', th' water in that sump kept me guessin'. I couldn't figger where it all come from. I had tried for sumps nearer to th' shack, of course, but got nothin'. Then I found water a-plenty when I dug *this* one." He jabbed at Ft. Kearney and waved his other arm. "I kept gettin' curiouser all th' time, an' yesterday, when th' idea hit me all of a sudden, I went back down th' crick bed twenty paces an' started diggin'. No water; an' yet, sixty feet up stream was more'n I could handle. I just sat down an' wrastled it out."

Tex leaned over and drew another line, one starting on the great curve. "Th' Salt Lake branch run up here, didn't it, Blascom? Th' ones th' troops used, near Old Julesburg, goin' out to lick th' Mormons?"

"How'd you come to know so much about that old trail?" demanded the miner. "It shore did—an' it was a bad section for stages. Well, I cut me a pinted stick an' after it got dark I went out an' jabbed it inter th' crick bed between th' wet sump an' th' last one I put down. About five feet below th' wet one I hit rock, not more'n six inches under th' sand, an' it sloped sharp, both ways, I'm tellin' you. Sort of a sharp hog-back, it is. Humans are blasted fools, Marshal: we can set right on top of a thing that's fair yellin' to be seen, an' not know it's there till somethin' knocks it inter our fool heads. Do you know what I got up there at that sump?"

Tex shook his head and grabbed the stick, a trace of vexation on his face. "You got it all wrong, Blascom," he declared loudly, drawing another line. "Th' old, original Oregon Trail never went up th' Rocky Ridge a-tall. It followed th' North Fork of th' Platte, all th' way to Ft. Laramie. It crossed th' river at Forty Islands, about twelve miles south of th' Fort. I crossed it there with a herd, myself. If you don't believe me, ask Hawkins—he was apprenticed to th' harness-maker at Old Julesburg, on th' South Fork."

"I got you there," laughed Blascom. "Th' Oregon Trail didn't cross at Forty Islands; but a lot of trail herds did. There was a waggin ferry at th' Fort that th' chuck waggins often used."

"It crossed either at Forty Islands or between 'em an' th' Fort," asserted Tex.

"Well, mebby yo're right, Marshal," admitted Blascom. He took the rod again. "That sump of mine is located in a rocky basin that's full of sand. Th' downstream side is that hog-back. That means that there's a thunderin' big, natural riffle in th' bed of th' crick, an' it's stopped and held th' sand till th' basin was full. Every freshet that comes along riles that sand up, lots of it bein' washed over th' riffle, an' carried along. More sand settles there as th' water quits rushin'; but here's th' pint." He jabbed at Denver and drew a line into the Gilpin County country, stopping at Central City. "Gold is heavy, an' it don't wash over riffles if it can settle down in front of 'em. While th' sand is soft from bein' disturbed by a strong current, it can settle. Ever since that crick has been a crick, gold has been settlin' in front of that riffle, droppin' down through th' sand till it hit th' rock bottom. Great Jehovah, Marshal—can you figger what I got?"

Tex roughly took the cleaning rod, traced a line in sud-

den vexation, slammed the rod on the floor behind him, and
fanned his face with his hat.

"An' how long you been settin' on that?" he asked in
weary hopelessness.

Blascom waved his arms and slumped back against the
chair. "Three years," he confessed, and went off into a profane description of his intelligence that left nothing to
imagination.

Tex laughed heartily. "If you was as bad as you just said
I'd shore have to take you in. Cheer up, man: it's there, ain't
it? You only have to git it out."

Blascom looked at him reproachfully. "Shore: that's all,"
he retorted with sarcasm. "Git it out before th' rain starts
again, an' do it without Jake catchin' me at it! If he learns
what I got, I'm in for no sweet dreams; an' if this starvin'
bunch of gold hunters learn about it, I'll be swamped in th'
rush! Good Lord, man! It'll take me a week to git th' water
out, an' then there's th' sand!"

Tex stretched, caught sight of a rider bobbing along the
C Bar trail and looked reflectively at Williams' Mecca.
"You got to get some dynamite or blastin' powder. Dynamite's better. Put some sticks on th' downstream side of that
rock riffle an' wait till Jake comes into town. You crack
that riffle open an' th' water will move out for you. Then
you can dig down th' other face of it an' get to th' pocket a
lot quicker." He laughed suddenly. "Do that blastin'. Then
when Jake gets back to his shack, saunter over with a jug of
whiskey an' forget to take it home with you. That'll give you
a solid week for yore diggin' without him botherin' you."

"Good idea," said Blascom, arising. "I'll go over an' see
if Williams has got any sticks. That's th' way to handle it,
Marshal. You ever do any prospectin'?"

Tex pushed him back again. "No, I ain't; but I've been
doin' a lot of thinkin' these days. Sit still. What does a

miner want explosives for? To get gold, of course. Bein' a placer worker don't make no difference: th' connection is there, just th' same. It'll only make 'em that much more curious. You go buyin' any dynamite an' th' parade will start for yore place before night. I'd get it for you, only me not havin' no reason to buy th' stuff, it would be near as big a mistake as you buyin' it. *I* ain't got no call to want any dynamite. Sit still: you ain't in no hurry!" He leaned over and put his finger on the map in the sand. "They hit Ft. Hall about here," he explained. "We got to get somebody that ain't connected with you, gold diggin', or Buffalo Crick, that won't make no troublesome connections. They usually left their waggins at Ft. Hall an' went up this way. If this feller comin' down th' trail is young Watkins, an' I'm sayin' he is, we got th' way. I reckon he can buy dynamite for th' ranch. That'll be all right, but suppose somebody else from that outfit comes ridin' in an' gets pumped dry? Lean back, stick yore feet on th' Overland, an' don't look so cussed tense. Here: I got it! Th' railroad uses dynamite! I shore got it, Blascom. Tim Murphy can buy it as innocent as you can buy chewin' tobacco!"

"But I don't know him well enough!" expostulated Blascom. "Anyhow, what excuse can I give him?"

"None at all," said Tex. "Wait till yore feet are in th' stirrups before you spur a hoss! You don't have to know him. *I* know him, an' that's a-plenty. Here, you listen close to every word I say, an' act careless-like while yo're doin' it." The explicit directions were rich in details, but Blascom soaked them into his memory like water in a sponge. "Th' whole thing is gettin' to him nat'ral, an' then gettin' th' stuff from him afterward," Tex wound up. Thoughtful for a moment, he nodded in sudden decision. "Got it ag'in! It's near train time. You, bein' restless an' lonesome, hanker to watch it come in. Th' Lord knows nobody in towns like this ever needs any excuse to see a train come in. That's one of th' idle man's inalienable rights—an' it seldom weakens. An' now I know how yo're goin' to git it from him afterwards: you listen ag'in," and further directions came in rapid-fire order.

The rider was near enough now to dispel all doubts as to his identity. Blascom arose, gripped the marshal's hand and faced the Mecca.

"I'm goin' over to git a jug: much obliged, Marshal." He crossed the street diagonally and disappeared in the store.

The rider came nearer and nearer, a great dust cloud rolling behind him not much unlike the smoke of a moving locomotive. When even with Carney's he drew rein suddenly and in another moment had dismounted in front of the lazy Tex.

"I'll be cussed!" he exclaimed, staring from Tex to the sign over the door and then back at the new peace officer, cocking his head as he read the badge.

"Good for you!" he cried. "It's about time this dog's town had a white man to run it; an' they couldn't 'a' picked a better, neither!" His enthusiasm ebbed a little and he looked curiously and thoughtfully into the marshal's eyes. "How'd you come to get th' job?" he demanded.

Tex stuck his thumbs in the armholes of his vest and grinned. He knew the thought that had sobered his companion's face. "Pop'lar clamor, Thomas; 'an all that sort of a thing,' as Whitby used to say. My great popularity an' my pleasin' nature an' disposition, not to mention my good looks an' winnin' ways, seem to have turned th' balance in my favor. But, outside of that I don't know why I got it. Carney thought I'd mebby bring him more trade; Williams mourned th' lack of anybody to give him adequate police protection, an' th' harness-maker mentions Jack Slade. He admires Jack Slade, an' says I remind him of that person by th' way I let him fix up my left-hand holster. That suits me because Slade was lynched."

"Then Williams really made th' play stick?" Tommy asked with poorly concealed suspicion.

"Williams pinned on my nickel-plated authority," said Tex. "Nobody else had one. He reckons I'm wearin' his colors; but, my Christian friend, th' only colors th' new marshal wears are his own. I'm to keep order in 'this dog's town,' as you put it, an' I'm goin' to do it. Miners, railroaders, storekeepers, cattlemen, an' ornery punchers please listen an' be enlightened. Th' badge is only a nickel-plate affair; but there ain't no nickel, nor rust, neither, on my Cyclopean twins. They're my real authority. Now, then, don't walk all over Blascom's Overland Trail, but set down in th' chair he just vacated. Tell me all about yoreself."

"Marshal," began Tommy in some embarrassment, "I didn't get th' hang of that little mix-up in th' hotel till I got quite some distance out of town. My head was whirlin' a little, an' I'm nat'rally stupid, anyhow. I just want to say that yo're wrong about them Colts bein' some kind of twins. Mebby they are durin' these peaceful days; but if things got crowded they'll turn into triplets, th' missin' brother bein' right here on my laig. Besides that, you got a craggy lot of deputies out on th' C Bar any time you need 'em. Don't stop me while I'm runnin' free! I'm saying I never saw a squarer, cleaner piece of shootin' than you showed us all in th' hotel th' other day. An'—you keep off th' trail while I'm comin' strong!—an' I've been somethin' of a fool about us an' that little lady. From now on I'm afoot where she's concerned, an' you know what us punchers amount to, afoot."

"I'm glad you said you was stupid," replied Tex. "It saves me from saying' it, an' comin' from me it might sound sorta official." He glanced up the street and back to his companion. "Yo're not afoot, cowboy; yo're ridin' strong. I'm th' one that's afoot, an' I'll agree with you about a cowpunch amountin' to nothin' off his cayuse. Did you ever have a door slammed plumb in yore face, Tommy?"

Tommy wiped out Denver, Central City, Old Julesburg, and Ft. Kearney with one swing of his foot. "You—I—you *mean* that?"

The marshal nodded. "Every word of it. Outlawed steers should keep to th' draws an' brakes, Tommy. Besides, I'm over forty-five years old, an' I never was any parson. Keep right on ridin', Adolescence; an' I'm hopin' it's a plain, fair trail. Tommy, did you ever shoot a man?"

"Not yet I ain't; but I've come cussed near it. Seein' what's goin' on in this town, I has hopes."

"Don't yield to no temptations, Tommy; an' let yore hopes die," warned the marshal. "If there's any of that to be done, I'll do it. I reckon you'll shore have a easy trail."

"I—will—be—tee-totally—d—d!" said Tommy. He shook his head and leaned back against the front of the office. "Does she know all about it?"

"Everythin'; I owed myself that much," answered Tex, and then he helped to maintain a reflective, introspective, and emotional silence.

Blascom emerged from the Mecca with a two-gallon jug, empty from the way it jerked and swung. He looked at the silent pair leaning against the marshal's office, abruptly made up his mind, and strode over to them.

"You shore look sorrerful," he said.

"We've just been to a funeral," said Tex. "Th' corpse looked nat'ral, too."

"Sufferin' wildcats!" ejaculated Tommy in pretended dismay, his chair dropping to all fours. "Whiskey by th' jug! I'm plain shocked, but mighty glad to see you, Mr. Blascom." He turned to the marshal. "Here, Officer! Shake han's with

Mr. Blascom, of Buffaler Crick. Give th' gentleman a cordial welcome."

Tex regarded the newcomer and his jug with languid interest. "Huh! I reckoned th' drought would shore end some day, but I figgered on rain. However, facts are facts. Pleased to meet you, sir!" He waved at Tommy. "Pass it to our friend first. It's dry work, settin' here, listenin' to me."

"It's like workin' in pay-dirt," retorted Blascom. He tapped the jug and it rang out hollowly. "I ain't give Baldy a chance at it, yet. Anyhow, a man's got to have some protection ag'in' snakes," he defended.

"A protection ag'in' snakes!" repeated Tex, thoughtfully. "Yes; he has."

"I'll pertect you ag'in' 'em as far as th' hotel," offered Tommy, arising and whistling to his horse, "seein' as yo're temporary defenseless. Come on, Blascom. See you later, Marshal," and he grabbed at the jug, missed it, and led the way, Tex smiling after the grinning pair.

Tommy's stride was swift and long for a puncher, due to his agitated frame of mind, and he suddenly slowed it to make an observation to his companion.

"Blascom, th' new marshal is shore quick on th' gun—this town ought to be right proud of him. I'm admittin' that he's a reg'lar he-man."

"He's a cussed sight quicker with his head," replied the miner, "an' that's shore sayin' a large an' bounteous plenty. If he don't play no favorites he's shore as hell goin' to need friends, one of these days. I'm admittin' myself to that cat-e-gory: but it'll be my hard luck to be out on th' Buffaler when it starts."

Tommy nodded and spat emphatically. "I'll be a cat, an' gory, too," he affirmed. "Wild as a wildcat, an' gory as all hell. That's me!" He glanced up quickly. "Talkin' ceases, for here we are." He tossed the reins over his pony's head and followed his companion into the hotel, where half a dozen men lounged dispiritedly.

Baldy grinned and lost no time in filling the jug, his efforts creating pleasant, anticipatory smackings among the dry onlookers, who from their previous unobserving weariness suddenly snapped into Argus-eyed interest. The alluring gurgle of the wicker-covered demijohn, the *slap-slap, plop-plop* of the leaping, amber stream, ebbing and flooding spasmodically up and down and around the greenish copper funnel, truly was liquid music to their ears, and the powerful odor of the rye diffused itself throughout the room, penetrated the stale tobacco smoke, and wrought positive reactions upon the olfactory nerves of the staring audience. It was scarce enough by the glass, these days, yet here was a reckless Croesus who was buying it by the gallon!

Blascom, smiling with quiet reserve, leaned against the bar to the right of the jug; Tommy, grave and forbidding, leaned against the bar to the left of the jug, both making short and humorous replies to the gift-compelling remarks of the erect crowd. The jug at last filled, Blascom pushed the cork in and slammed it home with a quick, disconcertingly forbidding gesture, which was as cruel as it was final. He paid for the liquor with one of the bills he had won from Tex, nodded briskly, and went out, Tommy bringing up the rear.

Reproachful, accusing eyes followed their exit, hoping against hope. A lounger nearest the bar, thirsty as Tantalus, shook his head in sorrowful condemnation.

"A man can be mean an' pe-nurious up to a certain limit," he observed; "but past that it's plumb shameful."

An old man, his greasy, gray beard streaked with tobacco stains, nodded emphatically. "There *is* limits; an' I say that stoppin' before ye begin is shore beyond 'em!"

"Yo're dead right," spoke up a one-eyed tramp who honored himself with the title of prospector. "As for me, I never *did* think much of any man as guzzles it secret. Show me th' man that swizzles in public, an *I'll* show you a man as can be trusted. Two whole gallons of it! A whole, bloomin' jugful, at onct! Where'd he git all that money? I'm askin' you, *where'd* he git it? On Buffaler Crick?" His voice rose and cracked with avarice and suspicion.

"Naw!" growled the man in the far corner, slumping back against his chair. "He won it from that Tex Jones feller—th' new marshal—two hundred or more—playin' poker. Th' same Tex Jones as shot Bud Haines. There ain't more'n day wages on Buffaler Crick. I know, 'cause I been lookin' around out there, quiet-like." He stiffened suddenly and sat up, excitement transforming him. "Boys, this here marshal has got money—I saw his wad when he an' Blascom was a-playin'."

"Yo're shore welcome to it," pessimistically rejoined the man nearest the bar, his vivid imagination picturing the amazing death of Bud Haines. "Yes, sir; yo're welcome to *all* of it. I don't want none, a-tall!"

The discoverer of the marshal's roll regarded the objector with deep scorn.

"That's you!" he retorted. "Allus goin' off half-cocked, an' yowlin' calamity! This here marshal likes poker, don't he? An' he can't play it, can he? Didn't Blascom clean him? He's scared to bluff, or call one, no matter how brave he is with a gun. Who's got any dust? Dig down deep, an' we'll pool it, lettin' Hank an' Sinful do th' playin' for us. Where's Hennery?" he demanded of the bartender.

Baldy mopped the bar and glanced at the ceiling. "Upstairs, sleepin' off a stern-winder. He got drinkin' to th' mem'ry of th' dead deceased last night—an' his mem'ry is long an' steady. He's too senti-mental, Hennery is, for a man as can't handle his likker good. If you fellers are goin' after th' marshal's pile, I'm recommendin' stud-hoss. He's nat'rally scared of poker, an' stud's so fast he won't have no time to start worryin'. Draw will give him too much time to think. Better try stud-hoss," he reiterated, unwittingly naming the form of poker at which the marshal excelled.

"Stud-hoss she is, then," agreed Sinful, licking his lips. "I like stud-hoss. We'll bait him tonight; an' we'll *all* have jugs of our own by mornin', since Buffaler Crick's settin' th' style."

The meeting forthwith went into executive session, depleted gold sacks slowly appearing.

Outside, Blascom offered the jug to his companion, who pushed it away, and shook his head in sudden panic.

"Don't want to smell like no saloon where I'm goin'," he hastily explained. "Now that yo're safe from snakes I'll be driftin' to my cayuse."

"All right, Watkins; I'll treat next time," and the miner, jug in hand, strode toward the station as Tommy mounted and wheeled to ride in the direction of the Saunders' home.

Blascom had timed his arrival to a nicety, for Murphy was on his way from the toolshed to the station to await the coming of the train, the smoke from which could be seen on the eastern horizon.

Blascom held up the jug invitingly and grinned.

The section-boss came to an abrupt stop, saluted, and stepped on again with the bearing of a well-trained English soldier. "Hah!" he called. "'Tis better from a jug; an' 'twould be better yet if it had a little breath av th' peat fire in it; but 'tis well to be content with what we have. Thank ye: I'll drink yer health!" Handing the jug back to its owner Murphy wiped his lips with the back of his hand and seated himself on the bench at the prospector's side. "Have ye seen th' new marshal?" he asked, glancing from the distant smudge of smoke to his watch. "I hear he's fixed up in style."

"Yes; an' he gave me a message for you, if you'll lean over a little closer," replied Blascom, and, as Murphy obeyed his suggestion, he said what he had come for.

"It sounds like Tex," grunted Murphy. "All thought out careful. Have ye ever used stick explosive? It's treacherous stuff at any time above freezin', an' more so after this spell av hot weather. Ye have? Then there's no use av me tellin' ye to handle it gintly. If I was knowin' th' job ye have, I might help ye in th' number av sticks. But if yo're used to it, ye'll know. I'll get it after Number Three pulls out; an' after dark tonight ye'll find it where he said—but deal gintly with it, Mr. Blascom. I've seen it exploded by impact—it was a rifle ball fired into it—this kind av weather. Ye might even do better to load th' shots, this kind av weather, after th' sun goes down. Carry it as ye find it, without unpackin' th' box."

Blascom nodded. "If I leave th' jug for you to put away when you go down for th' box, would you mind puttin' it out tonight with th' dynamite? No use of me makin' two trips to my cabin, an' I don't want to tote it around till dark."

"I will that, an' be glad to. There she comes now, leavin' Whiterock Cut. Casey's late ag'in; but that's regular, an' not his fault, as I've told them time an' time ag'in. Th' grades are ag'in' him comin' west, an' with his leaky packin's an' worn cylinders it's a wonder he does as well as he has. 'Economy,' says th' super. 'No money for repairs that are not needed on this jerkwater line.' I wonder does he ever figger th' fuel wasted through them steam leaks? An' poor Casey gets th' blame—though divvil a bit he cares."

Number Three wheezed in, panted a moment, and coughed on again. Murphy took a package consigned to him, picked up the jug and went down the track toward the toolshed, Blascom wandering idly over to the Railroad Saloon to pass some of the time he had on his hands. In a little while the big Irishman, a small wooden box under his arm, sauntered carelessly down the street, nodded politely from a distance to the sleepy marshal and went into the Mecca.

"Good day, Mr. Williams," he said with stiff formality. "I'll be havin' six dynamite sticks if ye have them, with th' same number av three-minute fuses. Handle it gintly, if ye don't mind. Th' weather is aggravatin' to th' stuff, an' it's timpermental enough at best."

Williams glowered at him. "Don't you worry about me handlin' it gentle, because I ain't goin' to handle it at all. If you want any I'll give you th' key to th' powderhouse an' wish you good luck. Th' sun beatin' down on that house, day after day, has got me plumb nervous. I wish you'd come for it all!" He shook his head. "I wouldn't let you even open th' door if it wasn't for gettin' that much more of it out of th' way."

"Is it ventilated well?" demanded Murphy, smiling a little.

"As well as it can be," sighed Williams. "You'll never catch me carryin' anythin' but powder over th' summer any more. I'm afraid a thunderclap will set it off every storm. What you got in that to pack it in?"

"Sawdust. While yo're cuttin' th' fuses I'll be gettin' th' stuff."

"You'll not come back for any fuses! Wait an' take 'em with you! An' when you are through with th' powder-house, throw th' key close to th' back door: I don't want no man with six sticks of dynamite hangin' around this store today. Want a bill?"

Murphy nodded. "Two av them is th' rule av th' company. You can mark 'em paid an' take it out av this."

The receipted bills in his pocket, he threw the fuses over his shoulder, their wickedly shining copper caps carefully wrapped in a handkerchief, took up the bunch of keys and the box, and grinned. "If ye hear an explosion out back, ye needn't come out to gimme any help. I'm cleanin' up some bad cracked rocks hangin' from a cut west av town, over near Buffalo Crick. I'm tellin' ye th' last so ye won't think it's thunderclaps on their disturbin' way to town. But ye'll sleep through it, no doubt, an' never hear th' shot."

"Blastin' at night?" exclaimed Williams in incredulous surprise.

"I don't like th' sun shinin' on th' darlin's while I'm pokin' 'em in th' hot rocks, so I may load her an' shoot her after dark," replied Murphy. "I've a lot av respect for th' stuff, much as I've handled it. Good day, sir," and he left behind him a man who was nervous and jumpy until after the keys had tinkled on the ground near the rear door; indeed, such an impression had been made on him that he mentioned it, with profane criticisms and observations, at the table that night in the hotel.

The marshal moved his chair farther around in the shade and on his tanned face there crept a warm, rare smile. " 'Lo, I will stand at thy right hand, and keep the bridge with thee!' Well said, Herminius! Yonder you go in spirit: Tim Murphy, you'd make complete any 'dauntless three'!"

The shadows were growing long when Tommy came into sight again, buried in thought as he rode slowly down the street. He stopped and swung to the ground in front of the lazy marshal.

"They shore do beat th' devil," he growled, throwing himself into the vacant chair and lapsing into silence.

Tex nodded understandingly. "They do," he indolently agreed, a smile flickering across his face. "Black is white an' red is green—they're the worst I've ever seen," he extemporized. "They're intuitive critters, son; an' don't you let anybody tell you that intuition hasn't any warrant for existing. It has. It's got more warrant than reason. It was flowering long before reason poked its first shoot out of the ground. Reason only runs back a few thousand generations, but intuition goes back to the first cell of nervous tissue—I might qualify that a bit and say before nervous tissue was structurally apart from the rest. Reason starts anew in every life, usually upon a little better foundation—often a poorer one. It is nursed and trained and cultivated an' when its possessor dies, it dies with him. Not so our venerable friend, intuition. He, or rather she, is cumulative. She is th' sum of all previous individuals in the life chain of th' last. She picks up an' stores away, growing a little each time—an' while she is vague, an' can be classified as a 'because,' or 'I don't know why,' she operates steady. Don't ask me what I know about it, for it has been a long time since I gave any study to things like this. I might guess an' say that it's th' physical changes in th' thought channels due to experience, or in th' structure of th' brain cells or th' quality of their tissues. Anyway, so far as practicability is concerned, you've summed up th' whole thing: 'They shore do beat th' devil.' "

Tommy was looking at him, puzzled and intent; but puzzled intelligently. There is a difference.

"With me an' you, two opposites in thought result in th' cancellation of one of them. We don't say of th' same object: 'This is white, this is black,' at th' same time an' believe 'em both. Th' words themselves are intelligible; but th' conception ain't. We can't do it. One is chosen an' th' other dies. But I won't bet you that a woman cancels. She may not get a dirty white or a slate gray, but she gets a combination, all right. That's where intuition's family tree comes in. No matter how absurd its contentions may be they have force because of th' impetus, coming from age. What did she get out th' colors for you?"

"Yo're th' easiest man to talk to that I ever met," said Tommy wonderingly. "I don't know how you do it. Why, she

got a bright red with a dull green cast—said you was justified, 'but a life's a life': an' then she cried!"

Over Tex's face came a light which only can be compared
to the rising sun seen from some lofty peak, for in the radiance there were shadows.

XIII

♦

Outcheating Cheaters

Gus Williams left the supper table, where he had held
forth volubly upon the subject of dynamite, in his almost lecture to the other diners, some of whom knew more
about it than he did, and walked ponderously toward the
poker table for his usual evening's game. Seating himself
at the place which by tacit consent had become his own, he
idly shuffled and reshuffled the cards and finally began a
slow and laborious game of solitaire to while away the
time until his cronies should join him. This game had become a fixture of the establishment, played for low stakes
but with great seriousness, and often ran into the morning
hours.

The rest of the diners tarried inexplicably at the plate-
littered table, engaged in a discussion of stud poker and of
their respective abilities in playing it, and of winnings they
had made and seen made. It slowly but surely grew acrimo-
nious, as any such discussion is prone to among idle men
who are very much in each other's company.

The new marshal sat a little apart from the eager disputants, taking no share in the wrangling. Finally Sinful,
scorning a shouted ruling on a hypothetical question concerning the law of averages, turned suddenly and appealed

to the marshal, whose smiling reply was not a confirmation of the appellant's claim.

Sinful glared at his disappointing umpire. "A lot you know about stud!" he retorted. "Bet you can't even play mumbly-peg!"

"That takes a certain amount of skill," rejoined Tex without heat. "In stud it's how th' cards fall."

Hank laughed sarcastically. "Averages don't count? We'll just start a little game an' I'll show you how easy stud-hoss is. Come on, boys: we'll give th' marshal a lesson. Clear away them dishes."

All but Sinful held back, saying that they had no money for gambling, but they were remarkably eager to watch the game.

Sinful snorted. "Huh! Two-hand is no good. I'm honin' for a little stud-hoss for a change. It's been nothin' but draw in this town. Reckon stud's too lively to suit most folks: takes nerve to ride a fast game. A man can have a-plenty of nerve one way, an' none a-tall another way. Fine bunch of paupers!"

Hank's disgust was as great. "Fine bunch of paupers," he repeated. "An' them as ain't busted is scared. You called th' turn, Sinful: it shore does take nerve—more'n mumbly-peg, anyhow. A three-hand game would move fast—*too* fast for these coyotes."

"Don't you let th' old mosshead git off with that, Marshal!" cried a miner, "Wish *I* had some dust: I'd cussed soon show 'em!"

Tex was amused by the baiting. Hardly an eye had left him while the whole discussion was going on, even the two principals looking at him when they spoke to each other. He looked from one old reprobate to the other, and let his smile become a laugh as he moved up to the table, a motion which was received by the entire group with sighs of relief and satisfaction.

"I reckon it's my luck ag'in' yore skill," he said; "but I can't set back an' be insulted this way. I'm a public character, now, an' has got to uphold th' dignity of th' law. Get a-goin', you fellers."

Sinful and Hank, simultaneously slamming their gold bags on the table, reached for the cards at the same time and a new wrangle threatened.

"Cut for it," drawled Tex, smiling at the expectant, hopeful faces around the table. Williams' irritable, protesting cough was unheeded and, Hank dealing, the game got under way. Tex honorably could have shot both of his opponents in the first five minutes of play, but simply cheated in turn and held his own. At the end of an hour's excitement he was neither winner nor loser, and he shoved back from the table in simulated disgust. He scorned to take money so tragically needed, and he had determined to lose none of his own.

"This game's so plumb fast," he ironically observed, "that I ain't won or lost a dollar. You got my sportin' blood up, an' I ain't goin' to insult it by playin' all night for nothin'. I told you stud was only luck: That skill you was talkin' about ain't showed a-tall. If there's anybody here as wants a *real* game I'm honin' to hear his voice."

"Can you hear mine?" called Williams, glaring at the disappointed stud players and their friends. "There's a real game right here," he declared, pounding the table, "with real money an' real nerve! Besides, I got a hoss to win back, an' I want my revenge."

Tex turned to the group and laughed, playfully poking Sinful in the ribs. "Hear th' cry of th' lobo? He's lookin' for meat. Our friend Williams has been savin' his money for Tex Jones, an' I ain't got th' heart to refuse it. Bring yore community wealth an' set in, you an' Hank. Though if you can't play draw no better'n you play stud you ought to go home."

"I cut my teeth on draw," boasted Sinful. He turned and slapped his partner on the shoulder. "Come on, Hank!" he cried. "Th' lone wolf is howlin' from th' timber line an' his pelt's worth money. Let's go git it!"

They swept down on the impatient Williams, their silent partners bringing up the rear, and clamored for action. Tex lighting a freshly rolled cigarette, faced the local boss, Hank on his right and Sinful on his left, the eager onlookers settling behind their champions. The thin, worried faces of the miners appealed to the marshal, their obvious need arousing a feeling of pity in him; and then began a game which was as much a credit to Tex as any he ever had played. He rubbed the saliva-soaked end of his cigarette between finger and thumb and gave all his attention to the game.

Williams won on his own deal, cutting down the gold of the two miners. On Hank's deal he won again and the faces of the old prospectors began to tense. Tex dealt in turn and after a few rounds of betting Williams dropped out and the game resolved itself into a simulated fiercely fought duel between the miners, who really cared but little which of them won. Hank finally raked in the stakes. Sinful shuffled and Tex cut. Williams forced the betting but had to drop out, followed by Tex, and the dealer gleefully hauled in his winnings. Again Williams shuffled, his expression vaguely denoting worry. He made a sharp remark about one of the onlookers behind Tex and all eyes turned instinctively. The miner retorted with spirit and Williams suddenly smiled apologetically.

"My mistake, Goldpan," he admitted. "Let's forget it, an' let th' game proceed."

Tex deliberately had allowed his attention to be called from the game and when he picked up his cards he was mildly suspicious, for Williams' remark had been entirely uncalled for. He looked quickly for the nine of clubs or the six of hearts, finding that he had neither. He passed and sat back, smiling at the facial contortions of Hank and the blank immobility of Sinful's leathery countenance. Hank dropped out on the next round and after a little cautious betting Sinful called and threw down his hand. Williams spread his own and smiled. That smile was to cost him heavily, for in his club flush lay the nine spot, guiltless of the tobacco smudge which Tex had rubbed on its face in the first hand he had been dealt.

Tex wiped the tips of his sensitive fingers on his trousers and became voluble and humorous. As he picked up his cards, one by one as they dropped from Hank's swiftly moving hand, he first let his gaze linger a little on their backs, and his fingers slipped across the corners of each. Williams had cheated before with a trimmed deck and now the marshal grimly determined to teach him a lesson, and at the same time not arouse the suspicions of the boss against the new marshal. With the switching of the decks Williams had set a pace which would grow too fast for him. Marked cards suited Tex, especially if they had been marked by an opponent, who would have all the more confidence in them. After a few deals if he wouldn't know each card as well as a man like Williams, whose marking could not be much out of the ordinary, and certainly not very original, then he felt that he deserved to get the worst of the play. He once had played against a deck which had been marked by the engraver who designed the backs, and he had learned it in less than an hour. So now he prepared to enjoy himself and thereafter bet lightly when Williams dealt, but on each set of hands dealt by himself one of the prospectors always won, and with worthy cards. Worthy as were their hands they were only a shade better than those held by the proprietor of the hotel and the general store. One hand alone cost Williams over eighty dollars, three others were above the seventy-dollar mark and he was losing his temper, not only because of his losses, but also because he did not dare to cheat too much on his own deal. Tex's eyes twinkled at him and Tex's rambling words hid any ulterior motive in the keen scrutiny. Finally, driven by desperation, Williams threw caution to the winds and risked detection. He was clever enough to avoid grounds for open accusation, but both of the miners suddenly looked thoughtful and a moment later they exchanged significant glances. Thereafter no one bet heavily when Williams dealt.

The finish came when Tex had dealt and picked up his hand. Sinful stolidly regarded the cheery faces of three kings—spades, clubs, and hearts. Williams liked the looks of his two pairs, jacks up. Hank rolled his huge cud into the other cheek and tried to appear mournful at the sight of the queen, ten, eight, and five of hearts. Tex laid down his four-card spade straight and picked up the pack.

"Call 'em, boys," he said.

Sinful's two cards, gingerly lifted one at a time from the table, pleased him very much, although from all outward signs they might have been anything in the card line. They were the aces of diamonds and clubs. He sighed, squared the hand, and placed it face down on the table before him. Williams gulped when he added a third jack to his two pairs, and Hank nearly swallowed his tobacco at sight of the prayed-for, but unexpected, appearance of another heart. All eyes were on the dealer. He put down the deck and picked up his hand for another look at it. After a moment he put it down again, sadly shaking his head.

"Good enough as it is," he murmured. "I ain't havin' much luck, one way or th' other; an' I'm gettin' tired of th' cussed game."

"Dealer pat?" sharply inquired Williams, suspicion glinting in his eyes.

"Pat, an' cussed near flat," grunted Tex. "Go on with her. I'll trail along with what I got, an' quit after this hand."

Notwithstanding the dealer's pat hand and his expression of resignation, the betting was sharp and swift. On the first round, being forty-odd dollars ahead, Tex saw the accumulated raises and had enough left out of his winnings to raise five dollars. He tossed it in and leaned back, watching each face in turn. Sinful was not to be bluffed by any pat hand at this stage of the play, no matter how craftily it was bet. He reflected that straights, flushes, and full houses could be held pat, as well as threes or two pairs, all of which he had beat. A straight flush or fours were the only hands he could lose to, and Williams had not dealt the cards. Pat hands were sometimes pat bluffs, more terrifying to novices than to old players. He saw the raise and shoved out another, growling: "Takes about twenty more to see this circus."

Williams hesitated, looking at the dealer's neat little stack of cards. He was convinced from the way Tex had acted that the pat hand was a bluff, for its owner had not been caught bluffing since the game started, which indicated that he had labored to establish the reputation of playing only intrinsic hands, which would give a later bluff a strong and false value. He saw and raised a dollar, hoping that some-one would drop out. Hank disappointed him by staying in and boosting another dollar. They both were feeling their way along. Hank also believed the pat hand to be worthless; and worthless it was, for Tex tossed it from him, face down, and rammed his hands into his pockets.

Sinful heaved a sigh of relief, which was echoed by the others, squinted from his hand to the faces of the two remaining players, and grinned sardonically. "Bluffs are like crows; they live together in flocks. I never quit when she's comin' my way. Grab a good holt for another raise! She's ten higher, now."

With the disturbing pat hand out of it, which was all the more disturbing because it had belonged to the dealer, Williams gave more thought to the players on his left and right. He decided that Hank was the real danger and that Sinful's words were a despairing effort to win by the default of the others. He saw the raise and let it go as it was. Hank rolled the cud nervously and with a sudden, muttered curse, threw down his hand. A flush had no business showing pride and fight in this game, he decided. Sinful grinned at him across the table.

"Terbaccer makin' you sick, Hank?" he jeered. "I'm raisin' ten more, jest to keep th' corpse alive. He-he-he!"

There was now too much in the pot to give it up for ten dollars and Williams met the raise, swore, and called, "What you got, you devil from hell?"

"I got quite a fambly," chuckled Sinful, laying down a pair of aces. "There's twin brothers," he said, looking up.

Williams snorted at the old man's pleasure in not showing his whole hand at once, and he tossed three jacks on the table. "Triplets in mine," he replied.

Sinful raised his eyebrows and regarded them accusingly. "Three jacks can tote quite some load if it's packed right," he said. "Th' rest of my fambly is three more brothers, an' they bust th' mules' backs. Ain't got th' extry jack, have you?"

Slamming the rest of the cards on the table Williams arose and without a word walked to the bar. Sinful's cackles of joy were added to by his friends and they surrounded the table to help in the division of the spoils, in plain sight of all.

"Win or lose, Marshal?" demanded Sinful shrilly above the hubbub of voices.

"Lost a couple of dollars," bellowed Tex.

"Much obliged for 'em," rejoined Sinful. He looked at Hank, winked and said: "Marshal's been real kind to us, Hank," and Tex never was quite certain of the old man's meaning.

Williams looked around as Tex leaned against the bar. "How'd *you* come out?" he asked, his face showing his anger.

"I lost," answered Tex carelessly. "Not anythin' to speak of: a few dollars, I reckon. I told 'em two dollars, for they're swelled up with pride as things are. They must 'a' got into you real heavy."

Williams sneered. "Heavy for them, I reckon. I ain't limpin'. They got too cussed much luck."

"Luck?" muttered the marshal, gazing inquiringly at the glass of whiskey he had raised from the bar, as though it might tell him what he wanted to know. "I ain't so shore of that, Williams," he slowly said. "Them old sour-doughs get snowed in near every winter, up in th' hills; an' then they ain't got nothin' to do but eat, sleep, swap lies, an' play cards. Somethin' tells me there wasn't a whole lot of luck in it. I know I had all I could do to stay in th' saddle without pullin' leather—an' I ain't exactly cuttin' my teeth where poker is concerned. Listen to 'em, will you? Squabblin' like a lot of kids. I reckon they had this cooked up in grand style. They're all sharin' in th' winnin's, you'll notice." He paused in surprise as a dull roar faintly shook the room. "What's that?" he demanded sharply. "It can't be thunder!"

His companion shook his head. "No, it ain't; it's that Murphy blowin' up rock, like I was sayin' at supper. Hope he went up with it!" He laughed at a man who was just coming in, and who stopped dead in the door and listened to the rumble. "Yore shack's safe, Jake," he called. "Th' Mick's blastin' over past yore away. You remember what I've told you!" he warned.

Jake looked from the speaker to the careless, but inwardly alert, city marshal, scowled, shuffled over to a table, and called for a drink, thereafter entirely ignoring the peace officer.

Henry came in soon after and joined the two at the bar. "Yes, I'll have th' same. You two goin' ridin' ag'in, Marshal?" he asked.

Tex shrugged his shoulders. "It shore don't look like it. She mebby figgered me out. Anyhow, she slammed th' door plumb in my face." He frowned. "Somehow I don't get used to things like that. She could 'a' treated me like I wasn't no tramp, anyhow, couldn't she?"

Henry smiled maliciously, and felt relieved. "They're shore puzzlin'. I hear that coyote Watkins was out there this afternoon. There wasn't no door slammed in *his* face." His little eyes glinted. "I see where he's goin' to learn a lesson, an' learn it for keeps!"

"Oh, he got throwed, too," chuckled Tex, as if finding some balm in another's woe. "He stopped off on his way home an' told me about it. Got a busted heart, an' bellyachin' like a sick calf. That's what he is; an' it's calf love, as well. Shucks! When I was his age I fell in love with a different gal about every moon. Besides, he ain't got money, nor prospects: an' she knows it."

Henry took him by the arm and led him to a table in a far corner. "I been thinkin' I mebby ought to send her a present, or somethin'," he said, watching his companion's face. "You, havin' more experience with 'em, I figgered mebby you would help me out. *I* don't know what to get her."

"Weakenin' already," muttered the marshal, trying to hide a knowing, irritating smile. "Pullin' leather, an' ain't hardly begun to ride yet!"

"I ain't pullin' no leather!" retorted Henry, coloring. "I reckon a man's got a right to give a present to his gal!"

"Shore!" endorsed Tex heartily. "There ain't no question about it—when she comes right out an' admits that she *is* his gal. This Saunders woman ain't admittin' it, yet; an' if she figgers that yo're weakenin' on yore play of ignorin' her, then she'll just set back an' hold you off so th' presents won't stop comin'. This is a woman's game, an' she can beat a man, hands down an' blindfolded: an' they know it. I tell you, Hennery, a wild cayuse that throws its first rider ain't no deader set on stayin' wild than a woman is set on makin' a man go through his tricks for her if she finds he's performin' for her private amusement, an' payin' for th' privilege, besides. It ain't no laughin' matter for you, Hennery; but I can't hardly keep *from* laughin' when I think of you stayin' away to get her anxious, an' then sendin' her presents! It's yore own private affair, an' yo're runnin' it yore own way—but them's *my* ideas."

Henry stared into space, gravely puffing on a cold cigarette. His low, furrowed brow denoted intense mental concentration, and the scowl which grew deeper did not suggest that his conclusions were pleasant. The simile regarding the wild horse sounded like good logic to him, for he prided himself that he knew horses. Finally he looked anxiously at his deeply thinking companion.

"It sounds right, Marshal," he grudgingly admitted; "but it shore is hard advice to foller. I'm plumb anxious to buy her somethin' nice, somethin' she can't get in this part of th' country, an' somethin' she can wear an' know come from me." He paused in some embarrassment and tried to speak carelessly. "If you was goin' to get a woman like her some present—mind, I'm sayin' *if*—what would you get?"

Tex reflected gravely. "Candy don't mean nothin'," he

cogitated, in a low, far-away voice. "Anybody she knew at all could give her candy. It don't mean nothin' special, a-tall." He did not appear to notice how his companion's face fell at the words. "Books are like candy—just common presents. A stranger almost could give 'em. Ridin' gloves is a little nearer—but Tommy, or me, could give them to her. Stockin's? Hum: I don't know. They're sort of informal, at that. 'Tain't everybody, however, could give 'em. Only just one man: get my idea?"

"I shore do, Marshal," beamed Henry. "You see, livin' out here all my life an' not 'sociatin' with wimmin—like her, anyhow—I didn't know hardly what would be th' correct thing. Wonder what color?"

Tex was somewhat aghast at his joke being taken so seriously. "Now, you look here, Hennery!" he said in a warning voice. "You promise me not to send her no stockin's till I says th' word." He had wanted to give Jane more reason to dislike the nephew, but hardly cared to have it go that far. "Stayin' away, are you? You make me plumb sick, you do! Stayin' away, hell!"

A roar of laughter came from the celebrating miners and all eyes turned their way. Sinful and Hank were dancing to the music of a jew's-harp and the time set by stamping, hob-nailed boots. They parted, bowed, joined again, parted, curt-sied and went on, hand in hand, turning and ducking, backing and filing, the dust flying and the perspiration streaming down. It seemed impossible that in these men lurked a bitter race hatred, or that hearts as warm and happy could be incubating the germs of cowardly murder. Not one of them, alone, would be guilty of such a thing; but the spirit of a mob is a remarkable and terrible thing, tearing aside civilization's training and veneer, and in a moment hurling men back thousands of years, back to the days when killing often was its own reward.

XIV

◆

Tact and Courage

Things were going along smoothly for the new marshal until two of the C Bar punchers, accompanied by two men from a ranch farther from town, rode in to make a night of it. It chanced that the C Bar men had been with a herd some forty miles north of the ranch, where water and grass conditions were much better, and they had become friendly with the outfit of another herd which grazed on the western fringe of the same range. A month of this, days spent in the saddle on the same rounds, and nights spent at the chuck wagon with nothing to vary the monotony of the cycle, had given the men an edge to be blunted at the first opportunity; and their ideas of working off high-pressure energies did not take into consideration any such things as safety valves. Action they craved, action they had ridden in for, and action they would have. The swifter it started, the faster it moved, the better it would suit them. So, with an accumulation of energy, thirst, and money they tore into Windsor one noon at a dead run, whooping like savages, and proclaiming their freedom from restraint and their pride of class by a heavenward bombardment which frightened no one and did no harm.

It so chanced that when they passed the new marshal's office they were going so fast, and were so fully occupied in waking up the town, that the lettering over the door of the lean-to escaped their attention. And they were past, bunched in a compact group, and nearly hidden in dust before the mildly curious officer could get to the door. He watched them whirl up to the hotel, the stronghold and stamping ground of Williams and the miners and, dismounting with shrill yells, pause a moment to reload their empty guns, and then surge toward the door.

Tex rubbed his chin thoughtfully as he considered them. Carney's was the cowman's favorite drinking place, yet these four cheerful riders had not given it a second glance, judging from the way they had gone past it. This was no matter for congratulation, but bespoke rather, a determination to show off where their efforts would create more interest. Who they were, or what they came in for, he neither knew nor cared. They were celebrating punchers from somewhere out on the range and they were going to hold their jamboree in the miners' chosen place of entertainment. A less experienced marshal, filled with zeal and conceit, might forthwith have buckled on his guns, and started for the scene of the festivities, to be on hand as a preventive, rather than a corrective, or punitive, force; and very probably would have hastened the very thing he sought to avoid. Tex hoped to take the edge from the class feeling, and determined to be openly linked with neither one side nor the other. His place was to be that of a neutral buffer and his justice must be impartial and above criticism. So, after turning back to buckle on the left-hand gun, he did not sally forth to blaze the glory of the law and precipitate a riot; he sat down patiently to await the course of events.

Williams poked his head out of the door of his store and looked anxiously down the street at the dismounting four. As they went into the hotel he hurried across to the marshal's office and stopped, panting, in the doorway.

"See 'em?" he asked excitedly. "Hear 'em?"

"What or who?" asked Tex, throwing one leg over the other.

"Them rowdy punchers!" exclaimed the storekeeper. "Nobody's safe! Go up an' take 'em in, quick!"

"What they do?" interestedly asked the marshal.

"Didn't you *see* an' *hear?*" demanded Williams incredulously.

"I saw 'em ride past, an' I heard 'em shootin' in th' air; but what did they do so I can arrest 'em?"

"Ain't that enough? That, an' th' yellin', an' everythin'?"

"Sinful and his friends made more noise th' other night when they left town," replied the marshal. "I didn't arrest them. Hank was of a mind to see if it was true that a bullet only punches a little, thin-edged hole in a pane of glass an' don't smash it all to pieces. Bein' wobbly, he picked out yore winder, seein' they was th' biggest in town; but Sinful held him back, an' they had a scufflin' match an' made more noise than sixteen mournful coyotes. There bein' no pane smashed I didn't cut in. A man is only a growed-up boy, anyhow."

Williams looked at him in frank amazement. "But these here fellers are punchers!" he exploded.

"I shore could see that, even with th' dust," confessed the marshal. "That ain't no crime as I knows of."

"It ain't th' four to one that's holdin' you back, is it?" demanded Williams insinuatingly. "They're punchers, too: bad as hell."

Tex languidly arose and removed the pair of guns and the belts, laying them gently on the floor. He pitched his sombrero on the bunk and faced his caller.

"Mebby I didn't understand you," he coldly suggested. "What was it you said?"

Williams raised both hands in quick protest, one foot fishing desperately behind him for the ground below the sill. "Nothin' to make you go on th' prod," he hastily explained.

"Listen to me, Williams," said the cool peace officer, his voice level and unemotional. "Anybody callin' me a coward wants to go into action fast, an' keep on goin' fast. That includes everybody from King Solomon right down to date. I'm responsible for th' peace in this town, an' when *anybody* starts smashin' it I'll go 'em a whirl. Yellin', ridin' fast, an' shootin' in th' air, 'specially by sober men, ain't smashin' nothin' in a town like this. I don't aim to run no nursery, nor even a kindergarten. I ain't makin' a fool out of myself an' turnin' th' law into a joke. Once let ridicule start an' hell's pleasant by contrast. They ain't shootin' now. Th' first shot fired inside any buildin', or dangerously low, an' I inject myself an' my two guns. I can't make no arrests on a blind guess, mine nor yourn. You better go back to th' store an' keep th' vinegar from sourin' on its mother."

Williams' jaw dropped. This was not Tex Jones at all, at least it didn't sound like him. "As th' owner of th' most valuable property in town I want them coyotes stopped from ruinin' it. I——"

"When they show any signs of ruinin' *any* property I'll step in an' stop 'em," the marshal assured him. "I got my ears open, an' had my authority buckled on—which I'll now resume wearin'." He picked up a heavy belt and slung it around him, deftly catching the free end as it slapped against him. "We'll have law an' order, Williams—even if I have to fill some fool as full of holes as a prairie-dog town; but I ain't goin' out an' trample on a man's pride an' make him get killed defendin' it, unless I got good reason to. This is a long speech, but I'm goin' to make it longer so I can impress somethin' on yore mind. Bein' a busy merchant you've mebby never had time to think about it much; but me, bein' a marshal, I *got* to think of everythin' like that. This is one of 'em: When bad feelin's exist between two classes, helpin' one ag'in' th' other, without honest reasons, is only goin' to make more bitterness. It can be held down only by impersonal justice. That's me. I don't give a damn what a man is as long as he behaves hisself." Picking up the second belt he slung it around him the other way and buckled it behind him. As he shook them both to a more comfortable fit a yell rang out up near the hotel, followed by a shot. Grabbing his hat from the bunk he pushed Williams out of his way and dashed through the door, flinging over his shoulder: "I'm in-jectin' myself *now!* You'd better go look to th' vinegar!"

He saw Whiskey Jim, the man whom he had caught beating the dog, in his blind terror run against the side of the harness-shop, recover from the impact and, stupefied by fear, frantically claw at the bleached boards. A spurt of dust almost under one of his feet made him claw more frantically. The hilarious puncher walked slowly toward him, raising the Colt for another shot. Behind him, laughing uproari-ously, stood his three friends, solidly blocking the hotel door.

"Hold that gun where it is!" shouted the marshal, dropping into a catlike stride. He was coming down the middle of the street, not more than forty paces, now, from the performing puncher.

The gun arm stiffened in air as the whiplike, authoritative phrase reached its possessor and, grinning exultantly, the puncher wheeled to get a good look at his next victim. He saw a grave-faced man of forty-odd years walking to-ward him, a bright star pinned to the open vest, two guns hanging low down on the swaying hips, the swinging hands brushing the walnut grips at every lithe, steady step.

"See what we got to play with!" exulted the surprised puncher, calling to his friends. "I want his badge: you can have th' rest!" His hand chopped down and a spurt of dust leaped from the ground at the marshal's side.

Disregarding it, the peace officer maintained his steady, swinging stride, his eyes fixed on those of the other, intently watching for a change in their playful expression. Another shot and the dust spurted close to his left foot. The hilarious laughter of the three in the doorway died out, and their friend in the street stood stock still, trying to figure out what he had better do next. The deliberate marshal was now only five paces away and at the puncher's indecision, plain to be seen in the eyes, he leaped forward, wrested the gun from the feebly resisting fingers, whirled the nonplussed man around and then kicked him his own length on the ground.

Ignoring the three men in the doorway, thereby tacitly admitting their squareness, the marshal calmly ejected the cartridges from the captured weapon and, as the angry and astonished puncher arose, handed it to him.

"It's empty," he said in a matter-of-fact voice. "Keep it that way till you leave town; an' when you come in again, intendin' to likker up an' raise hell, either unload it or leave it with me, unless you promise to behave yoreself." He turned to Whiskey Jim, who appeared to be frozen into a statue. "Come over here, Jim," he commanded, and again turned to the puncher, who did not know whether to laugh or to curse. "I reckon Jim's th' only injured party. His feelin's has been trampled on to th' tune of about five dollars. Pay him before he takes it out of yore hide. He's a desperate bad man, Jim is!"

The three men in the door, who were nowhere near drunk yet, knew sparkling courage when they saw it, and they shouted with laughter at their crestfallen friend, who grudgingly was counting the fine into the eager hand of the aggrieved citizen.

"Hey, Walt!" burbled one of them, a beardless youth on one end of the line. "Still want to play with that badge?"

"If you do," jeered the man in the middle, laughing again, "better rustle, *pronto,* 'cause I'm buyin' its boss a drink."

Walt grinned expansively, shoved the money into Whiskey Jim's clutching fingers, took hold of the quiet marshal, and turned toward the hotel. "You come along with me, officer," he said. "I'll pertect you. That fool says he's buyin' you a drink—mebby he *is,* but I'm payin' for th' first one. Yo're about th' best he-man I've seen since I looked into a lookin'-glass. I'm obliged to you for not losin' yore valuable temper." He waved a hand at the unbelieving Jim, who doubted his reeling senses. Five whole dollars, all at once! Gosh, but the new marshal was a hummer. "Now don't you lay for me, Jim," laughed the puncher. "We're square, all 'round, ain't we?"

The cheerful three in the door grabbed the marshal of Windsor and hauled him in to the bar, where he pushed free and surveyed them.

"Four cheerful imbeciles," he murmured sadly. "Don't you reckon you better quit drinkin', or else empty them guns?"

"Now don't you be too hard on us, Marshal," chuckled the eldest. "We're so dry we rattles, an' th' dust, risin' out of our throats gets plumb into our eyes. Here," he said, dragging out his gun and gravely emptying it, "these are shore heavy. I'll carry 'em in my pocket for a change," and he made good his words. The others laughingly followed his example, Tex's smile growing broader all the time.

"This ain't nothin' personal, boys," he said. "It's only that th' law has come to town. Knowin' you'll leave 'em empty till after you get out, I'll have one drink an' go about my business." He made no threats and his voice was friendly and pleasant; and it did not have to be otherwise. He had made four friends, and they knew that he would go through with any play he started. "Know Tommy Watkins?" he asked as he put down his glass.

"Shore!" answered Walt. "He's workin' with my outfit—C Bar. Ain't seen him for a month, him bein' off somewhere when we rode in for our pay. Marshal, shake hands with another C Bar rider—Wyatt Holmes. These two tramps is Double S punchers—Lefty Rowe, an' Luke Perkins. My name's Butler—Walt Butler. What's Tommy up an' done?" he finished somewhat anxiously.

"Glad to see you, boys," said Tex, heartily shaking hands all around. "My name's Tex Jones. Come in ag'in," he invited. "Oh," he said in answer to Walt's question, "Tommy ain't done nothin', yet. I was just wonderin'. Good boy, Tommy is. Sort of wild, I reckon, bein' young. Busy after th' gals. Most young fellers are hellers anyhow, or think they are. But he's a likable pup."

Walt laughed and the others grinned broadly. "You've shore figgered him wrong, Marshal. He's scairt of th' gals— won't have nothin' to do with 'em; an' I ain't never seen him nowhere near drunk; but" he hastily defended in loyalty to his absent friend, "he's all right, other ways. Yes, sir—barrin' them things, Tommy Watkins is a good man, an' I can lick any feller that says he ain't."

"Which won't be me," replied Tex, smiling. "I like him, first-rate. We been gettin' acquainted fast. Well, boys," he said, turning toward the door, "have a good time an' come in often. I like a little company from th' outside. It relieves th' monotony. So-long."

"You shore had th' monotony busted wide open today," chuckled Walt. "But Tommy's a good boy—whatever th' hell he's been doin' since I saw him last." Watching the marshal until out of sight past the door he turned and regarded his companions. "I'm tellin' you calves there's a man who'd spit in th' devil's eye," he said. "We was playin' with giant powder like four fools. Here's to Tex Jones, Marshal of Windsor!"

Lefty, tenderly putting the glass on the bar, looked thoughtfully around the room and then at the partially stunned barkeep. "How's friend Bud takin' th' new marshal?

Bud an' him shore will have an' interestin' Colt fandango some of these fine days."

Baldy sighed, wiped off the bar, and looked sorrowfully at the group. "Bud's planted on Boot Hill. They done had th' fandango, an' he did th' dancin'. My G—d, I can see it yet! It was like this—" and he left the bar, walked to the door, and painstakingly enacted the fight. When it was finished, he mopped his head and slowly returned to his accustomed place.

Wyatt Holmes reached out and gravely shook hands with his friends and finished by shaking his own. "You allus was a fool for luck, Walt," he said thoughtfully. "Giant powder?" he muttered piously. "Giant hell! It was dynamite with th' fuse lit. Here," he demanded, wheeling on the startled Baldy. "I *need* this drink! Set 'em up!"

Walt shook his head. "Now, what th' devil has Tommy done?" he growled.

Baldy, remembering Tommy's share in the altercation, maintained a discreet silence.

XV

♦

A Good Samaritan

Out on Buffalo Creek, Blascom, haggard, drawn, gaunt, and throbbing with an excitement which was slowly mastering him, scorning time to properly prepare and eat his food, drove himself like a madman. The creek bed at the old sump showed a huge, sloping-sided ditch from bank to bank, the upper side treacherous dry sand, the lower side a great, slanting ridge of rock, riven through in one place by the force of the dynamite, which had blown a great crater on the down-stream side of the natural riffle. In the bottom of the ditch a few inches of water lay, all that had saved him from fleeing from the claim because of thirst.

For year after weary year the miner had labored over the gold-bearing regions of the West, South, and North, beginning each period full of that abiding faith which clings so tenaciously to the gold-hunter and refuses to accept facts in any but an optimistic manner. A small stake here, day wages there, grubstakes, and hiring out, he had persistently, stubbornly pursued the will-o'-the-wisp and tracked down many a rainbow of hope, only to find the old disappointment. From laughing, hope-filled youth he had run the gauntlet of the years, through the sobered but still hopeful middle age, scorning thought of the twilight of life when he should be broken in strength and bitter in mind. Teeming, mushroom mining camps, frantic gold rushes, the majestic calm of cool canyons, and the punishing silences of almost unbearable desert wastes had found him an unquestioning worshiper, a trusting devotee of his goddess of gold. It was in his blood, it was woven into every fiber of his body, and he could no more cease his pursuit than he could stop the beating of his heart, or at least he could not cease while the goal remained unattained. Now, after all these years, he had won. He had proved that his quest had not been in vain.

Before the sun came up, even before dawn streaked the eastern sky, his meager, ill-cooked breakfast was bolted, and his morning scouting begun. First of all he slipped with coyote cunning down to the lower fork to see if Jake still kept his drunken stupor. The cold chimney of the miserable hut was the first eagerly sought-for sign, and every furtive visit awakened dread that a ribbon of smoke would meet his eye. A nearer approach made with the wariness of some hunted creature of the wild, let him sense the unnatural quiet of the little shack. A stealthy glance through a glassless opening, called a window, after the light made it possible, showed him morning after morning that his jug had not failed him. The unshaven, matted, unclean face of the stupefied man lay sometimes in a bunk, sometimes on the floor, and once the huge bulk was sprawled out inertly across the rough table amid a disarray of cracked, broken, and unwashed dishes. On the fifth morning the anxious prowler, fearing the lowered contents of the jug, had left a full bottle against the door of the hut and, slinking into the scanty cover, had run like a hunted thing back to the riven riffle and its unsightly ditch and crater.

Feverishly he worked, scorning food, unconscious of the glare of a molten sun rising to the zenith of its scorching heat. Shovel and bucket, trips without end from the ditch to a place above the steep bank where the carried sand grew rapidly higher and higher; panting, straining, frantic, worked Blascom. Foot by foot the ditch widened, foot by foot it lengthened, inch by inch it deepened, slide after sandy slide slipping to its bottom to be furiously, madly cursed by the prospector.

Then at last came the instant when the treasure was momentarily uncovered. Dropping the blunted, ragged-edged shovel, he plunged to all fours and thrust eager, avaricious fingers, bent like the talons of some bird of prey, into the storehouse of gold. Noiselessly responding to the jar and the impact of the groveling body, the great bank of sand had collapsed and slid down upon him, burying him without warning. The mass split and heaved, and the imprisoned miner, wild-eyed, sobbing for breath after his spasmodic exertions, burst through it and, raising quivering fists, cursed it and creation.

Hope had driven him remorselessly, but now that he had seen and felt the treasure, his efforts became those of a madman. More buckets of sand, jealous of each spilled handful, more punishing trips at a dogtrot, more frantic digging, and again he stared wildly at the pocket under his knees. Suddenly leaping erect, he cast anxious glances around him and a panicky fear gripped him and turned him into a wild beast. Yanking his coat from the rock riffle he spread it over the treasure and then, running low and swiftly, gun in hand, he scouted through the brush on both sides of the creek, and then bounded toward the lower fork. Approaching the hut on hands and knees, cruelly cut by rock and thorn, he studied the door and the open window. The bottle was where he had left it, the snores arose regularly, and once more he was reassured. Had there been signs of active life he would have murdered with the exultant zeal of a religious fanatic.

The day waned and passed. Night drew its curtains closer and closer, and yet Blascom labored, the treacherous sand turning him into a raving, frenzied fury. Higher and higher grew the sand pile on the bank, a monument to his mad avarice. With gold in lumps massed at the foot of that rock ridge, yet he must save the sand for its paltry yield in dust, pouring out his waning strength in a labor which, to save pence, might cost him pounds. At last he stumbled more and more, staggering this way and that, his tortured body all but asleep, forced on and on by his fevered mind, flogged by a stubborn will. Then came a heavier stumble, following a more unbalanced stagger and his numbed and vague protests did not suffice to get him back on his feet. When he awakened, the glaring sun shocked him by its nearness to the meridian, and the shock brought a momentary sanity; if he scorned the warning he would be lost—and another shadowy prompting of his subconscious mind was at last allowed to direct him. Calmly, but shakily, he weakly crawled and staggered toward his shack, from which came a thin streamer of smoke, climbing arrow-like into the quiet, heated air.

He stopped and stared at it in amazement, doubting his senses. Had he seen it the day before it would have enraged him to a blind, killing madness; but now, suspicious as he was, and deadly determined to protect his secret, the reaction of the high tension of the last six days made him momentarily apathetic. The abused body, the starved tissues and dulled nerves, now took possession of him and forced him, even though it was with gun in his hand, to approach the door of his squalid, disordered habitation erect and without hesitation. At the sound of his slowly dragging steps a well-known, friendly voice called out and a well-known, friendly face appeared at a window.

The marshal was nearly stunned by what he saw and then, surging into action, leaped through the door and caught his staggering friend.

The well-cooked, wholesome breakfast out of the way, a breakfast made possible only by the marshal's forethought in bringing supplies with him from town, he refused Blascom's request for a third cup of coffee and smilingly offered a glass of whiskey, over which he had made a few mysterious passes.

"Don't want none," objected the weary miner.

"But yo're goin' to overcome yore sudden temperance scruples an' drink it, for me," persuaded Tex. "A good shock will do you a lot of good—an' put new life into you. As you are you ain't worth a cuss."

The prospector held out his hand, smilingly obedient, and downed the fiery draught at a gulp. "Tastes funny," he observed, and then laughed. "Wonder I can taste it at all, after th' nightmare I've had since th' smoke of that blast rolled away. Where'd you think I was when you came?"

Tex chuckled and stretched. "I didn't know, but from th' glimpse I got of th' crick bed I was shore I wasn't goin' huntin' you, an' mebby get shot accidental. Did you find it, Blascom?"

"My G—d, yes!" came the explosive answer. "There's piles of it, all shapes an' sizes, layin' on a smooth rock floor. When that sand stops slidin' I can scoop it up with a shovel, like coal out of a bin. Half of it belongs to you, Jones: go look at it!"

"I don't want any of it," replied Tex with quiet, but unshakable, determination. "If you divide it, no matter how much there is, by th' number of years you've sweat an' slaved and starved, it won't be too much to pay you. You set here a little while an' I'll go on a scout in th' brush an' watch it till you come out. Better lay down a few minutes, say half an hour, an' give that grub a chance to put some life into you. I'll shake you if you fall asleep."

"Feel sleepy now," confessed the prospector, yawning and moving sluggishly toward his bunk. "Seein' as how yo're here, I'll just take a few winks—don't know when I'll get another chance. That sand shore is gallin' an' ornery as th' devil. Go up an' take a look at it—I'll foller in a little while."

Tex, closing the door behind him, slipped into the brush, where he made more than a usual amount of noise for Blascom's benefit, and as he worked up toward the ditch he chuckled to himself. There had been no need for a full dose, he reflected, and he was glad that he had not given one. Blascom's drink of whiskey had just enough chloral in it to deaden him and give his worn-out body the chance it sought; besides, he was not too certain of the effect of a full dose on a constitution as undermined as that of his friend.

The ditch, again slowly filling with sand, showed him nothing, and he stood debating whether he should disturb it for a look at the treasure, when he suddenly thought of

Jake and the whiskey jug. He remembered that Jake had been almost senselessly drunk when he had left the hotel on the night of the blast and that he had not been seen by anyone since. It would do no harm to go down to the lower fork and see what there was to be seen. The thought became action, and he was on his way, down the middle of the creek bed, where the footing was a little more to his liking.

The hut appeared to be deserted and the bottle of whiskey outside the door brought a frown to his face, which deepened as nearer approach showed him that the door was fastened shut by rope and wire on the outside, and that the snoring inmate virtually was a prisoner. There was a note in the snores that disturbed him and aroused his vague, half-forgotten professional knowledge. Hastening forward he pushed the bottle aside with an impatient foot and worked rapidly with the fastenings on the door. At last it opened, and gun in hand against any possible contingency, he entered the hovel and looked at its tenant, sprawled face down near the jumbled bunk. A touch of the drunken man's cheek, a tense counting of his pulse, sent Tex to his feet as though a shot had nicked him. Running back to Blascom's hut, where he had left his horse, he leaped into the saddle and sent Omar at top speed toward town.

His thundering knock on the doctor's door brought no response and, not daring to pause on the dictates of custom, he threw his shoulder against the flimsy barrier and went in on top of it. Scrambling to his feet, he dashed into the rear one of the two rooms and swore in sudden rage and disgust.

Doctor Horn lay on his back on a miserable cot and his appearance brought a vivid recollection to his tumultuous caller. Tex turned up a sleeve and nodded grimly at the tiny puncture marks and, with an oath, faced around and swept the room with a searching glance. It stopped and rested on a heavy volume on a shelf and in a moment he was hastily turning the pages. Finding what he sought he read avidly, closed the book, and hunted among the bottles in a shallow closet. Taking what he needed, he ran out, leaped into the saddle and loped south to mislead any curious observer, only turning west when hidden from sight of the town.

When night fell it found a weak and raving patient in the little hovel on the lower fork, roped in his bunk, and watched anxiously by the two-gun man at his side. The long dark hours dragged, but dawn found a battle won. Noon came and passed and then Tex, looking critically at his patient, felt he could safely leave him for a few minutes. Glimpsing the filled bottle of liquor at the door of the hut he grabbed it and hurled it against a rock.

Blascom was up and around when Tex reached the upper fork, dragging heavy feet by strangely dulled legs.

"Just in time to feed," he drawled. "Didn't sleep as long as I thought," he said dully, glancing at the sun patch on the floor. "Must be near two o'clock—an' I felt like I could sleep th' sun around."

Tex would not correct the mistake and nodded. "You must 'a' slept some last night," he suggested. "Looked like you had when I saw you from th' window this mornin'."

Blascom nodded heavily. "Near sixteen hours. I feel dead all over."

"A long sleep like that often makes a man feel that way," responded Tex. "Th' muscles are stubborn an' th' eyes get a little touchy, too," he added.

They ate the poorly cooked dinner and leaned back for a smoke, Blascom allowing himself to lose the time because he felt so inert.

"Have any visits from friend Jake?" carelessly asked the marshal.

Blascom laughed. "Not one. You see, Jake come home

that night about as drunk as a man can get an' walk at all. I planted th' jug, a full bottle of gin, an' near half a quart of brandy in his cabin where he'd shore see it. He's been petrified for a week steady. To make shore I put another bottle of whiskey ag'in' his door."

Tex nodded. "I busted that, just now. You come near killin' him. I just about got him through. Don't give him no more. I sat up all last night with him, draggin' him back from th' Divide, an' only left him a little while ago. Get yore gold out quick an' you don't have no call to want him drunk. Cache it, an' then spend a week takin' things easy. You wasn't far behind Jake when I saw you."

Blascom was staring at him in vast surprise. "I never thought good likker would hurt an animal like him!"

"I didn't say it was good likker," rejoined Tex. "Even good likker will do it when drunk by th' barrel; an' there's no good likker in Windsor, if I'm any judge. Well," he said, arising and taking up his hat, "I'll drift along for another look at Jake an' then head for town. Seein' as how you got him that way, through my suggestion, I'll admit, you better look in at him once in awhile an' see he has what he needs. Take some of yore water with you: his stinks."

XVI

♦

Buffalo Creek in the Spotlight

What instinct it is and how it operates, that leads vultures from over the horizon to a dying animal, has never been satisfactorily explained to a lot of people; no more than the instinct which led Sinful and Hank to go prowling around Buffalo Creek when by all rights they should have been hanging around their own camp or loafing in the hotel; but prowl they did, their cunning old eyes missing nothing, certainly nothing so new and shining and high as the sand heap above the creek bank.

Sinful saw it first and he nudged his companion, whose cud nearly choked him before he could cough it back where it belonged.

"Glory!" he choked. "Jest look at it! Come on, Sinful: we got to inwestigate. Nobody's diggin' all that out an' totin' it up there for th' fun of it. But why's he luggin' it so far?"

Sinful snorted scornfully. "Too busy totin' to pan it," he snapped. "Rain's due 'most any time an' he's workin' to beat it. I don't have to inwestigate it—anybody that's workin' like that knows what he's doin'; an' I ain't never heard it said that Blascom's any fool. If he didn't know it was rich, he wouldn't be workin' so hard in th' sun."

"Well, mebby," doubted Hank, always a cold blanket in regard to his companion's contentions. "Looks like he ain't got no water for pannin', like everybody else. He ain't lazy like you, an' instead of wastin' his time around th' hotel like us he's totin' sand so he can work while th' crick's floodin'. When th' floodin' comes everybody else'll have to set down an' watch it till it gets low enough. Me an' you would be doin' somethin' if we follered his example. Where you goin'?" he demanded as his sneering companion walked away.

Sinful flashed a pitying glance over his shoulder. "To git a handful of that sand an' prove you ain't got no sense, that's where. You keep yore eye open for Blascom while I raid his sand pile. Here's a can," he said, stooping to pick it up. "It'll mebby tell us somethin' when we gits it to some water. If you see him a-comin' out, throw a pebble at me. 'Twon't take me long, once I git my boots off."

Hank obeyed and scouted toward the hut, finally stopping

when he could see its door. Watching it a few minutes he saw Blascom pass the opening, and after another few minutes, the watcher slipped away, hastening toward the sand pile. Reaching it, he saw no signs of his partner and backed into the brush to await developments. He no sooner had stopped behind a patch of scrub oak than he caught sight of Sinful carefully picking his way across the stony ground in his socks, one hand carrying the can, the other a pair of boots. On his leathery face was an expression of vast surprise and pious awe. He seemed almost stunned, but he was not so lost to his surroundings that he ignored a bounding, clicking pebble which passed across his path. Clutching can and boots in a firmer grip, he sprinted with praiseworthy speed and agility toward the somewhat distant railroad track. In his wake sped Hank, an unholy grin wreathing his face at the goatlike progress of his old friend over the rocky ground. To Sinful's ears the sound of those clattering boots spelled a determined pursuit and urged him to better efforts. At last, winded, a cramp in his side and his feet so tender and bruised that he preferred to fight rather than go any farther in his socks, he dropped the boots, drew his gun, and wheeled. At sight of Hank's well-known and inelegant figure a look of relief flashed over his face, swiftly followed by a frown of deep and palpitant suspicion.

"What you mean, chasin' me like that?" he shouted.

"Gosh!" panted Hank as he drew near. "That was shore close! An' for an old man yo're a runnin' fool. Jack rabbits an' coyotes can cover ground, but they can't stack up ag'in' you. Did you see him?"

Sinful, one boot on and the other balanced in his hand, looked up. "No, I didn't; did *you?*" he demanded, suspicion burning in his old eyes.

"Shore," answered Hank, lying with a facile ease due to much practice. "He suddenly busted out of th' door with a rifle in his hands an' headed for his sand pile. I dusted lively, heaved th' pebble; an' here we are." He cast an apprehensive glance behind him and then sharply admonished his friend. "Hustle, you! Yo're settin' there like there ain't no mad miner projectin' around in th' brush with a Winchester! Think I want to git shot?"

"I reckon mebby you ought to," retorted Sinful, struggling erect and trying each tender foot in turn. "Stone bruises, cuts, an' stickers, an' all because you git in a panic!" he growled. "Come on, you old fool: there's a pool of water in th' crick, t'other side of th' railroad bridge. Yo're too smart, you are. Mebby yore eyes'll pop out when you see what's in this here can. Great guns, what a sight I've seen!"

Panning gold in a tomato can might be difficult for a novice, but Sinful's cunning old hands did the work speedily and well. After repeated refillings and mystic gyrations he carefully poured out the last of the water and peered eagerly into the can, bumping his head solidly against his companion's, for Hank was as eagerly curious.

Sinful placed it reverently on the creek bank and looked at his staring friend.

"An' only a canful," he muttered in awe.

"Glory!" breathed Hank, and looked again to make sure. "Nothin' but dust—but Good Lord!" He packed a vile pipe with viler tobacco, lit it, and arose. "No wonder he grabbed his gun an' dusted for his sand pile! Come on, Sinful: we got a long walk ahead of us, some quick packin' to do, an' a long walk back ag'in. If we only could get a couple of mules, we'd load 'em with three-hundred pounds apiece an' go down th' crick a day's journey. It'd be worth it."

Sinful looked scornfully at his worrying companion and slowly arose. "No day's journey for me, mules or no mules," he declared, spitting emphatically. "I ain't shore it would be worth it, considerin' th' time an' th' trouble; but it's worth pannin' right where it is. I've jumped claims before in my life an' I ain't too old to jump another. When I looked over that bank an' saw that wallopin' big rock a-stickin' up in th' crick bed, from bank to bank; an' th' ditch he's put down on th' upstream side, I purty near knew what th' sand pile would show. I'm bettin' he's got *bushels* of gold at th' foot of that riffle. If his location don't run up that far, an' mebby it don't, we got somethin' to keep us busy. An' if it does, we've mebby got more to keep us busy. Come on, you wall-eyed ijut: we got to be gittin' back to camp. Great Jerus'lam!"

The marshal of Windsor, riding slowly toward town south of the railroad track after a long detour to mask his trail, saw two scarecrows bumping along the ties, bobbing up and down jerkily as they tried to stretch their stride to cover two ties and repeatedly fell back to one. They were well to the northeast of him and to his left, but he thought they looked familiar and he pushed more to the south to remain hidden from them while he rode ahead. When he finally had reached a point south of the station he turned and rode toward it, timing his arrival to coincide with theirs.

Sinful grinned up at the smiling rider, his missing teeth only making more prominent the few brown fangs he had left. Two dribbles of tobacco juice had dried at each corner of his mouth and reached downward across his chin, giving him an appearance somewhat striking. He mopped the perspiration from his face by a vigorous wipe of his soiled shirt sleeve and lifted each palpitating foot in turn.

"Been ridin' far?" he asked in idle curiosity and in great good humor, considering the aches in his body and the soreness of his feet.

"Oh, just around exercisin' Oh My," answered Tex. "I thought you two was located out on Antelope, west of town?"

"We are," replied Hank, ignoring his partner's furtive elbow. "Been gettin' sorta tired of it, though, not havin' nothin' to do but set around an' look at th' same things. Thought we'd take a look at th' Buffaler, south of th' track; but it ain't much better, though there is some water in th' pools. Anyhow, Antelope's kinda crowded. We may shift our camp. Jake's out on Buffaler som'er's, ain't he?"

Tex nodded and glanced at the can. "Been fishin'?"

"If we had enough bait to fill that can we'd 'a' ate it ourselves," chuckled Hank.

"Naw, there ain't no fish left now," said Sinful. "Hardluck coffeepot, that's all it is. Good as anythin' else, an' shore plentiful. Punch a hole in each side of it an' shove in a piece of wire, an' she'll cook anythin' small. Ain't it hot?"

"Hot, an' close," replied the marshal. "Well, I reckon I'll be gettin' along. Feels like rain is due 'most any time, though I don't reckon we'll get any before th' moon changes. Still, you can't allus tell."

"Can't tell nothin' about it at all, this kind of weather," observed Hank, the can now against the other side of his body. "But one thing's shore—it's gettin' closer every day. So-long," and the grotesque couple went bobbing down the track toward their own camp.

Tex looked after them, humorously shaking his head. "'It's gettin' closer every day,'" he mimicked. "Shore it is. Pair of cunning old coyotes, an' entirely too frank about Buffalo Creek." Just then Sinful leaped into the air, cracked his sore heels together and struck his companion across the shoulders. This display of exuberance awakened a strong suspicion in the marshal. "I'll keep my eye on you two old codgers," he soliloquized, thoughtfully feeling of the handcuffs in his pocket. Wheeling abruptly he rode up to the station, where Jerry grinningly awaited him. "Let me know when those mossbacks go west, Jerry, if you see them," he requested. "They're too cussed innocent an' happy to suit me. How are things?"

Jerry shook his head. "I'll be cussed if I know. But I know one thing, and that is that I'm apologizing to you for the way Jane shut the door in your face. I don't know what's the matter with her lately."

"There's never any tellin' about wimmin," said Tex, smiling. "An' don't you ever apologize to anybody for anythin' she does. Wimmin see things from a different angle, an' they ain't got a man's defenses. A difference in structure is likely to be accompanied by differences in nature, in this case notably in the more delicate balance of th' nervous system. Their reactions are both more subtle an' more extreme. I wasn't insulted, but just folded my tents like th' Arabs, an' as silently stole away. Which I'm now goin' to repeat. See you later, mebby."

Jerry watched his visitor ride off and a puzzled frown crept over his face.

"Wish I knew more about you, Mr. Tex Jones," he muttered. "You're either as fine a human as I have seen, or the smoothest rascal: and I'm d—d if I can tell which."

The marshal rode to his office and sought the chair outside the door, his thoughts running back over recent events. Blascom's find and the physical condition of the man naturally brought to mind Jake's narrow escape. The latter bothered him, notwithstanding the certainty that Blascom would keep a good watch over the sick man. While he anxiously ran over his scant knowledge of Jake's illness and the remedies he had employed, he glanced up to see Doctor Horn nervously hurrying toward him. The doctor, in view of what he now knew of him, became a very interesting study for the marshal.

"Marshal!" cried the physician while yet a score of paces away, "somebody burst down my door during my absence and took some drugs which by their nature are not common out here and, consequently, hard to obtain. I am formally reporting it, sir."

"Doctor," replied Tex, "when a patient comes to you for help you naturally expect him to be frank and truthful. It is the same with a peace officer, who endeavors to cure not the ills of a single unit of society, but the ills of society as a whole. Here, as in your own field, a refractory or diseased unit may, and generally does, affect the body of which he is a part. So, as a social physician, I must ask of you that frankness so valuable to a medico. First, what drugs did you miss?"

"Your analogy, while clever, is sophistical and is entirely unwarranted," retorted the physician, taken somewhat aback by the words and attitude of a "cowhand," as he contemptuously characterized punchers. "Leaving it out of the argument, except to say, in passing, that your 'social physician' does not exercise a corrective influence, but rather a punitive one, I hardly see how the naming of the missing drugs will give any enlightenment to a layman. There still exists the forcible breaking into, and the unlawful entry of, my residence."

"For purposes of identification it might be well to know the drugs that were stolen; but I'll waive that. What time would you say this occurred?" asked Tex with professional interest.

"Some time yesterday," answered the physician.

"You certainly are not very specific, Doctor," commented Tex. "I'm afraid we must come closer to it than that. You say you were away at the time?"

"Yes: I did not return until quite late."

"In body or in spirit, Doctor Horn?"

"Sir, I do not understand you!" retorted the complainant, flushing slightly and gazing with great intensity into the marshal's eyes.

"There have been many others who did not understand me," replied Tex, calmly rolling and lighting a cigarette. "I'm mentioning that so you won't think you are an exotic variation of our large and interesting species. The study of man is the greatest of all, Doctor. The words were more of a joke than anything else. Have you ever suffered from hallucinations, Doctor? I've heard it said that too close confinement, too close an application to study, and too intimate relations with chemicals, volatile and otherwise, operate that way in these altitudes. Hothouse gardeners, for instance, notably those engaged in raising poppies, have slight touches of mental aberration. You are certain that your house was entered while you were away?"

The doctor, arms akimbo, was staring at this calm mind-reader as though in a trance, too stunned to be insulted.

Tex continued: "The value of the missing drugs and the damage to the door undoubtedly will be paid to you, Doctor, in a few days. In fact, I am so confident of that that I will pay you just damages now, taking your receipt in return. Do you agree with a great many people that a physician to the body has much the same high obligations as those belonging to a minister or a priest, who are physicians to the soul? That his work is of a humanitarian nature before it is a matter of remuneration; that he should hold himself fit and ready to answer calls of distress without regard to his own bodily comfort?"

Doctor Horn still stared at him, rallying his thoughts. He nodded assent as he groped.

"There are professional secrets, Doctor, which need not be divulged," continued Tex. "I understand that you have a horse?"

The physician nodded again.

"Then use it. I have reason to believe that a man named Jake, a miner, who is located on the first fork of Buffalo

Creek, west of town, urgently needs your professional services. I understand that he has been brought back from death from alcoholic poisoning, but will be much safer if you look at him. Did you say you are going now? And by the way, before you start, let me say that the old idea of peace officers being corrective forces, in a punitive sense only, is rapidly becoming obsolete among the more intelligent and broader-minded men of that class. While punishment is undoubtedly needed as a warning to others, the cure's the thing, to paraphrase an old friend of mine. Is there any connection between the natures of the missing drugs and alcoholic poisoning, Doctor? But we are wasting time. This little problem can wait. Just now speed's the thing. Drop around again soon, Doctor: I always enjoy the companionship of an educated man," and the marshal, slowly arising, bowed and entered his little office, the door softly closing behind him.

XVII

♦

The Rush

The marshal was leaving the hotel after breakfast the following morning when he saw Jerry walking briskly toward him from the station and he waited for the agent to come up.

"Those two old prospectors just passed the station, going west along the track," Jerry informed him. "From the way they were loaded down it looked as though they are moving their camp. And how men as old as they are can carry such packs is beyond my understanding."

"Thanks, Jerry," said the marshal. "Go back to th' station. I've got to take a ride. Trouble's brewin', I reckon."

Passing the hotel on his way to Carney's stable, Tex saw a running miner hurrying into it and in a moment an excited half-score of armed prospectors poured into the street, shouting and gesticulating. The little crowd picked up additions as it passed along the street and headed westward to strike the railroad at an angle. Some of them had partners with them and, when the tracks had been reached, quite a number turned and ran eastward toward their camps to pack up belongings and supplies.

"Mental telepathy?" murmured Tex, watching them in some surprise. "Hank and Sinful are too clever rascals to tell anybody anything of value that they might know. Huh! That's only a name, I guess, for subconscious weighing of facts subconsciously received: instinctive deductions from observations too vague to be definitely recognized. Instinct, I'm afraid you have more names than most people recognize. But it does beat the devil, at that! An animal does seemingly wonderful and impossible things because of the keenness of its scent, which passes our understanding; birds of prey have eyes nearly telescopic in power—but how the knowledge of this gold strike has spread about so quickly when everyone concerned in it naturally would be secretive, is too much for me. One thing is certain, however: it is known, and I have work to do, and quickly!"

Omar welcomed him and soon was stringing the miles out behind him as smoothly almost as running water. There was no need to urge the animal at its best speed, for it was doing two miles to the miners' one and easily would beat them to the scene of action.

When he reached the second fork, Blascom was not at the hut and, leading the roan into a brush-filled hollow, the marshal took his rifle from its scabbard and went up to the scene of the miner's operations. His hail was followed by a startled crouching on the prospector's part and a rifle barrel leaped up to the top of the ditch.

"Don't shoot: It's Jones," called the marshal, slowly emerging from his cover. "I come up to warn you that th' rush has started. Hank an' Sinful ought to get here in about half an hour, th' others a little behind them. I'm aimin' to be referee: th' kind of a referee I once saw at a turf prize fight: he had to jump in an' thrash both of th' principals—an' he did it, too. Get that bonanza cleaned out and cached yet?"

Blascom swore as he stood up again. "Yes: but nobody's goin' to git *this* without a fight! How th' devil did they find out I'd struck it rich?"

"Shore this claim is staked an' located?" demanded Tex.

"Yes; an' there's work enough done on it to make it stick. But how did they find out I'd struck it?"

"Don't know," answered the marshal. "You better climb out an' go off an' hide somewhere in th' brush from where yore rifle will cover th' cache. They're keen as hounds an' there's no use takin' chances of losin' th' greater to save th' less. I'll handle this end of it. If you hear a shot you better slip back an' look things over. Get a rustle on you—time's flyin'."

In a few minutes the creek bed and the little hut appeared to be deserted. Blascom lay on his stomach at a point from which he could see his cache and the ditch as well. After a short silence there came the sound of a snapping twig and a few minutes later Sinful's greedy eyes peered over the creek bank down at the big ditch. He slid a rifle over the edge and looked around eagerly. To his side crept Hank, who added his scrutiny to that of his partner. Sinful spoke out of one corner of his mouth as he gazed intently down the creek bed, where one corner of Blascom's hut could be seen through the scrawny timber on the little point. Hank nodded, crawled to the edge of the bank and was about to slip over it when a low warning from the brush at their side froze them both.

"Stay where you are," said a well-known voice, cold and unfriendly. "That claim's got one owner now, an' he ain't lookin' for no partners, a-tall. Better shove up yore hands an' face th' crick. You know me—an' so far you ain't seen me miss, yet."

Tex emerged from his cover, a Colt in one hand, a pair of shining handcuffs clinking from their short chains as they swung from the other. Snapping one over Sinful's wrist he curtly ordered Hank to his partner's side and linked the two together. Disarming them he unloaded the weapons, appropriated the cartridges, and searched them both to make certain they could do him no injury.

"Sit down," he said, "an' keep quiet. Th' real show is about to start. Who all did you chumps tell about this strike?"

Hank glared at Sinful, Sinful glared at Hank, and then both glared at their captor. "Nobody, so strike me blind!" snapped Sinful. "Hank ain't been out of my sight since we left here yesterday. Think we're fools?"

"Anything but that," grimly rejoined Tex. "Shut up, now: I want to listen. Any play you make that don't suit me will call for a gun butt bein' bent over yore heads. If I need you, I'll call: an' you come a-runnin'. Hear me?"

"We could come faster if we was loose from each other," whispered Sinful in bland innocence. "*Couldn't* we, Hank?"

"Can't come fast, a-tall, hooked up this way," said Hank earnestly.

"Shut up!" snapped the marshal in a low voice.

A winged grasshopper rasped up over the bank and rasped back again instantly. A few birds chirped and sang across the creek bed and chickadees flashed and darted in an endless search for food. Several birds shot suddenly into the air from the fringe of timber and brush on the farther bank halfway between the ditch and the cabin, quickly followed by vague movements along the ground. Then more than a half-score of men popped into sight and, leaping from the steep bank, landed in the bed of the creek and scurried to different points, fooled by the numerous sumps which Blascom had dug in his quest for water. None of them had the knowledge possessed by Hank and Sinful, and the weather conditions had been such that the ages of the various sumps could not be quickly determined. Each man, eager to grab a hole while there was one left to grab, and to become established chose a mark and appropriated it without loss of time. No sooner had the scurrying crowd selected their grounds than the marshal, who had crept along the top of the high bank, jumped over it and held two guns on them, guns which they had good reason to respect.

"Han's up!" he roared. "*Pronto* an' high! You-all know me—don't gamble! I drop th' first man that makes a gunplay. *Hank! Sinful!*" he shouted. "Come a-runnin'!" Crouched, he faced the scowling crowd, his steady hands before his hips, his steady guns ready to prove his mastery. The handcuffed pair, squabbling as they came, shuffled up to him.

"You yank me any more an' I'll bust yore fool head!" growled Sinful to his bosom friend. "Just because yore laigs is longer is no reason for playin' kite with me! Knock-kneed old fool! Here we are, Marshal: what you want?"

"Hold yore han's close," ordered Tex, his left gun slipping into its sheath, his right becoming even more menacing. With the free hand he fished out the key, handed it to Hank and waited until he had made use of it. It went swiftly back into the pocket and the left hand again held a gun. "Slip around an' take their weapons!" he snapped. "Don't get between them an' me. Lively!"

"We ain't goin' to spoil yore aim, Marshal," Hank assured him with great fervor. "Come on, you baldheaded old buzzard—git them guns for th' marshal! He gave his companion a shove forward. "He done us a good turn—an' one good turn deserves another. Come on!"

"Who you shovin'?" blazed Sinful, starting away.

"You ain't got no right, cuttin' in here!" shouted a red-faced, angry miner, his companions growling and cursing their hearty endorsements. "Yo're a town marshal, not a county sheriff! Turn them guns off us!"

"I got a wider range than marshal," rejoined Tex grimly and not for an instant relaxing his alertness. "Gus Williams said so when he 'pinted me; an', besides, I got th' very same authority out here as I have in town: twelve sections of th' Colt statutes as made an' pervided. Blascom has legally established his claim, drove his stakes, and done his work on it. When he comes he'll p'int out his boundaries. Hold still, you two! Git 'em all, Sinful; don't overlook nothin', Hank! No use turnin' this crick into a slaughterpen."

"I ain't likely to overlook nothin'," replied Sinful, moving more rapidly, "though I'm shore bothered by these here cussed contraptions on my wrist. You'll notice Hank unlocked *his* end of 'em! D—d claim jumpers! A man's rights ain't safe no more these days. Hank an' me shore would 'a' planted some of this passel if they'd bothered us. How th' devil did they find out about it, *I* want to know?"

"What you reckon yo're goin' to do with us all?" sneered a wrathy prospector, his hands slowly coming down toward a harmless belt.

"I'll tell you that after I see Blascom," answered the marshal, firing a shot into the ground. He ordered Sinful and Hank to pile the weapons at his feet, locked them together again and ordered them to get closer to the rest of the miners. The shot brought Blascom as rapidly as he could get there with a due regard to caution. Obeying Tex's terse command he slid down the bank and went to him.

"Shore yore claim takes in th' ditch an' th' riffle?" asked Tex in a whisper.

"Th' new one does," answered Blascom. "I sent off th' papers with Jerry, like you said, th' day I got th' dynamite."

"Th' old one any good?"

"Not much; not much better'n day wages. 'Tain't no good without water; but neither is th' other, now."

"This crowd is fooled by yore old sumps," explained Tex hurriedly. "If we drive 'em off they'll be back ag'in, an' mebby add yore murder to th' rest of their crimes. I can't stay here day an' night; an' if I could, they'd get us both after dark, or at long range in daylight. You got to let 'em stay. By tomorrow there'll be twice as many. I'm scared some'll come slippin' up any minute an' turn th' tables on us. You let Sinful an' Hank divide a quarter of th' sand pannin' between 'em—they'll commit murder for half that, an' you've got to have partners in case of a rush. Besides, rain's due any day now, an' you need 'em to beat it."

"I hate like—" began Blascom stubbornly.

"We all has to do things we hate!" cut in his companion. "You can't do anythin' else. If you can, tell me quick!"

Blascom shook his head. He could do nothing else. He turned and faced the crowd, telling it to go ahead and stake out claims where each man had started to, on condition that there was to be no more jumping and that they join him in putting up a solid front against any newcomers other than partners. The scowls died out, heads nodded, and the hustle and bustle began again from where it had left off.

Tex called the Siamesed pair to him and they listened, with their eyes glowing, to Blascom's offer of limited partnership, Hank nearly swallowing his cud when asked if he was satisfied with the terms. Sinful smelled a rat and looked properly suspicious, his keen old mind racing along on the theory that no one ever gave away anything valuable. Suddenly he grinned so expansively that a generous stream of tobacco juice rolled down his sharp chin.

"Us three ag'in' that gang," he mused. "Huh! Fair enough, *I* says. Hank an' *me* can lick 'em by ourselves. *Can't* we, Hank?"

"Shore!" promptly answered the other weather-beaten old rascal. "We shore kin, Sinful!"

Tex smiled at the cheerful old reprobates, bound closer together now than ever they had been before. "I ought to dump th' pair of you in th' new jail," he said, "though it shore wouldn't get no benefit from it. Yo're a pair of land pirates an' you both ought to be hung from th' yardarm of some cottonwood tree. Hold out yore hands till I turn you loose. You two youngsters want to keep th' bargain, or I *will* hang you!"

"Glad to git shet of them cuffs," growled Sinful. "Hank takes sich long steps an' walks sideways, th' old fool. We'll play square, *won't* we, Hank? There; he said so, too. We allus has felt kind of friendly to Blascom, *ain't* we, Hank? Shore we has. An' he needs us to keep our eyes on them blasted claim jumpers. 'Sides, he's a friend of yourn, Marshal: an' we ain't forgettin' them few dollars we won from you t'other night—*are* we, Hank?" His shrewd old eyes baffled Tex's attempt to read just what he thought about the poker game.

"We ain't!" emphatically replied Hank, spitting copiously and vehemently. "We'll make these claim jumpers herd close to home; yes, sir, by glory!" He paused a moment and leaned nearer to his companion's ear. "*Won't* we, Sinful?" he suddenly shouted.

"Who you yowlin' at that way?" blazed Sinful, and then his eyes popped wide open in frank surprise. "Cussed if th' doc ain't got th' fever, too!" he ejaculated. "Here he comes up th' crick! Beats all how news does spread! An', great Jerus'lam: if he ain't as sober as a watched Puritan!"

Nodding right and left Doctor Horn rode slowly among the busy claim jumpers and drew rein in front of Tex and his companions.

"How do you do, gentlemen?" he said, smiling. "I see you're quite busy, Marshal, which seems to be a habit of yours. I happened to have a patient out this way, down on the lower fork, and while I was in his vicinity I thought I would drop in and compliment Blascom for his care of Jake. While the efficient treatment he first received un-doubtedly saved his life, Blascom's nursing comes in for well-earned praise. He is still a sick man, although out of danger. I hope you will disregard our former conversation, so far as my part of it is concerned, Marshal. Good day to you all," and wheeling, he rode up a break in the creek bank and slowly became lost to sight among the bowlders and timber.

Sinful had watched both men carefully while the doctor spoke, and now he covertly glanced at the marshal, who was gazing after the departing physician. Then he looked at Blas-com, and from him to his own, disreputable partner.

"Come on, Hank," he said. "If any of these gold thieves start swappin' claims, we'll play 'em a smart tune for 'em to dance to. There's shore been a-plenty of lives saved on this crick plumb recent—our own, mebby, among 'em. An' who do you reckon yo're a-starin' at?"

"You, you pore ol' fool!" retorted Hank. He blew out a bleached cud, rammed in a fresh one, nodded at Blascom and the contemplative marshal, and followed his impatient partner toward their packs and guns.

Tex slowly turned and looked after them. "Hey, Sinful!" he called. "You still makin' coffee in old tin cans? If you are, you want to watch 'em close on account of sand gettin' in 'em!"

Sinful nudged his companion, stopped, scratched his head, and then grinned.

"Don't have to use 'em *now*. We got all our traps along, an' th' old coffeepot is with 'em, kivver an' all. Anyways, *we* don't mind a little sand once in awhile—*do* we, Hank?"

"No, sir, by glory!" cried Hank. "Not no more, we don't, a-tall!"

XVIII

◆

"Here Lies the Road to Rome!"

A few nights later Tex awakened to feel his little lean-to shaking until he feared it would collapse. A deafening roar on the roof made an inferno of noise, the great hailstones crashing and rolling. Flash after flash of vivid lightning seemed wrapped in the volleying crashes of the thunder. A sudden shift in the hurricane-like wind drove a white broadside against his front windows, both panes of glass seeming spontaneously to disintegrate. Another gust overturned a freight wagon in the road before the office and tore its tarpaulin cover from it as though it were tied on with strings, whisking it out of sight through the incessant lightning flashes like the instant passing of some huge ghost. The teamster, who saw no reason to pay for hotel beds while he had the wagon to sleep in, went rolling up the slatted framework and down again, bounced to his knees, and crawled frantically free, beaten by the streaking hail and buffeted by the shrieking wind. He was blown solidly against the lean-to, almost constantly in the marshal's sight because of the continuous illumination. Groping along the wall, he reached the shattered window and, desperate for shelter, promptly dived through it and rolled across the room.

Tex laughed, the sound of it lost to his own ears. "Yo're welcome, stranger!" he yelled. "But I'm sayin' yo're some precipitate! Better gimme a hand to stop up that window, or she'll blow out th' walls and lift off th' roof. Grab this table an' we'll up-end it ag'in th' openin'. I'll prop it with th' benches from th' jail. That's right. Ready? Up she goes."

After no mean struggle the window was closed enough to give protection against the raging wind, the two benches holding it securely. Then Tex struck a match and lit both of his lamps.

"We don't hardly need any light, but this is a lot steadier," he shouted, turning to look at his guest. His eyes opened wide and he stared unbelievingly. "Good Lord, man! You look like a slaughter-house! Here, lemme look you over!"

The teamster, cut, bruised, and streaked with blood, held up his hand in quick protest, shouting his reply. "'Taint nothin' but th' wallerin' I did when th' wagon turned over, an' th' beatin' from th' hail. I've seen it worse than this, friend. These stones are only big as hens' aigs, but I've seen 'em large as goose aigs, an' lost three yoke of oxen from 'em. I was freightin' in a load of supplies for a surveyin' party, down on th' old Dry Route, southwest of th' Caches. One ox was killed, his yokemate pounded senseless, an' th' others couldn't stand th' strain an' lit out. I never saw 'em again. I was under th' wagon when they left, which didn't turn over till th' hail changed into rain, an' I wouldn't 'a' poked out my head for all th' oxen in th' country. This here's a little better than a fair prairie hail storm. Gosh," he said, grinning, as he glanced at the badge on his companion's vest. "I got plenty of nerve, all right, bustin' into th' marshal's office! Ain't got any likker, have you?"

Tex handed him a full bottle and packed his pipe. The deafening crashing of the hailstones grew less and less, a softer roar taking its place as the rain poured down in seemingly solid sheets. The great violence of the wind was gone and the lightning flashed farther and farther away.

"Feel better now," said the teamster, passing the bottle to his host and taking out his pipe. He accepted the marshal's sack of tobacco and leaned back, puffing contentedly. "Sounds a lot better, now. I'd rather drowned than be beat to death, any time. There won't be a trail left tomorrow an' not a crick, ravine, or ditch fordable. Some of 'em with sand bottoms will be dangerous for three or four days. I once saw th' Pawnee rise so quick that it was fetlock deep when I started in, an' wagon-box deep before I could get across—an' a hull lot wider, too, I'm tellin' you. An' yet some fools still camp in dried crick beds!"

"That's just what I been thinkin' about," said the marshal, a look of worry on his face. "Out on Buffalo Crick there's near two dozen miners with claims staked out on th' dried bed. It shore would be terrible if this caught 'em asleep!"

"Don't you worry, Marshal," reassured his guest, laughingly. "Them fellers may have claims in a crick bed, but they don't sleep on 'em. They know too much!"

Tex related what a hail storm had done to a trail herd one night years before, and so they talked, reminiscence following reminiscence, until dawn broke, dull and watery, and they started for the hotel, to rout out the cook for hot coffee and an early breakfast.

All day it rained, but with none of the fury of the darker hours, and for the next ten days it continued intermittently. There was no special news from Buffalo Creek except that it had changed its bed in several places, and that two miners had been forced to swim for their lives. It was noteworthy, however, that the prospectors of the country roundabout began to spend dust with reckless carelessness. The hotel was well patronized during the day, and the nights were times of great hilarity. Drink flowed like water and old quarrels, fed by fresh fuel, added their share of turbulence to the new ones.

Sleeping late in the mornings, the marshal was on his feet until nearly every dawn, stopping brawls, deciding dangerous contentions, and once or twice resorting to stern measures. The little jail at one time was too full for further prisoners and had forced him to resort to fines, which brought his impartiality and honesty into question. He had been forced to wound two men and had been shot at from cover, all on one night. He grew more taciturn, grimmer, colder, wishing to avoid a killing, but fearing that it must come or the town would turn into a drunken riot. Then came the climax to the constantly growing lawlessness.

Busy in repairing washouts along the railroad and strengthening the three little bridges across the creeks of his section of track, Murphy and Costigan, reinforced by half a dozen other section-hands from points east, who had rolled into town on their own hand car, had scarcely seen the town for more than a week when they came in, late one Saturday afternoon. The extra hands were bedded at the toolshed and at Murphy's box car, and took their meals at Costigan's, whose thrifty wife was glad of the extra work for the little money it would bring her. Well knowing the feeling of the Middle West of that time against his race, the section-boss cautioned his crew to avoid the town as much as they could; but rough men are rough men, and wild blades are wild. Knowing the wisdom in the warning did not make it sit any easier on them, added to which was the chafing under the restraint and the galling sense of injustice.

Sunday morning found them quiet; but Sunday noon found them restless and resentful. The lively noise of the town called invitingly across the right-of-way and one of them, despite orders, departed to get a bottle of liquor. He drew hostile glances as he made his way to the bar in the saloon facing the station, but bought what he wanted and went out with it entirely unmolested. The news he brought back was pleasing and reassuring and discounted the weight of the section-boss' admonitions, and later, when the bottle had been tipped in vain and thirsts had only been encouraged by the sops given them, some wilder soul among the crowd arose and announced that he was going to paint the town. There was no argument, no holding back, and the half-dozen, laughing and singing, sallied forth to frolic or fight as Fate decreed.

The first saloon they entered served them and let them depart unharmed and without insult, raising their spirits and edging their determination to enjoy what pleasures the town might have for them. They were as good as any men in town, and they knew it, which was right and proper; but soon it did not satisfy them to know it: they must tell everyone they met. This, also, was right and proper, although hardly wise; but in the telling there swiftly crept a fighting tone, a fighting mood, a fighting look, and fighting words; yet they were behaving not one whit different from the way gangs of miners had behaved since the town was built. The difference was sharp and sufficient: The miners had been in the town of their friends; the section-gang was in the town of its enemies.

The half-dozen entered the hotel barroom, jostled and elbowed, jostling and elbowing in return, their tempers smoldering and ready to burst into flames. Calling for whiskey at the bar they drank it avidly and turned to look over the room, where all sorts and conditions of rough men and ready fighters were frowningly watching them. The frowns grew deeper, and here and there a gibe or veiled insult arose above the general noise. The gibes became more bitter, the insults less veiled, and finally a huge miner, belted and armed, stood up and shouted for silence. Sensing trouble the crowd obeyed him, waiting with savage eagerness to hear what he would say, to see what he would do.

"I'm goin' to tell you a story," he cried, and forthwith made good his promise. It was not a parlor story by any stretch of imagination, and it ended with St. Peter slamming shut the gates of heaven as he repeated one of the then popular slogans of the country along the roadbeds, "No Irish need apply." It was not couched in language that St. Peter would use, and suitable epithets of the teller's own gave added weight to the insult of the tale. Still swearing the miner sat down, an ugly leer on his face, while shouts, laughter, catcalls, and curses answered from every part of the room.

"Run 'em out of town!" came a shout, which swiftly became a universal demand.

The track-layer nearest the door, a burly, red-haired, red-faced fighting man, leaped swiftly to the miner's table, kicked the half-drawn gun from his hand, and went to the floor with him. "St. Peter will open no doors to th' like av ye!" he shouted. "I'm sendin' ye to hell, instead!"

The bartender, fearing pistol work, whipped his own over the counter and yelled his warning and his demand for fair play. "I'll drop th' man that draws! Let 'em have it out, man to man!"

This suited the crowd as an appetizer for what was to follow, and chairs and tables crashed as it surged forward to better see the fight, the five section-hands their broad backs against the bar, forming one side of the pushing, heaving ring, their faces set, their huge fists clenched, in spirit taking and giving the flailing blows of the rolling combatants, so intent, so lost in the struggle that consciousness of their own danger gradually faded from their minds. They had faith in their champion and were with him, heart and soul.

The miner could fight like the graduate he was of the merciless, ultra-brutal rough-and-tumble of the long frontier, biting, kneeing, gouging, throttling as opportunity offered, and he was rapidly gaining the advantage over his cleaner-fighting opponent until, breaking a throat hold, barely escaping the fingers thrust at his eyes and a wolflike snap of murderous jaws, the Irishman broke free, and staggered to his feet to make a fight which best suited him. Great gasps of relief broke from his tense friends, their low words of advice and encouragement coming from between set teeth.

"Steady, Mac, an' time 'em!" whispered his nearest friend. "He fights like a beast—lick him like th' man ye are. He's as open as a book!"

Panting, his breath whistling through his teeth, the miner scrambled to his feet, needlessly fearing a kick as he arose, and rushed, his great arms flaying before him as he tore in. Met by a straight left that caught him on the jaw a little wide of the point aimed at, he rocked back on his heels, his knees buckling, and his arms wildly waving to keep his balance. Before he could recover and set himself, a right flashed in against his chest and drove him back against the ring of men behind him. Gasping, he bent over and threw himself at his enemy's thighs, missing the hold by a hair. The Irishman retreated two swift steps and waited until his opponent had leaped up and then, feinting with his left at the swelling jaw, he swung his right shoulder behind a stiffening right arm and landed clean and squarely above the brass buckle of the cartridge belt. The crash shook the building, for the miner's feet came up as he was hurled backward and he struck the floor in a bunched heap.

The bruised and bleeding victor, filling his lungs with great gulps of foul air, started backing toward the bar to regain his breath among his friends, but he staggered sidewise on his course, coming too close to the first line of the aroused crowd and one of them leaped on him, the impact toppling him over, just as the five friends charged. Chaos reigned. Shouts, curses, the stamping of feet, bellows of rage and pain filled the dusty air with clamor as the crowd surged backward and forward, the storm center ever nearing the door. The valiant half-dozen, profiting by experience, resisted all efforts to separate them, keeping in a compact group, shoulder to shoulder, with their rapidly recovering champion in their middle. They had passed the end of the bar, which had been a sturdy bulwark against their complete encircling, and the crowd was pouring in to attack from that once-protected side when a hatless figure leaped through the deserted rear door, bounded onto the long bar without changing his stride, dashed along it and jumped, feet first straight at the heads bobbing nearest to the stout-hearted six. It was Costigan who, not finding Murphy, was acting on his own initiative and according to his lights. In his hand was a broken mattock handle and under its raining blows an opening rapidly grew in the crowd. Had he been given arm room, where his full strength could have been used, Boot Hill would have reaped a harvest. Audacity, that Audacity which is the fairest child of Courage, the total unexpectedness of his hurtling, spectacular attack won more for him and his friends than the deadly effectiveness of the hickory handle. The astonished crowd drew back in momentary confusion and Costigan, cursing at the top of his panting lungs, shoved the nearly exhausted handful through the door and into the street. As the last man staggered through and pitched to the ground, the club wielder leaped to the door, barring it with his body. He was about to tell the crowd what he thought of it when the situation changed again.

A hand clutched his shirt collar and yanked him back and he went striking with the club as he sprawled beside a battered friend. The change had been so sudden and the crowd just recovering from its surprise at Costigan's flaying attack that it looked like magic. One instant a red-shirted Irishman, his clothing torn into shreds, lovingly balancing his favorite weapon; the next, a calm, cold-faced, blue-shirted, leather-chapped gunman, bending eagerly forward behind the pair of out-thrust Colts, his thumbs holding back swift death in each hand.

"The devil!" growled a miner.

"Aye!" snapped Tex. "An' I'll find work for idle hands to do! *Why do you stop and turn away? Here lies th' road to Rome!*" he laughed, exultantly, sneeringly, insultingly; and never had they heard a laugh so deadly. It chilled where words might have inflamed. There was not a man who did not shrink instinctively, for before him stood a killer if ever he had seen one.

"I only got twelve handy—which dozen of you want to open th' way for th' rest?" asked the marshal. His quick eye caught a furtive movement in the crowd and the roar of his flaming Colt jarred the room. The offender pitched forward before the paralyzed front line, rocking to and fro in his pain. "Th' next man dies!" snapped the marshal, his deadly intent fully revealed by his face.

The crowd gazed at impersonal Death, balanced in the two firm hands. They saw no hesitancy reflected between the narrowed lids of those calculating eyes, no qualifying expression on that granite face; and they were standing where Bud Haines had stood, facing the man he had faced. A restless surge set the mass milling, those behind pushing those in front, those in front frantically pushing back those behind. Tense and dangerous as the situation was, a verse of an immortal fighting poem leaped to the marshal's mind and a sneering smile flashed over his face. *Was none who would be foremost to lead such dire attack; but those behind cried "Forward!" And those before cried "Back!"* He seemed to tense even more, like some huge, deadly spider about to spring, and his clearly enunciated warning, low as it was spoken, reached the ears of every man in the room. "Go back to yore tables, like you was before."

The surge grew and spread, split following split, until the dragging rearguard sullenly followed its companions. The dynamic figure in the door slowly forsook its crouch, arising to full height. The left-hand gun grudgingly slid into its sheath, reluctantly followed by its more deadly mate. Casting a final, contemptuous look at the embarrassed crowd, each unit of it singled out in turn and silently challenged, the marshal shoved his hands into his pockets, turned his back on them with insolent deliberation and stepped to the street, where a bloody, battered group of seven had waited to back him up if it should be needed.

"Yer a man after me own—" began Costigan thickly between swollen lips, but he was cut short.

"That'll keep. Take these fellers back where they belong, an' *keep* 'em there," snapped Tex, the fighting fire still blazing in his soul. He watched them depart, proud of every one of them; and when they had reached the station he wheeled and went back into the hotel, had a slowly sipped drink, nodded to his acquaintances as though nothing out of the ordinary had occurred, and then sauntered out again without a backward glance, turning to go to the station.

When he reached the building he stopped and looked toward the toolshed where Murphy, just back from a run of inspection up the line, and Costigan, had turned the corner of the shed and stopped to renew their argument, which must have been warm and personal, judging from their motions. Finally Costigan, looking for all the world like a scarecrow, hitched up what remained of his trousers, squared his shoulders, and limped determinedly toward his little cottage, glancing neither to the right nor to the left. Murphy, hands on hips, gazed after him, nodded his head sharply, and was about to enter the shed when he caught sight of the motionless two-gun man. Snapping his fingers in sudden decision, he started toward his capable friend, his frame of mind plainly shown by the way his stride easily took two ties at once.

"God loves th' Irish, or 'twould be diggin' graves we'd now be doin'," he said. "An' me away! But they'll be mindin' their P's an' Q's after this. I was goin' to skin Costigan, but how could I after I learned what he did? It ain't th' first time he's tied my hands by th' quality av his fightin'. But 'twas well ye took cards, an' 'twas well ye played 'em, Tex."

"I have due respect for Costigan, but if he leaves th' railroad property he'll lose it quick," replied the marshal. "I turned that mob into a mop, but there's no tellin' what might happen one of these nights. Tim, I wish his family was out of town. It's no place for wimmin an' children these days, not with ten marshals. I can't be everywhere at once, an' I'm watchin' one house now more than I ought to."

"They're leavin' on tomorry's train east," said Murphy, breathing a sigh of relief. "I've Mike's word for it, an' if he can't get 'em to go without him, then he's goin' with 'em, superintendent or no superintendent! I'm sorry that it's my fault that ye had th' trouble, Tex; I should 'a' stayed close to them d—d fools."

"There's no harm done, Tim, as it turned out. It was comin' to a show-down, gettin' nearer an' nearer every day. Now that it's over th' town will be quiet for a day or two. I know of marshals who were paid from eight hundred to a thousand dollars a month—I'm admittin' that I've earned my hundred in just about five minutes today. For about fifteen seconds th' job was worth a hundred dollars a second—it was a close call."

"But look at th' honor av it," chuckled Murphy. "It's marshal av Windsor ye are, Tex—an' ye have yer Tower, as well!"

Tex laughed, glanced over the straggling town from Costigan's cottage to another at the other end of the street. "I'm not complainin'. I'm only contrastin' and showin' that Williams didn't pull any wool over my eyes when he offered me my princely salary. I agreed to it, and I'm paid enough, under th' circumstances."

"Aye," said Murphy, following his friend's glance, a sudden smile banishing his anxious frown. "Money ain't everythin'. Perhaps yo're not paid much now, Tex—but later, who can tell?"

XIX

♦

A Lecture Wasted

That evening Tex had a caller in the person of Henry Williams, who seemed to be carrying quite a load of suspicion and responsibility. He nodded sourly, and nonchalantly seated himself on a chair at the other side of the door. His troubled mind was not hidden from the marshal, who could read surface indications of a psychological nature as well as any man in the West. No small part of his poker skill was built upon that ability. Should he lead his visitor by easy and natural stages to unburden himself; make a hearty, blunt opening, or make him blurt out his thoughts and go on the defensive at once? Having anything but respect and liking for the vicious nephew, he determined to make him as uncomfortable as possible. So he paid him the courtesy of a glance and resumed his apparently deep cogitations.

Henry waited for a few minutes, studying the ground and the front of his uncle's store and then coughed impatiently.

"'Tis that," responded Tex abstractedly; "but hot, an' close. I was thinkin'," he said, definitely.

Henry looked up inquiringly: "Yes?"

"Yes," said the marshal gravely. "I was." His tone repulsed any comment and he kept on thinking from where he had left off.

Henry shifted on the chair and recrossed his legs, one foot starting to swing gently to and fro. To put himself *en rapport* with his forbidding companion, he too, began thinking; or at least he simulated a thinker. The swinging foot stopped, jiggled up and down a few times, and began swinging more energetically. Soon he began drumming on the chair with the fingers of one hand. Presently he shifted his position again, recrossed his legs, grunted, and drummed alternately with the fingers of both hands. Then they drummed in unison, the nails of one set clicking with the rolling of the pads of the fingers of the other hand. Then he puckered his lips and began to whistle.

"Don't do that!" snapped Tex, and returned to his cogitations.

"What? Which?" asked Henry, starting.

"That!" exploded the marshal savagely and lapsed into intense concentration.

Henry's lips straightened and he looked down at the drumming fingers, and stopped them. Squirming on the chair, he uncrossed his legs and pushed them out before him, intently regarding the two rounded grooves in the dust made by his high heels. Then he glanced covertly at his frowning companion, cleared his throat tentatively, and became quiet as the frown changed into a scowl.

The marshal thought that his visitor must have something important on his mind, something needing tact and velvety handling. Otherwise he would have become discouraged by this time and left. Was it about Jane? That would be the natural supposition, but he slowly abandoned it. Henry never had shown any timidity when speaking about her. It must be something concerning the riot in the hotel.

"I say it can't be nothin' else!" fiercely muttered the marshal, his chair dropping solidly to all fours as he rammed a fist into an open palm. "No, sir! It *can't!*" He glared at his companion. "What did you say?"

"Huh?" demanded Henry, his chair also dropping to all fours because of the impetus it had received from his sudden start. "What for?" he asked inanely.

"What for what?" growled Tex accusingly. "Who said: 'What for'?"

"I did: I just wanted to know," hastily explained Henry in frank amity.

"That's what you said!" retorted Tex, leaning tensely toward him; "but what did you *mean?*" he demanded.

"What you talkin' about?" queried Henry, truly and sincerely wondering.

"Don't you try to fool me!" warned Tex. "Don't pretend you don't know! An' let me tell you this. You are wrong, like th' ministers an' all th' rest of th' theologians. That's th' truest hypothesis man ever postulated. It proves itself, I tell you! From th' diffused, homogeneous, gaseous state, whirlin' because of molecular attraction, into a constantly more compact, matter state, constantly becomin' more heterogeneous as pressure varies an' causes a variable temperature of th' mass. Integration an' heterogeneity! From th' cold of th' diffused gases to th' terrific heat generated by their pressure toward th' common center of attraction. Can't you see it, man?"

Henry's mouth remained open and inarticulate.

"You won't answer, like all th' rest!" accused Tex. "An' what heat! One huge molten ball, changing th' force of th' planets nearest, shifting th' universal balance to new adjustments. 'Equilibrium!' demands Nature. An' so th' struggle goes on, ever tryin' to gain it, an' allus makin' new equilibriums necessary, like a dog chasin' a flea on th' end of his spine. Six days an' a breathin' space!" he jeered. "Six trillion years, more likely, an' no time for breathin' spaces! What you got to say to that, hey? Answer me this: What form of force does th' integration postulate? Centrifugal? Hah!" he cried. "You thought you had me there, didn't you? No, sir; not centrifugal—centripetal! Integration—centripetal! Gravity proves it. Centrifugal is th' destroyer, th' maker of satellites—not th' builder! Bah!" he grunted. "You can't disprove a word of it! Try it—just try it!"

Henry shook his head slowly, drew a deep breath and sought a more comfortable position. "These here chairs are hard, ain't they?" he remarked, feeling that he had to say something. Surely it was safe to say that.

Tex leaped to his feet and scowled down at him. "Evadin', are you?" he demanded. Then his voice changed and he placed a kindly hand on his companion's shoulder. "There ain't no use tryin' to refute it, Hennery," he said. "It can't be done—no, sir—it can't be done. Don't you ever argue with me again about this, Hennery—it only leads us nowhere. Was it Archimedes who said he could move th' earth if he only had some place to stand? He wasn't goin' to try to lift himself by his boot straps, was he, th' old fox? That's th' trouble, Hennery: after all is said we still got to find some place to stand." He glanced over Henry's head to see Doctor Horn smiling at him and he wondered how much of his heavy lecture the physician had heard. Had he expected an educated man to be an auditor he would have been more careful. "That was th' greatest hypothesis of all—the hypothesis of Laplace—it answered th' supposedly unanswerable. Science was no longer on th' defensive, Hennery," he summed up for the newcomer's benefit.

"Truly said!" beamed the doctor, getting a little excited. "In proof of its mechanical possibility Doctor Plateau demonstrated, with whirling water, that it was not a possibility, but a fact. The nebular hypothesis is more and more accepted as time goes on, by all thinking men who have no personal reasons strong enough to make them oppose it." He clapped the stunned Henry on the back. "Trot out your refutations and the marshal and I will knock them off their pins! Bring on your theologians, your special-creation adherents, and we'll pulverize them under the pestle of cold reason in the mortar of truth! But I never thought you were interested in such beautiful abstractions, Henry; I never dreamed that inductive and deductive reasoning, confined to purely scientific questions appealed to you. What needless loneliness I have suffered; what opportunities I have missed; what a dearth of intellectual exercise, and all because I took for granted that no one in this town was competent to discuss either side of such subjects. But he's got you with Laplace, Henry; got you hard and fast, if you hold to the tenets of special creation. Now that there are two of us against you, I'll warrant you a rough passage, my friend. 'Come, let's e'en at it!' We'll give you the floor, Henry—and here's where I really enjoy myself for the first time in three weary, dreary years. We'll rout your generalities with specific facts; we'll refute your ambiguities with precisions; we'll destroy your mythological conceptions with rational conceptions; your symbolical conceptions with actual conceptions; your foundation of faith by showing the genesis of that faith—couch your lance, but look to yourself, for you see before your ill-sorted array a Roman legion—short swords and a flexible line. Its centurions are geology, physics, chemistry, biology, astronomy, and mathematics. Nothing taken for granted there! No pious hopes, but solid facts, proved and reproved. Come on, Henry—proceed to your Waterloo! Special creation indeed! Comparative anatomy, single-handed, will prove it false!"

"My G—d!" muttered Henry, forgetting his mission entirely. His head whirled, his feet were slipping so rapidly that he did not know where he was going. He stared, open-mouthed at Doctor Horn, dumbly at the marshal, got up, sat down, and then slumped back against his chair, helpless, hopeless, fearing the worst. Over his head hurled words he thought to be foreign, as his companions, having annihilated him, were performing evolutions and exercises of their verbal arms for the sheer joy of it. Finally, despairing of the lecture ever ending, he arose to escape, but was pushed back again by the excited, exultant doctor. Daylight faded, twilight passed, and it was not until darkness descended that the doctor, finding no opposition, but hearty accord instead, tired of the sound of his own voice and that of the marshal, and after profuse expressions of friendship and pleasure, departed, his head high, his shoulders squared, and his tread firm and militant.

Henry's sigh of relief sounded like the exhaust of an engine and he shifted again on the chair and tried to collect his scattered senses. Before he could get started the marshal sent him off on a new track, and his unspoken queries remained unspoken for another period.

"Seen Miss Saunders yet?" asked Tex, struggling hard to conceal his laughter.

Henry shook his head. "No; but I ain't goin' to wait much longer. I don't see no signs of her weakenin', an' that C Bar puncher is gittin' too cussed common around her house. For a peso I'd toss him in th' discard. I reckon yore way ain't no good with her, Marshal. I got to do somethin'—got to get some action."

"I know about how you feel," sympathized Tex. "I know how hard it is to set quiet an' wait in a thing like this, Hennery, even if action does lose th' game. Who was it you aimed to have perform th' ceremony?"

"Oh, there's a pilot down to Willow—one of them roamin' preachers that reckons he's found a place where he can stick. He'll come up here if th' pay's big enough, an' if I want any preacher. He'll only have to stay over one night to git a train back ag'in. Anyhow, if we has to wait a day or two it won't make much difference, as long as we're goin' to git hitched afterward."

Tex closed his eyes and waited to get a good hold on himself before replying. "He'll come for Gus, all right," he said. "Think you can hold out a few days more—just to see if my way will work? It'll be better, all around, if you do. Where was you aimin' to buy them presents for her?"

"Kansas City or St. Louie—reckon St. Louie will be better. Gus gets most of his supplies from there. You still thinkin' stockin's is th' proper idea?"

Tex cogitated a moment. "No; they're a little embarrassin': better try gloves. I'll find out th' size from her brother. Nice, long white gloves for th' weddin'—an' mebby a nice shawl to go with 'em—Cashmere, with a long fringe. They're better than stockin's. You send for 'em an' wait till they come before you go around. You shouldn't go empty-handed on a visit like that. An' you want th' minister with you when you go after her—you can leave him outside till he's needed. Folks'll talk, an' make trouble for you later.

There's tight rules for weddin's; very tight rules. You don't want nobody pokin' their fingers at yore wife, Hennery. It'll shore mean a killin', some day."

"I ain't so cussed anxious to git married," growled Henry. "It's hard to git loose ag'in—but I reckon mebby I better go through with it."

"I—reckon—you—had," whispered Tex, his vision clouding for a moment. He grew strangely quiet, as though he had been mesmerized.

"A man can allus light out if he gits tired of it," reflected Henry complacently.

The marshal arose and paced up and down, thankful for the darkness, which hid the look of murder graven on his face. "Yes," he acquiesced; "a man—allus—can—do—that." This conversation was torturing him. Anything would be a relief, and he threw away the results of all his former talking. "What was on your mind when you come down to see me today?"

"Oh!" exclaimed his companion a little nervously. "I plumb forgot all about it. You see," he hesitated, shifting again on the chair, "well, it's like this. Us boys admires th' way you handled things in th' hotel this afternoon, but somebody might 'a' been killed. 'Tain't fair to let a passel of Irish run this town—an' they started th' fight, anyhow. Th' big Mick kicked Jordan's gun out of his hand an' jumped on him. Then th' others piled in, an' th' show be-gun. We sort of been thinkin' that th' marshal ought to back up his town ag'in' them foreigners. Gus is mad about it—an' he's bad when he gits his back up. He thinks we ought to go down to th' railroad an' run them Micks out of town on some sharp rails, beatin' 'em up first so they won't come back. Th' boys kinda cotton to that idea. They're gettin' restless an' hard to hold. I thought I'd find out what side yo're on."

Tex stopped his pacing, alert as a panther. "I ain't on no

side but law an' order," he slowly replied. "I told that section-gang to stay on th' right-of-way. They're leavin' town early tomorrow mornin', an' may not come back. A mob's a bad thing, Hennery: there's no tellin' where it'll stop. Most of 'em will be full of likker, an' a drunken mob likes bright fires. Let 'em fire one shack an' th' whole town will go: hotel, Mecca, an' all. It's yore best play to hold 'em down, or you an' yore uncle will shore lose a lot of money. Th' right-of-way is th' dead line: I'll hold it ag'in' either side as long as I can pull a trigger. You hold 'em back, Hennery; an' if you can't, don't you get out in th' front line—stay well behind!"

"Mob's do get excited," conceded Henry, thoughtfully. "Reckon I'll go see what Gus thinks about it. See you later."

Tex watched him walk away, silhouetted against the faintly illuminated store windows, and as the door slammed behind him the marshal shifted his heavy belts and went slowly up the street and into the hotel, where he received a cold welcome. Seeing that the room was fairly well crowded, accounting for most of the men in town and all of the afternoon crowd, he sat in a corner from where he could see both doors and everything going on.

In a few minutes Gus Williams and Henry entered and began mixing with the crowd, which steadily grew more quiet, but more sullen, like some wild beast held back from its prey. Henry sat at one table, surrounded by his closest friends, while his uncle held court at another. The nephew was drinking steadily and his glances at the quiet marshal became more and more suspicious. Around midnight, the temper of the crowd suiting him, Tex arose and went down the street toward his office, passed around it and circled back over the uneven plain, silently reaching the railroad near the box car.

Murphy quietly crept out of his bunk, gun in hand, and slipped to the door, pressing his ear against it. Again the drumming of the fingers sounded, but after what had occurred earlier in the day he wanted more than a tapping before he opened the door or betrayed his presence in the car. Soon he heard his name softly called and recognized the voice. As quietly as he could, he slid back the door and peered into the caller's face from behind a leveled gun.

"Don't let that go off," chuckled Tex, stepping inside. "Close th' door, Tim."

Murphy obeyed and felt his way to his visitor and they held a conversation which lasted for an hour. Tex's plans of action in certain contingencies were more than acceptable to the section-boss and he went over them until he was letter-perfect. To every question he gave an answer pleasing to the marshal and when the latter left to go up and guard the toolshed and its inmates he felt more genuine relief than he had known since he had become actively engaged in the town's activities. Things were rapidly approaching a crisis and the knowledge had filled him with dread; now let it come—he was ready to meet it.

Silently he chose a position against the railroad embankment close to the toolshed and here he remained until dawn. Murphy and Costigan passed him in the darkness on a nearly silent hand car, going west, but did not see him; and he did not know that they had returned until the sky paled. For some time he had heard a bustling in the building, and just as he was ready to leave he saw the section-gang roll out their own hand car and go rumbling up the line toward Scrub Oak.

Plans Awry

For the next few days a tense equilibrium was maintained in the town, the marshal, grim, alert, and practically ostracized by nine-tenths of the population. He could feel the veiled hostility whenever he went up and down the street, and silence fell abruptly on groups of men conversing here and there whenever he was seen approaching. Hostile glances, sullen faces, shrugging shoulders greeted him on every side, and he felt more relieved than ever when he reviewed his arrangements with the section-boss.

Henry Williams was growing openly suspicious of him, impatiently awaiting the arrival of the presents from St. Louis, which he had ordered through Jerry's telegraph key, and he was drinking more and more and keeping more and more to himself, his only company being two men whom Tex had been watching since the death of Bud Haines. The marshal felt that with the coming of the presents trouble would begin, and he had asked Jerry to keep a watch for them, and let him know the moment they arrived. Fate tricked him here, for when they did come they were packed in a large consignment of goods for Gus Williams, and since he regularly was receiving shipments there was nothing to indicate to the station agent that Henry's gifts had passed through his hands.

Henry's suspicions of the marshal were cumulative rather than sudden. Never very confident about what Tex really thought and what he might do, certain vague memories of looks and of ambiguous words and actions recurred to the nephew. He was beginning to believe that the marshal would shoot him down like a dog if he pressed the issue as he intended to press it in regard to Jane Saunders, and he was determined that Tex should have no opportunity to go to her defense. Several methods of eliminating the disturbing marshal presented themselves to the coyote-cunning mind of the would-be lover. He could be shot from cover as he moved about in his flimsy office, or as he slept. He could walk into a rifle bullet as he opened his door some morning, or he could be decoyed up to Blascom's while Henry's plans went through. This last would taste sweeter in the public mouth than a coldly planned murder, but on the other hand the return of the marshal might end in cyclonic action. There was no doubt about Tex's feelings in regard to killing when he felt it to be necessary or justified. He would kill with no more compunction than a wolf would show. Then from the mutterings of rebellion and the sullen looks of discontent among the hotel habitués a plan leaped into the nephew's mind. It solved every objectionable feature of the other schemes; and Henry forthwith went to work.

The nephew was no occult mystery to a man like the marshal, who almost could see the mental wheels turning in any man like him. Tex was preparing for eventualities and part of the preparation was the buying of a pint flask of whiskey from Carney—a bottle locally regarded as pocket-size. When night fell he emptied into the liquor a carefully computed amount of chloral hydrate, recorked it, shook it well, and placed it among sundry odds and ends in a corner of the office, where it would be overlooked by any thirsty caller, whose glance was certain to notice the bottle of whiskey in plain sight on a shelf. Against the consciousness of sixteen men that innocent-looking flask would tip the scales to its own side with an emphasis; and the marshal not only knew the proper dose for horses but also how to shove it down their throats with practiced ease and swiftness. Buck

Peters had paid him no mean compliment when he had said that Tex could dose a horse more expertly than any man he ever had known. Having put all of his weapons in order he marked time, awaiting the pleasure of the enemy.

He did not have long to wait. To be specific he waited two days more, which interval brought time around to the last day on the calendar for that month, the day which railroad regulations proclaimed to be the occasion for making out sundry and numerous reports, a job that kept many a station agent writing and figuring most of the night. Having sense and imagination, the agent at Windsor did what he could of this work from day to day and as a consequence saved himself from a long, high-tension job at the last minute; but he did not have imagination enough to know that a packing-case of formidable dimensions which he had received that noon from the west-bound train and later saw hauled to the Mecca, held the watched-for gifts that Henry Williams would eagerly present to Jane.

Contemptuous of any interference that Jerry might make in a physical sense, Henry nevertheless preferred to have him absent when he made his determined attempt. The brother doubtless would have great influence on Jane by his protests, and that would necessitate drastic measures which only would make the matter worse. If Jerry were detained by force, injured, or killed to keep him from the house it would cause a great deal of unpleasantness, from a domestic standpoint, to run through the years to come. There was only one night a month when the agent remained away from his house for any length of time, and this must be the night for the action to be carried through.

The mob was being slowly, but surely, inflamed by the nephew and his two friends, its anger directed against Murphy and Costigan since the section-gang had not returned to town. The section-boss and his friend came in every night while they worked along Buffalo Creek, and were careful not to give any excuse for a hostile demonstration against them. They were even less conspicuous because they walked in instead of rolling home on the hand car. But on this last night of the month the whole crew, rebelliously disobeying orders, came in on their crowded hand car, much to Henry's poorly concealed delight, and to Tex's rage. Murphy had promised otherwise.

Here was oil for the flames Henry had set burning! Here was success with a capital letter! The mob now would surely attack, divert Jerry's attention, and perhaps rid the town of its official nuisance. He would act on the marshal's kindly warning, for he would not be in the front rank of the mob; in fact, he would not be with the mob at all. He had other work to do.

The sudden look of joyous expectation, so poorly disguised, on Henry's face acted on Tex like the warning whirr of an angry rattlesnake and he quietly cleaned and oiled his guns, broke out a fresh box of cartridges, and dumped them into his right-hand pocket. The remaining chloral-filled shells he slipped in the pocket of his chaps. Shaking up the flask of whiskey to make certain of the crystals being dissolved and the drug evenly distributed throughout the fluid, he hid it again and, seating himself in his favorite place, awaited the opening number.

Darkness had just closed down when Tommy loped in from the ranch and stopped to say a few careless, friendly words, but he never uttered them, for the marshal's instructions were snapping forth before the C Bar rider could open his mouth.

"This is no time for pleasantries!" said Tex in a voice low and tense. "Turn around, ride back a way, circle around th' town an' leave yore cayuse a couple of hundred yards from Murphy's box car. Tell him trouble's brewin' an' to look sharp. Then you head for her house, actin' as cautious, an' go up to it on foot, an' as secretly as you know how. Lay low, outside. Don't show yourself at all—a man in th' dark will be worth five in th' light tonight. Stay there no matter what you hear in town. If she should see you, on yore life don't let her think there's any danger—on yore life, Tommy! Mebby there ain't, but there's no tellin' what drunken beast will remember that there's a woman close at hand. You stay there till daylight, or till I relieve you. Get-a-goin'—an' good luck!"

Tommy carried out his orders, gave Murphy the warning, and was gone again before the big Irishman, seething with rage at his crew's disobedience, could say more than a few words. Murphy had been forced to construct a plan of his own, and he wished to get word of it to the marshal's ears. Tommy having left so quickly, he could not send it. Convincing himself that it was not really necessary for the marshal to be told of it, and savagely pleased by the surprise in store for him and every man in town, the section-boss went ahead on his own initiative. Going to the toolshed he went in, frowning at the thoroughly cowed and humbled crew, blew out the lamps and with hearty curses ordered the gang to put their car on the rails and to start east for the next town.

"Roll her softly, by hand, till ye get out av th' hearin' av this hell-town, an' then board her, an' put yore weight on th' handles," he commanded. "An' don't ye come back till I send for ye. Costigan an' me are plannin' work for ourselves an' will not go with ye. Lively, now—an' no back talk. A lot depends on yer doin' as yer told. One more order disobeyed an' I'll brain th' pack av ye with a crowbar. Ye've raised hell enough this night. Now git out av here, an' mind what I've told ye!"

The orders quickly obeyed and the car quietly placed on the rails, the gang went into the night as silently as bootless feet would take them, pushing the well-greased car ahead of them, and as gently as though it were loaded with nitroglycerin. When far enough away not to be heard by anyone in town, they put on their boots, climbed aboard, and sent their conveyance along at an ordinary rate of speed. They hated to desert their two countrymen, and began to talk about it. Finally they made up their minds that Murphy's orders, in view of their recent disobedience, were to be followed, and with hearty accord they sent the car rolling on again, the greater part of the grades in their favor, toward the next town. The distance was nothing to become excited about with six husky men at the handles to pump off the miles.

Up at the station a single light burned in the little office where Jerry worked at his reports. Outside the building in the darkness Murphy lay on his stomach in a tuft of weeds, a rifle in his hand, and a Colt beside him on the ground. Within easy reach of his right hand lay a coatful of rocks culled from the roadbed, no mean weapons against figures silhouetted by the lamp-lighted windows of the buildings facing the right-of-way; and close to them were half a dozen dynamite cartridges, their wicked black fuses capped and inserted. Tim Murphy, like Napoleon, put his trust in heavy artillery.

Costigan was nowhere to be seen. Down the track lights shone under the cracks of the doors of the toolshed and the box-car habitation of the section-boss, and one curtained window of Costigan's rented cottage glowed dully against the night. Crickets shrilled and locusts fiddled, and there were no signs of impending danger.

In the hotel the tables were filled with lowly conversing miners in groups, each man leaning far forward, elbows on the table, his shoulders nearly touching those on either side. Gus Williams and his closest friends had pulled two tables together and made a group larger than the others. Henry and his two now inseparable companions were at a table near the back door, talking earnestly with Jake, who by this time had recovered from his recent sickness. The Buffalo Creek miner was quieter and more thoughtful than he had been before Blascom had nearly killed him, and his mind for several days had been the battle ground of a fiercely fought struggle between contending emotions, which still raged, but in a lesser intensity. He listened without comment to what was being said to him, swayed first one way and then another. His last glass of liquor was untasted, which was something of no moment to Henry's whiskey-dulled mind. Finally Jake nodded, tossed off the drink with a gesture of quick determination, hitched up his cartridge belt and, forgetting his sombrero on the floor, arose and slipped quietly out of the door. As he left, another man, peremptorily waved into the vacated chair, also listened to instructions and also slipped out through the rear door. He set his course toward the right-of-way, whereas Jake had gone in the other direction, toward Carney's saloon and the marshal's office.

The last man stopped when even with the line of shacks facing the railroad, noted the dully glowing shade in Costigan's house, the yellow strips of light around the rough board shutters of the box car, and the broader yellow band under the toolshed door. Satisfied by his inspection he slipped back the way he had come and made his report to Henry.

Jake crept with infinite caution toward the marshal's office, but when nearly to it he paused as the battle in his mind raged with a sudden burst of fury. The marshal had humbled him in sight of his friends and acquaintances and had boasted of worse to follow if his victim forced the issue; the marshal had saved his life in the little hut on the lower fork, laboring all night with him. Doctor Horn had said so, and Blascom, playing nurse at the marshal's request, had endorsed the doctor.

Ahead of him, plain to his sight, was the marshal's side window, its flimsy curtain tightly drawn; and silhouetted against it were the hatted head and the shoulders of the man he had been sent to kill. Again he crept forward, the Colt gripped tightly in his right hand. Foot by foot he advanced, but stopping more frequently to argue with himself. A few yards more and the mark could not be missed. He, himself, was safe from any answering fire. A heavy curse rumbled in his throat and he stopped again. He fought fair, as far as he knew the meaning of the term in its generally accepted definition among men of his kind. He never had knifed or shot a man from behind, and he was not going to do it now, especially a man who had no reason to save his sotted life, but who had done so without pausing. Jake arose, jammed the gun back into its holster and walked briskly to the door of the flimsy little office, which he found locked against him. He knocked and listened, but heard nothing. Again he knocked and listened and still there was no answer.

"Marshal!" he called in a rasping, loud whisper. "Marshal! Git away from that d—d window: th' next man won't be one that owes you for his life. I'm goin' back to Buffaler Crick. Look out for yoreself!" and he made good his words, striding off into the dark.

Back of the hotel, lying prone behind a pile of bleached and warped lumber, the marshal watched the rear door. He saw Jake leave, recognizing the man in the light of the opening door by certain peculiarities of carriage and manner. He smiled grimly when the man turned toward the north, and he waited for the sound of the shot which would drill the window, the shade, and the old shirt hanging on the back of a chair. He wondered if the rolled-up blanket,

fastened to the broken broom handle, which made the head
and held Carney's old sombrero, would fall with the impact.
Then the door opened again and the second man hurried
out, turning to the south. He came back shortly, left the door
open behind him and with his return Henry's voice rang out
in an impassioned harangue. The hotel was coming to life.
The stamp of heavy boots grew more continuous; loud voices
became louder and more numerous, and shouts arose above
the babel. The protesting voice of Gus Williams was heard
less and less, finally drowned completely in the vengeful
roar. Sudden noises in the street told of angry men pouring
out of the front door, simultaneously with the exodus
through the rear door. Oaths, curses, threats, and explosive
bursts of laughter arose. One leathern-lunged miner was
drunkenly singing at the top of his voice, to the air of *John
Brown's Body,* a paraphrase worded to suit the present situation.

The marshal leaped to his feet, secure against discovery
in the darkness, and sprinted on a parallel course for an
opening between the row of buildings facing the right-of-
way. His sober-minded directness and his lightness of foot
let him easily outstrip the more aimless, leisurely progress of
the maudlin gang, which preferred to hold to a common
front instead of stringing out. Drunk as they were, they were
sober enough to realize, if only vaguely, that a two-gun
sharpshooter by all odds would be waiting for the advance
guard. In fact, their enthusiasm was largely imitation. Henry's mind had not been keen enough to take into consideration such a thing as anticlimax; he had not realized that
the psychological moment had passed and that in the interval of the several days, while the once white-hot iron of
vengeful purpose still was hot, it had cooled to a point where
its heat was hardly more than superficial. The once deadly
purpose of the mob was gone, thanks to Gus Williams'

efforts, the ensuing arguments, and the wholesome respect for the marshal's courage and the speed and accuracy of his two guns. Instead of a destroying flood, contemptuous of all else but the destruction of its victims, the mob had degenerated into a body of devilish mischief-makers, terrible if aroused by the taste of blood, but harmless and hesitant if the taste were denied it.

Tex, sensing something of this feeling, darted through the alleyway between the two buildings he had in mind, dashed across the open space paralleling the right-of-way, crossed the tracks, and slipped behind the toolshed to be better hidden from sight. Its silence surprised him, but one glance through a knot hole showed the lighted interior to be innocent of inmates. He forthwith sprinted to the box car and a warped crack in one of the barn-door shutters told him the same tale. A sudden grin came to his face: Murphy had done what he could to offset the return of his section-gang. He glanced at Costigan's house and its one lighted curtain, and at that instant he remembered that he had not noticed the gang's hand car in the toolshed. He brought the picture of its interior to his mind again and grunted with satisfaction. Its disappearance accounted for the disappearance of the gang.

The mob would now become a burlesque, having nothing upon which to act. Chuckling over the fiasco, he trotted toward the station to see that Jerry got away before the crowd discovered its impotence to commit murder as planned, and to stay on the west side of the main street in case the baffled units of the mob should head for Jerry's house. There was no longer any shouting or noise. He knew that it meant that the advance guard of rioters was cautiously scouting and approaching the lighted buildings with due regard to its own safety; and he reached the station platform before he saw the sudden flare of light on the ground before the toolshed which told of its doors being yanked open. Figures tumbled into the lighted patch and then milled for a moment before hurrying off to join their fellows on the way to attack the other two buildings.

"That you, Tex?" said a low voice close to him. "This is Murphy."

"Good!" exclaimed the marshal. "You've beat 'em, Tim. They're like dogs chasin' their tails; an' from th' beginnin' they didn't sound very business-like. But there's no tellin' what some of them may do, so you go up an' join Costigan while I take a look around Jerry's house. Where is he? His light's out."

"He went home when he heard th' yellin'," answered Murphy, "to git th' lass out av th' house an' to Costigan in case th' mob started that way. 'Tis lucky for them they didn't, an' pass within throwin' distance av me! 'Tis dynamite I'd 'a' fed 'em, with proper short fuses. Look out ye don't push that lighted cigar too close to th' darlin's!"

Tex stepped back as though he had been stung. "I'm half sorry they didn't give you a chance to use th' stuff," he growled. "Well, I reckon mobs will be out of style in Windsor by mornin'. This ain't no wolf-pack, runnin' bare-fanged to a kill, but a bunch of coyotes usin' coyote caution. We'll let Costigan stay where he is, just th' same. You better join him as soon as these fools go back to get drunker. Th' woman in this makes us play dead safe. I'll head up that way an' look things over. If I hear a blast I'll get back fast enough. Don't forget to throw 'em quick after you touch 'em to that cigar!"

"I'll count five an' let 'em go," chuckled Murphy. "I got 'em figgered close."

"Too close for me!" rejoined the marshal, moving off toward the Saunders' home.

"I'd like to stick one in Henry's pocket," said the Irishman, growling.

"Damn me for a fool!" snapped Tex, leaping into the darkness.

XXI

◆

An Equal Guilt

Tommy Watkins, after delivering his message to Tim Murphy, hastened to the Saunders' home, where he carried out his orders, with but one exception; but the exception nullified all his efforts for a stealthy approach and a secret watch. The best cover he could find around the house was a little building near the back door in which firewood, kerosene, and odds and ends were kept. Despite the kindling and the darkness his entrance had been noiseless and he was paying himself hearty compliments upon the exploit when his head collided with a basket of clothespins which hung from a peg in the wall, and sent the basket and its contents clattering down on the kerosene can and a tin pan. He started back involuntarily and his spurred heels struck the side of a washtub which was nearly full of water, kept so against drying out and falling apart. Into this he sat with a promptness and abandon which would have filled the heart of any healthy small boy with ecstasies. Bounding out of the tub, he fell over the pile of kindling and from this instant his rage spared nothing in his way. Had he deliberately started out with the firm intention of arousing that part of Kansas he scarcely could have made a better job of it. While he cursed like a drunken sailor, and burned with rage and shame, the door was suddenly flung open and Jane, lamp in hand, stared at him in fright and determination, over the trembling muzzle of a short-barreled .38.

"Oh!" she exclaimed, the hand holding the gun now pressing against her breast. "Oh!" she repeated, and the lamp wobbled so that she tremblingly blew it out. For some moments she struggled to get back to normal, Tommy thankful that the lamp no longer revealed him in his present water-soaked condition. He felt that his flaming face would give light enough without any further aid.

He sidled out of the door, tongue-tied, crestfallen, miserable, and placed his back against the shed, intending to slip along it, and dash around the corner into the kindly oblivion of the black night.

"Wait!" she begged, sensing his intention. "Oh, my; how you frightened me! Whatever made you get into this shed, anyway? What were you trying to do?"

Here it was, right in his teeth. Tex fairly had hammered into him the warning not to frighten her—on his life he was to keep from her any thought of danger if she should see him. She had seen him, all right. She had seen entirely too much of him—and he was not to frighten her! Holy Moses! He was not to frighten her! He resolved that plenty of time should elapse before he allowed Tex Jones to see him. Not to frighten her—it was a wonder she had not died of fright.

"What on earth ever made you go in there?" she demanded, a little acerbity in her voice.

"Why, ma'am, I was hidin' from you," said the culprit. "Let me light th' lamp, ma'am, an' straighten things out in there. Everythin' slid that wasn't nailed fast. That tub, now: was you savin' th' water for anythin', ma'am? If you was I plumb spoiled it."

"No; it was only to keep the staves swelled tight—for heaven's sake, do you mean that you fell in it?" She reached out and grasped his coat, and suddenly collapsed against the building, shrieking with laughter. When she could speak she ordered him to feel for and pick up the lamp, and to lead the way into the house. "Go right into Jerry's room and change your clothes—I hope you can get his things on. But whatever made you go in there, anyway? What was it?"

"Like I done said, ma'am," he reiterated, flushing in the dark. "I was goin' to play a joke on Jerry when he came home—but I didn't aim to do no damage, ma'am, or scare you!" he earnestly assured her.

"Oh, but you were willing to scare Jerry!" she retorted.

"I don't reckon he'd 'a' been scared," he mumbled. "Here's th' lamp, ma'am, on th' step; I'll see Jerry at th' station. I'm fadin', now," and before she could utter a protest he had put down the lamp and disappeared around the house. But he did not go far. Wet clothes meant nothing to him, nothing at all in his present state of mind, and he intended to stay, and to keep his watch faithfully. And it was to his present flurried state of mind that he owed his more serious misadventure of the night, for he blundered around the second corner squarely into two figures hugging the wall and a descending gun butt filled his mental firmament with stars. He sagged to the ground without even a sigh and was quickly disarmed and bound. A soiled handkerchief was forced into his mouth and he was rolled against the wall, where he would be out of the way.

One of the two hirelings nudged the other as they stood up, putting his mouth close to his companion's ear. "Hey, Ike!" he whispered. "This fool is wet as a drownded pup—wears a gun an' cowpunch clothes. He ain't the agent!"

"Hell no!" responded Ike; "but he meant us no good, bein' here. We'll git th' agent, too. He'll be comin' soon, an' fast. Git over by th' path he uses."

Jane, somewhat vexed, had picked up the lamp and entered the house. The constantly repeated "ma'am" and the stammering explanations, which she put but little stock in, made her suddenly contrast this big, overgrown boy with a man she knew, and to Tommy's vast discredit. She had hit it: one was no more than an overgrown boy, coarse, unlearned, clumsy, embarrassed; the other, a grown man, cool, educated, masterful, unabashed. One was in his own way; the other, unobtrusive in manner but persistently haunting in his personality. She might not be able for good reasons to see Tex Jones in a room filled with people, but she could not fail to sense his presence. But the marshal was no longer to be thought of; he had taken a human life and was forever beyond the pale of her interest and affections. He had blood on his hands.

Suddenly she started and cast an apprehensive glance toward the window which faced the town. A low, chaotic roaring, indistinct in its blurred entirety, but fear impelling because of its timbre, came from the main street. A shot or two sounded flatly and the roaring rose and fell in queer, spasmodic bursts. Before she could move, a knock sounded on the door and, fearing bad news about her brother, she took a tight grip on herself and walked swiftly toward the summons, flinging the door wide open.

Henry Williams, a smirk on his face, bowed and entered, not waiting for an invitation. He forgot to remove his hat in his eagerness to place his packages on the table where she plainly could see them. Selecting the easiest chair, he seated himself on the edge of it, and tossed his sombrero against the wall.

"Nice evenin', ma'am," he said, flushing a little. "I was hopin' for more rain but don't reckon we'll git none for a spell. What we had has helped wonderful. You an' Jerry feelin' well?"

"It doesn't feel like rain, Mr. Williams," she replied, torn between her fear and mirth at the presence of this unwelcome visitor. "Both my brother and myself are as well as we can expect to be. If you'll go to the station you'll find him there—this is report night and he may not be home until quite late."

"I ain't waitin' for Jerry," explained Henry, leering. "It's just as well if he is a little late. My call is shore personal, ma'am; personal between me an' you."

She was staring at him through eyes which were beginning to sparkle with vexation. She was now beginning to accept her first, intuitive warning.

"I am not aware that there is anything of a personal nature which concerns us both," she rejoined. "I believe you must be mistaken, Mr. Williams. If you will close the door behind you on your way out I will be duly grateful. Jerry is at the station." She stepped back to let him pass, but he ignored the hints.

There came an increase in the roaring from the direction of town and she started, casting an inquiring and appealing glance at her visitor.

"Th' boys are a little wild tonight," he said, smiling evilly. "They've got so much dust that they're bustin' loose to paint th' old town proper. There ain't nothin' to be scared about."

"But Jerry: my brother!" she exclaimed fearfully. "He's alone in the office!"

"No, he ain't ma'am," replied Henry with an air meant to reassure her. "I got four good boys, deputized by th' marshal, watchin' the station in case some fool gets notions. Jones, hisself, is settin' on a bench outside, an' you know what *that* means. I allus look after my friends, ma'am." He smiled again. "'Specially them that are goin' to be real close to me. That's why I'm here—to look after you now— now, an' all th' time, now an' forever. Just see what I brought you—sent all th' way to St. Louis for 'em, an' shore got th' very best there was. Why," he chuckled, going to the table, and so engrossed in his packages that he did not see the look of revulsion on her face, a look rapidly turning to a burning shame and anger.

"These here gloves, now—they cost me six dollars. An' lookit this Cashmere shawl—you'd think I was lyin' if I told you what *that* cost. I told th' boys you'd show 'em off handsome an' proper. Put 'em on and let's see how they look on you." He held the gifts out, looking up at her, surprised by her silence, her lack of pleased exclamations, and paused, dumbfounded at her expression.

Mortification yielded place to shame and fear; shame and fear to anger with only a trace of fear, and then rage swept all else before it. The colors playing in her cheeks fled and left them white, her lips were thin as knife blades and her eyes blazed like crucibles of molten metal. She struck wildly at the presents, sending them across the room and raised her hand to strike him. Never in all her life had she been so furious.

"Why—what's th' matter?" he asked, not believing his senses. He put out a hand to pacify her. It touched her arm and turned her into a fury, her nails scoring it deeply as she struck it away.

"What's th' matter with you?" he demanded angrily, looking up from his bleeding hand. "Oh!" he sneered, his face working with anger. "That's it, huh? All right, damn you! I'll cussed soon show you who's boss!" he gritted, moving slowly forward. "If you won't come willin'ly, you'll come unwillin'ly! Puttin' on airs like you was too good for me, huh? I'll bust yore spirit like you was a hoss!"

She flung a quivering arm toward the door, but he pressed forward and backed her into a corner, from where she struck at him again and again, and then felt his arms about her as he wrestled with her. Her strength amazed him and he broke loose to get a more punishing hold. "Ike!" he shouted. "George! Hurry up: she's worse'n a wildcat!"

Ike's head popped in through a window, George dashing through the door, and with them at his side Henry leaped for her. She clutched at her breast and crouched, as savage and desperate as any animal of the wild. He shouted something as he closed with her and then there came a muffled roar, a flash, and a cloud of smoke spurted from between them. Henry, his glazing eyes fixing their look of fear, amazement, and chagrin, spun around against his companions, his clutching hands dragging down their arms, and slid between them. For him the mob had been incited in vain.

His two friends, stupefied for an instant, gazed unbelievingly from Jane to Henry and back again, vaguely noticing that her horror and revulsion were unnerving her and that the short-barreled Colt in her hand was wobbling in everwidening circles. Ike recovered his self-possession first and, reaching out swiftly, knocked the wavering weapon from her hand. Shouting savagely he leaped for her as a streak of flame stabbed in through the window he had entered by, the deafening roar filling the room. He stiffened convulsively, whirled halfway around and pitched headlong under the table, dead before he touched the floor. His companion's arms jerked upward with spasmodic speed.

"Keep 'em there! Sit down, Miss Saunders," came an even, unflurried voice from the window as the marshal, hatless and coatless, hoping that George would draw, crawled into the house behind a steady gun. "Good Lord!" he muttered, glancing over the room, his eye passing the fallen .38 without betraying any recognition. "Steady!" he cried as Jane's knees buckled and she slid down the wall. "Keep 'em up!" he snarled at George as he swiftly disarmed him. "Face th' door!" As the frightened man obeyed, the marshal stepped quickly to a shelf on which stood a bottle of brandy and some glasses. He changed his gun to his left hand, snatched a cartridge from his chaps' pocket and, yanking out the lead with his teeth, emptied the shell into a glass. Quickly filling this and another he wheeled and thrust one out at the rigid prisoner. "Drink this," he ordered. "You shore need it; an' if you don't I'll blow you apart." George's stare of amazed incredulity changed to one of hope and relief and he downed the drink at a gulp. Tex slipped a pair of handcuffs over his wrists and ordered him to sit down. "Sit down in that big chair, an' close yore eyes. I got somethin' for you to do—relax!"

As he bent over Jane she stirred, opened her eyes, glanced at him, and then fixed them on the men on the floor, shuddering and shrinking from the sight; but she could not look away. "I killed him! I killed him!" she sobbed hysterically, over and over again.

"Drink this," ordered the marshal, forcing the glass between her lips. He nodded with quiet satisfaction. "Shore," he replied in an assumed matter-of-fact voice, as though it were an everyday occurrence. "Good job, too. I should have done it, myself, days ago." He held up the glass again. "Can you drink a little more of this, Miss Saunders? There are times when a little brandy is very useful." His low, even, unemotional tones were almost caressing, and she thankfully put herself in his capable hands. Slowly growing calmer she began to see things with a less blurred vision and the slow slumping of the sleepy man in the chair took her wondering attention.

"Why, is he—killed—too?" she asked shuddering.

"Oh, no; he's only half asleep," replied Tex, smiling. "Three more minutes an' he'll be sound asleep, for a dozen hours or more. Brandy has an hypnotic effect on some people, Miss Saunders, while it stimulates others. Will you please collect a small valise of your most valuable and indispensable possessions, all the money in the house, a good wrap of some kind, and allow me to escort you to Murphy and Costigan? You are leaving town, you know, never to return."

"But I've killed a man, and you are an officer of the law! Do you mean—" she paused unbelievingly.

"You shot a mad skunk in plain self-defense," he replied. "He has powerful friends and influence to avenge him. The jury would be packed and justice scorned. I'm marshal no longer, Miss Saunders. I accepted the appointment on the definite understanding that I would be marshal only as long as I could. The term has automatically come to an end. So far as this town is concerned I'm a rabid outlaw." He tore the badge from his vest and threw it on the table. "Ah! George is sleeping more soundly than he ever slept before. There's no need of gagging him, for he'll give no alarm. Please fill that satchel, Miss Saunders—time presses."

"You are a good friend, Mr. Jones; and I have wronged you," she said, her words barely audible. "My hands are as bloody as yours—and I scorned you for taking life! Take me away from here—please—please!"

"As fast as I can," replied Tex, soothingly. "You help me by filling a satchel and getting your wrap. Put your mind on your possessions, please; think what you wish to take with you, and then get them. Money? Jewels? Miscellaneous valuables, intrinsic or sentimental? Documents? Apparel? Please—you must aid me all you can if I'm to aid you. We have no time to lose!"

"But my brother—he is safe?"

"Waiting outside, tied, and gagged. I couldn't stop to free him," Tex answered. "Watkins, likewise. They laid their plans well, but the mob was a misfire and didn't keep me as busy as they counted on. Will you obey me, Miss Saunders,

or must we leave bare-handed? I'll give you just three minutes by that clock—then we go."

A pious, shocked exclamation came from the window
where Murphy stared suddenly into a magic gun before he
was recognized. "Holy Mother!" he whispered, and then:
"I found Tommy—where is Jerry?"

"Don't you ever do that again!" snapped Tex, a little
white showing in his face. "I don't know how I kept th' hammer up! You look around by that clump of scrub oak, where
the path goes around the big bowlder. I nearly fell over him.
Take them both with you—we'll follow close. Any signs of
anyone coming from town?"

"Not yet—but ye needn't stay here all night! Hurry, miss,
or there'll be a slaughter that'll shake this country!"

As Jane obeyed, Tex walked over, drew up one of
George's eyelids and smiled grimly. Then he placed a hand
on each of the figures on the floor and nodded, a sneer flickering over his face. In a moment Jane, still a little unsteady,
returned and found the ex-marshal pinning the nickeled
badge on the lapel of Henry's coat, and while it meant nothing to her then in her agitated state of mind its significance
came to her later. When that badge was found she would be
freed of blame for Henry's death. Opening the door Tex
blew out the light and led the way. They hurried over the
uneven, hard ground and soon reached the railroad, where
a hand car, with Murphy, Costigan, and Tommy at the handles, waited to run them over a trail where no tracks would
tell any tales.

"Head for Scrub Oak, an' stop outside th' town till Jerry's party gets away," ordered Tex. "Th' grades are mostly
against you an' all of you came from th' east, where Mike's
family went. They'll figger you went th' same way, if they
think of th' hand car at all. It ain't likely they will, because

I'm aimin' to give them something plain to read, when they're *able* to read it. Got money? Got enough to buy three good cayuses with saddles, grub, an' everythin' you need? Good! Tommy, when you get to town, go in alone, get three outfits, an' take Miss Saunders an' Jerry to Gunsight as fast as they can travel. When you get there, ask for Nelson, an' tell him Tex Ewalt says to hold off h—l an' high water before givin' up these two. I'll join you there as soon as I can. Here, listen close," and he gave a description of Gunsight's location sufficient for a rider of the plains. "Off with you, now—let her roll gently near Buffalo Crick—she'll rumble deep crossin' that bridge an' Jake *may* be at home. So-long— get a-goin'!"

"But you?" cried Jane. "Where are you going? Surely not back into that town!" The distress and anxiety brought a smile to the ex-marshal's lips. "You must come with us! You must! You must!" she insisted almost hysterically. "You can't fight the whole town!"

"I'm bettin' he can," growled Murphy. "Here, Tex! Better take a couple av these little firecrackers! Count five an' let 'em go; but *you* better count sorta fast."

"No, thanks, Tim," laughed Tex. "I can't go with you, Miss Saunders. I've got a pack of coyotes to make fools of— see you at th' SV in four or five days. Don't you worry—it was clean self-defense. He brought it on himself. All right, Tim: get a-goin'!"

He listened to the sounds of the cautiously propelled car, the clicks of the rail joints growing softer and softer. When they had died out, he walked swiftly back to the house, where he got his hat and coat and then went on to town. Going to where the roan patiently waited for him he led it to John Graves' stable and reconnoitered the building. John was not at home on this night of excitement.

Tex forced the door, and quietly saddled the sorrel and the gray, threw a sack of corn across the latter and, leading them forth, led the three animals back of a deserted building and then went toward the hotel.

XXII

◆

The False Trail and the True

The maudlin crowd was ugly and did not accept the marshal's appearance with any enthusiasm. While he had not opposed them he had warned and sent away their hoped-for victims. Frank scowls met him wherever he looked. He stopped at the table where Gus Williams and a dozen cronies, the bolder men of the town, were drinking and arguing.

"Blascom's cussed sick," he announced. "Sick as a dog. I rode out to spend th' night with him, knowin' that when that coyote section-boss sent his pack out of town there wouldn't be no reason for me to stay here an' make myself unpopular. I got a good job in this town, an' I've got a right to have friends here. Anyhow, I told Murphy that if his men came back they'd have to do their own fightin'. Reckon that's why he sent 'em along. Him an' Costigan follered 'em on th' other hand car." He glanced over the room. "Where's Hennery?" he asked. "I heard he wanted to see me."

Williams roused himself and looked up through blood-shot eyes. "Th' fool's gone courtin', I reckon; an' on a night like this, when I needed him. Don't know when he'll git back. He mus' be enjoyin' hisself, anyhow."

John Graves chuckled and endorsed the sentiment.

Tex nodded. "I reckon mebby he is, his star bein' bright tonight. Much excitement in town after I left? Station agent make any trouble?"

"A lot of chances he'd 'a' had to make any of us any trouble," sneered a miner. "I reckon he cut an' run right quick. We've been figgerin' he's better off in some other town. Been thinkin' of chasin' him out. Any objections from th' marshal of Windsor?"

"Not a cussed one," answered Tex. "He's a troublemaker, stayin' here. Chuck him on th' train tomorrow an' send him back East, where he comes from. An' his sister, too, if you want."

Williams shook his head. "Not her," he said. "Henry'll never let her git away from him. He's aimin' to take care of her; an' he shore can handle her, *he* can."

"I reckon he can," agreed Tex. "I just come in to get th' doc to go out an' look at Blascom. Since he's struck it rich he's been feedin' like a fool. Them as live by canned grub, dies by canned grub, says I; an' he's close to doin' it. I got a bottle of whiskey for him, but I reckon gin will be better for his stummick. Yes, a lot better. Hey, Baldy!" he shouted. "Put me out a bottle of gin an' set up th' drinks for all hands. We'll drink to a better understandin' an' to Hennery an' his bride." He pulled the pint flask from his pocket and winked at his companions. "I got a little somethin' extra, here. Th' smoke of Scotch fires is in it. Might as well use it up," and he quickly filled the glasses on the table, discovering when too late that he had none left for himself. "Oh, well; whiskey is whiskey, to me. I'll take some of Baldy's with th' boys," and he swaggered over to the bar, tossing a gold piece on the counter.

"Where's yore badge, Marshal?" asked Baldy, curiously.

Tex quickly felt of his coat lapel and then of his vest. "Cuss it!" he growled. "I knowed I'd lose that star—th' pin was a little short to go far enough in th' socket. Oh, well," he laughed, holding up his glass, "everyone knows me now; an' they'll know me better as time goes on. Here's to Hennery!" he shouted. "Drink her standin'!"

The toast drunk to roaring jests, he took the gin and went back to Williams. "Goin' after th' doc," he remarked. "Lost my badge, too; but lemme say that anybody found wearin' it shore will have bad luck. See you all tomorrow. He's sick as a pup, Blascom is. Good night, an' sleep tight, as th' sayin' is!" he shouted laughingly and nodding at the crowd he wheeled and went out.

Once secure from observation of any curious inhabitants of the town, he ran to the horses, mounted, and rode up to the Saunders' house, a home no longer. Entering it he quickly collected a bag of provisions and then, milling the horses before the door to start a plain trail, he cantered toward the station, where he crossed the tracks and struck south for the old cattle trail.

All night he rode hard, sitting the sorrel to keep his own horse fresh, and at dawn, giving them a ration of corn each, he ate a cold and hurried breakfast and soon was on his way again. During the forenoon he let the sorrel go, riding the gray with the depleted corn sack tied to the pommel. Several hours later he threw the still further depleted sack on the roan, changed horses again and turned the gray loose. After nightfall he came within sight of the lights of a small town and, waiting until the hour was quite late, rode through it casually to lose the tracks of his horse among the countless prints on its streets. He left it along a well-traveled trail leading westward, one which would take him, eventually, to Rawlins.

In the town of Gunsight, Dave Green was polishing glasses behind his bar when a dusty, but smiling, stranger rode up

to the door and called out. Grumbling, Dave waddled forth
to answer the summons.

"Which way to th' SV?" asked the stranger. "I'm lookin'
for my friend Nelson."

"What is it—a house-raisin' or a christenin'?" asked
Dave, grinning broadly. "Th' SV's gettin right pop'lar these
days—as it ought to be." Dave cogitated a moment. This man
said Nelson was a friend of his; but if not, there would be no
harm done to anyone on the SV. Dave was quite certain of
that, with Hopalong, Red, and the outfit at Johnny's back.
Still, his curiosity was aroused. "Yore name Jones, or Ewalt?"
he asked.

"Ewalt," replied Tex, grinning.

Dave left the door and gravely held out his hand. "Heard
tell about you, long ago," he said. "We're good friends till
you horn into a poker game that I'm settin' in. Heard about
you this mornin', too. A tenderfoot, a cowpunch, an' a
reg'lar picture in skirts stopped an' asked me what you did.
Also wanted to know if I had seen Jones or Ewalt. You just
foller that Juniper trail," and he gave a description tiresome,
and needlessly detailed, to a man to whom compass points
would have sufficed. "Jones comin', too? Don't know I ever
heard of him."

"Jones is dead," said Tex with touching sorrow. "Th'
pore ol' soul, we'll never see him more. He had buttons runnin' up his back, an' buttons down before."

"Too bad," replied Dave, but he was suspicious of the
other's grief. He shook his head. "Life shore is uncertain.
You tell Johnny if he's havin' a party that I ain't too fat to
ride that far, not if I'm invited. I ain't much on dancin',
but I'll do my best."

Tex nodded, thanked him for his information and went on,
gradually becoming lost in introspective musings.

"Omar," he muttered, shaking his head sadly, "I ain't got

no right. I'm hard-boiled, an' I've reached purty low levels th' last twenty years. There ain't no human meanness, no human weaknesses, hardly, that I ain't seen. My view of life is so cynical that it near scares me, now. I lost my illusions years ago, an' I'm allus lookin' for th' basest motives for a man's actions. Besides, I'm forty-odd years old—an' that's *too* old.

"Now you take Tommy Watkins. He's fresh, young, chock-a-block with illusions; trustin', ambitious, steady. He's clean, body an' mind. When he grows up, ten years from now, he'll be a purty fair sort of a young man. It shore does beat all, Omar."

A little farther along he drew a deep breath and patted the roan. "Omar, I've made up my mind: Youth should be for youth; illusions, for illusions; freshness, for freshness; innocence, for innocence. Her purity deserves better than my mildewed soul—if a man's got one." After a moment's silence he patted the horse again. "Omar, yore name brings somethin' back to me:

> *Ah Love! could you and I with Him conspire*
> *To grasp this sorry Scheme of Things entire,*
> *Would not we shatter it to bits—and then*
> *Remould it nearer to the Heart's Desire!*

Raising his head he saw a rattlesnake sunning itself on a rocky patch of ground near the trail and his gun leaped into crashing life. The snake writhed, trying in vain to coil. A second shot stretched it lifeless.

"There, damn you!" shouted Tex, shaking his fist at the quivering body, "that's how I feel!" and, the burst of passion gone as quickly as it had come, he shook his head and rode on again, calm and determined. At last he came to the top of the last hill hiding the ranchhouse and drew rein as he looked down into the north branch of the SV valley. A boy was riding along the bottom of the slope and Tex hailed him.

"Hey, sonny!" shouted the ex-marshal. "I'm lookin' for Hopalong Cassidy. Know where he is?"

"He's at th' house!" replied the boy. "Yo're Tex Ewalt! Foller me, an' I'll beat you to him!"

"Bet yo're Charley!" responded Tex. "Yo're shore goin' to ride some, cowboy, if you aim to beat me!" and a race was on.

There came a flurry of movement at the ranchhouse door and three men ran to their saddled horses. A sudden cloud of dust rolled up and the three, bunched leg to leg, raced toward the galloping newcomer. Heedless of Charley's vexatious appeal they shot past him and kept on while he swung his pony around and saw them sweep up to the slowing roan and surround him and his rider. More soberly, after a hilarious welcome, the four, with Charley endeavoring to wedge into shifting openings not half large enough for his pony, they rode up to the ranchhouse, where Jerry had run out to meet them, Margaret Nelson at his heels. As soon as he could Tex asked for Jane and learned that she was resting.

"She has been under a very heavy strain, Mr. Ewalt," Margaret told him. "She asked that you see her as soon as you came; but she is sleeping, now, and it will be better for her if you wait. Her remorse is as great as her horror and fatigue."

"I suppose so," replied Tex. "That's the woman of it. She shot a beast in plain self-defense and now she's remorseful. Shucks—it's all my fault. I should have done it, myself, days before."

"I didn't say just what I think is causing her remorse," replied Margaret, smiling enigmatically; "but that is something a man should find out for himself," and, turning quickly, she entered the house.

Tex stared after her and then around the circle of happy, grinning faces. An answering smile crept to his own, a smile wistful, but shaded with pain.

The next few days were busy ones from a conversational standpoint, for there was a great deal to talk about. Tex learned the history of the SV's rejuvenation, and his friends eagerly listened to the news he brought from Montana, and to the messages he brought from their friends; while Jane, much better because of the rest she had had, sat by the cheerful group, smiling at the perfect accord between its units and rapidly changing her ideas of western men. Here she saw friendships which seemed to be founded on the eternal rock, unshakable, unquestioning. She found it almost impossible to believe that these thin-lipped, yet kindly and smiling men, whose trick of looking out through narrowed lids at first made her wonder, each had killed again and again, as Margaret had told her. To her they were gravely kind, courteous, and deferential, accepting her without question, their manner a soothing assurance as to her safety. Jerry and Tommy were unquestionably accepted and made part of the happy circle—they were friends of Tex Ewalt, whom she now knew by his right name. Johnny's boyish enthusiasm and mischievous smile made it hard for her to believe that he, single-handed, had overcome the odds against him and cleared this range of its undesirable inhabitants. Margaret's proud account of his deeds rang true, and Jane knew that they were true.

There they all sat on the front porch, telling anecdotes on each other which amazed Jane, speaking of remarkable exploits in matter-of-fact voices. She learned of Tex's part in the saving of Buck Peter's ranch, and gradually pieced together the story of his activities in Windsor. Prodded by Tex, at last Johnny and Hopalong gave a grudging exhibition of revolver shooting which made her catch her breath. Tex Ewalt had been right: these two cheerful men could ride into Windsor and wipe it from the map; and she no longer feared the appearance of any of the Williams' friends. If they could find and follow the trail, let them!

Tex was the quietest man in the party, and she was pleased because he spoke only in the vernacular. She had not heard him deviate from it for one instant. He had no wish to "show off" at the expense of his roughly speaking friends. Tommy's garrulity, considering how little he really had to say, sounded like the prattle of a child among grown-ups; but he was a good, well-meaning boy. Daily he spoke of getting work on the Double X, where Lin Sherwood could use another rider; but he had made no attempt to go, preferring to stay where *she* was and to follow her about at every opportunity.

Then came the afternoon when Johnny volunteered to show his guests about the ranch and they had set out, Tex remaining behind. Jane had felt a restraint at the thought of how close she and the ex-marshal would be thrown together on this ranch, but soon found it to be groundless. Deferential, reserved, friendly, he had not obtruded, and apparently had not noticed Tommy's attentions. They rode off, Jerry with their host, Tommy at the side of Jane. When down in the main valley Johnny had turned off to look at the fenced-in quicksands, Jerry going with him to see the now harmless death trap, and Tommy remained behind with her; and when they returned they found a flushed Jane and a despondent Tommy. The following morning when she sat down to a late breakfast with Mr. Arnold, Johnny's father-in-law, she learned quite casually that Tommy had gone to the Double X and that the rest of the men, her brother included, had ridden up to the north wire to make some repairs. Arnold explained about the difficulty of keeping the posts up along the bottom of the ravine where he had suffered his broken leg, and he told her of the fondness of the cattle for the wilderness of brush and of the difficult task of running a round-up on that part of the ranch.

"Let me throw a saddle on yore horse, Miss Saunders," he suggested. "It will make a pleasant ride for you; an' you can take 'em up some lunch if you like. They've got a bigger task than they think, for th' ravine floor is solid rock. I'll send Charley with you—he's on th' rampage because he overslept and I wouldn't let him go up and bother them. But he might as well go."

She thought for a moment, and then turned a grave and pitiful face to him.

"I feel that I can ask you anything, Mr. Arnold; and I'm so upset."

"You certainly can, Miss Saunders," he replied, abandoning the vernacular in response to her way of speaking.

She hurriedly told him of the killing of Henry Williams, of the blood on her hands, but avoided the real appeal, the question she must find her own answer to. He heard her through, and, arising, placed a fatherly hand on her shoulder.

"Jane," he said, slowly shaking his head. "Environment, circumstances, change all things. There's not a man on this ranch that doesn't feel proud of what he knows about you. A woman has as much right, and often a greater need, to defend herself, as a man has. Don't you worry about that beast; and don't you worry about anyone coming down here after you. We can muster forty fighting men, if we need them, purely on Johnny's say-so. We're all proud of you. Now I'll saddle your horse while Peggy puts up the lunch. You and Charley can easily carry it between you. There's no place down here where you can't safely go; but please keep in the saddle while you're on the range. These cattle are dangerous to anyone afoot."

While the simple preparations were being made she heard Charley's exultant whoops and soon she rode with him toward the upper end of the small valley, listening to his worshiping chatter about his heroes. Now he had a new one, the man who could pull poker hands out of a fellow's nose, eyes, and ears.

"He'd 'a' got that Hennery feller, too," he averred, "only you beat him out. Gee, Miss Saunders! Wish I'd 'a' been there! I ain't never shot nobody yet—but you just wait, that's all! I heard Tex say he'd 'a' shot up th' whole d—d town if they'd tried to bother you—an' Hoppy said he could 'a' done it, *easy!* Hoppy knows, too. Why don't you like Tex, Miss Saunders? I think he's aces-up!"

"Why, I do, Charley. Whatever made you ask me that?"

"Well, if you do, Tex don't think so," he grumbled. "You know that pile of rock, up on th' hill where th' Gunsight trail winds like a letter S?"

She nodded. She could see it plainly from her window.

"Well, I was layin' up there, keepin' watch for that Williams' gang, an' he never even reckoned anybody was near him!" he boasted. "Takes a good man to find me when I don't want him to, I tell you. Injuns can't, an' they're cussed acute, Hoppy says."

"Who was it who didn't see you?"

"Tex," chuckled the boy. "He come walkin' along like there wasn't nobody around, an' he sorta slammed hisself down on th' rock next to th' top one. You an' Tommy an' Jerry was ridin' back from th' main valley. We could just see you, me an' him, only he didn't know *I* was there. After awhile we could see plain. Jerry rode off to look at somethin', an' kinda fell back, leavin' you an' Tommy goin' on without him. I was watchin' Tex, because he had a funny look on his face. He just looked steady, an' when he saw you two ridin' along together, he threw out his arms an' said somethin' about bein' like Jerry. Somethin' about falling back an' seein' you an' Tommy ridin' through life together—as if anybody would ride as long as that! Tell you what: These grownups say some cussed foolish things. There was tears in his eyes—him, a grown-up, gun-fightin' son-of-a-gun! Huh! An' they used to tease *me* when *I* cried! What you think about that?" He looked eagerly at her for the answer and then snorted in frank disgust. "Cuss it—an' yo're snifflin', too! I'll be a son-of-a-gun!"

"You mustn't tell anyone about it, Charley!" she pleaded. "They won't understand!"

"I won't," he promised. "Don't blame you for bein' ashamed. Tex would 'a' been, too, if he knowed I saw him. Then mebby he wouldn't go up there every night an' watch yore window till the light goes out, an' I wouldn't have nobody to trail. Reckon he's scared that Williams gang will trail you down here? Huh! With him settin' up there, me roamin' loose, an' with Johnny, Hoppy, an' Red in th' house, I shore wish they *would* come a-pokin' their noses around here! I tell you, things'd shore pop. If Tex could clean out their whole town all alone, they'd shore have a pleasant time down here ag'in' him an' his friends! Gee!"

After supper the nightly gathering on the porch passed a pleasant hour or two and then dwindled as its members retired, the two women and Charley going first. Jerry followed soon afterward and not much later Red and Hopalong left to go to the bunkhouse, where they now were berthed. Arnold soon went into the house, to the room which Tex stubbornly had refused to occupy, the latter preferring the bunkhouse with his old friends. After a cigarette or two Johnny said good night and left his companion alone.

Tex arose, paced restlessly to and fro across the yard and, wheeling abruptly, went toward the corral. He had not been gone very long when Charley, noiselessly crawling out of the window of the room he shared with his father, froze in his tracks as he heard a noise beyond the summer kitchen. He had Red's Winchester, which he had taken from the gun rack in the dining-room, and he scouted cautiously toward the suspicious sounds. The moonlight let him see plainly, and he drew back behind the corner of the building as Jane rode away, leaving the light burning brightly in her room.

Charley frankly was puzzled. "Somethin's goin' on," he cogitated. "I was goin' to stalk Tex—now I dunno. Shucks! He can look out for hisself, but she might get lost. Reckon I'll foller her." He suited action to the words and soon was riding after her, keeping out of her sight with a woodcraft worthy of his elders.

She led him along the Gunsight trail, closer and closer to the S it made up the rocky hill, and because of the view commanded by the rocky pile on the summit, he had to dismount, picket his horse, and proceed on foot, working from cover to cover, often on hands and knees.

Tex had taken his time, buried in thought, oblivious to everything outside of himself. He followed the well-marked trail instinctively and soon reached the top of the hill, where he sat quietly in the saddle for a few minutes. Finally, shaking his head, he dismounted and listlessly walked to the place of his nightly vigil. Seating himself on the top-most bowlder he gazed steadily at the yellow light of the distant window and, like many men of his class, given to solitude, he argued his problem aloud. It seemed that often he could think more clearly that way.

This could not go on. Tomorrow he would start back to Montana, and he soon arose to return to the SV, to spend his last night there. As he went back to his horse another verse came to his mind, a verse of finality, and one fitting the present situation. He laughed bitterly and flung out his arms:

> *And when like her, O Sákí, you shall pass*
> *Among the Guests Star-scatter'd on the Grass,*
>   *And in your blissful errand reach the spot*
> *Where I made One—turn down an empty Glass!*

Suddenly he stiffened, his hands leaping instinctively to his guns. Then he let them fall to his sides and stared unbelievingly: "Miss Saunders!" he exclaimed in amazement. "Why—what are you—?" and ceased, tongue-tied.

"You are—going away?" she asked, her voice breaking, speaking so low he barely could hear her words.

"Tomorrow."

She hung her head for a moment and then turned a wistful, anxious face up to him. "I—I heard what you have been saying. O Tex—I—I am going with you!"